THE CHILDREN OF THE GODS SERIES BOOKS 50-52

DARK POWER TRILOGY

I. T. LUCAS

Also by I. T. Lucas

THE CHILDREN OF THE GODS SERIES SETS

MEGA SETS

INCLUDE CHARACTER LISTS

TRY THE CHILDREN OF THE GODS SERIES ON AUDIBLE

2 FREE audiobooks with your new Audible subscription!

CONTENTS

DARK POWER UNTAMED

DARK POWER UNLEASHED

DARK POWER CONVERGENCE

DARK POWER UNTAMED

THE CHILDREN OF THE GODS BOOK 50

1

CASSANDRA

"*L*ook at that ass," whispered the guy standing in line behind Cassandra. "I want to sink my teeth into those fleshy cushions."

She rolled her eyes but didn't react. It wasn't the first time guys had made lewd comments behind her back, and most times she pretended not to hear them and did not engage.

"I want to sink something else between them," his friend said, without even trying to lower his voice.

Her hands fisted at her sides.

It was one thing to whisper vulgarities to a friend. It was another thing to make sure that she heard it. It was rude in the extreme and a call to battle.

One the jerks would not win.

Her temper rising, Cassandra considered her options. She could turn around and lash out at the buttheads, releasing some of the negative energy that had built up and preventing it from reaching an explosive level, or she could pretend that she hadn't heard them. The problem with that was if her anger kept building, she would lose control over it.

Bad things happened when she allowed the pressure to accumulate without releasing at least some of the steam. At best, electronic devices around her malfunctioned, inanimate objects toppled and shattered, or glass cracked and exploded. At worst... she didn't want to think about that. Letting herself dwell on it would ruin what had been so far a relatively decent day.

The artwork for the next Surprise Box launch was finally done, which is why she'd allowed herself a small break and had gone out of the office to grab a cup of coffee. But instead of enjoying a few moments of peace, she had some jerks standing behind her and talking about what they would like to do to her ass.

"That's a really fine piece of ass," said a third one as he joined her club of admirers.

Out of the three, his comment was the least offensive, but it was the last straw.

Turning around, she glared down at them. "You know that I can hear you, right?"

Her intimidating pose had the pimply teenagers take a step back. With the three-inch heels she had on, Cassandra was over six feet tall and towered over them. Combine that with her hard glare, and the little jerks were probably shaking in their fashionable sneakers.

The boys were sixteen or seventeen at the most, and seeing how young they were, some of her anger dissipated, enough to significantly reduce the danger of things exploding in her vicinity.

Still, they should know better than to trash talk about a woman, especially one who was old enough to be their mother. Well, only if she had had triplets at seventeen, but still, if they were hers, they never would have dared to talk like that.

She blamed their parents. They had done a piss-poor job of raising them.

One of the three lifted his hands in a sign of peace. "We meant no disrespect. It's just guy talk."

As the other two took another step back and cowered behind the leader, she leaned down to level him with one of her deadly stares. "How would you like it if a bunch of girls commented on the shape of your butt and what they wanted to do with it?"

He smirked. "I would love it."

She had to give him points for guts. Her glares had grown men cower before her, and yet the skinny, pimply boy looked her straight in the eyes and kept smirking.

"What if a bunch of pimply whelps made comments like that about your mother or sister?"

His smirk melted away. "I wouldn't like that."

"There you go. A word of advice that will save you a lot of grief in the future. Don't say anything that you wouldn't want others to say about the important women in your life."

"Yes, ma'am." He lowered his eyes.

"Cassy," the barista called. "Your usual?"

She turned around and smiled. "How are you doing, Dylan?"

"I'm good." Leaning sideways, he peered at the three boys, who were keeping a proper distance from her. "Were they bothering you?"

"They needed a lesson in manners."

He chuckled. "I bet you gave them one to remember."

"I hope so." She handed him her card. "One venti mocha Frappuccino, please."

"A venti? Are you celebrating?" He swiped it and then gave it back together with the receipt.

The thing was probably a thousand calories, but she'd earned the right to indulge. "Yeah, I'm celebrating having a few moments to myself."

"Good for you. Every minute that is not miserable is worth celebrating."

"Amen to that." She collected her drink and waved at Dylan. "I'll see you again tomorrow, and if not, have a great weekend."

"You too."

Outside the wind had picked up, whipping the few strands of hair that had escaped her messy bun into her face, and as she crossed the street back to the office, it started raining. Cassandra ran the rest of the way, careful not to spill her drink or slide and land in a puddle. That would certainly ruin the rest of her day.

Once inside, she climbed the stairs to the second floor and opened the glass double doors. Striding through the firm's large common room, she ignored the unfriendly glares some cast her way, and the indifference of others, as well as the fake smiles of those who thought to gain favor with the firm's VP.

Cassandra had almost made it to the sanctuary of her private office when Kevin's personal assistant waved her down. "Cassandra! The boss was looking for you. He wants to see you in his office."

"Crap," she muttered under her breath and turned to walk in the other direction.

She loved Kevin, but the guy liked to talk, and right now she didn't have the patience for his so-called brainstorming, which was mainly about him throwing ideas around and using her as his sounding board. She planned on leaving at a reasonable time today and not taking work home with her. Perhaps she would even humor her mother and join her to watch that mini-series she was obsessing about.

"You wanted to see me?" Cassandra walked into Kevin's sprawling office, pulled out one of the fancy Art Deco chairs, and plopped tiredly onto it.

Whoever thought that the job of a creative director was glamorous didn't know how difficult it was to be in charge of ten unmotivated snowflakes, who for one reason or another kept dropping the ball on her left and right. Picking up the slack, she was working sixteen-hour days, taking work home, and barely making it in time for the monthly mystery boxes rollouts.

Kevin flashed her one of his charming smiles. "I hope you don't have any plans for Saturday evening."

"Why?" She narrowed her eyes at him.

"I need you to accompany me to the charity gala." When she opened her mouth to protest, he lifted his hand to stop her. "Josie can't make it. She has a concert the same night, and I need a stand-in."

If his wife had a performance scheduled, he would have known about it months in advance.

Cassandra wouldn't be surprised if Josie just wasn't in the mood to do the whole dog and pony show again. The woman was a saint for tolerating being paraded around and presented as her husband's muse, the inspiration for the company's *Fifty Shades of Beauty* cosmetics line.

Kevin was a businessman to his core, and he used every advantage available to him, including his beautiful wife who was a world-renowned cellist. He loved telling the story of how he'd been inspired to create foundations to match every skin tone because of her. When Josie couldn't find the right one for her dark olive complexion with reddish undertones, he'd had an aha moment.

In reality, that moment had been more about realizing the marketing potential of a unique angle than formulating a perfect shade for his wife.

5

"And you find out about it now? What the hell, Kevin?" Cassandra pushed to her feet. "Find someone else to go with you."

Who else had turned him down that he waited until the last moment to ask her?

Besides, Cassandra's days of posing for the camera were over. She still looked good, but she couldn't compare to the young girls they used to model their cosmetics. Kevin could ask any of them, and they would be thrilled to attend the gala with him and have their pictures plastered all over social media.

"Cassy, please, sit down. I need you to do this for me."

Damn him and his pleading tone. She hated when he did that, but after all that Kevin had done for her, she couldn't refuse him, and the bastard knew it.

"I don't want to be a stand-in for Josie. What are you going to tell the crowd? That you created the line for me?"

"I did."

She rolled her eyes. "You hired me after that. Besides, your wife is famous, and everyone knows what she looks like. I can't pretend to be her."

"I'm not asking you to." Leaning back, he crossed his arms over his chest. "Since even now you are wearing my foundation on your beautiful face, I can slightly alter my regular speech and say that I created it for you." He smirked. "Just not exclusively."

Ugh. Being paraded around by Kevin, her face stretched in a fake smile for hours, was Cassandra's personal definition of hell.

She probably wasn't going to win the argument, but that didn't mean that she was going to stop until she had exhausted every excuse possible to wiggle out of the damn event.

"Take one of the models. They all use your cosmetics, and they would love to hobnob with the rich and famous at a posh charity gala."

Assuming a sheepish expression, Kevin raked his fingers through his thinning hair. "I can't take an eighteen-year-old to the event. The media would eat me alive. The damn gossip magazines would publish articles about me taking advantage of the young women working for me, or worse, that I'm cheating on my wife with them. You are my vice president and the company's creative director, and other than Josie, you are the only one I can take. Besides, just like my wife, you embody the type of woman I created the line for. Strong, successful, and absolutely stunning."

Finally, she realized what he was after. He was going to use her to promote their best-selling foundation shade.

He was such a greedy, manipulative prick, but he paid her generously and gave her near-complete autonomy over the marketing creatives.

She owed him.

"I get it. My spice latte skin tone is a perfect match for your bestselling foundation. You want to show me off to promote it."

He didn't deny it. "Come on, Cassy, say yes."

Huffing out a breath, she uncrossed her arms and picked up her Frappuccino. "I don't have anything appropriate to wear."

"Take a day off tomorrow and use the company credit card to buy everything you need. Dress, shoes, jewelry, the works."

She arched a brow. "Budget?"

"Up to ten grand." He smiled. "But knowing you, you'll find stuff on sale at a fraction of the cost. You just can't stomach wasting money."

"That's because I didn't grow up with a silver spoon in my mouth."

"Neither did I, but I worked hard for what I have, and I don't mind spending it on the things I like."

She shrugged. "It's your money. You can do with it as you wish. But I'm not going to treat it any differently just because it doesn't come out of my own pocket."

"I know. But do me a favor and don't buy a dress at a thrift store. For this Saturday evening, you represent the company. Get something that will have the media photographers chasing you around like a bunch of rabid dogs."

She grimaced. "Calling them rabid dogs is uncalled for. Most are just trying to make a living like everyone else."

"I have a love-hate relationship with the media," Kevin admitted.

"Of course, you do. You want the free publicity when it suits you, but you don't want them around when it doesn't."

His mouth twisted in distaste. "Some of them are nasty bastards."

"Regrettably, that's true."

Cassandra had met some slimy photographers, but even as an eighteen-year-old model, she'd known how to deal with them. If they pissed her off, their pricey cameras had suffered irreparable damage.

Kevin shrugged. "I want your picture plastered over all the beauty magazines."

"I get it. You want to generate free publicity, and my story is interesting." The model turned executive who'd helped *Fifty Shades of Beauty* grow exponentially.

Kevin smirked. "Precisely."

"You are aware that the entire staff is going to hate me even more for this."

"Refusing to come is not going to make them like you better. You have a nasty attitude, and they are resentful because I let you get away with it. But mostly, they are just jealous of your success."

"That's why I don't bother trying to be nicer. It's not going to help anyway, and I'd rather they feared me."

The staff had a lot of reasons to hate her. She'd joined the company at eighteen as a model, but Kevin had recognized her talent early on, and he had promoted her ahead of people with college degrees and much more experience in the field. When he'd made her his VP and raised her salary to a quarter of a million, two other senior staff members had quit.

Her bitchy attitude didn't win her any popularity contests either, but she wasn't about to apologize for that. Cassandra demanded from others a fraction of what she demanded from herself, and yet they routinely failed to produce even that.

What did they expect? Praise?

Not from her.

Kevin was the politician, the one who smoothed things over and calmed the hysterical snowflakes after she'd melted them with the heat of her wrath.

Several petitions had been submitted to have her fired, and when Kevin had refused, they had started whispering that she was his lover. Some even went as far as saying that she had him bewitched.

Given what she was capable of when her temper flared, she might indeed wield dark magic, just not the kind that could bewitch a guy into loving her. If she could do that, she wouldn't be single at the ripe old age of thirty-four.

Besides, Kevin was happily married, and her relationship with him was purely professional.

Well, that wasn't entirely true. He and Josie were also her friends, and Cassandra valued that no less than the incredible break they had given her professionally. Just like her, the two of them had risen from nothing and had worked their fingers to the bone to get to where they were today.

"Do you really care that they'll become even more resentful?" he asked.

"No, I don't. Just don't complain to me when you receive the next petition demanding my dismissal."

He laughed. "Agreed."

2

ONEGUS

After reading the changes Bridget had made to his speech, Onegus shook his head. "The language is too strong for this type of event. The rich and famous come to these charity events to mingle, to be seen, and to have a good time. They don't want to have the horrors of trafficking shoved down their throats."

The parts Bridget had added had been taken from the speech she'd delivered in front of the clan's big assembly. Her no-nonsense blunt words had struck a chord with the retired Guardians, motivating most of them to return to the force and join the war on trafficking. But motivating rich humans to donate to the cause required a more diplomatic approach.

Thankfully, the doctor didn't seem offended. "I thought that was what Kian wanted me to do. Your speech lacks the punch to the gut that will make them pledge generously to the cause."

He chuckled. "I'm afraid that your verbal punch would just sour their stomachs and induce nausea. Trust me, I know what I'm doing. Talking about the transformative power of the rehabilitation we provide to the victims will put a positive spin on the ugly subject that the donors will feel comfortable rallying behind."

Leaning back, Bridget crossed her arms over her chest. "I trust your instincts. Feel free to remove the entire opening paragraph. What about the other changes I made?"

"Those are good. I'll keep them." Onegus collected the pages they'd worked on and put them in his briefcase. "Any chance that I can convince you to accompany me to the gala? I need a shield against the socialites. They swarm all over me at these events."

"That's the price of being so handsome," Bridget mocked.

"Yeah, right. They think that I'm the rich philanthropist in charge of the international conglomerate that runs the charity organization."

Bridget laughed. "You'll survive. You can pretend to be nasty, and maybe they'll leave you alone."

"Are you kidding me? That will only make them bolder. Besides, I'm there to solicit donations, which means that I need to be charming and smile at everyone."

Her expression turned apologetic. "I don't like going to events without Turner. It just feels wrong to get all dolled up and not have him by my side. When you find your one and only, you'll understand."

"Fat chance of that." He let out a breath. "Always the groomsman never the groom, which is fine with me. All my head Guardians are mated, and it's making things difficult. I can't send them on out-of-town missions because they can't stand being away from their mates. A military organization can't function like that."

"Most of our missions are local." Bridget glanced at her computer screen. "We've been running an average of fifteen missions a week for months now, and we haven't made a dent in the local problem. I don't see us venturing out of the Los Angeles area anytime soon, and if we do, it would be farther south, to San Diego, which is only three hours away. Being so close to the border, the city is a major hub for traffickers."

Onegus was well aware of that, and he had even contemplated approaching Kalugal about using his men to expand the operations. The guy would most likely refuse, and Kian wasn't keen on the idea either, but it was a possibility.

In the meantime, though, Onegus had the Kra-ell problem to deal with.

"Kian wants to send Arwel with a couple of Guardians to China, and to do that, he needs to convince Jin to go as well. That's just wrong. She's a civilian, and she has no business going on a reconnaissance mission that might get dicey."

Bridget shrugged. "Eleanor is a civilian as well, and yet you had no problem letting her go on a reconnaissance mission."

"That was different. First of all, Eleanor has experience in undercover work. Secondly, she's training with Kri and is in top physical condition. And thirdly, infiltrating a cult on US soil and investigating its leader was a very low-risk assignment, especially given Eleanor's compulsion ability. We had no way of knowing that Emmett was an immortal, or rather a long-lived distant relative of ours. Not only was he immune to her compulsion, but he also was much too strong for her to fight off."

Bridget winced. "Eleanor was lucky that he didn't kill her. She was powerless against him."

Onegus nodded. "So was Peter, and he's a trained Guardian. The Kra-ell are dangerous, and we need to find out what their plans are." He tapped his fingers on her desk. "Emmett is not a bad guy, but his people sound no better than the Brotherhood. They keep humans enslaved in their compound, using them for breeding hybrids and as a source of nourishment. They also treat the hybrids as second-class members, and their leader sounds like a ruthless tyrant."

Bridget sighed. "They have a different set of values and beliefs, and their social structure is very different from ours. That doesn't make what they're doing acceptable, but it also doesn't make them evil."

Onegus raked his fingers through his short hair. "That's an old philosophical dilemma. The fact that they don't think of themselves as evil doesn't mean that what they do isn't wrong. I don't accept cultural or religious beliefs and practices as an excuse for mistreating people, their own or others. I also don't care if their own people think that's the way it should be because it was drilled into their heads that it is. If their actions cause suffering, then those actions are unacceptable. End of story."

"I agree. But it's not our job to go in and forcefully change things for the better. Our job is to provide information and nudge humanity toward equality and democracy." She leaned forward. "Navuh and his scores of warriors are a much bigger problem than Emmett's people, and we haven't made any meaningful progress dealing with that threat, and not for lack of trying. Frankly, I don't understand why Kian is freaking out about the Kra-ell. Their numbers are insignificant, and they haven't caused us any trouble yet."

Bridget was brilliant, and she ran the rescue operations efficiently, but her lack of military background was evident.

"Navuh is a known adversary. We know what he wants, how he thinks to achieve that, and we also know how to thwart his efforts for world domination. The Kra-ell are an unknown. We don't know how many groups like Emmett's are scattered around the world, and we don't know what their agenda is."

Bridget pursed her lips. "That's where Jin's special talent might come in handy. She's the perfect spy, and she can blend in, provided that she masters Mandarin by the time they head to China."

Onegus shook his head. "She has no training, and she's hotheaded. I don't feel comfortable sending her out on a mission even with Arwel and a couple of other Guardians to keep her safe. She might endanger them all."

"It's true that Jin is a civilian with no combat training, but she has skills that are much more valuable than any Guardian's. The problem I see with that is her unwillingness to go. If she refuses, Arwel might turn down the assignment, and you will have to find someone else for the mission."

Onegus grimaced. "You see what I have to deal with? No other chief has to worry about his troops refusing to go out on missions because they can't be away from their mates."

"Don't forget that they are all newly mated," Bridget said. "Perhaps in a couple of decades, they will have no problem leaving their mates for weeks at a time."

"I don't have decades to wait, and besides, I doubt that the bonds will ever loosen. I have nightmares about the entire Guardian force being mated and having no one to work with."

Smiling, Bridget put her hand on his shoulder. "Have faith, Onegus. When the time comes, and everyone is mated, we will find a solution. We always do."

3

BOWEN

"*Y*ou really don't have to do that." Margaret stood next to the open front door, leaning on her crutches. "I will be perfectly comfortable on the bench."

"Right." Bowen lifted one of the armchairs and carried it out to the front porch. "You'll be more comfortable sitting on this." He set it down in a sunny spot near the railing, where she would be warm.

"Thank you." Margaret lowered herself carefully onto the seat and leaned the crutches against the wooden railing.

It was a beautiful day in the mountains. The sky was clear, the sun was shining softly, and the excited chirping of birds was announcing loudly that spring had arrived and it was time to mate.

Regrettably, he wouldn't be joining the mating frenzy anytime soon. He wanted Margaret, but she was off-limits. First of all, she was in a cast, healing from an injury. But even if she was perfectly healthy, it would be a bad idea. He'd befriended her, cared for her, and he could never treat her like one of his random hookups, enjoying her and then vanishing without giving it a second thought.

The situation Bowen found himself in was frustrating.

He couldn't have Margaret, and he couldn't go hunting for sex in the usual places where he found willing partners until he returned her to Safe Haven. Not that he was looking forward to the old, tired routine and the revolving door of sex partners. It reduced sex to a necessity like eating and drinking, stripping it of the emotions that made it so much more meaningful for mated couples.

For Leon, the chase was over, and even though Bowen was happy for him and Anastasia, he couldn't help but envy the guy.

Thank the merciful Fates, Anastasia had transitioned successfully and with no complications, was feeling great, and the couple was on their way back to the cabin, which meant that he'd better start on lunch.

Newly transitioned Dormants were not supposed to eat anything heavy, but Leon had already warned him that Anastasia was ravenous and craved hamburgers.

Lifting the long-necked lighter, he glanced at Margaret. "Are you sure the smoke is not going to bother you?"

If the smell made Margaret nauseous, she wouldn't eat, and he wanted to fill her belly with meat. She needed to get stronger.

"I like the smell." Margaret smiled up at him. "And I also like watching you grill."

"You do?" He lit the barbecue.

"You're so meticulous, and you take pride in it. You enjoy doing things well."

He could think of several things that he did exceptionally well, but they had more to do with licking and fondling than with cooking.

"Yes, I do." He couldn't help the nearly full octave drop in his voice.

Getting his meaning, she lowered her eyes as if he'd made her uncomfortable, but the slight scent of her arousal said otherwise.

Damn. He needed to get a grip. The poor woman had suffered enough. She didn't need to pine after a guy who couldn't return the sentiment no matter how much he wanted to.

"I'm going to get the meat." He walked back inside.

In the kitchen, Bowen loaded a tray with the steaks that he'd left marinating in the fridge overnight, a pack of seasoned hamburgers, a beer for him, and a bottle of water for Margaret.

After putting the tray down on the wooden cart he'd placed next to the grill, he took the bottle and walked over to Margaret. "You need to stay hydrated." He handed it to her.

"Thank you." She took it without lifting her head from her phone.

After finally learning how to use the search function, Margaret was surfing the internet like a pro, collecting articles for her workshop and saving them to a note application he'd downloaded for her.

Bowen was happy to see her doing what she enjoyed, but it was also a reminder that she would be going home soon, and he would probably never see her again.

When the gate opened and Leon pulled the car up in front of the house, Margaret reached for her crutches. "They are right on time. Are the steaks about ready?"

"They are." Bowen helped her down the stairs.

As the passenger door opened and Anastasia got out, he was taken aback. He'd expected her to look exhausted, but she looked radiant and beautiful. If he hadn't known that she had just been through a difficult transition, he would have thought that she'd been to a beauty spa instead.

"You look amazing," Margaret echoed his thoughts. "Are you sure it was food poisoning?"

"Yeah." Anastasia hugged her friend. "I wonder whether the doctor put some magic elixir into the IV that I was hooked up to."

Good one.

Evidently, Anastasia had learned from Leon how to twist words around, so she didn't actually lie but didn't tell the truth either.

"I hope you're hungry." He started loading the steaks onto a platter. "I made enough to feed a small army."

Inhaling deeply, Anastasia closed her eyes. "They smell divine, and I'm starving."

"Then let's eat." Leon took the platter from Bowen and headed inside.

"I wish we had a table on the porch." Margaret followed Anastasia. "It's such a nice day."

Bowen closed the door behind them. "We can have one delivered."

Margaret let out a soft sigh. "I'll be going home soon, and I guess that the three of you will leave as well." She looked at Anastasia. "I assume that you are not coming back to Safe Haven with me?"

"I'm not. But I'll come to visit you whenever I can. I'll probably go back to school and finish my law degree. I'm thinking about switching to nonprofit organizations."

"Good for you." Margaret waited for Bowen to pull out a chair for her. "Is there a chance that you'll visit me too?"

"Of course." He forced a smile.

Probably not. It was going to be difficult enough to say goodbye without dragging it out. A clean break would be best.

4

KIAN

"Mother." Kian bent nearly in half to embrace Annani's petite frame. "How was your trip?"

"Pleasant." She kissed both his cheeks before pushing him away to open her arms to Syssi. "And how is my favorite daughter-in-law?"

"I'm your only daughter-in-law." Syssi chuckled. "But I'm doing great."

Their embrace was a bit awkward given the big pregnant belly Annani couldn't wrap her arms around, and then it started moving this way and that as Allegra responded to all the excitement.

"Oh, wow." Annani released Syssi to put her hands on her belly. "That was one mighty kick, little one. Have mercy on your poor mother."

"I don't mind," Syssi said, her voice tender with love for their daughter. "When she's active, I know she's okay. Sometimes, I get anxious when she sleeps, and I poke her awake to make sure she's okay."

Alena put her hand on Syssi's shoulder. "I still remember each of my pregnancies and the irrational worry that gripped me whenever the baby was inactive for a while. But thank the merciful Fates, they were all born healthy."

"You're a pro." Syssi smiled. "Let's move the party to the dining room. I'm sure you're hungry after your trip."

As Kian followed the procession, he wondered about his eldest sister's miraculous fruitfulness. She'd had all of her eleven children in relatively quick succession and then stopped. It had been many centuries since her last daughter had been born.

Had she been actively avoiding pregnancy? Or had her body decided that eleven children were enough?

Alena had done her part ensuring the clan's future, and no one expected her to keep on producing babies. As it was, she deserved the title of Clan Mother no less than Annani.

"Are Amanda and Dalhu joining us for lunch?" Alena asked.

15

Kian pulled out a chair for his mother. "Amanda had a faculty meeting this morning that she couldn't get out of, but she'll join us for dinner."

"Thank you." Annani gathered the long skirt of her gown and sat down. "Any new developments with our newest dungeon guest?"

Kian hadn't spoken with her since Saturday, but he had no doubt that she was on top of things and had heard about the latest developments from Syssi and Amanda.

"How much do you know?" he asked.

His mother smiled indulgently. "The last time we spoke, you had not interrogated Emmett yet, and you were entertaining the idea that he might be a confused or insane immortal. Is that still a valid hypothesis?"

Kian shook his head. "Regrettably, it's not likely. If it was, I could have put the entire thing behind me and concentrated on the upcoming celebrations. Stella came forward with a story that confirmed Emmett's. It's still not a hundred percent conclusive, but it seems that Emmett is telling the truth. In addition, I suspect that his group is not the only one, and that there might be many more of them."

"Syssi told me about Stella's confession." Annani sighed. "Poor woman has kept the secret of who fathered her son for over twenty years. It must have been eating away at her." Her eyes smiled as she looked at him. "I am surprised that you are not angry at her."

"She vowed on Vlad's life never to reveal who his father was. It was the only way she could convince the Kra-ell hybrid to let her go. I can understand her fear of breaking such a vow. In her shoes, I would have done the same. Just as there are no atheists in a foxhole, I bet most parents would not be willing to gamble on their children's lives even when it's only a superstition."

"What are you going to do about the Kra-ell?" Alena asked. "Are you going to search for them?"

He nodded. "Emmett provided us with the exact location of their compound, but chances are that they are no longer there. After he escaped, they probably moved locations so he couldn't sell them out. And if they hadn't moved back then, they certainly did that after receiving his email about us. That being said, we might find clues that will lead us to them, which is why I want to send a team to investigate."

"What if they didn't get the email?" Syssi asked. "They could have sold the company, and whoever opened the email might have sent it to the trash folder, thinking it was junk mail or a prank."

"That's possible. If we are lucky, they didn't, and we'll find them where Emmett left them."

"Who are you planning to send?" Annani asked.

"We have no one who speaks the language fluently and knows the local customs. Turner is providing us with a human team that has worked in China before, and I'm supplementing it with several Guardians. I want Arwel to lead our team. His empathic abilities will be useful, and if Jin agrees to accompany him, her tethering ability could be invaluable to the mission."

"Did you speak with them?" Syssi asked.

"Not yet. I plan to call Arwel later today or tomorrow."

Annani eyed him sidelong. "I thought that you would take me to see Emmett later today."

Of course she did.

"Tomorrow works better for me, and you need to rest after your journey."

"I do not." She huffed. "But if you are busy, I will find ways to pass the time productively."

Was that an implied threat?

He narrowed his eyes at her. "What are you plotting already?"

"I want to talk to Stella. Did she tell Vlad about his father?"

Kian shrugged. "I don't know. But just in case she didn't, I suggest that for the time being we keep quiet about it. I don't want the rumor to spread and for the kid to hear about it from someone other than his mother."

Vlad had enough on his plate as it was. Kian didn't know whether he was still planning on visiting Wendy's father and getting him to confess what he'd done to the mother, and he didn't want to know.

Personally, Kian supported Vlad's quest for answers and even his need to avenge the wrongs that had been perpetrated against his mate. But as regent, he couldn't do that.

It was against clan law to thrall humans for personal gain.

There were only a few instances in which it was allowed, and Vlad's investigation wasn't one of them.

5

VLAD

$\mathcal{D}$espite moving out of his mother's house many months ago, Vlad still felt awkward about knocking on the door of what used to be his home. His mother wouldn't mind if he just walked in, but she had a mate now, and the fact that Richard used to be Vlad and Wendy's roommate and probably wouldn't mind didn't make it okay either.

Richard was still at the construction site, though, and he wouldn't be home for another couple of hours.

His mother opened the door. "You don't need to knock. No matter where you live and how old you are, this will always be your home."

"I love you too, Mom." He leaned and kissed her cheek.

She looked tense, and Vlad wondered what was going on. It wasn't unusual for her to call him and ask him to stop by on his way home. He would bring a tasty treat from the bakery, and they would have tea together. Today though, she'd sounded anxious on the phone, saying that there was something she needed to talk to him about.

The only thing that came to mind was that Stella and Richard were having a baby, but that shouldn't make her so nervous. Vlad wouldn't mind having a baby brother or sister. In fact, he would love it.

Except, maybe it was about his plans to pay Wendy's father a visit?

Richard might have said something, or maybe Wendy had.

"I brought muffins." He lifted the brown bag. "Blueberry, your favorite."

She smiled tightly. "I'll make tea."

He followed her to the kitchen. "What's going on, Mom?"

Her shoulders slumped. "I need to tell you something, and I hope that you won't be too upset."

He let out a relieved breath. It didn't seem like anyone had told her about his plans, so it had to be a baby.

"Why would I be upset? Perhaps I will be happy for you?"

Her forehead furrowed. "Happy for me? What do you think this is about?"

Vlad pushed his bangs back. "Apparently not what I expected."

"What did you expect?"

Now that he was about to say it out loud, it seemed silly. His mother and Richard hadn't been together long enough to have a baby. Then again, neither had Kalugal and Jacki, and they were expecting.

He chuckled nervously. "I thought that you and Richard were having a baby, and I got excited thinking about a little brother or sister."

Her eyes softened. "Fates willing, one day we will, but that's not what I need to tell you." She poured boiling water into the two mugs she'd prepared and handed him one. "It's about your father."

Vlad had never given much thought to the human who had contributed his genetic material to create him. He had been just an unknowing sperm donor. Vlad didn't even know that his mother had kept tabs on the guy.

"What about him? Did he die?"

She shook her head. "Not as far as I know. Your father wasn't human, so it's unlikely that he died."

Vlad's blood turned cold. Unless his mother had broken the taboo of having relations with another descendent of Annani, her only option for an immortal lover was a Doomer. "Was my father a Doomer?"

"No. He was Kra-ell."

That was it. His mother had officially lost it. She was confusing reality with the Krall virtual adventure she and Richard had experienced.

"The Krall are not real people, Mom. They were invented by Syssi for the Perfect Match virtual studios. I know that the virtual adventure felt like real life, but it wasn't."

Stella leaned over and put her hand on his chest. "Syssi is clairvoyant, Vlad, and the Krall aren't a figment of her imagination. She saw them in a vision. She got some of the details wrong, and her imagination filled in the gaps, but the real Kra-ell are very similar to her fictional Krall. Did you hear about the cult leader who kidnapped a Guardian?"

Vlad's blood went from cold to boiling in an instant. "I didn't hear anything. How did it happen?"

Richard was getting inside information from Kalugal, who was getting it from Kian, and Stella had heard about it from Richard. That didn't mean that the entire clan knew about it.

"The cult leader is one of them, I mean the Kra-ell, and he's also a powerful compeller who can compel other immortals. The Guardian was rescued, and Emmett Haderech was captured and is locked in the keep's dungeon, so that's over, but his capture opened up a whole new can of worms."

"Like what? And how does it affect me?"

"I hope it doesn't. You got the immortality gene from me. The Kra-ell are long-lived but not immortal, and other than your incredible strength, it doesn't seem like you have inherited anything else from your father. You don't crave or need blood for nourishment."

"They are really like the Krall? Are they vampires?"

"In that regard, they are. But according to Emmett, they never drain their

19

victims. Also, their main source of blood is animals, not humans, and they don't drain the animals either. They only take what can be replenished in a few days."

"Or so he claims. Did the one who fathered me claim the same?"

"Vrog didn't tell me much about himself or his people. My first thought was that he was a Doomer, but he didn't know what I was talking about, so I assumed that he belonged to an unaffiliated group of immortals, maybe the descendants of other survivors."

She pushed a strand of hair behind her ear. "I should have paid closer attention to what he said. He told me that he wasn't immortal, only long-lived, but I thought he only meant that immortals were not impervious to catastrophic injuries. He also told me that his people were ruled by a ruthless female who treated the males as her personal slaves, but again, I thought she was just a bitch, and that he was a fool for not leaving. I even offered him the option to join the clan, but he had made a vow never to betray his leader and couldn't leave."

"Where did you meet him?"

"In Singapore. Until he bit me, I thought that he was just an attractive human."

"Did he drink your blood?"

"I don't know. I blacked out." She smiled sheepishly. "It was my first venom bite."

"Yeah, that's too much information, Mom."

She lifted her hands, her many bracelets jingling. "You asked."

"I know. How come you never told me about him?"

His mother's eyes misted with tears. "Somehow, Vrog knew right away that we'd created a life, and he was terrified of what his leader would do if she ever found out. He wanted me to get an abortion. I was alone, in a foreign country, and Vrog was incredibly strong. I needed to come up with something to persuade him to let me go, and since he took vows so seriously, that's what I did. I vowed on the life of my unborn child that I would never reveal his secret."

Vlad wasn't a big believer in the power of vows, but his mother was superstitious. "You kept your vow for nearly twenty-two years. How come you broke it now?"

She sighed. "Richard figured it out after our Krall adventure, but I wanted to believe that didn't count as vow breaking. And then Emmett was caught, and Kian thought that he was making the entire story up after participating in a similar experience at one of the Perfect Match studios. I couldn't keep quiet and let him think that. Emmett had sent an email to his leader telling her about us and how our males could activate their Dormants. That was why he kidnapped Peter. He wanted to use him for that. Without the ability to activate their Dormants, they are facing extinction. They would do anything to get their hands on our males, and Kian needs to safeguard our people, which he wouldn't have done if he still believed that Emmett had made the story up."

"Wasn't Emmett's need to consume blood evidence enough?"

"They thought it was a fetish. But even if Kian eventually believed that the Kra-ell were real, there was another complication. Since according to Emmett, the Kra-ell females have fangs and venom, they were all talking about the connection to Mey and Jin, and how their peculiar traits could be explained by a Kra-ell father. It was only a question of time before they figured out that you weren't a typical immortal male either. I didn't want you to find out about it from someone else."

His eyes widened. "Jin and Mey were also fathered by a Kra-ell?"

"Isn't it obvious? Otherwise, why would they have fangs?"

"Damn. They might be my cousins."

Stella smiled. "Their mother must have been a Dormant, our kind of Dormant, but she wasn't Annani's descendant. So yeah, they might be your cousins on your father's side."

"Did you get to see Emmett?"

"I did."

"What do you think of him?"

"He's arrogant, and he has a penchant for theatrics, but he doesn't strike me as evil."

"Can I talk to him?"

She tilted her head. "Why would you want to?"

"To find out more about the blood coursing through my veins."

"Emmett is imprisoned in the keep. You'll need to ask Kian."

6

KIAN

Kian pulled out two new earpieces from his pocket and handed them to Annani. "You need to put these in."

She looked at the devices as if they were a couple of worms. "You said that Emmett is in chains. Why do I need to put these in? If he tries to compel me, Arwel can stop him with the push of a button. I would rather go in without them and test my compulsion on him."

"He could compel you to order everyone to stand down, and then Arwel wouldn't be able to do anything. I'm not willing to risk it."

She rolled her eyes. "Arwel is wearing his earpieces, so he will not be affected by my compulsion any more than he will be by Emmett's." She pushed his hand away. "I am going in without them."

"You promised me that you would wear them."

She looked down her nose at him. "I changed my mind. I need to test Emmett's susceptibility to my compulsion."

Annani was right, but Kian hated to put her in danger even if it was minimal. Not that he had much choice in the matter. Given her stubborn expression, his mother was not going to back down.

"How are you going to test it?"

"I will ask him to tell me everything he knows about his people."

"We have no way of verifying whether it's true, and even if it is, he might reveal the information voluntarily." Kian chuckled. "Given how terrified he is of his leader, he might be too scared to lie to you."

"That is possible." Annani turned to Arwel. "You have spent some time with Emmett. Is there anything he holds dear that I can ask him to reveal and it can be verified?"

"The wealth he's accumulated over the years seems to be more precious to him than anything else. You can ask him to tell you the numbers of his offshore bank accounts. We can verify those."

"Excellent idea. Thank you, Arwel." Annani turned to Kian. "Any more questions and instructions before we go in?"

"I think we have it covered." He looked at Arwel. "Set the remote to stun. The moment he tries anything, zap him."

"Understood."

Kian put his earpieces in and activated them.

As Arwel engaged the door mechanism, Kian put his hand on his mother's slim shoulder. "Wait until I say it's okay to go in."

"As you wish."

If only she could be so agreeable more often.

When the door swung all the way out, Arwel went in first, followed by Kian.

Emmett was seated in the same armchair as before, chained, and Alfie stood across from him with his hand on the gun. But unlike the other times Kian had visited him, Emmett didn't complain about the shackles or pretend nonchalance.

The guy looked nervous, which wasn't really surprising. He was about to meet the goddess, and given what he'd told them about his leader, he had good reason to fear his visitor.

Emmett lifted a worried pair of eyes to Kian. "Shouldn't I be on my knees?"

"The Clan Mother doesn't demand obeisance. Keep your tone respectful, and you should be fine."

"Of course."

Kian stepped back outside. "He's ready for you, Mother."

"Thank you, my son."

It was disturbing to hear his mother through the devices, sounding like a male. William had promised to work on a new design that would adapt to the speaker's voice, but he hadn't been successful yet.

Perhaps Annani was right about the low risk of Emmett trying anything.

Discreetly, Kian removed the devices from his ears and put them back in his pocket. For once, his longish hair would be useful for something other than pleasing his wife. It would cover the fact that he wasn't wearing the compulsion-blocking earpieces.

As Annani glided into the suite, Emmett sucked in a breath and bowed his head. He remained frozen like that, not moving a muscle and not saying a thing.

"You may gaze upon my face, Emmett." Annani lowered herself regally into the armchair across from him. "It is not forbidden."

Very slowly, Emmett lifted his head. "It's an honor to be in your presence, Clan Mother."

She nodded. "Tell me about your people, Emmett. Everything you know."

As Kian felt the soft caress of her compulsion, he wondered how Emmett's and Kalugal's felt. Luckily, he'd been spared from enduring either, but he was sure they felt nothing like Annani's.

"There were twenty of them to start with," Emmett said. "I don't know where they came from, but I was born in a rural area outside of Beijing."

It was difficult to tell if Annani's compulsion was working on Emmett. Kian paid attention as the guy repeated the same things he'd told them already, poised to catch any inconsistencies.

By the time Emmett had left, he said, the community had grown, but not significantly. Six pureblooded children had been born to the original settlers, two females and four males. Twenty-four hybrids had been born to human mothers and Kra-ell fathers, of which only two were females and the rest males. Children born to hybrid males with human females had been born human, and Emmett didn't know whether the hybrid females took human lovers.

Annani lifted her hand to interrupt him. "If you are like us, which I suspect you are in many ways, the children born to Kra-ell hybrid fathers and human mothers do not carry your longevity genes. Only the female hybrids can pass it on to their children, who can be activated with venom. You were fortunate that we captured you before you delivered Peter to your leader. He would have been useless for activating your second generation of hybrids, and she might have ended your life for bringing her a false promise." Annani smiled sadly. "My understanding is that she is not a forgiving female."

Emmett swallowed. "I was so excited to find a possible solution that I didn't pause to think it through. Peter told me that only the females transmitted the immortal gene." He looked at her with pleading eyes. "Can you tell me more about my origins? My father and the other purebloods refused to tell us anything. They considered us second-class members of the community."

She nodded. "My parents were the same, and I am not a hybrid, and I definitely was not considered a second-class anything either. I was born a pureblooded goddess, the daughter of the leading couple and the chosen heir to my father's rule. I suspect that their past was shameful, and they wanted a fresh start free of the taint of past deeds. They wanted the next generation to believe the gods were benevolent, only wishing to help humanity evolve into a free, democratic society like their own. It was a noble goal, one which I took upon myself to propagate after the demise of my people."

Emmett tilted his head. "If the gods were benevolent and taught their children well, how did your enemies, the Doomers I believe they are called, come to be?"

Annani smiled sadly. "How do you think the gods' era ended? The thirst for power is corruptive. It is poison. One ambitious god wanted to run things differently and rule over the other gods. He turned against them, and when he attacked, he perished alongside them. His son continues his evil legacy to this day. My clan and his followers have been fighting over the future of humanity for thousands of years."

"Who is winning?" Emmett asked.

Was it a genuine question? Or was it meant as sarcasm?

By now, Emmett must have figured out that Annani wasn't a terrifying tyrant, and he might have felt emboldened.

Annani lifted her chin. "Despite their superior numbers, we are winning, but it is not a smooth progression. There are setbacks, and sometimes the Brotherhood manages to thwart and even undo our efforts, rewinding humanity's progress by hundreds of years. Still, we keep pushing forward. Without us, humans would still be in the Dark Ages and probably enslaved to the followers of Mortdh."

For the first time since Annani's arrival, Emmett turned to look at Kian. "The followers of Mortdh have been actively working against you for thousands of years, and you are worried about my people being your adversaries? They don't even know that you exist, let alone bother you."

"Not yet. But they might."

"Unlikely," Annani said. "Given their social structure and the scarcity of females, the Kra-ell cannot multiply at the rate the Doomers do, and their numbers will remain insignificant."

"I agree that number-wise they are not a threat," Kian said. "But the days of needing brute force to take control of people are over. With today's technology, a small group of people with compulsion ability and advanced technological knowhow could take over the world."

Annani nodded and then turned to Emmett. "How advanced were your people?"

"Frankly, they did not strike me as more advanced than humans. We didn't have any interesting gadgets or weapons. I don't know that for sure, but I think that they obtained the knowhow needed to start Kumei telecommunications from compelling humans to give it to them."

Annani looked at Emmett skeptically. "How is it possible that people who traversed the universe to get here have no advanced technology?"

Kian crossed his arms over his chest. "We don't have the technology or ability to build an interstellar ship either, and yet, our ancestors got here some-how. Being passengers on a ship doesn't make them engineers. They might have been dropped off on Earth, for whatever reason, and their ship returned home."

Or was still orbiting the Earth, hidden by a cloaking device, or simply hiding behind the dark side of the moon.

Annani adjusted the folds of her long skirt. "The technology could depend on materials we do not have on Earth. The gods did not build anything techno-logically advanced either. Whatever they had, they must have brought with them, and the devices slowly deteriorated over time. We only had a few flying machines, and the same was true for the tablets. I remember my Uncle Ekin, who was the only one among the gods I knew with technological knowhow, working on inventive solutions using what was available in the world back then. I guess the Kra-ell were faced with the same difficulty." She looked at Emmett. "One last question before we part. Please tell us the bank location of your largest offshore account, and recite the number along with your personal access code."

This time, the compulsion she used was not a gentle caress. It was more like a chokehold, so oppressive that Kian felt the mental pressure even though it hadn't been directed at him. It was a struggle to pull out his phone and get ready to write down the information Emmett was about to reveal.

Looking as uncomfortable as Kian felt, Emmett did as she commanded, wincing with every letter and number leaving his mouth. When he was done, sweat beaded on his forehead. "You are a powerful compeller, Clan Mother."

"Indeed." She smiled apologetically. "Do not worry, no one is going to take your money. This was just a test to make sure that I can compel you."

As access was granted, Kian whistled. "You have done pretty well for your-self, Emmett. Is that all from running the Safe Haven retreats? Or did some of your community members bestow their inheritances on you?"

"I'm a savvy investor, and I had a long time to do it."

Kian put his phone back in his pocket. "No doubt by compelling people to give you insider information."

Emmett shrugged. "Are you going to hold that against me as well?"

"It's immoral, and it's a crime, but it's not a crime against the clan."

Besides, Kalugal had done the same thing and was probably still doing it, and yet Kian had invited him to join the clan.

Annani pushed to her feet. "It was a very interesting meeting, Emmett. Good day."

He bowed his head. "Good day, Clan Mother."

When they were at the door, Annani paused and turned around. "One last thing before I go, Emmett." She walked closer to him, halting several feet away from the prisoner, and unleashing her godly power on him. "You will never attempt to compel any of my clan members, and you will not do anything to harm them physically or otherwise. You will not attempt to escape, either."

Once again, Annani's compulsion felt like a vice around Kian's throat even though it had been directed at Emmett.

The guy must have felt it tenfold, and yet he took it without averting his eyes or slumping in his seat.

When the power winked out, both Emmett and Kian let out a relieved breath.

Annani smiled sweetly. "Goodbye, Emmett."

7

ARWEL

*W*hen the interview ended, Kian motioned for Arwel to follow them outside. "After you move Emmett back to his cell, come to my office. Annani and I will wait for you."

Arwel arched a brow. "Does it have anything to do with my prisoner?"

"In a way. Finish with Emmett first." Offering his arm to the goddess, Kian started toward the elevators.

She smiled up at her son. "The last time I visited your old office was under similar circumstances. It was when I came to see Lokan."

Anandur and Brundar followed behind mother and son, and as the four entered the elevator, Arwel opened the door and walked back into the suite.

Alfie had already unlocked Emmett's leg shackles, and as he tossed them on the floor, Emmett's eyes followed, his mouth curling with distaste.

"You did well." Arwel clapped him on the back.

"I didn't expect the Clan Mother to be so powerful, or so kind, or so beautiful."

The order of adjectives was telling. Emmett wasn't as impressed with beauty as he was with power and kindness.

Emmett stretched his arms over his head. "Do you have a book about the history of your clan that I can read?"

After the initial shock and awe of seeing the goddess, the guy had gone back to his usual act of a bored, harmless intellectual.

"We don't."

Edna kept records, but they weren't in story form, and they weren't accessible even to clan members. If anyone wanted to go through the records, they needed to ask Edna's permission and give her a reason for the request.

"That's a shame. I would have liked to learn more about you. Any other books that you can lend me? I'm bored."

"You can watch television." Arwel walked Emmett out into his own cell. "Or play video games."

"I enjoy reading more. I would really appreciate some books."

"I'll see what I can do. What do you like to read?"

"Anything that's well written. Fiction and non-fiction."

"Did you read *Game of Thrones*?"

Emmett grimaced. "It was too cruel and bloody for my taste. I read to relax."

Arwel arched a brow. "A pacifist bloodsucker? That's a contradiction in terms."

"I'd rather avoid conflict when I can. I guess I inherited my peaceful nature from my human mother."

Arwel wanted to ask Emmett more about his experience growing up as a hybrid in the Kra-ell compound, but Kian and Annani were waiting for him.

"I need to go. We can talk more when I come back."

Emmett nodded. "I'm looking forward to it. Our little talks are the highlight of my day."

Even with his empathic ability, Arwel wasn't sure whether that was meant as a compliment or as sarcasm. Emmett was a natural actor, and sometimes it was difficult to tell the difference between what was an act and what was real, probably because the lines were as blurred for Emmett as they were for his audience.

The guy was a condescending prick and a know-it-all, but the truth was that Arwel enjoyed their talks as well. Emmett had a good grasp on human nature and on politics, and he'd even read the works of all the major philosophers.

Nevertheless, if Kian had a new assignment for him, Arwel would jump on it. Jin was tired of the dungeon, and so was he.

As the elevator doors opened and Arwel stepped out on the office's level, he saw Anandur heading his way.

"I'm going up to get coffees from the vending machines. Do you want anything?"

"No thanks." Arwel grimaced. "Living here, I've had too much of the café's limited selection already."

As he walked into Kian's office, his boss motioned to the chair next to him. "Take a seat, Arwel."

"How are you enjoying your post here?" Annani asked.

Arwel sat down. "Emmett is not a difficult prisoner, but I'd rather get out of the dungeon."

She tilted her head. "I thought that you preferred living underground. It filters the human emotions that bother you topside."

"It does, but living in the village is better. Immortals don't broadcast their emotions nearly as much as humans, and I'm exposed to humans only when I go out on missions, which is tolerable. My quality of life has improved significantly since we moved out of the keep."

She smiled indulgently. "I am sure that having a mate has a lot to do with it as well. How is Jin taking all this? Has she met with Emmett?"

"Jin expressed no desire to do so."

Annani looked surprised. "Is she not curious about her father's people?"

Arwel shrugged. "She saw Emmett on the surveillance feed, and I told her everything I learned listening to the interrogation and also from talking to him.

At first, we were worried about the Kra-ell shorter lifespans and how it might impact Jin and Mey if they are related to them, but since their mother must have been a Dormant, that's no longer a concern."

Huffing out an impatient breath, Kian was done waiting out their small talk. "I want you to be in charge of the China team," Kian said. "Your empathic abilities might be useful on an information-gathering mission."

Arwel was the right guy for the job, but that was not the kind of mission he'd been hoping for. Leaving Jin behind would be tough. Hopefully, he wouldn't have to be gone for more than a few days.

"Who else is going?"

"Turner is supplying a human team that is familiar with the local culture and knows the language. I want you to work with them, and you can take as many Guardians as you deem necessary. But since this is a reconnaissance mission, less is probably better."

"How long do we need to plan to be there?"

"A couple of weeks." Noting Arwel's barely stifled grimace, Kian tapped his fingers on the table. "What do you think about taking Jin with you?"

"As my companion or as a spy?"

"Both."

Arwel shook his head. "She doesn't want to use her ability for spying."

"I know, but the results of this investigation have direct implications for her and Mey. Aren't they curious about their biological parents?"

"The father or fathers who discarded them as if they were garbage? I don't think so. They consider the Levins their parents and rightfully so."

"I get it about the biological father or fathers, but the mother didn't have a choice. She was forced to give them up. If she's still alive, and we don't have a reason to think that she's not, she would be overjoyed to see how well her daughters have turned out."

"I can ask Jin."

Kian nodded. "Good. I want you to hire a tutor to teach you and your chosen Guardians Mandarin. It will be faster than learning from an audio course."

Arwel pulled out his earpieces. "We can use these to translate what is said to us, but it would be beneficial to be able to speak it. Do we have anyone in the village who speaks it fluently?"

"Stella does," Annani said. "But I do not know if she is fluent. You might want to check with Morris. When he is not flying the clan's jet, he translates flight manuals into different languages. Perhaps one of them is Mandarin."

Arwel chuckled. "We should include Carol in the class. Isn't she supposed to accompany Lokan to China?"

"She won't come back for that," Kian said. "She's staying in a hotel in Washington until Lokan is ready to leave. She refuses to be apart from him."

"Can't blame her." Anandur walked in with two cardboard trays filled with paper coffee cups. "She and Lokan can use a Rosetta Stone to learn." He started distributing the drinks. "And so can Arwel and his team."

Arwel shook his head. "Unlike other immortals, Jin is not good with languages. It's probably because she transitioned as an adult. It would appear that the ear for languages develops at a young age. If she agrees to join me on the mission, she'll need a one-on-one tutor."

8

ONEGUS

"Is that the tux?" Connor's eyes lit up as Onegus walked in with the garment bag slung over his shoulder.

The tux had been ordered a month ago with input from his roommate, who considered himself a fashionista and would no doubt want to examine the finished product.

"It is." Onegus sniffed at the aromas coming from the kitchen. "What's cooking? I don't recognize the smell."

Connor was gracious enough to cook for both of them, but his repertoire consisted of six recipes that he cycled throughout the week. Not that Onegus was complaining. If not for Connor, he would have been subsisting on sandwiches and pastries from the café.

As the chief, Onegus was entitled to a house all to himself, but he preferred to share it, just not with one of the Guardians. His position created a natural distance between him and those he was in charge of, and cohabiting with one of them would have been awkward.

Connor had been a good choice. He was a composer and worked from home, while Onegus spent most of his waking hours in his office or traveling as Kian's representative.

"I'm trying one of Callie's recipes," Connor said. "She posted it on the clan's website last weekend."

"Then I'm sure it's delicious." Onegus headed to his room.

"I want to see you in the tux," Connor called after him.

"You'll see it tomorrow."

"I need to get one for myself, and I want to check the craftsmanship."

Onegus stopped and turned around. "What's the occasion?"

Connor was an excellent score composer, but he hadn't gotten nominated for an Emmy or an Oscar yet.

"It's not a nomination, if that's what you were thinking. Regrettably." Connor sighed. "I've been invited to speak at an event." He cast Onegus an accusing side-long glance.

Was he offended that Onegus hadn't invited him to be his pretend date?

He'd jokingly asked Brandon and had made the mistake of telling Connor about it.

"Fine. I will try it on for you." Onegus ducked into the bedroom.

When he emerged a few minutes later, Connor whistled. "That's one hell of a well-tailored tux. You look dashing." He chuckled. "Good luck with the gold-diggers."

"I'll be fine. It's not my first rodeo, and I've refined the technique of brushing them off politely."

"Oh, yeah? How?"

"I pretend not to notice that they are flirting with me. I just smile and keep talking about how important the charity is and how much the contributions collected at these events help us rehabilitate more rescued trafficking victims. Eventually, they get bored with me and move on to the next eligible bachelor."

"What do you do when they just flat out proposition you? You can't pretend not to get it."

"You'd be surprised. I tell them how flattered I am but that I have so much work and can't possibly make time for pleasure."

It wasn't a complete lie. He worked insanely long hours.

Amusement dancing in his eyes, Connor cast him a pretend stern look. "Tell me the truth, Onegus. When they get really pesky, aren't you tempted to push them away with just a smidgen of a thrall?"

"Tempted, yes. Do I do that? No. I'm the chief. If I break the law or even bend it a little, how can I demand compliance from you civilians?"

Connor smiled. "Come on. No one would know. It's not like a little thrall can do much harm."

"I would know." Onegus ran his fingers through his short hair. "I need to get a haircut."

"Don't. It's short enough. Just gel it. If you want, I can do that for you."

"Thanks. It will save me a trip to the barber."

The look of disdain on Connor's face was comical. "A barber? That's who cuts your hair? No wonder it's a mess."

"What's wrong with it?"

"Everything. You need a stylist, not a damn barber."

"Well, since I don't have one, the job is yours."

9

CASSANDRA

"Cassy? Are you home?" her mother called from downstairs.

"I'll be down in a moment." Cassandra unzipped the garment bag, pulled out the dress she'd bought, and laid it on the bed.

At first glance, it might not have looked like much to the untrained eye, which was probably why she'd gotten it at a bargain price, but Cassandra had known it was the one the moment she'd laid eyes on it. And when she tried it on, it looked as though it had been custom-made for her.

The color was a very dark purple, nearly black, the dress was sleeveless and had sheer panels that precluded wearing a bra, but that wasn't a problem. Her breasts were small and perky enough to get away with it. The dress was sophisticated and daring without being too showy or trashy.

Kevin would be furious if he found out that she'd gotten it at a boutique specializing in used designer attire, but hopefully he wouldn't check the receipts from her purchases.

She just hadn't had the heart to spend a fortune on a dress for one night. So what if some celebrity had worn it once? It was absolutely gorgeous and had been dry cleaned.

Everything else she'd gotten was new, and the shoes had cost twice as much as the dress. Opening the box, she pulled out the black velvet Louboutins and gazed at the masterpiece of craftsmanship.

"Hello, gorgeous." She pulled them out, slipped them on her feet, and walked over to the full-length mirror attached to the back of her bedroom door.

Wearing only a pair of skimpy bikini bottoms, a lacy bra, and the shoes, she looked hot if she said so herself, and she couldn't resist striking a pose and admiring herself in the mirror.

Not bad for a thirty-four-year-old.

It was a shame, though, that she didn't have anyone to model for. Not in her underwear anyway. The last time anyone had seen her without her clothes on had been over a year ago.

With a sigh, she turned around, lifted the dress off the bed and pulled it on. As evening gowns went, it was very comfortable. The fabric was stretchy, and it molded to her body perfectly.

"Cassy?" Her mother knocked on the door. "Can I come in? I want to see what you got."

Smiling, Cassandra opened the door. "What do you think?"

Her mother's hand flew to her chest. "Oh, Cassy, you look so beautiful. I wish your father could see you like that."

She stifled the urge to roll her eyes.

Cassandra had never met her father and didn't even know who he was. Her mother's stories about him changed according to her mood. Sometimes he was a surgeon whom she'd met while recovering from an injury in a hospital. Other times he was an astronaut in training she'd met in a bar, or an ambassador from Ethiopia whom she'd met on the beach, and so on.

Her mother had always lived in a fantasy world, and yet she'd somehow managed to raise Cassandra well and provide her with everything she needed. They had lived in a one-bedroom tiny apartment, but it had been in a good area with decent schools. Cassandra had never felt like she lacked for anything.

Now that she was making excellent money, she'd bought a house and was taking care of her mother.

"Who is he this time, Mom?"

"What do you mean?"

It was pointless to challenge the stories, but sometimes she just couldn't help it. "Never mind. Aren't you going to your book club meeting tonight?"

Cassandra doubted that her mother's outings were always as innocent as book club meetings or bingo night with her girlfriends, especially since she often came home in the early hours of the morning.

She was a beautiful woman, who didn't look old enough to have a daughter Cassandra's age, and she was most likely more sexually active than her daughter.

Not that that was difficult to achieve. Cassandra didn't do hookups, and she'd broken up with her last boyfriend over a year ago. If not for her trusty BOB, she would have turned into a virgin again.

"It's tomorrow." Her mother sat on the bed. "Just look at you." She sighed. "I just wish you were going to the gala with a nice young man instead of your boss."

"I don't have time for dating."

"You work too hard."

"I work as hard as I have to. Kevin is not paying me a quarter of a million salary for a nine-to-five job."

Her mother leaned her elbows on her knees and rested her chin on her fist. "I know that you don't have time to go to clubs or wherever young people go to mingle these days. But what about those dating apps everyone is talking about? You could try those."

Cassandra had tried a couple, and her mother had known that, but Geraldine's memory was spotty, especially long-term memory, and she'd probably forgotten.

It was best to ignore it. Her mother got upset when anyone noticed her memory issues or commented on them, and she tried to cover up for the lapses by making up stories.

"I tried, Mom. It was a colossal waste of time. People lie on their profiles, post pictures that are a decade old or Photoshopped, and it was one disappointment after another."

"Perhaps you are too picky?"

"I'm not going to lower my standards. I'm not looking for a dashing billionaire, but I want a guy to be in reasonably good shape, have a paying job, and be able to hold an intelligent conversation for more than five minutes. I don't think that makes me picky."

There were other requirements as well. Like respect and fidelity. Cassandra had met a few players in her life, and she'd dropped them as soon as she'd figured out the pattern. If a guy only wanted to hang out around her place or his, didn't introduce her to any of his friends or family, and found excuses for not taking her out, it meant that he wasn't serious and was probably seeing other women at the same time.

The right guy also shouldn't mind that she still lived with her mother and had no intentions of moving out anytime soon. Or ever. Her mother needed to be taken care of, and she had no one other than Cassandra.

Geraldine had many friends but no relatives, or at least none that Cassandra was aware of. Her mother might have forgotten them.

All they had was each other.

"I just don't want you to end up alone, Cassy."

Neither did she, but what were the chances of her finding a man who checked off all her boxes?

Cassandra sat on the bed and wrapped her arm around her mother's shoulders. "I'm not alone. I have you."

BOWEN

"Good morning." Leon saluted Bowen with his mug. "Coffee?"

"Definitely." Bowen pulled out a stool and straddled it. "Is Anastasia still sleeping?"

As an immortal, she would need no more than four hours of shuteye, but she was still recuperating from the transition.

"My mate is not an early riser, and I don't think that's going to change even when she's fully transitioned." Leon handed him a steaming mug. "I wish I could stay in bed with her longer, but waking up at dawn is a habit that I can't seem to break." He sat next to him.

"When she recuperates fully, I'm sure she'll need less sleep."

Leon smiled. "I hope so. I'm looking forward to early morning walks and other fun activities before our workday starts."

"You are one lucky bastard." He took a sip from the piping hot coffee.

"I know." Leon swiveled the barstool to face him. "But maybe you are too."

Bowen lifted a brow. "Meaning?"

"Eleanor made an interesting observation. On the face of it, Ana and Margaret have nothing in common. But despite the age difference and their very different backgrounds, they became best friends in no time. Eleanor thinks it might be affinity at work. Margaret might be a Dormant."

For a brief moment, his heart leaped at the kernel of hope, but then it dropped back down and sank low.

"I wish. But she doesn't have any paranormal talents. I know that not all Dormants have them, but it would have been helpful to have a big-ass hint like that. Margaret is fragile, and she went through hell before joining Safe Haven. I don't want to hurt her any more than she's already been hurt by giving her hope and then taking it away."

"Do you have feelings for her?"

"I think that's quite obvious."

Leon seemed to be mulling over something, but then shook his head and said nothing.

"What do you want to ask?"

"It's none of my business." He took a sip of his coffee.

"What's on your mind, Leon? We've been friends and partners for a long time. You are like a brother to me, and nothing you can say will offend me."

"I'll remind you of that when you swing a punch at me." He put his mug down and pushed it aside before turning back to face Bowen. "When I met Ana, all I could think about was making her mine. I was fighting it with everything I had, but she obliterated my resistance because she felt the same. I know that you and Margaret like each other, but I don't sense that overpowering need to get naked together from either of you."

"She's recuperating from surgery, and she has a cast on her entire leg. I can't think of her as a sexual being when she's hurting and so breakable. And as for Margaret, I think that she doesn't believe in her own appeal, so she's afraid of letting herself feel anything other than friendship toward me."

Seeing that no punch was heading his way, Leon lifted his mug and took another sip. "Unless you try, you won't know. Don't let Margaret return to Safe Haven without making sure. She might be your one."

Bowen shook his head. "How do you propose I do that?"

"Easy. Make love to the woman, just be gentle."

Bowen winced. "I'm afraid to touch her the wrong way and undo all the progress she's made. Besides, I know nothing about wooing a woman, romancing her. All I know is how to seduce women for hookups."

Leon pulled out his phone. "I'm sending you a link."

Bowen chuckled. "What for? Dating advice?"

"How to make love to a woman whose leg is in a cast."

"Don't tell me there is an instructional YouTube about that."

"It's an article written by a woman who had surgery on her knee just like Margaret, and how she managed to have sex safely despite the cast. She gives a lot of practical advice."

Arching a brow, Bowen crossed his arms over his chest. "Did you actually research that?"

"Anastasia did on the way here."

"Oh, that's just great. You two had nothing better to do than to plan how to get Margaret and me in bed?"

"Ana is really excited about the possibility of her best friend being a Dormant. She's already making plans for how the two of them will live in the village and get to hang out together."

"It still doesn't solve my problem of how to approach Margaret. I've been playing the role of the Good Samaritan. How do I switch to being a romantic interest?"

"You can start by asking her out on a date. Margaret would love that. And then you seduce her. Come on, Bowen, you're not a kid. I don't need to explain the birds and the bees to you."

Bowen groaned. "If she's a Dormant, I don't want to induce her transition without her consent, and I can't ask her consent before I'm sure that she's the one for me."

"You said that she's easy to thrall."

"So?"

"Use condoms until you are sure of your love for her and her love for you, and then get her consent before going bareback."

"I don't have any."

Smirking, Leon rose to his feet. "Lucky for you, you have a friend who thinks of everything. Ana and I stopped at a Walgreens on the way, and I got you enough condoms to last you a couple of weeks." He headed for the bedroom he shared with Anastasia. "I'll get them for you."

Bowen shook his head. "I don't know if I should be mad at you or thank you."

"Thank me. You are definitely going to thank me."

11

ONEGUS

Onegus tossed the key to the valet. "Take good care of my baby."

"I will." The young guy eagerly sat behind the wheel of Onegus's borrowed black Porsche and drove away.

Onegus had a room reserved at the hotel, but he still hadn't decided whether he was going to spend the night there. The drive to the village wasn't long, and staying in the hotel was more a safety precaution than a convenience. The paparazzi would certainly try to follow him, and some would lurk in the vicinity throughout the night, but there would be fewer of them tomorrow, and losing them would be easier during the day, using Turner's mall parking lot trick.

Fixing his bow tie, Onegus strode through the front doors and headed straight for the podium. As the official host of the event, he was the first speaker, and therefore had arrived early, but he wasn't the first one there. About a quarter of the guests were already sitting at the tables, the men in black suits and tuxedos, the ladies in evening gowns and sparkling jewelry.

Waiters in white jackets and black bow ties circled between the tables, taking drink orders and serving hors d'oeuvres.

As people turned to look at him, Onegus flashed them his signature broad smile, waved at those he recognized, and scanned the faces of those he didn't for potential trouble later on.

So far, it seemed like not many young socialites had made it to the event, but he knew he wouldn't be that lucky.

"Onegus." Brandon waved him over. "Meet my very dear friend Mrs. Warbleton."

"Enchanted." Onegus leaned and took the matron's gnarly hand, brushing his lips over the back of it.

"I'm sure." She flashed him a smile full of pearly white teeth. "I'm looking forward to hearing your speech." She leaned closer. "I hope it's not too long."

"It isn't. I promise."

"Good. When you're done, come back to my table. I want you to meet my granddaughter. She's a lovely young lady, and she's single." The matron winked.

He forced a smile. "It would be my pleasure."

Great. The evening hadn't started yet, and he was already getting propositioned.

Well, at least the woman's granddaughter wasn't a gold-digger. Mrs. Warbleton was one of the richest women in the country, but not many knew her by her married name, which was how she preferred it.

At the podium, Onegus pulled out his notes and read over them one more time. By now, he had them memorized and could deliver the speech without looking at them, but it never hurt to keep them at the ready.

When he was done, he lifted his eyes to scan the crowd again, glancing at Mrs. Warbleton's table to see if her granddaughter had arrived. Perhaps if he flirted with the woman, her grandmother would make a larger contribution.

Onegus didn't like the idea of pimping himself out, but he could stomach a little innocent flirting for a very deserving cause.

The matron's table was filling up, but none of the guests was a young woman, and he moved his eyes to the next table over.

Now, that was a woman he wouldn't have minded doing more than flirting with. Tall and willowy, she had a model's body and posture but not the vacuous stare so many beautiful women wore. She looked regal, confident, and a little bitchy, which he didn't mind in the least.

A gorgeous woman like her was probably accustomed to fending off overzealous male advances, and the sneering expression was her defense against unwanted attention. She reminded him a little of Rihanna, just minus the curves, and she was taller, towering over the guy she was with. She was all sharp angles, except for her ass. It was small, but perfectly rounded.

The woman was simply spectacular.

The top of her dress had sheer panels, but it wasn't immodest, just a little daring, her hair and makeup were impeccable, and her jewelry perfectly matched her outfit. She either had an exceptional stylist or great taste.

He recognized the guy she was with, the founder of a cosmetics company that had been growing exponentially over the last several years. He'd attended the gala last year, but Onegus couldn't remember who his companion had been. It certainly wasn't the stunning beauty he'd brought this time.

Onegus would have remembered her.

The only reason he remembered the guy was the generous contribution he had made last year, and the name of his company that was a clever play on those books that had been all the rave a decade ago—Fifty Shades of Beauty. The name was easy to remember, not only because of the books bearing a similar name, but also because of the monthly boxes full of his company's cosmetics that had been arriving like clockwork at the sanctuary and the halfway house ever since last year's gala.

Was she his wife? His lover?

She smiled at something the guy had said, and then turned to the woman sitting on her other side and struck up a conversation. It was hard to tell whether the two were romantically involved.

Onegus was staring, and at some point she must have felt his eyes on her and turned, pinning him with her intense dark eyes.

He flashed her one of his practiced charming smiles, but she didn't smile back. Her eyes lingered on him for a moment longer, and then she turned back to her companion as if Onegus wasn't worth her time.

Damn, it hurt.

Usually, women undressed him with their eyes and salivated over his good looks, even when they were with someone else.

Onegus wasn't used to being ignored.

Perhaps she was in love with the cosmetics guy, which would be a damn shame.

CASSANDRA

*W*ow, talk about a punch to the gut.

Cassandra averted her eyes to sever the sizzling electrical current the guy's smile had sent straight to her core.

He was seriously gorgeous, but when he smiled, he was devastating.

She leaned toward Kevin. "Who's the guy on the podium?"

"That's Onegus McLean. The head of the 'Save Them' charity foundation."

She'd heard about him from Kevin. The elusive billionaire who only showed his face to the public to solicit donations for the charity his international conglomerate had started.

Except, the guy didn't look like any billionaire she'd ever seen on television or in the news. Elon Musk was handsome, but he had nothing on Onegus McLean. Billionaires who looked like that could only be found on the covers of romance novels.

Kevin smirked. "Handsome fellow, isn't he?"

"I guess." Cassandra pretended indifference. "Since when is the charity called Save Them? What happened to Save the Girls?"

"Some of the trafficking victims are boys, so they changed the name to Save Them."

"They could have called it Save the Girls and Boys. 'Save Them' sounds weird."

Kevin arched a brow. "Are you putting your foot in your mouth again, Cassy? That's not PC. What if some of the victims don't identify as either?"

"Right." She crossed her arms over her chest. "They need to reinvent the language and call everyone they and them. As is it now, it's too damn confusing."

Cassandra was only thirty-four, but she was already too old to understand the new generation and its new rules of propriety. Half of her altercations with her employees and coworkers were over perceived offenses. At least she was spared being called racist, but it was only a matter of time before someone found a way to pin that on her as well.

Kevin, who was more than a decade older than her, had a good grasp on all that PC stuff. She wondered if he had secretly researched the latest guidelines or was just better at absorbing them than she was.

"Distinguished guests!" Onegus's rich baritone sounded over the loudspeakers. "It's a great pleasure for me to be here today."

He looked straight at Cassandra as if he was addressing her alone.

"First, I want to share with you the tremendous difference your contributions have made in the lives of the rescued victims of trafficking. Without your help, we would have been forced to limit the number of residents in our sanctuary and in the halfway house, sending these young people back into the world before they were ready. Instead, they can stay for as long as they need to, allowing time for healing and recovery. The support we provide is so much more than just a temporary shelter. We are providing them with the tools necessary to not only survive, but also to flourish, so when they are ready to spread their wings, they can do more than fly away. They can soar."

There was a round of applause, after which Onegus told a few personal anecdotes, and how he had been inspired to help trafficking victims after a friend's daughter had been lured into a trap but saved in the nick of time.

He finished with a couple of jokes and then encouraged the guests to donate lavishly, pledging to match each contribution to double the evening's proceeds.

The guy was charming, funny, compassionate, and looked like a movie star. The audience was eating it up, and Cassandra wasn't immune, catching herself gazing at him dreamingly and imagining what it would be like to have a man like him.

Except it was all a show, and the guy was probably a spoiled playboy who hadn't worked a day in his life. The international conglomerate most likely belonged to his family, and he was just the pretty face that they used for public speaking.

She was willing to bet that all that charm was an act, and that in real life, the guy was a stuck-up snob with a stick up his ass the size of a flagpole.

When he was done and people rose to their feet and applauded him, he bowed his head politely, and smiled that panty-melting smile of his.

"Thank you." He dipped his head again.

As Onegus stepped down, someone else got up on the podium. "Let's give it up one more time for Mr. Onegus McLean."

Everyone clapped again, and then it was Kevin's turn to give his speech.

"Come on, Cassy. Do your part."

Plastering a smile on her face, she followed him up to the podium and struck a pose. That was her damn part. To be Kevin's prop for the evening, and for her so-called Cinderella story to provide him with free publicity.

"You owe me big time for this," she hissed.

He kept on smiling while the photographers went into a snapping frenzy. "Whatever you want, it's yours. You're worth it."

13

ONEGUS

*O*negus pretended to listen to Kevin Brunswick's speech, smiling politely and clapping when everyone else clapped, but his entire focus was on the stunning lady standing next to the guy.

When Kevin turned and smiled at his companion, though, Onegus snapped to attention.

"I would like to introduce my Fifty Shades of Beauty creative director, Cassandra Beaumont."

Everyone clapped again.

"Cassandra started in my company as a model, but she soon proved to be so much more than that. If there is one person I should credit with my company's rapid success, it is my beautiful and incredibly talented vice president. Give her a round of applause."

As the guests clapped and the photographers snapped away, Cassandra forced a smile and dipped her head. "Thank you," she said to the microphone and then moved aside, giving the stage back to her boss.

She was comfortable in front of the cameras, striking a well-practiced pose and turning her head to just the right angle so they would get her best side. Still, Onegus could tell that she didn't like being up there and was struggling to hide how pissed she was. Her smile never reached her eyes, and she glared daggers at her boss.

Evidently, she hadn't been on board for his little publicity stunt. A beauty rising from rags to riches thanks to hard work and extraordinary talent made a good story, and the free publicity Fifty Shades of Beauty would get out of it was priceless.

He had her name now, and she wasn't just a pretty face, a piece of eye-candy on Kevin's arm. She was a creative director of a large cosmetics company and Kevin's vice president. Pretty impressive for such a young woman.

No wonder she radiated confidence.

Cassandra wasn't a kid, though. Onegus estimated her to be in her late twenties or early thirties, which made her absolutely perfect. He liked his women to be more mature and to have a mind in addition to looks.

And as an added bonus, she wasn't at the gala to snatch a rich husband or a sugar daddy.

Not that he had any objections to being the latter, but she didn't need his money. He had no doubt that the position Cassandra held in Kevin's company came with an appropriate salary.

The only question was whether she was taken.

Several rings adorned her long, elegant fingers, but none looked like a wedding or an engagement ring. Except, that didn't mean a thing these days. She could be married and not wear a wedding ring, or she could be cohabiting with a partner.

Onegus had a rule against seducing married women, and that included those who had live-in boyfriends.

When all the speeches were done and everyone had made their pledges, dinner was served, and after that the mingling part of the event finally arrived. Usually that was the part of the evening he hated the most, but not tonight.

Excusing himself from his dinner companions, Onegus beelined straight to where Cassandra and Kevin were standing and talking with several of the other guests.

"Good speech." He clapped Kevin on the back and smiled at Cassandra.

"Yours was too." The guy offered Onegus his hand. "How much was collected tonight?"

"I have no clue." He offered his hand to her. "It's a pleasure to make your acquaintance, Ms. Beaumont. I'm Onegus McLean."

"I know who you are, Mr. McLean."

She reluctantly put her slender hand in his, and it was like getting zapped with a high-voltage current, but not in a sexual way.

"Wow." She pulled her hand out of his. "Static electricity." She smoothed it over the side of her dress. "It must be the fabric. Or maybe the shoes."

As she stuck one dainty stiletto-clad foot out from under the long skirt, Onegus had the absurd urge to kneel on the floor, wrap his hand around her ankle, and remove the shoe.

Why?

He had no clue. It wasn't as if he had a shoe fetish, and he'd never gotten excited over a woman's foot, but hers was just so perfectly shaped, and her skin so perfectly smooth that he wanted to lick it all over.

"If you'll excuse me." She smiled nervously. "I need to powder my nose."

Onegus stifled a chuckle. That used to be a polite way for ladies to say they needed to use the bathroom, but nowadays it had a very different meaning that had to do with a certain drug that was in powder form. He wondered whether Cassandra knew that. She was too young for the old expression, but perhaps a little too old to realize what the latest generation of young humans used it for.

In Cassandra's case, though, it was probably neither. For some reason, she wanted to get away from him.

Perhaps the curious sparks between them had unnerved her.

She arched one perfectly shaped brow. "What's so amusing? Did I miss a joke?"

He leaned closer. "I'll tell you when you return from powdering your nose."

As her lush lips thinned out into a stubborn expression, he expected her to insist that he tell her now and not later, but she must have thought better of it and forced a polite smile before turning to start toward the bathrooms.

Damn, she had a fine ass. And that runway walk was causing him all kinds of trouble.

With an effort, Onegus tore his eyes away from her sashaying hips.

He had no intentions of letting her escape. She couldn't run off without Kevin, who was most likely her ride home, and Onegus planned on keeping him engaged until Cassandra's return.

Perhaps while she was gone he would coax more information about her from her boss, specifically whether she was married or had a steady boyfriend.

14

CASSANDRA

*A*s Cassandra turned away from the infuriatingly handsome billionaire, she let out a muted relieved breath. Walking toward the restrooms, she could feel his heated gaze on her back, and the contrary part of her decided to give him something worth looking at, a version of a runway walk that would leave him panting for what he couldn't get.

Damn, the guy was hot. If he made a move on her, it would take all her formidable defenses to keep him at arm's length.

And what in the name of the devil was that electrical current that had arced between them?

Cassandra was attracted to Onegus, so she'd expected some reaction when she put her hand in his large paw, but instead of a pleasant tingling or excited butterflies in her stomach, she'd produced an energy zap that had nearly knocked her off her Louboutins.

Hopefully, it wasn't her witchy power reacting to him. Or perhaps it was?

Other than being too handsome, too tall, too rich, and too charming, Onegus McLean hadn't done anything to aggravate her enough to cause such an instant spike.

It must have been her subconscious thought process that had caused her power to suddenly unleash, and now that she had allowed those thoughts to surface, her anger simmered close beneath her skin. It was good that she'd released some of it earlier, or she would have been in trouble.

The guy probably thought he could get any woman he wanted, but if he tried anything with her, he would discover that wasn't so. Cassandra didn't do hookups, and she didn't compromise on anything less than a man's full and dedicated attention, and a genuine effort to win her heart. Onegus was too smooth and too everything else to be anything other than a player.

It was a shame, and a tiny part of her hoped that she was wrong, but her rational mind knew better. If McLean ever had a serious relationship, it would be with an heiress, someone just as rich as he was. People like him didn't marry for love. They married for political gain or business advantage or both and had lovers on the side.

Prejudice much? A small voice in the back of her head whispered. Perhaps he was a perfectly nice guy who was looking for the love of his life?

Right.

Onegus wasn't freaking Prince Charming, and she wasn't freaking Cinderella.

It was true that she'd come from basically nothing, but Cassandra had made something of herself with hard work and dedication. If anyone was her Prince Charming, it was Kevin, and thankfully he'd done it not because he'd fallen in love with her, but because he'd recognized her talent and believed in her.

His gamble on her had paid off big time. From a small company that had been barely making it, Fifty Shades of Beauty had become a national brand, and it wasn't thanks to how great the products themselves were, but thanks to her cohesive branding and marketing.

After finishing in the restroom, Cassandra fixed her lipstick, checked her updo for any strays, and when there was nothing else to justify her prolonged stay in the ladies' room, she squared her shoulders and walked out.

Hopefully, Onegus had moved on to his next victim, and she could grab Kevin and tell him that she wanted to leave. Josie's concert should have ended a long time ago, and he was no doubt eager to go home to her.

No such luck.

Onegus and Kevin were still standing in the same spot she'd left them.

Cassandra huffed out an annoyed breath. So be it. She wasn't embarrassed about asking Kevin to take her home in front of their host.

Onegus must have sensed her approaching and turned around, flashing her that beautiful panty-melting smile of his. "Here you are. I thought that you got lost."

She arched a brow. "I'm surprised you're still here." It was rude, even she knew that, but he was pushing her buttons without intending to.

Onegus leaned closer, his breath tickling her ear. "I promised to tell you why powdering your pretty nose amused me, and I never break my promises."

"Really?"

"Really. Come dance with me and I'll tell you."

She crossed her arms over her chest. "Tell me now."

Kevin chuckled and then waved at someone. "I'm going to say hi to Bob Grinberg." The traitor walked away, leaving her alone with their host.

"Come on, Cassandra. Just one dance. I promise not to bite." He winked. "For now."

He was so full of himself. But to refuse was to admit that he scared her. Well, not that he was scary. It was her attraction to the bad boy billionaire that was frightening.

"Fine." She put her hand in his and let him lead her to the dance floor. "But just so you know, I have two left feet, and I don't know these kinds of dances."

He looked down. "Your feet look absolutely perfect to me."

Finding them a spot on the crowded dance floor, he put his hand on her waist while holding the other. "Just let loose and follow my lead."

The man knew how to dance, and he was being a perfect gentleman, not trying to bring her too close against his body or holding her too tightly, and after a minute or two she started to relax.

Well, she wouldn't call it relaxed when her body hummed with need, and she was reining in the traitorous rioting hormones with sheer willpower.

"Where did you learn to dance like that?" she asked just to break the silence.

"My mother taught me."

"Are you close to your mother?"

"We talk once a week, and I visit her at least twice a year. She lives in Scotland."

A man who cared about his mother couldn't be too bad.

"What about your father? Are you close to him?"

"He passed away a long time ago."

After leaving his fortune to his son, but still, the fact that Onegus hadn't pissed it away indicated that he was at least a decent businessman.

"I'm sorry."

He shrugged. "As I said, it was a long time ago. How about you? Are you close to your mother?"

Cassandra smiled. "Very. I still live at home." That usually cooled down most guys.

"That's lovely."

She eyed him from under lowered lashes. "I'm thirty-four."

"So?"

"So, most men find it strange that I still live with my mother."

"I see nothing wrong with a daughter taking care of her mother. I value family above all."

"How do you know that I take care of her?"

"You didn't mention a father, so I assume he is not around and your mother has no one else. Otherwise, you wouldn't have stayed. You are too strong-willed and independent for that, and it's not a financially driven decision either because you must be making a very good living."

"You don't know me."

"True, but no one achieves the level of success you have by being meek." He leaned closer. "I bet that you are supporting your mother, financially and emotionally."

He was either a very good judge of character, or what was more likely, he'd learned all of that from Kevin the traitor.

"I see that you had an interesting conversation with my boss. What else did he tell you about me?"

Onegus grinned. "Nothing that I didn't know already. He said that you are one of a kind and that he's very fortunate to have you. Then he threatened me with bodily harm if I tried to steal you from him."

Cassandra laughed. "He's so full of it." Kevin was in good shape, but he was tiny compared to Onegus who seemed to be built from solid rock. "Nevertheless, I love him for saying that."

15

ONEGUS

*O*negus's good mood had gone straight to hell. "Is there anything going on between you and your boss?"

Her lips a thin line, Cassandra glared at him and then smiled wickedly. "A lot. We spend hours together nearly every day, our heads bent together as we whisper secrets to each other."

She was mocking him, taunting, but that didn't answer his question and he had to make sure. "Are you in love with Kevin?"

Cassandra tilted her head, her dark eyes so intense that he half expected to see flames in them. "You are lucky that you didn't ask if I was sleeping with him, because I wouldn't have deigned to answer and would have just walked away. But you asked whether I was in love with him, so I'll humor you. I love Kevin, and I also love his wife. They are like family to me. Kevin was already married when he took me under his wing, believed in me, and supported me when I doubted myself, and I'm grateful to him for it. But there were never any romantic feelings between us, and all he ever wanted from me was my talent and work ethic. Kevin thinks of me as his little sister and has never hinted at anything else."

Despite all her bluster, Cassandra was naive.

"Kevin seems like a good guy, and he might love his wife with all his heart, but unless he's known you since you were a little girl, I doubt that he can think of you as a sister. Males are just not built like that."

She shrugged. "What he thinks is irrelevant. His actions are what matters." She chuckled. "If I was held responsible for the thoughts running through my head, I would have been arrested on several counts of attempted murder. I feel like killing someone at least once a day, but since I don't actually do it, I'm still a free member of society."

"Very true, and talking about illegal activity reminds me that I haven't told you what powdering your nose means these days."

It took her a couple of seconds to figure it out, and then her eyes widened. "No way. Are you sure? I've never heard that before." Her beautiful lips twisted in a grimace. "But then I don't get out much. I'm all work and no play."

He nodded. "I'm afraid so. If you don't want people to think that you are going to the bathroom to snort cocaine, you need to find another polite expression for excusing yourself."

"That's so twisted." She shook her head. "I don't get this new generation. Perhaps it's because I skipped the last two years of high school and never went to college. I wasn't exposed to all those changes."

He was surprised. Cassandra was way too smart to drop out of high school. She must have opted for homeschooling and had acquired her marketing skills in other ways. There were so many online courses these days, some even from fully accredited universities, that attending a brick-and-mortar institution was no longer the only or even best way to get an education.

"What made you switch to homeschooling?"

She smiled. "I'm glad you didn't assume that I dropped out."

Her stiff posture softened, and as the song ended, Cassandra made no move to pull out of his arms. When the next one started, they resumed dancing.

"You're too smart for that." His hand on the small of her back, he drew her a couple of inches closer to his body, but not close enough so their chests were touching.

She didn't resist. "Thank you. We lived in a decent area of the valley, but the local high school was nevertheless overrun by a bad element. I didn't feel safe attending, and I told my mother that I preferred to finish the last two years at home. She agreed provided that my grades wouldn't take a turn for the worse. I graduated a year early with perfect grades."

"Why didn't you continue to college? Was it because you needed to take care of your mother?"

Onegus didn't have a high school diploma or college education either, but that was because those hadn't been available to him when he was a young lad.

His mother and his uncles had taught him what he'd needed to know, and the rest he'd learned on his own and was still learning. Knowledge wasn't a stagnant thing, and continuous education was a must.

Cassandra's expression turned thoughtful. "That wasn't the reason. I don't want you to get the wrong impression of my mother. She's not disabled. She just has memory problems from time to time, but she can mostly take care of herself. I couldn't go away to college, but I could've gone locally. I went for one semester, decided that it was a waste of time and money, and quit. I learned what I needed from online courses."

"Smart and frugal. I like it."

She gazed at him from under lowered lashes. "What would a rich guy like you know about being frugal?"

"A lot more than you think."

16

CASSANDRA

"*A* frugal billionaire. Well, I guess it's possible. I read that Warren Buffett lives in a modest house and drives an old pickup truck. How about you? Do you live in a mansion?"

"Nope. I live in a nice two-bedroom house, which I share with a roommate." He smiled. "Who's a guy, in case you are wondering whether I'm single."

"Are you?"

"Very."

"I find it hard to believe. You are a rich, handsome guy."

"I'm also very busy, and I don't get out much. We have that in common."

He probably used that line on all the hookups he collected. "Let me guess. You probably travel a lot as well."

That was another line that guys used to explain why they were not available. It was a perfect excuse for when they were testing the waters with someone else or just wanted to keep things casual.

"I travel for work, that's true, but lately not that much. Most of my days are spent in the office, either staring at a computer screen or in meetings. Occasionally, I meet with business associates on their turf, and once in a while, I attend events like this one." His hand on the small of her back caressed her gently through the sheer fabric. "Usually, I don't look forward to them, but I'm glad I came tonight." He drew her a fraction of an inch closer.

Onegus was about to say more, when Kevin got on the dance floor and headed their way.

"I just came to tell you that I'm going home." His eyes twinkled with mischief. "Obviously, you don't have to leave because I do. You can call a taxi, or perhaps Onegus could give you a lift." Kevin jerked his chin toward the photographers who were snapping pictures of her dancing with the dashing billionaire. "They love you."

Damn, she'd been so consumed by Onegus and his overwhelming presence that she hadn't noticed the photographers.

Kevin was practically salivating over the free publicity. Tomorrow, all the gossip magazines would post her picture in Onegus's arms and publish speculative articles about their non-existent fling.

"I'll take you home," Onegus said and then turned to her boss. "Good night, Kevin, and thank you for your generous contribution."

The nerve of the guy.

She cast him a saccharine smile. "Thank you for the offer, but I'd rather Kevin took me home."

Her boss paled. "And miss out on all that?" He pointed at the photographer with his chin again.

Smirking, Onegus leaned to whisper in her ear. "I promise to be a perfect gentleman."

She wasn't worried about him trying anything without her active encouragement. He wasn't the problem. The photographers and reporters were. If she left with him, they would make a story out of it even if all he did was to drive her home.

Kevin put his hand on her exposed shoulder. "Stay a little longer, Cassy, have some fun." His eyes were pleading with her to do as he asked. "It would be better if we didn't leave together if you know what I mean."

Damn him and his pleading eyes. "Same goes for me. I can stay, but I'll take a taxi home."

"Thank you." He leaned and kissed her cheek.

Was it her imagination or had Onegus growled quietly?

"Good night, Kevin." She kissed her boss's cheek back. When he left, she narrowed her eyes at Onegus. "Did you just growl at my boss?"

Assuming an innocent expression, he shrugged. "I had something in my throat." He reached for her hand. "Would you like a drink?"

"I would love one. I'm parched."

As they made their way to the bar, Onegus leaned to whisper in her ear, "We don't have to leave the hotel together. In fact, we don't need to leave at all. I have a suite upstairs, and we can sneak out one at a time. I can order coffee, and we can keep talking in private."

Right. Talking.

Well, at least he was trying to be polite.

It would be a lie if she claimed his proposition wasn't tempting. Onegus was the sexiest man she'd ever met or ever would, and to be with him, she might have considered bending her no hookups rule a little. But there was no way she was staying the night and then doing the walk of shame the next morning in her gala dress.

"I need to go home soon. My mom will be worried if I'm not back by midnight."

He arched a brow. "Can't you call her? You're thirty-four, not fourteen. You can tell your mother that you're having a good time and will come home later than usual."

"Do you mean the next morning?"

He smiled. "If I'm very lucky."

"Well, you are not."

"What's wrong with me?"

"Nothing." He was perfect, but his ego was inflated enough as it was.

"What would you like to drink?" he asked as they reached the bar.

"Vodka Cranberry."

He told the barman their choices, and when their drinks were ready, led her out onto the terrace, where several of the guests were smoking fat cigars.

"Is it allowed to smoke out here?" She leaned against the railing.

Onegus shrugged. "It's not my job to enforce the rules in this hotel."

It was an odd answer, but she shrugged it off and took a sip of her drink.

Leaning against the railing next to her, Onegus sipped on his whiskey for several long moments. "Are you involved with someone?"

"No."

"Don't you like me?"

She rolled her eyes. "What's not to like?"

"Then why not come up to my hotel room?"

"I don't do hookups, Onegus. And even if I did, I wouldn't do that here with photographers and reporters following us around. There is only so much that I'm willing to do to generate free publicity for Fifty Shades of Beauty."

"Is that why you danced with me?"

She wondered whether the vulnerable note she detected in his voice was genuine or an act.

"I enjoy your company, Onegus, and I like you, but if you are interested in more, you'll have to do it the old-fashioned way. Ask me on a date, come to my house and meet my mother, call me, ask me on another date, and so on. I'm not going to settle for less."

17

ONEGUS

On a gut level, Onegus had known that Cassandra wouldn't be an easy conquest, but it was rare that a woman her age adhered to such old-fashioned standards of dating. Most were more than happy to engage in casual hookups and had very few expectations from him, if any.

Maybe he was old-fashioned as well. He liked that Cassandra was demanding, that she was confident enough to believe that she deserved the investment of time and effort, and that sex was not a casual thing for her.

When she shivered, he wrapped his arm around her. "Do you want to go back in?"

"No, I like it out here. Especially since the photographers and reporters stayed inside."

His doing, but she had no way of knowing that. One signal to the guy in charge of security, and no reporter or photographer was allowed to go out on the terrace.

"Hold my drink." He handed her his glass and shrugged his jacket off. "Here you go." He wrapped it around her shoulders. "Better?"

Her eyes roaming over his white dress shirt, she licked her lips. "Much, thank you."

He chuckled. "If you wish, I can drive you home, come in, and introduce myself to your mother. That would take care of one item on your list. Then you can change into something more comfortable but leave the shoes on. They are sexy as hell."

Stifling a smile, she huddled inside his much too large jacket. "Thanks for the offer, but it's still a no."

"Can't blame a guy for trying." He sighed dramatically

"Invite me on several dates, and after a couple of months, you can try again."

He groaned. "You're killing me, Cassandra."

"You'll live."

Shaking his head, he reached into the jacket pocket and pulled out his phone. "Give me your number. I'm going to start tomorrow."

"I'd rather take yours."

He narrowed his eyes at her. "Nice try, but I know that you are not going to call. Give me your number, Cassandra."

"Why do you think that I'm not going to call?"

"A gut feeling. You probably think that I'm a spoiled rich guy who needs to conquer every woman he meets, and you refuse to be one of many. You want to be the one I fall for."

She shook her head. "I'm not thinking that far into the future, and love is not what I'm after. Not to start with, anyway. I just can't imagine being intimate with anyone who I didn't get to know first. Respect is non-negotiable. I need to know that you respect me, and I need to respect you."

"I respect the hell out of you, Cassandra." He took her hand and brought it to his lips. "You are a worthy woman, and I want to get to know you."

"But?"

"No buts. Just give me your phone number. If you don't, I'm going to call your boss and get it from him."

She narrowed her eyes at him. "I have a better idea. Let's decide on a time and place right now, and I'll meet you there."

"Tomorrow, eleven in the morning, Venice Beach. But I need your number in case I'm delayed."

She looked surprised. "Why the beach? And why so early?"

He leaned toward her and smiled. "So you don't suspect me of asking you out only to seduce you. If we want, we can spend the entire day getting to know each other."

"And then go to your place, right?"

"It will be entirely up to you, my lady."

She smirked. "I love it. But I'm afraid that I'll have to disappoint you."

His forehead furrowed. "What now? If you want to meet somewhere else, just tell me."

"The beach is perfect, but I won't be wearing these sexy shoes for a walk on the sand." She wiggled her stiletto-clad foot.

"Naturally, I'm also going to take you to a restaurant, but it's not a fancy place, and you can wear sneakers if you wish."

She cast him a sidelong glance. "I finally meet a guy tall enough for me to wear heels, and he wants to take me to the beach. A girl just can't catch a break."

"Choose someplace else, then."

"No, I like your idea of spending the day together. If everything goes well, you will just have to take me out on another date somewhere that justifies getting dressed up for."

"Deal." He shook the hand he was still holding on to.

"It was a pleasure doing business with you, Mr. Onegus McLean." She shook it back and then pushed away from the railing. "But if we are to meet tomorrow morning, I need to go home and get some sleep." She started to take his jacket off.

"Keep it. You can get it back to me tomorrow." He smiled. "That will obligate you to actually show up."

Pushing one leg forward, she looked at him down her pretty little nose. "I don't make promises that I don't intend to keep." She pulled her phone out of her evening purse. "What's your number?"

When he arched a brow, she smiled and patted his arm. "I need it so I can call you and so you'll have mine."

1 8

ELEANOR

"Good morning, family." Eleanor walked into the dining room. "How is everyone feeling?"

Vivian cast her a curious look. "You seem in a good mood today."

Parker used the opportunity of his mother and Magnus's attention being diverted to slip Scarlett a slice of roast beef.

The dog snatched it from his fingers, swallowed it in one bite, and was looking at him with pleading puppy eyes, begging for more.

"I am in a great mood." Eleanor poured herself a cup of coffee and pulled out a chair. "And when you hear my announcement, you will be too. I'm moving in with Peter."

Leaning back, Magnus folded his arms over his chest and gave her the displeased father look. "That was fast. Since when did the two of you become an item?"

Stifling a chuckle, Eleanor shook her head. "Peter and I are not dating. Leon and Anastasia are coming to the village soon, and they will need a place of their own. Leon prefers to move into a new house, so there will be room in his old one, and Peter is okay with me as his new roommate. I also no longer need a keeper. Kian trusts me." She took a sip from her coffee. "To a certain extent."

Magnus didn't look happy, which was surprising. He should be glad to be rid of her. "Did you check with Kian or Onegus that you are allowed to move out?"

"Do I need to? I thought that my probation period was over. I'm allowed to come and go as I please, so I'm quite sure I'm allowed to choose where I live as well. I've imposed on your hospitality for long enough."

Vivian put her fork down. "Kian shouldn't mind. I think that Magnus just doesn't want you to leave."

Eleanor snorted. "You're too sweet. Magnus is going to throw a party when I'm gone, true?" She cast him an amused glance.

He shrugged. "I've gotten used to you. The house will feel empty without you."

"I'll miss you," Parker said.

"You can visit me anytime you want. It's not like I'm moving out of town. I'll be a ten-minute walk away."

"It's not the same." He patted the dog's head. "And Scarlett is going to miss you too."

"You can bring her along when you come to visit me."

The dog would probably be the only one who really missed her. Parker was busy with school, and the rest of the time he was hanging out with Lisa. The kid was head over heels in love with the girl, but she had no clue, thinking that they were just buddies.

Was she being as clueless as Lisa?

Moving in with Peter could be a mistake. He was an attractive guy, and she wasn't blind to his charms, but he wasn't her type, and she wasn't his. Still, cohabitation would bring them closer, and things might get dicey.

"When are you moving?" Vivian asked.

"I can move right away, but all of Leon's things are still at the house and I don't want to do the packing for him. I could wait until he and Anastasia come to the village and he takes his stuff to their new house, which will probably be in this section. On the other hand, I'd rather move sooner than later because of Greggory. There will be less of a chance of me bumping into him in the old village."

Magnus cast her a pitying look. "If you don't want to see him, I suggest that you stay away from the café. Now that he's single, he will be hanging out there a lot."

Vivian shook her head. "Eleanor can't avoid the café. Where is she going to meet males? She needs to find someone new."

"Don't worry about me. I meet plenty of people in the training center. The café is not the only hunting ground in the village."

"Gross," Parker murmured.

Magnus clapped him on the back. "Finding a mate is like a treasure hunt. If you don't look, you won't find her."

"Perhaps I already did." He pushed away from the table. "I'm taking Scarlett for a walk."

When he was gone, Vivian sighed. "Lisa is either blind or she's pretending not to see how in love with her Parker is."

"She probably doesn't want to hurt his feelings," Magnus said. "Besides, they are both just kids, and it's nothing more than infatuation."

He didn't sound convincing at all.

"How old were Romeo and Juliet?" Vivian asked. "The young feel everything more fiercely, and first love is the most powerful. Romeo and Juliet were willing to die for each other."

It was possible to fall deeply in love at fourteen, and just as quickly fall out of love. Teenagers saw the world in black and white, and they were either all in or all out.

"Romeo and Juliet weren't immortal," Magnus said. "We operate differently."

He reached for Vivian's small hand and put it on his chest. "We are bound to each other for eternity."

Lucky bastards.

Was there someone out there for her? Or were the fickle Fates ignoring her as usual?

Remembering Emmett's intense dark eyes, a shiver ran down Eleanor's spine. She sincerely hoped that he wasn't the one the Fates had chosen for her. She wanted a nice, uncomplicated guy who would treat her well and have her back, and that wasn't Emmett.

19

VLAD

*V*lad walked into the café expecting to find few if any people sitting at the tables, but it seemed that the pleasant spring weather had drawn many more customers than usual this Sunday morning.

There was no service on Sundays, but people could still buy coffees, sandwiches, and pastries from the vending machines that Jackson kept well-stocked, replenishing them with fresh supplies daily and sometimes twice a day.

Navigating between the tables, Vlad smiled and nodded to those he passed until he found a secluded one that was tucked against the wall of greenery.

He put his art bag down and pulled out a chair.

Coming out here to draw was just an excuse to get out of the house. Wendy had gone shopping with Sharon and Tessa, and Vlad wasn't in the mood to stay in the house or visit his mother and Richard.

He was still reeling from her revelation and hoping that she was wrong. Perhaps she'd gotten pregnant with him before meeting the Kra-ell male and had just assumed that he'd been the father.

After believing his entire life that his father was human, it was a difficult adjustment to accept that he was fathered by a member of another species of immortals.

He hadn't even told Wendy yet.

He hadn't asked Kian to allow him to see the captured Kra-ell either.

Maybe if he pretended that nothing had changed, nothing would. He was still the same guy, too tall, too skinny, and too strong. Had anything changed on the inside with the knowledge that he wasn't like other members of his clan?

He should find out more, ask the Kra-ell male to tell him all he knew about his kind, and figure out if any of it had shaped the man Vlad had become.

Perhaps he would do that after the business with Wendy's father was done. There was only so much that he could deal with at once.

Right now, he had a school assignment he hadn't even started, and it was due on Tuesday. Pulling out his drawing tablet, he moved his chair so the sun wasn't shining directly onto it. Vlad sketched a quick outline, saved it, and opened another layer on top of it for the more precise outlining. He was about to get started on that when he spotted Brundar's long blond ponytail next to the vending machines.

He still hadn't talked to the Guardian as Kian had suggested.

Leaving the tablet behind, he walked over to the coffee machine and swiped his card, pretending like that was what he'd come for.

"Good morning," he murmured to Brundar.

The Guardian only nodded.

"Do you have a moment?"

"For what?" Brundar unwrapped a pastry and took a bite.

"I need to ask you something."

"Ask."

The guy acted as if every word was precious, and he had to be frugal with them.

Vlad leaned closer to the Guardian and lowered his voice. "Kian said that you were once faced with the dilemma of knowingly breaking clan law to seek vengeance. I'm faced with the same dilemma, and I wondered if you can give me advice."

When Brundar just turned around and started walking, Vlad heaved out a sigh, but then the Guardian motioned for him to follow.

When they were out of the café's enclosure, Brundar cast him a sidelong glance. "Stop talking in riddles, and just spit it out."

"You are a Guardian. If I plan on doing something illegal, I shouldn't tell you about it."

A barely perceptible smile lifted one corner of Brundar's mouth. "Talking is not a crime. We will just treat it as hypothetical."

"Right." Vlad pushed his bangs out of his eyes. "Wendy's mother left her when she was a baby, and she's been missing ever since. Her father is a monster who abused his wife and daughter. I want to find out whether he killed Wendy's mother, and to do so, I need to thrall him to get him to talk. I know that thralling humans is allowed only under certain circumstances, and that's not one of them."

"What if you find out that he killed her?"

"I'll thrall him to walk into a police station and confess. Wendy doesn't want his blood on my hands. She wants to kill him herself."

Brundar's expression didn't change. "Would she still want to kill her father if he didn't kill the mother?"

"No."

"What are you going to do if he didn't?"

"I'll make him tell me all he knows about where she might be. If I can find the mother before our wedding and have her attend, it would be the best wedding present I can give Wendy."

Brundar nodded. "Both are worthy goals. My situation was a little different, though. I beat the shit out of Callie's murderous bastard of an ex-husband, forcing him to sign her divorce papers, and then I thralled him to forget me. I wanted her to be free of him. After I did that, I walked into Edna's office, confessed my transgression, and submitted to the punishment such an offense calls for, which is whipping."

Vlad winced. "Didn't Edna take into account the extenuating circumstances?"

"She did. Edna wanted to give me a reduced sentence of a few days of incarceration, but I preferred to be done with it as soon as possible and get back to Callie, so I chose the whipping. If you decide to go through with it, you can ask for the reduced sentence. Just try not to murder the human."

"Do you think I should do it?"

"Murder him?"

"I promised Wendy that I wouldn't, but what if I'm consumed by rage and Richard can't control me?"

"You plan on taking Richard with you?"

Vlad nodded. "He will have to bring a taser. He won't be able to restrain me otherwise."

"If you take him with you, he becomes an accomplice." Brundar turned his eyes heavenward. "Hypothetically speaking, if a civilian breaks the law, it's up to them if they wish to confess. If they are caught later, the punishment might be more severe, but they might also get away with it. And in this hypothetical case, if no bodily harm was done, it might count only as an infraction."

20

CASSANDRA

*C*assandra stood in front of the mirror and grimaced at her reflection. The black shorts were sexy and beach-appropriate, but they were showing too much ass, and Onegus might get the wrong impression.

Or the right one.

Last night, she hadn't been able to fall asleep for hours. Every time she'd closed her eyes, Onegus's gorgeous blue eyes and charming smile had popped behind her lids. Remembering how his large hands had felt on her while they danced had sent sizzling currents through her body, and the only way to release all the pent-up tension had been to pleasure herself while pretending she was with him.

She'd exploded like a firecracker, barely able to stifle the loud moan that had torn out of her throat.

Even now, thinking about him made her nipples stand to attention and her core tingle.

His effect on her was unprecedented and also dangerous.

For the first time ever, the build-up was caused by sexual attraction instead of anger or frustration, but the result was the same. If she didn't release it, things would start to explode. But after her self-righteous speech about needing to get to know each other before getting intimate, she couldn't drag him into her bed and have her way with him.

Cassandra hated playing the age-old game of luring a guy into seducing her and then pretending that she was helpless to resist. She'd never been that girl. Her no was a hard no, and her yes was a definite yes. She didn't send mixed messages, and she didn't play games.

Then again, she was a good-looking, successful woman who'd been without male companionship for most of her life. So maybe she was missing something?

Perhaps all those games other women played were a vital part of the interplay between the sexes, and without them, she seemed uninterested? Unapproachable?

Or was it just her abrasive personality that scared men off?

It hadn't scared Onegus though, which was a big part of her intense attraction to him. He was worthy, his lion strong enough to tame her lioness.

Or not.

Her bizarre destructive power was unpredictable, and its sudden connection to Onegus might put him in danger.

Or not.

Obsessing about what-ifs was pointless.

The shorts would have to do. Paired with a pair of white Keds, a black tank top, and a cute little bomber jacket that was made from fake leather and lace inserts, she looked sexy and casual. The outfit also showcased her long legs and pert bottom.

Onegus was going to salivate.

As Cassandra walked into the living room, her mother lifted her head from the magazine she'd been flipping through and smiled. "You look beautiful, Cassy. Are you meeting with friends?"

She hadn't met with friends since quitting high school, but for her mother, it probably seemed like yesterday.

"Actually, I have a date. I'm meeting a guy, and we are going for a walk on the beach."

"That's lovely." Her mother frowned. "Just stay away from the water. The ocean is dangerous."

Geraldine was terrified of getting even her feet wet at the beach, but she loved sitting on the sand and watching the waves. She also loved swimming in their pool at home, which didn't make sense to Cassandra. Her mother claimed that the vastness of the ocean scared her, and knowing that there were fish and other creatures in the water grossed her out.

"I'm not even wearing a swimsuit." Cassandra parted her jacket to show her mom the tank top. "We are going to a restaurant overlooking Venice Beach, and after that, we are going on a walk."

"Who is the young man? Is he someone from work?"

"You could say so. I met him at the charity event I attended with Kevin."

"Is he handsome?"

"Devastatingly so."

"Oh, my." Her mother's lips lifted in a smile and her hand lifted to her chest. "Just don't let him devastate you."

"It's just an expression."

"Do you have a picture?"

There were probably dozens of them all over the gossip magazines, but Cassandra refused to look. God only knew what kind of trash they had written about her and Onegus.

"I don't have a picture, but he's tall, taller than me with heels on, and built like a tank. He also has a charming smile, blond curly hair that he tries to tame with hair products, blue eyes that twinkle with mischief, and a square, strong jaw." Cassandra chuckled. "He looks like one of the models on your billionaire romance novels."

"Oh, dear. You sound like you are half in love with the man already."

"I'm not." Cassandra leaned and kissed her mother's cheek. "I might be gone the whole day, so don't worry about me. And if you do, just call me or text me, and I'll call you back."

Her mother smiled. "I'm not going to bother you on your date, sweetheart. Besides, I'm not staying home. The book club is meeting for lunch at Danny's."

Geraldine's book club must be the most active one in the entire nation, but Cassandra had a feeling that not all of her mother's book club meetings were about books.

"That's great. Have fun, Mom."

21

ONEGUS

$\mathcal{O}$negus parked his car in Hotel Erwin's self-parking garage and headed to the rooftop bar to wait for Cassandra.

He was half an hour early for their date, plenty of time to relax with a glass of whiskey and ponder the idiocy of asking her on a date.

When she'd made her attitude about hookups clear, he should have let it go, but he just couldn't resist. It was like she'd bewitched him, and he'd had to see her again.

Onegus had no intentions of making it to the second or third date, though. Meeting Cassandra during the day made seduction even less likely, which was why he'd chosen the time and location. His main purpose was to find out more about the peculiar current that had arced between them when they touched.

She'd explained it as static electricity, and he might have accepted that if not for the guilty look that had passed over her eyes. She'd known what had caused it and had tried to cover it up.

A good excuse, but who was he trying to convince?

Onegus was curious about much more than that zap. Cassandra intrigued him, challenged him, and staying away from her required willpower that he was apparently short on. Eventually he would flex that muscle, but today, he would enjoy her company and not think about why letting her go was the decent thing to do.

Sitting with his back to the bar, he watched the roof access as more humans arrived to enjoy the beautiful spring day and the views of Venice Beach below. Couples young and old, holding hands, friends meeting to hang out together, their carefree laughter enviable.

For at least a few hours of the glorious Sunday morning, they were able to forget their daily struggles, their troubles, and just enjoy being.

Onegus wished he could be like them, but despite his easy smiles and seemingly mellow nature, his mind was never at ease. Being in charge of the

Guardian force and the clan's security was a huge responsibility, and his occasional sojourns as Kian's stand-in were a welcome break.

Motioning to the barman with the empty glass, he asked for a refill.

It was a little early in the day for another shot of whiskey, but with his immortal metabolism, it would take much more for him to feel even a slight buzz.

When the barman handed him a fresh one, Onegus turned around and nearly dropped the glass.

Cassandra was even more beautiful in casual attire and minimal makeup than she had been when all decked out in her evening gown.

She smiled as she waved at him, sauntering over in her tiny black shorts and white sneakers. Her legs went on forever, the skin on them so smooth that it gleamed in the sun. Had she smeared suntan oil all over her legs? Or did her skin shine naturally?

"Good morning." He rose to his feet and leaned to kiss her cheek.

"Good morning to you too." She took a step back. "Are you sure that you are not a vampire?"

Onegus tensed. Were his fangs showing?

Usually, he had excellent control over every part of his body, including the scents that could reveal his emotions to other immortals. That was one of the things that made him such a good chief and negotiator for Kian. But it had been centuries since a female had elicited such a strong response from him.

"What do you mean?" He put his hand on the small of her back and led her to the table he'd reserved.

As they passed by the other guests, there was no male who didn't devour her with his eyes, and Onegus had to stifle the urge to growl a warning that would have them cowering beneath the tables.

"I didn't notice it last night, but you look like you haven't been out in the sun in years. You are so white that it's blinding." She pretended to shield her eyes from the glare. "I hope that you put sunscreen on before leaving your lair or you will turn red like a cooked shrimp."

Onegus couldn't get a tan even if he wanted to. His body's self-healing would take care of that. "I have to admit that I didn't." He pulled out a chair for her. "But I probably should have." He waited until she sat down before taking the seat next to her.

Lifting her large purse, Cassandra sifted through the contents and pulled out a small tube. "You're lucky that I always carry sunscreen with me. If there is one thing you can do to slow down aging, it's to put it on every morning even if you don't plan on being out in the sun. Especially with fair skin like yours, wrinkles and dark spots are not the only things to worry about."

She handed it to him. "At least cover your face, and don't forget your ears, your nose, and the back of your neck."

2 2

CASSANDRA

"*Y*es, ma'am." Onegus popped the cover and squeezed out a small dollop into the palm of his hand.

Thankfully, he was still smiling after her idiotic tirade about his paleness and sunscreen. Had she put her foot in it again by bringing up a taboo subject?

And then she'd made things worse by lecturing him about it.

Cassandra was socially inept on most days, but the impact of seeing Onegus with those powerful muscles of his on display had scrambled her brain, making it much worse.

He'd looked amazing in a tux, and when he'd taken his jacket off, she'd seen the outline of those biceps through his dress shirt. But the white short-sleeved button-down that was open at the throat was much more revealing. He looked good enough to eat in it, not to mention the jeans, which were lovingly hugging his muscular thighs.

Distracted by her thoughts, she hadn't noticed the strange way he was going about smearing the sunscreen on his face until he asked, "Am I doing it right?"

He had a big white spot on his nose and two more on his cheeks. The rest of the sunscreen was still on the palm of his hand, and he was using it by dipping a finger in it and dabbing it on his face.

She chuckled. "Do you mind if I do that?"

"Not at all."

Leaning over the table, she gently spread the sunscreen all over his face, including behind his ears. The guy didn't have any wrinkles or dark spots, and his skin was smooth and soft, as if he got daily facials.

"How do you manage to have such great skin when you don't even know how to put sunscreen on?"

"I spend most of my days in a windowless office." He smiled, and her core clenched. "I guess I live like a vampire. Usually, when I leave the office, it's already dark outside."

She arched a brow. "A billionaire working in an office with no windows? How come? Are you afraid of someone spying on you through the glass?"

As his smile faltered, Cassandra wondered whether she'd committed another faux pas. She was so bad at simple social interactions that it was pathetic.

Perhaps she should hire a coach.

He leaned over the table. "I'll let you in on a secret. I'm just an employee, and I don't own the family business empire. Are you disappointed?"

Actually, it was a huge relief. If he was just a regular guy, working for his family's business, there was a chance that they could have a normal relationship. Provided that she didn't blow it up, that is, figuratively speaking or literally.

"I'm terribly disappointed." She leaned back and crossed her arms over her chest, pretending to be mad. "I finally meet a billionaire who looks like the ones on the covers of romance novels, and he turns out to be just a poor schmo, whose office is in the basement."

Onegus's left brow lifted. "I didn't say that I was poor. I'm not a billionaire, but I'm quite wealthy. And as for my office, I choose to work underground for various reasons."

Bummer.

Uncrossing her arms, Cassandra let out a sigh. "That's a shame. I was hoping that you were an ordinary person like me."

"There is nothing ordinary about you." He reached for her hand and clasped it in his much larger one. "You are radiating with inner power, and I find it sexy as hell."

Yeah, sexy, until things started exploding.

So far she'd been lucky, but if he kept looking at her like that, she wouldn't be able to contain that energy for much longer.

Perhaps a quick trip to the ladies' room was in order?

Gross.

Besides, how did he know?

The most anyone ever suspected her of was being a jinx. Kevin often joked about the office gremlins who caused pottery to crack, or the phones to malfunction, and all the other small damages that her temper had been responsible for.

"What's that grimace for?" Onegus asked.

"What did you mean by power?"

"I can sense it. It's like your body is humming with an electric current. Can't you feel it?"

"I don't know what you're talking about."

"Liar." He smiled and lifted her hand to his lips. "Remember what happened when our hands touched last night?"

She shrugged. "It was static electricity. It's not happening now, is it?"

He eyed her from under his dense, blond lashes. "I can still feel it, and it turns me on."

Cassandra scrambled for a quick change of topic.

"By the way, I didn't forget your jacket. I have it in my car. Remind me to give it back to you before we leave."

"There is no rush." He lifted his hand and motioned for the waiter to come to their table. "You are mine for the entire day."

She pulled her hand out of his. "What if I have other plans?"

"Do you?"

"No, but you shouldn't assume."

He dipped his head. "My apologies. It has been a very long time since I last dated, and I'm out of practice."

With his admission, a warm feeling washed over Cassandra, which was very strange since she could think of only one reason a gorgeous man like him hadn't been dating. He must have been married, and it had ended recently. But she was comforted by the fact that he was also unsure and fumbled with social rules.

"Apology accepted. God knows that I have no right to preach about etiquette."

23

ONEGUS

*O*negus was enjoying himself way more than he should.

After a couple of drinks, Cassandra had loosened up, her smiles were coming in more easily, and she'd become less guarded.

Other than getting upset over the slow service and the waiter's dismissive attitude, Cassandra seemed to be enjoying his company as much as he was enjoying hers, but she was still far from trusting him.

So far, she'd refused to acknowledge the swirling energy he sensed in her, flat out denying that it even existed. One explanation could be that she wasn't aware of it, the other that she was afraid to admit it, which raised the question of why.

It had intensified when she'd gotten angry, leading him to believe that it was connected to her emotions.

As the waiter dropped their bill on the table and left, Onegus pulled a couple of hundreds out of his wallet and put them inside the folder.

"Are you ready for a walk on the beach?" He rose to his feet.

She was still eyeing the money he'd left. "We need to wait for the waiter to bring you the change."

"That's okay. He can keep the rest."

She shook her head. "That's a very generous tip, and it wasn't earned. The guy did a lousy job serving us, and he was cranky."

"True, but it wasn't his fault. He was the only waiter up here, serving all the tables by himself." He offered her a hand up.

"I don't think it's right to reward a subpar performance." She took his hand reluctantly, and just like the day before, the current arced between them.

"Did you feel that?"

She waved her other hand in dismissal. "Static electricity again. We must have opposite charges or something." She glanced in the waiter's direction. "He didn't even ask if we needed anything else before dropping the bill on the table, and you left him an eighty-dollar tip."

"How do you know that? You didn't see the bill."

"I didn't have to. I estimated how much our lunch and drinks cost given the prices on the menu."

He chuckled. "Let it go, Cassandra. It's not worth getting upset over."

"Yeah, you're right." She sent another baleful look at the waiter before lifting her bag and slinging the strap across her body.

As they started to walk away, someone dropped a glass, cursing as shards and liquids spread over the floor.

Onegus slowed his steps, but Cassandra ignored the incident as if nothing had happened and tugged on his hand, pulling him behind her.

"I want to see if anyone got hurt."

"It was just a glass. Nothing major." She kept walking.

For some reason, he had a feeling there was a connection between the drop of energy he sensed from her and the shattered glass.

Telekinesis?

He'd never met anyone who actually possessed the talent, and those he'd heard about sounded like charlatans. That didn't mean that the talent didn't exist, though.

Could Cassandra have somehow caused the glass to fall?

Only that didn't make much sense. If she wanted to get back at the waiter, she would have directed her power at a glass he was holding and not at some random customer. Then again, her intention might have been to create more work for him.

After all, the waiter would have to clean up the mess.

In all likelihood, she'd had nothing to do with it, and it was just his wishful thinking. A paranormal talent was a possible indicator of dormancy, and Onegus would have loved Cassandra to be one.

If she was a potential Dormant, he would be justified in seeking another date with her, seducing her, making love to her.

Fates, how he wanted to strip the hellcat naked, grab her succulent ass in his hands, and have his way with her. He had no doubt that she would be magnificent.

As they left the boardwalk and neared the waterline, Cassandra pulled the tube of sunscreen out of her purse. "You should reapply the sunscreen. It has been more than two hours since you applied it last."

Remembering how it felt to have her gentle fingers smearing the lotion on his face, he nodded. "Sure, why not?"

When she offered him the tube, he shook his head. "You'd better put it on me. You've seen how bad I am with that."

"Okay." She flipped the cap and squeezed a dollop into the palm of her hand.

Cassandra was tall, but without the stilettos she was still half a head shorter than Onegus, and as she looked up at him, her eyes zeroed in on his lips.

Did she want him to kiss her?

24

CASSANDRA

*D*amn, the guy had the most kissable lips. And those aquamarine eyes of his beheld her with such stark need that Cassandra found herself tilting toward him and parting her lips.

"You keep looking at me like that, and I'm going to kiss you regardless of who's watching."

Yes, she wanted to say. *Do it*. But that was such a bad idea.

After what had happened at the rooftop bar, some of the excess energy built up had been released, allowing her to breathe freely, and she would be a fool to let it accumulate again.

Except, they were on the beach, with nothing that could fall or explode in their vicinity.

Eh, what the hell. She only lived once.

Lifting on her toes, Cassandra quickly closed the distance between them and brushed her lips over his.

Sparks exploded, and she took a step back, quickly glancing around to check if anything had happened.

"That's it?" Onegus reached for her waist and pulled her against his rock-hard body. "That wasn't a kiss," he murmured against her lips. "That was a tease."

His mouth slammed over hers, and as her arms wrapped around his neck, she stifled a moan. Unapologetic, his tongue pushed past her lips, and she allowed it, leaning into his firm body and opening for him with a ravenous hunger that had roared to life once she released the leash.

Long minutes passed, and still he kissed her, and she didn't make a move to pull away or stop him, not until she was out of breath and it was either let go or pass out from lack of oxygen.

Someone behind them clapped, then whistled and made a lewd comment, but for once, Cassandra ignored the taunting, her eyes holding Onegus's gaze.

He smirked. "Now, that's what I call a kiss."

She lifted her sunscreen-covered palm. "I smeared it all over your neck."

He laughed. "I won't get sunburned there for sure." He took her hand. "Let's keep moving, or I'll go for another one. That kiss just whetted my appetite for more."

Hers too.

Cassandra had never been kissed like that, with such passion, such raw need, and she'd responded in kind.

She was tempted to drag Onegus back to that hotel and rent a room, tossing her rule about no hookups and caution to the wind.

"I should put some sunscreen on your face," she murmured.

"I don't think it's safe." He didn't look at her, keeping his eyes on the shore meandering before them. "Tell me more about yourself. Distract me."

Cassandra had a feeling that she needed distracting more than he did. Besides, she wanted to find out more about him, not the other way around. She still didn't know much about him other than his family owned the conglomerate he'd represented in the charity gala, and that he was just one of many owners. The quick internet search she'd done this morning hadn't revealed anything more than she'd already known, and curiously, there had been no stories about him dating heiresses or movie stars or hobnobbing with politicians. It seemed like he emerged once a year to attend the charity gala and then disappeared again.

"You know more about me than I know about you. Tell me something about yourself that you haven't told me yet."

He cast her a sidelong glance. "Only if you tell me something that no one else knows about you."

She laughed. "There are many things no one knows about me, and for good reason."

"Tell me one."

"I have a temper."

He chuckled. "I bet that's not a secret."

"It gets worse if I keep it bottled up. That's why people sometimes think that I'm rude." She looked up at him. "Your turn."

"I've never been in love. Have you?"

She nodded. "Twice."

"What happened?"

"I got disappointed. My mom thinks that my expectations are too high and that I'm picky, but that's not true. I have had requirements that I wasn't willing to compromise on, and when they were not met, I preferred to end things and move on. It kind of soured me on the whole dating thing. Besides, I don't have time to go out and meet people. I often work sixteen-hour days."

"What about the people you work with?"

She rolled her eyes. "Most of them are snowflakes a decade younger than me, and I have nothing in common with them." She sighed. "Frankly, I don't feel like I have a lot in common with anyone other than Kevin and Josie. Both of them are ambitious, hard-working, and nothing has been handed to them on a silver platter. They worked hard to get to where they are today, and they sacrificed a lot. More than I did."

"What do you mean?"

"They gave up on having kids. They are both in their late forties, so I assume it's no longer an option."

"Do you want children?"

"Very much so. How about you?"

He nodded. "With the right mate, of course."

She arched a brow. "A mate?"

"Significant other, wife, life-long partner. I'm tired of being alone." He smiled sadly. "I live with a roommate, even though I don't have to. I'm damn grateful to have a good friend who welcomes me home and asks about my day, but that's not the same as having a mate."

Onegus sounded even lonelier than she was. How was it possible? The guy was gorgeous, successful, and rich. Did he have some heinous hidden flaw she wasn't aware of?

"You must have women throwing themselves at you left and right. Why are you alone?"

"I could ask you the same question."

"In my case, that's kind of obvious. I'm opinionated, uncompromising, demanding, and I scare men away. I'm also all work and no play, and I live with my mother."

He laughed. "For someone with a natural knack for marketing, you are not doing a great job at selling yourself."

"I don't want to sell myself. You either like the package, the good and the bad, or not. I don't believe in false advertising."

Onegus lifted her hand and kissed her fingers. "I like the entire package very much. What are you doing tomorrow?"

"Working."

"I want to see you again."

"I want that too. What do you have in mind?"

He smirked. "I can come to your house, introduce myself to your mother, and then take you out on a date."

"Are you trying to knock out the items on my list of demands as quickly as possible?"

"Busted." He let go of her hand and wrapped his arm around her. "You are the boss, Cassandra. You decide the when and where. I decide the how. Just don't torture me for too long."

What did he mean by *I decide the how*? And why had his words excited her, making every female part of her tingle?

25

VLAD

"*Hi*, everyone." Wendy walked into Stella and Richard's home with two large bags in each hand. "I had a great time with Sharon and Tessa." She lifted the bags. "There was a huge sale at the outlet, and I went a little wild."

"The important thing is that you had fun." Vlad kissed her cheek and took the bags from her.

"What did you get?" Stella asked.

"I got three pairs of jeans, size four, five T-shirts, size small, and two dresses, also size small."

Vlad wanted to say that she was losing too much weight, but they'd had that discussion so many times that he'd gotten tired of bringing it up.

Perhaps he should ask Vanessa to intervene.

"I also got two pairs of shoes and a gorgeous pair of boots." Wendy lifted one of the bags. "Do you want to see?"

"Of course."

As the two grabbed the rest of the bags and ducked into the master bedroom, Vlad sat down on the couch next to Richard. "I talked with Brundar earlier."

"About?"

"Our plans. He basically told me that it's not a big deal if a civilian uses thralling as long as no one gets hurt. A few days in a dungeon is probably all we will get for thralling the information out of the bastard."

Richard put down his newspaper on the coffee table. "I heard that Brundar got a whipping for something similar. And if that's in the cards, I can tell you right now that I'm not on board for that."

"Brundar chose to get whipped because he didn't want to waste time in the dungeon. Edna gave him the option, and he turned it down. He'd also beaten up the guy, so more than thralling was involved. Besides, Brundar hinted that we don't have to confess. We just need to be careful not to get caught."

Richard shook his head. "I don't want to break any clan laws. I'm a new member, and I've just gotten my freedom back and can come and go as I please. I don't want to lose my privileges over this. If we do it, we will have to confess." He took a deep breath. "Even if all we get as punishment are a few days in the dungeon, I might lose my job over it. I'll have to tell Kalugal and ask whether he's okay with me missing several days of work."

"If we get caught, I'll take the blame and say that you tried to stop me."

"I still need to ask Kalugal for a few days off to go with you. How am I going to excuse it?"

"You can tell him the truth or just say that you need to keep an eye on me, so I don't do something stupid. I don't think Kalugal is going to spill the beans to Edna. Then again, he could blurt something to Rufsur, and the guy could tell his mate. You'll have to ask him to keep it confidential."

"Good point." Richard turned his head to glance at the hallway. "Did you tell Wendy?"

"About my father?"

"That too. But I meant about what you want to do to hers."

"No to the first, and yes to the second. She's okay with me thralling him to get the information, but she doesn't want his blood on my hands. I promised her that I won't kill him."

Richard nodded. "Then you definitely need me with you. I'll ask Kalugal first thing tomorrow morning, and if he doesn't mind losing me for a few days, I'll book us a flight for Wednesday. We've been pussyfooting about this for long enough."

"I agree."

"When are you going to tell Wendy about your father? And why didn't you yet?"

Vlad shrugged. "There is nothing to tell because I don't know anything about the Kra-ell."

"You know where you got your strength from, and your eyes."

"That's unimportant. I need to find out what kind of people they are, and what I heard so far doesn't inspire confidence. I was much happier believing that my father was some random human."

Richard chuckled. "When your mother acted all mysterious about who your father was, I thought that he might have been a criminal, and that was why she'd kept his identity a secret. A human father is not necessarily better than a Kra-ell. Emmett isn't evil. He's smart, cunning, and self-serving, but he didn't kill or harm Eleanor, although he could have. So even though he's a bloodsucker, he's not a murderous bastard."

"Yeah, I guess. But he is a bloodsucker, and that's disturbing."

Richard regarded him with a smile tugging at his lips. "I assume that you never had a craving for blood."

"Gross. I get nauseous just thinking about it."

Richard shrugged. "I don't know why. You bite during sex, and there is always a little blood that you need to lick. Does that gross you out?"

"Of course not. It's Wendy's blood, and it's just a few drops."

"Did it taste good?"

It didn't taste bad, but he didn't crave it.

"It does, but I never felt the need to take more."

"But you don't get nauseous from licking her blood, so the rest is probably all in your head. If you didn't think of bloodsucking as gross, you might have enjoyed it, at least a little bit."

"Why? Do you think you would have liked it?"

"I'm the type of guy who's willing to try almost anything at least once before I knock it down."

Vlad grimaced. "I really don't want to hear about your sexual preferences. You are mated to my mother."

"You asked, and I answered."

2 6

MARGARET

.

"*A*re you excited?" Ana lifted another section of Margaret's hair and wrapped it around the curling iron.

"I don't know what to think. Why is Bowen taking me out on a date?"

Ever since Ana and Leon had returned to the cabin, Bowen had been acting strange. He was as courteous and as helpful as before, but Margaret sensed a distance between them as if he was uncomfortable being around her.

At first, she'd thought that he'd figured out she was attracted to him and wanted to let her down gently, but then, out of the blue, he asked her out.

"Isn't it obvious?" Letting the curl she'd made cascade down Margaret's front, Ana separated another section to curl. "He likes you, and he wants to take your friendship to the next stage."

"What next stage? He hasn't given me any indications that he was interested. And why would he?" She waved her hand at the mirror she was sitting in front of. "Just look at me."

Ana released the curl and leaned over Margaret's head, looking at her in the mirror. "You are beautiful. You just haven't done anything to accentuate your beauty in ages. Once I'm done with you, you will look like a new woman." She sighed. "I wish I had told Leon to get some hair color when he and Bowen went shopping. Blond highlights would have brightened your face." She separated another section and wound it around the curling iron. "Except, God knows what he would have brought back. You can't send a guy to buy stuff like that."

Looking at the dark circles under her eyes and her hollow cheeks, Margaret doubted Ana would be able to pull off a miracle and transform her into a beauty with a curling iron and some makeup.

Even after more than a week of rest and being fed and pampered by Bowen, she still looked haggard. She wasn't attractive, not on the outside, and not on the inside. He just didn't know enough about her to realize that her lack of beauty was more than skin deep.

"Stop looking like you are getting ready for a funeral." Ana waved the iron around. "You are going to a nice restaurant with a handsome guy. Smile!"

When Margaret's smile turned out to look more like a grimace, Ana shook her head. "Close your eyes."

"Why?"

"Because I don't want to stare at your sad face when I'm trying to make you beautiful. Imagine happy things and try to relax. I'll tell you when I'm done."

"Yes, ma'am."

Margaret closed her eyes and imagined herself back at Safe Haven, teaching the workshop she'd started putting together in the cabin.

It was about making chocolates and truffles as an expression of love. What could be more satisfying than combining her favorite treat with craftsmanship and art? She doubted there would be even one community member who wouldn't want to participate.

The internet was a fabulous source of information, providing her with everything she ever needed to know about making chocolates. She'd watched YouTube videos, copied recipes and pictures, and neatly organized everything in the application Bowen had downloaded for her.

Perhaps now that Emmett was gone, she could convince Riley to allow community members to have computers and cell phones.

As time away from Safe Haven passed, Margaret's blind worship of Emmett and everything he'd preached was starting to fade. It made her sad to admit that Emmett hadn't been right about limiting the community's access to the internet. It was true that it was easy to get lost in it and get distracted away from productive endeavors, but there was so much information out there. So much to be learned. It was as if all of humanity's accumulated knowledge was accessible to everyone on the globe.

It was a revolution that had completely passed her by. But she was part of it now, and she wasn't willing to let it go. If Riley resisted, Margaret was going to fight her hard and put the issue to a community vote. With Emmett gone, they could become a real commune, where everyone had a voice.

At some point during her musings, Ana switched from doing her hair to applying makeup. It was like getting a massage or a facial. It was relaxing, and Margaret wasn't even curious to see the transformation. Given the canvas Ana had to work with, there was only so much she could do.

"You can open your eyes." Ana patted her shoulder.

"I don't want to."

"Why not?"

"Until I see myself, I can imagine that you've managed a miracle. When I open my eyes, I'll have to face reality."

"I think you'll be pleasantly surprised." Ana gently squeezed her shoulder. "Come on, Margaret. On the count of three. One, two, three!"

Cracking one eye open experimentally, Margaret looked at the mirror, but it was hard to see with just one eye and she opened both.

"Oh, wow." She leaned closer. "You're good."

Her hair was no longer dull and hanging limply around her shoulders. Instead, soft, shiny waves framed her face. The dark circles were gone, and her big brown eyes were framed with a delicate dark brown line and black eyelashes. Coral tone lipstick added a splash of color to her face, which no longer looked grayish.

She actually looked pretty.

"Thank you."

Ana beamed at her through the mirror. "Now, let's get you dressed."

"My options are very limited."

Ana walked over to the closet and pulled out one of the three dresses Bowen had gotten for her. "Don't worry. We will make it work."

27

BOWEN

*B*owen was as nervous as a teenage boy going on his first date. He hadn't even told Margaret how beautiful she looked because he'd been too stunned by the transformation to say anything.

She'd expected him to say something, he'd seen it in her eyes, and yet the only words that had left his mouth had been, "Let's go. Our reservations are for eight."

Suave. It was a miracle he'd managed as many hookups as he had.

But what could he have said? That she looked beautiful because her hair was done and her makeup hid the dark shadows under her eyes? Nothing about her had changed intrinsically, and to compliment the superficial seemed wrong on some level.

Sitting next to him in the car, Margaret fidgeted with the clasp of her purse. "It was nice of you to think of a way to give Ana and Leon some privacy. Given the long drive, we will be gone for more than four hours. I'm sure they appreciate it."

Bowen wanted to bang his head against the wheel. Of course, Margaret would think that. He hadn't given her any reason to think that he wanted to spend time with her, to woo her.

"That's not why I asked you out."

She chuckled nervously. "That's okay. You won't hurt my feelings by admitting the truth. I'm happy to do this for them, and I will enjoy an evening out with you even if it's not a real date."

The woman was too selfless and unassuming for her own good.

"Is it so hard to believe that I asked you out because of you and no one else?"

Smiling, she turned to him. "We spend all of our days together. You don't need to ask me out to get to know me. I think that by now, you know me better than most of my friends in Safe Haven."

If that was true, then she didn't have any real friends. He knew practically nothing about her, aside from the things he'd guessed, and those were just speculation. The only glimpses she'd allowed him into her life before Safe Haven had been her admission to an opioid problem she'd overcome and her cryptic remark about having seen evil.

Bowen wanted to know more, but as long as he was just a friend, she had no reason to confide in him. He hadn't told her much about himself either.

But if they were to become more than friends, someone had to make the first move, and that someone had to be him.

"What if I want to be more than your friend?"

She laughed. "Oh, Bowen. Did Leon put you up to this?"

In a way he had, but she couldn't have known that, and it was irrelevant. Leon had just given him a push in the right direction.

"He has nothing to do with it."

It took Margaret a long time to respond. "Why would a guy like you be interested in me?"

"Why not? You are smart, compassionate, and pretty."

"I'm nothing special. I have very little going for me, and I live in a community that you consider a cult. I really don't understand what's your game, Bowen. I have nothing you need or want." She turned her face to look out the window.

If Margaret was a Dormant, she had everything he needed, but he couldn't tell her that.

"I feel a pull toward you, and I know that you feel it too. All I want is a chance to explore it, and I'd rather have a nice talk away from the cabin over dinner in a restaurant." He turned toward her and smiled. "Besides, you've been cooped up in that cabin for days on end. I figured you would enjoy a night out."

"It was very nice of you to take me out to dinner." Margaret let out a breath. "It's just that you are doing so much for me, and I don't understand why. No one is that selfless."

He shrugged. "I told you my motives. I needed a vacation, and you provided me with a perfect excuse to take one."

She cast him a sidelong glance. "We both know that was just an excuse. You did it for Leon and Ana."

"In part." He took a deep breath. "So, here's the truth. Something about you called to me, and I couldn't bring myself to let go of you. In fact, every time I think about you returning to Safe Haven, I feel an ache right here." He rubbed a hand over his chest.

"I feel the same," she murmured. "It makes sense why I feel that way, but it doesn't for you."

"We are about to figure it out." He cast her an amused smile. "Relax, Margaret. We are only going to a restaurant, not eloping to Vegas."

MARGARET

For the rest of the drive, Margaret tried to keep things from getting too serious.

Bowen was right. It was just a date, and neither of them was committing to anything other than enjoying each other's company. So she talked about her workshop, and how she was planning to convince Riley to allow computers and cellphones for each one of the community members.

Bowen nodded. "The retreats generate enough money to allow for much more luxury than the community members enjoy. The question is whether people will keep coming without Emmett's charismatic presence adding to the mystic allure of Safe Haven."

She hadn't thought of that. "Perhaps we can keep pretending that he's still there."

Bowen chuckled. "Doing what? Meditating in his secret chapel?"

"Why not?" She lifted her arms. "We can claim that by meditating, Emmett is projecting his awesomeness to every guest of the retreat."

It was so much easier to talk with Bowen about anything other than their so-called relationship.

As long as he hadn't shown interest in her, Margaret had successfully stifled her attraction to him, and she would have preferred to keep it that way. Having him as a friend was better than losing him entirely because she desired a man she shouldn't. But now that Bowen was hinting at his interest, her subdued urges were bubbling to the surface.

"Unfortunately, they don't have a valet service at this place," Bowen said as he turned into the restaurant's parking lot. "It's not as fancy as I would have liked it to be." He cast her an apologetic smile. "But a place like that would have taken another forty-five-minute drive."

"I don't want anything fancy, and I can hobble to the entrance."

"I have the wheelchair in the trunk. Do you prefer that to the crutches?"

"Actually, I do. It will be easier for everyone if you just wheel me in instead of me hobbling on one foot. There'll be less staring."

He let out a breath. "I love how reasonable you are. If it were Anastasia, she would have insisted on walking."

He was probably right. Ana was prideful, while Margaret's pride had been stripped away a long time ago. When she insisted on fending for herself, it was because she didn't want to be a burden, not because she was embarrassed to accept assistance.

Help wasn't offered often or freely, and when it was, she'd learned to take it and say thank you.

Life was difficult enough as it was.

Bowen took the wheelchair out of the trunk, unfolded it, and then pushed it to her side of the car. When he opened the door and reached for her, Margaret didn't argue even though she could have gotten into the chair on her own.

She probably should have, though.

Being carried in his strong arms, inhaling his masculine scent, it was impossible to suppress her raw attraction to him.

He lowered her gently into the chair and then draped the coat Ana had loaned her over her knees. "Ready?"

"Yes, sir."

When they entered the restaurant, the hostess smiled at her. "Skiing accident?"

"I wish. Unfortunately, it was just a bad fall."

"I hope you get better soon," she said and turned her attention to Bowen. "This way, please." She sauntered in front of them, sashaying her shapely hips and butt for Bowen's benefit.

To his credit, his eyes hadn't shifted to her ass even once.

When they were seated, the hostess handed them the menus, flashed Bowen an inviting smile, and sashayed away.

"She couldn't have been more obvious if she tried," Margaret murmured from behind the open menu.

"She's just a kid."

Margaret lowered the folder. "She's no more than a couple of years younger than you."

"I'm not as young as I look."

She'd never asked him how old he was, but he couldn't be more than thirty. Should she ask?

"How old are you?"

He smiled. "Guess."

"Twenty-nine?"

"Guess again."

"Thirty?"

He shook his head.

"Twenty-seven?"

"You're getting colder."

"Just tell me."

"You have to guess."

The waiter's arrival stopped the guessing game, but after they ordered, it was on again.

"Thirty-one."

When he shook his head, Margaret kept going until she reached her own age. "No way." She crossed her arms over her chest. "You can't be thirty-eight."

He smirked. "I didn't say that I was."

"Thirty-nine?"

Bowen shrugged.

"Show me your driver's license."

"Why? Don't you believe me?"

"I don't. You just want me to feel more comfortable with you."

"I give you my word that I'm older than you."

"You don't know how old I am."

"Yes, I do. Did you forget that I was in the hospital with you when you were admitted? You filled out the questionnaire right next to me."

"You must tell me your secret then. How do you manage to look so young?"

He winked. "I work out a lot."

Other than lifting her and carrying her around, Margaret hadn't seen Bowen exercise even once in all the time they'd been together in the cabin. But then he usually woke up hours before her, so he might have finished his workout routine by the time she got up.

"That's it." She tapped the table. "Once this damn cast is off, I'm starting to lift weights every day. Apparently, my walks on the beach are not doing the trick."

"To build muscle, you need to eat protein, and you don't eat enough of it or anything else for that matter. Chocolate doesn't count."

"You are right. I should have ordered the steak in addition to the fish." She lifted her hand, pretending to summon the waiter.

"Don't forget a side of spinach." He flexed both arms without even lifting them.

The bulges were impressive enough to draw the attention of other diners.

How could he be older than her? He'd given her his word that he was, and Bowen wasn't the type of guy who would do that and lie.

Perhaps he was just blessed with incredible genes.

29

BOWEN

"*D*id you enjoy yourself?" Bowen asked as he pulled out of the restaurant's parking lot.

"I did. Thank you." Margaret readjusted her dress. "In fact, I don't remember ever enjoying myself as much."

It had been a very pleasant evening, especially after he'd convinced Margaret that he was older than her. Bowen had employed Leon's tactics, and they had worked remarkably well. All he'd said was that he was older and let her assume the rest. She'd stopped guessing at thirty-nine.

Still, if that was the most Margaret had ever enjoyed herself, her life must have been pretty dull. It wasn't surprising given how long she'd lived in Safe Haven, basically working herself to the bone.

"I'm glad." He reached over the center console and gripped her slim hand. "We should do it again tomorrow."

She didn't pull her hand out of his. "You're spoiling me, Bowen." She looked at their conjoined hands. "But the truth is that I'm well enough to return to Safe Haven, and I shouldn't keep you away from your work any longer."

"You still need help."

"Not really. I can shower by myself, and I can get dressed without help. I also suspect that Leon and Ana are staying in the cabin for my sake. We all need to get back to our lives."

"Not yet." He lifted her hand and brushed his lips over her knuckles. "Stay at least until next Monday."

"That's an entire week."

"It will give you time to get stronger. Besides, my goal of fattening you up hasn't been achieved yet. I want you to gain at least five pounds before you return to Safe Haven."

She chuckled. "There are no scales in the cabin. How would you know if I gained anything?"

"Easy. My arms will be the scales, and I'll weigh you every morning."

Given the soft curve of her lips, she liked the idea. "Frankly, I'm not in a rush to go back. I just don't want to keep the three of you from getting on with your lives."

He cast her a sidelong glance. "If you want to get rid of Leon and Anastasia, just say the word. I wouldn't mind having you all to myself."

She swallowed. "I don't think that's a good idea."

"Are you scared of being alone with me?"

"What? No! Of course not. You are the only man other than Emmett who I feel safe with." She looked at her cast. "I'm no good for you, Bowen."

"Because of that? That's temporary."

"It's still going to be there by next Monday. But that's not the only thing that's broken about me." She let out a sigh. "Do you really want to get involved with a former junkie?"

"As long as it is former and not current, it doesn't bother me. You've hinted at it enough times, so it's not like I didn't know. Getting over addiction and keeping clean is a monumental achievement. You should be proud of it rather than ashamed."

"There is nothing to be proud of. I was young, weak, and stupid, and I got addicted to painkillers. I wasn't able to stop, and I only sank deeper and deeper." She lowered her head. "It got so bad that I was willing to do anything for my next fix."

His heart broke for her.

Had she sold her body for drugs?

"It's not what you think," she whispered. "I didn't prostitute myself, but I deliberately sought injury to get hospitalized and prescribed more painkillers."

He didn't want to think about how she'd done that, but he had a good idea.

"How did you get out of it?"

"I was forced into rehab. While I was there, I met a woman who told me about Safe Haven. At the time, it seemed like my only option. I had nowhere to go and no money, and I was afraid for my life."

"Why were you afraid?" He had a good idea, but he needed to hear it from her.

Margaret shook her head. "That's a story for another time, or maybe never."

Bowen didn't want to press her. She was opening to him, telling him things she hadn't before, and if he insisted, she might clam up again.

"How did you get to Safe Haven?"

She smiled. "I hitchhiked. Even though I was a recovering junkie, I was still pretty back then. It took me nearly a week to get to Safe Haven, and when I did, I looked like a dirty, starved rat. Emmett took me in, no questions asked. Later, I told him everything, and he still gave me a home and a job. With Emmett's help, I was reborn in Safe Haven, becoming a completely different person."

"He did a good deed, but that doesn't compensate for what he did to you and the other females in your community. I'm surprised that you never suspected him of drugging you."

"Do you know what kind of drugs he used? Maybe they were just mild relaxants?"

"I have no idea. We should have searched his place, but there was no time."

Margaret nodded. "I don't know what he has done to your people directly, but if they ever catch him, tell them to be kind to him. I'm not mad at Emmett for what he has allegedly done to me, and I bet the others aren't either. In my opinion, Emmett's good deeds outweigh the bad."

Bowen wasn't sure of that. He hadn't heard the latest updates from the interrogation. He should call Peter and ask him what else had been uncovered. Most likely, it was nothing good.

30

ELEANOR

*I*t was early in the morning when Eleanor made her way to the office building, the cold air cooling her heated face. When she'd sent Kian a text message asking to speak with him, she hadn't expected him to invite her to come to his office right away.

What she needed to talk to him about wasn't urgent, and her text hadn't implied that it was.

The café was still closed, but a few people were already sitting at the tables, enjoying coffee and pastries from the vending machines. A couple of males even smiled her way, which was new.

It could be because they had heard of her breakup with Greggory, or perhaps people were starting to view her more favorably now that she'd proven her loyalty to the clan.

The office building's front door was open, but she didn't encounter anyone as she climbed to the second floor. The place was completely quiet, which meant that no one other than Kian started their workday that early.

As she reached his door, Eleanor took a deep breath and knocked.

"Come in." His gruff voice didn't sound welcoming.

Perhaps he was pissed about something else. The guy had a thousand balls in the air at all times, and she was just the thousand and one.

Depressing the handle, Eleanor pushed the door open and walked in. "Thanks for agreeing to see me." She closed it behind her.

"Take a seat." The gruff tone didn't soften, but he motioned to the chairs in front of his desk.

"Thank you." She pulled one out and sat down.

"How can I help you, Eleanor?"

She smiled nervously. "Perhaps the better question is how can I help you." She straightened her back and forced herself to look into his intense eyes. "Since

I am immune to compulsion, I think that I should be part of the team guarding Emmett."

"Annani compelled Emmett not to use his compulsion on clan members, so that's no longer an issue. Besides, you are not a Guardian yet."

"I'm training."

"You won't be ready for many years, and don't think I'm saying that because I don't trust you, it just takes that long to go through the training."

"Physically, I might not be anywhere near the Guardians' level of ability, but I have the kind of experience that's precisely what's needed in this case, and I believe that I can do a better job with Emmett than they can. Especially given my immunity and my other assets."

"Annani also compelled Emmett to tell her everything he knows about his people."

Eleanor smiled. "Compulsion is good for many things, but not for getting information unless you know exactly what to ask. If you don't believe me, ask Peter. He managed to avoid answering many of Emmett's questions."

"I hadn't considered that, but you are right." Leaning back, Kian regarded her for a long moment. "Perhaps you can be part of a team. I'll have to discuss this with Onegus."

"So, is it a yes or a maybe?"

"It's a maybe."

"When will you have an answer for me?"

He leaned forward. "First, tell me why you want to guard Emmett. Do you want to get back at him for what he did to you?"

"I'm madder about what Emmett did to Peter than what he did to me, but revenge is not my motive."

"Then what is? I know that you are not doing it out of the goodness of your heart or because you believe that you are the best woman for the job."

Damn. She didn't mind telling Peter or even Magnus why she needed to do this, but admitting her real motives to Kian would be awkward in the extreme.

"Well?" He arched a brow.

"Actually, I do believe that I'm the best woman for the job. Emmett is attracted to me." She pushed her chest out. "When Kri suggested I volunteer for the job, she put it quite crudely. She said that boobs make men stupid, meaning that as a female, I have a better chance of getting Emmett to reveal information that he would never have shared with the male Guardians."

Kian looked surprised. "Do you plan on seducing him?"

Eleanor shrugged. "I'm single again, so why not? I can scratch an itch and help the clan at the same time. It's a win-win."

He nodded. "I'm sorry that things didn't work out between you and Greggory."

"Yeah, well. Me too. But it is what it is, and I'm ready to move on."

"To Emmett?"

"Maybe." She chuckled. "It's so like me to go for the worst possible candidate. First, I choose a former Doomer, and then I move on to a member of another potentially hostile immortal species, who is locked up in a cell indefinitely. I need a third option. A nice clan member who doesn't think that I'm a shrew."

Kian cracked a smile. "I'm sure there are plenty of those. But in case you develop feelings for Emmett, you won't be falling for a lifer. I promised him a place in the village provided that the information he gave me about the last location of his people is true."

"What if they moved to a different location and didn't leave any traces behind?"

"Then the deal is off. Emmett will have to earn his freedom some other way."

31

KIAN

ood morning, boss." Onegus strode into Kian's office and pulled out a chair. "How is your day going so far?" He spread his long legs in front of him.

"You seem in a good mood. I assume that the gala was successful?"

"Very much so. Brandon says that the contributions were even larger than the year before." Onegus flashed him his signature smile. "I would like to think that it was my speech that made the difference."

"Bridget said that you dismissed most of her suggestions."

Onegus shrugged. "I only took out the tearjerkers. I left everything else in. People come to events like that to enjoy themselves, to hobnob, to mingle, to be seen. You can't douse them with depressing stuff and expect them to be in a charitable mood. The best way to encourage them to donate is to show them how much good their money will do, insert a little humor and humility, and sprinkle it with some individual success stories to bring it home."

Kian hadn't seen Onegus this upbeat in a long time, and he doubted the generous pledges were solely responsible for it.

"Did you enjoy yourself?"

The grin splitting Onegus's face was infectious. "More than I expected."

He had probably met someone whose company he'd enjoyed, but Kian wasn't interested in the details.

"Eleanor came to see me earlier. She wants to be part of the team that guards Emmett."

"Why? Does she want revenge?"

"That was my reaction as well, but that's not what she's after. Kri convinced Eleanor that she has a better chance of getting Emmett to open up than any of us, and she might be onto something."

Onegus shook his head. "Once was not enough for her? Eleanor already played that part with Emmett in Safe Haven, and it didn't end well for her."

"Indeed." Kian nodded. "She also lost Greggory because of it. Apparently, he couldn't handle what happened between her and Emmett, which would give the revenge hypothesis more credence, especially given Eleanor's personality. She's not the forgive and forget type. On the other hand, she admitted to feeling a strange attraction to Emmett, so it might be about her need to explore that."

Onegus rubbed a finger over the cleft in his chin. "That complicates things. It's one thing for her to go into it with a cold heart and manipulate Emmett to open up to her. It's another thing altogether if she falls for the bloodsucker."

Kian crossed his arms over his chest. "I don't see a problem with that. Carol fell for Lokan, but she never betrayed our trust even once. The clan came before her feelings for him, and him falling for her played a big part in his willingness to cooperate with us and reveal the location of the Doomers' island."

"Eleanor is not Carol. But we can mitigate the risk by assigning Peter to the case as well. He knows her, and he can keep an eye on her."

"I like your idea with one caveat. Peter also has a grudge against Emmett, even worse than Eleanor, and if I put him in charge, things could get ugly."

"Peter wouldn't do anything that wasn't sanctioned by you or me. And having him in charge might be another way to encourage Emmett's cooperation."

Uncrossing his arms, Kian leaned forward. "Are you comfortable with promoting Peter? It would be the first time he'd be in charge."

"He's experienced enough, and this is a low-risk assignment. I'm not worried."

Peter had failed his Safe Haven mission, but it hadn't been his fault. Kian, Onegus, and Turner were as much to blame as he was. The problem was that none of them had taken Eleanor's suspicion seriously. It had been a curiosity that Kian had wanted to investigate, and they hadn't put in place contingencies in the event that her suspicions were correct. They had also relied too much on Eleanor's immunity to compulsion. None of them could have suspected that Emmett was a different breed of immortal who was incredibly strong physically, on top of being a powerful compeller.

"Put Peter in charge, but have him report to Magnus or directly to you, and keep an eye on him."

"Done. When do you want him to start?"

"As soon as possible. I want to send Arwel to China, and Peter will need a few days to learn the routine."

"What about Eleanor? Do you want them to start at the same time?"

"First, let's summon them both and see if they are willing to work together."

"I don't see why not." Onegus pulled out his phone. "I assume that you want to see them right away?"

"Indeed." Kian opened the drawer and pulled out his cigarillo box. "I'm going to take a break on the roof. Text me when they get here."

32

ELEANOR

*O*ne advantage of working for Kian, Eleanor realized, was how fast he made and implemented his decisions. He'd promised her an answer right after he spoke with Onegus, and since they were meeting right now, she expected him to call her back soon.

It didn't make sense to go back home, and she decided to go for a walk around the old village instead. She could use the quiet time to sharpen her arguments in case the answer was no.

Eleanor needed this assignment, and not just so she could be close to Emmett and figure out what had caused her attraction to him.

The simple truth was that she needed a job, and being Kri's assistant in self-defense classes wasn't it.

She had plenty of money saved up, and now that she was free to leave the village, she had access to it, but having a job wasn't just about earning an income. She needed to be busy, and she needed to be challenged. Working out for hours a day had made her into a lean, mean fighting machine, but if she couldn't use it, then what was the point?

When the text from Kian came, Eleanor turned around and jogged back to the office building. After taking the stairs two at a time, she forced herself to slow down as she walked down the corridor and then knocked on Kian's door.

"Come in!"

When she walked into the office, Onegus flashed her his toothy smile. "How did you get here so fast? Were you waiting in the café?"

"I took a walk." She pulled out a chair and sat next to him at the oblong conference table.

"We need to wait for Peter." The chief leaned back and crossed his arms over his chest.

"What does Peter have to do with my assignment?"

"Since the two of you seem to work so well together, Kian and I decided to have you both stationed in the keep."

"What about Arwel? With all due respect to Emmett and his powers, he doesn't need so many people to guard him."

Kian lifted a hand. "Let's wait for Peter to get here. I don't want to answer every question twice."

"Makes sense." The problem was that now she would have to engage in small talk, and she sucked at it. "How did the gala go?" she asked Onegus.

His smile was so broad that he was all teeth. "Excellent. We collected so much money that we have enough to open another halfway house."

"Do we need more than one?"

"If we have more room, we can let the residents stay longer. Julian and Vanessa are complaining that they need to nudge them to move on before they are ready."

Eleanor shrugged. "Nudging is good. It forces them to become independent sooner, and once they are, they feel better about themselves. Dependency might feel safe, but it doesn't feel good."

"Not everyone is as tough as you, Eleanor," Kian said.

"Thank you. That's the best compliment you've ever given me."

Kian looked as if he was about to retort when a knock sounded on the door, and Peter walked in. "Apologies for the late arrival." He looked at Onegus. "I was under the impression that I was still on a leave of absence, and your text found me in bed." He pulled out a chair on the chief's other side. "Do you have a new assignment for me?"

"I might." Onegus turned toward Peter. "But first, I need you to tell me how you feel about Emmett. Specifically, do you have the urge to tear his throat out when you see him?"

"Not at all. I'm not one to hold a grudge. Besides, if I were in the guy's position, I would have done the same thing. The survival of my people trumps any other considerations."

"Good." Onegus clapped him on the back. "I'm putting you in charge of the team guarding him. Congratulations."

Great. Peter hadn't even asked for it, and they were putting him in charge as if he had done such a great job in Safe Haven. Then again, she'd messed up as well.

Eleanor crossed her arms over her chest. "What about Arwel? Isn't he in charge?"

"He will be in charge of checking the information Emmett gave us." Kian turned to Peter. "Are you okay with the assignment?"

"Sure. I just got promoted. Does that mean a raise?"

Onegus chuckled. "Let's see first how well you do."

"What about me?" Eleanor asked. "What's my status?"

Onegus looked at Kian. "Do we officially make Eleanor a Guardian in training?"

Kian nodded and turned to her. "Guardians in training are paid a salary. It's much less than full-fledged Guardians are paid, but it's enough to live on, and it makes your status official."

Onegus extended his hand to her. "Welcome to the force."

"Thank you." She shook it. "I'm truly honored."

In fact, it was quite unbelievable. From a prisoner to a Guardian in training in a matter of months instead of years. She'd thought it would take forever before people stopped giving her the evil eye.

"When do we start?" Peter asked.

"You can start tomorrow," Onegus said. "Arwel will show you the routine, and you'll work under his supervision until he's comfortable leaving Emmett's guardianship in your hands."

Eleanor's stomach clenched. She hadn't expected it to happen so fast, but she was glad that it had. Waiting and thinking and speculating would have driven her nuts.

"It's a pleasure working with you." She smiled at him and then turned to Kian. "Things go from concept to execution in a matter of hours or days. When I still worked for the government, everything took forever."

"That's the advantage of a small organization," Onegus said. "There's no bureaucracy to deal with."

33

ARWEL

"*A*re you sure about that?" Arwel rose to his feet and started pacing the length of the small living room.

He didn't like Kian's plan to put Eleanor and Peter in charge of guarding Emmett. The three had a history together, and it was never a good idea to have the prisoner and his jailers emotionally involved, either in a positive or negative way.

"Eleanor offered to use her feminine wiles on Emmett. I talked it over with Onegus, and he doesn't have a problem with that."

Arwel chuckled. "What feminine wiles? She is not a bad-looking woman, but she's not a seductress. Let's face it, Eleanor is not Carol."

"No one is like Carol, but as the saying goes, there is a lid for every pot, or is it the other way around? Anyway, Emmett might find Eleanor's assertiveness enticing since she's more like the females in his original community."

"Good point. I hadn't considered that. But since Annani compelled him to tell her everything about his people, what else can Eleanor learn?"

"Compulsion is not very effective for retrieving information. Unless you know exactly what to ask and how to phrase it, there are ways to work around it. That's how Peter managed to avoid telling Emmett our location or anything else that he could have used against us. Peter's experience taught us that compulsion is more effective at the physical level because the commands can be precise."

"You have a point. How do you want the transition to work?"

"Peter and Eleanor will be there sometime this afternoon, so you can give them an overview of what they are required to do. Perhaps it would be a good idea to have a talk with Emmett and tell him about the guard switch. They will start tomorrow morning, and you will need to stay for a few days to supervise. I want you to leave for China as soon as possible."

"We don't have a plan ready, and Jin hasn't given me her final answer yet."

"We will have to wing it. I don't want to waste time, and we need to collect information before Turner can devise a plan. He can do that while you are there."

"I can't argue with your logic. I'll talk with Jin when she comes over this afternoon."

Kian sighed. "I want to make myself clear. You are going with her or without her. I need you there at least for the initial investigation."

"She knows that."

"Good. Then we are all on the same page."

After Kian ended the call, Arwel kept pacing for several moments. It would be difficult to be apart from Jin, but he had a job to do, and he couldn't pick and choose his assignments based on her preferences.

Kian and Onegus accommodated the mated Guardians as much as they could, but Arwel had to agree that he was the best choice for this investigation. Well, if he had a mastery of Mandarin, that would have been better, but so far he hadn't made much progress with the Rosetta Stone. For immortals, learning a new language while being immersed in it was easier. Morris was fluent, though, and the pilot could be part of their team.

Arwel was still pacing when Jin walked into the suite an hour later. "Is this your new form of exercise?" She threw her purse on the couch and wrapped her arms around his neck.

He cupped her bottom and squeezed. "I much prefer a different form of physical activity."

She kissed him lightly on the lips. "Close the door, and it can be arranged."

"We need to talk."

Jin frowned. "About what?"

"China." He wrapped his arm around her waist and led her to the couch. "Kian is putting Eleanor and Peter in charge of Emmett, and as soon as I'm comfortable that they got the routine down, he wants me to head out there."

"I'm happy that you're getting out of the dungeon, but why Eleanor? She's not a Guardian, and frankly, I don't trust her."

"She's immune, and as Kian pointed out, she might be just the kind of woman Emmett would find irresistible. She would remind him of the females in his community."

"I don't know about that. Eleanor is full of bluster, but she's emotionally vulnerable, especially now that Greggory dumped her. Combine that with her intrinsic lack of moral compass, and the result could be the exact opposite of what Kian wants to achieve. Emmett might use her to either learn more about us or to get free."

"That's why they are putting Peter in charge." He clasped her hand. "If you don't want to come, that's okay. I won't be gone for more than a couple of weeks."

Jin shook her head. "I'm coming with you, but don't expect me to speak Mandarin anytime soon. I think that I'm linguistically challenged. I don't understand why it's so difficult for me. I'm already bilingual, but then I learned both English and Hebrew as a child." She sighed. "My adult brain is refusing to cooperate."

"It's difficult for me as well. I think immortals learn languages better by getting immersed in them. Perhaps our mental abilities let us absorb it from the humans we interact with."

"Like mental osmosis?"

"That's the idea. But that's just my hypothesis. I need to run it by Vanessa."

Jin shrugged. "She has enough on her plate. I guess we will find out when we get to China."

"I'm so glad that you decided to come with me. I don't know how I would've survived without you." Wrapping his arms around his mate, Arwel kissed her softly.

34

MARGARET

"We are off on a walk." Ana waved goodbye. "We won't be back before dinner."

Margaret lifted her head and smiled. "Have fun."

"Plan to be back by six," Bowen said. "I'm firing up the grill at five forty-five. If you're late, you'll eat it cold."

"No problem," Leon said before closing the door.

Bending to look at her phone, Margaret pretended to return to her internet research.

Things had been a little awkward between her and Bowen. After admitting that he wanted more than friendship with her, he hadn't done anything differently from what he'd done before. He was still friendly and eager to help in any way he could. He gave her space and didn't try to talk to her while she was reading articles or collecting recipes for her workshop.

Did he expect her to make the first move?

If so, he would be waiting for a long time. Not because she didn't want to, but because she didn't have the nerve.

Margaret had never actually initiated the few interludes she'd had with community members. And the only reason she'd responded to their flirting was to avoid being shunned for selfishness. The truth was that she hadn't been interested, and since she'd always seemed rushed, only a handful had bothered to flirt with her.

Those who had persisted had been disappointed with her performance and hadn't returned for seconds, which had been perfectly fine with her. The only one she'd enjoyed being with had been Emmett, and apparently even that had been chemically induced.

Bottom line, she was an unenthusiastic and less than mediocre sex partner, who treated it more as an obligation and a chore to be suffered through than something to relish and enjoy.

"Do you mind if I watch a movie?" Bowen sat next to her on the couch. "I can put headphones on if you wish."

Always so considerate and polite. How did he expect anything to happen between them when he kept acting so formal and proper?

Her own experience of being part of a couple shouldn't be the guideline for any sane person, but watching Ana and Leon together, Margaret had figured that the teasing and bickering meant that they felt safe enough with each other not to watch every word, and it made them closer.

All that politeness shored up the invisible wall between her and Bowen, keeping them in the friend zone.

She put her phone down. "Perhaps I'll take a break and watch a movie with you. What do you have in mind?"

"Something light." He smiled sheepishly. "You'd laugh, but romcoms are my favorite."

"What are romcoms?"

"Romantic comedies."

"That's really surprising since you like reading Stephen King."

"I don't like watching the movie adaptations of his books."

"Well, in that case, let's watch a romcom."

"Any in particular?"

Margaret smiled sadly. "Since I don't know any that are less than twenty years old, any would do."

"I have one." He clicked the television on and started scrolling through the selection. "It hasn't been released yet, but one of my cousins is the producer, so we have it on our servers."

Bowen and Leon used the term cousin loosely. It encompassed most of their extended family members, or the clan, as they referred to them, and Margaret suspected that it didn't imply any real family connection. It was nice, though. Even if the cousins weren't blood relatives, referring to them as such made them feel like family, and that was good.

"What's the movie's title?"

"*Shoeless Sally*. It's a humorous take on the classic Cinderella story."

"Sounds lovely."

"You'll laugh your pants off." He cast her a sheepish sidelong look. "If you were wearing pants, that is."

Margaret wished she had a teasing answer, or at least something funny to say, but nothing came to mind, so she adjusted her skirt and smiled instead.

"Found it." He clicked on the title and leaned back.

As the opening credits started rolling, Bowen wrapped his arm around her shoulders, and her first response was to stiffen, but then she forced herself to relax and leaned her head on his bicep.

After all, that was precisely what she craved—the closeness, the lightheartedness, the lack of formality. She wanted Bowen to tease her, maybe even make some suggestive remarks like Leon was constantly doing to get a rise out of Ana.

"Would you like me to make some tea?" Bowen asked. "I've already seen the movie, so I can miss the opening scenes."

Margaret would have loved a cup, but that would mean losing his arm around her and she didn't want to chance him not returning to the same position. "Maybe later." She cuddled even closer, signaling in the only way she could that she was enjoying the closeness and didn't want it to end.

His hand on her arm moved down and then up, gently caressing and raising goosebumps all over it.

Except, calling what she felt goosebumps was a gross understatement. It was more like the pins and needles she'd used to get after sitting with her leg folded under her for too long.

This time though, it wasn't just a numb limb awakening, it was her entire body.

35

BOWEN

*A*s Margaret snuggled closer, Bowen forced himself not to stiffen. Appearing relaxed became nearly impossible to do, especially after the faint scent of her arousal hit him.

He wasn't paying much attention to the movie, but maybe he should in order to take his mind off the woman pressed so trustingly against him. In her shy way she was signaling her interest, but he didn't know how to take it from there.

The damn cast was acting as a better chaperone than the strictest of matrons, and Margaret's fragility wasn't helping either. Whenever carnal thoughts filtered through his shield, Bowen felt ashamed. How could he imagine himself holding this highly breakable woman pinned against the wall and thrusting into her?

That was what the internet article had suggested as a suitable position for sex with a cast, and when he'd read it, for a brief moment Bowen's stifled libido had roared to life with need. Except, when he'd imagined himself with Margaret like that, the cast was gone, and she had her legs wrapped around his waist.

He needed her to be healthy and whole before he made love to her, but he couldn't wait that long. By then, she would be back to Safe Haven and out of his life, and he would never know whether she'd been his one.

Was making love really necessary to establish that she was the one for him? Wouldn't he know that even without it?

He might, but the only way to induce her transition, providing that she was a Dormant, would be to have sex with her. There was no way around it, and he couldn't wait five more weeks for the cast to come off.

But even if he seduced her tonight, he would only have one week to induce her and that was not enough. Unless he managed to convince Margaret to stay longer, she was scheduled to leave Sunday afternoon.

Maybe he could ask for an extended vacation and join the damn cult until Margaret was good to go? But what about that free-love philosophy they had?

He wouldn't let anyone near her. Then again, until the cast came off, she probably wouldn't invite anyone, and the bastards had to wait for an invitation. They were not allowed to pester the females, which he had to grudgingly give Emmett kudos for.

But what if he got invited? He would just refuse, maybe making up a story about some trauma he was working through. According to Anastasia, new members were allowed some leeway, which was how she'd managed to avoid inviting anyone to her bed until Leon had shown up.

Onegus wouldn't be happy about the long leave of absence. He'd already informed Leon that he needed him back by Thursday.

With the influx of clan members arriving for the wedding and Kian's birthday, Guardians had been allocated to their security, and the force would be stretched thinner than ever. Already some of the rescue missions had been canceled, and Onegus was calling in every available Guardian back to work. Vacations were officially suspended until after the celebrations.

Bowen was the exception only because Margaret might be a potential Dormant, and Dormants took precedence over almost everything. The question was whether Onegus would approve an even longer leave of absence.

After the celebrations were over, the plan was to increase the number of weekly rescue missions to compensate for the cancellations until they were all caught up.

Next to him Margaret laughed, jerking Bowen out of his thoughts.

He glanced at the screen, trying to figure out what she'd found funny, in case she commented on it and expected him to answer coherently. The truth was that he didn't remember much of the lighthearted romantic comedy, and the details were fuzzy.

"Here she goes again." Margaret waved her hand at the screen. "Trying to walk in her boss's large shoes."

He remembered it now. Instead of glass slippers, the story started with a pair of ill-fitting shoes. The prince was the grouchy owner of the company, and the big ball was a party at Sally's boss's penthouse. Sally borrowed a nice dress from her roommate, but she didn't have money to buy fancy shoes to match. When she got to the party, she snuck into the boss's closet and borrowed a pair from her, but they were too big. The actress had done a fantastic comedic job with Sally wobbling on the too-tall, too-big shoes, grabbing people on her way and apologizing profusely. Eventually she got the owner, causing him to spill his drink, and that's how their love story started.

"You're not watching." Margaret finally noticed.

"I was thinking."

"About what?"

"Going to Safe Haven with you. If you put in a good word for me, do you think the new management will accept me as a member?"

Margaret quirked a brow. "You're joking, right?"

"No. I'm serious. I know that you want to go back, but I'm not ready to be apart from you. I'll ask my boss for a leave of absence."

"Oh, Bowen." She cupped his cheek. "You are serious."

"Did you think I was making it up?"

"You are always so formal with me," she whispered. "I didn't know what to think."

Her lips were so close, and there was nothing broken or fragile about them. They were full and plump, and he knew he could taste them without fear or guilt. The problem was what would happen after that, but he would just have to figure it out.

If he hesitated, if he refused the invitation he saw in her eyes, she might never get the courage to issue it again.

Dipping his head, Bowen gently pressed his lips to Margaret's, and when she eagerly parted them for him, he swept in with his tongue. To finally hold her close, pressed against him, and to kiss her was like an electrical shock to his system, but he never loosened the tight control he had over his fangs and his eyes.

As she moaned and tilted her head to give him better access, some of his self-control slipped. Holding her with one hand on the small of her back and the other on her hip, he deepened the kiss, devouring her as if he was a starved man, which he was.

After a long moment she pushed on his chest, and he realized that she needed to breathe and released her mouth.

"I'm sorry."

"I'm not." Margaret brought a trembling finger to touch her lips. "I wish I didn't have to take a breath."

"Have you taken enough?"

"I have."

"Then, kiss me back."

She tilted her head up and did precisely as he'd commanded.

36

CASSANDRA

Onegus hadn't called yet.

It was after six o'clock, the staff were already gone, and the only ones left in the office were Cassandra and her boss.

She couldn't remember the last time she'd checked her phone every five minutes to make sure that she hadn't missed a call from a guy. But that was what she'd been doing throughout the day. Onegus had said that he would call as soon as he knew what time he would be done with work, and that should have been a while ago.

What if he didn't call?

He'd seemed interested enough, but what if he'd changed his mind?

Normally she didn't suffer from insecurities, but Cassandra was a realist, and Onegus was a much bigger catch than she was.

Even if he wasn't a billionaire, he was still rich, and he looked like a movie star. Scratch that, he looked like a god. If he could have any woman on the face of the planet, why would he bother with an obstinate, opinionated, and demanding one like her?

Not to mention her short temper and its destructive power, but he didn't know about that yet.

So yeah, she had a great body and a pretty face, and she had a well-paying job, but she wasn't young, lived with her mother, and she'd told him that she didn't do hookups. And to top it off, she'd also told him that he would have to come to her house and introduce himself to her mother.

What the hell had possessed her to do that?

Meeting her loony mother was a sure way to scare the guy away, and that was the last thing she wanted.

It had been a test, one of many she'd thrown at him to make sure that he deserved her time and attention, and she'd expected him to fail. But so far,

Onegus had passed each one she'd challenged him with. The question was whether he would pass them all.

Cassandra huffed out a breath.

Subconsciously, or maybe consciously, she'd created an obstacle course designed to weed out the half-hearted contenders and the flakes. The prize for the one who reached the finish line would be her love and devotion.

Except, she was no princess, and there was a serious dearth of worthy knights. Chances were that no one would be willing to work so hard to win her heart, and she would end up a spinster.

When her phone finally rang at 6:37 and Onegus's name appeared on the screen, she sagged in relief. Not to appear overly anxious, Cassandra let it ring three times before accepting the call.

"Hello?" She pretended as if she didn't recognize the number.

"It's Onegus."

She switched the phone to her other ear and leaned back in her chair. "Oh, hi. How are you doing?"

"Great. How about yourself?"

"I'm good."

"Are you still in the office?"

"Yes. I'm just finishing a few things." She could leave right away, but again, she didn't want to sound overly eager.

"When can you leave?"

"I have about half an hour's worth of work left."

"Are you heading straight home?"

Cassandra slumped in her chair. He hadn't called to ask her out after all. "I am. Why?"

"When are you going to get there?"

Maybe he wanted to pick her up at home? That was nice of him.

"Seven-thirty or eight."

"If you give me the address, I can come to pick you up at eight, and you can introduce me to your mother."

She chuckled. "I won't subject you to that. Let's meet somewhere in town."

"That's not what we agreed on yesterday. I'm picking you up at home and saying hello to your mother. You don't need to invite me for tea, but I want to introduce myself."

Perhaps she could make it quick and warn her mother not to say anything strange or embarrassing. If she kept refusing, Onegus would think that she was embarrassed about her home or about her mother.

She wasn't about either.

The house she'd bought wasn't a mansion, but it was in a new gated community, and she had it beautifully furnished. As for her mother, there was nothing wrong with Geraldine except the memory lapses and the crazy stories that she sometimes spouted. Her mother was a beautiful woman with impeccable manners.

"I don't know if she's even going to be home. My mother has a busy social life. But you can come over at eight, and if she's there, I'll introduce you."

"Fair enough."

"I'll text you the address. It's a gated community, so when you stop at the gate, tell the guard that you are visiting the Beaumonts."

"I remember your last name, Cassandra."

"Cassy. That's what my friends call me."

"I'm glad that you consider me a friend, but I love your full name. Cassandra," he purred.

She chuckled. "Of course, I consider you a friend. I don't let strangers or mere acquaintances kiss me."

Just thinking about that had her nipples tighten into two hard knobs. No man had ever rocked her world with just one kiss, and if Onegus made love the way he kissed, she was in for the experience of a lifetime.

"I'm also glad for that. I'll see you at eight."

"Wait. Where are we going? I need to know how to dress."

"Wear whatever makes you feel sexy, and we will take it from there."

"That's kind of vague. I felt sexy wearing those shorts, but that's not what I would wear to a dinner date."

He was quiet for a moment. "Dinner it is, then. Have you ever heard of a place called By Invitation Only?"

"I have, but I've never been there. Have you?"

"No, but I can get us in. My boss has a membership."

That was impressive as hell, but if he hadn't made reservations, there was no way he could get them a spot in a place like that.

"I doubt they will have a table available. Besides, it's too fancy for a weekday evening, second date."

"Nothing is too fancy for you, my beautiful Cassandra. I'll see what I can do, but even if I can't get us reservations at By Invitation Only, I'm taking you somewhere fancy. Dress accordingly."

ONEGUS

*B*eing the chief of Guardians had its advantages.

Gerard had tried to argue that he couldn't possibly find a table for Onegus and his date on such short notice, but it hadn't taken Onegus long to convince the prick that it was in his best interest to find them a table.

He didn't care if his cousin had to squeeze an additional table in or put it in the restaurant's covered patio in the back. One way or another, he and Cassandra were dining at By Invitation Only tonight.

The reservation was for nine-fifteen, and it was five minutes to eight when Onegus parked in front of Cassandra's manicured front lawn. The restaurant was only a twenty-minute drive away, which gave him plenty of time to chat with the mother and get that obstacle checked off.

Grabbing the bouquets of flowers he'd bought on the way, he got out of his car and walked up to the front door.

It opened before he had a chance to knock.

"Flowers? How gallant." Cassandra reached for the bouquets. "For my mother and me?"

"The tulips are for your mother. The orchids are for you."

"Thank you. Both are lovely."

She looked resplendent in a figure-hugging silver-hued dress that reached a little above her knees. The slightly shiny fabric accentuated her warm caramel-colored skin, and the sophisticated cut complemented her tall frame and long limbs. Spiky-heeled silver sandals adorned her slender feet, held only by narrow straps. Long silver earrings dangled from her dainty ears, and a chunky matching necklace gleamed around her long neck.

He didn't know much about makeup, but he'd seen her yesterday with barely anything on her face, so he knew she had it expertly applied now. Cassandra was a natural beauty, but all decked out, she was magazine-cover perfect.

"You look ready for the runway." He followed her inside. "Silver looks good on you."

She gave him a crooked smile, followed by a hooded eyed once-over. "You clean up nicely yourself."

He waved a hand over his charcoal suit. "This old thing?"

Cassandra laughed. "You stole my line."

"Is your mother home?"

"Let me first find vases for these, and then I'll call her."

"No rush. Our reservation is for nine-fifteen."

Looking at him over her shoulder, she arched a perfectly shaped brow. "Did you manage to get us a reservation for By Invitation Only?"

"Of course." He stuffed his left hand in the pocket of his slacks and looked around the beautifully decorated living area.

It wasn't professionally done like Ingrid's interiors, and not everything matched or was even in the same style, but it was still elegant and yet warm and inviting. Cassandra had impeccable taste, which explained her success as the creative director of Fifty Shades of Beauty.

"I'm duly impressed." She put the flowers on the counter and pulled two vases down from one of the shelves. "Who did you have to bribe?"

He chuckled. "My cousin is the owner. But it took threats of bodily harm to convince him to secure a table for us."

Her brows dipped. "I hope he doesn't spit in our food out of spite."

"Gerard is obsessed with providing his super-important guests with an incomparable culinary experience. He would never do something like that."

She cast him an appreciative glance. "You are well connected, but then I shouldn't be surprised. Your family owns a multinational conglomerate."

She didn't know the half of it, but that was how the clan needed it to be.

As Cassandra filled the vases with water and unwrapped the flowers, Onegus examined the artwork. Noticing her name scribbled at the bottom of one, he checked the other paintings and charcoal drawings, and sure enough, her name was on each one of them.

"You are a very talented lady, Cassandra."

She lifted her eyes and smiled. "Thank you."

When a door opened somewhere on the second floor, and a moment later light footsteps sounded going down the stairs, Onegus turned and prepared to flash a charming smile that would disarm the most protective of mothers.

The woman who entered the living room was nothing like what he'd expected, and for a moment he wondered whether she was a visitor, perhaps a friend whom Cassandra had forgotten to mention.

Dark hair cascading around slim shoulders framed a pale, unlined face that was much too young to belong to Cassandra's mother. Big blue eyes eyed him with curiosity, and her red-colored lips curved in a mysterious smile.

"You must be Onegus." She offered him her hand.

"Indeed." He shook it. "And you are?"

She laughed. "I'm Geraldine. Cassy's mother."

"Impossible. You can't be. A sister, maybe. But her mother? No way."

"Oh, dear. You are a charmer, aren't you? And so handsome. I thought that

Cassy was exaggerating when she told me you were a god among men. But every word was true."

"Mother." Cassandra walked over to the much shorter woman and wrapped her arm around her shoulders. "You are embarrassing me."

"I'm sorry." Geraldine lifted her face to look up at her daughter. "You two look perfect together." She giggled. "Like Ken and Barbie. You are both so tall and beautiful."

"The tulips are for you." Cassandra kissed her mother's cheek and then grabbed a small purse off the counter. "Let's go before my mom decides to show you my naked baby pictures to prove that she's indeed my mother." She walked over to Onegus and threaded her arm through his.

"It was a pleasure to meet you, Mrs. Beaumont." Onegus smiled at the woman.

"Just Geraldine." She walked over and patted his arm. "Thank you for the flowers. It was my pleasure to make your acquaintance as well. Enjoy your evening."

"Thank you."

38

CASSANDRA

*C*assandra had been to fancy restaurants before, where a couple could easily spend over three hundred dollars without even overindulging in exotic drinks or delicacies, but By Invitation Only was by far the most exclusive gig in town, perhaps even in the entire country.

It was a well-hidden gem that wasn't marked by a sign, and the only indication that there was anything happening beyond its sprawling gardens was the valet service, but even that was done so discreetly that only those in the know could find the place.

It was also run more efficiently than any of the other high-end restaurants she'd ever been to.

As soon as Onegus had given his name, they were quickly led by the hostess to one of the secluded enclaves. Candles burned on the tables they passed on the way, their light too faint to illuminate the patrons' faces.

She had no doubt that it was intentional, providing privacy to the movers and shakers who owned a membership.

As soon as they were seated, the hostess took their drink orders so they could sip on them while going over the menu. Looking at the offerings, Cassandra was glad of having taken French as a second language in high school. Otherwise, she would have been forced to guess what she was ordering. It also bothered her that the prices were not listed.

It probably didn't matter. Everything was no doubt so costly that her choice of entree wouldn't make a difference in the bill Onegus got.

She glanced at him over her menu. "Do you get a discount because your cousin owns the place?"

He chuckled. "No, but don't worry about it."

"I'm not worried. I'm just curious. There are no prices on the menu. Does he charge a lump sum no matter what we order? Or is the cost included in the membership? How does it work?"

Onegus leaned forward. "Frankly, I have no clue. It's my first time here."

That was surprising. "I know that this place is not new. Why only now?"

He flashed her one of his panty-melting smiles. "I've never met a woman whom I wanted to impress as much as I want to impress you."

"I see." Leaning back, she stifled the urge to fold her arms over her chest.

Should she feel flattered that the guy was so desperate to shorten the wait until he had sex with her?

"What does that mean?" Onegus asked. "What do you see?"

"A guy who, for some reason, can't wait to get into my panties."

"I don't think your panties will fit me."

She rolled her eyes. "You know what I mean."

"That's not why I brought you here."

"Oh, yeah? You admitted that you wanted to meet my mother as soon as possible just so you could cross off that item on my list of prerequisites."

"I don't deny that. But I didn't bring you here expecting to wow you into dropping your panties for me." Smirking, he leaned closer. "You will drop them, but only because you find me irresistible."

"Overconfident much?"

"No. Just confident."

Damn. Why did she find his cocky attitude so sexy?

Usually, that sort of response would have annoyed her because it would have been empty boasting. In Onegus's case, though, it was just a statement of fact.

The way her body was fighting her resolve to wait, she might only hold off until the end of dinner and then drag him to the nearest hotel and have her way with him.

His nostrils flaring, Onegus sucked in a breath. "What were you thinking about just now?"

"Wouldn't you like to know?" She lifted the menu to hide her flaming cheeks.

With her dark coloring and the amount of makeup she had on it was doubtful Onegus would notice her blush, but she needed a moment to catch her breath and think.

Should she lie? Try to play coy?

Men didn't like to catch their prey too easily. If they didn't have to work for it, they didn't appreciate it as much.

Then again, Onegus had come to her house so he could meet her mother, which none of the men Cassy had ever dated had offered to do on the second date. Then he had taken her to the most exclusive members-only restaurant, which was probably going to cost him thousands.

Guys these days didn't expect to work as hard for a hookup, especially not men like Onegus, who had women throwing themselves at them left and right.

The thing was, Cassandra wasn't playing games to make herself stand out from the crowd. She just didn't want casual sex. She wanted a relationship that led to intimacy, and not premature intimacy that would leave a bad taste in her mouth.

When she lowered the menu, he was still staring at her.

She arched a brow. "What?"

"You asked if I would like to know what you were thinking about, and the answer is yes, I would."

Smiling, she reached over the table and put her hand over his. "I'll tell you after dinner."

He groaned. "You are evil. Why not now?"

She shrugged. "A lady should always be a little mysterious. Otherwise, where's the fun?"

39

ONEGUS

*U*nexpectedly, Cassandra's hard-to-get act was indeed fun.

Onegus loved that she wasn't all over him and was making him work hard to gain her approval. He loved that she challenged him on every front, forcing him to bring forth the best version of himself.

It was like a blast from the past, and it was refreshing, especially since she wasn't doing it just to be difficult or to play games. Cassandra wasn't willing to compromise on what she wanted from a man, and he applauded her for it.

Except, he couldn't give her that, and if he were truly a gentleman, he would have walked away.

Cassandra wanted a relationship, she wanted love and closeness, she wanted a partner she could trust.

Onegus could be none of those things. He might be able to see her a few more times, but eventually, he would have to move on. Unless, of course, he was incredibly lucky and Cassandra was a Dormant.

She hadn't exhibited any paranormal talents yet, and the raw energy he could sense in her could be just a physical manifestation of her assertive character. Some humans projected their feelings with such force that it was uncomfortable being around them, but that wasn't the case with Cassandra. To Onegus, the energy was like an aphrodisiac, an irresistible pull.

Unless she could somehow shape it and wield it, though, it wasn't a paranormal talent.

When they were done with dinner, and they ordered coffee and dessert, he leaned forward and smiled. "You said that you would tell me after dinner."

"Tell you what?" She pretended not to remember.

They'd talked about many things throughout the evening, but he doubted she'd forgotten that flare of arousal he'd scented coming from her.

"I'll jog your memory. When we discussed whether I was cocky or confident, a lovely blush coated your cheeks, and you hid behind the menu. The entire evening, I've been waiting not so patiently for you to tell me what caused that blush."

She glanced around, checking if anyone was listening in. "I'll tell you when we are in the car."

"Na-ah, Ms. Cassandra Beaumont. Stop being a coward. Out with it."

Her eyes narrowed, sending jagged daggers his way. "I'm the opposite of a coward."

She was even more magnificent when her feathers were ruffled. Sexy lady, so full of fire. He couldn't wait to feel the burn.

Crossing his arms over his chest, Onegus challenged her. "Prove it."

She swallowed. "You said that you're just confident, not cocky, and you are right. Your confidence, in addition to everything else you are, makes you very attractive to me." She swallowed again but didn't back down. "The thought that caused that blush was that it would be difficult to force myself to keep you waiting much longer, and I debated who would win the battle, my body or my mind."

Her honesty and courage impressed him, and he wanted to repay her in kind.

"What is your mind telling you?"

Unfolding her arms, she put her hands on the table, her long, elegant fingers splayed, the red nail polish like drops of blood on the white tablecloth. "It tells me that I should get to know you better first. That if we jump straight into intimacy, it wouldn't be as satisfying as having an emotional connection first." She let out a breath. "I'm not built for hookups, but the pull I feel toward you refuses to be denied."

"Then don't." He reached over the table and gripped both of her hands. "I feel the pull and the connection as well, and if I were a better man, I would have taken you home, kissed your cheek, and said good night."

She tilted her head, the dangling silver earring catching the light from the candle. "But you are not going to do that."

He smiled, letting the predator inside of him peek through the thin civilized veneer he wore. "I want you, Cassy, with an intensity that I haven't felt for any other woman, and I've been with many. I feel like I will burn if I don't have you. I won't make empty promises just to seduce you, though. I don't know what tomorrow will bring. Hell, I don't know if I will still be here a week from now. My boss might send me to Europe or the East, and I might be gone for weeks."

The last part wasn't true, but he needed a ready excuse for when he would have to say goodbye and stop seeing her, which was inevitable. But unlike all the other times he'd done so, the thought caused a dull pain in his chest. He hadn't lied or even exaggerated when he'd told Cassandra that he'd never met a woman who intrigued him and ensnared him as completely as she had.

40

CASSANDRA

*O*negus's message was clear. And honest.

They had just met, and he couldn't promise her forever, but the thing between them was too powerful to deny.

He was strong, physically and mentally, and perhaps with him she could for once lower her shields and let the storm swirling inside her loose.

No, she could never do that. What was she thinking?

She wouldn't risk damaging this magnificent male just to test what happened if she let go of the tight leash that she had over the darkness that swirled and churned inside her.

"I can't make any promises either," she said softly. "Maybe I won't like you the next morning."

His smile was predatory. "Does it mean that you will spend the night with me?"

She nodded. "Your place or mine?"

Wow, talk about a surprise. Onegus had been pushing hard, but until the words left her mouth, Cassandra hadn't expected him to win.

He looked just as stunned at receiving the invitation as she was at issuing it.

"Is your place even an option with your mother there?" he asked.

"Good point. What about your roommate?"

"I have an apartment downtown."

She arched a brow. "A shag-pad?"

He laughed. "It's a brand-new place, and you are the first guest I'm going to take there."

It was on the tip of her tongue to ask where he'd brought the many other women he'd been with, but it was none of her business. She didn't own his past or his future, she could barely stake a claim on his present.

After Onegus paid the bill without batting an eyelid, they were escorted back to the valet station, where his car was already waiting for them.

118

"I'm afraid to ask." Cassandra reached for the seatbelt after the valet closed her passenger door.

"Ask what?"

"How much was the bill."

Onegus chuckled. "Do you ask all of your dates how much they paid for the meal?"

She cringed. "I can't help it. I hate wasting money even if it's not mine." She cast him a sidelong glance. "Kevin gave me a ten grand budget to buy the dress and accessories for the gala. Guess how much I ended up spending?"

It was probably the least appropriate topic of conversation she could choose on the way to a hookup, but she was nervous, and talking about budgets and money was safe and took her mind off what she was about to do.

"Double," Onegus said. "That dress was almost as exquisite as the woman wearing it."

She snorted. "My mother was right. You're such a charmer. But thank you. Anyway, I spent less than half, and Kevin was mad at me for not spending all of it. I didn't even tell him that the dress I bought was once worn by a celebrity on the red carpet."

God, she was babbling what Onegus probably considered nonsense. What did he care about where she'd bought her dress or how much she'd spent on it?

"Which one?" He smiled. "I can't think of any actress that could look as good as you in that dress."

His compliment sounded utterly genuine, and it made Cassandra feel a little less embarrassed about her nervous prattling.

"I didn't ask."

"But if you bought the dress secondhand, how did you still manage to spend five grand?" There was no judgment in his voice, only curiosity.

"The shoes cost nearly three thousand." She smiled shyly. "I have a weakness for shoes. That's the only wardrobe item that I don't buy at a bargain."

"Kevin is paying you well. Are you saving for something special?"

"I bought the house my mother and I live in, and I want to pay off the mortgage in ten years. I'm also investing in stocks to grow my money."

"Your mother looks very young," Onegus changed the topic unexpectedly.

Cassandra had been wondering when he would bring that up. Everyone who ever met her mother said the same thing.

"If you're asking me how old she is, the answer is that I don't know. The number changes every time I ask."

"What does her driver's license say?"

"She lost it years ago and never bothered with a replacement."

Onegus arched a brow. "How does she get around?"

"Nowadays, she uses Uber. Before I bought the house, we lived in an apartment building that was close to a bus station. She just used the bus." Cassandra glanced out the window, noting the wide boulevard and the high-rises on both sides of it. "My mother has a memory problem. I don't think she would be able to get a new license if she applied for it."

"She's too young to have Alzheimer's."

Cassandra didn't like talking about her mother's condition. It was no one's business. But for some reason, she felt like it was okay to tell Onegus about it.

He would never use the information to taunt her or hurt her like some of her school friends had done.

"It's not Alzheimer's. My mother suffered a head trauma a long time ago and had total amnesia. She had to relearn everything from scratch, including speech, and she did, but she still suffers from periodic memory lapses. She tries to cover up for that by making up stories, so if she tells you something outlandish, it's probably made up. The best thing to do is to just nod and pretend that you believe her. Confronting her with the truth just makes things worse for her."

Onegus nodded. "How did she manage to raise you and do such an excellent job of it?"

Cassandra smiled. "She and I are proof that love is more important than anything else. I knew from a very young age that my mother forgot things and that I needed to be alert and help her out. But I also knew that she loved me unconditionally and would do anything for me. She would eat ramen for weeks so she could buy me the art supplies I needed for my drawings and paintings. She also made most of our clothes, buying fabric remnants and creating beautiful things from them."

"No wonder that you are so frugal as well as creative, which is an unusual combination." Onegus turned into the underground parking of one of the highrises. "Your mother instilled both in you."

"That and many other good qualities. You won't ever hear me complaining about my childhood."

41

ONEGUS

$\mathcal{T}$he apartment Ingrid had designated for Guardians' use during the wedding celebration was fully stocked and ready for Onegus to move in, which was why he'd decided to bring Cassandra there. Usually, he took his partners to one of the keep's apartments or to a hotel.

The upside was that for now, he was the only one who had access to the apartment, so there was no risk of one of the Guardians claiming it first. The downside was that the surveillance cameras had been already installed, the feed going to the security office in the keep. There was no avoiding the guys seeing him taking Cassandra up to the apartment.

Normally he didn't care, but she was unlike any of the others, and it infuriated him to think about the lewd remarks the guys might make when they saw him with her.

He even considered disconnecting the security feed and sneaking her up there somehow. Except that would bring the Guardians running to investigate, which would achieve the opposite of what he wanted.

"Does anyone live here?" Cassandra asked as they exited the elevator on the nineteenth floor. "Everything smells brand new."

"Not yet. It used to be an office building. The conversion to apartments was just recently completed." He unlocked the door with his phone. "After you, my lady."

Sauntering on her spiky heels, her slim hips sashaying enticingly, Cassandra looked around the professionally decorated living room and then walked up to the wall of windows. "You don't live here," she said, facing the glass.

"No, not yet. But I will be staying here starting Thursday."

Turning around, she arched a brow. "What happens on Thursday?"

He'd misspoken. The upcoming wedding and the clan members, who were arriving soon and would be staying in the building, needed to stay confidential or as confidential as possible.

Fortunately, he'd had many centuries of practice in coming up with convincing lies. "The semi-official opening of the building is this Friday. We have a large list of preferential clients who get to experience the apartments during the week before we open them to the public. I'm their host, and I need to be here to entertain them."

As Cassandra narrowed her eyes at him, the energy vibrating under her skin intensified. "You're not a real estate agent, Onegus. Why are you feeding me stories?"

"I'm not." He pushed his hand into his pocket. "Can I offer you a drink?"

The energy crackled. "What's really going on in this place?"

"Precisely what I told you."

As a faint rattling noise snagged his attention, he started to turn, catching from the corner of his eye a crystal vase swaying on top of the pedestal it was precariously perched on. Lunging for it, he could have caught it before it hit the floor, but instead of falling it exploded, the shards flying toward him like pieces of shrapnel.

Onegus's lightning-quick reflexes had him lift his arm to shield his face, at the same time grabbing Cassandra's arm and flinging her behind him.

He groaned as a volley of shards hit his forearm and thighs, penetrating the fabric of his suit and embedding in his flesh.

Behind him, Cassandra trembled. "I'm sorry. Oh God, I'm so sorry."

Turning around, he inspected her from top to bottom. "Are you hurt?"

Cassandra's eyes were the size of saucers, and instead of the fresh scent of ozone he associated with her, he smelled fear.

"I'm fine." She looked at his arm. "Are you hurt?"

He smiled to reassure her. "The suit absorbed most of it. I'm fine." He wasn't, but once he plucked out the shards in the bathroom, his wounds would heal right away, and no sign of injury would remain.

"I'm so sorry," she murmured again. "I didn't mean it."

"It wasn't your fault." He looked at the pedestal and the crystal pieces that were strewn about. "Cheap, made-in-China crap. It must have had a defect, or maybe the frequency of our voices agitated it into exploding."

She let out a shuddering breath. "I thought that I knocked it over by mistake."

Taking her elbow, he led her to the couch. "Let me pour you a drink."

She looked at his shredded sleeve and the tiny pieces of crystal embedded in his pants. "I should get those out first." She reached for his sleeve.

Onegus caught her hand. "Don't. You'll only hurt yourself. I'll get you a drink and then check the damage in the bathroom."

Cassandra shook her head. "I'm coming with you. You might need help." She lifted her small bag. "I have tweezers."

Damn. He couldn't let her see him heal faster than humanly possible. "I'll tell you what. If you really want to be helpful, find a broom and clean up this mess while I'm in the bathroom."

She opened her mouth, no doubt to argue, but then closed it and nodded. "I can do that."

"Thank you." Onegus leaned and kissed her cheek. "I'll be right back."

In the bathroom, he plucked out the bigger pieces from his sleeve and then carefully peeled the jacket off, wincing as the shards dragged over his skin.

Underneath, his shirt sleeve was soaked with blood. As he looked at the many tiny particles that were embedded in the skin underneath, he thought about Cassandra's offer to use her tweezers.

Hopefully, Ingrid had included a pair in the basket of toiletries, and he wouldn't have to ask Cassandra for hers. She would offer to do the plucking, and if he allowed it, he would have to thrall the memory of his fast healing away, and then he couldn't thrall her again after biting her.

Not a good plan.

When he found the tweezers in the basket, Onegus let out a relieved breath.

It took him almost half an hour to dig all the shards out, and when he was done, he stepped into the shower to wash the blood away.

42

CASSANDRA

*W*hat a mess.

Cassandra's damn temper had done it again. She should have told Onegus to take her home instead of going with him to his new shag pad.

He hadn't lied when he told her that she was the first one he'd ever brought there, but that was only because he'd just gotten the place. And why the hell had he made up those ridiculous lies about showing apartments to potential clients?

Onegus might not be the head of his family's international conglomerate, but his position in the organization was important enough that he wouldn't have to do the job of a real estate agent. If he'd told her that he was selling the entire building to potential investors, it would have been somewhat believable, but to assume that she'd believe he was tasked with showing apartments to potential buyers had been an insult to her intelligence. It had gotten her so mad that she'd lost the battle of trying to keep her sizzling energy contained, and it had exploded into that crystal vase as if it had been drawn to it.

Even after all the years she'd been dealing with that power, Cassandra still had no idea why it chose certain objects and not others. It seemed that glass, crystal, and ceramic were its favorite conduits. Usually, only inanimate objects suffered the consequences, but that could be dangerous as well.

She shuddered. If Onegus hadn't reacted as quickly as he had, both of them could have gotten seriously injured.

The guy had incredible reflexes.

Still shaken, Cassandra opened the bar cabinet and surveyed the selection. There was also a built-in fridge at the bottom, and it was well stocked. She mixed herself a tall glass of gin and tonic, added a few ice cubes, and drank half of it in one go.

It had way more tonic than gin, so getting tipsy wasn't going to happen, but she felt a little better and went looking for a broom and dustpan.

She found both in the utility cabinet in the kitchen, along with the latest

Dyson model. Sweeping in high heels and an evening dress felt ridiculous, but with all the little pieces of glass she didn't dare take her shoes off. Once most of it was gone, she took out the Dyson and vacuumed the rest.

Altogether it hadn't taken her more than ten minutes, but she was starting to worry about Onegus. Maybe he needed help getting the shards out?

If he got seriously injured because of her, she would never forgive herself.

There had to be a way to control those damn power surges. One way she'd found was to go on a run, but that wasn't feasible in most situations. Self-talk didn't help and trying to meditate only added to her irritation.

Should she knock on the bathroom door and ask if he needed help?

After taking another long gulp from the gin and tonic, she dug the tweezers out of her purse and headed to the bedroom. It was just as beautifully done as the living room. A massive four-poster bed took up most of the space and was covered with a cream-colored duvet and a mountain of pillows. Across from the bed, a matching dresser had a large screen perched on top of it, and a chenille settee with two decorative pillows sat in the corner. Even the colors on the area rug and the artwork matched. The room looked like it belonged in a high-end hotel.

In the bathroom, the water was running in the shower.

So that was what was taking Onegus so long. He must have gotten bloodied to need a shower.

As guilt assailed her once more, Cassandra felt the urge to flee. She could leave right now, call an Uber, and never see Onegus again.

A coward's way out.

Eyeing the bed, she thought about all the ways she could make it up to him. Maybe she could kiss and lick all those nicks and scrapes better?

They had only shared that one kiss on the beach, but if that was an indication of the kind of lover Onegus was, Cassandra was up for one hell of a trip.

After she'd made up for the explosion, though. She didn't deserve getting pleasured until then.

Sitting on the bed, she kicked her sandals off and sighed with relief. They were pretty and matched her dress, but they weren't comfortable. Her toes were grateful to her for ending their torment.

Cassandra debated for a long moment whether she should undress or wait for Onegus to get out of the bathroom and peel the dress off her. Eventually, the soft duvet cover won the argument.

Pulling the dress over her head, she tossed it on the settee. The necklace and earrings were off next, and she put them on the nightstand. Leaving the tiny satin panties and matching bra on, she crawled under the duvet to wait for Onegus to come out.

43

ONEGUS

*A*s he stood under the spray, Onegus wondered about Cassandra's strange reaction to the vase shattering. She'd kept apologizing as if it had been her fault, but she'd been nowhere near the pedestal when the vase started rocking.

The scent of fear she'd emitted had been strong, but he'd also detected guilt. Had she really thought that she'd knocked into the pedestal? Or had something else caused it to move?

After the accident, Cassandra's energy had seemed dimmed. Was it possible that it had been somehow released into the vase?

Other than Sylvia, Onegus had never encountered anyone with telekinetic ability. Sylvia could fritz out electronics with a thought, and most of the time she could control it, but sometimes her energy just got loose and caused havoc. Was it possible that Cassandra possessed a similar talent? If she did, it was probably on a different frequency than Sylvia's, and she had no control over it.

It should be interesting to find out.

By the time Onegus finished showering, there was no sign of injury anywhere on him. His clothes, though, were ruined.

After removing his phone and his wallet, he wrapped the suit jacket around the bloodied white shirt, and together with the pants, tossed everything into the wastebasket.

Thankful for Ingrid's attention to detail, he pulled one of the two white terry-robes off the hook and shrugged it on.

It would do for now, but he needed a change of clothes to take Cassandra home tomorrow morning. She might want him to take her back tonight, but he had no intentions of being done with her before the sun came up.

A long text to Arwel took care not only of that, but also a change of clothes for Cassandra, courtesy of Jin. Onegus had known that she was staying with her mate at night, and even though it hadn't been approved by him, he hadn't objected.

In appreciation, Jin was more than happy to do him a favor.

Tucking the phone and the wallet into the robe's pocket, Onegus turned to the door. When a soft rustling from the other side hinted at Cassandra's presence in the bedroom, he smiled.

Was it too much to hope that she was waiting for him in bed?

Yeah, it was. She probably waited to see whether he needed help plucking out the crystal shards.

Nonetheless Onegus was hopeful, and as soon as he opened the door, he glanced at the bed. Only her head peeked over the duvet, but her shy smile was the best invitation imaginable.

"What a pleasant surprise." He prowled toward the four-poster.

He wondered if Cassandra would be on board with putting those posts to good use. Imagining her nude and spreadeagled, her limbs tied with soft silk scarves to the posts, Onegus hardened, and his shaft tented the robe.

Commanding it to stand down, he uttered a soft groan.

It was a stupid idea on so many levels. First of all, games like that required complete trust, and Cassandra didn't know him well enough or long enough to play. Secondly, he had no silk scarves on hand. And thirdly, he'd never played games like that before and had no idea why it had even popped into his head.

Smiling nervously, her eyes roaming over his body, Cassandra let the blanket slide down, revealing her small, satin-covered breasts. "You look good in a robe."

"I look even better without." He undid the tie and let the terry cloth part.

Cassandra's eyes widened at the sight of his nude body and the impressive erection that he'd sprung.

Her tongue darted out to lick her lips. "Yes, you do."

Lifting to her knees, she let the blanket drop all the way.

The two scraps of gray satin covering her breasts and her mound didn't leave much to the imagination. Cassandra's body was pure perfection. She was slim and athletically built, but she was all woman, nonetheless.

Her eyes darting to his erection, she walked her knees closer to the edge of the bed. Her intention was clear, but if she touched him, it would become impossible to keep his fangs from punching out, and he wasn't ready to thrall her yet.

As she reached for him, he caught her wrist and lifted her hand to his lips. "Not tonight, sweetheart. I don't want it to be over before it begins."

A lie, but a handy one.

"I want to make it up to you."

"You are." He climbed on the bed and kneeled facing her.

As he reached with his finger and traced the outline of her mouth, her lips quivered, and as he wiped off the silvery, cherry lipstick and slipped the tip of his finger into her mouth, she licked it clean.

"That's one way to take lipstick off." She chuckled.

"There is still plenty of it left." Dipping his head, he licked at her lips while drawing a circle around her satin-clad nipple with his wet finger. "I didn't want to stain your bra."

"Your consideration is much appreciated." She reached behind her and unclasped it.

His breath hitched as it fell on the bed, exposing her perky breasts and stiff nipples. She had no tan lines, and for a brief moment, he wondered whether she tanned in the nude or just used a lot of sunscreen to protect her perfect skin from damage.

44

CASSANDRA

*A*s Onegus stared at her breasts, Cassandra could barely breathe, waiting for him to do something, anything to ease the ache, to defuse the energy building up a new storm inside her.

Then his head dipped, and he flicked his tongue over her left nipple, nipped it lightly, and licked the small hurt away.

"Breathe," he reminded her.

As she sucked a breath into her oxygen-starved lungs, he switched sides and licked her right nipple.

She couldn't decide whether what he was doing was pleasure or torture. His tongue and his lips eased the ache but created a new one, and she wanted them everywhere and all at once.

His hands too.

Those large, masculine hands that were touching her so gently as he smoothed them over her back. Then he reached her rear, and the gentleness was gone as he kneaded her ass cheeks.

Letting go of her nipple, he lifted his head and angled his mouth over hers, and that too wasn't gentle.

Her hands shooting to his spiky hair, she pulled him closer, her naked breasts pressing against his powerful chest. His skin was smooth, hairless, but he was all man. She trailed her hands down his back, tracing every muscle, every ridge and valley, learning him.

He was still kissing her when his finger trailed the edge of her panties, teasing.

Please. She was too proud to give voice to the plea.

Then he left her mouth and trailed kisses down her neck, nipping, licking his way down, and as he reached her nipple, his finger pushed the scrap of fabric aside and found her wetness.

129

He hissed, his wicked finger pressing against that spot at the apex of her thighs, and when he sucked her nipple into his mouth, she bucked her hips and groaned, her head falling backward.

More, she needed more, but Cassandra was too proud to beg.

They were both still on their knees, facing each other, when Onegus's finger pushed inside of her, and the coil that had been tightening sprang free.

The sound leaving her throat sounded like a growl, and as she ground herself on his finger, riding out the orgasm, Onegus chuckled softly. "Greedy minx, aren't you?"

In response, she wrapped her arms around him and pulled him down with her.

His magic finger had gotten dislodged by the maneuver, but having his heavy body on top of her was worth it. His weight on her felt just perfect.

Sturdy, strong, solid.

Cupping her cheeks, he looked into her eyes and smiled. "You are magnificent, my Cassandra." He dipped his head and kissed her softly.

Given the fire burning in his eyes, the lust she'd sensed hiding behind the admiration, the guy had to have the self-control of a monk to kiss her so gently.

A lover's kiss.

Don't read too much into it.

And then he was sliding lower and taking her panties with him, exposing her to him unceremoniously.

"Just look at you." He leaned back on his haunches. "A goddess."

His hands smoothed up her legs, starting with her calves, going up to the outsides of her thighs, and when they circled in, parting her for his heated gaze, Onegus dipped his head and licked her where she needed it most.

A strangled moan left her throat.

It had been so long since anyone had touched her intimately that she felt like a virgin again, and for sure no one had ever touched her with such reverence and skill.

Plunging two fingers inside her moist heat, Onegus licked and nipped, kissed and sucked, and through it all, she wasn't sure who was making more animalistic noises.

He sounded like a tiger as he growled against her flesh, a happy tiger, though. She'd never been with a man who seemed to revel in feasting on her, and knowing that he enjoyed being the giver of pleasure just as much as she enjoyed being the receiver unfurled something inside her.

A ravenous tigress who'd been too shy to purr for others, purred like a well-oiled engine for Onegus.

As the coil inside her tightened until it could tighten no more, Cassandra fisted Onegus's hair, barely aware that she was probably hurting him, and as he closed his lips over her clit and sucked, the coil sprung. The release that barreled down her wasn't a wave, it was an explosion, wresting a scream out of her that would have startled the neighbors if there were any.

Pressing a soft kiss to her folds, Onegus slid back up and cupped her cheeks. "I will never tire of hearing you scream my name." He kissed her hard.

The taste of her was strong on his tongue, but surprisingly, she found it erotic rather than gross.

Cassandra had a feeling that everything this man did to her would feel right.

Heck, she couldn't believe that she'd screamed his name without being aware of it. She'd never screamed a guy's name before. In fact, she couldn't remember ever screaming her climax at all.

45

ONEGUS

$\mathcal{A}$ s Onegus looked into Cassandra's eyes, he wanted to be the man she believed he was. There was awe in her gaze, a dreaminess, and it wasn't just about the two orgasms he'd wrought out of her. There was trust and hope that maybe what they were sharing was more than just a hookup. That it was the beginning of something wonderful.

He wished he could give her that and much more, but for now, all he could give her was pleasure.

Gazing into her expressive eyes, he nudged her entrance, waiting as he always did for the final consent, but not really expecting to be denied.

"Stop," Cassandra said to his great surprise, and put a hand on his chest. "You forgot protection."

"Right." Onegus reared up on his haunches. "Sorry about that." He leaned down over the bed to retrieve his wallet from the robe pocket and took out a packet.

As he tore it open, Cassandra sat up. "Let me put it on you."

If she touched him, he would probably explode in her hand, but he handed it to her anyway.

"Impressive." Her fingers brushed over the sensitive skin.

"You say the nicest things, but if you don't hurry, I'm going to erupt."

She smiled apologetically. "I wanted to take a moment to admire. It's not every day that a girl gets to see such male perfection."

He wasn't sure whether she was teasing or serious. Onegus had enough trouble keeping his fangs from punching out prematurely, which was a bigger problem than coming all over her beautiful breasts if she didn't hurry up.

As her long fingers expertly sheathed him, he wondered how she'd gotten so good at it. If she didn't do hookups and had been in love only twice, those two times must have been long-term.

But now was not the time to think about that.

132

As Cassandra lay back, he prowled over her, nudged her legs apart with his knee, and settled himself between them.

Some of the momentum had been lost, on her part, not his, but as he kissed her mouth, her neck, and then paid tribute to each nipple, Cassandra's hips started churning beneath him in a blatant invitation.

Lacing his fingers through hers, he laid their joined hands over her head and guided the tip of his shaft into her.

After orgasming twice, Cassandra was slick, but it had been a long time since she'd been with anyone, and she was tight.

Rolling his hips, Onegus pushed a little further, and when she moaned and arched up, he fed her a little bit more.

"You're tormenting me." She arched up again.

Lifting his hips, he didn't let her impale herself. "Patience, beautiful. I don't want to hurt you."

"You won't." She tried to pull her hands out of his grip.

His self-control only went so far, and as he surged into her, seating himself to the hilt, they both groaned.

The fit was tight, but not uncomfortable, and yet he didn't move, letting her get accustomed to the intrusion.

Dipping his head, he took her lips, intending the kiss to be soothing, gentle, but Cassandra was impatient and nipped his lower lip.

"Move," she hissed.

Onegus chuckled against her mouth. "Your wish is my command."

He withdrew slightly, and pushed back in, going slow at first and increasing the tempo and power of his thrusts in small increments to gauge her response. When she was panting, urging him to go deeper by arching into every thrust, he let go of her hands and gripped her hips.

Holding her down, he pounded into her hard and fast, and she melted beneath him, surrendering to him in the most primal way.

He needed her mindless with lust before he could let his fangs punch out, and as the release barreled through her for the third time, he pushed a small thrall to have her accept his bite without fear.

When she turned her head, offering him her neck, the last of his control snapped and as he erupted inside of her, his fangs sank into her neck and she orgasmed again, and again, and again.

And then her eyes rolled back in her head and she passed out.

For long moments, he lay on top of her, holding her tightly to him as if he would never let her go, listening as her breathing evened out and her heart rate slowed down.

When his own heart stopped hammering against his rib cage, he pulled out gently and padded to the bathroom to dispose of the condom.

He was still hard enough to pound nails with his shaft, and as he stood under the spray in the shower, he gave himself another release while replaying what had happened only minutes ago.

That didn't do the trick either, and when he came back to the bedroom with a couple of wet washcloths, Onegus was still sporting an erection that refused to deflate.

He found Cassandra sprawled on the bed in precisely the same position he'd left her, a satisfied smile on her beautiful face. She didn't stir when he gently cleaned her, and her breathing didn't change cadence when he climbed into bed and scooped her into his arms.

Tomorrow, he would have to wake her up early and get her home so she could change into work-appropriate attire, but tonight, he planned to hold her for as long as she let him.

46

CASSANDRA

"Good morning," said a familiar male voice as the bed dipped.

A moment later the smell of freshly-brewed coffee registered, and Cassandra opened her eyes.

It was morning?

The room was still mostly dark, the dawn's early light just starting to illuminate the sky.

"What time is it?" She reached for the coffee mug.

"It's five-thirty in the morning." Onegus smiled. "I figured that the coffee smell would do the trick. When I tried to wake you up twenty minutes ago, you pulled the pillow over your head and showed me your beautiful ass."

"I don't remember it." She took a sip from the coffee.

In fact, she was confused, not sure which parts of last night she remembered and which she'd dreamt up. She'd had the most amazing dreams of soaring through the clouds above alien cities and waving to the people below. She'd also dreamt about Onegus biting her neck, but it hadn't been painful. On the contrary, it was the most pleasurable thing she'd ever experienced, and after the number of times she'd orgasmed last night, that was saying something.

"You were tired." He leaned and kissed her cheek. "I wish I didn't have to wake you up, but unless you can call in sick, I need to get you home so you can change."

"I wish I could." She took another sip from the coffee. "But if I'm not there, my snowflakes aren't going to do a damn thing, and I'll have to pull all-nighters to catch up."

He arched a brow. "Your snowflakes?"

"The employees in my department. A bunch of twenty-somethings who think that they are entitled to do as little as possible and not only get paid for it but also get promoted." Cassandra shook her head. "Forgive my rant. I'm cranky in the mornings, especially this early."

135

"You can rant to me as much as you want."

He flashed her his gorgeous smile and reached for the mug of coffee on the nightstand.

With the cobwebs of sleep dissipating, she noticed that he was dressed in a pair of jeans and a button-down. The closet door had been open when she'd walked into the bedroom last night, and there had been nothing in it. "Where did you get the clothes from?"

"I texted a friend last night and had him deliver a change of clothes for both of us. He left them by the door." Onegus lifted his leg, showing her that the jeans were too short. "Arwel is not as tall as I am, but his girlfriend is about your size, and she lent you a T-shirt and a pair of leggings."

That was embarrassing. Had he planned on her spending the night? Or had he contacted his friend after she'd passed out?

"That's very sweet of her, and please thank her for me, but it's not necessary. The building is vacant, and no one is going to see me leaving with my evening dress on."

"That's true." He smoothed his hand over his curly blond hair. "But since he was bringing things for me, I figured you might want to change into something casual as well."

"It was a nice thought. I appreciate it."

"I wish both of us didn't need to go to work today." He gazed at her from under his blond lashes, his blue eyes vivid even in the dim morning light.

The man was truly beautiful.

Surprisingly, things weren't as awkward between them the morning after as she'd expected. It almost felt as if they'd been longtime lovers, comfortable with each other, but still very sexually aware.

"I wish so too." She took a few more sips of coffee before handing him the nearly empty mug. "I need to use the bathroom."

"Of course." He didn't move.

She had three options. Fling the comforter off and parade naked to the bathroom, wrap the comforter around her body and drag it to there, or ask Onegus to give her some privacy.

Normally Cassandra wasn't shy, and even though he'd seen every bit of her already, it still felt like too much too soon.

Understanding flashing through his eyes, Onegus got up. "I'll get you a robe."

"Thank you." She clutched the comforter to her chest.

Alone in bed, she felt the gravity of what she'd done weighing on her. She shouldn't have gone to bed with him on their second date, or third if she counted the gala. It was too soon. And yet, she couldn't bring herself to regret it.

She would, though, if he never called her again.

Men were hunters, and once they caught their prey, they lost interest. Cassandra had never made it so easy for a guy before. If a man wanted her, he had to work hard on wooing her because she was worth it.

Onegus returned with a robe that was identical to the one he'd worn before. "I'll make breakfast while you get dressed. Any preferences?"

She smiled tightly. "A fresh cup of coffee will do. I usually don't eat breakfast."

"I'll make eggs and toast." He leaned and kissed her cheek again. "You rocked my world last night, Cassy. I want more of that soon."

"Me too."

She waited until he left the room to let out a relieved breath.

This wasn't the end. It was just the beginning.

47

EMMETT

Twelfth day in captivity.

Emmett wondered how long he would keep count. A month? A year? A decade?

Kian had promised to let him out of the cell, conditional on the information he'd provided proving useful in locating his tribe, but Emmett doubted it would be.

The Kra-ell were nomadic by nature.

Their numbers were small, so it wasn't difficult to keep moving from place to place, and it helped keep them hidden. If too many humans started disappearing in one area, people became suspicious, especially of those who were different.

It had been relatively easy to disappear in China, and during his time with the tribe they'd moved several times, never returning to the same spot twice.

Kian's people were not going to find anything at the location he'd given them. Their best chance was to follow the money.

If Jade had sold Kumei there should be a money trail, but he had a feeling that she'd kept at least some control over the company. That was why he'd sent the email there.

What else could he offer Kian in exchange for his freedom?

The sanctimonious prick would never release him to his precious human world, but under the circumstances, the immortal village sounded like a sweet enough deal.

If all the immortal females were as tasty as Eleanor, then he was in for a buffet of treats.

Seducing them wouldn't be difficult. According to Arwel, Emmett's only competition for female attention were the former Doomers, a bunch of crude, uneducated brutes.

Compared to them, Emmett was a catch. Hell, he was a catch compared to nearly all males, human, long-lived, and immortal. He was sophisticated, charming, and a great lover if he said so himself.

The fact that he nibbled on a little blood from time to time was inconsequential, a small price to pay for the incredible physical pleasure he provided his partners, not to mention the intellectual pleasure of his company. Any female should feel honored to be chosen by him.

Perhaps he could offer Kian money, provided that the prick hadn't emptied Emmett's largest bank account already. He had plenty more, but losing what he had in the one he'd given the goddess access to would be painful.

What a powerful compeller the Clan Mother was.

Compared to her, Jade was a weakling. And unlike Jade, the Clan Mother had treated him with respect. But then she'd forced him to give her access to his largest bank account, which was what Jade would have done. She owned everything that their community had, including its members.

But at least Jade never tried to appear as anything other than the ruthless bitch she was. It would be a sad joke if after all of Kian's preaching about morality, fairness, and the importance of consent, he stole the money.

The guy didn't seem to be after Emmett's fortune, but everyone, even a rich guy like Kian, could always use more.

Emmett had a lot more stashed away in foreign accounts, and he owned the Safe Haven property free and clear. Which was another problem he needed to solve. The future profits belonged to him, but if he didn't claim them, they would be lost, squandered by whoever had stepped up to take his place.

Was it Riley?

She was the most qualified, but she lacked charisma and the others wouldn't follow her. Worse, they would try to undermine her, and the internal squabbles would ruin the well-oiled money-making machine he'd created.

As the door mechanism activating snagged his attention, Emmett looked up, curious to see who was visiting him this time. It was probably just one of the Guardians with his breakfast, but as starved as he was for company, even the stoic Alfie would do.

He liked Jay better, but the one Emmett liked the most was Arwel.

The guy was intelligent and well-read, which was a rare find these days. Perhaps it was different with immortals, but young humans liked their information to be served in condensed bites, preferably in color and with sound. And if they bothered to read at all, it was all about I and I and more I. They should be called the I generation, not X or millennials or any of the other terms used to describe them.

When the door finished swinging open, Arwel walked in with a tray in his hands, and Emmett greeted him with a genuine smile. "Good morning. I'm glad it is you and not one of your helpers."

"Why is that?" Arwel put the tray on the coffee table.

"You're more fun to talk to, and I'm bored." He lifted the lid off the container of blood and took a sip. "Lamb." He smacked his lips. "My favorite."

Arwel pointed at the plate of beef tartar and another container of blood. "After you finish everything, brush your teeth and wash your mouth. There is a change of guard later on, and the sight and smell of blood might gross them out."

Emmett paused with the tall container mid-air. "Are you leaving me?"

Arwel chuckled. "Not yet, but soon."

"Why?"

"I'm needed elsewhere. But don't worry, you will like my replacements." He smiled. "Eleanor and Peter are here, and one of them or both will bring your lunch. I'm staying just until they have the routine down."

Eleanor.

As everything that made Emmett a male awakened, and not too gently, his mouth filled with saliva, and not for the animal blood in the cup he was holding in his hand.

But then reality came knocking, and he frowned. "Should I expect trouble?"

"Not unless you cause it. They will not harm you."

"They both have reason to seek revenge, and I'm helpless." He lifted his cuffed arms. "I'm bound by shackles, both tangible and intangible. Your Clan Mother compelled me not to use my powers against her clan members."

"I'm well aware of that. Otherwise, I would have never agreed to have a female guard you."

"Do you think so little of me? I didn't harm Eleanor. I just nibbled a little on her blood, and regardless of what she told you, she was most willing. I didn't use compulsion on her, and the spiked wine had very little effect on her."

Arwel's usually pleasant expression hardened. "She tried to stop you, but you held her down and kept sucking. That's not willing in my book or any other."

They were all a bunch of self-righteous pricks, even Arwel. "Spare me the holier-than-thou sermon. As if all the females you guys bite during sex are consenting to receive your venom. They might sign up for the sex, but not for the fringe benefits they haven't bargained for."

48

MARGARET

"I don't think I can eat one more hamburger or steak without getting nauseous," Ana whispered as Bowen closed the door behind him. "But I don't have the heart to tell Bowen that I'm sick of eating the same thing every day."

"You don't have much longer to suffer through it." Margaret looked at Bowen through the window, her eyes following his movements as he fired up the grill. "You and Leon are leaving Thursday morning."

Ana sighed. "Yeah, I know. I'll probably miss Bowen's cooking when I go back to living on frozen meals."

It would be hard to say goodbye, especially to Bowen, but everyone had to go back to work eventually, including her.

He'd offered to come with her to Safe Haven, but that would be a temporary solution as well, and it would make saying goodbye to him even harder. Bowen didn't belong in Safe Haven, and he didn't belong with her. If she had any decency, she would not only let him go but push him away.

If you love something, let it go. If it comes back to you, it's yours forever. If it doesn't, then it was never meant to be.

She could remove the middle portion of that saying. Bowen was suffering from an acute case of a savior complex, and once he was free of her, he would realize that and forget about her.

Margaret looked through the window at the two men on the front porch. Leaning against the railing, Leon was sipping on a beer while Bowen fanned the charcoal to ignite a larger flame.

He was so handsome, so masculine, such an incredibly good man.

Tearing her eyes from Bowen, she looked at her friend's flat stomach. "Maybe you are pregnant after all. You said that you missed your birth control shot."

"The doctor took a blood test. I'm not pregnant." Ana rubbed a hand over her belly. "But maybe my stomach is still sensitive."

"You've lost weight."

Ana had returned changed from the clinic, and aside from the very strange and sudden weight loss, she didn't look like someone who had to get antibiotics through an IV. Her hair was glossier, her skin smoother and blemish-free, and her eyes practically glowed, especially when she got excited. Ana herself joked about the miracle potion the doctor must have injected her with.

But joking aside, what had actually happened in that clinic?

Ana grinned. "At least one good thing came out from that damn infection. I finally lost those stubborn pounds on my hips and ass that I couldn't get rid of."

"If you say so."

"Or was it two things?" Ana lifted a brow. "You were different when I came back. I have a feeling that things were getting serious between you and Bowen." She smiled. "It's adorable the way he looks at you."

"What do you mean?"

"He follows you with his eyes like a lovesick puppy."

To compare that mountain of a man to a puppy was an insult. Besides, Margaret wouldn't call his fond glances lovesick.

"He does not." She lifted her glass of water and took a sip. "We are just friends."

Liar.

Ana pursed her lips. "Right. Tell it to someone who doesn't know you. Yesterday, when Leon and I returned from our hike, your cheeks were flushed, and you looked like you were floating on a cloud of happiness."

Ana was just fishing. Margaret didn't blush. Or did she?

"I don't know what you're talking about." She felt heat creep up her cheeks.

Damn.

Ana smirked. "Did you two do something naughty when Leon and I were gone?"

"Not what you're imagining, that's for sure."

"Then tell me what you did, and it better not be nothing."

"We kissed. That's all. Just one kiss." Actually, there were two or three kisses, and a lot of caresses.

She'd lost her mind yesterday, allowing herself to indulge in the fantasy for just a little bit.

Those few precious moments would have to sustain her for a very long time. Now that Emmett was gone, Margaret was going to insist on some changes, mainly no more shunning members for abstinence. She had no intentions of inviting anyone into her bed.

"Just one kiss?" Ana glanced out the window. "With that hunk of a man? What's wrong with you?"

"This." Margaret lifted her cast. "What could we possibly do with that?"

She had a few ideas, but she wasn't going to share them with Ana or Bowen. If she made love to the man, leaving him would destroy her.

"A lot," Ana said. "You just need to be creative."

"I'm not that imaginative."

Liar.

Margaret had spent half the night thinking about all the naughty things she could do with Bowen despite the cast, and she had fallen asleep only after giving herself a release while imagining those were his fingers between her legs and not her own.

"I think Bowen is in love with you."

"Think again. Why on earth would he love me? What's there to love?"

Ana looked as if she'd slapped her. "Margaret! I don't want to hear you say such nonsense. You are a wonderful woman, beautiful and compassionate. What's not to love?"

If she only knew.

"Forget I said that. I'm in a mood today." She rubbed her thigh above the cast. "I'm itchy, and I want this thing off already." It wasn't a lie, but it wasn't the truth either.

Her mood had little to do with the cast and a lot to do with the man she had to leave behind.

Ana's eyes softened. "You poor thing. Is there anything I can do to make it better for you?"

"I'm fine. As long as I'm busy, I don't think about it, and it doesn't bother me as much."

"I'll let you work then." Ana pushed to her feet. "I'm going to chop some veggies for a salad."

Margaret waited until Ana was in the kitchen before letting out a breath.

Why couldn't she just let herself enjoy Bowen?

If she could regard him in the same way she had the Safe Haven male members that she'd been with over the years, everything would be fine. Thoughts about the future would be irrelevant, and she could enjoy the days she had left with him, accepting the gift of him without feeling guilty about indulging in what she shouldn't.

49

ELEANOR

"*R*eady?" Peter put a hand on Eleanor's shoulder.

"Yeah. I'm just wondering if we should go in together. The idea is for me to get close to Emmett, which is not going to happen with you smirking from the sidelines. Maybe you should stay with Arwel and watch us through the feed."

"How is that different from me being in there with you? You will know that I'm watching, and so will Emmett."

She turned to look at Arwel, who was sitting on the couch with earphones on, learning Chinese.

At least he wouldn't listen in.

Maybe that was the solution. "Can you watch without the sound on? Arwel is busy, but I'm sure he wouldn't mind."

"He's still the boss. We need to ask him if that's okay."

Arwel waved a hand. "Go ahead. The Clan Mother compelled Emmett to behave. Just watch your neck. She didn't tell him not to suck blood."

"Very funny." If Eleanor wasn't holding a tray, she would have flipped him off. "By the way, do I want to know what's in here?"

"Just hamburger patties," Arwel said. "I didn't want to gross you out on your first visit, but you'll have to get used to the blood."

She grimaced. "I'll live."

"Come on." Peter walked out into the hallway. "I'll open the door for you, but I won't come in."

"Thank you."

When the door to Emmett's cell swung open, Eleanor took a deep breath, plastered a bored expression on her face and sauntered in.

Emmett rose to his feet and dipped his head. "It's a pleasure to see you, Eleanor. Can I relieve you of the tray?"

He looked different without the beard and the long, majestic hair. Gone was the charismatic cult leader, and in his place was just a very handsome, attractive man, who was still pretty damn charismatic even without the props.

"So gallant all of a sudden." Eleanor put the tray on the coffee table.

Behind her, the door started to swing closed, and she had a moment of panic thinking about being locked in with Emmett in the small room.

"I'm always gallant." He motioned for her to take a seat on the couch. "Are you going to join me for lunch?"

She snorted. "I'm not going to be your lunch, that's for sure."

He laughed. "Touché. I promise to never bite you without your permission again." He sat next to her, unfurled a paper napkin as if it was a fancy fabric one, and draped it over his pants.

"From what I understand, you couldn't bite me even if you wanted to. The goddess compelled you to behave."

"Ah, Eleanor." He lifted the lid off the container. "As a compeller, you should know that the wording needs to be very precise. Otherwise, it's possible to find loopholes."

"Where is the loophole here?"

"The Clan Mother commanded me not to harm any members of her clan, but I don't consider a bite that delivers pleasure harmful, nor the little nibbling I do. I took very little from you." His dark eyes flashed turquoise for a moment. "Your taste was exquisite."

Remembering how it had felt, a shiver ran down Eleanor's spine. And if she cared to be frank with herself, the momentary terror she'd felt when she couldn't dislodge his hands had only added to the fuel of her arousal. Or was it something else?

That's why she was here, to find out what caused that strange, unwanted desire she felt for Emmett.

She still missed freaking Greggory, and if he hadn't been such a jerk, she would have wanted him back. But that chapter was closed, and all she could do was to look forward.

Emmett speared a hamburger patty with a fork and transferred it to a paper plate. "Can I offer you at least one? They are not bad."

She looked at the nearly raw meat and shook her head. "I'll have lunch later. Go ahead, eat. Don't mind me."

Next time, she was going to bring a meal for herself as well. If she was to seduce him into trusting her, she needed to spend time with him. The trick was not to make herself too obvious.

That shouldn't be a problem.

Eleanor wasn't the flirtatious type, and Emmett was a hunter to the core. If she showed no interest, he would try to seduce her, and after a while, she could pretend to succumb to his charm and charisma.

Again, that wouldn't be difficult.

She looked around the small room and noted the pile of books stacked on top of the dresser. "I see you've been busy reading."

"There isn't much else to do here." He wiped his mouth with a napkin. "What do you do to pass the time?"

"I train."

"How about that partner you've talked about and Peter has mentioned? Do you spend time with her?"

She laughed. "That was a made-up story. Kri, my friend and trainer, was supposed to come with me to Safe Haven, and we pretended to be a couple. Kri is happily mated to a fellow Guardian in training."

"What about you?"

Her smile faltered. "I had a boyfriend, but things didn't work out between us. We ended it a few days ago."

"I'm sorry to hear that." He didn't look sorry at all. In fact, he looked like the cat who was about to abscond with the cream. "Did it have anything to do with what happened between us?"

She shrugged. "If he couldn't handle what I needed to do on the job, he wasn't the right guy for me."

"I agree a hundred percent."

50

BOWEN

"Tea?" Bowen clicked the electric kettle's switch on.

Margaret nodded. "I would love some, thank you."

As usual, Ana and Leon had gone on a hike right after lunch to give him and Margaret some alone time.

The kiss had changed things between them, but he wasn't sure if it was for the better. They could no longer pretend that their relationship was just friendship, which was what he'd wanted, but Margaret seemed to cling to the pretense as if her life depended on it.

She hadn't said a word about the kiss they'd shared the day before, and her smiles had been guarded, polite. She had, however, put a little more effort into her appearance, which gave him hope. Her hair was no longer hanging limply down her shoulders and was instead styled in soft waves that shone thanks to Anastasia's curling iron. It wasn't much, but combined with the healthier-looking skin color and the little weight she'd gained, her beauty shone through.

If he only had more time, he would peel away her layers despite her resistance and uncover the diamond buried underneath. But even after all the time they'd spent together, he didn't even know what those layers were about.

What was she trying to protect?

Her heart?

What was she afraid of?

He was running out of time, and accommodating Margaret's avoidance was not an option. He had to confront her, to get her talking, and he wished he was better equipped for the task. Margaret needed someone with Vanessa's skill set and experience, not a Guardian of a few words.

When the water boiled, Bowen poured it into the two cups, added teabags, and put a few chocolates on each saucer.

Margaret glanced at the chocolates and smiled. "Are you still trying to fatten me up?"

"Not trying. Succeeding." He sat next to her. "But my work is not done." He dipped the teabag in the hot water. "If you insist on going back to Safe Haven on Sunday, I need to come with you to make sure you are not forgetting to eat."

She lifted her phone. "I'm not going to give this up, and Ana showed me how to set up timers with reminders. I will not forget to eat."

The phone was clan issue, and Kian would not want it falling into enemy hands. The device had restricted access, but someone could realize that it wasn't an iPhone or any other known brand and try to reverse engineer it.

"I'll have to get you a new one. This device belongs to the organization I work for."

"Oh." She cradled it in her palms. "That's a shame. I've gotten attached to this marvelous thing. Now that I know what it can do, I can't imagine life without it."

He was so damn jealous of that piece of technology. She couldn't imagine life without it, but she had no problem imagining life without him?

"I wish you thought that way about me," he murmured.

Her smile wilted and a tear slid down her cheek. "Oh, Bowen. I will miss you terribly, but it's for the best."

"How can you say that? You can stay with me. We can explore our feelings for each other, let them grow. It's not like either of us is leaving someone so we can be together. There is no upside to you going back there without me, nothing worthy of the sacrifice, it's just your stubbornness that's in the way of our potential happiness. Why don't you want to give us a chance?"

She looked down, her wavy brown hair cascading and creating a curtain to shield her face from him. "Safe Haven is not the right place for you, Bowen. Eventually, you will need to get back to work, and saying goodbye will be even more difficult. That's why I said it was best if we parted now."

"I don't intend to leave Safe Haven without you." He reached for her hand and clasped it. "My plan is to make you fall in love with me and leave together."

She chuckled sadly, but still didn't look at him. "Falling in love with you is easy, Bowen. You are handsome, and wholesome, and everything that is good. I'm not worthy of you, and sooner or later you are going to realize that and leave."

"If you think that your opioid problem makes me think any less of you, you are wrong. It's in the past, and I will never hold it against you. On the contrary, you overcame the addiction and have stayed clean ever since. It shows a remarkable strength of character, and you should be proud of yourself for achieving something that many fail to do."

She shook her head. "The shame is not about the addiction itself. It's about how I got addicted in the first place, and what I did to support it."

His gut clenched as he thought about the trafficking victims he rescued. Most of them were addicted to drugs not because they chose them but because their captors forced them to use, so they would later do anything for a fix without giving them any trouble.

Had Margaret sold her body to support her addiction?

"Whatever you did, it's in the past. You've spent your years in Safe Haven helping countless people deal with their demons. It's time you forgave yourself."

"I can't."

When he opened his mouth to argue, she lifted her hand. "Please, Bowen, let it go. It's difficult enough for me as it is." She looked at her phone and sighed. "I need to get back to work. Immersing myself in it is my way to cope. If I give it up, this one thing that makes me feel good about myself, I will have nothing left."

51

CASSANDRA

*C*assandra closed the garage door and took a deep breath before opening the door to the laundry room.

This morning she'd managed to dodge her mother's barrage of questions about her date with Onegus, but there was no escaping it now.

She could have stayed late at work, hoping that Geraldine wouldn't be home by the time she got there, but she was tired, and finishing up what she needed to do while sleep-deprived was easier done in her pajamas.

"I'm home." She dropped her overstuffed satchel on the kitchen counter and walked over into the family room, where one of her mother's soaps was playing.

"You're home early, Cassy." Geraldine grinned. "We can have dinner together for a change." Her smile turned into a frown as she glanced at the bloated satchel. "I see that you brought work home."

"I always do." Cassandra leaned to kiss her cheek.

"You should have called. I would have prepared something."

"That's okay, Mom. We can order takeout." She headed for the stairs.

"You promised to tell me about your date with Onegus." Geraldine pushed to her feet. "You can do it while I make us something to tide us over."

Letting out a sigh, Cassandra turned around. With all the things her mother was forgetting, couldn't she have forgotten about that?

She walked over to the fridge and pulled out a soda. "He took me to a really fancy restaurant, we ate, we talked, we even danced a little, and then he took me to his place."

Geraldine grinned. "And how did that go?"

"I got angry and shattered a vase." Cassandra popped the lid and took a sip.

Her mother paled. "Oh, dear. I hope it wasn't irreplaceable."

"Is that what worries you? It was a crystal vase, and it exploded. The shards flew at us, and if not for Onegus's lightning-fast reflexes, both of us would have gotten hurt." She sighed. "I'm seriously contemplating taking relaxants again."

Pulling out a pack of frozen ravioli from the freezer, Geraldine shook her head. "You can't. They make you sleepy and dull your creativity. You should take up meditation, or yoga, or just learn how not to get angry over things you can't control."

"I don't have the patience for meditation or yoga, and I'm doing my best not to get angry." Cassandra took out her earrings and stuffed them in her pocket.

They'd had that same conversation many times. Geraldine might have forgotten she'd already given Cassandra that advice, but it didn't make it any less valid.

"Did Onegus suspect that you had something to do with it?" Her mother filled a pot with water from the filter and put it on the stove.

"He was very gracious about it. I took the blame, saying that I accidentally knocked it over. But he said there must have been a flaw in the crystal, and some frequency of our voices resonated with it. He also said that it was cheap Chinese crap, so at least I didn't feel guilty about ruining something valuable."

"What did you get angry about?"

"He lied to me. You know how much I hate that."

"About what?"

"About the apartment he took me to. It was brand new, and in a newly renovated building that no one lived in. He said that he's supposed to show it to prospective clients, but that was a bullshit story. I don't know why he lied about it."

Geraldine pulled out a stool next to Cassandra and leaned her elbows on the counter. "And yet you spent the night with him."

There was no disapproval in her mother's tone, only curiosity.

"I felt so guilty and grateful as well. He saved me from the flying shards, and his expensive suit got ruined. I don't know how he didn't get injured, but he could have, and he did it to protect me." She lifted her hands. "How could I have denied him after that?"

Her mother gave her a lopsided grin. "I'm sure that gratitude was your only motive to hop into bed with that gorgeous hunk of a man."

Cassandra's lips twitched with a stifled smile. "Well, there was that too."

"How was it?"

The thing about having a young, unconventional mother was that they were more like sisters and could talk about everything. And that was also a problem. Cassandra didn't want to discuss her sex life with Geraldine, but her mother would be offended if she brushed her off.

She had to give her something. "Spectacular. I feel so calm." She put a hand over her chest. "Instead of a stormy sea, it's a placid lake in here."

It was as if all of her excess energy had gotten discharged when her body had detonated with one climax after the other.

Geraldine laughed. "That's your cure, Cassy. You don't need relaxants or meditation, just great sex with Onegus."

151

52

ONEGUS

"*Y*ou are home early." Connor removed his headphones. "I didn't make anything today." He tapped his finger on his tablet. "Brandon gave a mile-long list of things he didn't like about my score for *The Destroyer*. Until I'm done, it's going to be sandwiches from the café."

"You don't need to apologize." Onegus walked up to the fridge and pulled out a beer. "I wish I could tell you that I'll take over the cooking, but I'm moving into the new building on Thursday, and I'm going to stay there until the festivities are over."

Connor smirked. "Not to mention the new lady friend you're seeing. What's her name?"

The guy was the epitome of a busybody, but he wasn't a distributor of gossip, only a collector. Onegus trusted his roommate not to spread rumors about the new lady in his life.

"Cassandra Beaumont. She works for Kevin Brunswick, the founder of Fifty Shades of Beauty. His company donates cosmetics to the sanctuary and halfway house, and he's also contributing funds to the charity."

"Is he related to Josephine Brunswick, the cellist?"

"He's her husband."

"I know her. She's a sweetheart." Connor shook his head. "Dating a lady who works for one of our contributors is dangerous. She's not just a random chick you picked up in a club."

"I'm well aware of that."

Connor eyed him with speculation gleaming in his smart eyes. "She must be something. Since you and I moved in together, it's the first time I've seen you return from a date in the morning, and you are done with work early the second day in a row, which means that you are taking her out again. You're asking for trouble."

"I know what I'm doing." Onegus pointed with the bottle. "I thought that you were pressed for time. Go back to your composition."

"Just don't fall for her." Connor put the headphones back on.

Onegus had never fallen for a woman before, and he wasn't about to now. Cassandra was one of a kind, but if she wasn't a Dormant, he had no business pursuing a relationship with her.

And even if she was a Dormant, she wasn't necessarily his one and only. Hell, he had no desire to get shackled with a mate, and not for the reason other males avoided commitment. Giving up other females would be a relief rather than a hardship, but he liked his autonomy. Having to share everything with another, to not be able to just get up and go when he pleased, and for whatever reason, that was definitely a hardship.

It was crippling. He'd seen it happening to all of his head Guardians. So yeah, the bastards were happy, but that happiness came at a price. For them, the gain must have been worth much more than the pain, but for him it was the opposite.

That being said, it wasn't going to be easy to let Cassandra go.

They clicked, and it wasn't just physical, although sex with her had seriously rocked his world. He liked her assertiveness, her no-nonsense attitude, her work ethic, her drive, her talent…

Damn, there was a lot to like about Cassandra Beaumont. So much so that he was inclined to reevaluate his gain versus pain ratio. She felt different than other women he'd been with, and that strange energy field she emitted might be an indicator that she was more than just human.

It was worth investigating, and it gave him a good excuse for seeing her again.

Walking toward his bedroom, he pulled out his phone and dialed her number.

"Hello," she answered after six or seven rings, pretending once again that she hadn't recognized his number.

He could play along. "Hello, beautiful. Are you still at work?"

"I'm home, but I brought work with me."

"Can you take a break?" Onegus sat on the bed and leaned his elbow on his knee.

"To do what?"

He couldn't thrall her again so soon, but he needed to be with her again, see that perfect body of hers naked and writhing in pleasure. He should have enough self-control to hold off biting her until the next day.

"I can come to your place and bring takeout, or we can go out."

"How about I come to your place instead? Not that apartment you took me to yesterday, but your real home."

Aha, so that was what she was after. She still doubted him and wanted to make sure that he didn't have another woman in his life.

"I thought that you were short on time."

"Do you live far away?"

"Quite. It's an hour's drive. Besides, I have a nosy roommate who thinks that he's my mother and asks too many questions."

"He sounds like fun. In fact, I would love to meet him."

Onegus's suspicions were confirmed. Cassandra either didn't believe that he actually had a roommate or didn't believe that his roommate was a he and not a she.

"I can put him on the phone." Onegus rose to his feet and walked back to the living room. "His name is Connor."

"What about me?" Connor took the headphones off.

"Cassandra wants to talk to you." He activated the speaker function.

"About?"

Onegus shrugged. "I think that she doesn't believe me that you are a guy."

"I didn't say that," Cassandra bristled.

He put the phone on top of Connor's tablet.

"Hello, Cassandra. As you can tell by my voice, I am male, but if you want, we can switch to Zoom, and you can see my handsome face. I'm much better looking than this giant brute."

"I'm sure you are." Cassandra's tone lost its edge. "But I'm in my pajamas, and my hair is a mess, so no video."

"That's such a damn shame." Connor looked the picture of disappointment. "I was just joking about being better looking than my brawny, blond-haired, blue-eyed housemate." He cleared his throat for emphasis. "I was curious to see the lady who has him wrapped around her little finger."

Onegus shook his head. It had been a mistake to give the phone to Connor.

She laughed. "He's too big to fit around my little finger."

Connor barked out a snort. "If I value my life, I'm not going to respond to that. Anyway, I wanted to tell you that I know your boss's wife. If you see Josephine, tell her that Connor says hi."

"How did you meet her?"

"I write scores for movies, and she was the soloist for one of my compositions. She's a lovely human being."

"Josie is amazing. She'll be tickled silly that you are Onegus's roommate."

"Housemate. We don't share the same room. That would be just awkward."

Cassandra chuckled. "Naturally."

"Say goodbye, Connor." Onegus took the phone back.

"Goodbye, Cassandra."

"Bye, Connor. It was nice talking to you."

Onegus turned the speakerphone off. "Are you convinced now?"

"I didn't doubt you before."

He laughed. "Liar. Ask your mom what kind of takeout she wants."

"You are serious. You want to eat dinner with my mother and me."

"It would be my pleasure."

"Chinese. My mom loves Chinese food. Orange chicken is her favorite."

"Chinese it is. I'll be there at eight."

"Thanks. I'll see you later."

When he ended the call, Connor was still grinning at him. "She sounds nice. Do you have a picture?"

"I do." Onegus pulled out one that he'd taken on the beach and handed the phone to Connor.

Connor whistled. "She's a knockout. No wonder you are smitten." He enlarged the photo with two fingers. "But she looks a little bitchy, pardon my French." He handed the phone back.

"I admit that Cassandra has an attitude, but that's one of the many things I like about her. She has spunk."

"A spunky lady to spank." Connor waggled his brows.

"Pervert." Onegus turned around to hide his smile, that and the erection that had popped up behind his zipper as he imagined his hand on Cassandra's perfectly rounded bottom.

53

CASSANDRA

*C*assandra absentmindedly sketched the layout for the cover of the brochure that would go in next month's Surprise Box, years of honing her skills making it possible for her to create while her mind was busy elsewhere.

She knew what the finished product should look like even before putting down the first stroke, and it was just a matter of tweaking the layout and the colors, choosing photos, and adding flourishes.

Despite the calm that usually accompanied her creative work, an echo of unease churned in Cassandra's stomach, and she couldn't figure out what it was. It had something to do with Onegus, something she knew that she should remember and couldn't. The feeling was like trying to recollect a line from a movie, or an actor's name that was on the tip of her tongue yet eluded her.

Had he said something she couldn't remember?

It felt like it was something important, and not being able to bring it up terrified her.

As panic threatened to choke her, Cassandra tried to beat it down by reciting the self-reaffirming convictions that usually helped in situations like that.

Her mind was orderly and sharp. She wasn't going to end up like her mother, losing entire chunks of her past or hours from her day. Her mother's memory issues were the result of head trauma. Cassandra's were just ordinary memory lapses everyone experienced from time to time.

Sometimes, though, she wondered whether Geraldine hadn't invented the trauma and resulting amnesia as well. It had happened long before Cassandra had been born, and given how young her mother was, it must have happened when Geraldine was still a child. She claimed not to remember her family, and yet she'd never mentioned a foster home or an orphanage either. Someone must have taken care of her, a child who'd had to relearn everything from scratch, including language.

When Geraldine mentioned it, which she rarely did, she talked about it as if she'd been an adult while it happened.

Heck, who knew? Her mother refused to reveal her age, claiming that a lady never should, but maybe she was in her fifties and only looked young?

Perhaps crazy people aged slower?

It was frustrating to know so little about the most important person in her life and the only family she had, or rather knew of. But whenever Cassandra complained, her mother just hugged and kissed her and said that 'love is what matters and everything else is just background noise.'

Respecting her mother's wishes, Cassandra hadn't dug into Geraldine's past even though she'd been tempted. When she'd started making good money, she'd even thought about hiring a private eye to look into it, mainly because she wanted to find out whether she had any family out there. But doing so behind her mother's back felt wrong. It would have been a huge betrayal of trust, and her mother didn't deserve that from her.

The woman had dedicated her life to raising Cassandra as best as she could, finding work that she could do from home and doing most of it at night, so her child wouldn't have to fend for herself during the day.

Whatever dark secrets her mother hid from the world and from herself, they belonged to her.

As someone who had her own skeletons in her proverbial closet, secrets that she couldn't share with anyone, she had no problem walking a mile in her mother's shoes. Cassandra wouldn't have wanted anyone digging into them or forcing her to seek psychological help.

The difference was that Geraldine knew her darkest secret, but Cassandra didn't know her mother's.

Perhaps that was how it was supposed to be.

If she ever had children, Cassandra would do her best to hide her witchy powers from them. Until she learned to control that energy, though, she had no business having kids. What if she got angry or frustrated and hurt them?

The thought was terrifying enough to consider getting her tubes tied.

"Cassy." Geraldine peeked into her study. "You should get ready. It's quarter to eight."

She glanced down at her jeans and flip flops. "I am ready. We are not going out. It's just a takeout dinner at home."

Her mother shook her head. "At least change your T-shirt. You have paint smudges all over it."

She chuckled. "It's not smudges, Mom. It's the shirt's design. I got it on sale, but the original price was close to two hundred dollars."

Geraldine's expression was doubtful. "If you say so. Just wear something nice for Onegus. It doesn't have to be fancy, but a lady does not accept guests in flip-flops and jeans."

Her mother sometimes seemed to forget what era they were living in, but arguing with her would only upset her and make things worse. The memory issues became much more obvious when Geraldine was upset.

"You have such old-fashioned ideas about propriety, but fine. I'll change."

Her mother beamed happily. "Now, was that so hard to do?"

157

"Not at all." Cassandra pushed to her feet. "Just do me a favor and don't spin tall tales or embarrass me in any way during dinner."

"I don't know what you mean." Her mother pushed her chin out. "It's one thing to talk freely and joke around with my daughter, and it's another thing altogether to do so in front of a gentleman caller. I plan to be the perfect hostess."

Cassandra stifled the urge to roll her eyes.

Her mother had embarrassed her plenty of times in front of her friends from school, until she'd stopped inviting them over.

"Since I've never had a *gentleman caller* before, you don't have practice being the perfect hostess, and your book club doesn't count. I heard you and your friends discuss romance books, and you were far from proper." She pulled a summer dress out of the closet. "Let's agree on a sign. If I clear my throat, you will stop whatever you're talking about and change the subject or let me do that. I don't want to talk over you and appear rude."

Geraldine huffed out a breath as if to say that Cassandra was offending her for no good reason. "I'll let you get dressed and go set the table."

"Thanks, Mom."

"You're welcome." Her mother hesitated for a moment. "I know that you are all grown up and that you don't need advice from your crazy mother. But just try not to seem too eager. Men like to chase, and if they catch you too easily, they don't appreciate you."

Geraldine had given her that same advice so many times that it was hard-wired into her brain. Nevertheless, Cassandra pretended it was the first time she'd heard it. "Thanks for the advice, Mom." She walked up to her mother, kissed her cheek, and once she left, closed the door and sighed.

Her mother's advice sounded so outdated, so old-fashioned. Even anti-feminist. Why should women play hard to get when they wanted sex just as much as men did?

They shouldn't.

But the world was not fair, and people played all kinds of games to get the upper hand. Cassandra hated playing games, but she hated losing even more.

54

ONEGUS

*T*he door opened even before Onegus had a chance to knock, but it wasn't surprising given that the guard had called the house before letting him through the gate.

He was glad that Cassandra and her mother lived in a gated community. Home invasions were much more commonplace than most people realized, and two women living alone were an easy target.

"Hello, Onegus." Geraldine beamed at him, or rather at the bag he was holding in his left hand. "The orange chicken smells delicious."

In his right, he was balancing a bouquet of flowers and a bottle of wine. It never hurt to go the extra mile, so to speak.

"Good evening. I hope it is as good as it smells." He handed her the bottle and flowers.

Geraldine looked lovely, her dark hair swept to the side and secured with a comb, and a pale blue summer dress accentuating her delicate build. The cat-eye eyeliner and pale pink lipstick made her look like a fifties model, but she was way too young to have grown up in that era. In fact, she looked no older than Cassandra, maybe even younger, because Geraldine's expression was softer.

Perhaps she wasn't Cassandra's birth mother?

Nah, that didn't make sense. No agency would let a young, unmarried woman adopt a child. Unless she was Cassandra's older sister. Perhaps siblings were allowed to foster their younger sisters and brothers?

But that didn't make much sense either.

Applying Occam's razor, the simplest explanation was that Geraldine had Cassy as a teenager, and she'd been lucky enough to age well.

He followed her inside. "Is Cassandra still working?"

"You guessed it. She insists on creating a new design for each new monthly Surprise Box, says it keeps them fresh, but that means that she has to reinvent the wheel every month anew."

It was a very lucid insight from a woman who was supposedly a little off.

He put the bags on the kitchen counter. "Cassandra knows what she's doing. Kevin is lucky to have her."

"Onegus." Cassandra flew down the stairs, her dress billowing around her hips, earrings dangling, and a bright smile on her gorgeous face.

"Cassy." He opened his arms, and she went right into them, wrapping her arms around his neck as if welcoming her mate returning from a long trip.

It felt too right.

Her enthusiastic welcome shouldn't make him feel so damn happy.

As he embraced her lightly and kissed her forehead out of respect for her mother, Geraldine cleared her throat.

"Let's eat before everything gets cold."

For some reason, Cassandra chuckled. "My mother seems uncomfortable with our display of affection. She's a little old-fashioned."

Geraldine smiled sweetly. "It's not that. I just can't wait to dig into my orange chicken." She took the bag and started putting boxes on the dining room table that was already set up for three.

He leaned and whispered into Cassandra's ear, "You look beautiful. Good enough to eat." The last sentence was delivered in a tone an octave lower than the first, and he interpreted the answering gleam in Cassandra's eyes as a *yes, please.*

"Later," he whispered.

Her mother cleared her throat again. "Cassy, could you please bring sodas from the refrigerator?"

"Of course." She winked at him before letting go and heading into the kitchen.

"I want to thank you," Geraldine said.

"You're welcome, but it's nothing." He waved a hand at the takeout boxes. "I hope you enjoy it. The Golden Dragon is my favorite place for Chinese."

"I'm sure Cassy and I will love it. But what I really wanted to thank you for is making my daughter happy." She narrowed her eyes at him. "Don't hurt her."

The message was clear, and he didn't doubt the potency of the unspoken 'or else.' The same energy he'd felt swirling inside Cassandra was also inside her mother, just at a much lower voltage.

He wondered whether sensitive humans picked up on that the way he had and what they made of it. In days long passed, mother and daughter could have been accused of witchcraft. Thank the merciful Fates those days were over, hopefully never to return, but one never knew with humans.

The us-versus-them chimp mentality was hardwired into the human race, as was blindly following their leaders, whether clergy, and or politicians. Nowadays there were also internet and social media influencers to follow. The twenty-first century was a brainwashing fest like no other, but the impetus hadn't changed. It had always been about power and money, and it was still about leaving as little of it as possible in the hands of the masses.

As long as it didn't lead to wars, though, Onegus didn't care. The problem was that at some point, someone always figured out that they could shift even more money and power from others to themselves by taking it forcefully.

"What are you thinking about?" Cassandra smoothed a finger over his forehead. "You're frowning."

He hadn't noticed that she'd returned with a six-pack of sodas and wine glasses for the wine he'd brought.

"Just random thoughts." He smiled. "Thank you for sharing your home with me tonight. I'm honored." He dipped his head to Geraldine.

"It's our pleasure." Cassandra's mother smiled sweetly as if she hadn't threatened him just a moment ago.

55

CASSANDRA

They were almost done with dinner, and so far Geraldine had behaved, but Cassandra had a feeling that her luck was about to run out when her mother smiled mysteriously, put her fork down, and pushed her plate away.

"This was excellent, but not as good as the one I had in Washington while dating Cassy's father."

Cassandra cleared her throat.

Disregarding her, Geraldine continued. "He was an analyst for the Ethiopian embassy."

So today, her father had been just the analyst. The other day he'd been the ambassador himself, and other times he hadn't been from Ethiopia but from Yemen or Senegal. And that was when he wasn't a visiting professor, a surgeon, or an astronaut.

As her mother lifted a paper napkin and dabbed it at her lips, Cassandra cast Onegus an apologetic sidelong glance.

"He was a descendant of the legendary Queen of Sheba." Her mother chuckled. "Or so he claimed." Her eyes became dreamy. "He was certainly majestic enough. Tall, broad-shouldered, and his smile." She fanned herself with her hand. "It was as beautiful as yours, Onegus."

Eager to interrupt the fantasy trip, Cassandra pushed to her feet. "Ready for coffee and dessert?"

Onegus followed her up. "I'll clear the table."

Geraldine remained seated for a moment longer, that dreamy expression still on her face. It would almost be a shame to bring her back to reality, but Cassandra feared that one of these days her mother would float away on the wings of her imagination and never come back.

"Mom, isn't Gwen supposed to pick you up at ten? It's nine-fifty, and you still need to change into something warmer."

Her mother shook her head. "I'll grab a sweater on my way out. It's not like we are going anywhere. We are just going to watch a movie at Gwen's."

"As you wish."

Geraldine pushed away from the table. "Do you need me to help clear the dishes?"

"No. We are fine, Mom. Go have fun."

"Thank you." She smiled at both of them. "It was a lovely dinner."

When Geraldine headed upstairs to get her sweater, Onegus smirked like a cat who had realized that the canary's cage was open. "We will have the house to ourselves," he said softly. "I feel like a teenager waiting for my girl's parents to leave, so I can have my wicked way with her."

Cassandra filled the carafe with water from the filter. "I'm sorry about my mother's stories about my father." She poured it into the coffeemaker. "I don't know if she makes them up because she can't remember who he was, or because she enjoys the fantasy." She smiled at Onegus. "For some reason, he's never just a schoolteacher or a plumber, which would make her stories more believable."

Onegus glanced toward the stairs, but her mother wasn't coming down yet. "As long as the fantasies don't make her dangerous to herself or others, they are harmless. Geraldine sounds lucid most of the time, she is intelligent, friendly, and seems to have an active social life."

"Yeah, she belongs to a book club that meets twice a week, sometimes three. My mother has a much more active social life than I do." Realizing how pathetic that sounded, Cassandra added, "But she doesn't work eighty hours a week and has the time to be social."

Onegus sighed. "We are a lot alike, you and I. I have never taken a proper vacation. I consider traveling for business my time off."

Leaning against the counter, she crossed her arms over her chest. "Do you enjoy what you do?"

"Very much so." He cast a glance at the hissing coffeemaker, which was spewing dark brew into the clear carafe. "Sometimes I don't even notice that I've been in the office for twelve hours straight."

"That's why you don't take a vacation," Cassandra said. "You enjoy working more than you enjoy time off."

It was also a sign of loneliness.

Cassandra hadn't taken a vacation since she'd started working for Kevin either. Neither of her two boyfriends had offered to take her on one, and going alone was just sad. After her high school friends had gone to college and she'd gone to work for Kevin, Cassandra had lost touch with them, so that wasn't an option either. Besides, they were no doubt married by now and chasing gaggles of kids around.

When the coffeemaker was done, she poured them both a cup. "Where would you go if you had someone to go with?"

He was about to answer when her mother came down the stairs.

"I'm off to Gwen's." She kissed Cassandra's cheek and then did the same to Onegus. "I hope to see you again." She tilted her head as if it was a question.

"I'm not going anywhere anytime soon."

Hopefully, that wasn't a lie.

"Good." Geraldine beamed happily.

Cassandra wondered if her mother was going to remember Onegus once he stopped coming over.

Probably not, which would be a blessing.

The guy was too good to be true, and something in his tone had told her that he wasn't planning on sticking around for long despite what he'd told her mother.

There were other indicators as well.

If he was serious about her, he would want to show her off to his friends, not take her to a deserted building where no one could see them together. So yeah, he'd taken her to his cousin's restaurant, and they'd even danced a little, but he hadn't introduced her to his famous cousin or anyone else.

Having her speak with his roommate on the phone didn't count.

If there was another date, she would insist that Onegus invite her to his house, the one he shared with the composer, or that he invite some of his friends to join them on an outing. If he tried to wiggle out of it, she would have proof that her hunch had been right, and she should end things before getting attached to him.

It would still be hard as hell to say goodbye to Onegus, but she could at least save her dignity and avoid even more pain down the line.

56

ONEGUS

*A*s soon as the door closed behind Geraldine, Onegus pulled Cassandra into his arms. "Let's skip coffee and dessert. I'd much rather snack on you." He smacked his lips.

Her smile was tense. "I still have work to do tonight."

"So do I, but there is always time for a quickie." He dipped his head and kissed her softly. "I can either eat my dessert here, sprawled on the dining table, or on the couch, or you can take me to your bedroom."

She hesitated for a couple of seconds. "Let's go to my room." She took his hand and led him up the stairs.

"That's my mother's room." She pointed at the double doors leading to what was no doubt the master bedroom. "And this is mine." She opened the next door and turned the lights on.

The room was small, but like the rest of the house, it was uncluttered and beautifully done. A queen-sized bed with a wrought iron headboard took up most of the space. The bedding was cream-colored cotton with embroidered accents, and a colorful quilt was folded at the foot of the bed. There was space for only one nightstand and a dresser that was tall and narrow, and there were no knick-knacks or framed photos like in most females' bedrooms. Cassandra also had no television or any other electronics in her room, not even a landline phone, and instead of pictures, an intricate quilt covered half the wall across from the bed.

The room was designed to promote peaceful sleep and nothing else. He applauded her decorating approach. Living in a city that had suffered a number of powerful earthquakes, having nothing in her bedroom that could fall over and break was a smart decision.

"You don't work in here," he stated the obvious.

She chuckled. "I wouldn't be able to sleep at all if I had my work stuff here.

The next bedroom over is my study, but I use its closet to store half of my clothes. There is not enough room in this one."

She sounded a little nervous, so he ran his hands over her back in soothing circles. "You bought the house, and yet you gave your mother the master bedroom. How come?"

She shrugged. "My mother worked very hard to raise me on her own. She deserves a little pampering from me. Besides, I only sleep in here, and I use the other bedroom as well."

He put his hands on her waist. "Under all your bluster, you are very sweet."

She scrunched her nose. "I am not sweet. I'm spicy."

He licked his lips. "Let's put it to the test."

He gathered her dress until it was bunched around her middle. "Lift your arms."

Smiling seductively, she did, and he pulled the dress over her head.

"Gorgeous." He lifted her by the waist, laid her on the bed, and then stood at the foot of it and just feasted his eyes on her.

"Get the lights, Onegus," she whispered.

"Are you being shy, Cassy?"

"No, but it's more romantic in the dark."

"If you say so." He walked over to the light switch and flicked it off.

Plenty of moonlight streamed through the open window, bathing Cassandra in a silvery light that made her skin glow like burnished copper.

Her bra and panties were white satin, simple yet elegant, just as the gray set she'd worn the day before. The woman had impeccable taste, and she paid attention to the smallest of details.

Even the bottle of moisturizer on the nightstand matched the color scheme of her room.

It gave him an idea. "Turn around on your belly. I'm going to give you a massage."

She grinned. "With a happy ending?"

"Of course."

As Cassandra turned over, he sucked in a breath. Her panties weren't a thong, but they didn't cover much either. The narrow triangle of satin barely covered the valley between her cheeks, and they were so enticing that he just had to kiss each one before sliding those panties down her long legs.

"I love your ass." He kissed each cheek again before reaching for the lotion.

"Only my ass?" Reaching behind herself, Cassandra popped the clasp of her bra, pulled it off, and tossed it on the floor.

"I love your breasts too, and your legs, and your arms." He squeezed out a dollop, rubbed it between his hands, and smoothed them over the back of her thighs. "I also love those pouty lips of yours, and your eyes, especially when they sizzle with power."

Cassandra stiffened. "What do you mean?"

"Your spunk, your energy." He smoothed his hands over her perfect bottom and kneaded. "You are strong, determined, uncompromising, and I find it sexy as hell."

"Some would summarize it as bitchy," she murmured.

"Not me." He slid a finger down her feminine folds, eliciting a throaty moan.

"What would you call it?"

He paused for a moment, thinking how to put into words the way he saw her. "I would call it majestic, my beautiful queen."

57

CASSANDRA

$\mathcal{C}$assandra laughed. "You are such a charmer, Onegus. But you are not original. I've been called a queen bitch before."

The smack landing on her bottom caught her by surprise. "What was that for?"

It hadn't been more than a love tap, and given how big and muscled Onegus was, he had barely touched her. Was it part of the foreplay?

"I just couldn't help myself." Another one landed on her other cheek, and then he was kneading them with his strong fingers, spreading the heat around. "This ass is driving me crazy. Men would go to war over this perfection."

"You're obsessed." Smiling into the pillow, she wiggled her bottom.

He smacked it again. "You're damn right I am. Can you blame me? Have you looked at that ass in the mirror?"

She laughed again. "I sure did."

Being playful in the bedroom was a novelty. The other men Cassandra had been with, the whole two of them, had taken sex way too seriously. She never would have expected to enjoy the banter with Onegus so much.

"Once or twice. But you promised me a massage, and all you're doing is talking and playing with my butt."

"Apologies, my queen."

She heard him squirt another dollop, and then his hands were on her calves, massaging, kneading.

Her toes curled as her muscles eased.

After strutting in high heels all day, her calf muscles were tight, and having his strong fingers on them felt almost orgasmic, which she freely expressed with several delighted moans.

He chuckled. "And here I thought that you would be hard to please." He lifted her foot and massaged each toe separately.

"If you promise to do this every night, I'll marry you as soon as we can get to a chapel." She regretted her words as soon as they'd left her mouth, and even more when his hands stopped massaging. "I'm just joking, Onegus. I have no intentions of marrying you or anyone else. I'm married to my job."

Liar.

She loved her work, but that didn't preclude having a man in her life, or even children—provided that she mastered her energy so it never acted out when it shouldn't. Her mother would help her raise them, and she could hire a nanny to help her. Geraldine would be thrilled to have babies to take care of. And as for her long workdays, Cassandra could do most of the work from home.

Kevin wouldn't mind. In fact, he would probably be overjoyed. It would save him from having to manage all the complaints from the other creatives about her bitchy attitude and her so-called unreasonable demands for timely production.

Yeah, dream on.

Time wasn't on her side as far as having children was concerned. If she didn't find someone soon, as well as learn to control her power, that would remain just a dream.

"I kind of liked the idea." His hands moved back to her calves. "But regrettably, I'm in the same boat as you. And on top of that, I also travel for work. Not a lot, but enough to make my lifestyle unsuitable for marriage. Unless my hypothetical future wife worked with me in my office and came along on my business trips, she would be alone most of the time."

Onegus had told her as much, so at least she knew that he wasn't making it up to explain why she shouldn't think of him as husband material, but it hurt nonetheless.

Cassandra let a single tear slide into the pillow, and then she shut her damn brain and heart down and concentrated on the sensation of his hands on her body.

He started a slow track up her thighs, his fingers tracing the inner side with feather-light strokes.

As her core responded, igniting with need and flooding with heat and moisture, she shamelessly parted her legs a little to invite more. If this was all he could give her, she would make the most of it as long as it lasted.

His fingers dipped lower, skimming the edge of her swollen petals and providing absolutely no relief.

This was dangerous.

The sexual frustration combined with the irritation from before provided combustive fuel for the volatile energy building up inside her.

When the bottle of lotion on the nightstand started shaking, she whispered, "Onegus."

"Yes?" His fingers continued their barely-there strokes.

The bottle fell down to the floor, the hard plastic making a thudding sound but not a splattering one, which was a relief.

"Touch me before I explode."

He chuckled. "That's the idea."

The lotion was the only item in her room that could have fallen victim to her energy. If he didn't defuse it somehow, Onegus would be next.

"I'm not joking."

Something in her tone must have gotten through to him, and those teasing fingers glided into her.

Her moan was one of pleasure and relief.

Then his mouth replaced his fingers and he gripped her hips, lifting her bottom to allow him better access.

Grinding herself on his tongue, his lips, she groaned into the pillow.

His grip on her hips tightened, holding her in place as his tongue found that most sensitive spot and flicked over it.

Behind her eyelids, her eyes rolled back in her head, and as his mouth closed around that needy, pulsating bundle of nerves, the climax exploded out of her in a rush.

"Onegus!" She shouted his name into the pillow.

Kissing her folds softly, he caressed her sides as the ripples subsided and her panting slowed.

She expected him to drop his pants and spear into her, but instead, he kissed her ass cheeks one at a time.

"No rest for the weary." He lightly slapped her bottom. "You have work to do."

She flopped around. "What about you?"

"I'm the master of delayed gratification."

"Are you sure?" She glanced at the erection pushing against his zipper.

He smacked his lips. "I got my dessert. I'll have a full five-course meal tomorrow."

58

VLAD

*A*s the plane touched down on the runaway at Milwaukee airport, Richard opened his eyes and yawned.

"Good morning." Vlad unbuckled his seatbelt.

Since Kalugal had given Richard only one day off, they'd decided to save time by taking the red-eye. They'd left Los Angeles Tuesday night, and were going back today. Unless Wendy's father wasn't where he was supposed to be, it should be enough time for what they were about to do.

Richard had slept through the entire flight, but Vlad had been too strung out to even close his eyes. The taser idea hadn't worked out because they couldn't take the device on a commercial flight, and getting one in Milwaukee would be too much of a hassle.

Vlad would have to rely on his willpower to refrain from killing Wendy's father. Richard wasn't strong enough to hold him back, and even if he was, Vlad didn't want to put him in the position of having to muscle down his mate's son.

The other thing that had kept him awake was that he still hadn't told Wendy the big secret about his own father. She was his mate, and he was supposed to tell her everything, and the more time passed since his mother had revealed the truth to him, the more guilty he felt for not sharing it with Wendy.

The truth was that there was no reason to keep it from her. The weak excuse he'd come up with to justify it was that he didn't want to add to her burden.

What he was about to do weighed heavily on both of them, and he figured that it would be better to save his news for after his mission was done.

Neither he nor Richard had checked-in luggage or even carry-ons, and since the airport wasn't big, they were out the door within minutes after landing.

As they waited for the Uber that Richard had called, his partner-in-crime checked the app for the car's progress. "It's five minutes away, or so it says. The damn thing keeps updating." Richard looked up. "I hope we catch Roger Miller at home. If he leaves to run an errand, we will be stuck waiting for him and might miss our flight back."

Roni had gotten all the latest details on Wendy's father. His address hadn't changed since Wendy had left home, and he was working as an insurance agent for a local company. Fortunately for their plans, most of the week he did it from home, working from the company's offices only on Tuesdays and Fridays.

It was only a little after nine in the morning in Milwaukee, so he should be awake. Vlad had debated long and hard whether it would be better to attack while Roger was asleep, getting into his head when he had no barriers up.

The problem with that was accessibility of long-term memories. Short-term memories were easy to access, but memories from nearly two decades ago would be buried deep, unless Roger thought about what he had done to his wife and daughter often and in detail.

Since that was unlikely, Vlad would have to use more crude persuasion methods to get him to reveal what he had done. If Roger resisted or tried to lie, he could then enter his mind and pluck the memories that the interrogation would undoubtedly bring up to the forefront of the maggot's mind.

He would do his best not to kill Wendy's father, but he probably wouldn't leave him unscathed.

"I wish we had Yamanu with us," Richard said as the Uber dropped them one street over from Roger's house. "What if he's going to scream murder? Can you thrall him not to do that?"

"I'm a good enough shrouder to put the three of us in a bubble of silence." Vlad felt his fangs elongate. "No one is going to hear him scream."

"Easy, kid." Richard put a hand on his shoulder. "Don't work yourself up before we even get there. You need to keep calm." He looked around him. "Maybe I should find something I can clobber you over the head with."

He was only teasing, trying to get Vlad to loosen up, but it wasn't a bad idea.

"When we get inside his house, look for something you can use. Just don't smash my brain. Even immortals can't recover from that."

"Got it."

As Vlad's phone buzzed in his pocket, he didn't need to look at the screen to know it was from Wendy. It was still early morning in Los Angeles, and she'd probably just woken up.

Are you there yet?

He typed back. *We are walking toward the house. We will be there in less than five minutes.*

Don't kill him.

I won't.

Her return text was a row of hearts.

I love you too. I'll call you when we are done.

59

ONEGUS

*A*s Ingrid walked into the apartment she'd designated as the chief's operation center, her eyes immediately zeroed in on the barren pedestal.

"What happened to the crystal vase that was there?" She pointed an accusing finger.

"It's gone." Onegus rose to his feet. "I bumped into it, and it fell before I could catch it."

Hand on her hip, Ingrid narrowed her eyes at him. "What really happened to it?"

He sighed dramatically. "Is it really important? It was just some Chinese-made crap that probably didn't cost more than twenty bucks."

"It was eighty-six bucks, and it wasn't crap." She tossed her purse on the entry table and sauntered toward the kitchen. "But I know that your reflexes are too fast to allow it to fall. Did you bring someone up here?"

He followed her into the kitchen. "It's none of your business, but yes. Cassandra must have bumped into it, and I was too late to catch it."

That wasn't how it had happened. The vase just exploded, and he had a feeling that Cassandra's ire had something to do with it, but he wasn't sure.

Arching a perfectly shaped blond brow, Ingrid pulled a soda out of the fridge. "Cassandra Beaumont? The one you danced with at the gala?"

"How did you know?"

She leaned against the counter. "Your pictures were plastered all over the tabloids. You're the chief, and you don't need my advice, but you shouldn't have brought her here. She's not some random chick you picked up at a club. You've been photographed together. Being seen with her again is asking for trouble."

"No one saw us coming up here aside from the guys in security." He rubbed a finger over the cleft in his chin. "I sense something special about her."

"Oh, yeah?" Ingrid's eyes sparkled with interest. "Do tell."

There was no harm in telling her his suspicions. She was a smart woman, and she wasn't prone to gossip. She would keep whatever he shared with her confidential.

"Cassandra emits energy like a high-voltage wire, especially when she gets agitated or excited. I have a feeling that the vase just exploded because Cassandra got mad at me."

"What did you do?"

"Nothing." He leaned on the counter next to her. "She thought this was my shag pad." He crossed his arms over his chest. "Cassandra has standards. She demanded that I introduce myself to her mother before agreeing to get closer."

"That's kind of old-fashioned. Did you actually do it? Or did you thrall that idea out of her head?"

He cast her an amused glance. "I'm the chief. I don't thrall humans willy-nilly. I met with her mother."

"And?"

"She's almost as lovely as Cassandra, and she emits similar energy, just not as potent."

"Do you think that they are Dormants?"

He smoothed his hands against his spiked hair. "I feel a pull to her that I haven't felt toward any woman before, and it scares the shit out of me. I wasn't looking for a mate."

Ingrid's lips twitched with a stifled smile. "Is the big bad Onegus afraid to face his feelings? Or are you afraid of the beautiful and bewitching Cassandra Beaumont?"

He chuckled. "When you meet her, you might be scared too. That strange power of hers is like a keg of dynamite, and she has a very short fuse."

"Well, if she feels so special to you, go for it. Try to induce her."

"I don't think that I'm in love with her yet. And until I do, I'm going to use damn protection."

"What happens once you realize that she's the one? Since you've already had fun with her, I assume that she's susceptible to thralling?"

"She is, but I don't want to overdo it and cause damage." He sighed. "I can't stay away from her, and it's driving me crazy. Spacing our encounters is torment."

"Yeah." Ingrid pursed her lips. "You need to get her somewhere secluded, tell her the truth, get her consent, and then have fun until she transitions. And if she doesn't, thrall the memory away. We also have the option of Kalugal compelling her silence. Even Eleanor would do for that."

Onegus shook his head. "I'm not overly keen on involving others in my private affairs." He cast her a sidelong glance. "I don't know why I'm even telling you all this."

She patted his arm. "Because even the chief needs someone to talk to. But if you don't want to involve anyone else, the vacation option is still there." She smiled. "The cabin becomes available soon. Leon and Anastasia are coming to the village tomorrow, and Anastasia's friend is going back to that cult place Sunday evening. If you are willing to do the cleaning yourself, you can take Cassandra to the cabin on Monday. The Odus have their hands full with driving the guests around and serving the Clan Mother."

"I can't take a vacation until everyone goes home."

"Then invite her for the next weekend. It's not like there is a rush." She chuckled. "Except for your insatiable craving for her, that is."

60

VLAD

"Take a deep breath," Richard said as they walked up to Roger's front door.

"I'm okay." Vlad fisted his hands inside his pockets.

That's where his hands were going to stay unless Richard couldn't handle Roger on his own, which wasn't likely with his immortal strength. They'd agreed that Richard would do the physical intimidation while Vlad reached into Roger's mind.

Secretly, he hoped that Richard would kill the bastard. Then blood wouldn't be on his hands, but Roger would be dead and unable to hurt anyone else.

There was no answer when Richard knocked on the door. He rang the bell.

"Hold your horses," Roger shouted, and a moment later, the door opened.

The guy was still handsome for a drunkard who was in his late forties, but Vlad could sense the monster inside even though he wasn't particularly empathic. Given Richard's icy demeanor, he felt it too.

"Roger Miller?" Richard asked.

"What do you want?"

"We have a few questions for you." He flashed the fake FBI ID that he'd printed from the internet. It wouldn't have fooled a ten-year-old, but Vlad reached into the maggot's mind and made him believe it.

"About what?" Roger still blocked the door.

"Your daughter." Richard took a step forward. "Let's get inside."

Reluctantly, Roger moved, letting them into his house.

The place was a mess. Newspapers and magazines covered every surface, including the couch and one of the armchairs facing it. Several pairs of dirty socks littered the carpet, and there were empty beer cans everywhere.

Roger collected the newspapers strewn over the couch to make space.

"The housekeeper quit on me." He motioned for them to sit down. "Did anything happen to Wendy?" There was a note of concern in his voice that surprised Vlad.

The monster who'd abused her until she'd managed to escape him couldn't possibly care for her.

"That's what we are trying to find out." Richard sat down and pulled a little notepad and pen out of his pocket. "When was the last time you saw her?"

"I've already answered all those questions. I haven't seen her since she was recruited. I have no idea where she is, and why she's thrown away a well-paying job. It was probably for some dick." He ran a hand over his thinning hair. "I did everything I could to raise her so she wouldn't grow up to be like her drug-addicted, whoring mother, but she turned out to be exactly like her."

Vlad's fangs punched out, but as he lunged for the maggot, Richard got in the way. "Stop right now, kid. I've got it."

"No, you don't." Vlad pushed him aside.

"What the hell?" Roger's horrified expression probably saved his life. "What are you?"

The satisfaction of seeing it cooled Vlad's murderous intentions. "I'm your worst nightmare."

Instead of tearing the jerk's throat out, he took hold of his mind, clamping invisible fingers on his cognition and bending it to his will. He had never done that before, but it came naturally to him. If he wanted, he could have fried Roger's brain, turning him into a vegetable. Would Wendy be mad at him if he did that?

Forcing his mental fingers to ease the pressure, he asked, "What did you do to Wendy's mother? Where is she?"

Roger sucked in a breath. "I don't know, and I don't care. She was a druggie and an unfit mother. I told her to stay away from me and from Wendy or I'd end her miserable life. I thought that I was protecting Wendy by removing the bad influence, but apparently that shit was in her genes and there was nothing I could do to fix that."

"Did you kill your wife?"

He shook his head. "She still had enough brain cells functioning to never show her face in this house again. Either that or she died from a drug overdose. I don't know where she went after I kicked her out."

Reaching into his mind, Vlad looked over the memories Roger had summoned. The abuse and humiliation he'd inflicted on the poor woman were enough to have Vlad's blood boiling in his veins, but he didn't see Roger killing Wendy's mother. Was it possible that he'd suppressed the memory of that?

Perhaps his monstrosity hadn't crossed the line into murder?

"And you think that you were a fit father?" Richard asked. "You abused your daughter."

"I was strict with her, so she wouldn't turn out like her mother. I did the best I could, but it wasn't enough."

"Why did you keep her if you didn't want her?" Richard asked.

"Who said that I didn't want her? I wanted to raise her right, to make sure that she never touched drugs, that she did well in school, and that she didn't sleep around. But despite my best efforts, she ended up being a disappointment."

"You consider abusing her your best effort?"

Roger waved a dismissive hand. "I don't know what she told those shrinks in the government program, but I never hit her in the face or did anything to disfigure her. What I did was nothing compared to what my father did to me, and I turned out all right." He lifted his shirt and turned around. "That's a souvenir from my asshole of a father."

Roger's back was crisscrossed with old welts, but that wasn't an excuse for what he had done to his wife and daughter.

Richard winced. "Your father was a worthless worm, and you followed in his footsteps." He clapped his hands. "Here is the applause."

Tired of the excuses, Vlad squeezed his mental fingers, knocking Roger out.

When the guy slumped, Richard reached to check his pulse.

"I didn't kill him. I just knocked him out. I'm debating whether turning him into a vegetable would upset Wendy."

Richard arched a brow. "I didn't know it was possible to do that with a thrall."

"Neither did I." Vlad pushed his bangs out of his face. "Maybe it's something that I inherited from my father."

"What did you see in his mind?"

"A lot of crap I wished I could un-see, but I didn't see him murder Wendy's mother."

"Did he abuse anyone else since?"

"I don't know. He didn't summon those memories, and I can only see recent ones."

"What do you want to do with him?"

"Kill him. Even if he's not a murderer, he's a twisted, sadistic monster. I'd be doing the world a favor."

Richard shook his head. "You promised Wendy that you wouldn't. Thrall him, make sure that he never hurts anyone again, and erase the memory of us ever being here." He smiled evilly. "You can always come back at a future time and finish the job."

61

CASSANDRA

"You're in a good mood today." Kevin perched on the edge of Cassandra's desk. "You haven't snarled at anyone yet. What gives?"

"I finished the design for the new brochure and handed it over to Brenda to put into production. Then I started working on next month's box. I made good progress, and I'm finally ahead instead of being behind."

Last night, after Onegus had left her satisfied but puzzled, she'd taken a shower and worked until two in the morning.

Why hadn't he wanted her to return the favor?

Or just finish what he'd started and make love to her?

What kind of man brings a woman to a shattering orgasm and just leaves?

"Why didn't you send the brochure to me for approval?"

She crossed her arms over her chest. "Since you never bother to check them, I stopped doing that months ago. Hadn't you noticed?"

Kevin's expression turned sheepish. "I didn't. You should remind me."

"Fine." Cassandra uncrossed her arms and picked up her pencil.

He didn't make a move to leave and was still looking at her as if she'd dyed her hair green. "Do you need anything? Or were you just bored and decided to waste my time?"

Kevin smiled. "And she's back. I just wanted to check on the design for the eyeshadow line ad campaign. Did you send that to me and I missed it too?"

"Not yet. I'm still playing around with it. And I need to run a comparison test to choose the best performing creative. I'll send it to you when it's done." She twirled the pencil between her fingers. "I almost forgot. Tell Josie that Connor says hi."

"Who's Connor?"

"A score composer she's worked with before. He's Onegus's roommate."

Kevin grinned. "That's what the good mood is about. Did you snag the most elusive eligible bachelor that all the socialites have been pursuing for years?"

She frowned. "How come no one did?"

"He's a mysterious fellow. He shows up for those big charity events and then disappears for months." Kevin leaned closer. "To tell you the truth, I thought that he was gay, but apparently I was wrong."

She snorted. "Very wrong."

"Do you know where he disappears to?"

Onegus had told her the truth about his position in the family business, but she wasn't going to betray that even to Kevin.

"He told me that he travels a lot for business. I thought that it was just an exit strategy for when he dumps me, but maybe it's true and that's why he's gone most of the year."

"Why would he dump you?"

Cassandra leaned back. "A guy like him is expected to marry an heiress or the daughter of a high-ranking politician. What would his family think if he brings home a woman who doesn't even have a college education?"

That was regrettably true even if he wasn't the head of the operation. He was still a member of an incredibly rich and influential family.

Kevin shook his head. "If that's a sore spot for you, you should just get that damn degree. You can do it online." He leaned closer and whispered, "That's what I did."

"I know." She rolled her eyes. "I don't have time for that, and I don't need it. But people judge you if you don't have it."

When her cell phone rang, she snatched it off the table and smiled. "It's him." She waved her hand at Kevin. "Go. Find someone else to bother."

"Fine." He pushed off the desk and walked out of her office.

She waited for him to close the door before answering. "Hi."

"Hi, yourself. I have a question. Can you take a vacation starting the following Monday?"

"No. Why? Are you going somewhere?"

"Not unless you are coming with me. I want to spend time with you away from work and all the hustle and bustle. I will be very busy starting tomorrow and all through next week, and I don't know if I will be able to make time to see you."

So that's what this was about. He was letting her down gently.

Cassandra wasn't going to make it hard for him. It was better to end this on a good note and at least keep fond memories from their very short time together.

That was what her brain said. Her heart, on the other hand, felt as if Onegus had stabbed it with a rusty knife.

She rubbed her chest. "I can't take more than one day off. I just have too much to do."

"You have a department full of employees. Have them earn their money."

Was he insisting because he knew she couldn't go?

"They won't lift a pencil if I don't tell them how to do it and when. I don't have anyone who can take over for me. I haven't taken more than a day off since I got promoted."

"That was more than ten years ago."

"Tell me something I don't know."

"I'll call your boss and admonish him for overworking you and hiring the wrong people for your department. I want you all to myself for at least a week."

He sounded sincere. Maybe she'd misjudged his intentions?

"Out of curiosity. If I managed to get away for an entire week, where would you take me?"

"My family owns a secluded cabin in the mountains. It's very romantic, and there are no other homes for miles around. We will have complete privacy."

As Cassandra's anger flared red hot, the pencil holder on her desk started rattling.

She'd expected Onegus to say Paris or Milan, and if not that, then at least New York. But a damn cabin in the woods?

"I see. You want to take me to another place where no one will see us together. What's the matter, Onegus? Embarrassed to be seen with a pleb?"

"What kind of nonsense is that?" He pretended to get mad. "Where have you gotten that idea from? I danced with you at the gala and our pictures were splattered all over the tabloids and the internet. I took you to the fanciest restaurant on the West Coast, or maybe even the entire country, and we danced there as well. How can you think that I'm embarrassed to be seen with you?"

"The gala was nothing. You didn't come with me and you didn't leave with me. And the restaurant was dark, and no one paid any attention to us. The damn place belongs to your cousin, and you didn't even introduce me to him."

"That's because Gerard is a prick, and if I had walked into his kitchen, he would have thrown a knife at me. You are being ridiculous, Cassandra."

"Am I? I invited you to meet my mother and introduced you to her, but you couldn't even invite me to your home and introduce me to your roommate?"

"I let you talk to him on the phone."

"Whoopty doo. I'm the kind of woman a guy should be proud to be seen with, a woman he would show off to his friends and introduce to his parents. I'm not a shameful secret to be brought in the middle of the night to an unoccupied building." She paused to take a breath. "I told you that I don't do hookups, and if that's all you have to offer, then I'm not interested. Goodbye, Onegus." She disconnected the call.

The tears started a moment later.

Cassandra really liked the guy, and pushing him away hurt, but everything she'd told him was true. If he wasn't willing to show her that he was serious about her, she wasn't going to waste any more of her time on him, or worse, fall in love with a man who didn't appreciate her.

ONEGUS

*D*umbstruck, Onegus stared at his phone. He couldn't believe that Cassandra had hung up on him without waiting for his reply.

The woman was nuts, and she had a huge chip on her shoulder. How could she think that he was embarrassed to be seen with her?

She was gorgeous, successful, smart, talented, had superb taste, and she was a potential Dormant. Naturally, she wasn't aware of the last one, but she was well aware of everything else. Had he really given her a reason to suspect he thought otherwise?

The woman was more than confident, she was prideful, and she had a shitty attitude.

For a brief moment there, he'd thought that she might be the one for him, and he'd even contemplated ways he could have a mate without compromising his work standards. But he'd been wrong about her, and she wasn't the one for him. Onegus didn't need the drama, and he didn't need tantrums. What he needed was a coolheaded, reasonable woman who had a life of her own and wasn't needy or dependent.

Aside from the short fuse, he'd thought Cassandra was all those things, but it seemed like that short fuse was a much bigger problem than he'd anticipated.

Angry and hurt, he threw the phone on the desk and headed out.

Ingrid intercepted him in the hallway. "I programmed the locks of all the rooms with the guests that will be staying in them and emailed everyone their room assignments. That will save us the trouble of handing out keycards and showing them to their rooms."

"Good." He kept on walking.

"What happened?" She fell in step with him, her high heels clicking along.

"Nothing."

"Don't nothing me, Onegus. I'm not one of your Guardians, and I smell girl trouble. Did she turn you down for the vacation idea?"

He stopped and turned to her. "She practically slammed the phone down on me."

"Why? What did you say to get her mad?"

"Nothing. She asked me where I wanted to take her, and I told her about the cabin. She exploded, accusing me of being embarrassed to be seen with her and hiding her from my friends and relatives."

Ingrid winced. "I can see her point. You didn't introduce her to your friends or family, just not for the reason she thinks."

"So, what am I supposed to do? Bring her to the village?" He turned and kept walking toward the elevators.

Ingrid rushed after him. "You could invite her to the wedding. That will put an end to any talk about you hiding her from the important people in your life."

"Are you serious?" He pressed the button.

"Completely. Gerard's human staff is serving at the event, and Yamanu is going to take care of their memories when it's over. He can do the same to Cassandra."

The elevator arrived, and the door opened, but Onegus didn't step inside. "If Yamanu will erase her memories, then what's the point of inviting her to the wedding? She won't remember it."

"Good point." Ingrid put a hand on her hip. "You will need to do it and only remove the incriminating stuff and where the event was held. You will also need to get her drunk so she will blame the holes in her recall on the booze."

"Too risky."

"Not really. The same was done with Nick when Eva insisted on inviting him to her and Bhathian's wedding. And just like in Nick's case, it's only a temporary fix until Cassandra transitions."

"What if she doesn't?"

Ingrid laughed. "She will. If the mighty chief is obsessing about a female, then she must be a Dormant."

63

VLAD

"You need a drink." Richard stopped at the corner of the street and pulled out his phone to call an Uber.

"Am I back to normal?" Vlad glanced down at his mother's mate. His fangs had retracted, but he had a feeling that his eyes were still glowing.

Richard chuckled. "You are back to looking as normal as you usually do."

"Thanks." Vlad grimaced. "And I don't mean it sarcastically. You were a great help in there. If not for you, I don't think I would have walked out of that house with his heart still beating."

"You're welcome, kid." Richard clapped him on the back. "We have three hours until our flight back. We can have that drink at the airport."

Vlad nodded. "I need to call Wendy."

"Wait until we are inside the car, and then do your silent bubble trick. It's a forty-minute drive to the airport."

Wendy was probably biting her nails, worried about what he might have done to her father and what he'd discovered about her mother. The good news was that Roger hadn't killed her mother. The bad news was that they still didn't know whether she was alive and if she was, where to find her. Roger hadn't lied about not knowing where she'd gone after he'd kicked her out of the house. Vlad had double-checked by going through the memories he'd brought back, looking for any clue, but there had been none. Roger had never bothered to search for the mother. In his mind she'd been as good as dead, most likely from a drug overdose.

As the Uber driver pulled up to the curb, Richard opened the back door and signaled for Vlad to get in. He then took the front passenger seat and started chatting with the driver about the best restaurants and bars in Milwaukee, keeping the guy's focus on himself and not on the strange dude sitting in the back and talking without making a sound.

After snapping the sound bubble around himself, Vlad dialed Wendy's number.

"Is he dead?" she shot at him.

"Regrettably, he's still breathing."

She let out a breath. "Thank God."

He chuckled. "It should be, thank Richard. He kept me from losing it."

"You sound like you are in a good mood. Did you find out what happened to my mother?"

"He didn't kill her, and he doesn't know where she went after he kicked her out. He told her that he would kill her if she didn't stay away from you and him."

"Why?"

"He said that she was a drug addict."

"Yeah, that's what he told me too, but I didn't believe him."

Vlad pinched his brows between his thumb and forefinger. "She was, but I don't blame her for escaping the nightmare of living with him in any way she could. It's a miracle that she didn't off herself."

"Maybe she did," Wendy whispered. "Otherwise, she would have come back for me."

"She might have been too scared. Roger meant it when he told her that he would kill her if she ever came back. And from what I've seen of his memories, he nearly did it several times, beating her up so badly that she ended up in a hospital."

"How did they let him get away with that? Why did no one intervene?"

He was quiet for a moment, remembering what she'd told him about her father. "You know how he did that. The same way he fooled your teachers and the nurse and anyone else who noticed that you weren't doing so well, or the people who you actually turned to for help."

"I don't get it. He's not a compeller."

"No, but he's a handsome, all-American-looking guy, and he knows how to play the part of the harmless, charming, ordinary man. People don't want to see the monster hiding behind the façade. They prefer to believe the lie and keep their heads in the sand."

"Yeah, I know. So what do we do now? We are back to square one, we can't find my mother, and you made the trip for nothing."

"Not for nothing. I made sure that the maggot will never hurt anyone again."

"How?"

"I thralled him to feel severe chest pain if he even thinks of hurting anyone. Anytime he has violent thoughts, he will be gripped by that pain and believe that his heart is going to give out and he's going to die."

"That's clever. How long is it going to hold?"

"Depends on how strong his brain is. I plan on reinforcing it from time to time."

"I don't want you to ever see him again."

"I won't. It can be done over the phone."

She was quiet for a moment. "I didn't know that thralling works long distance."

"It doesn't, but compulsion does."

There was another long pause. "Are you going to ask Eleanor to do that for us?"

"I think that I can do it myself. I discovered today that my thralling ability comes with a strange twist. I need to figure out exactly what it means."

"How come you didn't know you had it before?"

Telling her about his Kra-ell ancestry over the phone was far from optimal, but it was time. "There is something that I've been meaning to tell you after this thing with your father was over, but I wanted to do it in person. Can you wait until I'm back?"

"No way! You have to tell me now. I can't stomach another moment of stress and anxiety."

"My father wasn't a human. He was a Kra-ell hybrid."

"A what?"

"Kra-ell, like the Krall, like the cult leader the clan captured."

"How is that possible? And what does it have to do with your newly discovered ability?"

"To answer the first question, my mother had a thing with one of them and kept it a secret until the cult leader was found and their existence became known to the clan. And as for your second question, apparently my strange new ability, as well as my superior strength, came from my father. I was always aware of the latter, but not of the former."

6 4

MARGARET

$\mathcal{A}$fter lunch when Ana and Leon had gone on their daily hike, leaving Margaret with Bowen, she ducked into the bathroom like the big coward she was.

Yesterday she'd been saved from his probing questions by their return, but now they were gone, and he would no doubt use the opportunity to keep digging into her shameful past.

She should never have agreed to stay through the weekend. Tomorrow, Ana and Leon were leaving the cabin and going their separate ways for a while. Strangely, neither looked too distraught about that, so maybe their separation period was going to be short.

Margaret wished them the best of luck, and she also wished that they would stay until Sunday and not leave her alone with Bowen with no buffer.

If all he wanted was sex, she could've dealt with that, but he wanted so much more than that. She would have loved to give him all of it and more, but he wouldn't want any part of her if he knew how horrible she really was. A lifetime of helping others couldn't compensate for what she'd done, and once Bowen found out, he would want nothing to do with her.

She could keep it from him, pretend that the past didn't exist, and he would never find out. But she would know, and it would forever eat at her from the inside. Hiding it was akin to deceiving him, and it would cost her the last shreds of her dignity.

Margaret didn't have much left, and she desperately clung to the little she had. If she lost it, it would be the end of her. She would either find a way to end her miserable existence or succumb to the false oblivion drugs offered.

A soft knock on the door startled her.

"Are you okay?" Bowen asked. "You've been in there for almost an hour."

"I'm okay." She put a hand over her racing heart. "I'll be out in a moment."

"I'll make coffee."

"Okay."

Sitting on the edge of the tub for a moment longer, she tried to think of a good excuse for why she had to leave tomorrow. Perhaps she could call Riley again and ask if she was needed?

But what if Bowen insisted on coming to Safe Haven with her?

She needed to end his inexplicable infatuation with her. Bowen had a heart of gold, and his need to save her was clouding his judgment.

It was time he learned the truth about the woman he believed was such a saint.

Easier said than done, though.

The only one who had known all of her sins and hadn't judged her for them was Emmett. Her savior who had turned out to be a sinner himself.

No wonder he'd been so understanding.

God, she missed him. Not as a lover, but as a leader, a teacher, the man who had shown her a way to rise from the ashes and make something of herself. He'd been harsh, demanding, but by doing so he'd pushed her to do better, to excel, and to feel pride in her work when it had finally gotten his approval.

After flushing the toilet that she hadn't used, Margaret washed her hands, splashed some water on her face, and toweled it off. Taking a deep breath, she leaned on her crutches and hobbled out of the bathroom.

Bowen regarded her with worry in his eyes. "You look pale. Are you sure that everything is all right?"

Margaret nodded and took a seat at the counter. "I'm fine. I was thinking about Ana and Leon leaving, and I realized that we should leave as well. We've hogged this cabin for long enough. Maybe some of your cousins would like to use it over the weekend."

She was such a damn coward. She'd always been one, which was the main reason her life had turned out as horrible as it had. If she had been more assertive and less fearful, she would be in a much better place today.

Shaking his head, Bowen poured coffee into two cups and brought them to the counter. "Are you scared of being here alone with me? Is that why you want to leave early?"

"I'm not scared of you, Bowen. I never was. You are the best human being I know."

He chuckled. "Compared to the bunch of goody two-shoes you've lived with for the past decade or two, I'm probably the wickedest person you know."

"Not even close." She put a spoonful of sugar in her coffee, added milk, and stirred. "It's time, Bowen. You need to get back to your life, and I need to get back to mine." She swallowed. "I need you to book me a flight for tomorrow afternoon."

65

BOWEN

*B*owen wasn't buying it. Margaret was scared, the scent of her fear was unmistakable, but he didn't know what she was scared of. If it wasn't of him, then of what?

"If I'm booking you a flight, I'm booking one for myself as well." He rose to his feet and scooped her into his arms.

"What are you doing?" Her arms instinctively went around his neck.

"I'm getting to the bottom of this." He carried her to the couch and sat down with her in his arms, positioning her in his lap sideways, so her legs, the good one and the one in the cast, were stretched out comfortably. "What are you afraid of, Margaret?"

Avoiding his eyes, she looked down. "Of your reaction once you learn the truth about me."

"Unless you murdered someone in cold blood, there is nothing that would change my opinion about you."

That got a small smile out of her. "What if I murdered someone not in cold blood? What if it was a crime of passion?"

"Then I will hear you out and determine whether it was justified."

"You are very forgiving."

"Not at all. But I know you better than you think. You are incapable of hurting anyone."

"You might be right, but sometimes inaction is just as bad. I'm a coward, and my cowardice is at the root of all that has happened to me."

Cupping her cheek, he gently guided her head so that her other cheek was resting on his chest. "Tell me what happened to you."

"I'm ashamed."

"Don't be. I'm not going to judge your choices or what you had to do to survive."

Heaving a sigh, Margaret closed her eyes. "My mother died when I was

189

sixteen of a viral infection that she'd picked up in a hospital while having a minor operation. My father didn't last long after that. He died from heart failure. The only family I had was an uncle whom I didn't know and who lived in another state. He didn't come for me, and I was sent to foster care. It wasn't as bad as people think, and the couple who took me in were okay. But I was lonely, and frightened, and I used the only assets I had, which were a pretty face and a nice figure. I met a guy who was more than a decade older than me, had a paying job, and proposed after dating me for two months. I thought that my troubles were over, but they had just begun."

Suspecting where Margaret's story was going, Bowen's arms tightened protectively around her. "Go on."

"He started hitting me when I got pregnant. At first, it was just a shove here, a slap there, but it got progressively worse. He never hit me in the stomach or punched me in the face, it was always in places that I could hide under clothing, and like an idiot, I did. I was ashamed, I was scared, and I didn't know who to turn to for help. He always apologized, blaming it on the booze or on stress at work. And each time he promised that it would never happen again, but it did. Over and over, and no matter how hard I tried to please him, to avoid his wrath, he always found reasons to knock me around."

Bowen's fangs were itching to elongate, but he tamped down the urge. It wasn't about him and the rage he felt. This was about Margaret pouring her heart out and him showing his support.

He kissed the top of her head. "I'm so sorry for all that you've suffered. And I'm glad that you somehow managed to escape. It must have been very difficult."

She heaved another sigh. "When our daughter was born, he fell in love with her, and the violence stopped for a while. I hoped that we'd turned a new page and that we could be a normal family, but I should have known better. It started again soon enough, worse than before."

She lifted her head and looked at him. "I wasn't clumsy, and those broken bones were not accidents. That was how I got addicted to opioids. It started with the first hospital visit and a prescription that I abused. It was easy back then to get more. There was no awareness of how dangerous opioids were and that they were just as addictive as street drugs. I became an expert at manipulating the system and getting more prescribed, and when that failed, I bought them from dealers. I pinched pennies, skimming from the household budget. I barely ate, saving on groceries. I got nice baby outfits and toys second-hand for next to nothing and claimed that I'd spent a lot of money on them." She sighed. "I became very creative."

Bowen had a feeling that Margaret wasn't telling him the worst of it, but he wasn't going to press. She was finally confiding in him, and his heart broke for her. He would take only what she was willing to give, but he could encourage her with his support.

"You did what you had to do to survive. I'm not judging you."

She huffed out a breath. "That's not the worst part. I needed more and more to get that disassociated floaty feeling going, and saving on groceries and other household expenses wasn't cutting it." She swallowed. "He wasn't blind to what was going on, but he couldn't lock me in the house to prevent me from getting more, and beating me up was just making things worse. Eventually, he hired a nanny to take care of our daughter when he was at work because he didn't trust me with her." Margaret's eyes were full of tears when she looked up at him. "That's the only thing I was ever grateful to him for. I was spacing out, and I was afraid of being alone with our baby. The nanny was a young woman who didn't speak a word of English, and even as out of it as I was, I noticed that something was going on between them. When I confronted him, he put me in the hospital again."

Bowen couldn't help the growl that rose from his throat, and as Margaret looked up, she gasped. "Your eyes are glowing."

Thankfully, he was still able to control his fangs. "It's a light effect. Go on."

She lowered her eyes to her hands. "I was given opioids again," she whispered. "I had a Eureka moment, and a pattern began. As soon as I ran out, I provoked him into beating me up badly enough to get me hospitalized so I could get more. At some point, I just wished he would finish the job, and I wouldn't wake up again."

Bowen didn't know what to say to that. The things she was telling him were even worse than what he'd suspected. In a way, it would have been better if she'd prostituted herself to get the drug money. It would have done less damage.

"Anyway," she continued. "He almost did. He told me that if I didn't get my act together, he would have me committed to a psychiatric hospital, and he would make sure that I didn't ever see my child again. He searched the entire house and threw away every pill he could find, but I had more stashed away for an emergency. I tried to quit, but I was too weak to do it without help. When he found out, I was sure he was going to kill me. He nearly choked me to death. The baby screaming for me in the next room must have gotten through to him and he let go and stormed out of the house. The next morning, he waited for me in the kitchen with a bag that he'd packed for me. He told me to run and hide because if he found me, he was going to finish what he'd started the night before. I believed him. He wasn't drunk, he was completely lucid, and he had murder in his eyes. Nevertheless I cried, and I begged, and I pleaded, and I promised to go to rehab, but it only got him more furious, and the things he said..."

Margaret shook her head. "I was afraid that he would hurt our daughter to punish me. He loved her as much as he hated me, but he wasn't right in the head." She snorted. "And neither was I. I figured out that she was better off with him and the nanny than with me, and I left. I had no money, no friends, and nowhere to go. But I still had a full packet of Percocet stashed away. I decided to end my life and took all of them at once. Someone found me passed out behind the supermarket dumpster and called an ambulance. They pumped my stomach and called him. He did his usual shtick, pretending to be the wronged husband who had to deal with a horrible, druggie wife who whored herself out—that's how he explained the marks on my neck and the black eye he'd given me, it had been an unsatisfied client, not him. His act must have been convincing, or maybe they thought that it had been my fault, and I was sent to mandatory rehab. He came to visit once, just to deliver the same message. If I ever came anywhere near him or Wendy, even unintentionally, he was going to make sure that it was the last thing I did."

Bowen frowned. Her daughter's name was Wendy?

Suddenly, the pieces of the puzzle started falling into place. That was why Margaret had seemed familiar when he'd first seen her. She'd reminded him of Wendy. The big brown eyes, the smile, the face structure. But Wendy was short and plump, while Margaret was tall and slim.

Perhaps it was just a coincidence.

He didn't know Wendy's last name, but he could easily find out. He could call Wendy herself, but if his suspicion proved incorrect, it would upset her. He could probably get the information from Jin or from Eleanor.

"Did you change your last name?"

Margaret lifted her head. "Why do you ask?"

"I'm just curious. Your ex sounds like a dangerous scumbag. If I knew you back then, I would have advised you to get a fake identity so he could never find you. He could've changed his mind later and come after you."

Bowen would have killed the scum to keep her safe and get her daughter back to her.

"That was what Emmett said when I told him my story and he got me a new identity." She swallowed. "I never got a divorce because I never dared to contact Roger. Legally, I'm still married to him."

"Not for long. What was your married last name?"

"Miller. But what do you mean by not for long?"

"I have friends who can take care of that," he lied.

"How?"

"Hacking into official databases." That might have been true, but it wasn't how Bowen planned to end Margaret's marriage.

He was going to make her a widow.

66

MARGARET

*B*owen hadn't reacted as Margaret had expected. He hadn't been appalled by her drug addiction and what she had done to support it, not even by her greatest sin, which was leaving her daughter behind and running away and hiding like the coward she was.

He didn't regard her as a piece of trash, and his arms were still around her, supporting, encouraging.

Perhaps he hadn't internalized the gravity of her cowardice yet. A man like him could never understand a spineless mouse like her. He was strong, brave, he would have fought against all odds.

Why hadn't she?

"He might have divorced you," Bowen said. "I don't know much about the subject, but I'm sure no one expects a wife gone missing for eighteen years to sign divorce papers. One of my cousins is an attorney. She can check it for you."

Margaret shook her head. "I'm afraid to do that. What if he gets notified that someone checked? He will know it was me, and it's best that he thinks that I'm dead."

"There are ways to do that without alerting him. My cousin is very good at what she does."

Panic gripping her, Margaret felt her throat close up and breathing became difficult.

"What's wrong?" Bowen looked at her with worry in his eyes.

"I can't breathe," she croaked, her hand going to her throat.

"Don't be scared." He took her clammy hand in his. "I will never let anything happen to you. You are safe. No one is going to get you."

Slowly, his words penetrated the haze, and the tightness in her throat eased. When she sucked in a breath, Bowen released one as well.

"If you feel such acute panic after eighteen years, I can't imagine how scared you were back then."

"I'm still terrified. Why do you think I never left Safe Haven? When you took me to the hospital, it was the first time since my arrival there."

He frowned. "I thought that you were allowed to leave for doctors' visits and the like."

"Theoretically, yes, but I never needed to see a specialist. We had a doctor that came twice a year to give everyone a physical, and Shirley took care of the colds and the flus and the sore throats. The furthest I'd gone away from the lodge was the beach in front of it."

"Weren't you curious about Wendy?"

Here it was. Now that Bowen realized the extent of her cowardice, he would despise her.

"Of course, I was. We had no access to the outside world in Safe Haven, but I begged Emmett to check for me. He said it was dangerous, that any internet inquiry can be tracked, and looking for information about a minor would trigger some safety features that would alert Roger and enable him to find me. Emmett said it wasn't worth the risk to me and to the rest of the community. He said that Roger sounded insane, and that he might come with a machine gun and kill everyone in his path."

As the choking sensation started again, Bowen squeezed her hand. "Emmett lied to you, Margaret. Or rather exaggerated. It's true that everything you do on the internet can be tracked, but someone has to have a very good reason to do that, the resources, and the knowhow. Looking for information about Wendy wouldn't have triggered any traps unless your maniacal ex was a computer expert and a master hacker or has enough money to pay for one."

"Why would Emmett lie about that?"

"For the same reason he didn't allow community members access to the internet or even radio and television. By controlling the information, he controlled the community."

What he said made sense, but Emmett wouldn't have done that to her. Or would he?

Maybe he'd thought he was protecting her?

Or maybe he'd checked despite what he'd told her and found out that something had happened to Wendy?

As the panicky sensation threatened to steal her air again, Margaret tightened her grip on Bowen's hand. "Can you help me find out about my daughter?"

He hesitated. "I have a cousin who is an expert on those things. I can call him."

"Can you do it now?"

His eyes were full of pity as he looked at her. "To call him, I will have to let you out of my arms, and you are shaking like a leaf."

She hadn't been aware of how cold she was until he'd pointed it out. "I don't know why I'm so cold."

"Telling me your story was emotionally draining, and it has awakened old fears. You are in a system overload." He caressed her arm. "Close your eyes and rest your head on my chest."

His voice was so soothing, so compassionate.

She did as he instructed. "How come you don't hate me for what I did?"

"Why would I hate you? You were a victim. How old were you when your daughter was born?"

"I had just turned nineteen."

"You were still a child yourself, alone, abused, and frightened." His voice sounded as if it was coming down a tunnel, but his words eased some of the heaviness in Margaret's heart.

Heaving out a sigh, she drifted away, pieces of their conversation floating disjointed in her exhausted mind.

How had Bowen known that she'd left eighteen years ago? Had she told him that? Margaret couldn't remember, and as cognition faded, focusing on any one thought became impossible.

6 7

BOWEN

*W*hen Margaret's breathing had slowed and deepened, Bowen pushed to his feet with her in his arms and gently laid her on the couch. Remembering that she'd been cold, he covered her with the throw blanket before heading out to the front porch.

He needed a moment to breathe some fresh air and calm the fury her story had evoked. She'd been victimized for years, first by her husband, who'd abused her and robbed her of her child, and then by Emmett, who'd lied to her and compelled her to panic every time she thought about finding out what happened to her daughter.

The cult leader's motives might have been benevolent if he'd truly believed that he was protecting Margaret and his community from her psychotic husband. Or, they might have been malevolent, meant to keep Margaret from leaving.

Although why he had deemed her so important was unclear. She didn't have any money, and her work for the community could have been done by others.

Had her blood been a delicacy he hadn't wanted to lose?

Leon had told him that Emmett claimed Eleanor's blood was particularly tasty and potent. Perhaps that was also true of Dormants' blood?

It hit him then. If Margaret was Wendy's mother, she was a confirmed Dormant. Eleanor had been right about her.

Pulling out his phone, he dialed her number.

"Bowen, what a nice surprise," Eleanor answered. "Are you calling to congratulate me on my promotion?"

"What promotion?"

"Kian put Peter and me in charge of guarding Emmett. We've temporarily moved to the keep."

He couldn't care less who was guarding the guy, but he didn't want to hurt

Eleanor's feelings by ignoring her unexpected promotion. It must be a big deal for her.

"Congratulations. How did that come about?"

"It was Kri's idea. She said that Emmett might tell me things he wouldn't tell the guys. I suggested it to Kian, and he liked the idea. I'm now officially a Guardian in training, including the salary that comes with the position."

"I'm happy for you. How is it going with Emmett so far?"

"I've only seen him twice. Once yesterday and once today. I'm taking it slow, so it won't be too obvious."

"What exactly are you planning to do? Seduce him?"

"It's an option."

She'd tried to sound nonchalant, but Bowen detected the nervous undertone. "That's going above and beyond your job description."

"I know. If I do that, it would be for me, not for the job."

"Then I wish you good luck. I have a question for you."

"Ask, and I shall answer."

"Do you know Wendy's last name?"

"Yeah, it's Miller. Why?"

Should he tell her before he told Wendy and Margaret? It didn't feel right, but he needed a woman's perspective and advice on how to handle the situation.

"I think that Margaret is her mother."

There was a long moment of silence, and then Eleanor huffed out a breath. "Is her last name Miller?"

"It was before she had it changed, and she has a daughter named Wendy who she left behind with her abusive husband."

"Did you tell her your suspicion?"

"No, not yet. I wanted to make sure first."

"Good. Miller is a very common name, and so are Wendy and Margaret. It might be a coincidence. Before we raise their hopes, we need to make sure."

"How?"

"Blood test. Bridget already has Wendy's, and if she needs a fresh sample, she can make up an excuse for why she needs it. Julian or Gertrude can go to the cabin and collect Margaret's."

"Were you involved in Wendy's recruitment?"

"No, Simmons recruited her himself. Why?"

"Do you know her father's given name?"

"It was in her file, but I don't remember. Maybe Jin or Jacki know, but I doubt it. Wendy was a loner, and she didn't interact with the other trainees. But maybe Richard knows. He was her and Vlad's roommate until he moved in with Stella."

"I'll call him. If he says that the father's name is Roger, I think that's proof enough."

"Probably. But there is still a small chance that there is another Miller family that has a Margaret, a Roger, and a Wendy."

"Perhaps, but given that we suspect Margaret is a Dormant, the chance of coincidence is reduced to practically zero."

"Probably, but we don't know whether Margaret is a Dormant for sure. A blood test will be conclusive proof that she is Wendy's mother, and then you can bring her to the village without having to go through all that nonsense of inducing her and waiting to see if she turns."

"You are talking about a DNA test, and those take time. I need to know as soon as possible."

Eleanor sighed. "Do they look alike?"

"Not enough. They have the same eyes and smile, and the same hair color, but Margaret is tall and slim."

"That's not good enough. You need at least one more piece of information that can be verified."

"Like an address. Provided that her father didn't move, and if he did, that Wendy knows the old one."

"Did Margaret tell you where she's from?"

"I didn't ask. Right now she's asleep after I helped her relax with a little thrall." He ran a hand over the back of his head. "It was an emotionally draining experience for her."

"I bet. If I remember correctly, Wendy is from Milwaukee, but I'm not sure. I can ask her, make some excuse about why I need to know."

"I'll just call Vlad. I don't know why I didn't think of calling him first. Wendy is working at the café, so it's not likely that she will overhear the conversation."

"Good luck."

"Thanks. And do me a favor, don't tell anyone until Wendy and Margaret are told."

"Obviously."

68

VLAD

*V*lad was nursing his second beer at the airport bar when his phone rang.

"Wendy again?" Richard asked.

Vlad frowned at the screen. "It's Bowen." He accepted the call. "This is Vlad. Did you dial my number by mistake?"

"No mistake. I need to talk to you. Are you anywhere near Wendy?"

"No. Why?"

Vlad didn't elaborate on where he was at the moment. The less people knew about his and Richard's excursion, the better. He'd promised Richard to keep it confidential.

"I think that I found her mother, but I want to make sure before I tell either of them and raise their hopes for nothing. I need us to compare notes, so to speak."

Richard arched a brow. "I'll be damned."

Vlad lifted his face heavenward, wondering about the Fates' twisted sense of humor. Couldn't Bowen have called him a day earlier? He wouldn't have gone to pay Roger a visit and would have been spared from looking into the guy's ugly memories. Then again, his visit ensured that Roger Miller never hurt anyone again, so it wasn't a complete waste of time. Besides, Bowen could be wrong.

"What do you want to know?"

"Wendy's parents' names."

"Margaret and Roger Miller."

The Guardian let out a breath. "That's a match. Where is Wendy from originally?"

"Milwaukee."

"That's what Eleanor thought. I haven't asked Margaret yet, but I will when she wakes up."

"How did you meet her?"

199

"Do you know about the Safe Haven Cult rescue mission?"

"Yeah, the cult leader kidnapped a Guardian, and a bunch of you went there and rescued him."

"Correct. But do you know why the Guardian was there in the first place?"

"Something about an heiress that Turner was hired to retrieve. I don't know all the details."

"The heiress's name is Anastasia, and she turned out to be a Dormant and has already transitioned. She didn't go to the village yet because she wanted to stay with her best friend Margaret, who's recuperating in the cabin from an injury she sustained during our rescue mission."

"Our Cabin? The one Wendy and I stayed in?"

"One and the same."

"So, Wendy's mother was in the cult all these years?"

"It's a long story, but her husband abused her and then kicked her out and told her that if he saw her again, he would kill her. She ran to Safe Haven, the cult leader took her in and nursed her back to health. What he also did, though, was to compel her to fear looking for any information about her daughter. She suffered a panic attack when I suggested a simple internet search. She actually couldn't breathe."

Vlad shook his head. The Fates weaved a complex tapestry. He just wished he knew what their end goal was.

"How did you connect the dots?"

"From the very first moment, Margaret seemed familiar to me. I didn't know why until she told me her story about leaving a daughter with her abusive husband. Everything clicked into place the moment she told me that her daughter's name was Wendy. I just needed to make absolutely sure before I told Margaret that her daughter was safe and that she could see her today if she wanted."

"I can give you their home address. Roger Miller hasn't moved since Wendy was a baby. If Margaret gives you the same address, then that's the final proof."

"That's great news. Eleanor suggested we have them both take a blood test, but those things take time, and I'm running out."

"Why? What's the rush?"

"Margaret wants to return to Safe Haven tomorrow. But if she's indeed Wendy's mom, then she's a confirmed Dormant, and I can tell her everything and bring her to the village."

Finally, Vlad connected the dots. He'd been too distraught over the earlier interaction with Wendy's father to pick up the clues, but Bowen's comment about bringing Margaret to the village had been like a light beam through the haze.

"Is she your one?"

"I think so."

Vlad chuckled. "Welcome to the family, Bowen. I've always liked you."

"Same here, kid. Text me that address, will you? And also a picture of Wendy, or even better, the two of you together. If Margaret confirms the address, I want to be able to show her the beautiful, happy woman Wendy is today. And since a lot of it is thanks to her mate, Margaret should see a picture of her son-in-law as well."

Vlad wasn't sure about that. He wasn't what a human mother pictured as husband material for her daughter, but maybe it would be better if she was prepared.

"I will send the address and the pictures as soon as we end the call. Let me know if she confirms the address and it's conclusive. I would like to tell Wendy the good news."

There was a brief moment of silence before Bowen said, "Don't tell her yet. I have a feeling that it will be a shock for Margaret, and she will need some time before she'll be able to face Wendy."

Vlad looked at Richard, who nodded sagely, agreeing with Bowen.

"I'll wait until you tell me it's okay."

"Thank you."

"I need to thank you. Earlier today, I thought that Wendy's mother would never be found. The Fates have a strange sense of humor proving me wrong only a couple of hours later."

"Indeed. Sometimes I think that they push us around like chess pieces on a board and having free will is just an illusion."

69

MARGARET

"*M*argaret." A warm hand caressed her arm. "I need you to wake up for a moment."

She opened her eyes to Bowen's handsome face hovering a few inches above hers. "I'm awake." She tried to sit up, but her head hurt and she put it back down.

While she slept, Bowen had brought her a pillow from her bedroom and covered her with a blanket. He was still taking care of her, even after learning what a rotten person she was.

"I'll make you coffee, but first, I need to ask you something."

At that point, she had no more secrets to hide. She'd laid herself bare for him, expecting him to recoil with disgust, but he was still there, still looking at her with soft eyes that seemed just a little troubled.

"What do you need?"

"Do you remember the address of the house you shared with your ex?"

How could she forget?

"Why do you need to know that?"

"I just do."

She put a hand on his forearm. "You can't go kill Roger. As bad as he is, Wendy doesn't have anyone else."

"That's not why I need the address."

She looked at him skeptically. "I saw your eyes when I told you what he'd done to me. You saw red. I know that you are a soldier, and that you've seen combat. You're a good man, a protector, and it's an instinct for you to take out the bad guys."

"I swear on my honor that I don't need the address so I could go kill your ex."

She had a feeling that honor meant a lot to Bowen. He wouldn't swear on it in vain. But just in case, she would start with the street name and omit the house number. "It was on West Tesch Avenue in Milwaukee, Wisconsin. But he might have moved since then."

"He didn't." Bowen sat next to her on the couch. "I have something important to tell you."

"What is it?" She pushed up, leaning against the armrest.

Bowen opened his mouth to answer when the door opened, and Ana came in with Leon.

"Are we interrupting in the middle of something?" Ana asked.

Bowen nodded. "Can you give us a few more minutes?"

"I'll just grab a couple of water bottles from the fridge." Leon headed to the kitchen.

"Get two for Margaret and me as well."

"No problem."

As Leon tossed him the two bottles on his way out, Margaret was sure at least one of them would hit her, but Bowen caught both like a circus performer.

When the door closed behind the two, he uncapped one bottle and handed it to her, then did the same for his.

"What were you going to tell me?" She took a sip.

"Wendy is no longer with Roger. She is safe and sound in our village, mated to one of my cousins. I needed the address to confirm that you are really the mother of the Wendy I know." He lifted his phone and showed her a text message from someone named Vlad.

She must be still sleeping, and this was a dream.

Margaret lifted the bottle and took another sip. If it was a dream, it was damn realistic. "Can you pinch me? I must be dreaming because that's just impossible."

He sighed. "It's fate. Do you want to see her picture?"

Margaret swallowed, her throat suddenly dry even though she'd just drunk water. "Yes, please," she whispered.

He tapped on his phone and handed it to her. "This is Wendy today."

Tears started streaming down Margaret's cheeks. The beautiful, smiling young woman in the picture was her Wendy. She had absolutely no doubt. Wendy was a perfect mix of her and Roger, who had been as handsome on the outside as he was twisted on the inside.

"She's perfect."

"I agree."

"Do you know her?"

"Quite well. She and her mate stayed in this very cabin with Leon and me."

Her eyes widened. "They were the couple you guarded?"

He nodded. "They found love here. Just like Anastasia and Leon." He wiped away her tears with his thumbs. "And just as we did."

"Knowing what I did, how can you love me?"

"What you told me didn't change anything. I feel the same as I did this morning and as I felt the day before, and the one before that. And now that I know your story and how the threads of our lives were weaved into one tapestry, it is clear to me that the Fates have been planning this for a very long time." He took her hand and kissed it. "We belong together."

70

BOWEN

*I*t must have been too much to process, and Margaret just fell apart. Sobbing uncontrollably, she pushed at his chest, and when he yielded, she flung both legs around and hopped on her one good leg toward the bedroom, nearly falling on her face if not for Bowen's quick reflexes.

She let him help her to the bed, but then lifted her hand. "Please. I need to be alone for a little bit."

"I understand." He didn't, but he did as she asked nonetheless.

She should have been overjoyed, her tears should have been of happiness and not of devastation.

The front door opened a crack, and Anastasia poked her head inside. "Is it safe to come in?"

"Yeah." He walked to the refrigerator and pulled out a beer.

"What happened?" Leon asked.

"You're not going to believe it." Bowen gave them a quick summary, omitting many of the details he thought Margaret would prefer to keep private.

"I'll be damned." Leon shook his head. "How did I miss it? She looks a lot like Wendy."

"Who's Wendy?" Anastasia asked. "I mean apart from being Margaret's daughter, who I never knew existed."

When Leon was done telling his mate an abbreviated version of Wendy's story, Anastasia walked to the kitchen, pulled out a bottle of wine, and uncorked it. "Let me handle this." She took a glass, filled it to the brim, and took it to Margaret's room.

"Let's give them some privacy." Leon pulled out a beer for himself and headed out the front door.

As Bowen followed, he heard Anastasia huff out, "Oh, Margaret, just stop it and grow a set. Bowen has a lot he can tell you about Wendy."

Closing the door, he didn't hear Margaret's response.

"Congratulations." Leon offered him his hand. "You found your mate."

Bowen shook it. "Who would have thought that when I gave Wendy fatherly advice, I would one day become her stepdad." He grimaced. "Not that it's going to happen anytime soon. Margaret is too fragile to handle any more surprises right now, and I don't know whether she should even attempt transition in her state."

"The timing is actually perfect." Leon leaned against the railing and crossed his legs at the ankles. "The Clan Mother is here for the wedding and birthday celebrations, and she'll still be here two weeks from now. If you hurry, Margaret could enter transition while Annani is still here, and if things turn south, the Clan Mother can give her a blessing."

"The blessing is good only for giving the mates hope." Bowen took a long swig from his beer. "It doesn't do shit for the transitioning Dormant."

"I disagree. Each time the Clan Mother has given her blessing, the Dormants have enjoyed a miraculous recovery. Coincidence? I think not."

Bowen shrugged. "Nothing is going to happen between Margaret and me during the next two weeks. I just can't bring myself to make a move on a woman recovering from surgery. The cast needs to come off first."

Surprisingly, Leon nodded in agreement. "It didn't occur to us before, but we should have remembered that the body needs to be healthy before transition can occur." He lifted his bottle in a salute. "But at least you can now tell Margaret the truth and bring her to the village. There is no doubt that she's a Dormant."

If only things were as simple as that. Bowen had thought that he understood people, men and women, but he hadn't foreseen Margaret's reaction. Her response to his declaration that they had found love in the cabin had been to start sobbing. She hadn't denied it though, so maybe she felt the same and had just gotten overly emotional.

"I can't tell Margaret anything right now because she's already overloaded and won't be able to process it. The problem is that she wants to return to Safe Haven tomorrow, and I can't let her do that." He shook his head. "Well, I can, but I will have to go with her, and she doesn't want me to."

"Why the hell not?"

"She thinks that she's not good enough and I don't know how to convince her otherwise." He took a long swig from the beer, emptying it. "I've never had problems with women. I thought I understood them, but apparently I'm just as clueless as the rest of my gender."

Leon nodded in commiseration. "Maybe she needs more time. She's just learned that her daughter is within reach, and then you drop the love thing on her. It was too much?"

"I thought that you and Anastasia were giving us privacy."

"We tried, but other than sticking fingers in our ears, we couldn't help hearing you talk."

The door opened and Anastasia stepped out, holding the half-empty glass of wine in her hand. "Margaret has calmed down a little, but she wants to stay in her room and think. She says she's not ready to face Wendy." Anastasia joined Leon, leaning against the railing. "She's scared that Wendy will reject her."

"It's possible," Leon said.

Bowen frowned. "Do you think that I should talk to Wendy first? Explain why her mother never contacted her?"

Anastasia shook her head. "It's Margaret's story to tell."

"But she doesn't know the whole story, and if I don't tell her about Emmett, she won't know it before talking to Wendy."

"What does Emmett have to do with anything?" Anastasia asked.

"He compelled her to be terrified of looking for her daughter."

"Are you sure?" Leon asked.

"Every time I mentioned searching for information about Wendy on the internet, Margaret had a panic attack. Maybe that's why she's so scared of meeting her."

"We need that guy who helped Peter," Anastasia said. "He can remove the compulsion like he did for him. If it's still messing with Margaret's head, no wonder she's so spooked."

Bowen pushed away from the railing. "I need to check with Kalugal to see if he's willing to do it. He's a character, and he might demand my firstborn in exchange for the favor. But maybe he can do something over the phone. A video call should be enough."

71

MARGARET

*M*argaret had stopped crying long enough for Ana to leave, but as soon as the door closed behind her friend, she grabbed a pillow and pressed it to her face to muffle her sobs.

It was hard to breathe, but she welcomed the suffocating sensation. If only she was strong enough to go all the way and end her miserable life.

How could she possibly face Wendy? She wasn't strong enough to survive her daughter's anger, her anguish. It would have been so much better for Wendy to believe that her mother was dead.

That was what she probably believed already, no doubt thanks to Roger, and she'd made peace with that, laid it to rest. Digging up her not-so-dead mother would only cause her pain.

Wendy would wonder why Margaret had left her, and why she hadn't cared enough to come back to check on her.

All the literature that Margaret had read claimed that antagonizing abusers could have catastrophic results, and that it was best to seek shelter before proceeding with legal action. The problem was that sometimes that wasn't good enough, and the abusers found their victims and hurt not only them but also the people who sheltered them.

But those were all excuses, and Wendy would be justified in scoffing at them.

Had Roger abused Wendy as well?

He'd loved her as a baby, so perhaps he hadn't, and Wendy had grown up in a decent home? Maybe Roger had divorced Margaret in her absence and married the nanny? She'd been kind to Wendy. She would have made a good stepmom.

Nevertheless, Margaret should have fought for her daughter and not run away like a spineless coward, hiding away and hoping that Roger and Wendy thought her dead, convincing herself that it was best for everyone's sake that they did.

When the bed dipped on her left side, Margaret nearly jumped out of her skin. With the pillow over her head, she hadn't heard the door open.

"I brought you tea," Bowen said.

She clutched the pillow to her face. "Please, leave."

"I'm not going anywhere. Talk to me, Margaret."

What could she possibly tell him? All she wanted was to be left alone so she could crawl back to her little hidey-hole in Safe Haven, where she was as good as dead to the rest of the world.

"Don't you want to meet your daughter?"

Panic seizing her throat in a choking sensation, Margaret flung the pillow away. "Did you tell Wendy about me?"

"No, not yet."

Letting out a breath, she slumped back on the pillows. "Thank God for small mercies. Don't ever tell her that you've found me. She's better off believing that I'm dead."

"How can you say that?" Bowen lifted a corner of the duvet and wiped the tears off her face. "She is getting married in a few months. Don't you want to be at her wedding?"

Margaret's eyes widened. "She's getting married? Is she insane? She's too young."

"At her age, you were already a mother."

She winced. "Yeah and look where it got me. Marrying at eighteen was the worst mistake of my life, and I'm still paying for it."

"Your mistake was marrying the wrong man. You were just a kid, alone, with no one to guide you, to offer you advice, or to see past Roger's veneer. You can't keep punishing yourself for what he did."

"I'm not punishing myself. I'm trying to save my daughter even more anguish. Believing that her mother is dead is better than knowing she was abandoned."

"You shouldn't decide that for her. After hearing your story, she might forgive you or she might not. But I believe she will. Wendy is a good kid. She was a little moody when I first met her, but she's changed so much after moving in with Vlad. She's happy."

"How do you know that? Maybe she's faking it?"

Bowen shook his head. "She's not. She doesn't need to. I know Vlad well, and he's the kindest, most mellow guy you can imagine. He's studying to become a graphic artist, and in the meantime, he works part-time in his best friend's bakery. Wendy works at the village café, so I see her almost every day. There is always a smile on her face. She's confident, friendly, and everyone likes her."

Bowen's description of Wendy's life eased some of the heaviness in Margaret's chest. "It sounds like she's really happy, which is more reason not to dump my existence on her head. The best thing I can do for her is to remain dead."

BOWEN

rustrating woman.

Bowen wished he had some psychological training, something that would help him get through to Margaret. But all he knew was what would have worked for him, and that would probably not work for a woman who'd spent half of her life in hiding, hoping the world had forgotten about her and thought her dead.

Perhaps telling Margaret about her possible immortality and Wendy's transition would change her perspective? Make her less fearful and more hopeful?

After all, Margaret had lost nearly eighteen years of Wendy's life, but if she transitioned, she would have eternity to make up for it. Nothing could compensate for Wendy's entire childhood that she'd missed, but that was water under the bridge.

Margaret had to grow a set, as Anastasia had put it, and face the music.

Since he was taking her with him to the village no matter what, she was going to meet her daughter whether she wanted to or not.

"Then Roger wins." He thrust the mug at her hands. "Drink."

She winced, either at his tone or at what he'd said about her ex winning, and then looked at the tea suspiciously. "What's in it?"

"It's just tea, but if I could pour courage into it, I would."

More tears ran down her cheeks as she lifted the mug to her lips with trembling hands, took a sip, and sighed. "How did you meet Wendy? And how did she end up in this cabin with Vlad, you, and Leon?"

Was this progress? Or was it an evasive maneuver to steer the conversation away from facing her daughter?

"It's a long story, and it's not mine to tell. Wouldn't you prefer for Wendy to tell you her story in her own words?"

"I'm terrified," Margaret admitted. "She might refuse to see me. Or she might agree to meet me only to spit in my face and tell me to go to hell. I deserve both, but I wouldn't survive it." She touched a trembling hand to her temple. "Whatever I managed to piece back together with Emmett's help would shatter. I wouldn't survive the rejection."

"I have a friend who might help you." Bowen pulled out his phone.

He'd spoken with Kalugal, and the guy had graciously agreed to help, telling Bowen to call him when Margaret was ready.

She shook her head. "I don't want to talk to a shrink."

"My friend is not a psychologist. He's a hypnotist and a motivational speaker. He will help you calm down and be less fearful."

"I don't want to lean on yet another crutch."

"It's not like that. Give him just one minute of your time." When she kept shaking her head, he added, "For me."

Lifting her sad eyes to him, she nodded. "I'll do it for you."

Bowen dialed the number. "I have Margaret with me here, and you are on speakerphone. Do you need me to activate the video function?"

Margaret's eyes widened, and she shook her head vehemently while pointing at her face.

"No need. My voice is enough. Hello, Margaret. My name is Kalugal. How are you doing today?"

She sagged. "Hello. I've been better."

"I bet. I want you to listen to me and repeat what I say. Are you ready?"

She nodded. "Yes."

"I have no reason to be afraid. Say it and believe it."

She whispered it.

"I am surrounded by friends who care for me, protect me, and will not let anything happen to my daughter or me. Say it."

This time around, her voice was a little above a whisper.

"Now say this. I am strong, I am a survivor, and I can handle anything life throws at me."

As she repeated the words, out loud this time, Margaret straightened her back.

"That's it. My job is done," Kalugal said. "Best of luck with the rest of your life." He ended the call before Margaret murmured a thank you.

Lifting her eyes to Bowen, she took a deep breath. "He's really good. I actually feel stronger, more confident."

Later, after he'd told her the entire story, Bowen would explain what Kalugal had actually done, but for now he was going to take it one step at a time.

"Can I call Vlad now to have him deliver the good news to Wendy?"

Margaret shrank into the pillows, but she didn't say no. "Does he know about me?"

"Yes. He gave me the address to verify that it was really you. I asked him not to tell Wendy until you were ready."

"Thank you." She put the mug on the nightstand and wrung her hands. "Do you think that's the best way to do it? For her boyfriend to tell her?"

"I'm not sure. Would you like to consult with Anastasia and Leon?"

"Yes, I think that's a good idea."

73

MARGARET

*A*fter washing her face, brushing her teeth, and combing her hair, Margaret felt a lot better. Or maybe it was the result of the short, yet very effective pep talk she'd gotten from Bowen's friend?

He must be a powerful hypnotist to effect such profound change in less than a minute. For lack of a better description, it felt as if he'd unlocked something inside her, some hidden reserve of courage or maybe zest for life that Margaret had thought was lost forever.

Though still terrified of Wendy's rejection, she no longer experienced the choking sensation that usually accompanied any thought of contacting her daughter, even checking on her covertly from afar.

When Margaret opened the door and stepped into the living room, her friends were waiting for her with fresh coffee and a plate of sandwiches.

"Feeling better?" Ana asked.

She was sitting in Leon's lap and looking stupidly happy and in love, especially for someone who was leaving tomorrow and parting with her boyfriend for at least a little while.

"Much better. Thank you."

Bowen got up and helped her to the couch.

Glad for the help, Margaret didn't shoo him away like she usually did. The meltdown and following sobbing fest had left her so exhausted that she could barely hold on to the crutches.

She glanced longingly at the coffee. "I don't know how Kalugal did it, but I feel like I've gotten a new lease on life."

Bowen poured her a cup, added milk and sugar, and handed it to her. "I'm very thankful that he agreed to help."

"Thank you." She took a sip. "What he did for me was nothing short of a miracle. He must be making a fortune selling his services."

Leon chuckled. "Kalugal is rich enough not to need to sell those particular

211

services, and he's not kind enough to offer them for free either. You are lucky he's our cousin."

"How many cousins do you guys have?"

Ana chuckled. "A lot. They call every extended family member a cousin. I met a few of them, and I can't wait to meet the rest." She grinned at Margaret. "I'm moving in with Leon."

"I thought that you wanted to go back to law school."

"I might do that later." She kissed Leon's cheek. "Maybe I'll even finish my degree online. I can't be apart from my one and only, the love of my life."

As envy and regret gripped Margaret's heart, she glanced at Bowen, who had an unreadable expression on his face. He'd told her that they had found love in the cabin, and instead of telling him how she really felt about him, she'd had another panic attack and had run off sobbing.

Well, hopped off. She wouldn't be running anytime soon.

Tearing her gaze from him, she looked back at Ana. "So what do you think? What's the best way to break the news to Wendy that her mother is not dead?"

Ana leaned against Leon's chest. "I vote for a surprise reunion. Vlad can bring Wendy over here under false pretense, something about visiting Bowen and Leon for old times' sake. That way, you get to tell her your story yourself. If I were in Wendy's shoes, I would like that better. It will spare her all the guessing and agonizing on the way here."

"What if it's too much for her to process?" Leon asked. "If Vlad warns her, she'll be better prepared."

Ana shook her head. "This cabin holds fond memories for her. Wendy and Vlad fell in love here. Besides, if she needs to clear her head and cool off, this is the perfect place for that. There is nowhere to run to, she will have to face you."

Margaret nodded. "Either way is not perfect, but I'd rather tell her my story myself. There is so much I need to explain."

"We are here for you," Ana said. "I can attest to the influence Emmett had on you, and how he was able to convince you that hiding and letting the world believe you were dead was your best option and in Wendy's best interest."

"How did you know that he did that?"

Ana shrugged. "I figured it out. One way or another, he did that to all the community members. He convinced me that my father would destroy my life if I let him. There was a kernel of truth in that, which was why I believed him, but I didn't need to hide in Safe Haven to assert my will and not let my father dictate how I lived my life. I could have done it on the outside just as well, probably better."

"Emmett had the same hypnotic quality as Kalugal," Bowen said. "Think how easy it was for Kalugal to free you from fear. That's how easily Emmett instilled it in you."

The truth of his words slammed into Margaret with a force that had her slumping against the couch pillows. "Why would he do that to me?"

"Control," Bowen said. "As long as you were terrified of leaving, you were his to exploit."

"I'm not such a great find."

Bowen growled. "You were twenty years old when you got to Safe Haven."

He was right. She was pretty back then, and Emmett had shown a lot of interest in her. At first, it had been to help her heal, but once she'd gotten better, his interest had turned more carnal in nature.

Over the years though, the guilt and sorrow eating her from the inside had turned her into a walking skeleton, making her look older and more haggard than her years or type of work justified. Emmett's interest in her had slowly faded along with her waning beauty, but the fear he'd instilled in her had remained.

Margaret shook her head. "How am I going to explain that to Wendy?"

"You are not alone." Bowen wrapped his arm around her shoulders. "We are here to support you."

74

VLAD

*V*lad wasn't sure at all that Bowen's idea to surprise Wendy was the best way for her to be reunited with her mother.

He hated lying to her, although technically he wasn't. He was just omitting what he knew about Bowen's new girlfriend.

The excuse for driving up to the cabin at night, right after his return from his trip to Milwaukee, was a reunion with the Guardians who'd been assigned to her and Richard after she'd betrayed their other location to her uncle.

"Remember not to mention my trip to Milwaukee to Bowen or Leon. Richard wants to keep it hush-hush."

"I know." Wendy curled up in her seat. "When did they come up with the reunion idea?"

"Today. They are leaving the cabin tomorrow afternoon, so today was the last day to do it. They were talking about us and how we fell in love at the cabin, and Leon wanted Anastasia to meet you. Just don't say anything about immortals because Anastasia's friend doesn't know yet."

Wendy's eyes sparkled. "Yet? Is she a potential Dormant?"

Vlad just nodded.

"I'm so happy for those two." She shifted in her seat to face him. "Leon and Bowen were really nice to me when they had no reason to be." She chuckled. "After you told me about being immortal, Bowen gave me a fatherly-sounding speech. I thought he was going to warn me not to hurt you again or else. Instead, we talked about people changing, and about my fear that you might become controlling or violent. You know how terrified of relationships I was. He helped me realize that I shouldn't be."

Not knowing how to respond to that, Vlad nodded again.

"Anyway, Bowen did a good job of reassuring me. He said that you're golden and that immortals were good people. He was also the one who told me about fated mates. I really hope that Anastasia's friend is a nice person. Bowen deserves to be happy."

"I'm sure she is."

"What's her name?"

"Margaret."

"That's easy to remember." Wendy turned to look out the window. "I don't think we are ever going to find my mother. She probably died from a drug overdose like my father said."

Vlad had told her a watered-down version of what he'd seen in Roger's mind, but perhaps he shouldn't have. If Wendy knew what her mother had suffered, she might be more forgiving.

"That maggot doesn't deserve to live. If not for my promise to you, I would have killed him, bled him slowly while he screamed in pain."

Wendy recoiled, and he regretted what he'd said even though it was true. He, who had never hurt a fly, would have delighted in tormenting Roger Miller for days, paying him back for all he had done to his wife and daughter.

"I'm sorry." He put a hand on her thigh. "It's still fresh in my mind. I didn't tell you the half of it, but just so you know, your mother had good reason to run and hide and never come back. He would have killed her on sight, and in his rage, he might have accidentally killed you as well, even though he loved you."

In his own twisted way, Roger Miller had believed that he cared for Wendy.

Wendy shivered. "I don't believe that he's even capable of love. In my mind, I don't blame her. But in my heart." She put a hand over her chest. "I ache because I've been abandoned by my mother. My life is good now, and I have no complaints. I just want to know whether she's alive and whether she found happiness elsewhere."

"Your wish might come true sooner than you think," he murmured.

"What do you mean? How?"

"The Fates work in mysterious ways."

75

MARGARET

Margaret was on her third glass of wine when Bowen got up and walked up to the front door. "They are here."

A moment later she heard the car engine, and her stomach did a somersault.

"It's going to be okay." Ana sat next to her on the couch and took her trembling hand in hers. "Try to act natural, see if she recognizes you."

"How could she? Wendy was a baby when Roger kicked me out. She won't remember me, and we don't look alike enough for her to figure it out. What am I going to say to her?"

"It will come to you." Ana patted her hand. "Don't freak out."

Easier said than done. Her entire body was trembling.

"I have no reason to be afraid," she murmured quietly. "I am surrounded by friends who care for me, protect me, and will not let anything happen to my daughter or me. I am strong, I am a survivor, and I can handle anything life throws at me."

Margaret kept repeating the words Kalugal had given her like a mantra in her head until Wendy walked in the door, a very tall, gangly young man at her side.

Then the words left her, lodged in her throat like a rock, and tears started streaming down her cheeks.

"What's wrong?" Wendy walked up to her. "Why are you crying?"

Margaret was trembling so badly that Ana had to pry the wineglass out of her hand because it was sloshing all over her.

"Wendy," she whispered. "My sweet Wendy."

Confusion in her eyes, Wendy crouched in front of her. "Do I know you?"

Margaret nodded. "I'm your mother."

For a long moment, no one talked, no one breathed, and the oppressive silence was choking the life out of Margaret.

As her vision started to tunnel, Wendy pushed up and wrapped her arms around her. "Breathe, Mom. I've got you."

Margaret sucked in a breath, and with the oxygen in her lungs replenished, she started sobbing on her daughter's shoulder. "I'm so sorry. So, so sorry. I didn't want to leave you. I'm sorry, so, so sorry."

"Shh, it's okay. I understand." Wendy pulled back a little and smiled, and it was the most beautiful smile Margaret had ever seen. "I thought that you looked familiar. Now I know why. Have you been hiding in that cult for all these years?"

Margaret nodded. "I'm sorry for being such a coward. I thought that you'd be better off thinking that I was dead."

"I've never believed that you were." Wendy sat on the couch on Margaret's other side, wrapped her arm around her shoulders, and looked at her fiancé. "How long have you known?"

He pushed his long bangs aside, revealing a pair of mismatched eyes. There was boundless love in them as he looked at Wendy. "Bowen called me today and told me that he might have found your mother. He needed a little more information to make sure that it was her. He called me later and told me that the information checked out but asked me not to tell you. He wanted to tell Margaret first. Then he called me again and asked me to bring you here but not tell you the real reason. Your mother wanted to tell you her story in person."

Ana rose to her feet. "I know it's dark outside, but let's go for a walk and give these two privacy."

Margaret gripped her hand. "Don't go. I'm done being scared and ashamed, and you are my friends. I trust you with my ugly secrets." She turned to Wendy. "Unless you prefer otherwise."

BOWEN

*B*y the time Margaret had finished telling Wendy her side of the story, all three ladies had tear-stricken faces, the men were fighting a losing battle with their fangs, and other than Margaret and Wendy, everyone had eaten several sandwiches and drunk a shitload of alcohol, even Anastasia.

Bowen's decision to end Roger Miller's life had solidified, and not because he wanted to terminate her marriage. He was going to do that regardless of whether Roger had divorced Margaret in her absence or not.

"I can't believe how forgiving you are." Margaret wiped at her tears. "How did you grow up to be so kind?"

Wendy glanced at Vlad. "I didn't. I was either scared or apathetic, selfish and indifferent, and I vowed never to fall for a man. All of that has changed thanks to Vlad. He showed me that not all people are bad, he showed me a community of people who had each other's backs, and they welcomed me even though I wronged them terribly."

Margaret's eyes widened. "How? What could you have possibly done?"

Wendy sighed. "I almost got some of them captured, and I still have nightmares about what would have been done to them if they hadn't managed to escape."

"Captured by whom? And why?"

When Wendy looked at Bowen, he nodded. "It's okay. You can tell your mother everything. I think she can handle it now."

"Isn't it something a mate does? I don't want to deprive you of the privilege."

"Margaret and I are not there yet, we are just getting to know each other, and this is a unique situation. I think you deserve the honors more than I do."

Wendy huffed. "Don't be ridiculous. If not for you, I wouldn't have found my mother, and you are her mate. You deserve to do it."

Margaret watched the exchange with curiosity mixed with fear in her expressive eyes. "Would someone please tell me what's going on? And why is everyone referring to a significant other as a mate?"

Bowen waved at Wendy. "Let's do it together. You start, and I'll supply details and proof when needed."

Chuckling, Anastasia patted Margaret's good knee. "My advice is to keep an open mind. I was in your situation just a few days ago, and I can tell you that everything is true, and no one is pulling your leg." She rose to her feet. "In the meantime, Leon and I will serve dinner."

Wendy took in a long breath. "So here goes. I have a low-level paranormal talent. I'm an empath, which means that I can read people's emotions." She smiled. "Do you have any special talents?"

Margaret shook her head.

"Usually, paranormal talents run in families. Anyway, dear Uncle Simmons had one day shown up at our house and offered me a very lucrative government job at their new paranormal talent department."

Simmons was Wendy's uncle?

Bowen shot a glance at Vlad, who nodded. "I only found out after Jacki's wedding, and it no longer mattered."

Margaret bared her teeth. "Edgar was my uncle, and the bastard didn't even bother to show up at his sister's funeral."

"I'm not surprised," Wendy said. "He was a selfish, power-hungry pedophile."

"What did he do to you?" Margaret whispered, her eyes filled with horror.

"Nothing. But I'm an empath. I saw what he wanted to do to me. That was revolting enough."

As Wendy continued her story, Bowen walked to the kitchen and pulled a couple of beers out of the fridge. He handed one to Vlad, who followed him there.

"You're in the way." Anastasia shooed them out.

It took another fifteen minutes for Wendy to get to where Vlad had revealed who and what he really was.

Margaret looked shell-shocked, but she heeded Anastasia's advice and didn't voice disbelief. There was awe in her eyes as she glanced at Vlad, then Leon, and finally when she leveled them at Bowen.

"How come I didn't see anything?" she whispered. "Did you thrall me?"

"Twice, but both times were to put you to sleep. Once when we took Anastasia to the clinic, and the other one was earlier today after you told me your story."

Anastasia dragged Leon into the living room. "I can demonstrate if you want." She kissed him hard, and when she let go, his eyes were glowing and his fangs had elongated, but not fully.

Margaret gasped.

There were many more gasps as the story continued, and when it ended, it was past midnight.

"You should spend the night here," Margaret said to Wendy and Vlad. "It's too late for you to drive home."

"It's okay, Mom." Wendy leaned and kissed her cheek. "Immortals only need a few hours of sleep, and our night vision is excellent. For Vlad and me, and these three." She waved her hand over Leon, Anastasia, and Bowen. "Midnight feels like eight in the evening. You have nothing to worry about."

"When will I see you again?"

Smiling, Wendy glanced at Bowen. "You'll see me tomorrow when Bowen brings you to the village. Did you think that you were going back to Safe Haven after everything that I told you?"

"I guess I can't." Margaret wrung her hands. "What am I going to do in your village?"

"Anything you want." Wendy kissed her again. "The important thing is that we are a family again, and we have all the time in the world to get to know each other."

Bowen's gut clenched.

Margaret was thirty-eight years old and not in the best of health. Transition would be difficult for her. Then again, he had to believe that the Fates wouldn't take Margaret away from him and Wendy after going to all the trouble of maneuvering them all together.

Margaret had definitely suffered enough to earn the reward of a true love mate, and Bowen hoped that his many good deeds had earned him some good-will from the Fates as well.

77

CASSANDRA

*A*fter Cassandra had ended things with Onegus the day before, he had called at least five more times. Not right away, and not before she'd cried her eyes out in her office and snarled at anyone who'd dared to knock on her door. His first call had come at seven in the evening, but she'd let it go straight to voicemail. He called again, and after letting that one go as well, she'd checked whether he'd left a message, but he hadn't.

After three additional calls, she'd turned her phone off and had tried to go to sleep. It had been a miserable night, but at least nothing had exploded. She wasn't angry, just sad, and the swirling energy inside of her felt subdued.

She'd finally found an antidote.

Depression.

Thank you, but no thanks.

She would let herself mope around for a couple of days, eat excessive amounts of ice cream, and then shake it off.

Sounded like a good plan when she'd tossed and turned throughout the night, but when she turned her phone back on in the morning, a message from Onegus was waiting in her voicemail, and ignoring it was not happening.

Sitting cross-legged on her bed, she pressed play.

"Upon further reflection, I realized that I might have given you the wrong impression. Nothing could be further from the truth, and I'm going to prove it to you. Call me."

How was he going to prove it? Invite her to meet Connor?

She'd pass.

Except, her bravado didn't last long, and after drinking three cups of coffee and feeling like she could personally power the entire state with the energy swirling inside her, Cassandra called Onegus back.

He answered right away. "Give me one moment, please."

It was noisy in the background, people talking, phones ringing, but it was fading as if Onegus was walking away from the source of the noise.

"Thanks for calling me back. I was ready to drive over to your office and make a scene."

She chuckled nervously. "Then I'm glad I called."

"You hurt my feelings yesterday," he said softly. "No one has ever hung up on me before. That was rude."

"I know, and I apologize for acting so immaturely, but I felt hurt too."

She still did, and he hadn't told her how he was going to prove to her that she'd gotten the wrong impression, but there was hope in her heart that hadn't been there before.

"You punished me for an imagined crime that I haven't committed," Onegus said softly. "I owe you a spanking for your ungrounded accusations and for hanging the phone up on me."

He hadn't sounded mad, which was a huge relief, and his teasing affected her in a most unexpected way.

She laughed. "First, you will need to prove your innocence as well as my guilt."

"I can do that in one fell swoop."

"How?"

"I'm inviting you to a family wedding. My cousin is getting married, and the entire clan is gathering to celebrate. I will introduce you to everyone as my partner. Will that end the nonsense about me being embarrassed to be seen with you once and for all?"

And then some.

"Yes."

"Then it's settled." He sounded smug.

"When is the wedding?" If he said a year from now, she was going to hang up on him again.

"This Saturday."

Oh, wow. She needed to get a new dress.

"Where?"

"I can't tell you for security reasons. It's a private affair, and we don't want anyone outside the family to catch wind of it."

Aha. It was probably a tiny thing, and his entire so-called clan meant twenty people.

"Is it a small wedding?"

He chuckled. "Is over seven hundred guests considered small?"

"You have a big family."

"I told you that the entire clan was gathering. A clan implies a large family."

She had run out of rebuttals and had to concede defeat. Her bottom clenched, and not in an unpleasant way.

"Are you going to pick me up?"

"I have to be at the venue early to make sure everything is ready. I'll send a car for you. Or is that not good enough either?"

"No, that's fine. I guess I need to rush to get a dress. You didn't give me much notice."

"More complaints?"

"No. I think I'm done for a while."

"Good. Plan to be ready by eight on Saturday."

"Will I see you before that?"

He chuckled. "Are you eager for that spanking I promised you?"

"Nope. Saturday is good."

DARK POWER UNLEASHED

THE CHILDREN OF THE GODS BOOK 51

1

KIAN

Six o'clock in the morning was too early for a smoke, but since Kian hadn't actually slept, it could be argued that it wasn't really morning for him. Syssi was in the shower, and while he waited for her to get ready for breakfast, he could sneak outside for a few minutes and get his fix.

As usual, too much was going on all at once, and his mind was spinning in circles trying to make sense of it.

What were the damn Fates up to this time?

"Good morning, master." Okidu bowed. "Would you like a fresh cup of coffee? It has just finished brewing."

"Yes, please."

A steamy mug of coffee in hand, Kian opened the living room sliding doors and walked out into the backyard. Sitting down on his favorite lounger, he put the mug on the side table and picked up his box of cigarillos.

Lighting up, he took a grateful puff and leaned back.

The Fates had played another of their games, bringing yet another Dormant into the clan's fold, and not just any Dormant, but Wendy's long-lost mother.

The text message from Bowen had arrived a couple of hours ago.

The Guardian probably hadn't expected Kian to read it right away, so he hadn't elaborated beyond the basic facts. But Kian could piece it together from what he already knew.

The irony wasn't lost on him.

Margaret had been under their noses for nearly two weeks, but Bowen had figured it out on the same day Vlad and Richard had traveled out of town to have a talk with Wendy's asshole of a father and find out what he'd done with the mother.

If Bowen had figured it out a day earlier, he would have saved them the trouble.

Had Wendy's bastard of a father been left to sully the earth with his presence for another day?

If Vlad had managed not to kill him, the kid had much better self-control than Kian. If he were in Vlad's shoes, Kian would have torn the jerk's throat out, and no one would have been able to stop him. It wouldn't even have mattered if Wendy's father had killed her mother or not. He deserved to die for the abuse he'd inflicted on his family. But Vlad was a gentle soul, and he'd made a promise to Wendy not to kill her father, so maybe the scum was still alive.

In any case, Kian wasn't going to ask or even hint that he knew about Richard and Vlad's trip.

Plausible deniability and all that.

Then there was Onegus and his unconventional request to bring a date to Sari and David's wedding. The chief had met the lady at the annual charity ball, and it seemed like he was seriously smitten, which was uncharacteristic of him. Onegus was a player who never hooked up with the same woman more than twice, which was how it was supposed to be for immortals engaging with humans.

As Kian heard the sliding door open, he turned and smiled at his wife. "That was quick." He extinguished his cigarillo.

"Isn't it too early for a smoke?" She lowered herself onto his lap with effort, her pregnant belly nestling against his. "What's troubling you?"

"Nothing major. Just many little things." He wrapped his arms around her to keep her warm. "Isn't it too cold for you out here?"

Syssi leaned her head on his shoulder. "Not when I'm lying on top of you. You are like a furnace." She lifted her eyes to him. "Are you nervous about Sari and David's arrival?"

Their flight was scheduled to land at LAX at twelve-thirty in the afternoon, and instead of them taking a taxi to the newly renovated building across from the keep, Syssi had insisted on picking them up at the airport.

"I'm nervous about most of the clan being here for their wedding. It's a logistical nightmare to keep everyone's arrival unnoticed. But that's just one in a long list of things keeping me awake at night."

"What else? The Kra-ell?"

"Yeah. That too. I want to get a move on it, but I have to wait until after the festivities. On top of that, Onegus has invited a human date to the wedding, and I was so shocked by the request that I said okay before thinking it through."

Smiling, Syssi cupped his cheek. "It was nice of you to allow it, and it's not a big deal. Gerard's human crew is serving at the wedding, and their minds will need to get wiped at the end of the night. One more human will not make a difference."

"True. But that's another annoyance. There will be too many humans working in the bowels of the keep to prepare and service this wedding, and later, having their memories wiped. Then there are the Chinese crews building our village, who will have to be wiped as well."

"You had every one of them checked for responsiveness to thralling, so it's not like some might be immune. You're fretting for no good reason." She lifted her head and kissed his cheek. "Relax, enjoy. These are happy times for us and for the clan."

Kian shook his head. "I feel like I've become complacent, and I'm taking too many risks." He ran his hand over her back. "The Kra-ell are wise to keep their communities small. They can pick up and go with ease."

"Perhaps they are nomadic in nature." Syssi put a hand on her belly. "I like staying in one place, and despite being an introvert, I love having a big community of people to interact with when I'm in the mood for it. I think I would have gone nuts with just a couple dozen people to talk to. For some reason, that seems more intimate and more intrusive." She rubbed her belly again.

"Is Allegra kicking?" Kian put his hand over hers.

"She's sleeping. I just like touching her. It's so cool that I can feel the contours of her little body through my belly." Syssi shifted, finding a more comfortable position. "Onegus's date must be special if he invited her to the wedding."

"He claims that he can sense some sort of strange energy from her that intensifies when she gets angry or excited. He says that her mother emits similar energy, but not as strong."

"Fascinating." Syssi sat up and put her hands on the small of her back. "I'm going to ask Lisa to sniff Onegus's date out at the wedding. After all, she was right about Anastasia being a Dormant."

Kian moved Syssi's hands aside and started massaging her back. "She was, and I regret not sending her to sniff out Anastasia's friend as well."

It was a gentle way to break the news to Syssi. He didn't want her getting overly excited in her condition.

"Why? Is she a Dormant too?"

"Confirmed."

Syssi turned wide eyes to him. "Did she transition and no one told me?"

There was no way to soften the delivery of what he had to tell her, so he attempted a softer tone. "Margaret is Wendy's mother."

Syssi gasped. "Impossible. How?"

"Apparently, she escaped her abusive husband when Wendy was a baby and has been hiding in Safe Haven ever since. Bowen somehow connected the dots, mother and daughter had an emotional reunion last night, and Bowen is bringing Margaret to the village today."

Syssi tried to push out of his arms. "We have to prepare lodging for them."

He tightened his arms around her. "There is no rush. Ingrid is too busy to deal with that right now, and if we let someone else do it for her, she'll throw a tantrum. Bowen and Margaret can stay with Vlad and Wendy for a week or two. I'm sure Wendy and her mother have a lot of catching up to do."

229

2

CASSANDRA

Cassandra glanced up at the rearview mirror to check her makeup. She'd been in a rush this morning and it showed. There wasn't much she could do about it while driving, though, except perhaps fixing her lipstick. Reaching over the central console for her purse, she was rummaging for the tube when her phone rang.

The familiar number popping up on her car's display brought a smile to her face. "Did you forget something?"

"Are you driving?" Onegus sounded like a stern schoolteacher, displeased with her supposedly reckless behavior.

"Yes, but don't worry. I'm not holding the phone, my hands are on the wheel, and I'm looking at the road."

Given that she'd had her hand in her purse and was about to apply lipstick while driving, Cassandra had been guilty of intent but not of actual infraction. So technically, she hadn't lied.

He chuckled. "How did you know that I was worried?"

"Your tone. You sounded like a policeman or a schoolteacher about to give me a lecture."

"If it turns you on, I can get into either of those roles with ease." His tone was teasing, but his voice had dropped by half an octave, stirring interest in her lady parts.

"I bet." She shifted in her seat.

On the face of things, Onegus appeared charming and easygoing, but she could sense the steel he was hiding under all those panty-melting smiles of his. He had a dominant streak, which would normally put him on her do-not-call list, but he wasn't overbearing and seemed more concerned with her pleasure than his own, so she didn't mind.

In fact, it was a big part of the attraction.

He was the kind of guy a woman could lean on, rely on, and he certainly wasn't a man who would fold under the slightest pressure.

Besides, he could handle her and wasn't intimidated by her, which was no small feat.

"Did you tell your mother about the wedding?" he asked.

"I didn't see her this morning, so no, I didn't tell her yet."

"Don't tell her or anyone else about it. It's crucial that the event stays confidential."

"Are you worried about paparazzi?"

He sighed. "I wish that was the extent of my worries. Our family has enemies, old feuds that go generations back. They would love to find out that nearly the entire clan is gathering in one location."

What the hell was he talking about?

Mafia wars came to mind. "You are kidding, right?"

"I wish I was, and before you jump to the wrong conclusion, it's not a mafia turf war. It really goes back many generations in time."

Onegus had a very slight Scottish accent, but Cassandra wasn't aware of any active feuds between Scottish clans. Then again, she wasn't a history buff, and what she did know came from her mother's Highlander romance novels. Not the most reliable source of information.

"Should I be worried?"

"Not with me by your side. I'll keep you safe."

She chuckled. "A warrior billionaire. It sounds like the title of a bodice-ripper."

"What's a bodice-ripper? It sounds intriguing."

"It's a sexually explicit romantic story that takes place in a historical setting. Highlanders are very popular in that genre."

"Is that so?" He let his Scottish accent come out full force. "I'm up for ripping your bodice anytime and in any setting."

She laughed. "I'll keep that in mind when shopping for a dress to wear to the wedding. No bodice."

"That sounds even more intriguing and fashion forward. But then I'd have to kill all of my male family members for looking at your breasts, and that would ruin everyone's fun."

"We don't want that." She chuckled. "A dress can cover up everything without having a bodice. How formal is the event?"

"As formal as they get. But you don't have to get a new dress. You can wear the same one you wore for the gala. You looked stunning in it. I'll be the envy of all my bachelor cousins."

She couldn't help the grin splitting her face. "Just the bachelors?"

"Yes." His tone changed from teasing to gruff. "We are a very traditional and loyal bunch, and mated males don't stray, not even with their eyes. Once we commit, it's for life."

"That's commendable, but I doubt it's factual. Forty percent of marriages end in divorce."

"Not in our community."

Cassandra had no idea what the official religion of Scotland was, but she was pretty sure it wasn't Catholicism.

"Are you Catholic?"

"It has nothing to do with religion."

"A code of honor then?"

"It's just the way it is. You will have to make do with just the bachelors' admiration."

He sounded cold, and Cassandra didn't like it. She liked the smile in his voice, his light-hearted banter. Had she put her foot in it again?

Perhaps Onegus had a history with an unfaithful girlfriend, and it was a sore point for him.

"I was just teasing. I hate players and cheaters with a passion, which was why I got so mad when I thought that you didn't want to be seen with me. That's the number one sign that a guy is dating several women at the same time. They don't want to get caught, so they find excuses for not going out."

"Has it ever happened to you?" His tone had warmed up a little, but he still sounded serious.

"Yeah, there is no avoiding it. It's not like guys have it written on their foreheads or in their dating app profiles. But as soon as I noticed the signs, I booted the two-timers out so fast that they didn't know what hit them."

"Good for you."

"What about you? Did you ever have a two-timing girlfriend?"

"I've never had a girlfriend."

She rolled her eyes. "Fine, a lady friend then, a woman you've dated. I don't care what you call them."

"I've never been with the same woman more than once, so the only terms that apply are one-night stands and hookups."

Great. So, he wasn't a two-timer, just a serial player. It was almost as bad.

"Fear of commitment much?"

"I just haven't met the right woman before."

Oh, he was smooth. "And I am her?"

"You are the first one I'm willing to explore the possibility with. When I commit, it's forever, Cassandra. I need to make absolutely sure that I'm committing to the right woman. My one and only."

3

MARGARET

*M*argaret stayed in bed long after waking up, afraid to go out of the room and face the others.

What if it had all been a dream? Or a drug-induced fantasy?

Except, she was clean. She hadn't touched opioids in over a week. Margaret also wasn't creative enough to dream up what she'd learned the day before. Somehow, Wendy had been turned immortal, and so had Bowen, Leon, and Anastasia, but Margaret didn't know how it had been done. Last night, she'd been too overwhelmed to ask.

Supposedly, they all had special genes that could be activated.

Anastasia had been turned with ease, so the activation process couldn't be too bad, and Wendy hadn't mentioned anything terrible either. Maybe it was as easy as getting some miracle elixir intravenously. Ana had joked about the doctor putting a miracle drug in her IV, and maybe that was what had been done to activate her dormant immortal genes.

If that was all it took, Margaret was willing to give it a try.

But did she really want to live forever?

Life was hard. Why would she want to drag it out indefinitely? Didn't the immortals get tired of living?

She wanted time to get to know her daughter, and maybe to explore a relationship with Bowen, who was actually much older than her but looked a decade younger.

Her mortal lifespan was long enough to do both.

If she became immortal, would the process reverse her aging and turn her young and beautiful again?

Could she start anew?

Margaret chuckled softly. The transition might shave ten years off her appearance, but unless Bowen thralled her to forget her ugly past, there was no getting rid of the memories she'd accumulated, and not many of them were good.

She'd learned not to feel too much, not to think about what she'd lost or about how meaningless it all was. She didn't want eternity to ponder the depressing reality of existence.

Margaret had learned to live in the moment, to keep so busy that she didn't have time to think. Idle moments were her enemy, as were the moments before falling asleep.

That was why she'd worked so hard, why she'd kept reading and researching material until her eyes burned from exhaustion and she knew that she would fall asleep as soon as she closed them. Anything less than that meant staying awake for hours and agonizing. To spend eternity like that would be hell.

When a soft knock sounded on her door, she wiped the few tears she'd shed with a corner of the duvet. "Yes?"

"Can I come in?" Ana asked.

"Sure."

Her friend walked in with a cup of coffee in hand. "Bowen is worried about you. He sent me to check on you." She sat on the bed and handed Margaret the cup. "How are you feeling this morning?"

"Strange. Did last night really happen, or did I dream it all up?"

"It happened." Ana smiled. "Your beautiful daughter came. She wasn't angry at you, she hugged you and kissed you, and she called you Mom. It doesn't get any better than that."

"It doesn't." Margaret took a sip from the coffee.

"So why were you crying?"

She shrugged. "I'm not sure that I want to live forever. I mean, I want time with Wendy, but I'm not old. I still have many years left to make up for those I lost."

Ana regarded her with puzzlement in her eyes. "Why wouldn't you want to live forever?"

"Because life is hard, and it's sad. Why drag out the misery?"

"It doesn't have to be miserable. You can learn to be happy." She leaned closer and whispered, "You have an amazing guy who wants to spend that eternity with you. What can be better than that?"

"Does he? When Wendy called him my mate, he told her that we were not there yet."

Anastasia rolled her eyes. "That's because you haven't had sex yet. It's like marriage. It needs to be consummated to be official. Bowen is in love with you, and you are in love with him. It's time you let yourself feel it."

Margaret opened her mouth to refute Ana's claim, to tell her that she wasn't in love with Bowen, but she closed it when she realized that Ana was right.

She'd fallen in love with Bowen from almost the very first moment. When he'd brought her to that ambulance and stayed with her, she'd felt the pull, the yearning. But she hadn't allowed herself to internalize it, in the same way she hadn't allowed herself to internalize anything else.

She'd been existing, not living.

To open her heart would have opened the gates not only to love, but also to misery, to the self-loathing, and to the horrible memories, and Margaret wouldn't have survived it.

Her capacity for pain had been maxed out a long time ago.

"You need to get up and get dressed." Ana patted her arm. "We can leave as soon as you are ready."

Margaret swallowed. "Do you mean the four of us?"

"Of course. There is no reason for us to stay here any longer. We are going to the immortals' village." Ana grinned. "I can't wait to see it. Leon has told me so much about it, and it sounds like a real haven, not the fake one Emmett created." She pursed her lips. "Which reminds me that there is one more piece of information that might shock you."

As panic constricted her throat, Margaret lifted her hand to her neck. "I don't know if I can handle any more shocking news."

"I think this piece will explain a few things, or at least make you see them more clearly. The clan has captured Emmett, and they have him locked up in their dungeon. Apparently, he's also an immortal, just from a different breed, and he used compulsion to make you and the others worship him. The guy who helped you, Kalugal, is not a motivational speaker. He is also a compeller like Emmett, and all he did was override what Emmett has done to you. The leader you admired so much compelled you to get panic attacks every time you thought of contacting Wendy or even just seeking information about her."

4

SYSSI

*B*y the time Okidu parked the limo in the underground garage of the building, Lisa and Ronja had talked up a storm, updating Sari and David on the latest village gossip.

Luckily, mother and daughter weren't aware yet of the one item that would most likely bother Ronja the most once she found out about it.

Syssi wasn't sure what kind of a relationship Ronja and Bowen had, or if it had developed into anything romantic, but even if it hadn't, the news about Bowen's newfound love would probably be upsetting to Ronja. Now that he belonged to another woman, he wouldn't be spending time with her like he used to.

Anandur, Brundar, and Kian had been busy talking about security and didn't pay attention to the prattle, but she'd caught Okidu stealing glances at Ronja through the rearview mirror.

Lately, he'd been acting even stranger than usual. Well, stranger for an Odu, but less strange for a human. Could it be that he was developing real feelings? Was he concerned for Ronja?

The butler knew everything that was going on, heard all the gossip, and stored it in his cybertronic brain.

Syssi shook her head. She was being silly, and it was all in her head. She'd gotten so used to Okidu that he seemed human to her.

"This building needs a name," Lisa said. "I'm tired of calling it the building across the street from the keep."

"What would you suggest?" Anandur asked.

Lisa shrugged. "I don't know. Anything would be better than that. Name it after one of the presidents or something. The Adams building, or Madison, or Monroe. Or the Shangri-La."

Syssi chuckled. "I like Shangri-La, but don't forget that we intend to lease

236

these apartments at some point. I don't think prospective tenants would like their building to be called after a fictional place."

"We can discuss this upstairs." Kian opened the passenger door at the same time Okidu opened the one on the other side. "Mother and Amanda are waiting for us with lunch."

As the eight of them headed toward the elevators, Okidu lifted Sari and David's luggage from the trunk and followed behind them.

"I shall wait for the next elevator, master." He bowed.

"Thank you for getting our luggage." Sari patted his arm. "I left Ojidu home to take care of those who volunteered to stay behind."

The perpetual shroud around the castle meant that those in charge of maintaining it couldn't leave. Usually, that wasn't a problem, but it was a shame that they couldn't take part in the celebrations. It was time to replace the shroud with technology, but, for some reason, Sari was dragging her feet about it.

Perhaps she wanted to move out of there. She had refused Kian's offer to join the village because she liked her independence, but that didn't mean that she couldn't move her people to another location in Scotland. The castle was beautiful, but it was old, and there was only so much that could be done to bring it into the twenty-first century.

"Your apartment is on the top floor." Kian pressed the button to call the elevator. "It's not a penthouse, because the building wasn't designed with residences in mind, but you'll still have a nice view."

Sari cast him an apologetic glance. "You've gone to so much trouble to make this event possible. We could have made the wedding a smaller celebration in the village."

As the elevator arrived and they all crammed in, Kian wrapped his arm around Syssi's shoulders. "The plans to convert the building from offices to apartments were made long before I decided to host the clan here. Your wedding only hastened the construction, so don't feel guilty about it. I just wish that you could stay in the village during your visit."

Sari shook her head. "I need to be near my people, and they are all staying here. But David and I will come visit the village on Sunday. Miranda can't wait to see it."

"When is she arriving?" Syssi asked.

"Later today." David held the elevator door open until all of them spilled out. "The logistics of bringing everyone here without attracting attention were complicated. Only a small group is arriving straight from Scotland, and not all from the same airport. Others are making stopovers at other major cities, in Europe and in the States, before heading here."

Kian nodded. "We are using delivery trucks to pick them up from the various collection centers they will Uber or taxi to."

Sari winced. "Please tell me those trucks have nice interiors. I don't want my people shuttled in like cattle."

"Of course." Syssi put her hand on Sari's arm. "This is a celebration not an evacuation."

As they started down the corridor toward the corner unit, the door opened and Amanda rushed out. "Sari!" She pulled her sister into a hug. "You look amazing." Amanda smiled at David. "Thanks to you, no doubt." She let go of Sari and hugged him too. "I'm so excited about your wedding. Especially since I didn't have to do anything. Gerard took care of all the details, including hiring the decorators and supervising their work."

Sari shook her head. "I don't know how you managed to rope him into organizing our wedding and Kian's birthday. You must teach me your magic spell."

Amanda pursed her lips. "Got guilt? That's my magic."

"I see." Sari turned to Kian. "Your birthday was supposed to be a surprise, but at some point, it was decided to include you in the plans."

Syssi lifted her hand. "That was my doing. Kian doesn't like surprises, but he loves big clan-wide parties. I figured that he would prefer to be included in the planning, especially since security was a major concern."

"You know me so well." He kissed the top of her head. "Let's not keep Mother waiting."

5

KIAN

*K*ian waited patiently for the emotional reunion between Annani and Sari to be done with and for everyone else to exchange greetings.

When it seemed to be done, he pulled out a dining room chair for his mother. "Oridu is wringing his hands in the kitchen, waiting for us to sit down so he can serve lunch."

Annani smiled up at him. "Oridu is not doing any hand wringing. Are you hungry, my son?"

"Starving."

"Then let us eat." She motioned for the others to join her.

"I thought that Andrew and Nathalie would come and bring Phoenix," Sari said as David pulled out a chair for her. "I can't get enough of that little girl. She just cracks me up with her grown-up talk. She sounds like a seventeen-year-old."

Syssi smoothed a hand over her belly. "Andrew had a big meeting at work he couldn't wiggle out of, and Nathalie didn't want to come without him."

"Why is he still working for the government?" Alena asked.

"He's not willing to give up the connections and the access to classified information that his job provides him with." Kian passed the basket of bread to Syssi. "Frankly, I haven't been encouraging him to leave. He's in the know, and he can alert us to new developments in real time. Right now, he's trying to get into UFO classified information. He might discover something connected with the Kra-ell's arrival. If what Emmett told us is true, then they arrived sometime at the beginning of the nineteenth century. Perhaps there are records of sightings from back then."

Leaning back, David crossed his arms over his chest. "Have any of you heard about the Tunguska event?"

The name sounded familiar, and after digging in his memory banks, all Kian could come up with was that it was something that had happened in Russia more than a century ago. "Was it a meteor?"

David nodded. "In 1908, there was a massive explosion near the Tunguska River in Russia. It flattened trees in an area of about a thousand square miles, maybe a little less. I don't remember the exact number. The theory is that the explosion was caused by a large meteoroid, or rather the airburst it created. It must have disintegrated at an altitude of several miles above the ground because no impact crater has been found. Based on the size and magnitude of the impacted area, the shock wave from the air burst would have been a 5 on the Richter scale. That's enough to destroy a large city. Fortunately, it happened over a remote, sparsely populated area, and only a handful of casualties were reported."

"What are you trying to say?" Annani asked.

David shrugged. "It's the largest impact event in recorded history, and there is no definite explanation for what actually happened. Perhaps it was an alien ship that went down, a large vessel that hadn't been supposed to enter the atmosphere and should have stayed in orbit. From what Sari told me, I understand that Emmett's group is small, and he was led to believe that they were the only survivors. It fits the narrative."

"I don't think they are," Kian said. "I have a feeling that there are many more of them scattered around." He unscrewed the cap from the large Perrier bottle and poured some into Syssi's glass and then his.

"There might have been several escape pods," David suggested.

Sari patted his back. "Is this the scientist talking or the sci-fi author?"

"Can't I be both?"

"Of course, my love. But this sounds like you've let yourself get carried away on the wings of your wonderful imagination."

Kian didn't think so. "Reality is often stranger than fiction, Sari. I'll mention the Tunguska event to William and see what he thinks of it."

"Speaking of William." Amanda shifted in her chair. "Is he making any progress with deciphering the Kra-ell language?"

"He is, but it's a slow process." Kian scooped a large serving of baked fingerling potatoes onto his plate. "William is not a linguist, and although we have many members who speak a lot of languages, no one is an actual philologist. He was able, however, to confirm Emmett's translation of the email he'd sent to his leader."

"The reason I'm asking, is that I had a great idea." Amanda paused for dramatic effect, looked around the table to make sure she had everyone's attention, and then smiled at Kian. "You are going to thank me for coming up with this one." She paused again. "You should send Mey with Arwel and Jin to China. Even if Emmett's people didn't leave any breadcrumbs, they still left echoes of conversations embedded in the walls of their former compound. She can listen to them and perhaps find out where they were planning to move to."

Annani clapped her hands. "That is a brilliant idea, Mindy. You are so clever."

The idea was solid, provided they could decipher the entire language and Mey could learn it in a couple of weeks, which wasn't going to happen.

Anandur chuckled. "You know what this reminds me of? The joke about the solution to the German U-boat problem during WWII. Someone came up with the bright idea that raising the ocean temperature by four degrees Celsius would make the U-boats inoperable. When asked how he proposed to do that, the guy said, 'I offered the solution, someone else will have to figure out the details.' Mey listening to the echoes in the walls will not achieve much if she doesn't understand what she hears. It's not like she can record it and then have Emmett translate it."

Amanda crossed her arms over her chest and jutted her chin out. "Then we should put her in the cell with Emmett and have her learn as much as she can until it's time for the team to leave for China."

Kian shook his head. "The question is whether she would agree, and even if she does, it will still take her a very long time to learn."

"Isn't it ironic?" Syssi sighed. "The two girls that the Kra-ell considered worthless and got rid of might lead to their capture."

"Yeah." Anandur grinned. "Payback is a b..." He cast an apologetic glance at Annani. "I mean, the Kra-ell will get what's coming to them."

6

ANNANI

"*P*erhaps that is why the Fates brought Mey and Jin to us." Annani turned to Kian. "How do you plan to use Jin's talent?"

"I'm not sure how her talent will be utilized, but given the circumstances, Jin and Mey could be our only hope of finding Emmett's group."

"I wish I had a cool talent like that," Lisa said.

"Yours is even cooler." Amanda patted her arm. "You were right about Anastasia. She was a Dormant, and now she's an immortal. I only regret that I didn't send you to sniff out her friend."

Lisa perked up. "I can still do that if you want me to."

Amanda waved a dismissive hand. "It's too late. We know that she's a Dormant for sure because she's Wendy's mom."

No one had mentioned Bowen's involvement yet, and Annani wondered whether it was intentional since Ronja was there. She liked David's mother even more than she had expected to and regretted that the news might pain her. Amanda suspected that Bowen and Ronja had been more than friends. If she was right about that, then Bowen finding a mate would no doubt disappoint Ronja.

"How did you hear about it already?" Kian asked. "I only found out about Margaret being Wendy's mother today, and that was at two o'clock this morning."

Syssi lifted her hand. "From me. I couldn't sit on news like that and not tell anyone, so I called Amanda."

"And I called Mother and Alena." Amanda cast Sari an apologetic glance. "I didn't call you because you don't know Wendy, so the news would have been meaningless to you."

Sari grimaced. "Discovering a new Dormant is never meaningless. I just wish some would find their way to my people." She lifted a pair of love-filled eyes to her mate. "I feel guilty about being the only lucky one so far."

Annani cast a quick glance at Ronja, but it seemed like she had not figured out yet that Margaret and Bowen had become an item.

Perhaps now was not the best time for her to discover that, and a change of subject was in order.

Syssi must have arrived at the same conclusion because she turned to Lisa. "I might have another sniffing mission for you at the wedding. Onegus is bringing a human date who he suspects might be a Dormant."

Lisa's eyes sparkled with excitement. "I'll be more than happy to sniff her. Just point me in her direction."

When a long moment of silence followed the exchange between Syssi and Lisa, and everyone kept sneaking glances at Ronja, Annani turned to Kian. "Has Jin agreed to take part in the expedition?"

Hopefully, her question would shift the conversation back to a neutral subject.

"She has. But to use her talent, she needs to learn Chinese, and according to Arwel, she's linguistically challenged. For an immortal, that is." Kian raked his fingers through his hair. "I wish we had more time for Mey and Jin to learn Mandarin and the Kra-ell languages properly. As it is, I'm afraid that they will have to make do with just rudimentary understanding."

"Fates willing, that will suffice." Annani smiled. "I also heard that Eleanor is becoming a useful asset to the clan."

"She's guarding Emmett," Syssi said. "Regrettably, things didn't work out between her and Greggory."

Annani had heard the news about the breakup. "If it was not meant to be, it is best that it has ended sooner rather than later. This brings me to my next question. Are there any new romances between Kalugal's men and our clan ladies?"

Amanda uttered a frustrated huff. "There are plenty of hookups, that's for sure. They are all acting as if they must sample every flavor available first. I guess having so many cookies in the jar makes it difficult to settle on just one."

Annani arched a brow. "Are you saying that none have formed relationships?"

"Not as far as I know." Amanda sighed. "It also doesn't help that Kalugal keeps his men busy in his downtown offices six days a week. By the time they get back to the village, the café is closed, and for now, that's the only meeting place we have."

Annani was not happy. The infusion of eligible males was supposed to result in many new pairings and hopefully a few pregnancies. What were the Fates thinking?

"Perhaps we should organize mixers. Are Kalugal's men invited to the wedding?"

Amanda shook her head. "Kalugal and Jacki are obviously coming, and so is Rufsur because he's mated to Edna. The rest are not part of the family yet." She glanced at Sari. "I didn't know whether you would want them at your wedding."

"I don't mind," Sari said. "It could be a good opportunity for them to mingle."

Everyone's eyes turned to Kian, who was shaking his head. "I need Kalugal's men to provide added security at the village while nearly all of us are at the keep. If we invite them, we will have to leave several more Guardians behind, which is not desirable on two accounts. The obvious reason is that the more Guardians can attend the wedding, the better. And secondly, we need them to secure the event and this building. They can take part in the celebration and safeguard the clan at the same time."

It was a valid point, but Kian was not using his emotional intelligence and thinking how the exclusion would affect Kalugal's men and their loyalty to the clan.

"If you want Kalugal's men to become an integral part of the clan, you need to treat them as such." Annani lifted her cup for Oridu to refill. "Since they are all trained warriors and therefore can be regarded as an auxiliary force to the Guardians, I suggest a lottery. Decide how many men are needed to maintain security in the village and have the Guardians and Kalugal's men draw lots in proportion to their numbers."

"Isn't it too late for that?" Syssi asked. "The wedding is in two days, and the Guardians have already been assigned their posts. I don't think it's a good idea to cause resentment among them because we want to include Kalugal's men in the celebration. There is enough of it going around already, especially among the males."

"I suggest a compromise," Amanda said. "We leave the wedding arrangements as they are, but we implement the lottery for Kian's birthday."

"It is a reasonable solution." Annani looked at Kian. "It is your birthday, my son. Is it agreeable to you?"

He looked conflicted. "I have nothing against Kalugal's men, but I prefer to have more of our Guardians attend the celebrations. I'll talk it over with Kalugal and see what he thinks. He might have a different take on this. Perhaps a small selection of his men can attend both events."

7

KIAN

*A*s coffee and dessert were served after lunch, Kian texted Kalugal to ask his opinion about inviting some of his men to Sari and David's wedding, and perhaps a larger group to Kian's bimillennial birthday celebration.

If he were a private man, Kian would have preferred to celebrate with his immediate family, but he was a leader, and his people needed as many reasons to celebrate as he could provide them. That's why his personal preferences regarding the attendance of Kalugal's men didn't really matter. If he could promote their integration into the clan by inviting them, then he was all for it.

Kian's end goal was for the offspring created by unions between clan females and Kalugal's men to belong to the clan and fortify its numbers, and for that, he needed the men to feel part of the community.

On the other hand, Syssi's argument was valid as well. Not everyone was happy about them joining the village, and having them attend might increase feelings of resentment rather than promote integration.

As he waited for his cousin's response, Kian observed his mother's interaction with Ronja. They were acting like old friends who hadn't seen each other in a long while, sharing gossip and talking about everything from Lisa's school experience to world politics and Ronja's conspiracy theories.

It was a shame that Ronja was too old to transition. She would have made a wonderful companion for Annani, maybe even freeing Alena to finally pursue her own interests.

His eldest sister had done a lot for the clan, birthing and raising thirteen children, and at the same time keeping Annani out of trouble. She had paid her dues and then some. It was time she started doing things for herself, living her life and finding her passion. Not that motherhood wasn't a worthy goal in itself, but it seemed like Alena's incredible fertility had been exhausted in her younger years and she could conceive no more. She needed something new to fulfill her.

After Kalugal had finally responded, promising to supply two lists of the men he wanted to bring along to each of the events, Kian pushed to his feet. "We should be heading back soon. I still have work to do today."

Annani looked up at him. "Is there an available apartment in this building that Alena and I could use? Our people will start arriving tomorrow, and I decided that we should be here with them."

Kian shook his head. "I don't know if there are any left, but even if Ingrid can rearrange things and free up an apartment for you, I'd prefer that you stay in the village. Otherwise, I'll have to beef up security in this building, and the Guardian force is already stretched thin as it is."

The stubborn tilt of Annani's chin didn't bode well. "I have made up my mind. Please check with Ingrid if she can reshuffle occupancy to make an apartment available for Alena and me."

He pinned her with a hard stare. "Beefing up security here means canceling even more rescue missions. Do you want that on your conscience?"

It was a low blow, but it was true. Besides, he really didn't want her to stay in the building.

Sari winced. "You are making me feel guilty for having the wedding here. I didn't know that you'd canceled missions because of us."

"I also had to cancel missions because of my birthday, so I should share the guilt. But neither of us has to feel guilty. The plan is to compensate for the reduction by doubling up after the celebrations are over and everyone goes home."

"There you go." Annani waved a hand. "This is the solution. Cancel all the missions until next week and then double up on the effort in the following weeks. I am sure the Guardians will appreciate a break for the duration of the festivities. Guarding me is not as taxing as what they usually do, and it is certainly not as depressing. It will also give them an opportunity to spend more time with their visiting relatives."

As the others all nodded in agreement, Kian knew that he'd lost the argument. "I'll speak with Ingrid and Onegus and see what can be done."

Annani didn't even try to hide her triumphant smile. "Thank you."

"Speaking of relatives," Sari said. "What's going on with Carol and Lokan? Are they joining us for the celebrations?"

"It's too dangerous for Lokan, and Carol has decided to stay with him in DC." Kian offered a hand up to Syssi. "They are flying out to China on Monday." He supported her back as she struggled to her feet.

Sari leaned back. "Together?"

Syssi nodded. "Lokan hired Carol as the marketing expert for the fashion label he's about to launch. They are flying out together, and he's reserved a two-bedroom suite for them in the Waldorf Astoria in Beijing."

"Fancy," Ronja said. "Does Lokan need a personal assistant? I would love to see Beijing and stay at the Waldorf."

"Me too." Lisa lifted her hand. "Does he need a teenage model for his fashion label?"

8

ONEGUS

*I*ngrid strode into Onegus's temporary headquarters looking as if someone had pissed on her designer shoes. "Annani wants an apartment in the building, and I don't have any furnished ones left. How am I supposed to reshuffle people as they are coming in?" She plopped down on the couch. "I need a drink."

Onegus walked over to the bar. "What would you like?"

"Whatever you make is fine." She waved a hand in dismissal. "Just not beer. I can't stand that vile stuff you guys drink."

He mixed her a gin and tonic. "You can give this apartment to Annani. I can move operations to my old office in the keep." He handed her the drink.

Ingrid lifted a pair of grateful eyes to him. "Are you sure? You said that you needed a place in the building for the Guardians to rest between shifts."

"They can rest in the keep. It's just across the street. Or we can section off part of the lobby for them. There is already a sitting area, and if you put screens around it and add a snack and drink bar, that should do it."

"I like it. I can make it look as if it's sectioned off for construction. That way, when people walk by, they are not going to wonder what's going on or try to get in to take a look."

As his phone rang, Onegus had a good idea who was calling. "Good afternoon, boss. Are you calling about the Clan Mother's request for lodging in the building?"

"I see that Ingrid beat me to it. Is she still freaking out?"

"We found a solution. Annani can have this apartment, and I'll move to my old office in the keep. We will also section off part of the lobby for the Guardians."

"Double the space you had in mind for that. With Annani in the building, we need to beef up security."

"We are already maxed out. I don't have enough Guardians."

"I know. We need to cancel the rest of the rescue missions until after everyone goes home and things return to normal."

"Did you speak with Bridget?" Onegus walked over to his desk and sat down on the swivel chair he'd brought from the keep just that morning.

"Yeah. She's on it. To compensate, we will double up starting next Monday."

"I don't like it, but I guess we have no choice." Onegus started collecting his notes and piling them up. "What the Clan Mother wants, the Clan Mother gets."

"That was my initial reaction as well, but Annani raised a valid argument. The clan is celebrating, and the Guardians have the same right as the others to take a pause from what they are doing and concentrate on happier things. I hate the thought of the victims suffering through one more week of torment while we are having fun, but we can't save everyone, and there will always be people suffering somewhere no matter what we do and how hard we try."

"Ain't that the sad truth. I assume that Annani wants the place by tomorrow?"

"She wants to be there when her people start arriving."

Onegus heaved out a sigh. "I'll pack my things and move to the keep today. Ingrid will have the place cleaned and ready sometime tomorrow." He glanced at the interior designer. "Do you have anyone other than the Odus to do that?"

The cleaning crews had left long before the guests had started to arrive, and they wouldn't be back until the guests were gone. The Odus were available only for emergency cleanups. Other than that, everyone was responsible for keeping their own place clean.

"As soon as you vacate the place, I'll get the cleaning crew in. They are very discreet, and they know not to ask questions. I can get it ready for Annani and Alena by tomorrow mid-morning." She reached for her purse and pulled out her phone. "I need to call the construction crew chief and get him back here to section off part of the lobby."

"Double the number of Guardians starting tomorrow morning," Kian said.

"Consider it done."

When Kian ended the call, Onegus rubbed a hand over the back of his neck. "I hoped to steal a few moments to see Cassandra, but evidently, it's not going to happen today."

Ingrid lifted a hand to indicate that she was still busy on the phone. When she was done, she dropped it back in her purse and pushed to her feet. "You can go for half an hour. I'll hold the fort for you."

He shook his head. "I need to reorganize the Guardian schedule, and then I have to greet my mother when she arrives tonight."

"You need to eat, right? You can eat with Cassandra. Have her meet you somewhere nearby. I'll cover for you."

"You are the best." He kissed her cheek. "I'll take care of the schedule and then call Cassandra."

"Give me fifteen minutes notice before you leave."

"I'll do that."

9

BOWEN

"It's like taking a ride into the future." Margaret glanced at the car's opaque windows. "I can't get over the car driving itself."

"Autonomous driving is going to be commonplace shortly." Bowen leaned over the center console and took her hand. "The technology is already incorporated into several car models, but the legislators haven't approved it yet."

"What about the windows?" She put her hand on the glass. "Is that a common thing too?"

"No. The technology is not new, but no one is implementing it the way we do. For us, it's a necessary precaution to keep our location safe. If a clan member is caught by our enemies, he or she won't be able to provide the village's exact location because they don't know it. Their cars drive in and out of the village autonomously, and the windows turn opaque so they won't see the entrance to the tunnel."

"We are in a tunnel?" She tilted her head to listen to the echoes.

"We are, and in a moment we will enter an elevator that will take us up to a parking garage."

"Do you know where the entrance is?"

He shook his head. "Only a few members have that information, head Guardians included, but I'm not one of them."

"Does it bother you?"

"Not at all. The clan's security comes first, and the fewer people who know how to get to our village, the better."

"But it's aboveground, right?"

He nodded.

"Then it can be seen from aircraft."

"You are correct, but we have ways to hide it from view by sophisticated camouflage technology."

When the car entered the elevator, the windows began to clear, and

Margaret pressed her nose against the glass, looking like a kid on an amusement park ride.

Bowen smiled. "Usually, when a new Dormant or immortal arrives at the village, there is a welcoming committee. But everyone is busy with the upcoming wedding and the arriving guests, so you are not going to get the usual treatment." As the elevator opened at the garage level, Bowen took over the driving. "But I think you'll like yours better." He drove into his parking spot, where Wendy and Vlad were waiting for them.

Leon and Anastasia, who had arrived a couple of minutes earlier, were waiting for them as well.

"Everyone I need is here." Margaret's voice quivered.

Wendy opened the passenger door and offered her mother a hand up. "Welcome to the village, Mom." She chuckled. "Well, you need to get out of the parking garage to actually be in the village, but that's what everyone says."

Bowen walked over to the trunk and pulled out the folding wheelchair. "The walk to Wendy and Vlad's house is long. It would be too difficult for you to traverse with the crutches."

"We brought a golf cart," Wendy said. "But it can be used for the luggage. If you're okay with the wheelchair, I can show you more of the village on the way, and maybe even introduce you to some people."

Margaret paled. "I don't know if I'm ready for that."

Wendy helped her into the wheelchair and then leaned and kissed her cheek. "I just want you to see where I work and to meet Wonder. Are you okay with that?"

"I guess so. But what about the other people in the café?"

"Don't worry about it." Wendy patted her shoulder. "I'll take care of them. You only need to smile and wave."

Cradling the front of her neck, Margaret still looked as if she had a frog stuck in her throat, but she nodded.

As Vlad helped with the luggage, taking some of the load from Leon and Bowen, Anastasia joined Wendy behind Margaret's wheelchair.

"Don't forget that I'm here as well." She put a hand on her friend's slim shoulder. "And people are going to want to say hello to me too. I'll deflect attention from you."

Margaret blew out a breath. "Thank you."

"No problem."

"Before I forget," Wendy said. "Syssi and Amanda apologize for not being here to welcome you both. They are having a family lunch with the bride and groom outside of the village and will try to stop by tomorrow afternoon."

"Who are Syssi and Amanda?" Margaret asked.

"Amanda is the goddess's daughter, and Syssi is married to the goddess's son," Wendy said. "They usually welcome the new Dormants and newly-turned immortals."

When Bowen's phone started buzzing the same time Leon's did, they exchanged worried looks, put the luggage down, and pulled out their devices.

"What's going on?" Vlad asked.

"It's a group message," Leon said. "All rescue missions are canceled until next

Monday, and we are to report to the keep tonight at eight-thirty for an orientation."

"Did something happen?" Anastasia asked.

Onegus was doubling security at the newly converted building, but he hadn't elaborated on why. Hopefully, it wasn't because a new cause for alarm had presented itself.

"It's probably about additional security for the wedding," Leon said. "With the entire clan gathering in one place, Kian must be freaking out." He put the phone in his back pocket and lifted the two suitcases. "I, for one, am happy." He glanced at Bowen. "My mother is arriving tomorrow. I'd rather spend time with her than go out on rescue missions."

Bowen groaned. "I completely forgot. I don't even know when my mother's flight is landing." He pulled out his phone and scrolled through his emails. "She's arriving tomorrow morning." He let out a relieved breath.

"What time?" Leon asked.

"Ten-fifteen."

"Then she must be arriving on the same flight as my mother. We can pick them up together."

Bowen shook his head. "We might get assigned a post at the meeting tonight. Besides, Turner has the entire transportation of arriving clan members nailed down. He doesn't want us to collect anyone from the airport."

"Right." Leon's smile wilted. "I guess we will have to wait to see our mothers after they arrive at the building."

10

MARGARET

*M*argaret felt her throat constricting again, and this time it wasn't Emmett's compulsion that was causing it.

"Your mother is coming to the village?" she croaked.

"She's going to stay in the clan's building downtown, but I'm sure she'll want to visit."

"That's awesome," Wendy said. "Bowen's mother can meet you, and Leon's mother can meet Anastasia." She leaned over Margaret's shoulder. "I never expected to have an extended family. Isn't it wonderful?"

Margaret forced a smile. "Yeah, it is."

It wasn't.

Bowen's mother was going to hate her, and rightfully so. She didn't deserve a guy like him, and if she had a son who was dating a woman like herself, she wouldn't have liked it one bit either.

"By the way." Wendy stopped in front of the elevators and pressed the button. "Vlad's mother and her boyfriend are at the house, waiting to meet you."

Margaret tried to swallow, but her throat was so constricted that she started to cough.

In an instant, Bowen was at her side, crouching in front of her. "Look at me, Margaret."

She tried, but the coughing was getting worse, and she couldn't catch a breath.

"Everything is going to be alright."

His words penetrated the haze of panic like a wave of calm waters, and suddenly, she was able to breathe. Had he thralled her?

"Better?" He cupped her cheek.

She nodded. "Did you thrall me?"

"Just a smidgen. I hope you don't mind."

"Thank you." She covered his hand with hers. "I'm sorry for falling apart like that over nothing. Everything is happening so quickly, and I feel overwhelmed."

"I bet. It's too much." Bowen lifted his eyes to Wendy. "Perhaps it wasn't a good idea to cram everything into one day. Your mother needs time to adjust."

"I can tell Stella and Richard to come some other time."

"It's okay." Margaret turned around to look at her daughter. "I'll be fine." She forced a smile. "I need to adjust to this new reality, and the sooner the better."

As the elevator door opened, Wendy wheeled her inside, and the others followed. It was cramped, but having them there, surrounding her, felt comforting. Everyone she cared for and who cared for her was in that elevator.

"You are going to love Stella," Wendy said. "She's so creative. She designs costumes for theater productions, and now she's also working on a fashion line. Richard is awesome too. I met him in the government program, and he was always nice to me even though I was a drag back then. When we escaped, and I betrayed everyone to the director, he stayed with Vlad and me in the cabin and was still nice to me despite that. Then we moved into the village, and he was our roommate for a while, but then he and Stella fell in love, and he moved out to be with her."

Apparently, Wendy talked up a storm when she was nervous, but Margaret didn't mind it in the least. She loved hearing her daughter's voice, and she was thirsty for every little bit of information about her past. They had so much catching up to do.

As the elevator doors opened, Wendy wheeled her out, and the others followed.

"This is the entry pavilion," Wendy explained. "The artifacts behind the glass belong to Kalugal, who's an archeology buff. I would have taken you on a tour, but Stella and Richard are waiting for us at the house."

"It's beautiful." Ana gasped. "Just look at how green everything is." She followed Vlad out the sliding doors.

"What do you think, Mom?" Wendy pushed the wheelchair out.

"It's paradise." Margaret wasn't referring to the lush greenery. "The place is beautiful, but what makes it special is that it's your home."

"It's your home too, Mom."

When the men were done loading the luggage onto the golf cart, Vlad hopped behind the wheel. "I'm going to drop off Leon and Anastasia's things at Leon's house first." He looked at Bowen. "Where should I take your and Margaret's things?"

"To my place." Bowen pulled out his phone. "I'll just let my roommate know that we are here."

"I thought that you were staying with us," Anastasia said. "What is Margaret going to do all alone in the house when you go to work?"

"Good point," Bowen agreed without argument. "I called Ingrid about getting us a place of our own, but she won't have time to take care of it until after the celebrations."

Anastasia shook her head. "Even when she gets you a place, you can't move in there until Margaret is independent."

Wendy looked conflicted. "I thought that you and Bowen would stay with us, but I'm working at the café, and Vlad is working at the bakery and attending classes in college. So maybe Mom can spend the days with Anastasia but come to our house in the evenings? Your place is in the new phase, right?" she asked Leon.

He nodded. "It's only a few minutes' walk away from yours. Even with the crutches, your mother can handle such a short walk."

Margaret cleared her throat. "Is no one going to ask me what I want?"

"Nope." Ana crouched next to her. "I know you. You'll say that you can manage on your own and argue that you don't want to be a bother. But I don't want to hear it. Leon is going back to work as well, and I don't want to be alone in the house either. You and I will brave this new world together."

11

CASSANDRA

Throughout the day, Cassandra's snowflakes had been sneaking curious glances at her. She hadn't chewed anyone out, hadn't criticized their work or lack thereof, and had been giving out more smiles than, well, ever.

They were probably whispering behind her back that she must have gotten laid, which wasn't far from the truth.

But it was much more than that.

Onegus, the most amazing guy she'd ever met, was serious about her. The invitation to his family wedding was the best proof she could have asked for. In fact, it was more than she'd ever expected. Getting invited to his home to meet his roommate or a dinner out with a couple of his friends would have sufficed.

Was she ready to meet his family?

Talk about intimidating.

Onegus seemed like a down-to-earth kind of guy. He wasn't a snob, didn't flaunt his family's wealth, and didn't act like a spoiled rich guy. That didn't mean, though, that his entire family was like him.

They might look down their noses at her, and she would have to smile and pretend not to notice for Onegus's sake. The problem would be reining in her temper. Perhaps she should take one of those relaxants that she'd experimented with a while ago. The problem was that they were probably expired, and it was too late to make an appointment with her doctor to get a new prescription.

Positive thinking would have to do.

She would have to focus on Onegus and how wonderful he was, reaffirm her self-confidence by reminding herself of all that she'd achieved and ignore any snide remarks or disapproving looks, or just not let them get under her skin.

Easier said than done, but not impossible.

When Cassandra's phone buzzed with Onegus's number on the screen, a happy grin spread over her face, and her heart gave a little flutter.

Did he miss her?

In the morning, he'd said that he would be busy until Saturday and wouldn't be able to see her.

"Hello, Onegus. What a nice surprise. I didn't expect another call from you today."

"I hope that I'm not interrupting, but frankly, I don't care. I need to hear your voice. When can you get away from the office?"

"At around seven. Why?"

"We could meet for a cup of coffee or a very quick dinner, and I mean fast-food quick. I can get away for half an hour."

He really missed her.

"I was resigned to not seeing you until the wedding. What changed your mind?"

He chuckled. "Do you want to hear me say that I can't stay away from you and that I need to see you?"

Switching the phone to her other ear, she crossed her legs and leaned back. "Only if it's the truth."

"Every word. I feel like a junkie who has to get his fix."

She arched a brow even though he couldn't see her. "Are we talking about a quickie or a coffee?"

He was silent for a long moment. "I won't lie. If a quickie was on the menu, I would have taken it. But seeing you, smelling you, and hearing your voice, that's all I need to tide me over."

Cassandra wanted to say that she felt the same, and that not seeing him until Saturday would be a torment, but that would reveal too much too soon and give him too much power.

Besides, Onegus was a man, and he would take sex over mushy declarations any day and twice on Sunday. Well, probably twice on any day. The guy had some stamina.

Heck, Cassandra would take sex with him over coffee or dinner anytime as well. She'd never craved a guy with such intensity.

"I can meet you at the apartment we spent the night in."

The groan he emitted sounded pained. "That's the best offer I could have hoped for, but, regrettably, that place is not mine exclusively, and right now there are at least three other people in there. Besides, I have a meeting at eight, and my mother arrives at eleven tonight, and she will expect me to spend time with her."

"Your mother?" Cassandra squeaked.

She'd never squeaked before.

"My mother is coming to the wedding."

"Are you going to introduce us?"

"Of course."

"Isn't it too early for that?"

"Why would you think that? I met your mother. It's only fair that you meet mine."

Oh God. She'd dug that hole for herself and had no way out of it. Could she fake a sudden sickness?

"Why so quiet all of a sudden?" Onegus sounded amused. "No snarky, witty comments?"

"Frankly, I'm speechless. It should have occurred to me that your mother was coming to the wedding, but it didn't, and I don't feel ready to face her. What if she doesn't like me?"

"She's going to love you. And even if she doesn't, which I can promise you is not going to happen, I'm a big boy, and I don't need my mother to approve of my choices."

"You might think so, but we all want our parents' approval. It means a lot to me that my mother likes you. Even though Geraldine has memory problems, she has good instincts about people, and I trust her opinion."

"Well, what's not to like, right? I'm every mother's dream guy for her daughter."

Cassandra laughed. "I'm sure that your modesty is what impresses them the most."

"It's only one among my many other exceptional qualities, but I will be more than happy to list them to you one by one when we meet. Can you get off a little earlier?"

"Six is the earliest I can manage. Does that work for you?"

"Have you eaten lunch already?"

"I never do. I live on coffee and candy until I get home."

"That's not good. Can you take a break and meet me for a late lunch around three o'clock?"

"That would actually work better for me. I can return to the office after we are done and finish what I need to do with no rush."

"If you don't mind, it will have to be somewhere close to where I am."

"No problem. Text me the address."

"I will. Until we meet again, my queen."

Long after ending the call, Cassandra was still grinning like a fool, but then she remembered that Onegus's mother would be at the wedding and her good humor evaporated.

Onegus might be every mother's dream guy for her daughter, but she wasn't every mother's dream for her son.

She would have to be on her best behavior, rein in her snarky comebacks, and definitely avoid making anything explode.

MARGARET

"We should go." Bowen put his beer down. "Margaret needs to rest."

"I'm fine." She waved a dismissive hand. "I can stay a little longer."

The truth was that Bowen was right, and she was tired, but Margaret wasn't ready to part with Wendy yet, or with Vlad, whom she was starting to adore, or even his quirky mother and her mate.

Vlad was a sweetheart, and his love for Wendy was evident in every glance, every touch, and every word, and the same was true for Wendy.

Stella was an interesting character. She was the typical creative type, a little flamboyant, a little dramatic, but she'd raised a really good man all on her own, and that spoke volumes about her character.

Richard, who was also a recently transitioned immortal like Wendy, was oddly protective of both Vlad and Wendy, and he acted fatherly toward them even though he was only thirty-four and hadn't known either of them long.

"We haven't talked about the wedding yet," Stella said. "Now that you are here, I'm sure you would like to take part in the planning."

Margaret shook her head. "I don't want to interfere. Whatever Wendy and Vlad decide is fine with me."

"You will need a nice dress," Wendy said.

"There is plenty of time for that. When is the wedding?"

"In about three months," Vlad said. "Annani is going to preside."

Wendy's eyes widened. "You are so lucky, Mom. Annani is presiding over Sari's wedding, and you'll get to see her even before your transition. That's such a rare treat."

Margaret still felt like she'd been cast into a fantasy novel. All that talk about the gods from mythology being real was difficult to believe, and the prospect of meeting one of the only two remaining goddesses made her nervous.

"Did you get to meet her?" she asked.

Wendy nodded. "Annani is indescribable. Prepare to be awed."

"Is she terrifying?"

"The opposite of that," Richard said. "Annani is powerful, but she uses her power for good, and you can actually feel it. Being in her presence is like being bathed in love." He chuckled. "But it takes a few minutes to get over the shock. She doesn't look human."

"Do you mean that she's inhumanly beautiful, or are you talking about the glow?" Wendy asked.

"Both. But it's more than that. She's like a force field. You can feel the energy emanating from her."

"True." Wendy nodded. "I thought that what I felt was awe, but you are right. When she enters a room, it feels like the air is sizzling with energy."

"That sounds scary," Margaret admitted. "I hope she'll be too busy to notice me."

"Don't worry about it," Stella said. "Annani will not seek you out. You will only see her from afar when she presides over the mating ceremony. When you transition, she might grant you an audience."

Margaret blew out a breath. "That's a relief. I'm barely ready to meet immortals. I'm not ready for a goddess."

"I want to meet Annani." Anastasia turned to Leon. "Can you introduce me?"

He shook his head. "The Clan Mother chooses who she wants to talk to. I can't initiate it."

"Since you've transitioned already, Annani will want to welcome you to the clan," Stella said. "Newly transitioned females are the key to our future."

Anastasia frowned. "In what way? I mean besides providing a child or two if we are lucky."

Stella turned to Leon. "Didn't you explain?"

"I thought that it was self-explanatory. All Annani's descendants are considered closely related. That's why we need the infusion of new genes, especially female because the heredity is determined by the mothers."

"We need genetic variety, period," Wendy said. "Both males and females can contribute."

Stella shook her head. "I see that my son didn't do any better job of explaining than Leon. Every new female immortal that is not Annani's descendant is a potential originator of a new maternal line. Her descendants can mate with Annani's, and the more lines we have, the better." She looked at Margaret. "You might be blessed with another child, and this time, you can actually enjoy raising it."

Margaret swallowed the lump that had formed in her throat. "I don't think I can have any more children. I've been taking contraceptive shots for years, and I can't even remember the last time I menstruated."

"The transition will fix whatever has gone wrong with your body." Stella chuckled. "You never know. I'm sure Wendy would love to have a little brother or sister."

Wendy wrapped her arm around Margaret's shoulders. "Babysitting will be good practice for Vlad and me."

Richard pushed to his feet. "With the way the Fates like to mess with us, you are both going to have babies at the same time." He offered Stella a hand up. "Let's go home and start working on a baby of our own."

Vlad groaned. "TMI, Richard."

Taking her boyfriend's hand, Stella cast her son a loving smile. "Wouldn't you like a little brother or sister to practice your parenting style on?"

"I would love it, and you know it. I just don't want to hear about you and Richard making it."

13

ELEANOR

"Good afternoon." Eleanor walked into Emmett's cell, holding a tray. "I have a treat for you. Alfie got fresh blood from the butcher."

The silent Guardian walked in behind her, looking appropriately threatening.

Emmett dipped his head. "Many thanks, my friend."

"Enjoy." Alfie turned to Eleanor. "If he gives you any trouble, I'll be here in a heartbeat."

"I know." She cast him a thankful smile.

The truth was that having the Guardians watching the feed from the other suite was far from ideal, and it limited what she could do with Emmett. For now, though, Arwel had agreed to mute the feed, so at least their conversations would be semi-private. But if things got heated between her and Emmett, they would have an audience.

As the door closed and they were left alone in the cell, she put the tray on the coffee table and sat on the small couch next to him. "Eat."

"Thank you for keeping me company." Emmett eyed the tall paper cup filled with blood but didn't reach for it.

"It's okay. Go for it. It's not going to gross me out."

He arched a brow. "Yesterday, you started gagging and had to leave. I don't want to lose your company."

"This time, I'm mentally prepared." She waved at the cup. "If we are to be friends, I need to get used to your culinary preferences."

Emmett's expression was the picture of surprise. "You want to be my friend?"

She shrugged. "It might come as a shock to you, but I don't have many friends, and most clan members still don't trust me. So I sympathize with you. You are all alone in here, and you don't have any friends either."

Lifting the cup, he held it between his palms. "It depends on who you consider a friend. I happen to like Arwel, and I enjoy his company. Does that make him my friend?"

She scoffed. "He's your jailer."

"So are you, my dear."

"True."

He shifted to face her. "Let me ask you a question if you don't mind."

"Ask away."

"If you haven't earned the clan's trust yet, how come Kian made you my Guardian?"

Damn. Way to go giving herself up.

"I'm not a Guardian yet. I'm a Guardian in training, and I'm supervised. But I was assigned to guard you because I'm immune to your compulsion."

"Arwel and the others wear those specialty earplugs that render my compulsion useless. Kian didn't need an immune to guard me. What's your agenda, Eleanor? Or should I ask, what's Kian's agenda?"

The guy was too smart to play games with. She had to give him something, or he would clam up and not tell her anything.

"I asked Kian for the position." She reached for the mixed nuts, which were supposed to be Emmett's dessert.

"Why?" He took a slow sip from the cup, careful not to let even a drop spill on his chin.

It was helpful, but it didn't solve the problem. She could still smell the blood, and her gag reflex kicked in.

Looking away, she popped another nut in her mouth in the hopes that it would drown the smell. When she was done chewing, she cast a quick sidelong glance at Emmett.

He was watching her like a hawk. "I'm still waiting for an answer."

Affecting the expression of a blasé attitude, Eleanor shrugged. "I felt something back in Safe Haven, and I need to figure out what it was."

Emmett's eyes shone with interest, the nearly black of his irises turning a lighter shade of a dark purple. "What did you feel?"

Fascinating.

Eleanor shrugged again. "You know what I felt. I bet your sense of smell is just as good as that of the other immortal males. What I want to know is whether you emitted some kind of potent pheromones that messed with my hormones, or whether I was genuinely attracted to you."

His smile could only be described as wolfish. "How about now? Are you still attracted to me?"

She'd been doing her best to suppress her reaction to him, mainly the horniness, but if his sense of smell was as acute as Greggory's, he'd probably sniffed it already anyway.

"You tell me," she challenged.

Putting the cup on the tray, he leaned toward her and smelled her neck. "Oh, yes. Definitely. The smell of blood masked your feminine scent, but I can smell it now." He shifted closer to her. "What are we going to do about this, my sweet Eleanor?"

Calling her sweet was like calling a badger cuddly.

She lifted a hand to stop his advance. "For now, nothing. I want to get to know you. And I want you to get to know me. I've traveled the road that started in a hookup and turned into a relationship. That hasn't worked well for me in the past, and you know what they say about repeating the same mistakes and hoping for different results."

Getting her meaning, he shifted a few inches away. "It's the definition of insanity."

She lifted her eyes to him. "Have you experienced the same?"

Emmett seemed conflicted. "All I ever wanted from women was sex and a little taste of their blood. Nothing else could have been possible because of the charade I had to maintain, and I definitely didn't want to father children that I would outlive. The friendship you propose is something I've never tried before." He pushed his fingers through his thick hair. "I've never had a real friend, either, let alone a partner, and I'm not sure I have what it takes to form a relationship." He eyed her from under lowered lashes. "That's what you're after, correct?"

14

EMMETT

*E*leanor looked unsure, but she nodded. "Yes. Well, I don't know. It depends on whether you are worthy. But since I have a terrible track record of determining who is and who isn't, I don't trust myself, and I don't know what I'm looking for."

Emmett might never have had a relationship, and given the way he'd been raised and the community he'd grown up in, he should know nothing about the special bond between loving partners, but he was an excellent observer, and he was well-read. He'd spent a long time pondering the philosophical topic of the human condition.

Eleanor yearned for love, that much was evident to him, and the question was how he could use that yearning to his advantage.

The clan's culture seemed to be more similar to the humans' rather than the Kra-ell's. They chose mates and formed lasting, exclusive bonds. Furthermore, Eleanor had been a human up until not too long ago, and she no doubt was still a human at heart, with all that implied.

He could use what he'd learned from fiction, psychology, and philosophy to manipulate her. A woman in love might go to extremes for her man, perhaps even betray her people to help free him.

Eleanor was a fighter. She was cunning and, to a degree, devoid of scruples. Also, she'd worked for the government, which meant that she had a lot of experience manipulating people to do her bidding.

Perhaps she'd even possessed some undercover spying skills.

She was a compeller, had been one even as a human, so it hadn't been difficult for her to manipulate her victims. But she couldn't compel immortals, and yet, only three months after getting captured by the clan while trying to entrap them, she'd managed to convince the suspicious Kian to let her go on a mission and then to give her a Guardian position.

Emmett couldn't have asked for a better ally.

The woman could be an incredible asset to him, provided that he could make her fall in love with him. The trick would be to make her believe that he loved her as well, and that wasn't going to be easy. She was jaded, had gotten jilted more than once, and was mistrustful by nature. If he was to convince her that he was worth saving, he would have to put up the best performance of his life.

Since she was wary, his best tactic would be reverse psychology. Instead of insisting that he was worthy, he would do the opposite, presenting himself as a lost cause and giving her a challenge.

Assuming a contemplative expression, he shook his head. "I'm probably an even worse bet than the others who've disappointed you. I come from a society that doesn't believe in love and scoffs at the concept of exclusivity. It's not that I'm enamored with the multi-partner lifestyle and can't see myself giving it up. I would do it in a heartbeat if I knew how to be different, but I don't."

She looked at him with sadness in her eyes. "Have you never been in love?"

The good news was that Eleanor hadn't gotten defensive, which meant that she'd bought his act, and that was the first step toward building trust. The bad news was that she seemed despondent.

He needed to give her hope.

"I've loved many, but I've never been in love with one particular woman."

She straightened her back and looked at him down her nose. "What do you mean by loving many?"

He spread his arms. "I was a shepherd, and I truly loved my flock, each and every one of them. Not equally, mind you, some I loved more than others, but they all had a place in my heart." He put his hand on his chest. "I can't say that they were like children to me because that would make me an incestuous pervert." He laughed. "I had sex with every woman who joined my community except for one, and it was only a matter of time before she too would have graced my bed."

"Are you referring to Anastasia?"

"The one you came to retrieve." Emmett chuckled. "Your mission was unnecessary. I don't know what stories her father told your friend, but Anastasia could have left whenever she wished. She was immune to my compulsion, so I can't be blamed for manipulating her to stay."

If looks could kill, he would be dead now.

Apparently, bringing up Anastasia had been a mistake.

Eleanor glared at him. "There are many forms of manipulation, and a young, vulnerable woman is putty in the hands of someone like you even without the help of compulsion. And once you had sex with her, how would you have made her forget about the biting? Drugs?"

He lifted his hands in surrender. "That's old news, Eleanor. Why are you getting upset over it?"

She blew out a breath. "I don't know. For a moment there, I forgot about the drugs, and your story about bedding every woman in your community reminded me of them."

He leaned closer to her. "I never used drugs or compulsion to manipulate a woman into my bed. I only used drugs to make them forget the details that would have incriminated me as a bloodsucker."

15

ELEANOR

"*Y*ou also used it to compel people to stay and worship you without question."

Emmett might have been able to pull the wool over the eyes of a more trusting soul, but Eleanor wasn't buying his act. He was well aware that his actions had been self-serving and manipulative.

Still, she wasn't looking for a saint.

Fates knew that she wasn't one.

Assuming an innocent expression, he puffed out his sensual lips. "Anastasia is a perfect example of someone I couldn't manipulate and who still decided to stay. Safe Haven was true to its name. For some, it was a lifeline, and leaving would have been detrimental to their well-being. I acted in their best interest."

"Are you referring to Margaret?"

"Among others." He narrowed his eyes. "What do you know about her?"

As far as Eleanor knew, no one had told Emmett about Anastasia's transition, and he definitely couldn't know about Margaret being a Dormant. The news was so fresh that only a few clan members were in the know.

Was Arwel one of them?

Probably not.

Should she tell Emmett?

Heck, why not. The news flash would wipe that smug expression off his handsome face.

Leaning back against the couch cushions, Eleanor crossed her arms over her chest. "Did you know that Anastasia and Margaret were good friends?"

"Of course. I knew everything that was going on in my community."

"Didn't it strike you as odd?"

"Why would it? Anastasia wanted to become a counselor, and Margaret was an experienced one. She took the younger woman under her wing, so to speak.

Also, Anastasia lost her mother at a young age, and Margaret yearned for a daughter. They adopted each other."

Eleanor shook her head. "Nevertheless, despite having very little in common, they were best friends rather than a mentor and an acolyte. There was a thirteen-year age difference between them. Anastasia was a rich heiress while Margaret had nothing, Anastasia attended a prestigious law school while Margaret has never attended college. What on earth did they have to talk about?"

"They both wanted to help people." Emmett drank the rest of the blood and wiped his lips. "Where are you going with this, Eleanor?"

Apparently, Emmett didn't know enough about Dormants and the affinity they had for each other to guess where she'd been leading him.

"Anastasia and Margaret were both Dormants. That's why they were drawn to each other."

His eyes widened. "How? I mean, how did the clan find out that they were Dormants? Peter said that they were extremely hard to find. He also said that Anastasia's father hired you to retrieve her. He didn't say anything about her being a Dormant, and he was under compulsion to answer my questions truthfully."

She'd definitely ruffled his feathers, and it was very satisfying. "Did you ask him whether she was a Dormant?"

He shook his head. "How was I supposed to know to ask that?"

"That's why he didn't tell you. You and I both know that compulsion needs to be phrased precisely to be effective, and thanks to me, Peter was aware of its limitations and how to work around it."

Emmett looked flabbergasted. "I should have suspected something. Margaret wasn't my type. She was a pretty girl when she came to me, but she was too timid, too weak. I prefer more assertive women. The taste of her blood, however, was delicious." He looked at her with hooded eyes. "Not nearly as exquisite as yours, of course, but better than that of other humans."

Eleanor felt stupid for taking his comment as a compliment, but she couldn't help it. Was her blood the most delicious he'd ever tasted?

"What about Anastasia?"

"I never got the chance to taste her blood, but her immunity should have raised my suspicion. In fact, if she weren't so wealthy, I wouldn't have invited her to join the community." He smiled sheepishly. "The taste of her father's money was almost as good as Margaret's blood."

Eleanor chuckled. "I bet you regret never tasting her. She might have been as delicious as I am."

He lifted his hand to her face, and she thought he was about to caress her cheek, but something passed over his eyes, and he dropped it. "I doubt that any woman would ever taste as good to me as you do." He sighed. "I wish you weren't repulsed by my bite."

"I'm not."

His eyes started to glow, and he lifted his hand again, this time making a feather-light contact with her cheek. "Are you sure? I saw you look away when I drank the blood."

When Emmett dropped his hand again, Eleanor fought the urge to lean into him. As annoying and as full of crap as he was, she still found him irresistible.

Maybe his potent Kra-ell pheromones were messing with her, but she was quite sure they weren't solely responsible for her reaction to him.

Emmett's masculine magnetism was about much more than a chemical reaction.

If Greggory was a Corolla—plain and reliable, Emmett was a Ferrari—sexy, sophisticated, powerful, and dangerous.

What was she, though?

Not a Corolla, because she was neither plain nor reliable, but not a Ferrari either, because she was neither sexy nor a great beauty. Perhaps she was a Harley-Davidson? Powerful, edgy, and opinionated?

Usually, she wouldn't have thought herself the type of woman a man like Emmett would go for, but he'd admitted to preferring assertive women.

She also had something even more desirable to him than beauty—delicious blood.

"I might have trouble watching you drink animal blood from a cup, but I'm not grossed out by your bite. Immortal males also bite during sex, and the sensation is so similar that, at first, I didn't even realize you were drinking my blood. It was pleasurable."

"And yet you tried to fight me off."

"I was taken by surprise and scared."

He lifted his eyes to the camera mounted near the ceiling. "What would happen if we tried that again?"

She followed his eyes. "It's probably not a good idea to try while we are being watched."

"Is there a way to solve this conundrum?"

As his fangs elongated, all the blood in Eleanor's body rushed to her core. She didn't feel fear. All she felt was an intense desire to once more experience his bite, but this time, along with everything else that came with it.

To hell with caution and waiting to get to know each other. Emmett was a captive audience. He couldn't leave even if he wanted to.

16

EMMETT

$\mathcal{E}$leanor was ripe for the taking, but if Emmett made a move, the males of her clan would come rushing in and beat the hell out of him.

Would he have enough time to get a taste before they stopped him?

He was sure that they wouldn't activate his cuffs when he was so close to Eleanor, but there would be retribution. Besides, the immediate gratification wasn't worth the sacrifice of his most valuable playing card.

His only card.

"I wish there was a way," Eleanor whispered. "I asked them to mute the volume so we could talk privately, but they'll never agree to turn the camera off. If only there was something that would convince them it was okay to give me privacy with you."

Eleanor was moving in the right direction, and with proper motivation, she might find a solution. Perhaps she would even think of a way to sabotage the recording. Emmett didn't know much about surveillance, but he'd watched enough movies to know that there were ways to circumvent it.

Pretending to be deflated, he sighed and shifted away from her. "This is a small room, and the only place where the camera can't see us is in the bathroom. I would never dare suggest intimacy there." He smiled sadly. "It's not very romantic, is it?"

Surprisingly, Eleanor didn't agree with him right away and seemed to contemplate the idea. But then she shook her head, dispersing the mist of hope her hesitation had offered. "Even if I was willing to do that, the Guardians will see us going in there. They won't let it happen."

"That's what I thought." He took her hand and lifted it to his lips for a kiss. "I'm afraid that our relationship will have to remain platonic until Kian allows me out of here."

It was a damn shame that he couldn't sample Eleanor's delicious blood again, but if he played his cards right, he could charm her into falling for him even without sex. Emmett didn't know enough about the clan customs, but there was a chance that mating Eleanor would be his ticket to at least partial freedom.

If Kian didn't find any clues as to the Kra-ell's whereabouts, the offer he'd made Emmett would be null and void, but mating Eleanor might grant him the same reward.

He needed to explore the possibility without showing his hand.

Eleanor leaned her chin on her fist. "Do you think he ever will?"

"Not really." Emmett brushed his thumb over her wrist, eliciting a shiver. "The information I gave him was correct, but knowing my people, they didn't leave any clues behind for anyone to track them. And unless Kian finds breadcrumbs to follow, he's not going to let me out of here."

She nodded. "Is there anything else you can think of that would help us find them?" She glanced at the empty cup of blood. "Maybe going from one butcher shop to another and asking who their most frequent customers are?"

"That's not going to help. Blood is used in many Chinese dishes, and it's not unusual for butchers' shops to sell it."

"The quantities would be larger, though."

"Restaurants buy large quantities. Besides, human minds are easily manipulated, and just like your people, mine ensure they are not remembered." He put his other hand on hers and caressed it. "Maybe Kian will learn to trust me like he did with you. How did you pull it off?"

"They needed me for the mission because of my compulsion ability, and Kri vouched for me. It helped a lot having a friend who's a Guardian."

"What about other newcomers to the clan? How do they earn their place in the clan's society?"

She chuckled. "They mate a clan member. The belief is that the bond between true-love mates is so strong that it takes priority over everything else. A mate will never betray her or his bonded partner."

That was both fascinating and useful. Mating Eleanor might indeed be his ticket out of prison. "Is it just a belief? Or is it real?"

"At first, I thought that it was all a load of crap, but I've witnessed enough to no longer shrug it off as a myth. Just think how improbable it was for us to find Anastasia and Margaret in Safe Haven. When Anastasia's father hired Turner, and we agreed to help retrieve her, no one suspected that she was a Dormant." Eleanor paused. "Well, that's not entirely true. Her father told Turner about the voices in her head, and a paranormal ability is one of the strongest indicators of dormancy. But Margaret wasn't on anyone's radar. The Fates, or some other higher power, had something to do with her being there in the first place, and subsequently us finding her."

Emmett wondered if the clan's Fates and the Kra-ell goddess were similar entities. The Mother of All Life was also believed to shape people's destinies. But that was a discussion for another time. Right now, he wanted to find out more about Anastasia and Margaret, how they were discovered, who they had bonded with, and whether the bonds were enough for them to get accepted into the clan.

"Have they both transitioned?"

Eleanor shook her head. "So far, only Anastasia has transitioned. Margaret broke her leg when we staged the fake fire at Safe Haven, so even though she and Bowen seem to be an item, they haven't consummated their connection yet."

"Does she have a paranormal talent?"

He knew the woman well, and she'd never exhibited anything unusual.

"I don't think so."

"So how do you know that she's a Dormant?"

Eleanor's smug smile promised an interesting revelation. "Since her daughter transitioned, there is no doubt that the mother is a Dormant."

Talk about a huge surprise. The daughter Margaret had left behind with her abusive husband somehow ended up an immortal.

"Wendy joined the clan?"

Eleanor nodded. "She's mated to a fine young immortal, and now she and Margaret are reunited."

"I'll be damned." He shook his head. "I'm starting to believe in those Fates as well. How did Wendy end up with the clan?"

"She was in the government program that I recruited paranormal talents for. The clan came to retrieve Jin, who as Mey's sister was a confirmed Dormant, and several of her friends jumped on the escape wagon and joined them. The team brought a compeller along, and he overrode the compulsion I had placed on them to stay loyal to the program. Otherwise, none of them would have been able to escape."

"Was it the same person who overrode mine?"

Eleanor shook her head. "His brother. Lokan is a weaker compeller than Kalugal, but he was good enough to override my compulsion. I doubt he could have done anything about yours. His younger brother is incredibly powerful, but their father is even more so."

The clan's Fates must be smiling upon him because Eleanor was giving him a lot of information that he might find useful in the future. And because she was romantically interested in him, the audio surveillance was turned off, so the Guardians had no idea that she was revealing more than she was supposed to.

"Jin is mated to Arwel, correct?"

With a nod, that knowing smile bloomed on her face again. "And she might be related to you. In fact, she almost certainly is."

17

ELEANOR

"*W*hat do you mean?" Emmett asked.

Given his shocked expression, Eleanor had a feeling that she'd said too much.

Why hadn't anyone told him about Jin and Mey? Wasn't Jin curious to meet Emmett?

"As I mentioned before, Mey and Jin were Dormants, and once they went through their transition, the sisters developed traits that were uncommon for immortal females. Also, their paranormal talents are unique and unheard of in the clan. It was suspected that they were descended from a different god or goddess, or that somewhere along the line the immortal genes have mutated. But now that we know about the Kra-ell, it's quite obvious that they were fathered by one of you."

Emmett's eyes blazed with excitement. "If that's the case, it means that our Dormants can be activated."

"I hate to disappoint you, but it's a no. First of all, the Kra-ell males probably can't transmit the immortal genes the same way our males can't. Mey and Jin wouldn't have them because you said only the Kra-ell males hooked up with humans, the females didn't. But even if the Kra-ell males could transmit the gene, they can't activate Dormants. If that was possible, Margaret would have transitioned a long time ago. The only way Mey and Jin could have been born Dormants and been able to transition was if their mother carried the immortal genes."

Leaning back, he smoothed his hand over his chin as if he still had a bushy beard. "What are the chances of one of our male hybrids encountering one of your female Dormants?"

"Probably none. It must have been fated."

He let out a breath. "Again with the Fates. Maybe it's the goddess."

"Annani?"

He waved a dismissive hand. "Annani might call herself that, and she might be very powerful, but she's not a real goddess. The Kra-ell believe in a female deity that is similar in power to the human God." He chuckled. "More similar to the biblical God of wrath the Hebrews believed in than the more modern interpretations of a benevolent deity that is full of love and compassion. Our Mother of All Life is vengeful and demanding like her Kra-ell female embodiments. She rewards fearless warriors who give their life in battle with heavenly mates who will cherish and adore them in a way their Kra-ell mistresses never did or would."

Eleanor tilted her head. "I thought that the Kra-ell didn't believe in love or even understand the concept."

He shrugged. "Believing in love is not practical for a society that has four males for every female, and since it's also very militant and aggressive, tender feelings are frowned upon. But I believe that the Kra-ell are similar enough to humans to have it in them to love. In order for us to be compatible and produce hybrid children, gods, immortals, humans and Kra-ell must have a common ancestry."

"Do you know that for sure? Or is it speculation?"

"It's an educated guess. Regrettably, the purebloods didn't share much with the hybrids, so I don't have the full story. They've never mentioned another species that was similar to them but even longer-lived. Still, I suspect that they knew about the people you call gods and were wary of them."

That was news to her, and probably also to everyone else who had interrogated Emmett. He hadn't said anything about his people suspecting that there were other immortals on earth, and neither had the guy who Stella had hooked up with twenty-something years ago in Singapore.

"What makes you think that?"

"I've often wondered about the need for extreme secrecy and the frequent moving from place to place. It seemed excessive if their only concern was discovery by humans. I thought it was because they knew of other Kra-ell groups and feared them, or just didn't want to be discovered by them. But after what I learned from Peter, I started thinking that maybe the purebloods knew about you."

If Emmett was right about the common ancestry, it was a logical assumption. If the gods and the Kra-ell came from the same planet or solar system, they probably had known about their neighbors' interstellar expeditions.

"It's a shame that your father didn't tell you anything about your origins." Eleanor pushed a strand of hair behind her ear. "I bet we could have learned a lot about ours from that."

A contemplative look passed across his eyes. "Just out of curiosity. What are Jin and Mey's special talents?"

She'd already told him a lot more than she should have, while he'd only disclosed a suspicion that he'd had about the Kra-ell being aware of the gods and their descendants.

"I'm not sure that I'm allowed to tell you that."

His thumb brushed over her wrist. "I'm only asking to see if their unique talents could be attributed to my people."

When she didn't offer him an answer, he continued brushing her pulse point with his thumb. "From what I could observe, the purebloods didn't have any special talents except for what you call thralling. So if Mey and Jin have uncommon talents, it could be that there is a third species of long-lived people on earth. Another explanation could be that those born to a Kra-ell male and a female descendant of gods are a superior breed."

18

ONEGUS

$\mathcal{T}$he café on Santa Fe Avenue was one of Kian's favorites, but it wouldn't have been Onegus's first or even fifth choice for meeting Cassandra, and the only reason he'd chosen it was its proximity to the keep and its outdoor patio.

Humans emitted too many smells, and whenever possible, Onegus preferred either outdoor dining or places that weren't overly crowded.

Hopefully, Cassandra wouldn't mind the vegan cuisine. It was actually pretty good, but not everyone appreciated the creative substitutes, like cashew macadamia cheddar cheese, or the espresso cashew flan with chocolate olive oil cake.

Onegus was still poring over the menu when he sensed Cassandra walking onto the patio. Something in the air sizzled, and he wasn't the only one who'd noticed. Every head lifted and turned to look at the stunning, statuesque beauty sauntering over to his table.

Dressed in a pair of palazzo white pants, a black blouse, black and white stilettos, and several gold necklaces of different lengths and widths, Cassandra looked classically elegant and every bit the cover model she used to be.

Rising to his feet, he greeted her with a smile and a chaste kiss on her cheek. "Every time I see you, I'm awed anew at your beauty and how well you accentuate it with what you wear." He pulled out a chair for her. "No wonder Kevin pays you so well."

She arched a brow. "Because of how I dress?"

"Because you have impeccable taste, and it translates into everything you create. There is a cohesiveness, a theme, and it's sophisticated and elegant." He waved a hand over her. "You are the most put-together woman I know, and that's saying a lot."

She rewarded him with a tentative smile. "Thank you. It's nice of you to notice."

"It's impossible not to." Onegus sat down and took her hand, just because he had to touch her, and that was the only way he could do so without causing a scene.

"Most guys just see the end result and have no clue what went into achieving it." She smiled. "And usually, I prefer that they don't."

"I'm not most guys." He winked. "And I have very discriminating taste as well." He leaned closer. "That's why I chose you. I love how creative you are, and that you apply it to everything you do."

"You are right about my personal style being an extension of my creativity and reflecting my eye for esthetics. It gives me pleasure to dress well. But some might say that I'm overdressed for today's casual work environment, or that a woman as tall as I am shouldn't wear high heels. Others might say that I'm vain for paying so much attention to my looks, and that I wear heels to intimidate people."

Lifting her hand to his lips, he kissed it. "It doesn't matter what anyone thinks. You should dress in a way that makes you feel good. I've seen you in shorts and sneakers, I've seen you in jeans and a T-shirt, and I've seen you in an evening gown and in a cocktail dress. You looked amazing in all of them. But, for some reason, this power look is my favorite so far." He leaned closer. "It's the sexiest."

That earned him a bright smile. "Sexier than nothing on at all?"

Tricky lady. "It's a hard choice." He leaned forward. "But it doesn't have to be. The sexiest thing would be for me to peel this beautiful outfit off you, one item at a time, until there is nothing left except for those gold necklaces."

As her fingers entwined in the delicate chains, her breathing became shallower, and her feminine scent flared. "They are not real gold." She shook her forearm, jingling the five bracelets on her left wrist. "And neither are these. I hardly ever buy real jewelry."

For some reason, Onegus didn't think it was because she was frugal. Gold jewelry wasn't that expensive, and Cassandra could definitely afford it. Maybe she had something against real gold?

"Why is that?"

She shrugged. "I like variety, and costume jewelry usually has more creative designs." She lifted her hand and wiggled her fingers. "Only the rings are real gold, but as you can see, they are devoid of precious stones. I chose them for the intricate designs."

"Beautiful." He didn't look at the rings. Instead, he gazed into her eyes.

She smiled. "Yes, you are."

The waitress stopping at their table disturbed the intimate moment. "What can I get you, folks?"

Tearing her eyes from his, Cassandra looked up at the girl. "I'm sorry, but I didn't have a chance to look at the menu yet. Could you give us a few more moments?"

"Certainly. In the meantime, can I get you something to drink?"

"I would like your chilled mint tea," Onegus said.

"I'll have the same." Cassandra lifted the menu, hiding her beautiful face from him. "On second thought, I'll have the cucumber juice."

19

CASSANDRA

*I*t was a cowardly move to hide behind the menu, but Cassandra wasn't ready to bare her soul to Onegus yet. Maybe she would one day tell him why she didn't buy precious jewelry for herself, but it wasn't going to be today or tomorrow or even a month from now.

Maybe not ever.

She thought of real jewelry as gifts of love, not something a woman bought for herself—an engagement ring, a diamond bracelet for an anniversary, a necklace for her birthday, and so on. If she told him, he might take it the wrong way.

So yeah, a successful, independent woman shouldn't wait for a man to buy those things for her, provided that she really wanted them, but Cassandra didn't crave possessions for their own sake. Unless they were gifts, an expression of love, gemstones were meaningless to her. She could enjoy cubic zirconia just as much as she would a diamond for a fraction of the cost.

Not that she was into that either. Pure metals, gold and silver, or imitations of them were her thing.

But that was beside the point. She couldn't tell Onegus any of it because it would sound as if she expected him to buy her expensive gifts, and she would never do that. If the time came and he proposed, she would love a beautiful engagement ring, but she wouldn't expect anything extravagant. She wasn't after his money. She was after everything else—his heart, his soul, and his body.

Those were much more precious than any gifts he could ever buy her.

"Have you decided what you want to have?" Onegus asked.

She hadn't even read through the selection. "It's difficult to decide." She moved the menu aside to peek at him. "What do you recommend?"

"Pretty much everything once you get over the weird substitutes. For starters, I recommend the warm rosemary butternut squash dip with radicchio, or the winter butter lettuce and endive salad. For an entree, I like the forbidden black rice bowl. The southwestern-style enchiladas are also good."

As she glanced at the menu again, it finally dawned on her that it was a vegan restaurant. "Interesting choices." She looked up at him. "Josie, my boss's wife, is vegetarian. I need to tell her about this place."

"Before you do that, you need to sample the offerings."

"Of course. I'll take the salad and the enchiladas. If I don't like them, you can eat them." She lifted her hand to summon the waitress.

When the waitress arrived, Onegus ordered for her and then added three more appetizers, two main courses, and two juices.

"Are you that hungry?" Cassandra asked when the woman left.

"Vegan food is not very filling."

"Then why did you choose this place? I've seen you demolish a filet mignon the size of a loaf of bread, so I know that you are not vegan."

"I'm not, but my boss is, and this is one of his favorite places. It's also close to the building I currently work in, and it has a nice outdoor patio."

"Who's your boss? An uncle? An older brother?"

"My cousin is the head of the family business in the US. I don't have siblings."

That reminded her of his mother, and that she was about to meet her at the wedding.

"Isn't it difficult for your mother to be so far away from her only child? She must be lonely."

"My mother is never lonely. She's surrounded by extended family, and we talk on the phone quite often." He winced. "She used to call me every day, but I've negotiated it down to no more than twice a week."

That was bad. Onegus's mother sounded like one of those tiger moms who were possessive of their sons. She wouldn't like sharing Onegus with another woman.

"Did she give you grief over it?"

"I'm a busy man, and I can't drop everything because my mother is bored and wants to chat. We had a long talk, and in the end, she understood that it wasn't because I didn't love her or didn't care about her, but because I held an important position, and I couldn't afford to spend hours on the phone." He folded his napkin and put it aside. "My mother is a strong-headed woman, and she can be unreasonably demanding at times, but she's smart and accomplished, and I have a lot of respect for her."

Fortunately, Onegus's mother lived in Scotland. Cassandra had a feeling that if the woman lived anywhere near her son, she would have been a major pain in her backside.

"Did you tell her about me?"

He shook his head. "I don't share my love life with my mother, and she doesn't share hers with me. Are you going to bite my head off for not telling her about you?"

"No, I get it. We've just started seeing each other. But she's going to see me at the wedding. How are you going to introduce me?"

He smiled, but the look in his eyes was indecipherable. "How would you like me to introduce you? My girlfriend? The lady I'm dating? My significant other?"

Perhaps there was tension between Onegus and his mother? His comment about not wanting to hear about her love life might have been a hint of that.

Not that it was a big surprise. It sounded like the woman wanted to domi-
nate her son's life, but Onegus wasn't the kind who would allow anyone to
control him, not even his mother.

Heck, maybe that was how he'd developed his resilience. It probably hadn't
been easy for him growing up.

"Any of those will do. You said that your father passed away a long time ago.
Has your mother remarried?"

It occurred to her that Onegus's mother might have eased up on the phone
calls because she'd found a new man.

He leaned toward her. "I'll let you in on a secret. She was never married, and
she doesn't even know who my father was."

That explained it.

"Oh, wow. We have that in common." Cassandra sighed. "I don't think my
mother knows who my father was either. That's why she keeps making up
stories about him. Or maybe she forgot who he was."

Except, her mother was a sweetheart, and it didn't sound like his mother
was. But then Cassandra had always taken care of her mother, while Onegus
had moved across the ocean from his. No wonder his mother felt neglected.

"Geraldine is a beautiful woman, and she looks incredibly young. How come
she never married?"

Cassandra grimaced. "I don't know. I could understand why she didn't date
when I was growing up, but I've been old enough to handle her having a
boyfriend for many years, and yet she hasn't brought anyone home even once."

He arched a brow. "Perhaps she's not into men?"

Cassandra laughed. "Oh, she's definitely into men. But unlike me, she's all
about casual hookups. She thinks I don't know that she's sexually active, and
that I believe her outings are all about book club meetings and hanging out with
her girlfriends. I'm just grateful that she's infertile and can't get pregnant again.
With her memory issues, she would have forgotten about birth control. I just
hope she remembers that pregnancy is not the only issue she needs to be
worried about."

Onegus's forehead furrowed. "How do you know that she's infertile? Did she
tell you?"

"She didn't have to. We used to live in a tiny apartment with only one bathroom, and until I got my first period, I never saw any of the feminine parapher-
nalia that's required to handle monthly cycles. My mother no longer gets
periods, and she can't get pregnant."

"Maybe she was very discreet about it and kept everything hidden?"

Cassandra shook her head. "I would have known."

20

ONEGUS

*G*oosebumps rose on Onegus's arms. Subconsciously, he'd known there was something odd about Geraldine, but with Cassandra's latest revelation about her mother, the pieces had finally snapped into place.

Geraldine was an immortal.

He felt it in his bones.

Her youthful looks, the story of her driver's license getting lost, and her never applying for a new one, the lack of menstruation, and the gentle currents sizzling underneath the surface, all pointed toward her being an immortal.

Then again, he might be jumping to conclusions because he wanted Cassandra to be a Dormant. Geraldine might have had her uterus or ovaries removed after a complicated birth or for any other number of reasons, her youthful looks might have been the result of good genetics, and her memory problems could explain the lost license and her inability to get a new one.

"What happened?" Cassandra asked. "You look even paler than usual." She chuckled. "I'm dating Casper the friendly ghost."

He was glad that the waitress arrived with their appetizers, and he didn't have to respond. What could he tell Cassandra that wasn't a lie?

"Is there anything else I can get you?" the woman asked.

"If you can bring out the main courses as soon as they are ready, I'd really appreciate it." Onegus cast her one of his charming smiles. "I'm a little pressed for time."

"I'll check with the kitchen."

"Thank you."

Cassandra lifted her fork. "Let's see if this tastes as good as it looks."

He waited for her to take the first bite before attacking one of his three appetizers.

"Not bad." Cassandra took a sip from her cucumber juice. "I might come back."

"I'm glad you like it."

For the next several minutes they ate in silence, but his reprieve didn't last long.

"You haven't answered my question yet." Cassandra pushed her plate away. "Why did hearing about my mother's infertility bother you so much?"

He affected an indifferent expression. "I was just reflecting on how similar our families are. You are an only child to an unwed mother, and so am I. Your mother looks incredibly young, and so does mine."

If he managed to get Cassandra drunk during the wedding, she might not notice the other oddities about his family, but no matter how inebriated she was, she would notice that his mother looked too young to have a son his age.

She nodded. "Were you wondering whether your mother became infertile after having you?"

It seemed that his remark about his mother looking young had gone unnoticed. Cassandra was more interested in the infertility part.

"It has never occurred to me."

"That's because you are a guy, and men don't think about stuff like that. But now that I've brought it up, do you think it's possible that she never married because she couldn't have any more children?"

He knew for a fact that wasn't so. "My mother has a full life. I don't think she's interested in sharing it with a man." That was true in regard to a human male, but he was sure she would be overjoyed to find a true-love immortal mate. In fact, if she found her one and only, she might even give him a little brother or sister.

"That's my mother's excuse too. But sometimes I think that her infertility is my fault, that it happened to her because of my birth. According to Geraldine, I was born a big baby, almost ten pounds. She's a small woman, delicate, fragile, and delivering a huge baby like me might have caused complications that resulted in the removal of her ovaries. Geraldine denies it, but what if she just can't remember it? Or worse, what if the memory problems are the result of the mental trauma of losing her ability to have more children rather than a head injury? I might have singlehandedly ruined her life."

Was that why Cassandra took such good care of her mother? Because she felt guilty?

"Oh, Cassy." He reached for her hand. "That's a lot of what-ifs, and I'm sure none of them are true. Your mother adores you, and she regards you as the best thing that ever happened to her."

She let out a breath. "I know. But it kills me that I don't know for sure. I'm always torn between wanting to find out the truth about her past and respecting her wishes. I bet a private detective could have found out everything in a few days, and it wouldn't even cost me an arm and a leg. But if I hired one, the guilt would be even worse."

"I might be able to help you with that."

She arched a brow. "How?"

Roni could find out everything about Geraldine Beaumont in less than an hour, but telling Cassandra about his in-house hacker was not advisable.

"One of my cousins is married to a guy who works for the government, and he has a pretty high security clearance. I could ask him to run your mother's name through the database and see what comes up."

Letting out a breath, Cassandra closed her eyes. "I don't know about that. It's still snooping into things that my mother prefers to remain private. And it doesn't matter that it is you doing the digging, if you are doing it for me."

2 1

MARGARET

"That's us." Leon stopped next to a house that was nearly identical to Wendy's.

"It's nice," Ana said without much conviction.

Margaret thought that it was beautiful. It looked brand new, and it had rosebushes in the front yard.

"Ready?" Bowen grabbed one side of her wheelchair, Leon the other, and together they lifted her over the stairs.

Once they set her down on the porch. Leon turned to Bowen. "Can you get the door?" He swung Ana into his arms.

Laughing, she wrapped her arms around his neck. "Carry me over the threshold, my love."

As he did, Bowen cast Margaret a tentative smile, and for a moment, she hoped that he would pick her up and carry her over the threshold as well. Instead, he put his hands on the wheelchair's handles and pushed her through.

Well, it was better than nothing.

Besides, they hadn't pledged their lives to each other like Leon and Ana had done. They weren't even officially a couple yet.

Or were they?

Despite voicing his intentions, most of the time Bowen was reserved with her. They'd gone out on a date and shared a few passionate kisses, but she didn't feel like his, and he didn't feel like hers.

Maybe she just didn't know what to expect. Her marriage had been a disaster, so that wasn't a good example. After that, she'd spent nearly two decades in a 'free love' community, where there had been no couples. Her only examples of what a loving couple was supposed to be like had been observing Leon and Ana, and now also Vlad and Wendy, Stella and Richard.

Her relationship with Bowen wasn't anywhere near that close, that loving, or that passionate.

Perhaps now that they had no more secrets between them, their relationship would flourish.

Emerging from the bedroom a little flushed, Ana waved a hand around the living room area. "This house is almost identical to Wendy and Vlad's. I like it, but it needs some redecorating."

Margaret had never lived in a house that nice. The one she'd shared with Roger had been okay, but she hadn't been allowed to make any decorating choices. Not that she'd been allowed to choose anything else. Roger had ruled over her with an iron fist. She couldn't do anything without getting his permission first, and if she'd dared to disobey, there had been consequences.

Shaking the bad memories away, Margaret shifted her focus to the furniture in the house. If it were up to her, she wouldn't change a thing.

Besides, she and Bowen would be staying with Ana and Leon only temporarily. Once the cast was off, they would move into a house of their own.

But what if things didn't work out between them?

What would become of her?

Perhaps she could get a job in the clan's sanctuary for rescued trafficking victims like they had discussed. If the position came with lodging, that would be a good plan B.

Ana paused her inspection of the living room to glance at her. "What do you think? Should we make it look a little more contemporary? I'm not a fan of all these boring earth tones. It's so nineties."

"I think it's gorgeous as it is. But if you want to decorate, go for it. It's your home."

Leon opened the fridge. "We need to get groceries." He looked at Bowen. "We can get some on our way back from the meeting."

"Right." Bowen cast a worried look at Margaret. "Are you going to be alright?"

She smiled. "Of course. While you are gone, Ana and I will unpack and put things away in the closets."

"I almost forgot." Anastasia slapped a hand over her forehead. "Wendy said that Syssi and Amanda are going to stop by tomorrow. Is there anything in the fridge that we can serve?"

Leon shook his head. "Make a list. Bowen and I will get everything you need on our way back from the meeting."

"It's going to be a long list."

Smiling, Leon pulled Ana into his arms. "It will be my pleasure to provide everything your heart desires."

As he followed with a passionate kiss, Bowen leaned down and pecked Margaret on the cheek. "You've had an exciting day. Try to get some rest."

Her gut squeezing, she nodded. "I need to unpack, but I don't plan on doing much else." They hadn't been apart since day one, and the thought of him leaving made her anxious. She cupped his cheek. "I'm going to miss you."

"Ditto." He smiled, but his facial muscles were tensed, making his jaw look even more prominent than usual.

"I'm going to wait up for you," she called after him.

"Don't. Onegus's meetings tend to be lengthy." He opened the door.

Tearing himself away from Ana, Leon followed his friend out the door.

Anastasia let out a breath. "It's difficult to be apart, but I will have to get used to that. We can't continue our honeymoon indefinitely." She cast Margaret a worried look. "Are you okay?"

"Yeah. I'm glad you convinced me to stay with you. It would have been scary for me to be left alone in a new place."

Wendy had to go back to the café, and Vlad had a school assignment he needed to work on. If she stayed at their place, she would have been all alone, counting the minutes until Bowen's return.

Ana smiled. "I'm glad that you are here as well. Let's check this place out. Do you want me to wheel you around, or do you want your crutches?"

"Definitely crutches. My bottom is feeling numb from sitting down for so long. I need to move."

Ana helped her up. "There are only two bedrooms in this house, but they each have their own bathroom and are about the same size. Leon says that the decor is slightly different, but I've only seen one so far, and we've rumpled the bed a little. I hope you don't mind."

Margaret was still stuck on the 'only two bedrooms' news flash.

She leaned on the crutches. "Am I supposed to share a bed with Bowen?"

Ana's forehead furrowed. "Is that a problem?"

"Of course, it is. We haven't had sex yet. It's going to be incredibly awkward. Perhaps I should stay with Wendy and Vlad after all. At least at night."

Ana shook her head. "What are you, seventeen? You are a grown woman, and Bowen is a grown man, and this is not the nineteenth century."

"I know. But we are not comfortable with each other yet. Bowen says that he wants more, but so far, we've only kissed. We need to date a little, get to know each other better."

"Nonsense." Ana waved a hand. "You've been together twenty-four-seven for almost two weeks. That's like dating three months. I say it's way past time for you to take it to the next level."

"It just doesn't feel right. Not for Bowen and not for me. Neither of us is ready."

Letting out an exasperated breath, Anastasia put her hands on her hips. "What are you going to do? Ask Bowen to sleep on the couch?"

"No. I can sleep at Wendy's place and come here in the morning. It's only a short walk away."

It was empty talk, and she knew that. Her defense mechanism was kicking in, trying to protect her from disappointment because she was afraid of rejection.

Grow a set, Margaret.

Was that what Ana would say?

"Suit yourself." Ana started toward the bedroom. "I'm going to unpack."

22

BOWEN

"I hope they are still awake." Leon hefted a bunch of grocery bags out of the trunk.

Bowen glanced at his watch. "It's past eleven. Anastasia is probably awake, but I doubt Margaret is." He pulled out the rest of the bags and closed the trunk.

It had been a long and exciting day for her, and she'd looked tired when he and Leon had left.

"It's a bummer that we need to return to work tomorrow." Leon broke into a fast walk, no doubt anxious to get back to Anastasia. "But at least we are stationed at the keep, so we can see our mothers when they arrive."

Bowen fell into step with him. "Did you tell Rowan about Anastasia?"

"I've sent her a long text from the cabin, telling her the entire story. She can't wait to meet her. What about you? Did you tell your mother?"

Bowen shook his head. "At first, there was nothing to tell because I didn't know whether Margaret was a Dormant. And then everything happened so fast that I didn't have time to even think about it."

"How about now?"

"I'll tell her tomorrow, but I wish I didn't have to."

"Why?"

Wasn't it obvious?

Everyone was so excited, taking Margaret's transition for granted, but at her age, it was dangerous. The clan hadn't lost a transitioning Dormant yet, but that didn't mean that their luck would hold up forever.

"Margaret is thirty-eight, Leon, not twenty-five, and besides, we are not at that stage yet. Because of her injury, things are moving super slow for us. I would have preferred to tell my mother about Margaret after her successful transition."

"Elise is a strong woman." Leon chuckled. "She had to be to raise a hellion like you. If things get rough, she won't fall apart. She will help you through it."

"I know. But I would rather spare her the anguish if I could." He cast Leon a smile. "After all I put her through growing up, my mother deserves only the best from me."

Leon laughed. "You were such a troublemaker. Who could have foreseen that you would grow up to be not only a Guardian, but the savior of damsels in distress and an all-around standup guy? When did that transformation happen?"

Bowen hadn't told anyone the story because it hadn't been one of his proudest moments. Most of the Guardians were much younger than him and therefore unaware of his past. He'd been an unruly teenager who had run wild, joining a gang of human boys and using his superior immortal strength to become their leader. He'd believed that the mischief they'd done had been mostly harmless, but it could have gotten them in a shitload of trouble. At the time, he'd thought that stealing sheep and chickens was hilarious, and that releasing horses out of the stables and having them run wild was fun. He hadn't considered the damage they had caused.

"My mother, Onegus, and Annani happened. Nowadays, it would have been called an intervention. I was given a choice between hard labor, working on the addition to the castle, or I could join the Guardian training program, which was even harder. The idea was to keep me busy from sunrise to sunset, so I would be too exhausted to even think about causing trouble. I chose the Guardian force because that suited my overinflated self-image better."

Leon nodded. "Now I get it. I couldn't understand why they let you join the force at such a young age. You said it was because they recognized your potential early on. But you lied. It was a punishment."

"I didn't lie. Onegus said that I was a born fighter and that the force was my destiny. I was strong for a fourteen-year-old, and I had great reflexes. He put the fear of the Fates in me, saying that squandering the gifts they had given me would anger them. He also told me that I needed to use these gifts to do good and not waste them on stupid behavior that causes much more harm than I'd realized. Then he listed all the potentially catastrophic consequences of my so-called pranks, shaming me and making me feel smaller than a flea. After the scolding was done, he clapped me on the back and promised to put me on the right path."

Onegus had done just as he'd promised, and Bowen had discovered that being a protector and a savior was much more satisfying than leading a bunch of delinquent hoodlums.

"Didn't you want to be a healer at some point?"

Bowen shrugged. "I like helping people. If I weren't built for fighting, I would have turned to medicine."

Leon snorted. "You're not studious or smart enough for that. Can you see yourself sitting on your ass for sixteen hours a day and poring over books?"

"You've got a point. Perhaps I could have been a paramedic. This reminds me that I need to talk to Onegus about putting all the Guardians through some basic medical training. Firefighters are trained paramedics, and if we ever need to pull a similar operation again, our lack of knowledge could give us away."

"We probably won't." Leon climbed the steps to the front porch and knocked on the door with his foot. "And if we do, we can take Julian with us. The training would take too long, and we have more important things to do.

But maybe it should become part of the curriculum for the Guardians in training."

"Good thinking. We don't need more than one person who knows what to do if a human gets injured. Margaret was lucky that Safe Haven had a nurse who helped her. If not for Shirley and the morphine shot she gave Margaret, she would have suffered needlessly. I don't think she would have made it to the hospital without passing out."

"You could have thralled her."

"True, but it would have been a damn intrusive thrall."

23

MARGARET

*B*owen was back.

Through the slightly opened bedroom door, Margaret heard him and Leon unloading groceries in the kitchen, and Ana commenting on what they'd bought.

She should have closed the door. The only reason she hadn't was the insane soundproofing of the house. When closed, no sounds penetrated the door or the walls, and the bedroom felt like a tomb.

She should have opened the window and closed the door, but it was too late to do it now.

If she got out of bed, Bowen would know that she was still awake, and she wanted to pretend to be asleep. That way, the decision to either join her in bed or sleep on the living room couch would be his, and she wouldn't have to invite him or comment on it or do anything at all. She could just pretend to sleep.

Damn, she was such a coward.

But it wasn't entirely her fault. Bowen was sending her mixed signals and confusing her. He claimed that he wanted her, but other than a few kisses, he hadn't initiated anything.

Maybe Ana was right, and they just needed to have sex and get it out of the way. They both wanted it, but they were both too reserved to go for it.

And then there was the cast.

Margaret had no clue how to maneuver around it, and even if they found a way, the sex would be awkward at best. That wasn't what she wanted, not for herself and not for Bowen.

She'd had enough awkward sex to last her a lifetime, even if it hadn't been more than a handful of times. Perhaps Emmett had done her a favor by spiking the wine he'd given her. It had taken care of the awkwardness, or maybe just her memory of it.

Roger, damn him all to hell, had been her first lover, and before he'd turned abusive, the sex had been quite good. After, she'd been too terrified to enjoy it even when he hadn't hurt her.

As the door opened a little wider, Margaret closed her eyes and forced her breathing to come out deep and even. She hadn't fooled Bowen, though.

"Would you like some tea?" he asked quietly.

Damn his immortal super senses.

"Sure." She opened her eyes and pushed up on the pillows. "How did the meeting go?"

Standing in the doorway and leaning against the doorjamb, the light from the living room framing him in a halo, Bowen looked like the warrior he was— big, strong, a rock she could lean on.

"As expected." He smiled. "Did you manage to rest?"

"A little. I can't fall asleep." She ran her hands over the mattress on both sides. "The bed is incredibly comfortable. I don't know what's keeping me from falling asleep."

Liar. She knew perfectly well what it was. She was too nervous about the sleeping arrangements.

"The tea will help." He pushed off the doorjamb. "I'll be right back."

Combing her hair with her fingers, Margaret arranged the blanket, so it covered her breasts. Her nightgown wasn't see-through, but without a bra, her breasts were a little saggy. They were still nice, nothing to be embarrassed about at her age, but Bowen had most likely seen nicer.

Also, it was cold in the room, and her nipples were standing at attention.

When he returned a few moments later with two teacups, she smoothed her hand over the blanket. "You can turn the light on if you want."

"I don't need it." He handed her the chamomile tea and sat on the bed next to her. "Do you?"

He'd left the door open, so the light from the living room was spilling in, and it was enough to see by. "No, I'm good." She took a sip from the tea. "It's just what the doctor ordered."

Had he left the door open on purpose?

"Anastasia told me that you were concerned about the sleeping arrangements."

She was never going to speak to Ana again. How could she?

"There are only two bedrooms." She looked down at the cup in her hands. "It's not that I don't want you sleeping in the same bed as me. It's just that we haven't been intimate yet, and it seems awkward."

24

BOWEN

"It doesn't have to be." Bowen reached for Margaret's hand. "Forget about what you think the rules are. You and I don't have to follow any of them. We can share a bed and just hold each other, or we can spoon, or we can lie on our backs and tell each other bedtime stories. And if we feel like kissing, we kiss. And if we feel like touching each other, we touch. I have absolutely no expectations. All I want is to be with you."

That got a smile out of her. "I want to be with you too. If not for the damn cast..." She lifted her eyes to him. "It's the cast, right? That's why you are holding off?"

He nodded. "I might be weird that way, and I know that most guys would have found a way to work around it, but I'm too afraid of hurting you." He lifted her hand to his lips and kissed it gently. "I want our first time together to be special, and I can wait patiently for the cast to come off." He smiled sheepishly. "Frankly, not so patiently, but I'd rather wait. There is only one first time, and I don't want to shortchange it for either of us. Are we on the same page?"

"I feel the same way. You know that I'm attracted to you, and if not for my injury..." Margaret lowered her eyes. "I'm not the type who is bold enough to initiate. I wish that I was assertive like Ana, but I'm not." She lifted her eyes to him. "I can't make the first move." She swallowed. "It will have to come from you."

It was her way of letting him know that he had her permission, but Bowen needed it verbalized better.

"That's perfectly fine with me." He kissed her hand again. "As soon as this cast comes off, the wait is over, and you are mine. Deal?"

She chuckled nervously. "Deal. I'm just...not sure that you really want me. I mean, most guys are not that patient."

Bowen arched a brow. "You think?" He took her hand and put it over his raging hard-on.

Her eyes widened. "Oh, my."

As Margaret's feminine scent intensified, his shaft responded by twitching against her hand.

She looked nervously at the opened door. "That's just...wow."

"Leon and Ana are in their room. They can't hear us." He removed her hand and gave it a little squeeze. "Do you still think that I'm not attracted to you?"

She licked her lips. "Now, I think that I want to do something about it." She sounded breathy. "May I?"

Her intention was clear, and as he imagined them pleasuring each other orally, his fangs started to elongate, and his venom glands swelled.

Margaret's breath hitched. "Your eyes are glowing."

He smiled, flashing her his partially elongated fangs. "Are you sure that you're ready for all that I am?"

She hesitated for a split second. "Yes."

Her yes hadn't sounded convincing, but as the smell of her fear mixed with that of her arousal reached his nostrils, the predator in him clawed to be let up to the surface.

That wasn't good.

If he didn't take the edge off before getting in that bed with her, he might do something he would regret, or worse, he might hurt her.

Leaning down, he kissed her forehead. "It was a long day, and I need a shower. You have until I come out of the bathroom to decide whether you are absolutely sure about being ready for me. If you are not, that's perfectly okay. We can do all those things that I've mentioned before. Spooning, or cuddling, or telling each other bedtime stories."

"Oh, Bowen." She lifted her hand and cupped his cheek. "How can you be so sweet?"

"Sweet?" He curled his lips back, letting her get a good look at his fangs. "I'm trying to do the right thing by you, but I'm still a predator. You should never forget that."

"I won't." She lifted on the pillows, letting the blanket slide down and expose the swell of her ample breasts. "I like that you are a fierce warrior. I feel safe with you because I know you will never use your strength against me, only for me. You can protect me until I transition and become strong enough to protect myself."

There would never be a situation in which Margaret would need to defend herself. That was his job.

"There is no safer place for you than this village, and as long as you are with me, which I hope is forever, I will protect you."

25

MARGARET

*L*ong moments after Bowen had gone into the bathroom, Margaret's heart was still pounding against her ribcage.

He hoped that she would be with him forever?

As what?

His life partner or just a fellow resident of the village?

She shook her head. That was stupid.

Back in the cabin, Bowen had said that they had found love there, and that he believed they were destined for each other. Perhaps it was time she stopped doubting his feelings for her and whether she was worthy of him.

She might be a broken doll who was held together by strings, but for some reason, the Fates deemed her worthy.

She knew next to nothing about statistics, but there was no way that their meeting hadn't been guided by a higher power.

The Fates had arranged for her to meet Bowen.

Thinking back to the woman who'd told her about Safe Haven, Margaret had a feeling that she hadn't been who she'd claimed to be. Perhaps the Fates that the clan believed in took over mortal bodies on occasion or compelled them to be their mouthpieces.

She wondered how Ana had first learned about Safe Haven, and if she'd also encountered someone who'd told her about it. Except, these days the Fates didn't need to use people to deliver their messages. They had the internet at their disposal, and instead of sending a human, or speaking through one, they could manipulate technology, sending the right Facebook ads or YouTube videos to those they wished to influence.

Wow, that was a profound realization.

What if those meddling Fates had helped create those channels of communication precisely for that purpose?

And that led her to another more disturbing thought.

Anyone with the right resources could do that through social media. As a novice, she might have paid more attention to the way it worked than those who had been using it since its inception, noticing that the ads she saw were definitely custom-tailored to her interests, and so were the videos YouTube suggested for her. She could see how easy it could be to take it a step further and use it to promote agendas that had nothing to do with commerce.

Margaret shook her head. That wasn't what she should be thinking about right now. What she needed to decide was whether she wanted to get intimate with Bowen tonight, or wait until the cast came off so they could make love no holds barred.

On the one hand, he excited her like no man ever had, and she wanted him. But on the other hand, she wanted to enter their relationship whole, and give it all she had. If she transitioned successfully, they would have eternity ahead of them and there was no need to rush things. They'd known each other less than two weeks, and although for some it might have been considered long enough, for her, it really wasn't even if she wasn't injured.

She'd let Roger take her virginity two weeks after meeting him, and that hadn't ended well for her. Bowen wasn't Roger, but it wasn't about him.

It was about her.

Margaret was no longer that naive eighteen-year-old girl who'd thought that her body was the only thing she had to offer. She might not be much of a catch, but she was wise and experienced enough to know that the love and companionship she brought to the table were no less valuable than sex, probably more.

Hey, how was that for a new-found self confidence?

She was making progress.

Perhaps she should write it down and later design a workshop around it.

Theoretically, that all made sense, but as the bathroom door opened, and Bowen stepped out with only a towel wrapped around his hips, logic flew out the window, and desire took over.

He was such a magnificent male.

She wanted to run her hands all over those defined muscles, feel that warm, smooth skin under her fingers, and kiss every inch of him.

He smirked. "Like what you see?"

"Like is too mild of a word," she breathed. "You are a god."

"Just an immortal." He sauntered over to the dresser and started opening drawers. "Where did you put my briefs?"

For a moment, she contemplated not telling him. If he couldn't find them, he would have to come to bed naked.

He looked at her over his shoulder. "Did you hide them on purpose?"

She shook her head. "I didn't. But maybe I should have."

Turning around, he dropped the towel. "Should I keep looking? Or should I get in bed?"

"Bed." She licked her lips. "Definitely get in bed."

26

CASSANDRA

$\mathcal{I}$t was after midnight, but Cassandra couldn't fall asleep. Her late lunch with Onegus had left her unnerved for several reasons. First, it had been the talk about her mother's murky past and Onegus's offer to investigate it, and then it had been the kiss goodbye that had left her hot and bothered.

Perhaps she should take the edge off with her neglected battery-operated boyfriend. Would it count as being disloyal to Onegus?

She snorted. Bob didn't count, and neither did her fingers, especially since she would be fantasizing about Onegus while pleasuring herself.

When her phone buzzed on the nightstand, a smile spread over her face. No one other than Onegus would be texting her in the middle of the night.

Lifting the device, she read the message. *Are you awake?*

She answered. *Yes.*

Her phone rang a moment later. "What are you doing awake after midnight?"

"Waiting for you to call." She pushed up on the pillows, dragging the blanket up to cover her bare shoulders. "How did it go with your mother?"

"We had a cup of coffee together, chatted for a little bit, and said good night. She was tired."

"Did you tell her about me?"

"Yes."

"What did you tell her?"

"That I met a sexy lady who is gorgeous, talented, smart, and has impeccable taste."

"What did your mother say to that?"

"That you must have great taste because you chose me."

Cassandra rolled her eyes. "Now I know why you are so full of yourself. It's your mother's fault."

"Isn't it every mother's job to think her child is the best there is?"

"I guess. Where are you now? Are you still at work?"

"I'm in bed, but I can't fall asleep."

"Why?"

"I can't stop thinking about you and how your lips tasted when I kissed you goodbye earlier today."

"How did they taste?"

"Like more. Are you naked?"

Cassandra laughed. "You sound like a pervert."

"Are you?"

"No."

"Can you get naked?"

"Quite easily. All I have on is an old T-shirt."

"No panties?"

"Nope."

He hissed. "Take it off."

"I'm not activating the camera."

"I'm not asking you to. My imagination can fill in the details."

"Oh, yeah?" She tugged the T-shirt up over her breasts, exposing them. "What did I just do?"

"Did you bare your beautiful breasts?"

"Good guess."

"Play with them."

She rimmed her left nipple with her finger. "I can only do one at a time because I'm holding the phone."

"Activate the speaker."

"Nah-ah. My mother might hear you."

"Right." He sounded disappointed.

"Are you naked?" She flipped the tables on him.

"I always sleep in the nude."

Imagining all those rippling muscles, she licked her lips. "Are you playing with yourself?"

"I wouldn't call it playing."

"What would you call it, then?"

"Strangling the snake, slapping the salami, waxing the eel, having a tug of war with a Cyclops."

She laughed. "I haven't heard any of those except for the salami one."

"I have plenty more. Choke the chicken, polish the knob, the five-knuckle shuffle."

"That's funny, but not very sexy."

"I agree. I'd much rather hear about what your fingers are doing."

"Nothing yet." She trailed her hand down her belly. "I'm inching my way down south."

He groaned. "Are you wet?"

"I don't know. I need to check."

She'd been aching since that kiss, so yeah, she was wet. Slipping a finger down her moist folds, she bit on her lower lip as she circled her throbbing clit.

Her hips arched of their own accord.

"Well, are you?"

"Very," she said on a hiss.

"Are you fingering yourself, Cassy?"

"Ah-hum." Sliding her fingers deep, she stifled a moan.

Imagining that it was Onegus's hand and his fingers that were plunging inside her, she repeated the move, but her own slender fingers couldn't compare to his, couldn't deliver the same kind of pleasure.

Trailing her hand back up, she cupped her breast and squeezed, then lightly pinched her nipple.

"Talk to me, Onegus. Tell me all the naughty things that you want to do to me."

"It will be my pleasure."

As his masculine voice whispered in her ear, Cassandra smoothed her hand down her belly until the tips of her fingers reached her moist center.

Spreading her legs wide, she closed her eyes and listened to his voice, imagining that he was there, doing all those naughty things he was describing in detail, and when she careened over the edge, it had been Onegus's hand that had brought the release.

On the other side of the line, she heard him groan, and as she imagined his strong hand pumping his manhood, his essence erupting and landing on his taut stomach, another release tore through her.

27

KIAN

"It's too early in the morning for a meeting." William walked into Kian's office with two tall cups of coffee in his hands.

"The Sanctuary people are arriving today, and some of the Scots arrive later tonight. I need to get everything out of the way as early as I can."

"My brain isn't fully awake before ten." He handed Kian one of the cups.

"That's because you work until two o'clock at night." Kian took a sip before putting the cup down. "How is the Kra-ell language coming along?"

"Slowly but surely." William sat down and put his briefcase on the conference table. "I put two of my assistants on it, but we are dependent on Emmett providing us with word lists, and he's taking his sweet time."

"Obviously." Kian sat at the head of the table. "He doesn't want us to decipher it too quickly. Maybe I need to pay him another visit and issue some threats."

"What's the rush? I've already deciphered the email he sent to his former mistress."

"Amanda came up with an interesting idea. We could send Mey with Arwel and Jin to China, so she can listen to the walls of the Kra-ell's old compound. The problem is that she needs to understand what she hears, and for that, she needs to learn the Kra-ell language."

William arched a brow. "Did she agree to go on the mission?"

"I haven't asked her yet. She and Yamanu are joining us for the meeting today, together with Jin and Arwel. Given that Jin has already agreed to go and lend her particular talent to the mission if needed, I assume that Mey won't say no. It would be like going on a family vacation."

"Can I go?" William lifted the cup to his lips.

"Why would you want to?"

"I've never been to China. I'm curious."

Kian shook his head. "I can't risk you. You are irreplaceable."

"So are Yamanu and Arwel and Jin and Mey."

"Of course. Each individual is precious. But I meant strategically. You are the only one capable of deciphering the gods' tablet and understanding the technical instructions, and you are far from done with that. Without you, all that knowledge will become useless to us."

"Speaking of the gods' tablet." William pushed his glasses up his nose. "I discovered a few common words between their language and the Kra-ell's."

"I'm not surprised," Kian said. "They either come from the same place or have a common ancestor. Otherwise, they wouldn't be similar enough to humans and to us to be sexually compatible and produce hybrid children."

William nodded. "I have a feeling that the Kra-ell language is much older than the gods'."

As a knock sounded on the door, Kian rose to his feet and opened the way. "Good morning."

"Yeah, about that," Jin grumbled. "Any reason you summoned us at the ungodly hour of six-thirty in the morning?"

Arwel cast her a warning glance, but she waved him off.

Kian chuckled. "You have to forgive me. My schedule is a bit crazy during the celebrations."

Mey, always the polite lady, smiled apologetically for her sister and dipped her head in greeting. Next to her, Yamanu grinned happily as if an early morning Friday meeting was his favorite thing to do.

"Please, sit down." Kian motioned to the conference table.

"You are probably wondering why I called you here today." Kian returned to his seat.

"I can guess," Mey said. "You want me to listen to the echoes of conversations left by the Kra-ell in their old compound."

"Correct." Kian clicked on the remote, activating the large screen hanging on the east wall of his office. "This video was shot with a drone by one of Turner's contacts in China. As you can see, the compound is no longer occupied by the Kra-ell and is used as a boarding school for international youth. It's bilingual, classes are taught in English and Chinese, and its goal is to foster integration between Chinese and Western cultures."

"When was the school established?" Arwel asked.

"1991." Kian clicked the video off. "Unfortunately, digging out information about who occupied it before and what happened to them is impossible. Roni can't hack into the Chinese government records because he's unfamiliar with the encryption protocol they are using. I believe that in time he will crack it, but for now, boots on the ground is our best bet for finding out more information."

Mey pushed a strand of hair behind her ear. "Yamanu and I can pretend to be prospective American parents who want their children to learn about their Chinese heritage. The problem is that I can't listen to the walls when there are other people in the room. We'll have to infiltrate the place at night."

"That's not the only problem." Kian drummed his fingers on the table. "Even if you hear echoes of Kra-ell conversations, you won't understand what's being said. You don't speak their language or even Chinese."

Mey's face fell. "Then there is no point in me going." She glanced at Jin. "I was actually looking forward to sharing an adventure with you and Arwel."

"How good are you at learning new languages?" Kian asked.

Mey winced. "Good, but not good enough to learn two extremely difficult ones in a few weeks."

"You don't have to get fluent. All we need to find out is where the Kra-ell moved to. If you spend a couple of hours with Emmett every day until it's time to go, you can learn most of the words associated with moving, trips, addresses, etc. And the same is true for Chinese. Actually, he can teach you both."

"You mean Jin and me?"

"I meant Kra-ell and Chinese, but having Jin with you is a good idea. She needs the lessons just as much as you do."

Jin groaned. "I wish there was a chip William could implant in my head that would translate what I hear. I've spent months studying Mandarin, and all I have to show for it are a few badly pronounced sentences."

Rubbing a hand over his jaw, Yamanu smiled. "What if we get Kalugal to compel you to learn faster? Do you think it might work?"

Jin shook her head. "Forget about it. I'm not letting him do that to me. It's enough that I have to suffer through learning this accursed language voluntarily. I can't even think about being forced to do it."

"And I'm not looking forward to spending time with Emmett," Mey said. "Those people got rid of Jin and me as if we were garbage."

"It wasn't Emmett's doing." Kian leaned his elbows on the table. "He was treated as a lesser being by his own father. Besides, he's an interesting fellow, and you might enjoy his company. Aren't you curious to find out more about your parents? He might know who they were."

"I don't give a shit about our father or fathers, but our mother is a Dormant." Jin looked at her sister. "If we find out where they moved to, we might be able to rescue her."

Mey nodded. "Not only her, but also the other humans they keep enslaved." She let out a sigh. "I'm in. I'll do what I can to help."

"You will both have to wear earpieces," Arwel said. "And I will be there to keep an eye on Emmett and make sure that he behaves."

"What about Stella?" Jin asked. "She's traveled extensively in that area. She must know Chinese."

"She probably does, but she could only function as a translator. I don't know how helpful that would be. I need to think it through."

28

MARGARET

*A*fter Bowen and Leon left for work, Anastasia stood with her back to the front door, her hands on her hips, and scanned the living room.

"Can you move and sit at the counter?" she asked Margaret.

"Why?"

"I want to push the couch closer to the wall." She looked at the fireplace. "Or maybe to the side. I don't like where it is."

"It's centered on the fireplace." Margaret used the crutches to push to her good foot. "Isn't that where it's supposed to be?" She collected her phone and her notes and hobbled to the kitchen counter.

"It's boring. This place looks like a hotel room. I want to make it feel homier."

"Perhaps you should wait for the men to get back and do the furniture moving for you."

"Nah." Ana waved a dismissive hand. "I'm strong now, and I'm getting stronger every day. I don't need help."

"Knock yourself out." Margaret touched the phone screen to wake it up.

Perhaps it was pointless to keep preparing the workshop she'd started working on in the cabin, but she had nothing better to do. Besides, if she were to get a job at the rescue center, or sanctuary, as they called it, she could modify the workshop to fit a mostly young female audience. Chocolate-making was sure to be a hit with the girls, but it would have to get approved by the therapist who was running the show.

Hopefully, she would like the idea.

The sound of Ana's phone pinging with an incoming message stopped her mid-shove. She left the couch in the middle of the living room to get it.

"We have visitors in fifty-five minutes," she said after reading the text. "Syssi and Amanda are coming over."

Margaret swiveled the barstool around. "Remind me who they are?"

"Syssi is the boss's wife, and Amanda is his sister. They both work in paranormal research, hoping to discover more Dormants."

"Are they scientists?"

"Leon told me that Amanda is a neuroscientist, but Syssi is an architect by profession. She started working for Amanda to learn more about her own paranormal talent, but after meeting Kian and transitioning, she decided to stay in the lab and help Amanda with the research instead of pursuing a career in architecture."

"Did they find many Dormants that way?"

"I don't know. We can ask them when they come over."

Margaret rearranged her skirt around her legs. "I wish I had something nicer to change into. I'm tired of wearing the same two dresses all the time." She chuckled. "I shouldn't complain. I've been wearing the equivalent of a uniform for nearly two decades. Those dresses are a vast improvement over that."

"You're waking up, discovering who you really are. Clothing is a form of self-expression." One corner of Ana's lips lifted in a smile. "Speaking of waking up. How did sharing a bed with Bowen go?"

Margaret felt heat rise up her cheeks. "It was nice."

"Just nice?"

It was the best night of her life, and given that what they could share had been limited by the cast, it was only a taste of what was still to come.

"That's all you are going to hear from me."

"Meanie." Ana shoved the couch back into place as effortlessly as if it was a chair. "The rearranging of furniture will have to wait for after the visit."

She'd become really strong. If Margaret had been that strong when Roger knocked her around, she could have beaten the crap out of him.

The thought made her smile.

Maybe after she transitioned and became as strong as Anastasia, she could go back and confront him.

Nah, he wasn't worth the aggravation. She was starting a new life with Bowen, she had her daughter back, and Roger was a pathetic loser she shouldn't waste even a single thought on.

As far as she was concerned, he was dead.

The lightness that filled her following that simple decision was like a breath of fresh air. She should forget that he'd ever existed, but that was impossible to do. They'd created Wendy together, and her daughter would always be a reminder of him. Thankfully, the resemblance didn't evoke any negative feelings. Wendy was beautiful, and some of it had come from Roger, but her character didn't resemble his in the slightest. She was pure sunshine and positivity.

Ana fluffed the pillows, unfolded and refolded the throw blanket, and took a step back to examine her work. "Maybe I'll just leave it like that."

Margaret rolled her eyes. "That's what I suggested."

"I should prepare some snacks." Anastasia walked into the kitchen. "I thought that they would come around noon, and I'd serve them lunch, but it's too early for that. Any suggestions?"

"Maybe some cut-up fruit and nuts would do as a mid-morning snack? Or you can just serve the chocolates Bowen got me along with tea or coffee. Everyone likes chocolate."

"I'll prepare a fruit and cheese platter and serve it with crackers."

"Even better."

29

ONEGUS

*O*negus glanced at his watch. It was nearly noon, and he hadn't planned on calling Cassandra, but he had to at least hear her voice to ease the irritation crawling over his skin.

Only she could calm that incessant itch.

Last night, he'd kept her awake past one o'clock in the morning, and the memory of her stifled moans had kept him up much longer than that. His hand had been busy, bringing him one release after another, but nothing save for Cassandra's slender neck could ease the pressure in his venom glands.

Perhaps he could meet her for lunch somewhere?

He fired her a quick message. *Are you free for lunch?*

Her return text came several minutes later. *Sorry for the delay. I couldn't hear the incoming message over the din in this store. What do you have in mind?*

She was shopping?

Wasn't she supposed to be at work?

Instead of texting, Onegus rose to his feet, closed the door to his office, and called her. "Where are you?"

"In Glendale. I took the day off to get a new dress."

"Why Glendale?"

"That's where my favorite store is."

Glendale was about half an hour away, provided that there was no traffic, but it was Friday, which meant the worst traffic of the week.

With a sigh, he leaned back in his swivel chair. "What about shoes? Are you going to wear the same ones you wore to the gala?"

She laughed. "I'm starting to think that you are even more into shoes than I am. Do you have a shoe fetish?"

"Not really. I just have a thing for those particular shoes on those particular feet. Are you about done with shopping?"

"I'm an efficient shopper, and I only needed a dress. I already have the shoes and the jewelry."

"You could've worn the same dress too. I don't know why you bothered. I'm wearing the same tuxedo to the wedding that I wore to the gala."

"No one remembers your tuxedo, and no one cares if you wear it to every function until it falls out of fashion. But whoever saw my pictures from the gala in the gossip magazines would recognize the dress. I needed a new one."

"Is it sexy?"

"Obviously, but it's also classy and elegant. Don't worry, I'm not going to embarrass you."

"The thought never crossed my mind. Can you meet me for lunch in the same place we met yesterday?"

She didn't answer right away. "Is your place still full of people?"

"Worse. I had to give it up for an unexpected guest, and now I'm sleeping on a cot in my underground office."

That was a lie. He'd spent last night in the Guardians' apartment in the keep. The place was like a frat house, so he might spend tonight in one of the renovated cells in the dungeon, but he couldn't tell Cassandra about either.

"Why are you the one in charge of taking care of the guests? It would seem to me that it's beneath your station."

Ouch.

"I'm part of a team of people who are in charge of coordinating everything, but I'm not in charge of the hospitality part. I coordinate the security, which is a huge headache with so many civilians coming in."

"Now I get it." She chuckled. "You are in charge of security and only moonlight as the face of your family business."

"You've got it. My cousin, who is the real head of the business, doesn't do well in social settings. I'm considered the charming one."

"Oh, you are charming, which is great for attending the annual gala, but your day job explains your bossy attitude."

"You like my bossiness, which reminds me that I still owe you a spanking."

"Well, you can't do that over lunch in a public place, so it's not happening."

Had he imagined it, or had she sounded a little breathy?

The hellcat was intrigued, and he was hard as a hammer. "How can we make it happen?"

"Instead of going out for lunch, you can come to my house. I'm walking toward my car as we speak."

"What about your mother?"

"She has a nail and hair appointment at one o'clock, and she won't be done until at least three."

That was plenty of time, but he didn't want her to miss out on time spent with her mother if that was the plan. "What about you? Aren't you joining her for the nail and hair thing?"

"Mine is tomorrow." She chuckled. "I feel like I'm on vacation. I took the day off to go shopping, and tomorrow I'm getting pampered in a salon."

"Speaking of vacations. You still didn't give me an answer about going away with me."

"To that secluded cabin? That's not my idea of a romantic vacation."

"What about a trip to Paris on a private jet?"

"Now you're talking."

She thought he was joking.

Paris wasn't a good destination as far as inducing Cassandra somewhere secluded, but she was going to love it, and that made the trip worthwhile.

"I'm serious. After the family festivities are over, I can take you for a weekend in Paris. I'm sure you can swing that."

"You said festivities? Is there something other than the wedding going on?"

It was so like Cassandra to latch on to the irrelevant part of what he'd told her. "My cousin's birthday is the following Wednesday. But forget about that. What about Paris?"

"How soon do you need an answer?"

Onegus shook his head. With any other woman, it would have been an automatic and enthusiastic yes.

"We can talk about it when I come over to your place."

She laughed. "I don't think we will be doing much talking."

30

MARGARET

"*Margaret.*" The tall brunette looked as if she wanted to pull her into her arms like she had done with Ana, but the crutches gave her pause. "It's a pleasure to finally meet you." She offered her hand instead. "I'm Amanda."

The boss's sister, who was way too gorgeous to be a neuroscientist, and who was very obviously pregnant.

"The pleasure is all mine." Margaret smiled as she took the woman's hand.

"And I'm Syssi." The other pregnant lady offered her hand. "Welcome to the village." She shook Margaret's hand and then Ana's. "I apologize for not welcoming you yesterday. With the entire family gathering for the wedding, Amanda and I had prior obligations we needed to attend to."

"Perfectly understandable." Ana motioned to the couch. "Please, make yourselves comfortable."

Margaret made her way to the armchair and lowered herself into it gingerly.

As Amanda and Syssi sat on the couch, Amanda turned to Ana. "I didn't have a chance to congratulate you yet. How does it feel to be an immortal?"

"Awesome." Ana grinned. "I'm so strong now, and it's not just physical. I feel like I can conquer the world."

"Good for you," Syssi said. "Do you plan on finishing your law degree?"

Ana nodded. "Eventually. For now, I want to play house with Leon for a little bit."

"What about the voices?" Amanda asked. "Are they still bothering you?"

Ana hadn't mentioned them, and Margaret felt bad for not asking. The voices had been the main reason Anastasia had joined Safe Haven. They had been a major disturbance in her life.

"I think Leon banished them." Lifting both hands, Ana crossed her fingers. "May they never return. I certainly don't miss them."

"Interesting." Syssi tried to reach for a piece of fruit, but her huge pregnant belly was in the way. "Maybe the sole purpose of the voices was to get you to Safe Haven so you could meet Leon. The Fates play a very long game."

Ana rose to her feet and lifted the tray for Syssi. "Then it was worth the suffering, and not just because I met the love of my life thanks to the voices. If I hadn't met Leon, I would have never found out about my dormant genes and wouldn't have turned immortal."

"About that." Margaret motioned for Ana to bring the tray to her. "How does it work?" She took a strawberry.

"The transition?" Anastasia asked.

"Yeah. I know that you received a transfusion. But what was in it?"

Syssi and Amanda exchanged glances, and then Amanda cast her a pitying look. "Bowen hasn't told you how a female Dormant transitions?"

She shook her head. "Is it different for males?"

"Oh, boy." Syssi groaned. "Should we tell her?"

That sounded ominous. "Please do. You are scaring me."

Amanda hesitated for about two seconds and then nodded. "Bowen should have told you, but with everything that was going on, he probably couldn't find the right time. Usually, it's the mate's job to do the explaining, but since you are a confirmed Dormant, I guess it's okay for me to tell you. You know about the fangs, right?"

"Of course." Margaret felt her cheeks heating up. Thankfully, her skin rarely reddened, and she was able to hide her embarrassment.

Last night she'd experienced her first bite, and it had been better than any drug she'd ever messed with. Bowen had pleasured her orally and then bitten her inner thigh, sending her on a trip no psychedelic could ever deliver, but it wasn't only about the intense pleasure and the chain of orgasms she'd experienced. The venom's lingering effects were therapeutic and invigorating.

Margaret felt better today than she'd felt in years.

"In addition to the venom's aphrodisiac and euphoric properties, it also acts as a catalyst, activating the dormant immortal genes." Amanda leaned forward. "Have you experienced it already?"

With all eyes on her, Margaret was sure that the rising heat was visible on her cheeks. "Yes."

"Did Bowen use protection?"

That was an intrusive question, but given Amanda's serious expression, Margaret figured that it was somehow relevant.

"We didn't get there yet." She pointed at her cast. "Bowen is afraid of hindering my recovery. Besides, condoms are not needed. Everyone in Safe Haven was checked for STDs, and I got regular contraceptive shots."

"I see." Amanda leaned back. "The reason I ask is that to induce transition, two things are needed. The venom bite and insemination. The contraceptive shot wouldn't have interfered with the process, but a physical barrier would."

Margaret couldn't believe that Ana had lied to her. Well, she could understand why Ana had done it initially, but she'd had plenty of time to correct the misconception after Margaret had learned about her transition.

She turned to her friend. "Did you make up the infusion part?"

"I received liquids intravenously, so I just went with your assumption." She chuckled. "I learned from Leon how to walk the thin line between not actually lying but not telling the truth either."

"You should have told me."

"I'm sorry. At first, I had no choice because I needed to keep it a secret, and later, I just assumed that Bowen had told you."

"In any case," Amanda continued. "I'm pretty sure that your knee has to heal before you can transition. The process is very taxing on the body, and we have learned from experience that a Dormant must be healthy before it can begin."

Syssi shook her head. "I don't think that a broken knee is the same as a body weakened by pneumonia. We should check with Bridget."

"It doesn't matter," Margaret said. "Anyway, Bowen is not going to have sex with me until the cast is off, and I'm in no rush. I can wait."

"You should see Bridget anyway." Amanda pulled out her phone. "Maybe Bowen's bite can speed up your recovery." She winked at Margaret. "How's that as an incentive for lots of fun time?"

31

CASSANDRA

"The Uber is here," Cassandra yelled from the first floor. "The guard just called."

"I heard the phone." Her mother came rushing down the stairs, her hair flowing behind her like a dark curtain.

"Have fun, Mom," Cassandra called after her. "And I'm sorry I couldn't drive you to the salon."

"That's okay." Geraldine threw the front door open. "Say hi to Onegus for me."

As the door closed behind her, Cassandra let out a breath. How had her mother known that she was expecting him? She hadn't told her about it, only that she needed to catch up on work. Had the mid-day shower she'd taken as soon as she'd gotten home given her away? Or was it her outfit?

She'd debated between a casual sundress and the black shorts she'd worn to their first date on the beach.

The dress was nicer, and Onegus appreciated her putting effort into dressing elegantly, but she remembered how he'd ogled her backside when she'd worn the shorts, so they won. A loose silk camisole with spaghetti straps went on top. It was dark blue, which allowed her to forgo a bra, and it draped very nicely over her small breasts.

It was a casual, slouch-around-the-house outfit, and Geraldine should have thought nothing of it.

Whatever.

Cassandra was a grown woman, and if she wanted to invite her boyfriend for an afternoon quickie, that was no business of her mother.

What she should be worried about was whether Onegus would make good on his promise to spank her and whether she'd allow it.

It was a sexy fantasy, and it got her tingly in all the right places. When her nipples stiffened, poking through the delicate fabric of her camisole, she cupped her breasts and breathed in and out slowly, trying to calm her raging hormones.

It didn't help, and as soon as the guard at the gate called to let her know Onegus was there, her breathing turned into panting.

Damn, she was like a cat in heat.

"Not a cat," she corrected herself. "A tigress." One that was about to pounce on Onegus as soon as he crossed the threshold.

When the knock sounded at the door, she threw it open, grabbed the front of his dress shirt, and yanked him down toward her.

Luckily, he didn't need to be told what to do next. Smashing his lips over hers, he cupped her bottom, lifted her up, and kicked the door closed behind him.

"Tell me that your mother is not home."

"She left a few minutes ago." Cassandra wrapped her legs around his waist, threaded her fingers through his tight curls, and attacked his mouth again.

He tasted of coffee and man, of desire and strength, and she couldn't get enough of him. His tongue swept in, plundering, and then he was carrying her up the stairs as if she weighed nothing while still kissing the living daylights out of her.

She expected him to tumble with her onto her bed, but instead, he pressed her against the quilt-covered wall, his body pinning hers, his manhood a hard length pressing against her core.

Letting go of her mouth, he traced a line down the column of her neck, licking, kissing, nipping. And when he clamped his teeth over the spot where her neck met her shoulder, she hissed, not from the slight ache, but from the surge of desire rushing through her. He let go, the hurt immediately soothed by a quick swipe of his tongue.

She had a fleeting thought that his teeth were damn sharp, but it eddied away as his lips traveled up her neck, kissing, his tongue licking, his hot breath tickling her ear.

Her breasts ached, needing the attention he was paying to her neck. Yanking the bottom of her camisole, she pushed it up, baring them to him in a blatant invitation.

Onegus groaned, and a moment later, she was hoisted higher on the wall, so her nipples were perfectly aligned with his hot mouth. He latched onto one, suckling it so hard that he made her see stars. Then he let go and soothed the ache with gentle swipes of his tongue.

How was he so strong? And how sexy was it that he could hold her up so effortlessly.

Onegus did the same with her other nipple, never halting the grinding movement of his hips and the press of that maddening hardness that Cassandra couldn't wait to feel inside of her.

She let her head drop back, saved from banging it hard thanks to the cushioning of the thick quilt she was pressed against.

Her mother would be tickled silly if she knew what her handiwork was being used for.

Perhaps a different mother would have been aghast, but not Geraldine. Heck, she might have made it especially for that purpose. After all, it had been her idea to hang it on the wall instead of using it as a bedspread.

With her camisole still bunched up under her armpits and hoisted up high, there wasn't much Cassandra could do other than thread her fingers through Onegus's hair. But that wasn't where she wanted to touch him.

She wanted to peel his clothes off, to kiss and lick every inch of his warm skin, and to run her hands over those perfect muscles it was stretched over.

"Let me down," Cassandra whispered.

Onegus let go of her nipple, looked up at her, then back at her straining nipples, and then up again. "Bed?"

"Oh, God. Yes."

32

ONEGUS

To bite, or not to bite, that was the question.

And the answer was a roaring, definitely bite.

Onegus had bitten Cassandra only once, had been inside her only once, and he needed to do both soon or he'd explode. He was a patient male with an iron will and firm control over his primal responses, but even he had his limit, and it seemed like he'd reached it now.

Fighting the urge to just toss Cassandra on the bed and rip those sexy-as-sin shorts off her, he laid her down gently and hooked his fingers in their waistband. Thankfully, there was enough stretch in the fabric to allow peeling them off her without bothering with the zipper.

She helped, lifting her magnificent bottom so he could pull them down. Her panties went along with the shorts, and as he tossed them on the floor, the only piece of clothing remaining on her was the bunched-up camisole.

Cassandra took care of that, yanking it over her head and tossing it on the floor to join her shorts and panties.

The lady wasn't shy, not with her body and not with anything else. Cupping her small breasts, she parted her legs, creating a perfect cradle for him.

"Your turn." Her hooded eyes roamed over his still fully-dressed body.

Smiling, he started on the buttons of his dress shirt, his fingers steady despite the urge to just rip the thing off. He lasted two buttons and then pulled it over his head and tossed it.

Cassandra sucked in a breath. "I will never tire of seeing you undress. You must train for hours every day to look that good."

His grin got wider. "Not really. I have good genes." Ones that she might be sharing. As he unbuckled his belt and dropped his pants, he might have flexed his abdominals a little.

Her eyes riveted on the bulge stretching his undershorts, Cassandra licked her lips. "Take them off."

"Bossy today, are we?" He hooked his thumbs in the waistband. "I still owe you a spanking, but luckily for you, I'm too impatient to get inside you to play games."

As he pushed the undershorts down and his shaft sprang free, Cassandra parted her legs even further and trailed one slender hand down to where she was already sleek and glistening. "Condom," she breathed.

"Right."

He'd almost forgotten, which wasn't like him. Unlike many other immortal males who thralled their human partners to think that they were using protection, Onegus had been using condoms faithfully ever since they'd come out on the market. Before the recent years of Dormant discoveries, it hadn't been about accidentally inducing a Dormant like what had happened to Eva. It had been about avoiding fathering a mortal child.

With Cassandra, however, it was a valid concern. She was almost certainly a Dormant, and he had no intention of inducing her transition without obtaining her consent first.

Bending at the waist, he retrieved his slacks and pulled a packet out of the pocket. "Do you want to put it on me?" He walked to the side of the bed, his shaft saying hello in person.

"Yes." Cassandra shifted up and took the packet from him. "But first, I need a taste."

He tensed, and when she wrapped her hand around him, he hissed. Her grip was surprisingly strong, just the way he liked it, and when she flicked her tongue over the head, his shaft rewarded her with a pearly offering.

"Hmm." Cassandra licked it off while looking up at him. "Tangy." Leaning down, she took nearly one-third of his length into her mouth.

Taken by surprise, Onegus nearly came. Gritting his teeth, he held his fangs at bay with a herculean effort, fisted her hair to hold her in place, and pulled out of the wet heat of her mouth.

"Perhaps I should give you that spanking after all."

She looked at him with a challenge in her eyes. "Didn't you like it?"

"I liked it too much." He motioned at the condom. "Put it on."

"Yes, sir," she said mockingly before tearing the packet open.

The minx could really use a good spanking, but it wasn't going to happen today. Regrettably, he had no time to play.

Somehow, despite her long, elegant nails, Cassandra managed to sheath him expertly without tearing the condom.

When she was done, Onegus pushed her back on the pillows and climbed in between that inviting cradle. "I'm not going to be gentle."

"I don't want you to be." Her eyes issued a challenge.

The beast in him wanted to rise to that challenge and surge into her with one swift thrust, but he stifled the urge and teased her opening instead, coating his shaft with her juices. Looking into Cassandra's eyes, he pushed in slowly, letting her body dictate the pace.

"I need you," she panted, lifting her hips and urging him to go deeper.

With a growl, he drove into her, seating himself fully.

Cassandra cried out, and as her long nails dug into his back, scoring it, the slight hurt snapped the last of his restraint.

Giving in to his baser needs, Onegus pounded into her without holding back. It was dangerous to let go like that with a human, but he knew that he wouldn't last long, and she was strong enough to take it for a short while, especially since he was going to bite her in the end.

Any bruising he might cause would be healed by his venom.

Cassandra took all he had to give, her moans and mewls accompanying the banging of the headboard against the wall to create the erotic music of abandon.

His favorite.

With her scent flooding his senses and shredding the last vestiges of civility, his seed rose up in his shaft, and when he was about to climax, she turned her head, offering him her neck.

Sending a slight thrall into her mind, Onegus struck, biting hard.

Her body jerked under his, reaching the peak and hurtling over it at the same time his did.

When he was spent, Onegus retracted his fangs and licked at the bite marks, sealing them, and then gently pulled out. He was still hard as a club, but regrettably, he had no time to wait for Cassandra to come down from soaring on the euphoric cloud so they could go for a second round.

After disposing of the condom, he covered her with the blanket and took a moment to gaze at her blissed out, beautiful face.

Perhaps Cassandra felt him looking at her because she smiled, but she didn't open her eyes.

After getting dressed, he kissed her cheek, her forehead, her parted lips, but it was to no avail. She didn't wake up, was probably still soaring, and it wasn't fair to shorten her trip.

He'd call her later, maybe in a couple of hours, to check on her and tell her... what? That he was grateful? That she'd rocked his world? Some witty combination of the two that his mind was too hazy at the moment to come up with?

Hopefully, by the time Cassandra woke up, he would figure it out.

33

BOWEN

"I'm leaving," Bowen told Leon as he returned from escorting guests to their suites. "You'll have to catch a ride back home with one of the guys."

Leon cast him a worried look. "What happened?"

"Amanda made an appointment for Margaret to see Bridget, and Margaret wants me to go with her."

"Did you get permission from the boss?"

"Of course."

Their shift was less than half over, but he'd texted the chief and asked to be released earlier. Onegus had accepted his request on the condition that Bowen found a Guardian to trade shifts with.

"Who is taking over for you?" Leon asked.

"Mason. He agreed in exchange for me taking over half of his night shift."

It was a steep price to pay, especially after last night and this morning. It had been revelatory to share a bed with Margaret, and he would have loved to do the same tonight, but he would have to settle for spending just half of it holding her in his arms.

"Is it about her cast?"

"Among other things." Bowen grimaced. "Amanda also explained the induction and subsequent transition processes, and Margaret wants to find out whether her healing injury is an obstacle."

"You didn't tell her what's involved?"

"When? There was no time."

Leon arched a brow. "You could have told her last night."

"Margaret was tired."

Leon's brow hiked even higher. "Really?"

If the guy was waiting for details, he could keep on waiting. "I'll see you later." Bowen headed to the elevators.

His mother's flight had been delayed, and she'd arrived only an hour ago. He'd barely had time to tell her a condensed and highly edited version of how he'd met Margaret and the story of her being Wendy's mother. Naturally, Elise couldn't wait to meet Margaret and wanted to come to visit right away. After explaining that Margaret was still shell-shocked and needed time to wrap her head around her new reality, he'd managed to convince his mother to wait until the wedding.

That reminded him that Margaret needed something nice to wear for the event, but he had no time to take her shopping, and it was too late to order online. Some items could be delivered overnight, but he doubted it included clothing.

Amanda could probably loan her something. Margaret was a little shorter and a little slimmer, but maybe Amanda had a dress that could fit her.

Except, he wasn't close enough to the princess to ask her for a favor. Who else was tall and slim but more approachable?

Sari. He'd gotten pretty friendly with her during the crisis with David's parents. She wasn't as slim or as tall, and her wardrobe wasn't nearly as robust as Amanda's. Besides, she'd probably brought with her only what she needed for the visit. Perhaps he could ask her to talk to Amanda on his behalf.

Nah. He was overcomplicating things. He would just take Margaret shopping after the doctor's visit. Hopefully, she wasn't too picky and would be quick about it.

When he parked the golf cart in front of Leon and Anastasia's house, he had a plan. He climbed the steps to the front door and knocked.

Anastasia opened the door. "Why did you knock?"

He shrugged. "It's your house."

"The four of us entered it yesterday evening for the first time together. For now, it belongs to all of us."

He found Margaret in the bathroom, brushing her hair. She turned and smiled at him. "Did I get you in trouble with your boss?"

"Not at all." He pulled her into his arms, lifted her, and sat her down on the counter. "It was torture to be away from you. Thank you for providing me with an excuse to come home early." He took her lips in a long, passionate kiss. "Are you mad at me for not telling you about what it takes to start your transition?"

She shook her head. "There was no time. Besides, it sounds like much more fun than an infusion, which is what I thought I was going to get."

He rested his forehead against hers. "I can't wait for this cast to come off."

"Neither can I."

"Let's see what Bridget says. Maybe it can come off sooner than we thought." He lifted her into his arms and carried her out to the golf cart.

"Amanda said that your bite can speed up my recovery." Margaret rearranged her dress over her legs and then waited until he got behind the wheel to whisper in his ear, "That's one hell of a bonus on top of the most intense pleasure I've ever experienced."

The grin that spread over his face stayed there until he parked the cart in front of the clinic. He had to force it off so he wasn't caught looking like a fool.

"It's embarrassing to be carried in," Margaret said softly.

"But it's more efficient. Besides, I enjoy it."

"So do I."

After last night, things had changed between them, and they were all good. Margaret was much less reserved, and she finally seemed to be embracing what they shared.

"Good afternoon," Bridget greeted them. "Let's go in there." She pointed toward a patient room. "You can set Margaret down on the exam table."

After he had done as she'd instructed, Bridget politely kicked him out. "You can wait in the front room or you can wait outside on the bench. I'll call you when I'm done."

"Can't he stay?" Margaret asked.

The doctor shook her head. "I'm going to remove the cast, and knowing how overprotective mates are, I'd rather Bowen wasn't there when I cut it off you."

"Oh." Margaret paled. "I wasn't expecting that." She cast a worried look at Bowen.

"I promise to behave." He crossed his arms over his chest. "I'll stand next to the wall and won't move from there."

Given her grimace, Bridget didn't like it, but she nodded. "One growl and I'm kicking you out."

"Deal."

34

MARGARET

"I feel so light." Margaret lifted her leg.

The cast was off, replaced by a light brace, and the doctor had said that it was okay to put weight on the foot of the injured knee.

"Are you up to doing some shopping?" Bowen carried her back to the golf cart only because she was missing a shoe.

Margaret laughed. "I don't think any store sells just one shoe."

"Very funny." Bowen set her down and hopped into the cart on the driver's side. "You need a dress for the wedding."

Her eyes widened. "Am I invited?"

"Of course."

"But you'll be working. What am I going to do there all alone?"

"You are not going to be alone, and I can be with you while keeping my eyes open for trouble and carrying concealed weapons. Being on duty only means that I can't get drunk. But since none of my friends can drink either, I don't mind." He cast her an amused glance. "You'll be missing out on lewd Scottish ballads."

"Can you sing me one?"

"You won't understand it."

"I want to hear you sing."

"Fine." He started so quietly that she could barely hear him over the wheezing noise of the golf cart's engine.

It still sounded beautiful to her. Bowen had a deep, masculine voice. Sexy, and as he got into it and upped the volume a little, his lilting accent and timbre raised goosebumps over her arms.

Now that the damn cast was off, there were no more excuses. Tonight, she was going to seduce him and make love to this magnificent male she could finally call her own and not feel like a fraud.

When the song ended, Bowen parked the cart in front of the house. "You can

319

wait here while I get your other shoe and one of the crutches." He turned to her and smiled. "That's all you need."

She frowned. "You were serious about the shopping."

"I have to wear a tux to the wedding, and everyone is going to be formally dressed. You need an evening gown, and there are only two ways you can get one on such short notice. One is to go to the mall, and the other is to borrow a dress from Amanda. The selection in her closet is probably better than any high-end boutique's, and it's all designer stuff."

"I can't ask Amanda for a dress. I barely know her. Do I really have to go? I don't know the bride or the groom, and they don't know me."

"You are my mate. Of course, you have to come. Besides, I promised my mother that she could meet you at the wedding. That was the only way I got her to agree not to come to the village this evening."

Margaret's throat constricted.

Damn, she'd been so sure that she would never be gripped by panic again, but here it was. First of all, Bowen had called her his mate. That was a big deal. And then he'd reminded her about meeting his mother.

Breathing through it, Margaret forced herself to relax.

She wasn't wary of meeting Bowen's mother. Not after what she and Bowen had shared. The sense of panic was a knee-jerk reaction stemming from her old self-doubt.

Something had changed in her last night.

Maybe it was the way Bowen had worshiped her body, or the incredible pleasure she'd experienced, or maybe it had been the bite's effect or the venom's, but she felt like a new woman.

She was happy and hopeful in a way she hadn't felt since before her parents had died and her world had dimmed. She hadn't realized it up until now, but she'd lived in darkness long before ever meeting Roger. Perhaps her despondency had drawn him to her, or perhaps she'd been too numb to notice how horrible he was. Margaret had no doubt that she would have never fallen prey to him if her parents had been alive and her world had been whole.

Turning to Bowen, she put a hand on his arm. "I need a dress, shoes, makeup, and a visit to a hairdresser. Can we manage all that in one afternoon? I want to look good when I meet your mother."

Bowen grinned. "I'll make it happen." He leaned and cupped the back of her neck. "You are beautiful to me as you are, but if you want a new hairdo, you are going to get one." He smashed his lips over hers.

The kiss was interrupted when the door opened and Anastasia stepped out. "Are you going to smooch for much longer? I want to know what the doctor said."

Reluctantly, Bowen let go of Margaret's lips. "Couldn't you have waited a few more minutes?"

Ana crossed her arms over her chest. "I was worried that poor Margaret would suffocate. She is still human, you know."

"Not for long." Margaret lifted her leg to show Ana the new brace. "The doctor said that my knee is mostly healed and that I can walk on this leg. She also prescribed as many venom bites as Bowen can manage to speed up my recovery."

A grin spread over Ana's face. "That's awesome. We need to celebrate with a bottle of wine." She uncrossed her arms.

"Later," Bowen said. "I'm taking Margaret shopping for an evening dress and to a hair salon."

Ana's eyes sparkled with excitement. "Can I come? I planned on wearing the black dress Amanda got me, but if you are going shopping, I might as well get something fancier."

Bowen didn't look happy, but Margaret lifted her hand to stop him before he could refuse. "Of course, you can come. I need your style expertise. Mine is terribly out of date."

35

BOWEN

*B*owen had expected to suffer through the shopping expedition with Margaret and Ana, but it turned out to be not as bad as he'd thought it would be.

Sitting in the food court, he was reading an article on his phone when he was interrupted by a call from Leon.

"How is it going?" his friend asked, a note of amusement in his voice.

"Better than expected. Your mate is an experienced shopper, and she's helping Margaret choose the dress and everything else. All I have to do is wait for them to be done."

He'd given Margaret enough cash to cover even the most extravagant gown along with everything else she needed. Naturally, she'd been shocked at the amount, saying that she wouldn't spend even a fraction of that, and once she got a job, she was going to pay him back.

To avoid further arguments, he'd nodded, but he had no intention of ever accepting her money. He had plenty, and it made him feel good to be able to pamper her. Fates knew that she deserved it after the miserable life she'd had.

"Have they been to the hair salon yet?" Leon asked.

"No." Bowen glanced at the time. "They have an appointment in less than half an hour, and the receptionist promised to have them out of there in an hour. My torment is almost over." Not that he was suffering.

"Which mall are you at?"

"The Oaks."

"I could join you there for dinner."

"It will have to be something quick. I need to get back for the night shift."

"Onegus is a bastard. He knows your situation. He should have just given you the time off with no trade-off."

"Not his fault. He told me to find someone to trade with, and Mason agreed to take over the rest of my day shift only if I took the first half of his."

"You'll be back by three in the morning. That's not so bad."

"Yeah. Margaret will be asleep, but at least I can wake up with her in my arms."

Bowen interpreted the silence that followed as Leon debating whether he should ask him about last night. Thankfully, his friend had more tact than that. "Anastasia told me that Bridget removed Margaret's cast and gave her a brace instead. That's good news."

"Yeah. She said that the knee is healing nicely."

Leon hesitated for another moment. "Then there are no more obstacles in the way of Margaret's transition. You can start the process."

Bowen's shaft hardened at the thought, but then as worry washed over him, it deflated. "I didn't tell her yet."

Leon chuckled. "Ana said that Amanda did that for you."

"She told her what's involved, but she didn't warn her about the risk. Margaret doesn't know that it can potentially kill her."

"It won't. The Fates didn't bring you together only to end it that way. You are a good guy, Bowen. They wouldn't do that to you."

"That's all superstition, and I can't put my faith in it. The risk exists, and I need to tell Margaret about it."

"Naturally. But I disagree with your lack of faith. We haven't lost a Dormant to transition yet. Not Andrew, who was forty at the time of his transition, and not even Turner, who was forty-something and not in good health. I think that we have enough circumstantial evidence in favor of affirming the Fates' involvement. It's not a superstition when it's proven true time and again."

Bowen raked his fingers through his hair. "What if Margaret gets scared and refuses to go through with it? She told Anastasia that she didn't want to live forever. That life was hard and sad and that she couldn't understand why anyone would want to prolong the misery."

"A lot has happened since."

"That conversation took place yesterday morning. How much could have changed for her since then?"

There was another pause. "Last night changed things for both of you. I could tell that just from looking at you and Margaret this morning at breakfast. She seemed like a different woman. There was a sparkle in her eyes that hasn't been there before, and her smiles were genuine rather than forced or polite. She looked happy. Hopeful."

Bowen had seen that too. And her excitement about getting a new dress and a hairdo was like a breath of fresh air. Before, Margaret hadn't wanted anything for herself.

It saddened him to think that after spending half of her life in Safe Haven, she had nothing worth retrieving from there.

"I'll tell her about the risk tonight before I leave for the shift."

"If you want, you can tell her over dinner, so Ana and I can support you if needed."

That wasn't a bad idea. "I might take your advice on that. Do you want me to check which restaurants are in the vicinity and make a reservation?"

"Nah. I'll do it. Knowing you, you'll choose a hamburger joint."

"As you wish. Make it for seven-fifteen in case the hair salon takes a little longer than expected."

"No problem. Any preferences?"

After the hamburger joint comment, he wasn't about to make any suggestions.

"Whatever you choose is fine."

"Good deal. I'll text you the name and address."

36

ELEANOR

"*L*et's go over the schedule." Arwel dropped a yellow pad on the coffee table.

Eleanor snorted. "What happened to the scheduling software you were testing?"

"Too much work." Arwel pulled out a pen. "It takes me less than five minutes to write it down, and there are no glitches where everything I worked on disappears because I pressed the wrong key."

Eleanor glanced at the monitor, checking on Emmett, who was supposed to write a dictionary of basic Kra-ell words, especially those that had to do with travel and locations. Kian wanted it done yesterday, which meant that her time with Emmett had been cut to nothing. Her job was to bring him food and leave right away, so he could work on the Kra-ell-English dictionary.

Peter opened the fridge and pulled out a bottle of water. "When are you heading out to China?"

Arwel cocked a brow. "Can't wait to get rid of me?"

Peter twisted the cap off and straddled a chair. "This is my first command. I'm eager to start."

The five of them were gathered around the small dining table in Arwel's suite, which served as their makeshift conference table. It was an intimate setting that she preferred to the one in Kian's office. For some reason, every time Eleanor participated in a meeting over there, she felt like she didn't belong. Here, everyone treated her as part of the team, and it felt good.

Jay cast him a look that Eleanor couldn't decipher. Was he mad that Peter had gotten promoted ahead of him? Or did he just doubt Peter's ability to be in charge?

Eleanor's first impression of Peter had been that he was a light-hearted, take-it-easy kind of guy who didn't take the initiative unless he was forced to. But she'd learned that there was more to him.

Perhaps Jay didn't know Peter as well as she did.

"Kian wants the team to leave after the guests are gone." Arwel leaned back in his chair. "My last day here is going to be next Friday, and I'm only working the first half of the day tomorrow." He picked up the yellow pad. "We need to work out a schedule for the wedding. Since it's right here in the keep, you can take turns. I suggest dividing it into one-hour shifts, so each of you gets to enjoy at least some of the party." He glanced at Eleanor. "By the way, several of Kalugal's men are invited to the wedding, so that's an additional level of security."

Great. If Greggory was one of those who were invited, she'd pass.

Alfie grimaced. "You think? I'd say that they are an additional level of complication."

"They pledged alliance to the clan, and it was cemented by Annani's compulsion. And unlike most of our civilians, they are trained warriors. I say that's an asset and not a liability."

"You're a head Guardian," Alfie said. "So you must know best."

As the two continued to argue and then Peter and Jay added their comments, Eleanor tuned them out.

She'd planned on attending the wedding, or at least some of it if possible. It would have been a great opportunity to mingle, maybe dance with some of the males and see if she responded to any of them.

Getting to know Emmett better, Eleanor was no longer distraught by her attraction to him, but she would've preferred to bond with a pleasant immortal clan member instead of the enigma who might be putting up an act to win her over to his case.

The problem was that she didn't have a date, which would have been fine as long as Greggory wasn't there. But if he was invited, the last thing she wanted was to see him dancing with other females and enjoying himself while she played the role of wallflower.

What if no one invited her to dance?

"I'll cover the wedding," she blurted. "You guys can go and enjoy yourself."

Arwel shook his head. "I can't leave you alone in charge of Emmett. Besides, why don't you want to attend the wedding?"

"Because someone decided to invite some of the ex-Doomers at the last moment, and Greggory might be one of them. I don't want to watch him having a splendid time with the clan females and gloating over my single status."

Peter put a hand on her shoulder. "We can go together and pretend to be a couple. Would that work for you?"

"Thanks for the offer, but no. That would defy the purpose. I planned on checking out other men, but with you by my side, no one would dare to approach me."

Alfie snickered. "They wouldn't dare even without Peter pretending to be your date. You're a scary female."

She flipped him the finger.

"What about Emmett?" Jay asked. "I thought the two of you were getting cozy."

"We're getting to know each other, but we are far from cozy. Besides, I want to keep my options open. Emmett is definitely not the guy of my dreams."

"Of course he's not." Peter wrapped his arm around her shoulders. "I am."

He was teasing, but there was a tiny kernel of truth in his words. The attraction was there, and if not for Emmett's magnetic pull, she might have given Peter a chance.

Except, their attraction to each other was so mild that there was no chance that they were fated mates.

She was female, and he was male, and that created an unavoidable sexual tension, but it was nothing either of them would write home about, so to speak. They were good friends, and they were sharing a home, which they weren't using at the moment because of the assignment in the keep.

Casting him a grin, she leaned into his arm. "Back to the schedule issue. I can guard Emmett on my own, and you can all enjoy the wedding without missing a thing. If you are worried about me being alone with him, I won't even go inside. We can give him a large meal before you guys leave, so I don't have to go in at all. And if there is an emergency, I can call one of you to come over."

Arwel nodded. "Since we will be right here in the keep if you need us, I'll consider that. But if I let you guard him alone, I don't want you opening his door under any circumstances, is that clear?"

"Crystal."

3 7

MARGARET

*A*s the hairstylist swiveled Margaret's chair to show Anastasia the final result, Ana gasped. "Wow. You look like a model."

The stylist joined Ana to admire her work. "You have a beautiful facial structure, but the dark hair made your cheeks look too hollow. The blond highlights soften your face."

"Thank you." She smiled at the stylist. "I'm glad I listened to you about that."

"And I'm glad that you are happy with the results."

"Your hair looks gorgeous too," Margaret returned Ana's compliment. "The guys' jaws are going to drop when they see us." She took the crutch that had been resting against the stylist's work counter and pushed to her feet.

It felt so good to actually walk instead of hobbling, to wear leggings instead of a dress, and to have shoes on both feet. New shoes that were black ballet flats instead of the white sneakers or snow boots that she used to wear in Safe Haven.

Anastasia grinned. "Bowen is going to faint." She lifted the shopping bags off the floor. "Let's go get him."

At the sight of those bags, guilt speared through Margaret.

Since the evening dress she'd gotten had been on sale and not nearly as pricy as Bowen had expected, Ana had convinced her to get some new everyday clothes, and once she'd started, she'd just lost it and bought a whole new wardrobe. Leggings, blouses, T-shirts, and jackets. Bras, panties, and shoes. It was good that Ana was an immortal now and had the strength to carry all of their purchases.

"I went overboard," Margaret said after paying for her hair. "I'm so embarrassed."

Ana snorted. "You think that's a lot? You've only spent a fraction of what Bowen gave you."

"It's still more than I've ever spent on myself. I'm writing down every penny he spends on me, and I'm going to pay him back as soon as I have a job." She groaned. "At the rate I'm going, I'll owe him a year's salary."

"Drama much?" Ana cast her an amused look. "Before Safe Haven, I would spend twice as much as you did today on every shopping run. You didn't buy that much, and everything you got was on sale. Besides, Bowen will never accept money from you, so you can just forget it."

"I'll make him take it. I don't want to be dependent on a man ever again. Not even Bowen."

Ana's eyes softened. "Oh, Margaret. I get why you feel that way, but if you say those words to Bowen, you are going to offend him. You're bundling him together with the likes of your ex. Don't do that."

Margaret swallowed. "I'm not. But I really want to be independent. How can I phrase it so it won't sound as if I'm comparing Bowen to Roger?"

Ana shrugged. "Just accept what he gives you for now, and as soon as you start earning an income, use your own money to buy groceries and things for the house. Don't make a big deal out of it. That's my advice."

"I don't want him to think that I'm a leech."

"Bowen will never think that. It makes him happy to buy things for you. It's his way of showing that he cares."

As they neared the food court, Margaret spotted Bowen sitting at a table, reading on his phone.

"Poor guy. He must be bored out of his mind."

"Shhh." Ana put a finger over her lips. "Don't let him hear you," she whispered. "I want to surprise him."

Margaret rolled her eyes. "Yeah, good luck with that. Bowen is a Guardian, and even while reading, he's alert and paying attention to what's going on around him."

A split second later, she was proven right as his head whipped around, and his eyes widened upon seeing her. A grin spreading over his face, he pushed to his feet and strode toward her.

"Stunning." He leaned and kissed her cheek. "Did you get a facial too?"

"No, it's an illusion created by the highlights." She fluffed her hair.

"I don't think so." His eyes roamed all over her, taking in the new outfit, the shoes. "It's everything together." He smoothed his hand over the sleeve of her new blouse. "I'm so glad that you bought more things for yourself. I should have suggested it, but I didn't think you'd have enough time."

"I'm going to…" She was interrupted by Ana clearing her throat.

"Leon is waiting for us in the restaurant," Ana said. "We should go."

Margaret closed her mouth.

Bowen took all the shopping bags from Ana, freeing her to thread her arm through Margaret's. "Are you okay to walk to the car?"

"I'm fine." She leaned on Ana's arm just a little.

The truth was that her body was tired, and she ached in multiple places. But she was also excited, energized, and hopeful. If not for the brace, she would have had a spring in her step.

Less than ten minutes later, Bowen parked the car in front of the restaurant.

Leon, who had secured a table out on the patio for them, rose to his feet and gawked the entire time it took them to reach him.

"You two look like you've stepped out of a fashion magazine." His eyes darted from Ana to Margaret and back to Ana.

Chuckling, Ana leaned and kissed his cheek. "Let's order some wine. We need to celebrate the cast removal."

Next to Margaret, Bowen tensed for some reason. Was he apprehensive about what that meant for them? It wasn't likely.

Last night, he'd proven to be not only a confident and dominant lover, but also superbly skilled. A man like him would never feel shy about taking that final step.

He pulled out a chair for her and took the crutch, leaning it against the patio's railing. "Do they serve whiskey here? I'm not a fan of wine."

"I can check." Leon waved the waiter down. "Do you have whiskey in your bar?"

The guy smiled and then listed all the brands they carried.

Bowen didn't look impressed by any of them, but he ended up ordering a Jack Daniels. Leon chose the same, while she and Ana ordered a glass of wine each.

The appetizers arrived together with the drinks, and after the toasts had been made, Bowen reached for her hand and looked into her eyes.

"There's one last thing I need to tell you." He glanced around at the other diners and then leaned closer to her. "The transition is difficult, and it gets more dangerous the older the Dormant is. For Anastasia and Wendy, the risk was minimal, but it's significantly higher for you."

She frowned. "What's the worst that can happen?"

"You might not wake up." When she sucked in a breath, he squeezed her hand. "It hasn't happened yet. All the Dormants we induced have transitioned successfully, and some were older than you. But I can't start your induction before making you aware of the risk."

"Do I have a choice?"

"It's entirely up to you. No one will force you to attempt transition."

"What's the alternative? Will I be allowed to stay in the village as a human?"

He nodded. "Kian has relaxed the rules lately, and now parents of transitioned Dormants are allowed to stay in the village. And as Wendy's mother, you qualify for that exemption. As for me, I love you, and I want to be with you. But if you choose not to risk your life for the chance of immortality, I will not try to persuade you. I'll take whatever years you can give me."

Margaret swallowed. "Can I take a day or two to think it through?"

"Take all the time you need. This is not a decision that should be taken lightly."

3 8

ANNANI

"Why didn't I think of inviting strippers?" Amanda accepted the virgin strawberry daiquiri Onidu handed her. "What kind of a bachelorette party is it without alcohol and strippers?"

Annani exchanged knowing smiles with Ronja. It did not matter that Ronja was younger than most of the immortal women in the room. She was a mother, and therefore had more in common with Annani and Alena than with the rest of the boisterous attendees of Sari's bachelorette party.

It had been decided to make the party alcohol-free on account of the three pregnant ladies and Lisa, who was still underage. Having the girl there also meant that the others needed to keep the sexy comments to a minimum, which would have been a problem if the girls got drunk.

There had been some grumbles, but no one was too upset about the lack of alcohol.

Syssi snorted. "Knowing Anandur, he's planning another performance to entertain us."

The men were at David and Sari's place, celebrating David's last day as a bachelor, and Annani had no doubt that the alcohol was flowing freely over there.

Wonder cast Syssi a mock angry look. "The only one Anandur strips for these days is me."

Hiding a smile, Syssi sipped on her virgin drink.

"We don't need strippers," Jacki said. "We have a full schedule of fun activities." She donned the colorful turban she'd brought for the occasion. "Who wants to have her fortune told first?" She sat on one of the big pillows thrown in the center of the living room and crossed her legs, pulling a fake crystal ball to nestle between them.

Her pregnancy was still in the early stages, so even if she got a real foretelling, it would not harm the child, but that was most likely not going to happen. Jacki's visions were rare, even more so than Syssi's.

Tonight, she was providing entertainment and nothing more.

"Sari is the bride," Amanda said. "She should go first."

Sari shook her head. "Miranda is dying to find a true-love mate. She should go first."

Her assistant got to her feet and lowered herself gracefully to the other pillow. "Tell me my fortune, oh great seer."

"Did you bring an object for me to touch?" Jacki asked.

Miranda removed a bracelet from her wrist and handed it to Jacki.

Closing her eyes, Jacki waved it over the plastic ball that was made to look like crystal. Humming, she swayed from side to side as if she was entering a trance.

"She's good," Ronja whispered in Annani's ear.

"I see a long journey," Jacki said. "To a faraway land. Lots of sand, the sun is blindingly hot, and in the distance, the ocean shimmers. A handsome man emerges from the water, his long dark hair plastered over his muscular chest, his green eyes blazing with desire." She opened her eyes. "For you, Miranda."

"When?"

Jacki lifted her hand and brushed it over the crystal ball. "Ten moons."

"Yay." Miranda clapped her hands, but then her smile slid off her face. "Does that mean none of Kalugal's men is the one for me?"

Jacki shrugged. "The future is always changing, and nothing is set in stone. Perhaps the gorgeous Aquaman will emerge from the water for someone else."

"Aquaman?" Miranda squeaked. "Did he look like Jason Momoa?"

Jacki smiled. "Yeah, he kind of did."

"Then it's worth the wait." Miranda pushed to her feet. "Onidu, another virgin margarita over here."

"Yes, mistress." He bowed.

"Who's next?" Jacki asked.

"I am." Veronica, one of Sari's good friends, jumped in before anyone else could volunteer. "I want Superman. The latest one. Henry Cavill."

Stifling a laugh, Jacki extended her hand. "An object, please."

She told two more fortunes before Ronja decided to take the hot seat.

"I don't have any particular requests." She crossed her legs and put her hands on her knees.

"Do you have an object for me to touch?"

Ronja pulled a compact mirror out of her purse. "I got this as a present from my first husband." She rubbed her hand over the engraving. "Michael gave it to me for my nineteenth birthday." Her expression turned wistful. "I loved Frank dearly, and he was a much better husband to me than Michael ever was, but Michael was the true love of my life, my passion, my obsession, and also the one who caused me the biggest pain. Regrettably, he didn't love me as much as I loved him." She cast an apologetic glance at Lisa. "I hope that you are not mad at me for saying that."

A tear slid down Lisa's cheek. "I can't get angry at you for telling the truth. The heart chooses who it wants to love, even if it's the wrong person."

Ronja nodded. "Even though Michael was much older than me, he was either immature, or just incapable of loving as fully and as completely as I was. Back then, I was young and naive, and I hoped that my love would be enough for both of us." She smiled sadly. "Now that I'm older and smarter, I know that's not how it works." She took in a deep breath. "What I want to know is whether I will ever experience that kind of love again, and more importantly, whether it will be reciprocated with the same fervor."

As Jacki closed her hand over the mirror and her eyes drifted shut, Annani straightened in her chair. Would Ronja's foretelling be real, or another one of Jacki's acts?

Jacki's forehead furrowed. "I can't see the man that will make your heart soar again, but I can sense that one was fated for you. You will know love again."

Ronja smiled. "I hoped you would see Aquaman or Superman in my future." She turned and winked at Lisa. "But I'll settle for loving again. Not right now, I'm not ready yet, but sometime in the future." She looked at Annani. "One is never too old to love, right?"

Annani nodded. "Never."

39

KIAN

"*H*elp yourself to the second finest cigars." Anandur placed the box on the coffee table. "Opus X."

"Why not the finest?" Kalugal reached into the box, pulled out one, and handed it to David. "The soon-to-be former bachelor goes first."

"Cuban cigars are banned in the United States," Kian grumbled.

"So?" Kalugal pulled out another one for himself. "You can get them on the black market."

"There are some online sellers that supposedly carry them, but you never know what you're actually getting." Kian slid the balcony doors open and stepped out. "Most are counterfeits."

Kalugal and David followed, and soon all ten were crowding the small balcony, with Okidu making rounds and refilling everyone's whiskey glasses.

Leaning against the glass railing, David puffed on his cigar. "Can you tell me more about the Kra-ell social structure?"

"You know the basics already. What else do you want to know?" Kian asked.

"I'll tell you what I know, and then you can fill in the blanks." David puffed on his cigar. "They are a different race of immortals who need blood for nutrition and have the ability to compel. They are relative newcomers to earth, and their society is matriarchal like the clan's. For every four Kra-ell males, only one female is born, so they don't form couple relationships. Instead, they live in small tribes, with two to four females sharing a group of males in a communal harem."

Kian tapped on his cigar, the ash falling into the big glass ashtray Okidu had put on the outdoor table. "Their compulsion or thralling abilities vary in strength from one individual to another, in the same way that ours do, they are long-lived, and they are genetically similar to us, but that's where the similarities end. Their society is very different than ours or any of the human cultures that I'm familiar with."

David smiled knowingly. "Then you are not familiar with the Mosuo."

"I've never heard of them."

"Their society is structured very much like that of the Kra-ell, and they are a subgroup in China. I remembered reading about them a long time ago, and when I heard about the Kra-ell and their society, I was reminded of the Mosuo and decided to refresh my memory."

Kian cocked a brow. "That's interesting. Maybe there is a connection."

"That's what I thought, but after reading more about them, I don't think there is. The Mosuo, or the Na as they call themselves, live in the Yunnan and Sichuan provinces, which are close to the border with Tibet. The women head the households, and inheritance is through the female line, but they leave the politicking to the males. That wasn't always the case, and in the past the matriarch was also the political head of the community. Still, even today, the matriarch, the Ah Mis, has absolute power over everyone in her household, assigns jobs to every member, and controls all the money."

Kian took a puff of his cigar. "So far, that sounds loosely similar to the Kra-ell. What about their mating habits?"

David smiled. "I saved the best part for last. The Mosuo men are primarily used as breeders. After the coming-of-age ceremony, which occurs at the age of thirteen for girls and boys..." David paused for emphasis. "The girls are given a private bedroom that is called the flowering room, and they can start inviting partners for what's called Walking Marriages. Those are basically sexual encounters, and the men are supposed to come at night and leave in the morning. Any resulting children stay with the mother. The fathers are granted visitation rights, but they are more involved with raising the children of their sisters and aunts in their own matriarch's house than they are with their own."

"That sounds a lot like the Kra-ell," Anandur said. "Why do you think they are not related? They could have picked up the customs from a neighboring compound."

"Because the Mosuo's tradition is thousands of years old, and the Kra-ell are supposed to be newcomers."

"Emmett thinks that his group arrived relatively recently." Kian lifted his empty glass for Okidu to refill. "But he deduced it rather than knowing it for a fact. Also, his group might not be the first one. It's possible that others came before."

"What are the Mosuo's religious beliefs?" Kalugal asked.

"The Mosuo have a hybrid faith. The Daba is their original religion, which has been handed down through the generations for thousands of years. It's based on the worship of a mother goddess and on their ancestors, functioning as both religion and oral history of their people. In recent years, Buddhism has gained ground in the Mosuo society, but it was adapted to suit their culture."

"The Kra-ell believe in a mother goddess." Kian took a puff of the cigar. "The leaders of their communities are supposed to be the goddess's embodiments. I need to ask Emmett if they also worship their ancestors."

Kalugal handed his glass to Okidu and extinguished his half-smoked cigar. "The ancestor worship is a big part of Confucianism and Taoism. It might have influenced the Mosuo beliefs in the same way that Buddhism did later. To me, that sounds too much like the Kra-ell for it to be a coincidence. The Chinese society is very patriarchal by nature, and for the Mosuo to develop such a divergent system, there must have been a strong outside influence." He smiled at David. "Your next task is to find out whether the Mosuo have vampire legends."

"As far as I know, they don't." David rubbed a hand over his jaw. "But they have an interesting legend regarding dogs. First of all, unlike other Asian cultures, eating dogs is strictly forbidden, and dogs are considered important members of the household. According to legend, long ago, dogs had much longer lifespans than humans—they lived to be sixty, while humans lived only thirteen years. At some point, humans traded lifespans with dogs in exchange for worship. During the coming-of-age ceremony, young Mosuo pray before the family dogs."

"Perhaps it's a loose reference to attaining longevity," Kalugal said. "Legends and myths get twisted over the millennia. It might have started as something else."

"Where did you say their communities are located?" Kian asked.

"The Sichuan and Yunnan provinces are on the eastern border of Tibet. Sichuan is more or less in central China, and Yunnan is to the south."

Kian glanced at Kalugal. "I think we should send a team to investigate that region as well."

Kalugal shook his head. "Even if the Mosuo were influenced by the Kra-ell, it happened thousands of years ago. What do you hope to find there?"

"Maybe there are some interesting archeological finds that would provide us with clues." Kian smiled at Kalugal. "That's actually your field of expertise. Perhaps you could do some digging."

Kalugal's eyes gleamed with interest. "Indeed."

40

SYSSI

*A*fter Jacki's fortune-telling, it was Callie's turn, and Syssi was grateful for the change in atmosphere.

Ronja's admission about her first husband having been the love of her life had been a mood downer, and more than one discreet tear had been shed. It must have been devastating to love a man who hadn't loved her back, and who'd cheated on her left and right. Syssi couldn't imagine the pain.

Callie emerged from the kitchen, followed by Okidu and Onidu, all three carrying trays loaded with the ingredients she'd prepared.

"This is going to be very simple." Callie pointed to the tray she'd put on the dining table. "We are going to prepare beautiful canapés and then eat them."

Amanda clapped her hands. "Perfect. I'm hungry."

For the next half an hour, they assembled small sandwiches, and then demolished them in less than ten minutes.

"That's the problem with cooking as an artistic expression," Amanda said. "In contrast, my contribution to this lovely evening is going to be a keepsake." She started pulling small bags from the large box Dalhu had hauled in before joining the men for their party. "Every bag contains several sheets of high-quality drawing paper and a packet of charcoals. All we need now is to choose a model, and I volunteer." She took her jacket off. "I can pose in the nude."

"Don't you dare." Syssi laughed. "Keep your clothes on. Besides, it's Sari's party, so I think she should pose."

Sari graciously agreed, pulling a barstool into the center of the living room. "Just so we are clear, I'm volunteering to be the model only because I can't draw for the life of me, and I'm not posing naked."

"That's a shame," Amanda grumbled. "You have a beautiful figure."

Sari dipped her head. "Thank you. But the clothes stay on."

They spent the next hour drawing and laughing at each other's fumbling efforts, and when everyone was done, Lisa's sketch was chosen as the best.

"I want to keep all of them." Sari collected everyone's sketches, insisting that each of them sign her creation.

"You should have Dalhu draw your portrait," Amanda said as she handed over hers. "You and David can come to his studio in the village, or you can just send him a photo to work from."

"I don't want to trouble him." Sari put the collection of drawings into the box the kits had come in.

"It's karaoke time." Wonder pushed to her feet. "I need help setting it up."

"I'll help you," Amanda offered. "I have lots of experience with these machines."

Syssi vaguely remembered Amanda buying a karaoke machine to entertain the all-female crew of the *Anna*. Alex's yacht had been used for trafficking young women that the corrupt immortal had been thralling into a stupor and selling for profit.

Back then, none of them could have anticipated that rescuing trafficking victims would become one of the clan's main humanitarian efforts. But the Fates must have started them on the path with that yacht.

When everything was set up, and Amanda took the microphone, singing along to Journey's '*Don't Stop Believing*,' everyone joined her.

Well, everyone save for Annani, who shifted closer to Syssi. "I was thinking," the goddess whispered in her ear, "that I like Ronja a lot, and I think that she deserves another chance at love."

"She sure does."

"Perhaps she should attempt transition after all."

Syssi turned to look at her mother-in-law. "I would have loved for Ronja to have another chance, and she'll get it, but not as an immortal. She can't transition at her age."

Annani smiled mischievously. "Perhaps with the help of my blessing, she can."

Syssi stifled the incredulity that threatened to show on her face. Annani's blessing was a great morale booster, but it couldn't guarantee a successful transition.

It wasn't as if she could argue with the goddess, though. That privilege was reserved for Annani's children, and perhaps in this case, also Bridget, who had medical training to back up her position. Then again, Annani regarded Syssi as her daughter, so perhaps she was allowed to voice her doubts, as long as she kept it respectful.

"As powerful and as generous as your blessings are, I'm not sure even that would be enough to pull Ronja through the transition. But I'm not an expert. Bridget is probably the one you need to talk to."

Syssi was kicking the can down the road, but she wasn't in a position to argue with the goddess, while Bridget had the authority to back up her argument. The doctor would no doubt shoot Annani's idea down and save Ronja from nearly certain death.

"You are right," Annani acquiesced. "I need to consult Bridget."

MARGARET

$\mathcal{I}$t had been difficult to say goodbye to Bowen when he left for his second shift of the day. Margaret felt guilty. If she hadn't been such a wuss, she could have gone to the clinic with Ana and waited for Bowen to come home.

But then he would have been too late to take her shopping, and she really needed an evening dress if she was to attend the wedding. Besides, she had a wonderful time.

When a knock sounded on the front door, Leon rose to his feet and opened the way for Wendy and Vlad.

"Is that you, Mom?" Wendy pretended not to recognize her.

"It's me." Margaret flipped her hair back and smiled. "Just improved."

"I'll say." Wendy sat on the couch next to her. "I don't know if it's the hair color or the clothes, but you look ten years younger."

The smile slid off Margaret's face. "Thank you. But it doesn't change the fact that my body is thirty-eight years old, and that transitioning is dangerous for me. Potentially deadly."

As everyone went quiet, Margaret felt bad for ruining everyone's good mood. She waved a dismissive hand. "I'm sure that everything will be okay. It's just that I didn't know that until a few hours ago, and it was a little bit of a shock to learn it."

"Does that mean you decided to go for it?" Anastasia asked.

"I don't know." She pushed a strand of hair behind her ear. "What do you think I should do, Wendy?"

Her daughter pursed her lips. "I say, go for it. Thirty-eight is not old, and I have no doubt that you will transition successfully." She turned to Vlad. "You said that so far, every Dormant who started transitioning has made it through."

Vlad nodded. "Correct." He glanced at Margaret. "But some had a really difficult time. I remember that Turner was in a coma for two weeks. Maybe even longer."

Leon chuckled. "That bastard would have wrestled death and won. He doesn't accept defeat."

"Who's Turner?" Margaret asked. "I keep hearing that name."

"It's a long story," Leon said. "Syssi's brother knew him from his special ops days, and when the clan needed to find a kidnapped clan member, he brought him in to help. Naturally, no one suspected that Turner was a Dormant, but he needed to be in the know in order to help us out. Kian gave the guy the bare minimum of information, but Turner is a brilliant bastard. He figured out that Andrew had turned immortal, and he demanded to be induced. The problem was that he had cancer, and that needed to be taken care of first. Kian sent him to Bridget for evaluation, the two fell in love, and the rest is history."

The shortened version left a lot out, but Margaret could ask Bowen to tell her the whole story some other time. Right now, she was more interested in how Turner had transitioned despite the cancer.

"Female immortals don't have fangs and venom. So, who induced Turner?"

"Kian," Vlad said. "Because he's Annani's son, he's the purest immortal we have, and his venom is the most potent. He was Turner's best chance. Also, Annani gave Turner her blessing, which many believe was what helped him pull through."

"A blessing?" Margaret whispered. "Does the goddess have healing powers?"

Leon and Vlad exchanged glances, and then Leon lifted his hands in the air. "Maybe. All I know is that every time she gave her blessing to a transitioning Dormant, it helped."

"Can I petition her to help me?"

Leon nodded. "It would be best if you started your transition while she's here. But since she's supposed to leave a week after Kian's birthday, I doubt that you'll make it in time. Still, if your transition gets dicey, Bowen can plead with her to fly over and give you her blessing."

When the silence that fell over the room was interrupted by another knock on the door, Wendy pushed to her feet. "That must be Stella and Richard." She walked over to the front door and opened it.

"Hello, everyone." Stella swept into the living room with Richard in tow. He was holding a humongous satchel that Margaret was sure had been custom-made. There was no way something that size and that embellished was sold in stores. It had Stella written all over it.

"I brought outfits and accessories galore." Stella stopped in front of Anastasia. "I love the hair." She turned to Margaret. "Yours too."

Wendy laughed. "Are we having a costume party?"

"Something like that." Stella took the satchel from Richard and plopped it on the coffee table. "I heard that you bought evening gowns for the wedding, but I bet that you didn't buy anything for Kian's bimillennial birthday, which is Wednesday. I thought that you could model my designs."

No one had mentioned the birthday, or that Kian was two thousand years old. Margaret hadn't met him yet, and now she was dying of curiosity.

Wrong phrase. She shouldn't mention the word dying in regard to anything until she transitioned successfully.

"Are we even invited to the birthday?" Ana asked.

"Of course." Leon wrapped an arm around her shoulders. "Everyone is. I should have thought about it when you told me that you were shopping for a dress for the wedding."

"Don't worry about it." Stella waved a hand. "I have it covered."

"Is it going to be as formal as the wedding?" Margaret asked.

"A little less."

As Stella started pulling dresses out of her satchel, Richard opened the sliding door to the backyard. "That's our cue, guys."

"Right." Leon walked to the kitchen. "I'll get the beers."

When the sliding door closed behind the men, Stella fluffed out a colorful dress. "This one will look great on you, Margaret. Try it on."

"Now?"

"Yeah." Stella unfurled another one and tossed it at Ana. "Right now, Sari is having her bachelorette party at the building across from the keep, and we were not invited." She pouted. "I figured we could have a party of our own."

"Splendid idea." Ana draped the dress over her shoulder. "I'll try on this beauty and then bring out the wine."

Stella gave her the thumbs up and then pulled a red dress out of the satchel. "I saved the best one for you." She handed it to Wendy.

As the three of them headed to the bedroom to change, Margaret felt tears prickle the back of her eyes.

Happy tears.

Grateful tears.

Life just didn't get any better than this. She had her daughter back, a great guy who loved her, and friends who were like family.

This was worth living for.

"I'm going to attempt the transition," she told Wendy.

"Oh, Mom." Wendy pulled her into her arms. "I've never doubted that you would, not even for a moment. You are a fighter."

341

42

ONEGUS

"Thank you." Onegus took the garment bag from Connor. "You're a life saver. I wouldn't have made it to the village and back on time."

"My pleasure." Connor put a paper bag on the desk and pulled out a Tupperware container. "Have you eaten yet?"

Onegus's mouth watered. "I didn't have time."

"That's what I thought. Dig in." Connor took a look around Onegus's spartan office. "You should spruce this place up a little. It's depressing."

"It's just temporary." Onegus motioned for his roommate to take a seat. "Can I offer you a beer?"

Connor shook his head. "I'm saving the drinking for the wedding. How is your lady getting here?"

"I'm sending one of the Guardians to pick her up." He opened the container and lifted one of the turkey wraps Connor had prepared for him.

"I can do that if you want. I know that your men are all busy guarding our guests."

"That would be a great help. Thank you." Onegus put the wrap down and pulled out his phone. "I'm texting you her address. Just be careful with what you tell her. She doesn't know anything yet."

Shaking his head, Connor glanced at the small fridge that served as Onegus's printer stand. "I think that I'll have that beer after all." He got to his feet and pulled a Snake Venom for himself. "Do you want beer or water?"

"Water. I'm on duty."

"Naturally." Connor put a water bottle on the desk and sat down with his beer. "How are you going to explain to Cassandra what she's about to see?"

"I hope she won't notice. People will have to keep up the pretense because of the human servers, so it's not like she's about to witness a lot of weirdness."

Connor arched a brow. "The servers will clear the banquet hall when Annani enters to preside over the ceremony. Do you think Cassandra will not notice a glowing goddess?"

"I plan to get her tipsy by then." Onegus twisted the cap off the bottle and took a long swig. "Hopefully, she will not notice the peculiarities, and if she does, I'll thrall the memory away."

There was no way Cassandra could miss a glowing goddess, but maybe he could convince her that it was a trick of the light?

"Right." Connor arched a brow. "And how are you going to get her tipsy while overseeing security?"

"Good point. You're seated next to her." Onegus saluted with the bottle. "You'll need to do that for me. I'll also ask Jackson, Roni, and Nick to keep offering her drinks."

"Why don't you just tell her? You must know by now that Cassandra is your one and that she is a Dormant."

"I suspect that she is, but I have a plan for when and how to tell her, and it's not during the wedding."

His eyes glowing with interest, Connor leaned forward. "What's your plan?"

"I'm trying to convince Cassandra to come with me to Paris after the festivities." He shook his head. "I was sure she would be thrilled and that I'd get an enthusiastic yes. But Cassandra is unlike any other woman I know. She said that she needs to think about it."

"And once she agrees, and you take her to Paris, how are you going to tell her?"

"I don't have all the details figured out yet, but I'm thinking a honeymoon suite in an exclusive hotel and a dinner for two on the suite's balcony."

"That's so romantic." Connor snorted. "I bet it wasn't your idea."

"It was Ingrid's. How did you know it wasn't mine?"

"Because you would have taken Cassandra to the cabin and thought that it was the most romantic getaway ever."

"I did suggest that. She got so mad that I had to invite her to the wedding to compensate. She thought that I didn't want to be seen with her, and that's why I chose a secluded cabin for our weekend getaway."

Connor leaned back and crossed his arms over his chest. "She thought that you were a player."

Nodding, Onegus pointed with the wrap at Connor. "The cabin was also Ingrid's idea, but that was a mistake. Next time, I'll come to you for advice."

"As you should. Let me ask you something. After you tell Cassandra the truth over a romantic dinner on the hotel suite's balcony, how are you going to keep her from running out and telling everything to whoever is willing to listen?"

"I didn't get that far. I'll figure something out."

43

KIAN

"This is so nice." Syssi leaned on the cushion Kian had put on her chair. "I love these family gatherings. I wish we all lived in the same place."

Annani reached over the dining table and patted Syssi's hand. "What makes them special is that we do not have them often. It takes a special celebration for us all to congregate in one place. If we were all living in the village, it would not have been as fun."

Kian agreed wholeheartedly, but he was smart enough to keep his mouth shut. Coming from his mother, it wasn't going to offend anyone, but if he dared to say something like that, his mother and sisters would think that he preferred them in small doses. Not that they would be wrong. Other than Alena, they all had big personalities, and having them all in one room was too much.

"Thank you for a lovely breakfast, Mother." Sari pushed to her feet. "But we have a wedding to get ready for, and the hair and makeup team is on its way." She looked at David. "You can stay for a little longer if you wish."

"I'll come with you." He rose to his feet.

"You are not allowed to see me before the wedding."

"That's a silly superstition. But if you want, I can stay in the bedroom and read while you are getting ready."

She smiled at him. "You know that I like you near me at all times."

Jacki leaned over and kissed Kalugal's cheek. "I'll see you tonight." She followed Sari up. "Thank you for inviting us, Clan Mother." She bowed to Annani.

Ronja, Lisa, and Alena also said their thanks and goodbyes, and then the five of them left to meet the beauty team in Sari and David's apartment.

Syssi and Amanda had opted out of the pre-wedding preparations and were going to change into their bridesmaids' dresses at home.

Annani, naturally, didn't require any preparations. There was no improving perfection. She never applied any makeup or styled her hair.

344

"How is Ronja dealing with Bowen finding his mate?" Annani asked.

"I'm not sure she knows." Syssi adjusted the pillow at her back.

"I thought that there was something going on between them, but I'm starting to doubt it." Amanda put her empty coffee cup down. "Ronja didn't even ask where he was and what he's been doing during the time he was gone."

Annani let out a relieved breath. "Good. I like her, and I do not want to see her hurt again. Ronja deserves a break." She looked at Kian. "Is there anyone else other than Bowen who's showing interest in her?"

"I'm not the right person to ask. Matchmaking is Amanda's department."

"She's friendly with many people," Amanda said. "But as far as I know, she isn't interested in anyone."

"That is a shame." Annani motioned for Ojidu to refill her coffee cup. "I would like her to attempt transition."

Kian had a feeling that was where Annani had been going. "Regrettably, she's too old, and it's too risky."

Annani leveled her eyes at him. "I will be there for her. I will give her my blessing, if needed, more than once."

Translation, his mother was willing to give Ronja more than one transfusion of her blood to help her transition. It might be enough, and it might not be. The risk was too high in his opinion. Besides, Ronja hadn't expressed an interest in transitioning.

Then again, as far as she knew, it wasn't an option for her, so she might have just resigned herself to mortality.

In any case, as much as Kian would have liked for his mother to have her new friend around forever, he wasn't willing to risk Ronja's life for that.

"Even if that was in the cards, Mother, Ronja needs to find a mate first," he said gently. "And she doesn't seem ready to get involved with anyone yet. She's still grieving for her husband."

"Yes, well." Annani dropped a cube of sugar into the coffee Ojidu had refilled and stirred it with a small silver spoon. "Normally, a year of grieving is to be expected, but Ronja is not getting any younger." She looked at Amanda. "Perhaps you can find her someone? You are so good at matchmaking."

"I'll see what I can do," Amanda said without much conviction.

If Annani noticed, she didn't let it show. "I will talk with Ronja and gauge her interest. Perhaps she has noticed someone but did not think it was appropriate for her to befriend a male so soon after Frank's passing."

"I'm so happy for Wendy," Syssi changed the subject. "Finding her mother must have brought her so much joy."

"I've thought of something," Dalhu said.

He usually spoke so rarely that everyone turned to hear what he had to say.

"If Emmett had sex with Margaret during the years she lived in Safe Haven, and I assume that he did, then it's proof that the Kra-ell don't have the ability to induce transition in Dormants." He looked at Kian. "From what I heard, everyone in there was checked for STDs, and the women received contraceptive shots. Therefore, there was no need for anyone to use condoms."

Kian had already deduced as much.

"What about the bond?" Amanda asked. "Perhaps Margaret didn't transition because there was no bond between her and Emmett."

Dalhu shook his head. "That's my point. We can't be sure that a bond is needed. Eleanor transitioned without a bond, and so did Eva."

"I've given it some thought." Amanda crossed her arms over her small belly. "Maybe it's only needed for those whose genes are highly diluted."

"Like me?" Syssi challenged.

"I don't think yours are weak. You are a strong seer, and Andrew is the only infallible lie-detector the clan has."

Syssi grimaced. "At least Andrew's gift is useful. My visions are mostly useless. The only time they were actually helpful was when I summoned a vision to find Ronja and Frank."

"You also saw the Kra-ell in a vision." Kian took her hand. "Once our baby is born, you can go back to training with Madam what's-her-name. What she taught you seemed to help with locating David's parents."

"Madam Salinka," Syssi reminded him.

"Yes, her."

"You want me to go back to training with her?"

"Only if you want to."

44

CASSANDRA

"You look so beautiful and classy." Misted with tears, Geraldine's eyes were full of pride. "My Cassandra." She wiped at them, smearing her mascara.

"Oh, Mom." Cassandra dipped her head and kissed her mother's cheek. "You always say that, and you always cry when you do."

Her mother wiped at her cheek even though Cassandra's lipstick was the kind that didn't come off. "That's because it's true, and seeing the amazing woman I raised fills my heart with pride and joy. But you still didn't tell me what's the occasion." She trailed her eyes over the floor-length black evening dress. "You are not dressed for just a date on the town."

It was so like her mother to get all emotional and yet notice everything. Despite her memory issues, there was no fooling Geraldine Beaumont.

"It's a private event, and Onegus made me promise not to tell anyone about it. I even had to lie to Kevin and tell him that I needed a day off because of a doctor's appointment. I couldn't tell him that I needed to go shopping for a dress for another event."

Geraldine was no stranger to secrets, and she didn't press for details. "Is Onegus picking you up?"

"He's sending someone. The event is so secret that he couldn't even tell me where it is."

Her mother glanced at her small evening purse. "I hope you have your phone with you."

"I'm sure he'll ask me to put it in airplane mode."

Geraldine waved a dismissive hand. "That doesn't prevent it from being tracked. He'll probably ask you to turn it off completely."

Cassandra narrowed her eyes at her mother. "How do you know that?"

"I read it in one of my billionaire romance novels and then checked the internet to see if it was true. It was."

As the house phone rang, Cassandra kissed her mother's cheek one more time. "That's probably Connor. Tell the guard to let him in."

She opened the door and walked out. The guy was doing Onegus a favor. She couldn't expect him to get out of the car and escort her out of her house like a prom queen.

Except, Connor was a gentleman, and as soon as he pulled up to her house and killed the engine, he got out and offered her his hand. "Hello, Cassandra. It's a pleasure to finally meet you."

"Same here." She shook his hand.

Connor matched how she'd imagined a score composer would look, only much more handsome. His shoulder-length dark brown hair curled at the bottom, framing a slim, smiling face with lush lips and merry blue-gray eyes. With her stilettos on, she was a couple of inches taller than him, which meant that without shoes, they were about the same height.

He opened the passenger door for her. "Onegus apologizes for not being able to pick you up himself."

"Does he?" Cassandra slid into the seat, careful not to snag her long dress.

"He would have if he weren't so busy."

"I want to tell Josie that I met you in person, but Onegus made such a big deal out of keeping this wedding a secret that I don't know what I'm allowed to disclose."

"You'd better not mention it." He smiled at her tightly. "I'm sure we will have many more opportunities to meet that you could tell Josie about."

She'd expected Connor to make light of Onegus's worries about the risk from some ancient enemies of his clan, but Connor seemed just as concerned.

As they reached the downtown area, Cassandra was surprised when Connor turned into the parking structure of the same building Onegus had brought her to.

"The wedding is in this building?"

"No, we are just using it for parking. A shuttle will take us to the venue."

Two guards stood at the entrance, and Connor stopped next to them. "This will take just a moment." He lowered the window. "Good evening, gentlemen."

The guy ignored Connor and looked only at her. "Who's your guest, Connor?"

"This is Cassandra, the chief's friend."

The guy nodded. "Good evening, ma'am." He motioned for Connor to move on.

"Onegus is the chief?"

Connor arched a brow. "He didn't tell you?"

"He told me that he's overseeing security for this wedding. What is he chief of?"

"You will have to ask him. It's not my place to say."

She rolled her eyes. Everything was steeped in so much mystery, and she wondered if it was really necessary.

On the way down the spiraling interior lane of the parking structure, she'd seen two more guards, and that was in addition to the cameras mounted on the walls in intervals of no more than ten feet.

"That's some serious security."

Connor cast her an apologetic sidelong glance. "Better safe than sorry, right?" He smiled. "Or the term that is now in vogue, out of an abundance of caution."

"In general, I'm all for caution, but this seems fit for a presidential visit."

For some reason, Connor found her answer amusing.

"Yeah, it does, doesn't it?"

The lowest level of the parking garage had its own gate, but it parted as soon as Connor pulled up to it. Did he live in the building?

Onegus had said that he and Connor shared a house, and that he was staying in the building only temporarily. Had he lied about that?

"How did the gate open? Do you have a sticker that allows you access?"

"I don't, but there is a camera up there." He pointed. "The people in the security office were notified of my arrival by the guards at the entrance. They read the car's license plate and opened the gate for me."

"Oh."

As he pulled in and the gate started closing, another car arrived, and the gate retracted once more.

Watching it in the rearview mirror, Cassandra didn't notice Onegus until Connor stopped the car.

He opened the door for her. "Good evening, gorgeous." He offered her a hand up.

Scanning her from head to toe as she straightened, Onegus let out a whistle. "I'm going to be the envy of every bachelor attending the event. How am I going to manage security tonight while keeping them away from you?"

Smiling, she leaned and kissed his cheek. "Don't worry about me. I'll put on my resting bitch face, and no one will dare to approach me."

"Don't forget me," Connor said. "I'll keep Cassandra safe."

"Come on." Onegus took her hand. "Let's find you a good seat before the transport gets full."

"What transport?" There were no buses or limousines waiting to shuttle guests from the parking garage to the venue.

"It's through that door." Onegus tugged on her hand.

Perhaps there was another garage on the other side or a corridor leading to the garage of the adjacent building.

Behind them, merry voices and the staccato of heels hitting concrete announced more guests arriving. Curiosity getting the better of her, Cassandra looked over her shoulder.

Two couples, but she wasn't sure who was with whom. The women were both beautiful and beautifully dressed, and they were holding hands. The two men walking behind them were no less good looking, and they were talking about some building project they were involved in.

"Are those relatives of yours?" she asked Onegus as he opened the door.

He glanced at the four. "Everyone attending tonight is in some way extended family. Even those two." He motioned with his chin at the men.

She wondered what he'd meant by that. Perhaps the men were more distant family. Second and third cousins. Or perhaps they'd just married into the family.

"Your chariot, ma'am." Onegus waved his hand at the so-called transport.

It was a long golf cart that looked like a golf limousine. She couldn't see inside, but it was long enough to seat eight people. The canopy enclosing the interior was decorated with ribbons and flowers and glitter, and a large banner hung at the back that said 'Sari and David are getting married.'

She chuckled. "That's my chariot? Does it turn into a pumpkin at midnight?"

"The celebration will last long into the night." Onegus offered her a hand up. "It can't turn back into a pumpkin before five o'clock in the morning."

He climbed in behind her, and the two of them sat at the back. Connor got in next, and then the four who had arrived behind them.

The driver's seat was separated from the back by a partition, just like it would be in a limousine, and the decorations covering nearly every inch of the canopy made it impossible to see what was outside the cart.

One of the women turned around with a face-splitting grin and offered her a hand. "Hi, I'm Gwen."

"Cassandra." She shook the hand she was offered. "It's nice to meet you."

"The pleasure is all mine." Gwen cast Onegus a knowing smirk. "Good luck."

"With what?" Cassandra asked.

"Taming Onegus, of course." She winked.

When he glared at her, Gwen giggled and covered her mouth with her hand.

"Ignore my nosy cousins." He took Cassandra's hand and held it in his lap. "It would seem that they've already started drinking."

45

ONEGUS

*D*uring the ride in the golf cart, Cassandra had chatted with Gwen and Elaine about this and that, the two doing an admirable job of keeping her too busy to notice where the cart was going, while avoiding incriminating topics.

When the cart finally stopped at the keep's underground garage, Gwen wiped invisible sweat from her forehead and mouthed behind Cassandra's back, *you owe Elaine and me for this.*

He dipped his head in acknowledgment.

"Where are we?" Cassandra asked.

The entire elevator bank was decorated for the wedding, with flowers and balloons and banners.

He pressed his thumb to the elevator button. "It's a portal to a fairytale land."

"It would appear so." Cassandra's forehead furrowed. "Did the button just scan your finger?"

"It did."

As the doors opened, he ushered her inside. Even the interior of the cabin hadn't escaped the attention of the overenthusiastic decorators. A large poster hung over the mirror with a picture of Sari and David kissing inside a big cutout heart, but just their silhouettes, so no one outside the clan could guess who they were.

Cassandra gave the poster a perfunctory glance before turning to him. "So, if I want to call the elevator, I can't?"

"Correct."

"What about them?" She waved her hand at Connor and the rest of their group.

"Every member of the family has their fingerprints taken and inputted into the system. They can all summon the elevator."

And that even included Kalugal's men, which Onegus wasn't entirely

351

comfortable with, but he was aware that his feelings on the subject were irrational.

They didn't pose a security risk.

If they had, they would have never been admitted into the village. But they were former Doomers, and he could never bring himself to trust them completely and without reservation.

"You are really taking security measures to the extreme."

Connor chuckled. "You've seen nothing yet."

"Show me." Cassandra looked up at Onegus. "Unless I'm not allowed to know that either."

She was irritated, and the energy swirling just under the surface was starting to crackle. Hopefully, it wouldn't affect the elevator's mechanism. If her energy operated like Sylvia's, just without the control, it might damage electronics.

Thankfully, they reached the banquet hall level without incident, and as the elevator doors opened, the noise of music and conversations was a welcome distraction.

Onegus put his hand on the small of Cassandra's back and led her to the table he'd chosen for them.

Sylvia and Roni were already there, and so were Nick and Ruth. Sharon, Robert, Jackson, and Tessa hadn't arrived yet.

The seating arrangement covered three objectives. First of all, except for Connor, every male at the table was mated, so no one would flirt with Cassandra. Secondly, most of them were either young immortals or newly transitioned Dormants. They were the least likely group to make Cassandra suspicious because they knew what to be careful about. And thirdly, he'd asked Sylvia to keep an eye out for Cassandra's strange energy and see if it felt similar to hers.

He'd explained the situation to them and had asked for their cooperation. Nick, who had attended Eva's wedding while still human, had been drunk through the entire party thanks to Jackson. He promised to goad Cassandra into doing the same, or at least getting tipsy.

Pulling a chair out for her, Onegus made the introductions. "Sylvia, Roni, Nick, and Ruth." He helped push her chair back in place. "Please meet Cassandra, my girlfriend."

The round table was too big to reach over and shake hands, so they either dipped their heads or waved as Onegus said their names, and Cassandra smiled and waved back.

The term girlfriend seemed so wrong in the context of what Cassandra was to him, but that was what she expected him to say.

As he sat down next to her, she put a hand on his thigh and leaned closer. "Are they your cousins?"

"Sylvia and Ruth are, while Roni and Nick are their partners."

Partners was a much better term than boyfriends, and maybe if he used it enough when talking about members of his family, Cassandra would deem it more appropriate than girlfriend as well.

"The reason I asked was that Roni seems familiar. I can't put my finger on it, but I know that I've seen him somewhere."

The kid had been on the news when he'd been caught hacking into the government confidential records, but Onegus didn't remember whether Roni's picture had been made public. If it had, Cassandra might have seen it. After the clan had helped him escape, there had been an APB on him, but he doubted it had been available for civilians to see.

"He might look like someone you know." Onegus sighed. "I wish I could stay, but I need to continue making rounds until all the guests arrive." He pushed to his feet. "Can I get you something from the bar?"

"No thanks." Cassandra reached for the water pitcher. "I'll stick to water for now."

"Allow me." Connor took it and poured her a glass.

"Who drinks water at a wedding?" Nick asked. "And a Scottish wedding at that. Everyone has to get drunk." He filled Cassandra's wine glass to the brim. "That's the tradition."

She lifted her eyes to Onegus. "Is it?"

"I'm afraid so." He patted her shoulder. "I'll be back as soon as I can."

46

ELEANOR

*A*lfie leaned over Eleanor's shoulder to look at the screen. "He's still reading?"

"What else do you expect him to do?"

She'd been watching Emmett for hours, waiting for the moments when he lifted his eyes to the surveillance camera, his intense gaze seemingly caressing her.

Did he feel her eyes on him?

Was that why he glanced at the camera every so often?

"He can watch television, play video games, or do some exercise." Alfie pointed to the pull-up bar he'd hung over the bedroom doorway.

He and the other Guardians used the contraption to do endless pull-ups, and even Eleanor had gotten in some during her shifts.

"You can't give him one of those because he could use it as a weapon."

"True, but he can do push-ups, lunges, and sit-ups. All he's doing is sitting on his butt all day and reading. At this rate, his muscles will atrophy."

That would be a shame. Emmett wasn't as buff as Alfie or the other Guardians, but he was lean and toned, just the way she liked it.

"Do you want to go in and keep him company?" Alfie asked.

Frowning, she turned to look at the Guardian. "I delivered his dinner two hours ago. I have no reason to go in again."

Arwel had decided against leaving her alone to guard Emmett, and Alfie had volunteered to stay with her. Apparently, the guy didn't like parties, and he didn't mind missing the wedding. Still, Peter had warned them to be extra careful. Everyone else was at the wedding, and although they could get to the dungeon level in minutes, no one wanted their fun interrupted.

Alfie shrugged. "I thought you wanted to spend time with him."

They all knew about her plan to befriend Emmett, and they also knew that her interest in him was not only professional. But Eleanor wasn't an exhibitionist, and there was no way they would let her be with him without the surveillance.

"I do," she admitted. "But I can't."

"You can." Alfie put a hand on her shoulder. "I'll keep an eye on you."

She snorted. "Are you hoping for a porn show?"

His smirk was confirmation enough. "I've watched you with him. He wants you, and you want him. What are you waiting for?"

She grimaced. "Privacy. I'm not an exhibitionist."

Alfie plopped down on the couch next to her. "I wish I could give you that, but it's not safe. The sound is already muted because I don't want to wear the damn earpieces all day long, but I have to watch."

She sighed. "I know."

"There is no camera in the bathroom…"

Eleanor cast him a disgusted sidelong glance. "That's gross. I'm not that desperate."

"It doesn't have to be. I've taken women into club restrooms—ladies' rooms, mind you, not the men's. Those are just as gross as you imagine. I've done it in closets, pantries, hallways, dark niches, you name it. It was exciting, for them and for me." He waggled his brows. "You should try it."

She shook her head. "The ladies' room might be cleaner than the men's, but it's still gross."

"You can always find at least one clean wall, and I'm sure that Emmett keeps the bathroom clean. He's not the messy type."

She'd noticed and liked that about him.

"I can't believe I'm having this conversation with you."

Eleanor was slowly losing her human inhibitions and adopting the immortals' attitude toward sex. Most of the change had occurred during the mission with Peter and Leon. To be treated as part of the team, she needed to act like a Guardian, and the only female example she had was Kri. The woman was as direct and as blunt about sex as any of the guys. Thankfully, the Guardians weren't crass or lewd. But they were unapologetic about their sexuality, and sometimes their talk still made her uncomfortable.

"Who else could you talk to?" Alfie waved a hand. "We are the only ones here, which is a golden opportunity for you to do what you want. I doubt you'd have the guts to go for it with Arwel or Peter watching."

He was right, but she really didn't want her first time with Emmett to be in the tiny bathroom.

"There must be another way. If it's okay for me to have sex with him in the bathroom, where you can't see us, then why not do it in the bed while you are not looking? I don't see a difference as far as security goes, but it will make a big difference to me."

Frowning, Alfie scratched his stubble. "Maybe there is a way. I can turn the screen brightness all the way down, so when you turn the lights off, I won't be able to see anything. And if you sense trouble, just say lights on."

She snorted. "If I can. The one time that Emmett bit me, I was helpless to do anything. I felt paralyzed."

Alfie's expression turned exasperated. "Do you want to do it or not? I can solve all your problems by going in with you. I wouldn't mind a threesome."

"Right." She narrowed her eyes at him. "Even if I was into that, how would you hold a gun while participating?"

His smile was lupine. "Oh, I know precisely how I would do that. Do you want me to describe the scene to you?"

She lifted a hand to stop him. "No need."

It was as if he had planted the image in her head, and she could see it. Her on all fours with Alfie in front of her, holding a gun trained on Emmett, who was thrusting into her from behind.

Alfie's nostrils flared, and his lupine smile turned into a hyena grin. "Evidently, you caught my drift."

47

CASSANDRA

$\mathcal{A}$s the guests continued to arrive, Cassandra realized what had been bothering her about Onegus's family. They all looked to be around the same age—mid-twenties to mid-thirties.

Where were the parents? The grandparents?

Perhaps Onegus's family had a respect-your-elders tradition, dictating that the young people had to be on time while the older generation arrived later. A Korean friend told her that she wasn't allowed to leave the dining table before anyone older than her, even by a month, was either done or gave her permission to leave. Different cultures had different traditions.

There were almost no children either.

She'd seen one cute toddler girl running around, one teenage boy who looked to be fourteen or fifteen, and one couple came with a stroller. But that was less odd than the missing elder generation. It was after nine in the evening, and the event hadn't started yet, so it made sense that nearly no one had brought their kids. The two exceptions probably couldn't find a babysitter for tonight.

When and if Cassandra got married, she would have a day wedding, so all the children could attend. A family should celebrate together, the young and the old.

Leaning closer to Connor, she asked, "Where are all the old people?"

"Gone," he deadpanned.

She rolled her eyes. "I'm serious. Where are the mothers and fathers, uncles and aunts, grandmothers and grandfathers? Were they not invited?"

Connor shrugged but didn't offer an answer.

"More wine?" Nick refilled her glass without waiting for her response.

Roni, who'd been eyeing her with the same curiosity she'd been eyeing him, rose to his feet. "Wine is boring. I'm going to the bar. Can I get you anything?" he asked her.

He hadn't asked anyone else.

Were they all trying to get her drunk for some reason?

"Thanks, but I'm fine with the wine." She lifted the glass to her lips and pretended to take a sip.

Maybe she should dump it in one of the flower arrangements and pretend to be drunk, so they would show their hand.

"I'll ask the bartender to mix you the same drink Sylvia and Ruth like."

So that was why he hadn't asked them. He knew what they wanted. Cassandra felt silly for being so suspicious, but she couldn't shake the feeling that something wasn't right, and it wasn't only about the missing older generation.

"Thank you. I'll give it a try."

As Roni walked away, a stunning brunette sauntered toward their table. She had a gorgeous face, eyes of such vivid blue that they must have been contact lenses, and lips that were painted red. The dress she wore was an Oscar de la Renta gold-hued gown from his latest collection. Cassandra had seen it in a fashion magazine and had ogled it, but the only way she would have bought it was if she found it in her favorite, used designer attire boutique. It cost a small fortune, and it was too showy even for the gala she'd attended.

The Grecian style loose gown was fit for the goddess-like creature wearing it.

It accentuated rather than tried to conceal the woman's pregnant belly, and it was also definitely the original and not a knockoff.

"You must be Cassandra." The woman sat on the chair Onegus had vacated. "I'm Amanda, one of Onegus's many cousins." She offered Cassandra her hand.

"Hi." She shook it. "I love your dress. Oscar de la Renta, right?"

"You have a good eye." Amanda grinned. "I'm so happy that Onegus is dating a fashionista. I will finally have someone to play with." She leaned closer and smoothed her hand over the skirt of Cassandra's dress. "And yours is a Versace. I had one just like it, but I donated it to charity." She smiled sheepishly. "I tire of outfits after wearing them only a few times, and I donate them to charity, so I don't feel as guilty for buying them in the first place."

Cassandra felt her ears heat up, and it had nothing to do with the wine. Well, perhaps the wine was partially responsible for her reaction, turning it from mild to exasperated.

Her anger wasn't directed at Amanda, though. She was mad at herself.

The gown was indeed Versace, but it was a three-year-old one that she'd bought second-hand. Most people wouldn't have noticed, but Amanda was precisely the type of woman who would.

Unlike the gala dress, which had been made by an unknown designer, the one she was wearing now was recognizable by anyone who followed fashion shows and magazines.

She should have considered that Onegus's family was rich, and that some of the ladies were bound to be fashionistas like Amanda. The best way to deal with that was not to try to cover it up, but to own it and turn it to her advantage.

Cassandra had nothing to be embarrassed about. In fact, she was proud of herself for being frugal. It wasn't as if she couldn't afford to buy the latest Versace. She just didn't want to spend so much on a dress that she would wear only once.

"It might be yours." Cassandra smoothed her hand over the straight skirt. "I got it in my favorite secondhand designer attire boutique."

For a long and awkward moment, Amanda and everyone else around the table didn't say a thing. Averting their eyes, they were probably desperately searching for something non-offensive and politically correct to say.

As the silence became oppressive, Cassandra took pity on them. "I like designer clothing. I love the precise cuts, the luxurious fabrics, and I get pleasure from wearing something that was created by a true artist. I just don't like the price tags attached to those beautiful outfits. Finding them on sale or buying a gown that was used only once satisfies the bargain hunter in me as well as the fashion junkie. It's a win-win." She smirked. "It gives me immense satisfaction knowing that I'm dressed to the nines but at a fraction of the cost."

Amanda laughed. "You have to meet my sister-in-law. Syssi can't stomach paying more than a couple of hundred for an outfit. The only time I saw her lose her cool and raise her voice at me was when I took her shopping in an exclusive boutique and bought her an entire wardrobe." She stood up and motioned for Cassandra to join her. "Come. I'll introduce you."

Reluctantly, Cassandra followed, expecting to be led to one of the nearby tables. Instead, Amanda kept walking toward the front of the banquet hall and stopped in front of a long, rectangular table, the only one in the room that wasn't round.

The bride and groom's family table.

"Everyone, this is Cassandra, Onegus's date for this evening and probably for many more to come." She walked up to the most beautiful man Cassandra had ever seen and put her hands on his shoulders. "This is my brother, Kian."

The god-like creature dipped his head in greeting but didn't smile.

Cassandra felt like offering a curtsy, but she stifled the impulse and forced a smile. "It's a pleasure to meet you."

"And this is his wife, Syssi." Amanda moved to a very pregnant blonde, who was smiling broadly and seemed like a sweetheart of a person.

"Nice to meet you, Cassandra," Syssi said. "I've seen your and Onegus's pictures in the gossip magazines, but you are even more impressive in person than in those articles."

"Thank you." Cassandra fanned herself. "You are making me blush." She looked at the other couples sitting at the family table. "Where are the bride and groom?"

"They are getting ready," Amanda said. "My sister Sari is the bride, and my other sister Alena is with her and the other bridesmaids." She rubbed a hand over her belly. "I figured that Sari had enough bridesmaids already so the pregnant ladies could sit this one out." She winked at Syssi.

The woman winced. "I can barely walk. I feel like a beached whale."

Cassandra laughed. "When are you due?"

"In three weeks."

"Good luck."

"Thanks." Syssi smiled. "I can't wait to meet my daughter."

"I bet."

The eyes of the terrifying god-like creature sitting beside Syssi softened, and he draped a gentle arm around his wife's shoulders. "All in good time."

"Anyway," Amanda said. "I wanted the two of you to meet because you have something in common."

Syssi arched a brow. "We are both artistic?"

"Well, yes, that too. But I'm referring to being frugal. Cassandra manages to look fabulous without spending a fortune on it like I do."

That was a nice way to put it.

Syssi chuckled. "No one spends as much as Amanda does. And in my case, it's hard to look fabulous when I'm the size of a whale."

"You're beautiful," her husband said.

"He's right." Cassandra offered the couple her best smile. "I should go back to my table. It was nice meeting you."

When Amanda escorted her back to her companions, the waiter arrived with another round of drinks for everyone.

"I ordered you a lychee martini," Roni said.

Cassandra grimaced. "It looks tasty, but I'm already a little tipsy. I don't think I should drink anymore."

"It's tradition to get drunk at a Scottish wedding." Amanda patted her shoulder. "Regrettably, Syssi and I will have to remain sober. You'll have to drink for both of us."

Lifting the goblet, Cassandra smiled. "When in Rome and all that. To the happy couple." She took a small sip.

48

KIAN

$\mathcal{K}$ ian watched Cassandra leave with Amanda and wondered who she reminded him of. Shuffling through two thousand years of memories wasn't an easy task, and after a couple of minutes, he gave up.

He might have seen her face in an advertisement back in the day.

Cassandra was a beautiful woman, and according to Onegus, she'd modeled for the cosmetics company she was still working for. So, it was possible that Cassandra simply reminded him of her younger self.

The thing was that her attitude seemed familiar as well.

She was confident to the point of being arrogant, and unlike most people, she hadn't been intimidated by him. No wonder that Onegus had fallen for her.

The chief needed a strong woman to stand up to him.

Onegus fooled most people with his easy smiles and his charm, but he was the chief of Guardians for a reason. He was a true commander, a great strategist, and he was also a stubborn bastard who didn't yield to pressure and didn't take bullshit from anyone. Not from Kian and not from Turner.

Cassandra was his match. The language she used was polite and eloquent, but she was a straight shooter who didn't mince words.

"Did you feel it?" Syssi asked.

"Feel what?"

"The energy coming off Cassandra." She smoothed her hand over her hair. "I felt my hair stand up on end."

"It didn't. You must have imagined it."

"I felt it too," Kalugal said. "But then I might have reacted to her feminine beauty."

"Do you miss your bachelor days?" Syssi asked.

"Not at all." Kalugal straightened in his chair. "So, who's the lady, and why did Onegus invite a human to the wedding?"

"He thinks she might be a Dormant, and he wants Sylvia to check out her

361

power, or at least that's the excuse he gave me. He thinks that the energy Cassandra has is similar to Sylvia's, but she doesn't know how to harness and direct it."

Kalugal looked confused. "Does Cassandra know that she's a potential Dormant?"

"She doesn't." Kian took a sip from his water goblet. "Onegus didn't tell her yet. He figured it was safe to bring her to the wedding because other humans would be here as well, and we couldn't do anything overly suspicious anyway."

Kalugal leaned back and pursed his lips. "Onegus could've asked me to compel her silence. Heck, even Eleanor could have done it. Why risk it?"

Kian put down his goblet none too gently, and some of the water splashed out. Stifling a curse, he wiped it off his sleeve. "He gave me some bullshit explanation about not being ready to involve others in his business. But by inviting her here, he involved all of us."

"I'll ask Lisa to sniff her," Syssi said. "I wish she was here."

Lisa and Ronja were part of Sari's entourage of bridesmaids, which was the size of a small army. His sister had a big heart, and she wanted to honor as many of the females close to her as she could. He suspected that Amanda and Syssi had bowed out so others could take their place.

That reminded him that he and Kalugal needed to take their places. Glancing at his watch, he turned to his cousin. "It's time." The groomsmen were supposed to meet outside the banquet hall in a few minutes.

He leaned and kissed Syssi's cheek. "Don't cry."

She got emotional at weddings, and the pregnancy made her even more vulnerable. Usually, Syssi found comfort in his arms, but he wouldn't be near her to offer it during the ceremony.

"I won't." She smiled at him. "Sari and David are already mated. This is just a party."

"Try to remember that when Annani makes her speech." His mother had a talent for tear-jerking.

"Don't worry." Syssi affected a wider smile. "Go already." She gave him a gentle push. "Stop hovering over me like a mother hen."

Pushing to his feet, he turned toward the room's double doors. Brundar and Anandur were already waiting for him there, not to guard him, but to join the other groomsmen.

"I wish Lokan was here," Kalugal said as they walked toward the door.

"Yeah, me too." Kian actually meant it. "And your mother as well. I wish there was a way to convince her to leave your father."

Kalugal sighed softly. "It's a lost cause. I stopped trying a long time ago."

"Do you still talk to her?"

"Twice a week."

"How is she?"

"Same as always. Loving, gentle, and totally misguided."

49

CASSANDRA

"So, I told the wife," Sharon leaned back and crossed her arms over her chest. "Your husband is not cheating on you with his secretary. He's cheating on you with his business partner."

Cassandra was still waiting for the punchline to Sharon's story. What did it matter who the husband cheated with?

"What did the wife say?" Roni asked.

"She rolled her eyes and said that she'd known the two had been lovers since college. She didn't mind, and the woman was so happy that he wasn't schtupping the secretary that she paid us a bonus."

Cassandra shook her head. "So, she didn't mind the one lover, but hired your firm to investigate whether there was a second one?"

"Yep," Sharon confirmed. "Humans are strange." She leaned toward Robert. "I can hardly stand it if Robert so much as looks at another woman with appreciation."

He wrapped his arm around her shoulders. "I only have eyes for you, my love."

Connor chuckled. "Let me guess. The partner was a guy, and that's why the wife was okay with it."

Cassandra was still stuck on Sharon's use of the word humans. Was that the new politically correct term for people? Cassandra couldn't for the life of her imagine what was wrong with 'people,' but these were strange times. Perhaps someone had decided that the word people was racist?

Could be.

After all, people might be from different ethnicities, but they were all human. She needed to remember that.

"Some people can be polyamorous," Tessa said. "Personally, I can't imagine living like that, but for some, it comes naturally."

Cassandra let out a breath. Apparently, the word people was still okay.

For now.

"Like the Kra-ell," Nick said and then winced. "I mean the Krall in the game."

"What game?" Cassandra asked.

"Have you heard about the Perfect Match Virtual Adventures Studios?" Ruth asked.

"I've heard about them, and I thought that it was all a big hype. Virtual technology is amazing, but it is still far from being realistic."

"It is very much so," Roni said. "If you ever get tired of Onegus, give it a try. It's pricey, but you can cram a two-week vacation into three hours. It's hard to beat that when you have a busy job."

"You don't have to dump Onegus to try," Sylvia said. "You can do it with him. Roni and I did it together, and it was the most fun we've ever had. We chose the winter spy adventure."

Roni smiled at his girlfriend. "We were already together when we went on the virtual spy adventure, but Cassandra and Onegus are not there yet." He turned to Cassandra and winked. "After all, it's called the Perfect Match for a reason. The software can find you a better match than him."

Roni had a sarcastic sense of humor that resonated well with hers. She lifted the wine glass Nick had just refilled and pretended to take a sip. "If things don't work out with Onegus, I'll give it a try."

He still hadn't made good on his promise to introduce her to his mother. In fact, he hadn't come to check on her at all. He'd said that he would join her after all the guests had arrived, but it seemed like every chair in the banquet hall was filled, and Onegus was still a no-show.

"Jackson and I need to give it a try," Tessa said. "But I'm scared. What if I don't like the adventure?"

"The technician is there to monitor you," Sylvia said. "If you get distressed, they will wake you up."

As the group continued discussing the wonders of virtual adventures, Cassandra listened with only half an ear. Not that the subject was boring, but observing her young companions was more interesting.

They were all about the same age as the snowflakes in her creative department, but they were completely different kinds of people. They all seemed to have busy careers, and Jackson, who looked no older than twenty, ran his own successful business.

The kid worked even harder than she did, and yet he couldn't be happier. He was excited to see his business grow and had no problem with the long hours he had to put into it. Naturally, his girlfriend wasn't happy about him working all of the time, but she accepted it as a temporary situation only until Jackson's business got big enough for him to delegate more of the work to others.

Cassandra had a feeling that Tessa would be waiting a long time. The guy's ambition would drive him to open yet another business and then another. At some point, though, he might get tired of the race and slow down.

The thing was, none of them complained about having to work too hard or about slights and offenses in the workplace, and for the first time in a very long time, Cassandra felt comfortable to speak her mind without having to double-check every word.

In fact, she felt like she was among longtime friends.

"Why aren't Vlad and Wendy sitting with us?" Tessa asked.

Jackson leaned back to scan the other tables, his chair perching precariously on its rear legs. "I see them sitting with Stella and Richard, Wendy's mom, Bowen, Leon, and the new girl. I don't know her name. Stella's mom is with them as well, as are Bowen and Leon's mothers. They have a full table." He leaned back.

Mothers? Cassandra glanced in the direction Jackson had looked, but she could see no one older than thirty-something. They either had an in-house plastic surgeon, or she'd stumbled into a nest of vampires.

She looked at her nearly empty glass. Perhaps she'd had too much to drink already, and her vision was blurry.

"Why isn't your mother sitting with us?" Tessa asked.

Jackson shrugged. "She decided to sit with Kalugal's men to keep them company so they wouldn't feel out of place. You know how she is. My mother always finds someone in need of help."

Cassandra emptied what was left of her glass. If mothers were supposed to sit with their children, then why wasn't Onegus's mother sitting at their table?

It wasn't that she particularly wanted her there, but she had to wonder why Onegus had chosen to seat her elsewhere.

Who had he thought to protect?

Her or his mother?

50

MARGARET

*B*owen's mother, a lovely woman named Elise who looked unnervingly young, held on to Margaret's hand as if she was afraid to lose her. "I'm giddy with joy that my Bowen found a mate." Using different words, she'd said the same thing at least ten times.

Margaret wondered if Elise would have been as happy if she knew about her past—a drug addict who had abandoned her baby daughter and hadn't gone back to look for her.

Wendy had forgiven her, but Margaret still had a hard time forgiving herself.

If what they had said about Emmett was true, then it really hadn't been her fault, but even that wasn't enough to eradicate her guilt. She should have fought harder.

Wendy had called her a fighter, but she wasn't. The best term Margaret could apply to herself was a survivor.

Leon's mother, Rowan, was more reserved than Elise. She snuck glances at Ana, and the two chatted a little about how Leon and Ana had met, but Rowan wasn't holding Ana's hand or gushing how happy she was that Leon had found a mate.

It was ironic. Leon had snagged himself a young, beautiful heiress, who was well educated and had no skeletons in her closet, but his mother wasn't over-joyed. Bowen was saddled with a former drug addict, abuse victim, and child abandoner, and his mother couldn't be happier.

Fate had a twisted sense of humor.

"Where is Eleanor?" Ana asked Leon. "I want to say hi, but I don't see her."

"She volunteered to guard Emmett," Bowen said.

Stella huffed out a breath. "I'm not surprised. Greggory is here, and he's sitting next to Vanessa. Eleanor would not have liked seeing that."

"Can you tell me more about Eleanor?" Leon's mother said. "I was under the impression that Kian wasn't at all happy to let her into the village, and now she's assigned guard duties?"

Bowen answered Rowan. "Eleanor helped Leon and Peter get Anastasia out of Safe Haven, and she was also instrumental in unmasking Emmett Haderech, the cult's leader. She's proven herself as not only trustworthy but also capable. Kian authorized her inclusion in the Guardian training program."

Stella snorted. "He must be desperate for new trainees to let her into the program. I don't trust her."

"Why?" Margaret asked. "I met Eleanor, and she might be rough around the edges, but she was nice to me, and Peter seemed to like her."

"Peter likes everybody," Elise said. "He has a good heart."

Margaret smiled at Bowen. "No one has a better heart than your son."

"I know." Elise smiled. "He was such an unruly child that I still can't believe what a good male he became."

Bowen had been a troublemaker?

"Is that true?" She looked at his smiling eyes.

He nodded. "I'm afraid so." He leaned, kissed her cheek, and then whispered in her ear, "If the Fates bless us with a child, I hope it will be a girl. I don't want to put you through what my mother had to endure."

Margaret was still reeling from the idea of having a child with Bowen when Elise said, "I heard that, and it's nonsense. You were a sweet boy who had a couple of hellion teenage years. I wouldn't have traded you for anyone. Margaret already has a wonderful daughter. I'm sure she wants a son."

"Well, in that case, whatever the Fates decide is fine with me." Bowen wrapped his arm around Margaret's shoulders.

Desperate to change the subject, she blurted, "Emmett is right here in the keep, right? Can I see him?"

Next to her, Bowen tensed. "Not tonight, that's for sure. Kian or Onegus have to approve it, and then you will need to wear earpieces that will nullify his compulsion."

"I've met him," Stella said. "He's not as bad as I thought he would be. He's polite, even charming."

"Villains often are," Ana said. "At least in movies. And being handsome doesn't hurt either."

Stella's mother, who was a very different person from her daughter, arched a brow. "Why did you go to see the cult leader?"

Margaret wanted to know that too.

For some reason, Stella glanced at Vlad before answering her mother. "Kian wanted me to help with the interrogation."

Vlad seemed relieved to hear her answer.

Was Stella hiding something?

"In what way?" Vlad's grandmother asked.

Margaret stifled the need to shake her head. None of the immortals looked old enough to be the parents of adult children, and definitely not anyone's grandparents, and yet some of them were ancient. Bowen included.

It was difficult to wrap her head around that.

"I speak Chinese, Stella said. "Both the Mandarin and Cantonese dialects, just not very well. I know enough to get by. But as far as I know, no other clan member does."

"Morris speaks it," Bowen said. "I don't know how well, though."

"He's fluent," Richard said. "He's teaching Mey and Jin Chinese in preparation for their trip."

Margaret shook her head. "Why did Kian need someone who spoke Chinese to interrogate Emmett?"

"There is still a lot you don't know about him." Bowen took her hand.

"Can you tell me?"

Bowen and Leon exchanged glances, and then Bowen shrugged. "You are a clan member now, so there is no reason to keep it from you. But now is not the time. Besides, I don't have all the details either. Only those who were involved with the interrogation do."

"I will fill you in," Stella said. "Just not tonight. This is a time to celebrate and rejoice."

51

CASSANDRA

$\mathcal{C}$onnor tapped Cassandra's arm. "Onegus is heading this way, which means that the ceremony is about to start."

She looked over her shoulder, hoping to see him walking toward her with an older woman that looked like him. Instead, he was holding a drink in each hand. The one with the lychees floating inside was probably for her, no doubt another attempt to get her drunk.

They were all drinking like fiends, but none of them seemed to be even tipsy, while she'd had to watch her step returning to the table. Then she'd had a martini, which had been delicious, and now her head was spinning.

She'd better not mention his mother and blurt out something that would sound bitchy. Besides, it wasn't as if she was eager to meet the woman. In fact, Cassandra would gladly skip it.

Perhaps Onegus was planning to introduce them after the ceremony?

That actually made sense even to her alcohol-addled brain. He'd been too busy before, and now that everyone had arrived, the ceremony was about to start.

"Thank you." She accepted the drink he handed her. "Are you free to finally join me?" There had been more bite to her words than she'd intended.

Watch the bitchy tone, Cassandra.

"Yes." He pulled out the chair next to her and sat down. "Now that everyone is here, I have the place locked down, so my team and I can sit down and enjoy the ceremony."

Lockdown sounded ominous; had Onegus locked the doors to the banquet hall?

"You shouldn't have done that. It's a fire hazard to lock the doors with so many people inside."

"The doors are not locked. The lockdown refers to the entry to the building."

Glancing at the closed doors, she noticed that all the servers were gone. "What's going on?"

"It's just a security measure," Onegus said. "We had every member of the serving staff thoroughly searched for bugs and weapons, but you never know what our enemies might come up with. This is just one more precaution to safeguard the bride and groom and the head of our clan."

"You mean Kian?"

Onegus cocked a brow. "Did you meet him?"

"Amanda took me to the family table and introduced me to her brother and sister-in-law."

"That's good." Onegus's expression and tone didn't match his words.

Was he upset that someone else had introduced her to his boss?

As the music was silenced, everyone turned to look at the closed doors, and a moment later they were opened by two burly men in tuxes.

A hush fell over the room.

It was as if they were all holding their breath, and Cassandra wondered whether it was in anticipation of the bride and groom. Perhaps their tradition didn't include the wedding song.

A small woman in a long white dress walked through the open doors, or rather floated because she moved with such fluidity that it didn't look like walking at all.

Was that the bride?

The dress looked more like a priestess's robe than a wedding gown, and the woman didn't wear a veil over her mane of flaming red hair, or hold flowers in her hands, and she glowed.

Cassandra wanted to rub her eyes to make sure that she wasn't hallucinating, but that would have ruined her makeup, so she just peeled them as wide open as she could and gaped.

It must be a trick of the light. Someone was shining a soft spotlight on the woman, or rather girl because she couldn't be more than eighteen, and the shiny fabric of her robe-like dress must be reflecting it, making it look as if her skin was glowing.

She wanted to ask Onegus who the beautiful angel was, but it was so quiet in the room that a needle dropping would have been heard. Cassandra barely dared to breathe, let alone whisper.

The woman floated up the three-rung platform at the back of the room, turned to face the guests, and lifted her arms. "It is with boundless love and joy that we gather here to celebrate my daughter and David's joining."

Cassandra closed her eyes and let that angelic voice wash over her.

Someone must have slipped her a roofie because she was hallucinating for sure. Angels weren't real, and the girl on the dais couldn't be anyone's mother.

But what if she was a priestess? Priests called everyone son or daughter, right?

Yeah, that made more sense than someone slipping her a roofie. Her boyfriend was the head of security. No one would dare to do that to his date.

The priestess just happened to be the most beautiful female Cassandra had ever seen, and she also happened to possess an angelic voice.

After all, the woman had no wings, and despite the glow, there was no halo floating above her head.

"Let us welcome Sari and David with the musical composition they chose for this joyous moment."

As the soft instrumental music started playing, the doors opened once more, and the groomsmen entered. She recognized Kian and the guy who had been sitting next to him at the family table. The other four were also inhumanly handsome, but next to those two, they looked almost ordinary.

All the members of Onegus's family could star in a soap opera. It was a shame that *The Bold and the Beautiful* title was already taken. It would have been a perfect fit for them.

When the men were in position, standing on the lowest rung to the priestess's right, the bridesmaids entered, and Cassandra stifled a surprised sound. One of them was an older woman who looked like a real mother, and one was a teenage girl.

Finally, some semblance of normality.

Perhaps she wasn't hallucinating after all, and Onegus's family weren't all beautiful vampires who never aged.

When all eight bridesmaids took their places to the priestess's left, all eyes turned to the banquet hall doors.

The music changed to another classical piece that Cassandra had never heard before, and the couple entered together holding hands.

The bride was gorgeous like her sister, but in a softer way. She was shorter, rounder, and her hair was auburn and not black. Her dress was simple and elegant, with no lace or embroidery or anything shiny. Just a perfectly cut bodice with a skirt that flared from the knees down and a train that trailed on the floor several feet behind her.

Cassandra had seen a similar dress at the Oscar De La Renta show, but this one was even more beautiful and had probably been custom-made for the bride.

Departing from tradition, the bride wore no veil and held no flowers. Her groom was a handsome blond man, who was grinning from ear to ear as if he'd won the lottery.

The couple walked up to the second rung of the platform and looked up to the priestess.

During the processions there had been several murmurs, but everyone hushed again, waiting for the priestess to start the ceremony.

52

MARGARET

$\mathcal{M}$ argaret stared at the goddess, willing her jaw to close. She wanted to see Ana's reaction, to say something to her friend who was sharing this revelatory moment with her, but to do that she would have to tear her eyes away from the glowing otherworldly being up on the dais.

When the door was opened once again and the groomsmen entered, murmurs started and some of the magic eddied, enough for Margaret to slide a quick glance at Ana.

Her friend was gaping just as stupidly as she was, but she still felt Margaret's gaze on her and turned to look at her. "Un-freaking-believable," she whispered. "The goddess is actually glowing."

Next to Ana, Leon and the other immortals smiled indulgently. Richard, however, nodded in understanding. "She's magnificent and terrifying to behold," he whispered. "But when you get to know her, the fear goes away. Annani is kind and friendly."

Taking another look at the goddess, Margaret could believe it. Annani looked like an ethereal angel, and her smile was benevolent, but her mane of fiery red hair hinted that there was a little bit of the devil in her as well.

The goddess's expression wasn't haughty or condescending, but Margaret wasn't convinced that it was all about Annani's love for her people. Annani radiated power, and she gobbled up their adoration, feasting on it in a similar way Emmett had done in Safe Haven.

Margaret wondered what Annani would have done if her people weren't as enamored with her, if they rebelled, or if they refused to follow the path she'd carved for them.

Would she have resorted to compelling them against their will like Emmett had done?

Under the tablecloth, Bowen reached for her hand and gave it a gentle squeeze. "You have nothing to fear from the Clan Mother."

He must have smelled her fear.

It was difficult to adjust to the new world she was living in, with immortals who could sniff her emotions, hear her heartbeat in another room, and perform other feats she couldn't even imagine.

She cast him a small smile and squeezed his hand back.

With Bowen by her side, she shouldn't fear a thing except for the goddess. He would protect her from everything and everyone, but he was as helpless against that immense power as she was.

As everyone in this room was, or perhaps in the entire world.

Well, that couldn't be true. The goddess had existed for over five thousand years, and if she was that powerful, she could have prevented wars and saved millions upon millions of people.

Annani probably wasn't powerful enough to smite entire armies, but she could have eliminated some of the leaders, the worst offenders in human history, and prevented the slaughter of so many.

Perhaps she couldn't do even that?

Maybe she was forbidden to tamper with destiny?

"Why are you suddenly so sad?" Bowen asked in a whisper. "This is a joyous occasion."

She waved a hand. "Don't mind me. Sometimes my mind wanders in twisted paths."

Across the table, Anastasia nodded.

As the music changed, the doors opened again, and the bride and groom entered holding hands. People smiled and waved at the couple, some offering air kisses as they walked by, but no one rose to their feet.

Come to think of it, they hadn't done that to honor the goddess either.

Maybe they had done away with that tradition because Annani was tiny. If everyone stood up, only those on both sides of the pathway would have seen her.

When the couple took their position on the platform, the music stopped, and the goddess lifted her arms again.

"It gives me great pleasure to have nearly my entire clan here to celebrate Sari and David's joining. They are blessed to have such a big, supportive, and loving family." She smiled down at the couple standing before her. "Are you ready to pledge your eternal love to each other?"

"We are," her daughter answered and turned to her groom. "Would you like to go first?"

He nodded. "I love you, my Sari. I wish there was a word stronger than love to express the depth of my feelings for you, but since there isn't, love will have to suffice. I, David, son of Ronja and Michael, pledge everything that I am to you, my life, my love, and my unwavering support."

Margaret wiped away a tear. It was such a simple and yet heartfelt pledge, and what made her tear up was the knowledge that nothing short of a major disaster would put a stop to that love. Immortals bonded forever, and abuse was unheard of in the clan. Hopefully, that would never change.

The groom pulled a ring out of his pocket. "Are you willing to share your life with me forever?"

"Yes, my love."

He slipped it onto her finger.

"My turn." Sari took his hands. "I, Sari, daughter of Annani, sister to Kian, Alena, Lilen, and Amanda, pledge myself to you, David, son of Ronja and Michael, brother to Lisa and Jonah. I will love you and support you and do my best to make you happy." She pulled a ring off her thumb. "Are you ready to share the rest of your life with me?"

"I am."

She slipped it onto his finger.

As the crowd erupted in deafening cheers and applause, the couple kissed, and the goddess waited patiently.

When they parted, she took her daughter's hand and then David's and put them one on top of the other. "May the Fates smile fondly upon this joining and shower your home with love, happiness, and as many children as your hearts' desire."

53

ONEGUS

*T*here were too many people around to discern Cassandra's scent, but Onegus could feel the crackling current under her skin intensifying. He kept casting her sidelong glances, trying to gauge her response to the glowing goddess standing upon the dais, but her expression was guarded. Her body was a better barometer of her feelings.

As soon as the ceremony ended, he would have to thrall her.

Right now, there was too much going on for her mind to be calm enough for him to be able to penetrate it.

"May the Fates smile fondly upon this joining and shower your home with love, happiness, and as many children as your hearts' desire."

As soon as Annani let go of Sari and David's hands, everyone got to their feet, applauding and cheering the now officially joined couple.

Next to him, Cassandra clapped while swaying on her stilettos, but as he reached to steady her, she cast him a withering look.

When the cheering and clapping subsided, Gerard made a rare appearance.

"I need everyone to calm down and take their seats so my servers can do their job. *Bon appétit.*"

In typical Gerard style, the request bordered on rude.

"That's my cousin the chef," Onegus said in Cassandra's ear. "Do you still want to meet him?"

Her eyelashes fluttered, and she looked at him down her nose. "His attitude doesn't scare me." She leaned closer, so her face was only a couple of inches from Onegus's. "I know how to deal with pricks like him." She lifted her hand and brought her thumb and forefinger together. "I can make him feel this small."

Onegus stifled a chuckle. Cassandra was way past tipsy and all the way to drunk.

"I'd sure like to see you cut the mighty Gerard down to size. But I don't think even you can do that. Kian avoids confrontations with him."

She arched one perfectly shaped brow. "That's because Kian cares. I don't." She started to push to her feet.

This time, Onegus couldn't contain the chuckle. "Sit down, Cassy. The servers are coming with dinner."

Glancing at the side doors that were opened to allow the servers in, she huffed and sat down. "It was a beautiful ceremony, and Gerard shouldn't have been allowed to come out and talk to the guests like that. Shame on him."

Next to her, Connor snickered, and their other dinner companions were all trying not to laugh. Thankfully, Cassandra was too drunk to notice or that energy swirling inside her would have unleashed its destructive power on Gerard's fancy china.

Perhaps she'd been too drunk to notice a glowing goddess?

"That priestess was something else." Cassandra lifted her water goblet and took a sip. "How did she make her skin glow? Did she smear sparkly lotion all over her skin? And that huge red wig was so over the top." She rolled her eyes. "Where did you find her? Hollywood?"

The first one to lose it was Sharon. Hiding behind Robert's broad shoulders, she giggled uncontrollably. Then Tessa joined in, and soon everyone except for Cassandra and Onegus was laughing.

He tensed, expecting plates to crack and glasses to explode. Instead, Cassandra waved a hand. "It wasn't that funny, but at least now I know I'm not the only drunk at the table."

The others took their cue from her comment and started pretending they were inebriated. Connor even started a lewd Scottish ballad, but he was interrupted by the flurry of servers who descended on their table like a flock of ravens, placing an artfully presented first course in front of everyone.

"What is that?" Cassandra eyed the culinary masterpiece suspiciously. "I don't know if I should eat it or take it home and put it on a shelf as a decoration."

Roni sniffed at the creation in front of him. It was shaped like a rooster, and by the smell, it was made from cheese and slivers of carrots, apples, green onions, and some other stuff that Onegus wasn't sure about.

"It has cheese in it," Roni said. "The rest are veggies and fruits."

Cassandra still stared at hers. "I can't eat that. It's too pretty."

"What I want to know is who made over seven hundred of these roosters." Sylvia lifted her plate to take a closer look. "There is no machine that could do that."

"Maybe Gerard had the Odus make them," Tessa suggested.

When Jackson threw a warning look at her, she covered her mouth. "I meant Oompa Loompas or gizmos."

Apparently, Cassandra was too drunk to notice the slip, and as Jackson lifted his rooster to his mouth and took a bite, she did the same.

Her eyes rolled back. "I forgot how good Gerard's creations are. He's forgiven."

Laughing, Onegus wiped nonexistent sweat off his forehead. "What a relief. The prick gets to cook another day."

54

EMMETT

*A*s the door to Emmett's cell started to swing open, he glanced at his watch. It was after nine at night, and no one ever visited him this late.

Eleanor.

He smelled her scent even before she stepped into his cell, one of the Guardians no doubt standing outside to make sure that he didn't make a run for it.

As if he were stupid enough to try it.

"Good evening, Eleanor. What a nice surprise." He looked her over.

She still wore the same clothes she'd had on when she'd brought in his dinner, and she had two large paper cups in her hands.

"Hi." She waited for the door to close before joining him on the couch. "I didn't bring you blood. But I thought you would enjoy some wine."

"I thought that I smelled wine." He reached for the cup. "Where did you get it?" He removed the plastic lid and took a sniff.

It smelled like good wine, which made drinking it from a paper cup even worse, but as the saying went, beggars can't be choosers.

"I swiped it from the kitchen." Eleanor flicked the lid off and lifted the cup. "Cheers."

"What are we drinking to?"

"Us."

"I'll drink to that." He tapped her cup with his.

While he sipped and savored, Eleanor gulped at least half of the large cup in one go.

"What's troubling you?" He regarded her with concern.

"Why do you think something is troubling me?"

"Do you usually gulp large quantities of wine?"

She looked at her cup. "No, but this one is good."

He doubted she'd even tasted it. "Talk to me." He reached for her hand. "We are friends, right?"

Eleanor glanced at the bed, then shook her head. "I'm not good at this."

He could sense her nervousness and wondered what had caused it. She wasn't fearful, just apprehensive.

"Good at what?"

"The whole seduction part."

She wanted to seduce him?

"What about the watchers?"

"It's only Alfie, and he's busy watching a movie." She glanced at the camera. "If we rotate the couch so its back is to the bed, it will block some of the camera's view." She avoided his eyes.

He had a feeling that she wasn't telling him the truth, but he didn't know about what.

Was it a trap?

Perhaps she'd been asked to seduce him so they would have a recording of him drinking from her?

But what could they possibly want it for? Obviously for leverage, but against whom?

"Even if we do that, and Alfie can't see what's happening on the bed, he will know what's going on and come to put a stop to it."

She shifted her eyes to him. "Why would he want to do that? I'm allowed to have sex with whomever I want."

"Even a prisoner whom you're guarding?"

Maybe someone had put her up to it to get her in trouble. She'd admitted to not being liked or trusted by many of the clan members. Someone might have devised a plan to get her kicked out of the training program, and if that happened, she would no longer be allowed to visit him.

He couldn't afford to lose her.

Eleanor's smile was tight. "The clan has its own laws, and human rules don't apply. It's not like I'm abusing my station to get you to do something that you don't want to."

"It could be interpreted that way. I don't want you to get in trouble."

She eyed him from under lowered eyelashes. "Perhaps you just don't want me?"

Releasing control over his fangs, he let them punch out and smiled. "Do you really think so?"

"That doesn't prove anything. You might be hungry or just crave a snack."

He shook his head. "You're an immortal. Use your sense of smell."

"I'm not good at interpreting smells."

"Then interpret this." He pulled her hand and pressed it against his erection. "Males can't fake arousal, Eleanor."

She sucked in a breath and ordered, "Dim lights!"

The system responded to her demand, dimming the lights, but Eleanor wasn't happy with it. "Dim lights by seventy-five percent."

"What are you doing?"

She leaned closer. "Making it much more difficult for Alfie to see us." She cupped his cheek. "Kiss me, Emmett."

55

ELEANOR

*A*s Eleanor stared into Emmett's dark eyes, she saw the hesitation and then the decision made.

He closed the distance between their mouths, not in a rush but with deliberate slowness, as if giving her time to change her mind. And then his soft lips were on hers, kissing her gently, as if she was fragile, precious, and then he withdrew and looked at the door.

"No one is coming to stop us, Emmett," she breathed. "Kiss me again."

He brushed a finger down her cheek. "I liked seeing you all flushed, wanting me." His finger trailed down her neck, stopping at where her pulse was beating wildly.

In the semi-darkness, his eyes flashed red, and his elongating fangs gleamed white. He looked like a beautiful demon, and an exquisite shiver of fear rippled down her back.

His finger continued its downward track. "Are your nipples hard, Eleanor? Shall I check?"

Her eyes closed, she couldn't breathe, couldn't respond, only pant in anticipation of his touch.

"Are they?" he whispered against her ear.

"Yes," she managed to hiss.

He nuzzled her neck, his tongue flicking over her pulsing vein. Was he about to bite her?

Her breath left her throat in a whoosh, her core spasmed, and moisture soaked the gusset of her panties.

Eleanor wanted Emmett to take her to his bed, to strip her naked and run his hands over every inch of her skin, but they hadn't moved the couch to block the camera's view yet, and she didn't want him to know that Alfie wasn't watching. As much as she wanted the sex, she didn't trust him yet.

He must have read her thoughts. Moving faster than she could process, he lifted her in his arms and shifted her to the bed, then turned the couch so its back was partially blocking the camera's view.

"I've fantasized about you naked in my bed for so many nights." He tugged her T-shirt up, and when she lifted her arms, he pulled it off her.

The red glow in his eyes eerie in the darkness, he gazed at her for a long moment before hooking his fingers in the elastic of her yoga pants. "Did you wear them knowing that I would take them off?" He pulled them past her hips.

She shook her head.

"I think you did." He pulled them all the way down and then tossed them over the back of the couch. "Gorgeous." He smoothed his hands over her outer thighs before dipping in, his thumb brushing over the soaked gusset of her panties.

"So ready for me. So lovely." Emmett leaned down and kissed her through the fabric. "Your scent is intoxicating." He moved the gusset aside and pushed a finger into her, then withdrew it and pushed back with two.

Eleanor was a hair away from climaxing. If he only touched the throbbing bundle of nerves at the apex of her thighs she was going to tip over.

Instead, he pulled her panties down her thighs, and then tossed them aside. Her bra was next, and then she was bare and didn't know whether to cover her breasts with her hands or let his eyes feast on her.

"Beautiful," he hissed. "Even more so than I imagined."

"I want to see you too."

His smile was conceited. "Have you imagined me naked when lying in bed alone at night?"

"Yes."

He started on the buttons of his shirt. "Have you been touching yourself, imagining that those were my hands and my fingers pleasuring you instead of your own?"

She searched her mind for something witty to say, but all that came out was the truth. "Yes."

He shrugged the shirt off, and she gasped.

"Do you like what you see?"

"You're beautiful." She didn't care that his ego was already inflated enough.

Emmett was perfect. His chest was all smooth, lean muscles and completely hairless.

Not bothering with the zipper, he pushed his jeans down his lean hips, and then he was standing in front of her in his boxer briefs, a massive erection obscenely stretching the fabric.

Eleanor licked her lips. "Take them off."

"Not yet, dove." He climbed on the bed and sprawled on top of her.

Dove? She was no dove. She was a bird of prey.

Lifting her head, she nipped at his lower lip.

He smiled, his fangs gleaming white. "A dove with teeth." He gripped her hands and pulled them over her head. "Do you want to wrestle with me, my little dove?"

She tried to pull her hands out of his grip, but it was like trying to break free from iron manacles.

"I didn't think so." He kissed her with surprising gentleness. "Don't fight me,

Eleanor. Aggression spurs instincts I'd rather remained dormant." He kissed her neck, nipping at it lightly. "If you let me, I'll pleasure you for hours. But if you fight me, this will be over too quickly for either of us to savor."

It dawned on her then that Emmett might enjoy her assertiveness, but any sign of aggression reminded him of his mistress and his near-slave status in the Kra-ell community.

When she let her arms go slack, he released his hold and watched her with a wary expression, probably expecting her to strike again and not looking forward to it.

Emmett needed her human softness and her willing submission. He didn't want to have to fight her for it.

Eleanor's muscled body and assertive attitude might have painted her as a hard woman, but there was a soft core hidden deep inside of her that the tough exterior protected.

Looking into his cautious expression, she made her decision.

Tonight, she would give Emmett access to that soft interior, and if he treated it with care, she might give him access to it again.

"Kiss me." She smoothed her hands up his arms, her touch gentle and caressing.

With a sigh that sounded like gratitude, he brought his lips to hers and licked into her mouth. He kept kissing her until she writhed under him, rubbing her aching nipples against his hard chest and her core against the tremendous bulge straining against the confines of his cotton briefs.

56

EMMETT

*W*hen Eleanor had bitten him, bringing out the Kra-ell savage in him, Emmett had fought against the instinct driving him to conquer and subdue.

He'd learned a long time ago that he preferred human females' softness and submission to the Kra-ell females' aggression, their sharp fangs and claws, their thirst for blood, their sadistic need to inflict pain, and the flip side of it, their masochistic need to be overpowered by the male.

It was a vicious dance that didn't allow for any feelings of closeness, or even fondness. It was primal and animalistic, deeply satisfying physically, but just as deeply disappointing emotionally.

Perhaps it was the fault of the human genes contributed by his mother that he didn't enjoy the Kra-ell savage sex games. Emmett enjoyed giving pleasure just as much as he enjoyed receiving it, and although he'd never been in love with any of his human partners, he'd been fond of most.

If he didn't like a female's personality, he didn't take her to his bed, and he definitely hadn't invited any rotten apples to join his community.

As he let go of Eleanor's lips and looked down at her, he found her staring at him with softness in her eyes, an acceptance that stirred something in his heart.

Eleanor knew who he was, what he was, and yet she accepted him, blood-sucking and all.

And then she lifted her hand and cupped his cheek. "You are so handsome."

He cocked a brow. "Even with the fangs?"

Her eyes became hooded. "Especially with the fangs. I know what these babies can do."

"In good time, dove." He slid down her body and licked at her nipple. "First, I want to taste you." He looked up at her. "Will you allow me to do that?"

She nodded, and as her thighs parted, her feminine scent hit him with a force that nearly knocked him out.

382

Licking her other nipple, he trailed his hand down her belly to the trove of pleasure between her legs.

As his fingers gently brushed over her wetness, her hips jerked upward, and she hissed, "I'm so close."

He pushed up and took her lips, licking into her mouth while his finger breached her entrance.

Eleanor moaned, her hips undulating to get more of his finger inside her. If he could make her come just with his fingers, he could make her come again with his tongue, preparing her to accept his size.

Adding another finger, he pressed his thumb to her clit and nipped her lower lip.

"Emmett," she groaned as a release washed over her.

"I love hearing you say my name." He kept stroking her, helping her ride out the aftershocks of the climax and watching her expression change from ecstatic to sated and content.

"I'm not done with you," he said when she opened her eyes.

"I know." She turned to him, her hand drifting down to stroke him over his briefs. "I want this inside me."

"Not yet." He slid down again and pushed her on her back. "Part your legs for me."

She obeyed without hesitation, and at the sight of her glistening sex, he dove down and treated himself to his first taste of her.

"Exquisite." He looked at her from in between her spread thighs. "Almost as good as the taste of your blood."

"Oh, dear merciful Fates." Her head dropped back on the pillows.

It did something to him that she was turned on by the thought of him taking her vein. The other females he'd been with hadn't known what was coming, and even though they had all orgasmed hard while he'd fed on them, it hadn't given him as much satisfaction because that first part, the wanting, the acceptance, had been missing.

He hadn't even realized that until now, until he saw the anticipation in Eleanor's eyes, heard it in her moans, and sensed it in the flare of her arousal.

She wanted him at her vein, craved it, and he couldn't wait to sink his fangs into her.

With a growl, he sealed his mouth over her sex, sucking, pulling, then licking and nipping, and back to sucking until she exploded over his tongue, her back arching like a bow off the bed. He didn't stop there, working her into another climax, and another, until she pushed on his head.

It took him less than a second to shuck his briefs, and then he flipped Eleanor's boneless body over and pulled her bottom up, baring her gleaming wet sex to him. Rising behind her, he gripped her hips and aimed his shaft at her entrance.

He wanted to spear into her with one mighty thrust, but even after all the orgasms he'd wrung out of her, Emmett feared that Eleanor might not be ready for his size. Pushing just the tip in, he waited for her response, and when she wiggled her bottom, he pushed in a few inches more.

Even with all the slickness, she was tight around him, but he couldn't wait a moment longer. Tightening his grip on her hips, he surged all the way in and then stilled as she whimpered.

Sweat beaded his forehead as he waited for her to adjust to his girth, and when she moved, encouraging him to do the same, the last of his control broke, and he pounded into her like a rutting beast.

It must have taken less than a minute for him to reach his climax, and as it erupted out of him, he let go of her hips, gripped her nape, and sank his fangs into her vein.

She orgasmed again, squeezing him tight, and as the first taste of her blood hit his tongue, he hardened again as if he hadn't just emptied a gallon of his essence into her.

Sucking and pulling, he started thrusting again, and as one orgasm after another rocked through Eleanor's body, Emmett had to remind himself to stop before he took too much.

With a Herculean effort, he retracted his fangs and sealed the puncture holes with a swipe of his tongue.

Her body slackened under him, and even though he could have climaxed again, Emmett pulled out, slid to the side, and tucked her into his chest.

Unfamiliar tenderness washing over him, he whispered in her ear, "Thank you."

57

CASSANDRA

*D*inner took forever. Seven courses had been served, each one small but delicious. Cassandra was pleasantly full, but not overstuffed, and if not for her spinning head, she would have enjoyed herself greatly.

Good food and good company made for a pleasant evening. The only problem she had with her dinner companions was their insistence on getting and keeping her drunk. She'd never consumed so much alcohol, and at the rate she was going, she would soon pass out.

"Coffee, cappuccino, or tea?" the server asked.

"Coffee. Definitely coffee," she slurred.

"Same here," Onegus told the server. "After we are done with coffee and dessert, I'll introduce you to my mother."

She wanted to shake her head, but it made her dizzy. "I'm sorry, but I don't think I can meet her now. I need to sober up first."

"You're fine," he said dismissively. "As long as you can string three words together in the right order, you are not considered drunk."

"According to which country rules?"

"Scotland, of course."

"That's right." Connor lifted his umpteenth glass of whisky and downed it in one go. "The night is still young, and I can still talk without slurring my words." He lifted the empty glass, signaling for the server to refill it. "They should just leave a couple of bottles here."

"They serve fine whiskies," Jackson said. "The bar tab alone must have cost Sari a fortune." He chuckled. "I'm sure Gerard is not donating his services or the supplies."

"He's not," Sylvia said. "Amanda paid for everything."

"What does she do to afford all that?" Cassandra asked.

"She comes from money." Roni leaned sideways as the server placed a plate with cake and ice cream in front of him.

385

Cassandra chuckled. "So do all of you, but I don't see Tessa or Sylvia wearing the latest gowns by Oscar de la Renta. Did Amanda marry someone rich?"

Maybe she was the wife or daughter of the head of their clan. No, Kian was the clan's head, and she was his sister. Now, that made more sense. The five siblings inherited the empire. Or was it four?

Cassandra vaguely remembered the bride naming four people. Two brothers and two sisters.

Robert, who had hardly spoken more than two words throughout dinner, shook his head. "Amanda mated a simple soldier."

There was that word again, mated. Was it the new politically correct term for married?

"I get it now." Cassandra smiled at Onegus. "It has taken a few moments for my inebriated brain to connect the dots. Amanda is one of the five heirs of the clan's business empire. I've met Kian, but not the other two Sari mentioned. I know that the third sister was one of the bridesmaids. Was the other brother one of the groomsmen?"

"Lilen is no longer with us." Onegus's eyes clouded. "He has passed to the other side of the veil."

"I'm so sorry. When did it happen?"

"A very long time ago." His eyes turned hard.

She wanted to ask how Lilen had died, but Onegus had gotten upset, so she decided to drop the subject and divert the conversation to another topic.

"I bet there is a fascinating story behind Amanda marrying a simple guy. How did the incredibly rich and gorgeous heiress end up with a soldier?"

Suddenly, everyone got busy with their coffees and desserts and avoided her eyes.

"What? Did I say something wrong? Did the snowflake police deem the term to marry discriminating and it was replaced with mated?"

The term mate kept popping up, and the priestess had talked about a joining, not a marriage.

Damn, she should have figured it out. Unlike husband or wife, mate was a genderless term like partner or significant other.

"I'm not aware of marriage or to marry getting booted out of the English language," Onegus said. "Did any of you hear anything about that?" He looked at their dinner companions, who all shook their heads.

"Damn." Cassandra huffed out a breath. "I can never figure out which words they will oust next. But if that's not the reason for everyone clamming up, then what is?"

"Amanda's story is hers to tell." Onegus lifted the tiny fork and scooped a small piece of the cake. "You should ask her."

58

ELEANOR

*A*s Eleanor drifted down from the euphoric cloud she'd been floating on, she wondered how long she'd been out.

She was on her side, her back tucked against Emmett's front, the stickiness of their releases gluing them together.

His deep and even breathing suggested that he was asleep, which gave her time to think over the experience.

He'd taken her blood, this time she'd been aware of it, and it had been a little scary but still erotic as hell. The effect was the same as Greggory's bite, which meant that Emmett had injected her with venom before sucking on her blood, and that his venom was either the same as Greggory's, or similar enough to be indistinguishable.

She wasn't as lightheaded as she'd expected to be after having her blood depleted, and the sexual satiety felt different than what she'd experienced with Greggory. It was more complete, which was surprising since she and Emmett weren't a couple.

Maybe it had been the vulnerability that he'd let her see, dropping his usual swagger and easy charm to show her the scars of his past.

"Don't fight me, Eleanor," he'd said. "Aggression spurs instincts I'd rather remained dormant."

She wasn't sure what he'd meant by that, but she could guess. From the little he had told them, she'd garnered that the Kra-ell females were cruel, savage, and that they reveled in inflicting pain on the males who fought so hard for the dubious privilege of breeding with them.

Apparently, those sexual games were not cultural but rather instinctual, driven by biology, necessary to ensure the survival of the species. By weeding out the weaker males and choosing the strongest, the species continually improved, at least physically.

It was common in the animal kingdom, but it was counterproductive for an intelligent species. The more evolved the society, the less valuable brute strength was. Cunning, intelligence, the ability to form alliances and work productively with others, those were the traits of the most successful humans, not how much weight they could deadlift or how powerful their punch was.

The Kra-ell must have come from a primitive society, and the technology used to bring them to earth probably hadn't been developed by them. Maybe they had stolen it, or maybe they'd conquered a more advanced but less militant species and had taken their technology.

What if that species was the gods? Perhaps the group that had arrived on earth thousands of years ago had been refugees from a war with the Kra-ell?

"Are you okay?" Emmett kissed her neck.

She turned in his arms to face him. "I'm better than okay. I'm perfect." She kissed his lips lightly. "I thought that you were asleep."

"I was. Your loud thinking woke me up." When she frowned, he laughed. "No, I can't read your thoughts. But the energy you were putting out felt like intense thinking."

"You can sense that?"

"Only when you are in my arms, and I can feel any minute change in your body. What were you thinking about?"

Emmett sounded a little anxious, and Eleanor debated whether to share her musings with him. Perhaps later. The topic was not really suitable for pillow-talk. Besides, they both needed a shower.

"If you are anxious about your performance, don't be. It was perfect."

He looked at her down his nose. "Anxious? Why would I be anxious? I'm an excellent lover."

Eleanor stifled a chuckle. The Emmett she knew and loved was back.

Well, love was too strong of a word. She'd been burned one time too many to let herself fall into that trap again. She and Emmett could be friends, lovers, maybe even confidantes, but they weren't in love, and they weren't each other's fated mates.

"Yes, you are." She kissed the tip of his nose.

"I'm surprised none of your Guardian friends has come in with guns blazing. Did you strike a deal with them?"

She smiled. "What if I did?"

"Nothing. I just wondered how you pulled that off."

"It wasn't as difficult as we both imagined." She pulled out of his arms. "Let's get in the shower. I can't put my clothes back on without washing first, and I still have a shift to finish."

CASSANDRA

"Come on." Onegus put his arm around Cassandra's waist, his hand resting on her hip. "My mother has waited patiently for hours. She wants to meet you."

"Can we do it tomorrow? I can barely walk. Besides, I have a hard time being pleasant when I'm sober. I'm afraid I'll say something wrong."

He stopped walking and turned to her. "I find your company very pleasant. I can't imagine anyone thinking differently."

The smile that bloomed on her face was way too big for the small compliment, but that was what alcohol did. Her mind was mostly fine, she was still as sharp as always, but maybe not as quick. Her body, on the other hand, was a different story. The movements of her legs and arms were too large and uncoordinated, her smiles were too broad, her frowns too pronounced, and she was probably too loud as well.

"You are so charming, Onegus." She lifted her hand and cupped his cheek. "I could so easily fall in love with you. Are you going to break my heart?"

"No." He smiled tightly. "Your heart is safe with me."

"Promise?"

"I promise." He resumed walking. "It's the second table from Amanda's. The blond with the curly hair is my mother. Her name is Martha."

Cassandra narrowed her eyes to clear the blur, but it didn't help. Martha still looked too young. Heck, she looked younger than Onegus. Perhaps it was time to see an optometrist. She'd been getting headaches lately, and it was probably from straining her eyes at work.

When they got closer, the woman rose to her feet and smiled. "Hello, Cassandra. I'm so glad to finally meet you." She offered her a hand. "I'm Martha. Onegus's mother."

Her Scottish lilt was lovely, but there was no way she was his mother. Were they playing a joke on her?

"No, you're not." Cassandra shook the woman's hand.

Martha was tall, and she was in heels, so they were more or less eye to eye, and Cassandra took a good look at the woman's flawless, pretty face. There was not even one wrinkle, and nothing was sagging. Even if she had him as a teenager, Martha would have to be at least forty-five. Not that forty-five was old, and women that age might not have wrinkles or saggy jowls, but they didn't look like pretty twenty-five-year-olds either.

"I assure you that I am." Martha's smile melted away, and she turned to Onegus. "A little help?"

Help?

With what?

"My mother had me when she was very young, and she takes good care of herself." He smirked. "Like your mother. That's yet another thing that we have in common."

"I doubt that," Martha said.

Cassandra's forehead furrowed. "What do you mean?"

Martha shrugged. "I doubt that your mother is anything like me, or I like her."

At her side, Onegus tensed, and his hand on her hip tightened. Was that a warning?

She brushed his hand off and struck a pose, shifting her body sideways and moving her right leg forward in a well-practiced modeling pose. "How would you know? You've just met me, and you don't know my mother or me."

Martha smiled tightly. "What I meant was that your mother and I grew up on different continents and in different cultures. It wasn't a comment meant to reflect my opinion of you or your mother. I'm sure you are both lovely ladies. I just find Americans a little rough around the edges, a little too loud, and too casual in their dress and in their manners, and that includes members of my family who have moved here."

Talk about a stuck-up Brit.

The sizzling energy crawling under Cassandra's skin had been numbed by the alcohol, but the verbal sparring with Onegus's mother had upped the voltage and cleared Cassandra's head.

If Martha was anyone else, she would have torn into her, but the woman was Onegus's mother, so she had to smile and act civil toward her.

"Well, I hope my mother and I will change your mind about Americans. Perhaps we could all meet for lunch."

Geraldine could give any stuck-up Brit a run for her money, but with her memory problems and her made-up stories, Cassandra wasn't sure that it was such a good idea. But she had to put it out there and hope that Martha would decline politely.

"I would like that very much." Martha's smile was genuine.

Onegus let out a breath.

What had he expected? That she would bite his mother's head off?

"I was looking for you." Nick swaggered over with a large wine glass in his hand. "There is a punch bowl the size of a witch's cauldron in the antechamber, and it's the best I've ever had. It's made with lots of fine whiskeys. You have to try it." He took a swig from his drink and smacked his lips. "Delicious."

The young girl Cassandra had seen on the platform walked up to Nick. "Can I have some?"

"You're not old enough, sprite." He patted her arm. "Next year."

She laughed. "I'm not going to be old enough by then either." She moved closer to Cassandra. "Hi, I'm Lisa." She extended her hand.

"Nice to meet you." Cassandra shook it. "I'm Cassandra."

"I know." Lisa smiled, turned to Onegus, and gave him the thumbs up.

Cassandra rolled her eyes. Had the kid just given her the stamp of approval? Well, at least there was that.

"When does the dancing portion of the evening start?" Martha asked.

"Given the change in music," Onegus said. "It's about to begin."

About a third of the chairs were vacant, but since no one was on the dance floor yet, Cassandra figured they were congregating in the antechamber and drinking punch. Damn Scots and their iron bellies. How could they drink so much and remain standing?

"Let's go." Martha threaded her arm through Nick's. "Lead the way to that punch, young man."

"I'm Nick," he said. "Ruth's mate."

"I know." Martha patted his arm. "Rumors about love matches spread fast through the clan, and they even jump over the ocean."

Love matches? Was there any other kind?

Well, duh. These people were rich. They probably married to make alliances with other rich people, either financial or political.

Cassandra did her best to walk properly, putting one stiletto-clad foot in front of the other. Despite having a somewhat clearer head, her body was still a little wobbly, and what was even worse, the current inside her was crackling like static electricity.

Holding it in would have been difficult under normal circumstances, doing so when her control was tentative required teeth gritting.

The damn static had been building despite her best efforts to tamp it down. Several petty annoyances had combined to create a volatile mixture that needed an outlet. She shouldn't have allowed it to build up like that, should have released it in small bursts, but it was too late for that.

Cassandra had to find a proper outlet and release it before she hurt someone. The problem was that a glass or a vase wouldn't be enough this time. She needed something that could absorb much more than her usual small blasts.

Perhaps she could excuse herself and go to the bathroom. Maybe a porcelain commode would do, or a large mirror. She would cause property damage, but at least no one would get hurt.

ONEGUS

*T*hat hadn't gone well.

Onegus should have known that his mother's strong personality would clash with Cassandra's.

It was ironic that he'd chosen a woman so similar in character to his mother. They were both alpha females, and therefore bound to lock horns. As a kid, he'd resented Martha's strictness, her haughty attitude, and her insistence on good manners. It hadn't been easy growing up as her son, but he had to admit that the things she'd instilled in him had served him well.

If not for his strict upbringing, he wouldn't have such strong self-control, the discipline that had helped him become Chief Guardian, and the manners that made him such a good stand-in for Kian.

In fact, compared to him, Kian was a brute.

But Kian was like that despite Annani's upbringing, not because of it. The Clan Mother hadn't been lenient with her sons or her older daughters. The only one who could get away with murder had been Amanda, who early on had figured out how to manipulate her mother and get anything she wanted.

"That's indeed a huge punch bowl." Martha stopped a good distance away from it. "I wonder what's in it."

"Lots of whiskey," Nick said. "But also champagne, orange juice, cranberry juice, some bitters, and cinnamon." He took another sip. "Maybe rum too."

"Sounds delicious." Martha eyed the long line. "Why is everyone here? The bar has plenty of other drinks."

"I don't know." Nick shrugged. "Maybe Gerard put something else in it that makes everyone crave it."

"Like what?" Cassandra asked.

"Magic." Nick snorted. "Although knowing that prick, it's something wicked." He let go of Martha's arm. "I need to find Ruth. She gets stressed in large crowds."

"Isn't she with Sylvia and Roni?" Cassandra leaned on Onegus's shoulder.

"Yeah, but it's not the same." Nick winked. "I'm her guy." He sauntered away without refilling his goblet.

"Are you okay?" Onegus asked quietly.

"My head's spinning." She looked up at him. "Can you point me in the direction of the lady's room?"

"I'll escort you." He was afraid she wouldn't make it.

"I can find it myself. It's not like you can go in with me."

"I can come with you," Martha offered. "You seem unsteady on your feet. How much have you drunk?"

Cassandra's energy surged, so much so that Onegus felt it sizzling against his arm.

"I lost count of how many drinks your son and his cousins kept pushing at me, but I assure you that I can get to the bathroom with no assistance from you or Onegus."

A clueless server stuck a tray with goblets full of punch in front of them. "Enjoy," he encouraged them to partake.

To Onegus's surprise, Cassandra took a goblet, and with a challenge in her eyes, brought it to her lips. "Nick said we have to try it."

"Indeed." Martha took another one.

"Well, I guess I have to taste it too." Onegus lifted the third. "Cheers." He clinked his glass with Cassandra's and then with his mother's.

"To many happy occasions," Martha said before drinking up.

"To the happy couple." Cassandra brought the glass to her lips.

She was still sipping on it when a guy backed into her to let a server through. The punch splashed over her face, not much of it, but enough to drip down her neck and into the neckline of her one-shouldered dress.

"Fruck," Cassandra cursed.

Thankful that she hadn't said fuck, Onegus took the goblet from her hand and waved a waiter over. "We need napkins."

"I'm so sorry," the offender apologized. He was one of the young Scots, and Onegus couldn't recall his name.

"I'll get you some napkins." He rushed off.

"Here." His mother pulled a handkerchief out of her small purse and handed it to Cassandra.

The waiter arrived at the same moment and handed her a stack of paper napkins.

"Thanks," Cassandra said to both and started patting at her neck and face. "The dress is ruined. Those stains are never going to come out."

"It's black, dear," Martha said. "No one is going to see the stains. You just need to fix your face." She took one of the paper napkins and lifted her hand. "You're covered with red and purple splotches."

Cassandra stayed her hand. "A napkin is not going to cut it. I'm sticky. I need to wash it off." She looked down at her cleavage and the sticky marks left by the punch.

"I'll take you to the restroom." Onegus put his hand on the small of her back.

He could take her to his office and let her use his private bathroom. She could take the dress off and shower if she wanted.

As the image of her standing naked in his shower flashed in his mind, he instantly hardened, a most inappropriate response given the situation. Cassandra was upset, his mother was standing right next to him, and people were watching them, curious about the commotion.

61

CASSANDRA

"I'll take you to the restroom." Onegus put his large hand on the small of her back.

Martha sneered. "Should we say our goodbyes now? I doubt the two of you will be back anytime soon."

From anyone else, Cassandra would have thought nothing of the suggestive remark, but coming from Onegus's mother, the woman who thought she was so prim and proper, it was annoying as hell.

Just another spark to ignite her barely contained energy.

She wished Onegus would hurry up and guide her to the bathroom, hopefully a private one.

His lips thinned for a brief moment, but then he smiled, and Cassandra realized that his charm was just one more weapon in his arsenal. It wasn't innate. It was practiced.

"I wish I could call it a night, Mother, but I need to be here to ensure all the guests get back to their respective lodgings safely."

"Of course." Martha smiled. "If you don't mind, I'll accompany you both to the ladies' room. I need to powder my nose as well."

Freaking great. That was the last thing Cassandra needed. How was she going to release the energy with Onegus's mother there? The one who had fueled it? If Martha was nearby, she would be like a magnet for it, and with how much Cassandra was packing, she would strike the woman dead on the spot.

"I'm going to take Cassandra to my old office. I have a private bathroom in there."

"Oh, well." Martha smirked knowingly. "Just be quick about it. I'm going to powder my nose and then join my friends on the dance floor." She sauntered away on her high heels, her curly, nearly white, blond hair swishing over her bare back, just skimming the top of her tight ass.

The woman was movie-star beautiful, and she was rich. No wonder she had a haughty attitude.

By now, the antechamber had partially emptied, with only a few people standing next to the tall round tables, chatting and sipping on their punch or coffee, some eating desserts on small plates. A server hovered nearby, collecting dirty cups, glasses, plates and used napkins.

"Thank you for the save." Cassandra smiled tightly.

Onegus arched a brow. "Save from what?"

Was he playing dumb? Or was he that clueless?

"Your mother. She's a bit much."

"I don't know what you're talking about. Other than that comment about Americans being uncouth, for which she apologized, she's been perfectly pleasant." He smiled sheepishly. "Or as pleasant as my mother can manage to be. She was doing her best."

If not for Cassandra's already elevated agitation, the tag-on at the end would have redeemed Onegus, but it was too little too late.

She could practically feel the last clamp holding her energy from erupting disintegrate. She was about to explode, and she needed a receptacle for the energy—preferably a sizable container, but there was no potted plant or statue in sight, not even one damn window.

Turning around, she had only enough time to focus her eyes on the punch bowl before the current zapped out of her with a force that had her staggering backward.

The bowl cracked, the thick glass holding up for a split second, and then it burst, big blue glass shards breaking off it and liquid spilling on the floor.

As before, Onegus shoved her behind his back, but this time they weren't close enough for the glass to hit him, or maybe the heavy weight of the thick glass had prevented it from getting airborne.

The disaster area was contained to the vicinity of the punch bowl, and the only one who got splattered was the poor server.

It didn't take more than a couple of seconds for a veritable army of broad-backed males to rush into the antechamber, Onegus's security team no doubt. Apart from their hard faces and muscled bodies, there was nothing to identify them as such. They were all wearing tuxedos and had run out of the ballroom, but the way their eyes quickly assessed the situation betrayed them as trained guards.

"How did that happen, boss?" One of them pushed a larger shard with his shoe toward the epicenter.

In the aftermath of the explosion, Cassandra felt faint, the blast emptying the excess energy together with what she needed to keep going. She held on to Onegus, her hand fisting the back of his tuxedo for support.

"No clue." Onegus wrapped his arm around her waist, propping her up. "I heard it crack, and then it just burst. I assume there was a flaw in the glass."

Cassandra sagged against his side, the relief further weakening her knees. He didn't suspect her. And if he did, he was covering up for her.

One of the men chuckled. "Perhaps the alcohol content was enough to erode the structural integrity of the glass."

Was that even a thing? Did glass even have structural integrity? Wasn't that a construction term?

A third guy offered another explanation. "Did anyone smoke near the bowl? Some idiot might have dropped a match into it."

"Given the alcohol content, the liquid might have caught fire, but there was none," Onegus said. "The thing would have burned, but I doubt it would have exploded. The bowl just cracked and then broke apart. Maybe it was the music. Sometimes a certain frequency can resonate with the glass. It's no big deal except for the cleanup."

"And the lost booze," someone bemoaned. "A lot of good whiskey went into that punch."

Cassandra wasn't an engineer, but even she knew that the bowl was too big and its glass too thick for the sound coming from the ballroom to shatter it. A noise cannon directed straight at it and tuned to its precise resonance frequency would have been needed.

Perhaps Onegus didn't know that, or maybe he was covering for her. Thankfully, none of the guys on his team knew that either.

62

ONEGUS

Onegus could feel Cassandra's body trembling with relief. If not for his arm around her, her legs would have given way.

"Liam, can you bring a chair out for Cassandra? She had quite a scare."

"I'm on it, boss."

"Roy. Get a cleanup crew here to clear the mess. Gerard has several people in charge of cleaning in the kitchen."

"Yes, boss."

Normally, he would have asked one of the Odus, but they were nowhere to be seen. He knew that Amanda wouldn't have excluded them from the celebrations, and she must have reserved seats for them. The Odus were treated as members of the family, and they were also an added level of security.

Perhaps they were helping Gerard and his crew in the kitchen. After all, the Odus were programmed to be helpful. Sitting around as guests would have probably fried their cybertronic brains.

Besides, Cassandra had just blown up the punch bowl. Until she learned to control her power, he didn't want the Odus anywhere near her. If anything happened to even one of them, Annani would be devastated.

Or worse, she might lose it and retaliate against Cassandra.

For now, he'd managed to cover for her, but he'd already told enough people about the power she possessed. It was only a question of time before someone figured out that the punch bowl hadn't exploded on its own.

Bridget came out of the ballroom and surveyed the damage. Finding the server, she walked up to him. "Are you hurt?"

He shook his head. "Just wet and sticky. I was lucky that none of the glass pieces got me."

"Indeed." She walked over to Cassandra. "How about you? Are you okay?"

"She's just rattled," Onegus said.

Bridget threw him one of her withering looks. "I didn't ask you, now did I?"

"I'm not hurt." Cassandra rubbed at the punch stains on her chest. "This is from before. Someone bumped into me, and I got splashed."

Bridget nodded. "Then if I'm not needed here, I'm going back inside."

"Thank you for checking on us." Cassandra lowered herself to the chair Liam had brought for her.

"You're welcome." Bridget waved before going through the doors into the banquet hall.

"In case you were wondering, that was our family's doctor."

"I figured. She sounded like one." Cassandra pushed to her feet. "If you don't mind, I could really use the bathroom."

"Of course." He took her hand and led her out into the hallway.

"Do you still want me to use the one in your office?" She didn't sound like it was something she wanted to do.

"It's up to you." He leaned closer to her ear. "I'm sure my mother is done powdering her nose."

"I didn't see her coming back, but then I was a little distracted." Cassandra smiled nervously. "I just want to wash this stickiness off me, have a cup of coffee to clear my head, and then go dancing."

"Sounds like a plan."

As they headed in the bathroom's direction, his mother walked toward them together with Sylvia.

"We heard that there was an incident with the punch bowl," Sylvia said. "What happened?"

"It must have been defective," Onegus said. "The bowl cracked and then broke apart."

"Did anyone get hurt?" his mother asked.

Cassandra shook her head. "Fortunately, no one was standing near it when it cracked, and the glass was too thick and heavy to go flying."

Sylvia looked at her with knowing eyes. "You need to learn to control it. This time you were lucky, and no one got hurt. Next time you might not be."

Cassandra tensed. "I don't know what you're talking about." She pulled her hand out of Onegus's and walked into the restroom.

"Someone is in denial," Sylvia said.

"Not really." Onegus rubbed a hand over his jaw. "She's just pretending that it had nothing to do with her, and that's what she should be doing. Imagine what would have happened to her if someone other than us figured out what she could do."

His mother grimaced. "Don't remind me. I lived during those horrible times." She put a hand on his arm. "You should tell her who and what you are. It's not right to bring her into our midst and keep her ignorant. You need to ask Kalugal to compel her silence."

"First, I want to tell Cassandra what's at stake and offer her options. Compulsion is just one of the ways to protect our secrets, and it's not my favorite."

63

CASSANDRA

$\mathcal{C}$assandra leaned closer to the mirror and examined the neckline of her dress. Miraculously, the stain hadn't penetrated the fabric, and she was able to rub it off with one of the cloth towels she'd wetted. The spot was wet, but because the fabric was black, it was barely visible.

Onegus's haughty mother had been right about that.

Wetting another one of the small rolled-up towels, Cassandra wiped the sticky residue off her skin, then took a dry one to finish the job. Everything was back to normal.

Right.

How had Sylvia guessed that she'd had something to do with the punch bowl incident? She hadn't been there when it happened. If Onegus hadn't realized the connection, how could she?

Maybe the girl was a psychic?

Whatever. Sylvia, Martha, and whoever else wanted to pin it on Cassandra had no proof, and as long as she kept pretending innocence, she was safe. Circumstantial evidence might make people suspicious, but it was not enough to incriminate her.

Squaring her shoulders, she took one last glance at her reflection. Her hair was fine, her newly reapplied lipstick didn't have any smudges, and her eyeliner was still intact.

Tucking her evening purse under her arm, Cassandra headed out of the ladies' room.

Thankfully Martha and Sylvia were gone, and Onegus was waiting for her, leaning against the wall and looking sexily debonair.

"Was the operation successful?" He walked up to her.

She waved a hand over her dress. "Good as new."

"I'm glad." He took her hand. "Are you up for dancing?"

"Coffee first. And maybe another piece of cake." She was no longer tipsy, but she felt depleted and tired. A boost of caffeine and sugar was in order.

"Sounds good to me." He led her back to the banquet hall.

Several couples were dancing, but most of the guests were sitting around the tables and chatting over coffees, desserts, and more drinks.

Again, she was struck by how uniformly aged everyone looked.

"Does your family own a fountain of youth?"

He chuckled. "In a way."

"In what way? An in-house plastic surgeon? Or just good genes?"

"The second one." He led her to their table. "I'm actually over five hundred years old, but I aged extremely well." He pulled out a chair for her.

"Ha-ha. Very funny." Cassandra looked at Roni, who was smirking and trying to hide it. "Let me guess, you are one hundred years old and only look nineteen."

She could feel Sylvia's eyes on her, assessing, speculating, but she didn't turn to look at the girl.

"No, I'm actually twenty," Roni said. "Good guess, though."

"What about the priestess?" Cassandra pointed with her chin toward the family table. "She looks like an angel, so I guess she could be as old as time and only appears to be eighteen."

Amanda and the red-haired priestess were chatting animatedly, and other than being too beautiful to be real, she seemed almost normal now that the spotlight wasn't directed at her.

"Annani is not a priestess," Onegus said. "She is the head of our clan."

The girl was too young to be the head of anything other than a sorority.

"Did the previous head of your clan pass away, and she inherited the position?"

Sylvia pushed to her feet and tapped Roni's shoulder. "Come dance with me."

He looked as if he was about to protest, but the intense look she gave him didn't leave room for argument.

As Roni rose to his feet, the rest of their companions followed suit, including Connor who didn't have a date.

"I'm going to mingle." He winked before beating feet away from their table.

"Did I say something to chase them off?" she asked.

"They wanted to give us privacy."

"For what?"

Was it about her questions regarding the mysterious head of their clan? What was the story with her?

Was the woman a vampire?

The glowing pale skin, the flaming red hair…

Right. This wasn't a movie, and vampires didn't exist.

Onegus let out a long breath. "To talk. But this is neither the time nor the place for that. Can you stay and spend the night with me?"

She arched a brow. "On the cot in your office in the basement? I'd rather get a hotel room if you don't mind."

It dawned on her then, that when Onegus had offered to take her to his office to clean up in his private bathroom, he hadn't mentioned leaving the building.

She frowned. "Is your office right here? In this building?"

He chuckled. "It is, but we don't have to spend the night there. I can secure a better place with a proper bed."

That sounded like an invitation to share that bed with him, which was way better than the ominous, *we need to talk.*

"Do you want to go now?" she asked.

"I do, but I can't. I have to stay until all the guests leave. I have to make sure that everyone gets safely to where they are going to spend the night, and that could take hours." He lifted her hand and kissed her fingers. "Can you last that long? Or are you tired and want to go home? If you are, I can ask Connor to take you."

She was drained. The release had left her devoid of energy. But at least she wasn't drunk anymore, and she didn't want to go before hearing what he had to say.

"I'm fine." Cassandra rose to her feet and offered him a hand up. "Let's dance."

64

ONEGUS

"I think I'm done," Cassandra admitted defeat after almost two hours of nonstop dancing. "My feet are killing me. I have to sit down."

It was a wonder she was even standing.

Given the tremendous energy she'd expelled, she'd lasted much longer than he'd expected. Someone less stubborn would have given up a long time ago, but Cassandra didn't know that she'd been competing against immortals, who were twice or thrice as resilient. Her competitive nature had driven her to push herself to the limit.

"No problem." Onegus wrapped his arm around her waist and led her back to their table.

The only one there was Connor. Tessa and Jackson were still dancing, Sharon and Robert had gone home, and so had Roni and Sylvia. Ruth and Nick were sitting at another table, talking with Vlad and Wendy and their extended family, which now included Wendy's mother.

"As much as I love these Louboutins, I can't stand them for another moment." Cassandra kicked the shoes off and let out a relieved breath.

"Do you want me to rub your feet?" Connor offered.

She narrowed her eyes at him. "Not a good idea. But I will be forever grateful if you get me a cup of coffee."

"I'm on it."

Onegus wondered whether she didn't want Connor to rub her feet because that was too intimate for her, or because she thought that he would get jealous.

The truth was that he didn't want any man's hands on her, not even Connor's.

As soon as his roommate left, Cassandra shifted the chair to the side, lifted her feet, and put them on the next chair over. "If I'm breaking any British etiquette rules, I don't care." She wiggled her dainty toes.

His mother might think so, but he didn't.

"You can do as you please." Onegus pulled out the next chair over, sat down, and took one of her feet in his hands. "I don't have a lot of time, but I can squeeze in a quick foot massage."

Her eyes rolling back in pleasure, she sighed. "I might never let you go. A man who offers foot massages is a keeper."

That was a loaded comment.

Connor had made the same offer a moment ago, and she'd refused.

As Onegus's hands on Cassandra's feet stilled for a brief moment, she opened her eyes. "Did I scare you? Don't worry. I was just teasing."

He shook his head and resumed massaging her toes. "You've got it all wrong. Your comment made me wistful, not fearful. I like the idea of you holding onto me."

Her eyes softened. "Don't say things you don't mean."

He put her foot down and picked up the other one. "I never say things that I don't mean."

Watching him kneading her foot with a pensive expression on her face, Cassandra didn't retort with a snarky comment as he'd expected.

Perhaps she was too tired to come up with one.

"The guests are starting to leave. I need to go." He put the foot down. "Are you going to be okay?"

"Of course she is." Connor put a steaming cup of coffee in front of Cassandra. "I'm here to keep her company." He looked at her feet that were still nestled in Onegus's lap. "I see how it is. I'm not good enough for your toes." He cast her a mock reproachful look. "But he is?"

Lifting Cassandra's feet off his lap, Onegus got up and then laid them down gently on the chair. "I hope it's not going to take long."

"Off with you." Connor waved at him before leaning closer to Cassandra. "Let's gossip."

Walking toward the exit, Onegus scanned the room to estimate how many guests were still there. About half were gone, and only a few were lingering in the antechamber. The rest were either dancing or sitting at the tables. It was nearly three o'clock in the morning, and it wouldn't be long before the rest left. Especially since David and Sari had already retired, as had the rest of the royal family as he liked to refer to them.

Annani usually didn't stay long, probably because she knew that her presence was intimidating to many of the clan members, and that they would have more fun and be less inhibited with her gone. Amanda, who usually stayed until the very end, was pregnant and tired easily, and the same was even truer for Syssi. She could barely walk.

He found Yamanu in the hallway, leaning against the wall next to the ladies' room. "Just the guy I was looking for. Are you waiting for Mey?"

He nodded. "I'm not going to make her stay until the end. She's going home with Jin and Arwel."

"Good thinking. I'm going to check on Gerard's people and see when they are ready to leave."

"I spoke with him already. The kitchen is done, but they still need to collect all the serveware from the ballroom. He thinks it will take them another hour to clean, and then they need to load everything including themselves into the vans, which probably will take another half an hour."

After the staff left the building, Gerard was going to have them stop up front for an inspection, and that was when Yamanu would manipulate their memories, changing the event's location and blurring the faces they had seen.

Onegus groaned. "It seems like you and I are not leaving here before four-thirty in the morning."

There was no way Cassandra would last that long.

He could have Connor take her home, but that meant that he would have to thrall her first.

Since Kalugal and Jacki had left already, asking him to compel Cassandra's silence wasn't an option. Eleanor could do that as well, but it meant taking Cassandra to the dungeon.

That was actually not a bad idea. The converted cells were as nice as any hotel room, and Cassandra wouldn't mind spending the night in one. She didn't need to know that they used to be prison cells. He could tell her that they were underground apartments or safe rooms.

She was probably too tired for having *the talk* tonight, but they could sleep in each other's arms and save it for the morning.

Following Ingrid's advice, he would tell Cassandra the truth and ask for her consent to induction in writing. After that was done, he would give her the option of either a thrall to forget what he'd revealed or compulsion that would force her to keep it a secret.

65

CASSANDRA

Sometime during Connor's endless prattle, Cassandra must have dozed off.

The next time she opened her eyes, she was sprawled over a row of chairs, and everyone except her and Connor was gone.

An older guy in a suit and a bow tie was vacuuming the floor, but she was too tired to ponder who he was or where he'd come from.

The noise he made with that infernal vacuum was probably what had woken her up.

Shifting up, she stifled a yawn. "How long have I been asleep?"

"A little over an hour," Connor said. "Onegus is almost done. He should be back any moment now."

"Thanks for staying with me." She picked up the cold cup of coffee and took a sip. "You didn't have to. I'm sure that I'm perfectly safe here."

"That's true, but I was afraid that you would roll off these chairs. My other option was to lay you out on the table, but I didn't think you would approve."

Cassandra chuckled. "No, I wouldn't. I can't believe that I didn't wake up when you laid me out on the chairs."

"You were out like a rock. People stopped by to say goodbye, and you snored right through it."

"I did no such thing. I don't snore."

"Yes, you do. Tiny little snores like a kitten."

She was about to answer when Onegus walked in, looking as fresh and as energetic as if it was the middle of the day.

"I'm sorry it took so long." He patted Connor on the back. "Thanks for guarding my lady."

"Anytime." Connor pushed to his feet. "I'll see myself out." He leaned down and kissed Cassandra's cheek. "Good night."

"Good night, Connor." She watched him walk away before turning to Onegus. "What now?"

He crouched next to her and picked up her shoes. "You have two options. I can put these shoes on your feet, and you can walk, or I can put them in my pockets and carry you."

"There is a third option. I can walk barefoot."

He shook his head. "I'm not letting you walk without shoes through that antechamber. Small glass shards might have remained after the servers cleaned the mess. They didn't do a thorough job."

Cassandra considered her options.

Just thinking about putting the shoes back on made her feet throb with pain, and other than the guy with the vacuum, there was no one else around. Besides, being carried in Onegus's strong arms sounded very appealing.

"Will they fit in your pockets? If not, I can hold them."

Given the satisfied grin on his face, that was the answer he'd hoped for.

"Let's see." He pushed up with a shoe in each hand, then spun them like a gunslinger before shoving them into his pockets, the spiky heels sticking out like gun handles.

"Show-off."

"You have no idea." Onegus bent at the waist and picked her up effortlessly.

She wrapped her arms around his neck. "I'll tell you a secret." She nuzzled his neck. "I like it when you carry me."

He chuckled. "I know."

Cassandra had never met a guy who could be so charming and full of himself at the same time. It was an art form.

"Where are you taking me?" she asked as he stopped in front of the elevators.

"A place not many get to see." He held her up with one hand while pressing his thumb to the button.

"Your secret lair?"

"Yes."

"Oh, wow. Is it like Batman's cave?" She laughed. "The guy who was vacuuming in a suit, is he your Pennyworth?"

"He's a butler, but he's not mine. He is Kian's." Onegus carried her into the elevator and pressed his thumb to one of the down buttons.

"So, if Kian is Batman, are you Robin?"

He gave her a scornful look. "I'm no one's sidekick."

"No, you are not." She kissed his neck. "You are Captain America."

"I like that much better."

As the elevator door opened, Onegus stepped out and turned into a wide corridor, which was lined with many doors. It looked like a dormitory or a school. There were no windows to the outside, and the ones on the doors were on the bottom instead of on the top.

Her arms tightened around his neck. "What is this place?"

"We have safe rooms down here."

"Safe from what?"

He stopped in front of one of the doors, hoisted her up with one arm, and punched a series of numbers on the keypad. "Safe from our enemies." He stepped back.

As the door started moving, its mechanism making a low buzzing sound, it became very apparent that it wasn't an ordinary door. The thing was a foot thick and made from some kind of alloy.

Was he taking her into a safe or a nuclear shelter?

"Put me down," she demanded.

"What's wrong?"

It was an instinctive response that hadn't been rooted in logic.

If Onegus wanted to imprison her inside that room, she would be helpless to do anything about it, and it wouldn't matter whether she was on her feet or in his arms. She couldn't outrun him, and even if she could run fast enough, she couldn't use the elevator.

"Hi, Chief," a woman behind them said. "What are you doing here?"

"What does it look like I'm doing?" He turned so Cassandra could see her. "This is my girlfriend, Cassandra."

"Hi." The woman smiled. "I'm Eleanor. Nice to meet you, and good night." She ducked back into the room she came out of.

Eleanor had looked amused, not troubled or alarmed, and knowing that there was another woman around made Cassandra feel less apprehensive.

"Who is she?"

"A member of my team." He walked into the room, which was decorated like any upscale hotel room, but it didn't have a window. Maybe it was indeed a safe room.

"As promised," Onegus said. "A queen-sized bed with a comfortable mattress."

He didn't take her to the bed, though. He put her down on the small sofa.

Damn. It seemed like she was going to get the talk after all.

66

ONEGUS

*C*assandra had had a nice long nap, and she seemed wide awake, which meant that they could have the talk tonight instead of waiting for the morning.

Except, now that Onegus had her where he wanted her, he didn't know how to broach the subject.

How had the other men done it? Four out of his six head Guardians had found love with Dormants, but each case was different. Brundar hadn't told Callie anything until she'd started transitioning because he hadn't believed she was a Dormant.

Arwel had had it easy because Jin had already learned the truth from her sister. And Kri also had had it easy because Michael already learned he was a Dormant from Kian and Amanda. Wonder was already an immortal when Anandur had met her, so the only one who'd had to jump through hoops had been Yamanu. How had he done it?

He'd asked Kian's permission to bring Mey into the village, but had he told her before or after?

Perhaps opening with Cassandra's power was the way to go.

Her denial had been a lie, and he knew that she was aware of the destructive power she possessed and feared it.

She might be more positively predisposed to what he was about to tell her if it offered an explanation and possibly even a solution for something that must have been giving her trouble for years.

"Can I offer you something to drink?" Onegus asked.

Hopefully, Okidu kept the small fridge stocked with fresh bottles of water and soft drinks. If not, he would have to go up to the lobby and get her something from the vending machines. Or better yet, he could send Eleanor or Alfie to get it.

"Coffee would be nice." Cassandra leaned sideways to look at the small bar he was blocking from her view. "I see a Nespresso coffee maker. They are easy to operate."

That's right. He'd forgotten about that. "Coffee coming up." He examined the pods. "I assume that you want a strong cup of java?"

"Yes, please. The strongest you have."

He filled the small container with water from the faucet, inserted a pod into the slot, put a mug under the spout, and turned the device on. It took moments to produce a decent cup of coffee, and he repeated the process to make the second one.

"Cream and sugar?"

"Yes, please."

He opened the cabinet and pulled out a container of sugar packets and another one of powdered creamer.

"I hope that's okay." He brought everything to the coffee table. "These rooms are not used very often, so everything in here is of the long-lasting variety."

Cassandra took a look around. "Someone must be keeping them clean. There is no dust."

"The butler you saw upstairs comes here twice a week."

He sat next to her on the couch, still not sure where to start.

She emptied two packets of sugar and one creamer packet into her coffee, stirred them with a spoon, and then took a long sip. "It's better than I expected."

"I'm glad."

After several long moments of silence, Cassandra put the cup down and leaned back. "Is it that bad that you can't bring yourself to get it out?"

He forced a smile. "Not at all. It's all good. I just don't know where to start, which is surprising. I'm rarely at a loss for words."

"Does it have anything to do with your mother? She doesn't seem to like me. Is that a problem?"

"In a way, it has to do with my mother, but not with her liking you or not. And just so you know, that was Martha trying her best to be nice. Usually, she's much worse, which leads me to believe that she likes you."

"Oh, my. I can't imagine what she's like at her worst."

He chuckled. "Imagine yourself when one of your snowflakes annoys you."

She arched a brow. "Are you saying that your mother and I are similar?"

"In more ways than you realize. You are both alphas, which is why you locked horns. Just like you, Martha is smart, capable, assertive, and doesn't take shit from anyone."

Cassandra grimaced. "It must be true that men seek out women who are like their mothers."

"It would seem so." He turned to face her. "There is one major difference, though. Not counting a sharp tongue, my mother doesn't have any special powers."

It wasn't entirely true. Martha could thrall to some extent, but nothing else.

Her back stiffening, Cassandra picked up her coffee cup. "What are you talking about?" She took a sip and kept looking at it, most likely to avoid his eyes.

"You know what I mean. When you get angry or overly excited, you emit energy that makes things explode. The glass at the rooftop bar, the vase at the apartment where we spent the night together, and now the punch bowl. Your power is dangerous, and you need to learn to control it."

6 7

CASSANDRA

*T*hat was what Sylvia had said.

Fear twisted Cassandra's gut.

Did they all know that the punch bowl incident had been her fault?

That didn't make sense. Onegus had covered for her, and Sylvia couldn't have learned it from him because he hadn't left Cassandra's side until they met Sylvia and his mother in front of the bathrooms.

She must have guessed it as well. But how? No one had ever suspected before because outside of movies and books, people weren't supposed to have such powers.

"Why do you think that I had anything to do with those incidents? Other than being a jinx, that is."

Smiling indulgently, he took her hand. "I can feel the power swirling inside of you. I know that it intensifies when you get angry or irritated, and I know that sex helps defuse it." He winked at her. "I volunteer to be your defuser."

Pursing her lips, she regarded him from under lowered eyelashes. "Let's assume for a moment that you are right. Doesn't it bother you? Most people would be scared, thinking that I'm a witch or a dangerous freak."

He chuckled. "You are a dangerous freak, but so am I, as well as most of the people you met at the wedding. I don't blame you for hiding what you can do and denying culpability. Humans are not known for their tolerance, especially when they fear you. My people and I hide our freakishness as well, but we do a better job of it than you."

She had no idea what Onegus was talking about, but he'd given her the opening to turn the tables on him.

"In what way are you and your people dangerous freaks? Your good looks? Your mother's freakishly young appearance?" She narrowed her eyes at him. "Or the exclusion of the older generation from taking part in your events so they don't spoil the family photos?"

She'd been mocking him, but to her surprise he nodded.

"We are immortal. We are stronger, faster, and we can manipulate human minds. That makes us dangerous."

Was he insane?

The oddities she'd noticed suddenly started making sense. The people at the wedding weren't really Onegus's family. They were a strange cult of people who believed they would live forever. The gorgeous glowing priestess was obviously their leader, using her beauty and charisma to lure her followers. Onegus had even said that she was the head of their clan, but what he'd meant was the head of their cult.

Cassandra should have gotten a clue then.

Onegus's relatives weren't really related to him. They'd been recruited into the cult, and they didn't just look about the same age, they were indeed in their early twenties and thirties. Those were the age groups that the glowing beauty recruited from. She only accepted the best-looking people, which also explained why Cassandra hadn't seen even one unattractive guest.

Furthermore, Martha wasn't Onegus's real mother, only his cult mother.

What a mess. Could she save Onegus from wasting his life by living a delusion?

The better question was how she was going to save herself.

What did they want with her? Was she a new recruit? Was the invitation to the wedding about getting the cult members' approval? She must have passed the scrutiny if he was telling her that nonsense.

"What's going through your head, Cassandra?"

"I assume that you are telling me this now because you want to recruit me into your cult. Was tonight a test? Did the other members approve of me?"

Tilting his head, he made a face that was part perplexed and part amused. "A cult? You think that my family is a cult? I'm curious to hear how you arrived at that leap of logic."

Cassandra knew all about plausible deniability, had been playing that game for years. Did Onegus think that his dumb act was going to work on her?

Crossing her arms over her chest, she looked down her nose at him. "It's quite obvious. A large group of twenty to thirty-something individuals, all attractive, led by a charismatic woman-child of unparalleled beauty, who think of themselves as family and believe that they will live forever. Was Martha your recruiter? Is that why she's considered your cult mother?"

Onegus's shoulders started shaking, and a moment later, he burst out laughing.

She glared at him. "There is nothing funny about it. You are brainwashed, and you're wasting your life living in delusion."

"It is funny." He wiped tears from his eyes. "I'm just stunned. If you ask me, vampires would have been a more logical suspension of disbelief than a cult."

He was mocking her, which was a great tactic for discrediting her observations. That's how they'd dealt with all those people who'd reported UFO sightings. The strategy was incredibly effective, convincing millions of people that those reports were made by loonies.

She'd been one of those who'd ate it up and thought those people were either crazy or prone to hallucinations. But then the former head of the French equivalent of NASA had come out with a statement that a small percentage of those sightings couldn't be explained as anything other than alien crafts, operating on alien technology. No aircraft made by humans could accelerate that fast or move in such a manner.

That had changed everything for her, and not only about UFO sightings. From that moment on, she doubted any statements made by people who had something to gain or lose by making them. The only ones she deemed credible were retired scientists and military personnel who were too old to care about what the government would do to them for spilling the beans, and who had nothing they could be blackmailed for.

"Making fun of my observations is not going to change my mind about what I saw and what I deduced. Save it for the weaklings who cave under social pressure."

68

ONEGUS

*S*tubborn, smart woman.

Cassandra's deduction wasn't crazy. In fact, it was the most logical explanation she could have come up with, given what she'd observed.

Onegus tugged on her arm, uncrossing it, and took her hand. "I'm not mocking you, and I'm not discrediting what you saw. I'm merely offering a different explanation. The glowing priestess, as you call her, is a goddess. One of the only two remaining from those you're familiar with from different mythologies. We are her descendants. When gods mated with humans, their children were born immortal, possessing some of the gods' powers, but to a lesser extent. But when immortals mated other immortals or humans, the children born to them were born human, but all was not lost. The immortal genes passed through the mothers, and the children born to immortal females possessed the genes in a dormant form. They found a way to activate them. Later, they discovered that those genes could pass in dormant form from mother to daughter throughout many generations and still could be activated."

He paused, waiting for Cassandra to ask questions or dispute what he'd told her, but she was looking at him wide-eyed, either thinking that his tale was incredible or that he was insane.

"Many of the dormant carriers possess supernatural abilities," he continued. "Which is why I believe that you are a Dormant, and so is your mother. Although in her case, I suspect that someone activated her a long time ago, and she's already immortal. You are too close to her to realize it, but Geraldine doesn't look any older than Martha, and you had a hard time believing that she was my mother."

Cassandra narrowed her eyes. "Why does that make sense to me?"

"Because you are smart, and you are already connecting the dots. Your mother's memory lapses could be real, or they could be her way to hide that she is much older. Just think about her manners. She acts like someone who grew up in the fifties."

Cassandra huffed. "She's definitely not a prude."

He smiled. "That's because immortals are inherently intensely sexual beings. She couldn't help it. Then there is the story about her losing her driver's license and not bothering to renew it. She might be avoiding doing that because it would give her away. Besides, she's probably using an alias."

"It can't be true."

"Which part? My story or your mother being immortal?"

"Everything."

"I'm not a hundred percent sure about your mother, and I can't prove that she's immortal without further investigation, but I can prove that what I told you about myself is true. I'm an immortal."

"How can you prove it?"

"One of the many benefits of being an immortal is our rapid healing. If I make a small cut on my arm, the wound will close in front of your eyes. The other way to prove it is to show you how different I am from a human male."

"Start with the last one, and I hope it doesn't involve your dick and some weird tentacles it can sprout during sex." She shuddered. "As much as I like you, that's a deal-breaker."

He laughed. "What the hell have you been reading?"

"One of my mother's sci-fi romances." She grimaced. "Talk about disturbing."

"Fortunately, I don't have tentacles, and I'm glad this is the only thing that you consider a deal-breaker." He lifted his finger and tapped her nose. "Remember that you said it when I show you my fangs."

"Fangs?" She shifted away from him. "What fangs? You don't have fangs."

"They elongate when I'm aroused or in response to aggression."

Her hand flew to her neck. "Are you a vampire? Did you suck my blood?"

"My fangs deliver venom. I don't consume blood."

Her face twisted in a horrified expression. "Venom? Like a snake's? Is it poisonous?"

"The venom acts as an aphrodisiac and euphoric when used during sex. In battle, it can be used to immobilize an opponent, and either put him in stasis or stop his heart, depending on the dose."

Cassandra shook her head. "I don't understand. How can it do one thing during sex and then another during a fight?"

"The venom glands react to stimulation, and the venom produced is different depending on the stimuli."

"What if you get aggressive during sex?"

"As long as I'm aroused, my glands will only produce the stuff that induces orgasms and euphoria." He leaned closer. "You've experienced it twice so far, and you loved every moment."

The good thing about the direction their conversation was taking was his rising arousal. Without forcing his body to stifle its reactions, his eyes were probably already glowing, and his fangs tingled, indicating that they were elongating. In a moment, he would have proof for Cassandra.

The bad thing about it was her reaction to finding out she'd been bitten twice already.

"How come I don't remember that?" She rubbed her neck at the exact spot he'd bitten her.

Her subconscious remembered it, and all he had to do was to release those memories and let them float to the surface. It would serve as additional proof.

"I thralled you to forget my two bites. But I can release those memories."

"What do you mean when you say you thralled me? Is it like hypnosis?"

"It is, and it's not. I don't need to speak to you to affect your mind, and I can also see your most recent memories. A hypnotist can't do either. When I entered your mind, I pushed the memory of my bite below the surface of consciousness. That's why your hand is rubbing the exact spot I bit. Your body remembers it. You might also have dreamt about it."

"I haven't. But I have a big problem with you entering my mind without my permission."

"I didn't look at anything other than the sex we shared. It would have been a violation."

"Weren't you tempted to take a look at how I feel about you?"

"I don't need to infiltrate your mind to know that." He leaned closer and sniffed. "There is one more thing immortals can do that I forgot to mention. Our sense of smell can discern strong emotions. I know when you are aroused, and I know what pleases you. That's one of the things that makes me such a great lover."

Her lips twitched with a stifled smile. "You are so full of yourself." She lifted her finger and pointed it at his face. "Your eyes are glowing."

He smiled, letting her see his partially elongated fangs. "That's what talking about sex with you does to me. I'm aroused."

Unafraid, she leaned closer to examine his fangs. "I know for a fact that you were aroused at other times, but your eyes didn't glow, and you didn't sprout fangs. How come it's happening now?"

"I'm not actively suppressing my reactions. I have very good control over my body."

She looked down at the erection pressing against his slacks. "You don't seem to be able to control that."

"I could if I wanted to. But since it's not strange for a male to get a hard-on, I don't bother. My only concern is hiding my immortality. The very existence of my people depends on no one discovering that we exist."

CASSANDRA

*C*assandra didn't know what was more unbelievable, the story Onegus had told her, or the fact that she was inclined to believe him.

"Aren't you taking a risk by telling me?"

"I can make you forget."

"So why tell me in the first place?"

"Because I need your consent to induce you. I won't do it without getting it first."

"What are you talking about?"

"You are a dormant carrier of immortal genes, I'm willing to bet my right hand on it, which means that those genes can be activated, and you can turn immortal. But I won't do it unless you agree to it. There are some risks involved."

Shaking her head, she lifted a hand. "First, tell me how this induction is done. Because if it's anything like Bella had to go through when Edward was saving her life, I'm out."

Relying on a movie was the epitome of stupidity, but since what Onegus had told her was partially covered by myth and turned out to be true, maybe the author of *Twilight* had based her story on a myth that was actually a true account as well.

When Onegus looked like he had no clue what she was blabbering about, Cassandra rolled her eyes. "It's from a movie about vampires called *Twilight*. Don't tell me that you haven't heard of it." She snorted. "That could be used as proof that you're an alien."

"I've heard of *Twilight*, but I didn't read the books or watch the movies. Many of my female relatives did, though, and there was this whole silliness going on about team Edward versus team Jason."

"Jacob, not Jason. But to make a long story short, Bella was dying after giving birth to a half-vampire daughter, and Edward saved her by biting her all over and injecting her with his vampiric venom. She made it, but she suffered through hellish pain while her body transitioned from human to vampire."

"Really?" He cocked a brow, but his lips were twitching with a stifled smile. "You would give up immortality to avoid a little pain?"

"That's a lot of pain, mind you." She shifted away, creating some space between them. No way was she going through that.

Besides, he'd said the process was risky, just like in *Twilight*, which meant that she could die. She'd rather live out the remainder of her human life than submit to torture that might or might not result in her gaining immortality.

"Then you'll be glad to know that our induction process is much more pleasurable. All that's required is unprotected sex and venom bites, which you've enjoyed greatly. I can't contract or transmit diseases, so that's not a problem, and if you are worried about pregnancy, contraceptives other than condoms and spermicides don't interfere with the process."

"What about the risk?"

"Our doctor warns that older Dormants might not make it through the transition, but so far, we haven't lost even one, and some were much older than you and not in as good health."

She frowned. "Hold on a moment. You said that it's all fun and sex, although I will need my memories back to determine whether it was as fun for me as it was for you. So, what's the risky part?"

He took her hand in both of his. "The induction is the fun part. When the transition process actually begins, it's not as fun. It starts with symptoms of mild flu, fever, muscle aches, etc. and after that, most transitioning Dormants lose consciousness, some for a few hours, others for days. Each case is different. The moment the transition starts, though, you will be admitted to our clinic and monitored by our doctor, who by now is very experienced with the process. Other than the flu-like pains, it doesn't hurt. Well, for females. Males have to grow fangs and venom, and that's painful as hell."

Judging by his grimace, he'd experienced that and remembered it vividly.

"Did you go through that? You said that children of immortals are not born immortal."

"Correct. I was induced at thirteen. That's when Dormant boys go through their transition. It's treated like a rite of passage, and there is a small ceremony."

"What about the girls?"

"They transition at a much earlier age. Usually as toddlers."

"How come?"

"That's how it was always done."

"That's not an answer, but I get it. Tradition doesn't always make sense. How many Dormants have your people discovered so far?"

"Not many, and all of them recently. The Fates have neglected us for a very long time, and then suddenly decided to smile upon us. Syssi, Kian's wife, was the first. Amanda discovered her about four years ago."

"How? Does Syssi have a paranormal talent?"

Onegus nodded. "Precognition. Amanda is a neuroscientist, and when Syssi volunteered for testing, she scored off the charts. Amanda hired her as a lab assistant and introduced her to Kian. The rest is history."

"I bet there is much more to it."

"There is, and the other Dormants' stories are no less fascinating, but now is not the time for them. I need an answer from you. Do you consent to induction or not?"

"I need to think about it. That's not an easy decision."

"It's not." He rubbed his hand over his jaw, looking vulnerable for the first time since he'd started his incredible tale. "There is another part to this. Usually, when the Dormant is a female, her inducer is her chosen mate." He lifted his glowing blue eyes to her. "Am I your chosen guy?"

Cassandra hesitated.

Her gut's answer was an unequivocal yes, but he'd just dropped on her a load the size of an aircraft carrier. It would take time to process it.

"We haven't been together long enough, and now with all that you've revealed, I need time to think."

"What does your gut tell you?"

"That you're the one for me, fangs and glowing eyes and all. But despite my short fuse, I'm not an impulsive person. I don't want to make promises that I would later have to break."

"Fair enough." He'd either taken her hesitation in his stride or had read through it, realizing that she was just stalling because she was scared. "Do you want your memories back? They might help you make up your mind."

"Aha, so that's the ace up your sleeve. Go ahead. I'm ready."

"Look into my eyes."

"Easy enough."

His eyes were gorgeous, even more so than usual, now that they were glowing.

Cassandra's only warning was a gentle squeeze of her hand, and then the memories flooded her mind in a rush, as if a dam had collapsed. At first, the pressure was too much, and she pulled her hand out of Onegus's grip to press the heels of both hands into her temples.

Thankfully, he hadn't suppressed a lot of memories, and the flood ended in a few seconds.

Closing her eyes, she let them wash over her, and the erotic images flashing before her eyes, as well as her body's recollection of the sensations she'd experienced, had her grow moist and needy in an instant.

"You weren't kidding," she breathed. "No wonder I can't get enough of you."

ONEGUS

*A*s the scent of Cassandra's arousal flared, Onegus hissed, "You are killing me." He reached for her and lifted her into his lap. "All I want now is to make love to you, but I didn't secure your consent yet."

"It can wait for the morning." She wrapped her arms around his neck. "I want to experience that bite again, and this time, don't make me forget."

Closing the distance between their mouths, she licked at the seam between his lips. "Let me in."

He gripped her nape to hold her back. "Careful. You might get your tongue nicked by my fangs. They are very sharp."

"I want to touch them."

He'd never let a woman kiss him, penetrate his mouth with her tongue, and the idea of Cassandra being his first was like dousing a fire with gasoline.

"I've never had a woman's tongue anywhere near my fangs."

She smiled against his lips. "How exciting. I'm going to take your fangs' virginity."

As she licked into his mouth, Onegus groaned, and as she folded her tongue around his right fang, he nearly exploded in his pants. Then she licked the other one, and it took every ounce of self-control to stop himself from taking over, throwing her on the bed, and tearing her dress off.

Onegus lasted for about ten seconds before taking over the kiss, his tongue sweeping in and conquering Cassandra's mouth.

She moaned, and it was his undoing. Gripping her nape even tighter, he kept kissing her while his other hand pushed the one strap holding her dress up down her arm.

Except, the dress was too form-fitting for him to tug it off without ripping it. Some semblance of restraint had him search for the zipper and lower it slowly enough not to destroy it.

As the bodice finally fell away, he discovered that Cassandra wasn't wearing a bra, and the last of his self-control snapped.

Lifting with her in his arms, he crossed the two feet to the bed and put her down.

"Is it a yes?" he asked as he shrugged his jacket off and tossed it on the couch.

"Yes." She shimmied out of the dress and pushed back against the headboard in her panties.

He needed to know precisely what she was agreeing to. "Yes to sex, or yes to sex without a condom?"

"Condom. I need more time."

It was disappointing, but he wasn't in a position to argue. All he wanted was to bury himself in her heat, and if it had to be with a damn condom, he'd take it.

"Take off your panties," he commanded as he tore off his bow tie and attacked the buttons of his shirt.

Onegus would have torn that off too, but he had nothing to change into. After the first two buttons were open, he remembered the cufflinks and pulled them out before tugging the shirt over his head.

"You move so fast." Cassandra's eyes roved over his bare chest. "Have you been holding back before?"

"You still have those panties on."

Her long fingers traveled to the gusset, and she pulled it aside, just enough for him to take a peek at the glistening slickness. "I want you to take them off me."

"Of course you do." He toed his shoes off along with the socks and dropped his pants.

Cassandra sucked in a breath. "No wonder you look like a statue of a Greek god. You have their damn genes."

He was on her between one heartbeat and the next, his fingers replacing hers in the slick heat, sliding in and out of her.

She was soaked, ready for the taking, but even though she didn't need any preparation, he needed a taste of her.

Sliding down her body, he tugged the panties off and then pushed her legs apart and dove between them.

As he treated her to the first lick, Cassandra jerked up, her bottom lifting and opening her further for his tongue to plunge.

He fucked her with his tongue, savoring her taste and her moans and her undulations, but he was too close to climaxing to torment her for much longer. He needed her to come so he could bury himself in her to the hilt.

Replacing his tongue with two fingers, he sucked the bundle of nerves at the apex of her thighs into his mouth.

With a growl, Cassandra bowed off the bed, her climax tearing through her like an explosion. He kept on licking and sucking, wringing every last drop of pleasure out of her. At some point her fingers threaded in his hair, and she tugged on his curls hard enough that the slight pain penetrated his sex-addled brain, and he let go.

71

CASSANDRA

*I*f not for the memory of that bite, Cassandra would have let herself drift off to sleep.

The orgasm Onegus had wrung out of her had left her sated and boneless, and given how tired she'd been before he'd carried her to bed, it was a wonder she wanted more.

He kissed her inner thigh, one side and then the next, and as she lifted her head and looked at him, he smiled and licked his lips.

"Come here." She tugged on his hair.

He didn't need to be asked twice.

Kissing up her belly, he reached her right breast and licked the nipple, then moved to the other one before settling in the cradle of her legs.

Poised above her, he was all muscles, fangs, and glowing eyes, and he was hers. Somehow, he didn't look alien to her, or scary. He was her Onegus, too gorgeous to be real, too charming, too much of everything, but he was hers, and she was not giving him up.

As the tip of his shaft nudged at her entrance, she debated whether to remind him to sheath himself in a condom or to pretend that she'd forgotten as well and just let it happen.

"I almost forgot." He leaned over the side of the bed and lifted his slacks. "We need this."

He pulled a condom packet out of his pocket, tore it open with his teeth, or rather fangs, and pulled the rubber on.

The whole maneuver had lasted only a couple of seconds, and then he was at her entrance again, pushing into her and kissing her at the same time.

Cassandra was so wet from her climax that he didn't need to go slow, but he did anyway, inching into her until he seated himself fully.

They both groaned.

Lifting his head, Onegus withdrew and then surged in, all the time watching her face with an intensity that made her feel like she was precious to him.

She wrapped her arms around his muscled back, her long legs around his powerful hips, and lifted to take him even deeper.

And still, that wasn't enough.

She wanted him wild and unrestrained, but despite all her bluster, she wasn't comfortable asking for what she wanted.

He'd said that he could read her needs, smell them, couldn't he tell that she needed him fast and hard?

Onegus smiled, his fangs gleaming white in the darkened room. "Tell me what you want, Cassy."

So, that was the game he was playing.

She could play as well. "Can't you guess?"

He pulled almost all the way out and then slammed back, propelling their bodies toward the headboard.

Stilling again, he looked into her eyes. "Is that what you want?"

"Yes. Don't stop."

He pulled out again, going to the very edge, and then slammed back in. Gripping her hips, he started pounding into her with abandon, and all she could do was to hiss, "Yes, yes!"

That kind of pounding would leave marks, and Cassandra knew she would be sore and bruised in the morning, but she didn't care.

This was Onegus unleashed, and he was magnificent. She wanted to take all he had, to give herself to him completely like she'd never given herself to any man before.

For tonight, he could be her master, and she relished the submission, so rare for her that she doubted she could do it again.

When his pounding became even stronger and faster, and his shaft swelled impossibly larger inside her, she knew it was time for what she'd been waiting for and turned her head, offering him her neck.

Except, he didn't bite her right away. Even though he was seconds away from climaxing, he licked the spot, preparing it for his bite, and when it came, the slight pain was just enough to hurtle her over the edge.

Cassandra climaxed, her sheath tightening around Onegus's impossibly thick shaft, and as the venom entered her system, she climaxed again, and again, until she must have passed out.

Soaring on a cloud of euphoria, she let herself drift away into the magical lands the venom had opened up for her.

72

ONEGUS

*A*fter Cassandra had drifted off to wonderland, Onegus had lain awake for a long time.

Last night had been a turning point in their relationship, but he wasn't satisfied with where it was. He hadn't told her that he loved her yet, and she hadn't said the words to him either.

Did he love her?

Did he even know what love was?

Onegus was an old immortal, and the only real love of his life was his work. While others had pined for mates, lamented about their loneliness and the never-ending revolving door of lovers, he'd been happy with his life. The tight control he had over himself meant that he didn't have to spend much of his time and energy hunting for sex partners, and when he did, it was mostly enjoyable and quite satisfying.

He hadn't been looking for an emotional connection.

Perhaps Cassandra had been right when she'd accused him of being a player at heart.

The thing was, she'd changed all that, and he had no problem envisioning life with her as his partner. She had her own career, was her own woman, and she wouldn't put unreasonable demands on his time.

They could make it work.

But that wasn't what Cassandra was after. She wanted his heart, his soul, and he wasn't sure he had it in him to surrender them to her.

Even if he and Cassandra bonded, love was not really part of the equation. Contrary to what most clan members believed, the bond wasn't some mythical thing ordained by the Fates. It was a biological reaction, hormones, or pheromones, or some other chemical process that created that insufferable need for mates to be together.

Love was different. Love came from the soul, and he wasn't sure that he was wired for love. Falling in like, or rather in lust, was the best he could hope for, and for him, that was enough.

It wouldn't be for Cassandra, though, and she wasn't the type of woman who would compromise on anything less than everything.

She'd told him that she could easily fall in love with him and had asked if he would break her heart.

He'd promised Cassandra that her heart was safe with him.

He would never betray her, and if she transitioned and became his mate, he would stay with her forever. But he couldn't promise her love without it being at least partially a lie.

To make her happy, though, he would have to do it. Onegus hated liars, didn't want to be one, but the alternative was to let her go, and he couldn't do that either. If she didn't turn, he would be forced to, but if she transitioned, he wanted to keep her.

Perhaps love would come later. Or maybe it was already there, but he didn't recognize it.

Turning to look at Cassandra's beautiful face, Onegus knew that he would love waking up next to her each morning, love talking to her over breakfast, and then love meeting her again in the evening after their workday was done. The other kind of love would come later.

He pressed a soft kiss to her cheek and then got out of bed.

It was five o'clock in the morning, and the Guardians would be switching shifts in an hour. He had to go up to the apartment, change into his day clothes, and get breakfast for him and Cassandra.

After he washed up and got dressed, Onegus stopped by the bed and spent a long moment looking at Cassandra's beautiful face. Her expression was one of bliss, and he loved that he'd put it there.

He should leave her a note in case she woke up before he returned.

Taking a napkin from the minibar, he wrote her a short message and put it on the pillow next to her where she couldn't miss it.

As Onegus opened the door with his phone, the mechanical whizzing sound didn't wake Cassandra or even make her stir.

Taking one last look at her before stepping out, he smiled. He would be back before she woke up.

Cassandra was probably going to sleep until noon, but in case she didn't, he left the door open, just enough for her to squeeze through, but not enough for someone walking by to see her sleeping in the nude.

After all, she wasn't a prisoner, and if he closed her in, she might panic.

Heading toward the elevator, he dialed Bhathian's number. Onegus had left him in charge of the night shift, not expecting any trouble, and hopefully, there had been none.

"Good morning, Chief," the Guardian answered.

"Good morning. Anything to report?" Onegus entered the elevator.

"Nope. All the guests made it safely to their beds last night, although some later than others. Several of our buddies from Scotland stayed with us in the lobby to chat. They left less than an hour ago."

"No news, good news."

"You got it, Chief."

When he reached the apartment, Onegus entered it as quietly as he could, trying not to wake the Guardians sleeping there. Six of them were crammed into the two-bedroom apartment, but it was a temporary situation, and no one was complaining.

After a quick shower and a change of clothes, he walked into the kitchen and started making breakfast, which inevitably woke nearly everyone up, but it was fine. Their shift was starting at six o'clock, and it was time for them to get ready.

73

CASSANDRA

*C*assandra was cold, which was what had woken her up. Onegus was gone, and with him his warmth.

He'd left her a note written on a napkin, saying that he went to check on things and would be back with breakfast.

Shifting to her back, Cassandra pulled the blanket up to her chin and tucked it around her. She was still bone-tired, and if not for the jumble of thoughts swirling in her head, she would have gone back to sleep. But too much was going on for her to let it go.

Onegus was an immortal, and he suspected that her mother was as well. Not only that, but her dormant immortal genes could also be activated as soon as she consented.

Seemed like a no-brainer, especially since Onegus downplayed the risks, saying that his clan hadn't lost a transitioning Dormant yet. They even had their own clinic and an experienced doctor to supervise the transition.

So why was she still hesitating?

Not enough information, that's why.

It all seemed too good to be true, and there must be a downside. Like the mysterious enemies that necessitated all that cloak-and-dagger secrecy and security around the wedding. How dangerous were they? And what beef did they have with Onegus's clan?

Would she have to disappear and live in hiding?

If Geraldine was immortal as Onegus suspected, then she'd done a very good job hiding in plain sight. There was no reason for them to go into hiding.

And then there was the process itself.

Onegus had said that her inducer needed to be her chosen mate, and he'd asked her if he was the guy for her. He hadn't asked her if she loved him, hadn't told her that he loved her, and yet he expected her to marry him? Or mate him?

What if after she transitioned, they came to the conclusion that it wasn't working out? What would her options be?

Cassandra needed answers before she could give Onegus her consent. She'd promised him an answer by morning, but she would have to ask for an extension until she had all the facts and could make an informed decision.

As the door started moving, she pushed up on the pillows and tugged the blanket with her.

What if it wasn't Onegus?

Other people were staying down there. She'd met Eleanor, one of Onegus's security team members. There were probably more of them on this level.

He walked in, wearing a fresh outfit and holding a large tray in his hands. "Good morning, beautiful. I didn't expect you to be up." He put the tray down on the coffee table. "I thought that I would have to wake you up."

"I was cold. This place is freezing."

"I'm sorry." He pulled out his phone. "I'll turn the heat up."

She eyed the tray from the bed. "I don't have a change of clothes, and I don't want to eat breakfast in my evening gown."

Without a moment's hesitation, he pulled his dress shirt over his head and handed it to her.

"Thanks." Her eyes roamed over his muscled chest. "That's a nice view to have over breakfast." She pulled the shirt on and swung her legs over the side of the bed.

"Same here." His eyes blazed with an inner light. "It looks much better on you than it does on me."

"Give me a moment to freshen up." She ducked into the bathroom.

After using the facilities, she washed her hands, and then opened the first vanity drawer to see if there was anything she could use to clean up her smeared makeup.

She found a pack of makeup removal towelettes, a new toothbrush still in its store wrapping, a tube of toothpaste, and even a selection of lotions. Whoever equipped the little suite was definitely a woman, and she had Cassandra's thanks for thinking of all the essentials.

When she was done and walked over to the couch, Onegus pulled her onto his lap. "I need one kiss before I let you eat."

"Just one?" She cupped his freshly shaved cheek.

"For now." He took her lips in a gentle kiss, his hands roving over her back, her exposed outer thighs, and up her ribs, brushing the sides of her breasts.

Breakfast forgotten, she kissed him back, expecting to find sharp fangs, but even though he was very obviously aroused, Onegus kept them from elongating.

"Did I dream about you having fangs?"

He smiled, showing her a row of perfect pearly whites with canines that were just a little on the pointy side. "Unlike many immortal males, I have excellent control over my fangs and the glow in my eyes." Lifting her off his lap, he set her down next to him. "Coffee?"

"Yes, please."

He poured them both a cup from the thermos and then added cream and sugar to hers. "Just as you like it." He handed her the cup.

She took a sip. "Perfect."

"Yes, you are."

ONEGUS

$\mathcal{O}$negus bided his time, waiting for the right moment to ask Cassandra for her consent again, and to explain why she couldn't leave without him either thralling away the memory of everything he'd told her or forcing her silence with compulsion.

She was a smart lady, so she'd probably figured that out already, but she seemed in no hurry to finish her breakfast and have the talk she knew was coming.

When there was nothing more she could nibble on, and the coffee thermos was empty, she leaned back, crossed her arms over her chest, and cast him a wry smile. "Okay, let's hear it."

"That should be my line. Do I have your consent or not?"

"Not yet. I need to get to know you better, I need to learn much more about what I'm getting myself into, and I have to find out whether my mother is immortal."

It was a sensible approach.

Onegus couldn't fault Cassandra for being careful and not jumping headfirst into the deep before finding out precisely what was in the water.

Still, he couldn't help the pang of disappointment. "I understand." He sighed. "I'll have to either erase the memory of everything I've told you or compel you to keep it a secret."

She frowned. "Making me forget doesn't make sense. How am I going to think it through if I don't know what I'm supposed to do? And why bother getting my consent if I won't remember it?"

"I thought that I would get your consent in writing, then suppress your memories, and when you started transitioning, I would show you the written agreement so you wouldn't get mad. The other option was for you to come with me to the cabin, and we would have stayed there until you started to transition. That's why I suggested it. Not because I didn't want to be seen with you, but because I needed to take you somewhere secluded where you couldn't tell anyone what you've learned."

She smiled sheepishly. "I'm sorry for accusing you of being a player. I had no way of knowing."

He nodded. "Apology accepted."

"What if I don't transition?"

That was the hard part to admit, but there was no way around it. "It pains me to say it, but immortals and humans can't have long-term relationships, Cassy. It's just too complicated. First of all, because of the need for secrecy, and secondly, because it's just too painful."

"I get it." She looked away, and he suspected that it was to hide tears. "I don't like it, but I get it. Still, even if I don't transition, and we have to go our separate ways, I don't want to forget any of it. I'd take compulsion over memory wipe any day."

"If you don't transition, forgetting the entire thing will be easier for you. You could go on with your life without being aware that the promise of immortality was dangled in front of you and then taken away. It could mess you up." He shook his head. "But why are we even considering the possibility? I know in my gut that you are a Dormant. You have an incredible paranormal ability that's very rare. In fact, I know only one other immortal who has a similar power."

"Let me guess. Sylvia?"

"You guessed right. How did you know?"

Cassandra shrugged. "She made comments about my inability to control my energy. It wasn't hard to figure out that she knew what I was dealing with."

"Sylvia can't blow things up, but she can make electronics malfunction."

"Can she teach me how to control my energy better? It's a major pain," Cassandra admitted. "When I feel it rising, I panic, which makes it worse, and I have to find a receptacle. I can hold on for a little bit, but eventually I need to release it or it becomes uncontrollable."

"Sylvia can teach you how to channel it, but I don't think she can teach you how to discharge it." Smirking, he took her hand, lifted it to his lips, and kissed her wrist. "That's my job."

She chuckled. "With sex?"

"You are much calmer after orgasming a couple of times."

"True." She cast him a suggestive smile. "But that also means that you can't tease me for long. Then the energy builds up, and I become dangerous."

He nodded. "Duly noted. Also, don't forget about your mother. If she is an immortal, then there is no question that you are a Dormant."

"Speaking of my mother." She leaned to lift her purse off the table. "I need to text her. With all the excitement, I forgot to let her know that I'm spending the night with you." She pulled her phone out and typed up a short message. "Do you want to see the text before I send it?"

"Why would I?"

"Oh, I don't know," she mocked. "Maybe I texted her your secrets."

"Who's going to believe Geraldine? It would be just another fantastic story she added to her repertoire. Besides, I trust you."

"Really? Then why thrall my memories or compel me to silence? I can just promise to keep quiet."

"It's done to ensure that you don't blurt it out unintentionally, and that you can't reveal the information even under duress."

"Right. You need to tell me about those enemies of yours. That's also something I need to consider before I give you my consent."

Was she implying that he couldn't protect her?

"You have nothing to fear from them. I'll never let anything happen to you."

"Nevertheless, I need to know what I'm getting myself into."

"Does it have to be now?"

"No. There is no rush."

As Cassandra sent the text, he leaned over the phone. "I'm not reading your text. I just wanted to see Geraldine's picture, but there are none."

"My mother hates having her picture taken. In the few I managed to snap, she either looks away or turns her back to the camera."

"Didn't you find that suspicious?"

She shrugged. "Some people are camera shy."

"Immortals more than anyone else."

"Why?"

"Just think about it. We don't change. A picture taken fifty years ago would look exactly like a picture taken today. It's a dead giveaway."

"I just had a thought. What if my mother is a Dormant like me and just looks young? Can she go through transition?"

"I don't know. She might be too old even though she doesn't look it."

"Who makes that call?"

"Our doctor."

"Right. You told me that you have one who specializes in transitioning Dormants."

"Among other things."

"How can we find out whether my mother is an immortal?"

75

CASSANDRA

Onegus let go of her hand and got to his feet. "If we can get a good picture of her face, our in-house hacker can run it through DMV records using a facial recognition program." He pulled two bottles of water from the fridge. "If a driver's license with her picture pops out more than once, decades apart, that would prove it." He handed her a bottle.

"Thanks." She unscrewed the top and took a long swig. "You assume that she changed her name."

"She would have had to. That's what we do."

"We might have to corner her and take it when she doesn't expect it."

Onegus sat back on the couch, braced his elbows on his knees, and leaned forward. "There is also the cut or scratch test I told you about. If she heals rapidly, that's even better proof than the driver's license. Does she get sick? Flu? Colds?"

Staring at his bunching biceps, she had a hard time concentrating. Perhaps she should give him his shirt back and put on the dress.

Taking another sip from the water, she tried to focus on his face and not ogle his chest and arms. "Frankly, I don't remember her ever getting sick, but that's not a proof either. She might just have a good immune system. And as for your other suggestion, I can't just go up to my mother with a knife in hand and cut her or scratch her. What about the super hearing? We can go up to my room and talk about immortals. If my mother can hear us, she would get anxious."

Onegus winced. "Provided that she knows and remembers that she's not aging."

Yeah, with her memory issues, she might have come up with a fantastic story to explain her youthful appearance.

"Could the memory loss be the result of the transition?"

Onegus rubbed his jaw. "Not likely, but stasis can."

"What's that?"

"Immortals can go into stasis and stay in that state for thousands of years. We have a clan member who was buried alive in an earthquake. She woke up over five thousand years later, when they built an apartment complex over the place she was buried in, and a pipe burst. Emerging from her stasis, she didn't know who she was or where she came from. Somehow, the Fates guided her to us, and with time she regained her memories."

Cassandra shook her head. "My mother can't be that ancient. Could a short stasis have done that?"

"Maybe. I don't know."

"How did she turn immortal in the first place? Did she hook up with some random immortal male who didn't use protection?"

He nodded. "It's possible. We have a clan member who was induced by a random hookup. Many immortal males don't use condoms because we can't get or transmit diseases, and our fertility rate is so low that pregnancy is not an issue either. I'm just more cautious than others."

"Right." She rubbed her temple. "I'm getting a headache from all this speculating. I need to go home, take a shower, and sleep until noon."

"I also need to get back to work." He looked at her with those intense blue eyes of his. "So, what will it be? Thralling, compulsion, or staying here until you transition?"

She looked around the small room. "Definitely compulsion. I would go nuts in here, and I need to be at work on Monday."

"Very well." He pushed to his feet. "I'll call Eleanor."

"What for?"

"She's a compeller, and she happens to be down the corridor."

"Can't you do it?"

"Compulsion is a very rare talent, which I don't possess. I can only thrall. Do you still want to be compelled?"

"Yes. I want to own my memories, good and bad. After watching my mother suffering from memory issues all my life, I can't tolerate the thought of losing my memory. It terrifies me."

"Oh, Cassy." He crouched next to her and took her hands. "I should have realized that memory is precious to you."

"That's okay. Just call Eleanor in here, and let's get it over with. Compulsion is scary too, but not as scary as the alternative."

"The cabin is still on the table."

"Yeah, well. You can't leave until after your boss's birthday, and I can't wait in this room until you can. Besides, I can't take a vacation that long."

He nodded. "I'll get Eleanor."

"Hold on." She pulled his shirt over her head and handed it to him. "I don't want her ogling my guy."

His eyes riveted to her bare breasts, he swallowed. "Now, I can't move."

Laughing, she gave him a slight shove. "Go. I need to get dressed."

76

ONEGUS

*O*negus found Eleanor in Arwel's suite, alone.
"Where is Alfie?"

She looked up from the monitor she'd been staring at. "He went upstairs to shower and change."

"He shouldn't leave you alone here."

She rolled her eyes, which he found disrespectful. It was okay when Cassandra did that, but not from an underling.

"I know not to open the door to Emmett's cell without backup. Alfie is going to get his breakfast, and I'm going to bring it to him."

"Has Emmett been behaving?"

"Yep. He hasn't given me any trouble at all."

Onegus glanced at the screen. Emmett was up, sitting on the couch with a book in his hands. "What's he reading?"

She shrugged. "I don't know. Arwel brought him a bunch of books. He likes to read."

"Good for him." Onegus rubbed a hand over the back of his neck. "I need your help. I need you to compel Cassandra not to reveal anything about us."

A smile bloomed on Eleanor's thin face. "Sure thing, boss. Is she your one?" She rose to her feet.

"I don't know yet. Cassandra is great. She's everything I ever wanted in a woman, a mate, but love is a foreign concept to me. At least romantic love. And she's not going to settle for anything less than everything."

He had no clue why he was sharing his inner struggle with Eleanor. Perhaps because he still viewed her as an outsider, an objective observer who would not interject her own feelings into the situation.

"Cassandra shouldn't settle for anything less than your love and devotion, and neither should you. Take your time. That's the only advice I can give you."

She smiled sadly. "My romantic track record doesn't qualify me as an expert."

"Yeah, mine neither."

"What's Cassandra's talent?"

He chuckled. "She blows things up when she gets mad."

Eleanor grinned. "My kind of girl."

When they walked into the room, Cassandra rose to her feet and offered Eleanor her hand. "Good morning." She smiled. "I hope Onegus didn't drag you out of bed."

She was dressed in her evening gown and the stilettos with the red soles, looking like a magazine cover model, even without any makeup and her hair in a messy bun.

"I was already up." Eleanor shook her hand. "Let's get comfortable." She motioned to the couch.

As the two women sat down, Eleanor lifted her eyes to Onegus. "Compulsion needs to be very precise. Do you want me to exclude you from the compulsion not to mention immortals, Dormants, and this place?"

"Good idea. Also include fangs and venom. And an override clause. Cassandra can talk about everything when I'm around and approve."

"Okay. That's going to be a bit tricky. I need a moment to formulate it precisely."

"Take as long as you need," Cassandra said. "I don't want you to compel me to do or not do anything other than what's absolutely necessary."

Eleanor nodded. "Look into my eyes and listen carefully. Until I release you, you are not allowed to say, write, type, whisper, or mime the following words: immortal, Dormant, fangs, and venom. You are not allowed to tell anyone the location of this building. If anyone asks, you were driven here, and you didn't pay attention to where you were taken. You are allowed to say that it was somewhere downtown. Also, don't repeat any of the names you've heard while attending the wedding. However, if you are with Onegus and he allows it, you can talk about all those things that you are not allowed to mention when he's not around."

"Is that all?" Cassandra asked.

Eleanor turned to Onegus. "I think I covered everything. Anything you want me to add?"

"We forgot gods and goddesses, but that's fine. It's meaningless without the rest."

"Let's test it." Eleanor smiled at Cassandra. "Tell me what's special about Onegus."

"He's handsome, charming, smart, bossy, and he has teeth that elongate and eyes that glow." Cassandra smirked. "You didn't think of everything."

"Oops." Eleanor looked at Onegus. "Should I include that?"

He shook his head. "That's fine. Who's going to believe it, right?"

"I'm not going to tell anyone." Cassandra pushed to her stiletto-clad feet. "If we are done, I would like to get home before my neighbors wake up and see me arriving in the morning wearing an evening dress."

CASSANDRA

"*Y*ou know what I'm thankful for?" Cassandra opened the passenger side window to let the fresh morning air in.

Onegus turned to look at her and smiled. "Letting Kevin persuade you to attend the gala so that you could meet me?"

"That too." He was so full of himself, but in a charming and disarming way that she had to admit she adored. "Contrary to what you believe, not everything revolves around you. This one is about me. I'm glad to finally understand where my strange power comes from, and that I'm not a witch."

He arched a brow. "Is that what you thought it was?"

"What else could I think? It terrified me. I could hurt people." And she had, but she wasn't ready to share that with him yet. "I was desperate to get rid of it, or at least learn to control it. I tried meditation, I even tried relaxants. But I didn't have the patience for meditating, and relaxants made me sleepy. I even read books on magic, but they were either a bunch of nonsense or impossible to understand."

"You should talk to Sylvia. Perhaps she can train you."

"I would like that."

His expression turned serious. "There is still so much I need to tell you. I wish we could go away for a few days."

"I would like that too." Cassandra sighed. "I feel like a slave to my work."

"You said that you often take work home."

"What about it?"

"We could go away together someplace nice, and you could dedicate a few hours a day to work, but we can have fun the rest of the time."

"That's a great idea, except I can't do everything that needs to be done in a few hours a day. It's not going to be fun for you to wait for me to finish my work."

"True." He turned to look at her again. "Then maybe you can stay with me for a few days? You'll do your work, and I'll do mine, but at least we will be together."

It was on the tip of her tongue to say that she would try to make it work, but then her mother's face flashed in front of her, and she knew she couldn't do that.

"I can't leave my mother alone."

"Not even for a few days?"

"Two or three, but no longer than that." She pushed a loose strand of hair behind her ear. "That's another thing you should consider. My mother and I are a package deal."

He grimaced. "Does that mean that she would have to live with us?"

"Either that or next door. She needs me."

"I'm okay with next door."

Cassandra shook her head. "Look at us. We are planning the rest of our lives as if everything is settled when, in fact, nothing is."

He reached over the center console and took her hand. "One step at a time, Cassy. First, you need to decide when you want to start working on your transition."

It wasn't only about the when, but also about the who. Was Onegus the one?

He squeezed her hand. "A penny for your thoughts."

"You said that my inducer should be the man, or immortal, who I chose to spend the rest of my life with. What if things don't work out between us?"

For a brief moment, Onegus looked as if she'd slapped him, but he recuperated quickly, and when he spoke, he sounded as calm and collected as usual. "We are great together, and I don't foresee that changing, but if, Fates forbid, something happens, and we part ways, you can choose someone else. Eleanor wasn't romantically involved with the guy who induced her. He was just a hookup, but later they gave a relationship a try. It didn't work out, and now she's on the prowl, looking for her one and only."

Cassandra blew out a breath. "I hope our relationship will keep on growing stronger, but knowing that agreeing to the induction doesn't mean a life-long commitment is a relief."

When he stopped at the gate to her community, she waved at the guard who recognized her and let them through without asking to see Onegus's driver's license.

A couple of moments later, Onegus pulled up in front of her house and turned the engine off.

A muscle ticked in his jaw when he turned to look at her. "Other than Eleanor, there was only one other female Dormant who didn't mate her inducer. Neither of them had known that she was a Dormant, and when she started transitioning, he was long gone. All the other transitioned Dormants are happily mated to their inducers."

He hadn't told her he loved her yet, but he was upset because she needed an exit clause?

Sometimes it was difficult to understand the way men thought, and apparently, that included immortals who'd been around long enough to think with their brains and not their male hormones.

"I hope we will be one of those happy couples, but we are not there yet." She pinned him with a hard stare. "Do you love me, Onegus?"

When he swallowed, she shook her head. "That's what I thought." Leaning toward him, she put her hand on his arm. "It's okay. I don't believe in love at first sight, and I don't expect you to fall in love with me in one week. By the same token, you can't expect me to commit to you after such a short time."

He nodded. "I've never been in love, so I don't know whether what I feel for you is love. What I know, however, is that I've never enjoyed being with a woman as much as I enjoy being with you, and that when I'm not with you, I can't wait until we meet again."

"I feel the same." Leaning over, she kissed his cheek. "For now, that will do, and it's a good start."

DARK POWER
CONVERGENCE

THE CHILDREN OF THE GODS BOOK 52

1

KIAN

In a rare moment of peace and contentment, Kian flipped through the wedding pictures posted on the clan's website that morning. The photographer had captured beautifully the heart-warming slices of life.

So far, Kian's favorites were Syssi dancing with Andrew and Phoenix, the girl riding on her father's shoulders and beaming with happiness, David and Sari gazing into each other's eyes as they stood in front of Annani on the podium, Wonder laughing at Anandur's goofy dance moves, and Kalugal toasting the happy couple with a glass of whiskey.

First thing Monday morning, Kian was going to ask Shai to add these to the compilation on his screensaver.

Putting the highlights from past clan celebrations on Kian's computer had been one of his assistant's better attempts at helping him to reduce his stress levels.

As he found himself gazing at the compilation throughout his workdays, it never failed to bring a smile to his face. The pictures he loved the most were of Syssi, some from their own wedding, others from Andrew and Nathalie's and other celebrations. Their trips to Hawaii and to Scotland provided many more.

He could spend all day looking at pictures of her beautiful face and lush body, but it would be even better to get up from his chair and go find her.

They were hosting a family Sunday brunch, and although Syssi was supposed to leave all the work to Okidu, Kian had no doubt that he would find her in the back yard, fussing over the final details, and making sure everything had been done according to her instructions.

As he entered the living room, he spotted her standing on the back porch, her fists pressed into the small of her back, a pose she assumed a lot lately because her muscles strained with carrying her very pregnant belly.

Kian walked up behind Syssi, leaned over her back, and kissed her neck. "Why are you out here?"

"I wanted to make sure that everything is ready."

He wrapped his arms under her huge belly and hoisted it up. "You were supposed to let Okidu handle everything."

"He has his limits. If I let him handle the music, Fates only know what he would choose. I still remember the polka compilation he put on the last time."

The soft instrumental piece playing through the outdoor loudspeakers was definitely a better choice. It added to the festive mood but wouldn't overwhelm the conversation.

"I concede in regards to the music. What else does he need help with?"

"Nothing. I just wanted to make sure that it wasn't too hot out here. The day has turned out to be perfect, though. The breeze is enough to cool down the air but not strong enough to blow away the decorations."

Kian looked up at the stuff Okidu had salvaged from the wedding and hung from tree branches and bushes around their backyard.

Had that been his own idea?

Probably not.

Someone must have suggested it to him because Okidu couldn't make decisions like that on his own.

That wasn't how his programming was supposed to work.

Or at least that was what Kian used to believe. Reading about the latest developments in artificial intelligence had made him reevaluate his opinion.

He wasn't a computer expert like William, but from what he'd read, he had garnered that the latest artificial intelligence design was based on neural networks that mimicked the multi-dimensional connections in the brain. When the network was presented with a tremendous amount of data and given an objective, it could learn and make decisions.

That made intuitive sense to him.

What Kian found strange was that the inner workings of the artificially made system were just as mysterious as the inner workings of the living brain, and the

researchers didn't actually know how the A.I. arrived at its decisions.

Over the millennia of Okidu's existence, he'd accumulated an enormous amount of data, and his neural networks were probably incalculably more advanced than those found in even the most robust present-day artificial intelligence systems. Could he have reached some level of sentience?

What exactly constituted sentience?

Kian shook his head.

Philosophy wasn't his forte, and he should leave it to those much smarter than he was.

Turning her head to look up at him, Syssi smiled. "Did you come out here just to hoist up my belly? Or did you have something that you needed to tell me and forgot?"

He chuckled. "I might be two thousand years old, but I'm not senile. You were standing with your fists pressing into the small of your back. I figured you needed help carrying our daughter around."

She kissed the underside of his jaw. "Can you do this all day long? I feel so much lighter."

"Two and a half weeks to go, love." He kissed her cheek. "You should take it easy."

She snorted. "If I take it any easier, I won't get out of bed in the morning. I need something to do other than worry."

Thankfully, his stubborn wife had listened to the doctor, who'd advised her to take a leave of absence from work for the last four weeks of her pregnancy. Bridget's argument was that labor might start unexpectedly, and if it happened while Syssi was en route to work or at the university, it might complicate things.

The argument had been convincing, but it had added another layer of anxiety that Syssi could have done without.

As Phoenix's happy squeal announced their first guests' arrival, Kian kissed Syssi's neck and let go of her belly.

A moment later, the toddler bounced into the backyard and unceremoniously flung herself into his arms.

"Uncle Kian." She cupped his cheeks. "Can we play horsey?"

Plucking the girl off his chest, he lifted her behind his back and deposited her over his shoulders. "Hold on tight."

"Yes!" She wrapped her little arms around his neck, choking him with a surprisingly strong grip. "Horsey, jump!"

Leaping over a lounge chair, Kian elicited an excited squeal from her, and when he leaped over the next one, Phoenix shouted, "Jump higher, horsey!"

"I can't watch this." Nathalie covered her eyes with her hands.

"Don't worry." Andrew wrapped his arm around his wife's waist. "Kian would never let anything happen to her."

"Damn right." Kian lifted the protesting Phoenix and handed her to Andrew. "That's enough horsey for today." He ruffled her hair.

"I want a pony," Phoenix said. "I want to teach him to jump over stuff like Uncle Kian does."

"When you're older." Andrew patted her back.

If her parents wanted her to train with horses, they would have to take her to a human equestrian center. Personally, Kian had nothing against the animals, but Amanda would lose her shit if they brought one to the village, especially now that she was about to have another child. Ever since she'd lost her son, she couldn't stand seeing kids anywhere near horses.

"Hello, everyone." Annani floated into the backyard, followed by Alena, Sari, David, and Ogidu.

"Good morning, Mother." Kian leaned down and kissed her cheek, then turned to his newlywed sister. "How does it feel to be a married woman?" He kissed Sari's cheek as well.

"Nothing's changed in the way I feel, except for being relieved that the wedding is behind me, and I can go back to my routine."

When he arched a brow, his sister cast him an apologetic glance. "That sounded ungrateful. The event and the ceremony were beautiful. David and I truly appreciate all that went into making it happen, and for enabling nearly the entire clan to attend."

"I get it." Syssi patted Sari's arm. "For me, it's draining to be the center of attention, but I thought that you were more extroverted."

"I am. I love being surrounded by people, but I'm also a creature of habit. Routine calms me down."

David took Sari's hand. "I want to thank you for hosting our wedding and for inviting us to your home today."

"You're welcome," Kian said. "It's our pleasure, and that's not a platitude. As far as I'm concerned, life doesn't get better than when celebrating happy occasions with my family."

2

CASSANDRA

*C*assandra's bed felt as hot as an oven, but she wasn't ready to get up yet. Instead, she flung off the duvet, flipped her pillow around, and turned to her side. Given the sweltering heat of her bedroom, it was probably around noon, but since she'd gotten home in the early hours of the morning, she was in no rush to start her day.

The slight headache was a reminder of how much she'd had to drink last night. Could she have dreamt up the bizarre events that had taken place after all that drinking?

A part of Cassandra wished that she had, and another part wished that all of it was true. Like the revelation about Onegus's fangs and what they could do.

They were a little scary but also exciting, especially after he'd released her memories of his previous bites and the orgasms that had followed and then given her a live demonstration. Those mean babies delivered the kind of ecstasy poems could be written about.

Regrettably, Cassandra couldn't write hymns in their honor or even tell anyone about them because she was under compulsion not to reveal anything she'd learned last night.

Onegus was immortal, and so was his entire family. Not only that, but he also suspected that her mother was immortal as well.

If not for a lifetime of living with a strange power capable of blowing things up, Cassandra would have had a much harder time believing Onegus's story despite the proof he'd presented her with.

And as if all of that wasn't enough to send her head spinning, he'd told her that she was most likely a dormant carrier of the immortal genes, and he wanted to induce her transition into immortality.

Cassandra was in no rush to give her consent.

It wasn't that she didn't want to be immortal, but she would be a fool to jump in the deep end without checking all the facts first. To make a well-informed decision, she had to find out precisely what she was getting into and what she would be giving up.

According to Onegus, no blood drinking was involved, and the transition was difficult but not painful. It sounded a little too good to be true.

Her overly creative imagination provided her with a slew of potential pitfalls that Onegus had deliberately omitted. Some of them were relatively benign, although significant, like the low fertility he'd mentioned. Others were nastier and too fantastic to take seriously, but she couldn't help where her mind was going.

If keeping her immortality involved human sacrifices or devil worship, she was out.

Snorting, Cassandra got out of bed and padded to the bathroom.

That was probably taking it too far, but his comment about fertility could mean that she wouldn't be able to have children, and that was a big deal.

Would that be a deal-breaker for her?

Maybe. Did immortals adopt children?

Probably not.

She needed to call Onegus and ask him a gazillion questions. She also needed to figure out a way to find out whether her mother was immortal, and if she was, how it had happened.

Given what Onegus had told her, the only way Geraldine could have turned immortal was if she'd had unprotected sex with an immortal male. Her mother could have hooked up with a random guy, neither of them realizing who the other was, and transitioned without knowing what was happening to her.

That was enough to mess with anyone's head. Could that be the reason for her mother's memory issues?

So many questions. So few answers.

Once Cassandra was done in the bathroom, she changed into a pair of yoga pants and a cami and headed downstairs to the kitchen.

"Good morning." Her mother beamed at her. "The coffee just finished brewing."

"Thanks." Cassandra poured herself a cup and took it to the dining table.

"How was your date?" Geraldine pulled a carton of eggs and a tub of butter from the fridge.

"Great."

"I heard you opening the front door this morning, but I figured you would tell me all about it after you'd gotten some sleep."

Sipping on her coffee, Cassandra considered what she could tell her mother. The event was over, so security was no longer an issue. She could tell her about attending the wedding. Besides, she needed to tell Geraldine about Onegus's mother because the four of them were supposed to have lunch together.

"It was a wedding." She smiled apologetically. "I'm sorry I couldn't tell you before, but Onegus made me promise to keep it a secret. His family has enemies, and it was important that no one found out about the event."

Cracking another egg into the pan, her mother turned to look at her. "What kind of enemies?"

"I don't know. He didn't say. Anyway, I met his mother."

As she'd expected, that got Geraldine more excited than the cloak and dagger secrecy around the wedding.

"Did you like her?" her mother asked. "What's she like?"

How to answer that?

"She's beautiful, like in a runway model beautiful, and she looks way too young to be Onegus's mom." Cassandra smiled. "Kind of like you." She observed Geraldine's expression closely, looking for any sign that the comment made her uncomfortable.

But there was none. "That's nice. Onegus is a very handsome man. I'm not surprised that his mother is a beautiful woman." Geraldine scooped the scrambled eggs onto a plate, added some toast, and brought it to the table. "Here you go, sweetie." She smiled. "You must be hungry after partying all night."

"Thanks." Cassandra took a bite out of the buttered toast. "Aren't you going to eat too?"

"I've already had breakfast." Geraldine refilled her cup with fresh coffee and joined Cassandra at the table. "Tell me more about Onegus's mother."

Aha. So her curiosity had been piqued.

"She's blond, like Onegus, and her hair is also curly, but she keeps it long. She's tall like me and has a killer figure. She's also a snotty Brit, or rather Scot, who thinks that Americans are loud and obnoxious. I told her that you and I will change her mind about that."

Geraldine arched a brow. "Me?"

"Yeah, you. You can give Martha a run for her money." Cassandra waved a hand. "You know all about being prim and proper. I suggested that we meet for lunch, and she liked the idea."

Hopefully, that wasn't a mistake, and her mother wouldn't slip into storytelling mode. Cassandra had no doubt that she'd do that eloquently, adding charm and humor to her stories, but the effect would be the same. Martha would think that Geraldine was nuts.

"When?"

"Soon. Onegus's mother is going back home next Sunday."

3

ONEGUS

*A*s the door to Onegus's office opened, he lifted his head ready to scold whoever it was for not knocking before entering.

Seeing who it was, he said, "Good morning, Ingrid."

After working together over the past couple of weeks and him sharing things with her he normally didn't share with anyone, they'd become buddies. That didn't entitle her to just walk in whenever she pleased, but he would let it slide this time. He owed her for all the good advice she'd given him.

"How did it go last night?" Ingrid pulled a chair out and sat down. "You didn't introduce me to your lady friend."

"You were busy with one of Kalugal's guys." Ingrid had been expecting an introduction, and Onegus had promised her that he would, but it had slipped his mind. Luckily, he'd noticed her locking lips with the former Doomer and could use that as an excuse. "What's his name? Dandor?"

A sly smile bloomed on Ingrid's face. "Yeah, that's the one." She crossed her legs. "Nevertheless, I wasn't busy with him the entire evening, but whatever. Just don't forget to introduce us during Kian's birthday celebrations."

"I haven't invited her yet. Should I?"

She shrugged. "Ask Kian if that's okay with him." The sly smile was back. "Just make sure that Gerard doesn't plan on bringing another punch bowl to the party."

Onegus shouldn't be surprised that Ingrid had figured out the punch bowl incident had been Cassandra's doing. She'd known about her energy and about the vase that had fallen victim to her temper. It wasn't difficult to connect the dots.

"Did you tell anyone?"

Ingrid affected an affronted expression. "What do you take me for? A snitch? I heard that you covered up for her. I wouldn't betray you." She leaned forward. "But it doesn't take a genius to figure out that it was Cassandra's fault. If you've told Kian about her energy, he probably suspected that she had something to do with it."

"Kian knows, and so does Sylvia, and probably Roni. I just don't want it to become the next item on the gossip-grapevine express. Kian and I talked about it briefly last night, and he wants Sylvia to train Cassandra to control her power."

Ingrid arched a brow. "Did you finally tell her who you really are?"

He nodded. "I told Cassandra the gist of the story last night, and I gave her the option to choose between written consent and thralling away her memories as you suggested, or compulsion to keep quiet. Cassandra chose compulsion, and I asked Eleanor to do it."

"Good." Ingrid pulled out her phone to check an incoming message. "It seems that my break is over." She pushed to her feet. "Another group of guests wants to visit the village, and they need me to arrange a ride."

"Do you want me to check if any of the Guardians are available?"

"No need. I was planning on going back shortly, so I might as well take them with me." She cast him a smile. "I wish you and Cassandra the best of luck." Tucking her purse under her arm, she headed for the door.

"Cassandra didn't consent to the induction yet."

Ingrid paused mid-step and turned around. "Why not?"

"She's cautious. I only told her the bare minimum last night, and she feels that she needs more information before making her decision."

"Makes sense." Ingrid pursed her lips. "Well, as I said before, best of luck."

When the door closed behind her, Onegus leaned back in his chair and crossed his arms behind his head.

Cassandra wasn't in a rush to commit to anything, which normally would have suited him just fine, but not this time. Seemingly, there was no urgency, but letting things drag on while her head was full of clan secrets was not a good idea.

He needed to speed up the process, and the best way to do that was to show Cassandra the wonderful community she and her mother could join as soon as she transitioned. Also, she needed training, and the only one who could help her with that was Sylvia, who had a similar talent.

With Annani currently visiting the village, security at the keep and the building hosting the guests could be easily handled by Bhathian, freeing Onegus to take Cassandra on a tour.

Perhaps he could also arrange a meeting with Sylvia if she wasn't busy.

When his phone rang, he knew it was Cassandra even before looking at the screen. He figured she would probably sleep late, but as soon as she woke up, she would remember last night and want more answers from him.

"Good morning, beautiful."

"Good afternoon is more like it. Did you get any sleep at all?"

"I don't need as much."

"Is that part of being..." She stopped, probably because she wanted to say immortal but couldn't before asking his permission. "Long-lived?"

Clever lady.

She'd found a synonym that Eleanor hadn't included in the list of forbidden words.

"It is, but that's not something we should discuss over the phone. Your line is not secure."

"Really? You told me about the wedding over the same unsecured line."

"That was different." The words wedding and enemies were not trigger words for the echelon system. Immortal and compulsion were. "I hope you don't have any plans for later today."

"Why? What do you have in mind?"

"It's a surprise. Can you be ready in an hour?"

"Ready for what?"

"I want to take you somewhere special."

"You need to tell me more so I'll know how to dress. If it's lunch with your mother, I'm putting on one of my power outfits."

He chuckled. "We are not meeting my mother. You can dress casually."

"Can you be more specific?"

He smiled. "Dress as you would for visiting good friends on the weekend."

She was quiet for a moment. "Are you taking me to your place? The one you share with Connor?"

Smart lady.

"You figured it out."

"Awesome. I'm looking forward to that. I like Connor a lot."

"Good. I'll see you in an hour." He ended the call and placed another one to his roommate.

"What's up?" Connor sounded sleepy.

"Are you still in bed?"

"What's it to you?"

"I wanted to give you a heads up that I'm bringing Cassandra over in about an hour and a half."

"To the village?"

"Where else? I told her part of our story last night, and Eleanor compelled her to keep silent about it. I need Cassandra to start training with Sylvia, so I'm inviting her and Roni over as well. Do you want me to get takeout, or do you want to whip something up?"

"I'll make lunch."

"Thanks, Connor. You're the best."

His roommate sighed dramatically. "You're saying that now, but in a week or two, I'll be looking for a new place to live."

"Why?"

"Because Cassandra will move in with you."

"Even if she does, you don't have to move out. We can share the place."

Connor chuckled. "For an old guy, you are incredibly naive. Cassandra wouldn't want to share you with anyone."

"Why wouldn't she? She likes you."

"Whatever, dude. I just woke up, and I need to tidy up the place and start cooking. We will talk later."

4

KIAN

"It's getting hot out here." Syssi fanned herself with her hand. "I vote for having coffee and dessert inside the house."

"Of course, love." Kian pushed to his feet and offered her a hand up.

Their living room was spacious, enough to fit the fifteen adults, but he doubted it was big enough to contain Phoenix. Thankfully, Ethan was a quiet little guy. At eighteen months, he could be running around like his overactive older niece, but he was content observing her or playing with his toys and didn't like leaving Eva's side.

Across the table, Kalugal helped Jacki up as well. She wasn't even showing yet, but his cousin liked to act gallantly.

He stopped next to Kian. "If everyone is going inside, we can enjoy a cigar out here."

Jacki lifted one brow. "Isn't it too early for that?"

Kalugal shrugged. "I don't enjoy cigars by myself, and I doubt Kian will invite me again this evening. So it's now or some other time."

Kian didn't contradict him because Kalugal was right. He loved his family, but he could take them only in small doses.

"Fine." Jacki patted Kalugal's arm. "But no whiskey."

"Can I join?" Eva surprised him.

"Of course. I didn't know you smoked."

"I don't. But I like the smell."

"I'll take Ethan inside," Nathalie offered. "Come on, sweetie, give your older sister your hand."

Ethan regarded her with his too-smart eyes and then looked at Eva. "Mommy."

She leaned and kissed his chubby cheek. "Go with Nathalie, baby. I'll come in a few minutes."

When Ethan gave Nathalie his hand, and the two stepped inside, Eva let out a breath. "He's a sweet child, really, but sometimes I need a little breather, and with Bhathian helping Onegus at the keep, I don't have a moment to myself."

"You don't have to apologize," Alena said. "It's perfectly understandable."

"I used to love the smell of cigars," Syssi said. "But now that I'm pregnant, I can't stand it. My body is telling me that it's not healthy for the baby."

"You are both weird." Amanda wrapped her arm around Syssi's shoulders. "I've always hated it."

"Are you coming, Mom?" Lisa asked Ronja.

"I'll stay out here for a little while longer." She looked at Annani. "Are you going inside?"

"I will stay with you." His mother motioned for Ronja to sit next to her.

Perhaps Annani would manage to cheer the woman up.

Throughout brunch, Ronja had seemed subdued. Her smiles, which usually came easily, had been forced, and she hadn't participated in the conversations unless someone asked her a direct question.

Kian had a good idea of what was troubling her.

Ronja had probably seen Bowen fussing over Margaret during the wedding and had figured out that they were a couple. Apparently, she'd had feelings for the Guardian despite Bowen insisting that there had been nothing between them.

Once everyone who was either too hot or didn't want to smell cigar smoke had gone inside, Kian opened the box of cigars Okidu had rushed to bring from the humidor.

"Help yourself, ladies and gentlemen."

Ronja opened her purse and pulled out a pack of cigarettes. "Would it bother you if I smoked?" she asked Annani.

"Not at all, dear. But you should not smoke. You are not immortal, and your body can not heal the damage these things cause. It is unhealthy for you."

"I know." Ronja sighed. "I don't indulge often, but sometimes I just have to have one."

David, who'd decided to partake in the cigar fest, leaned over his mother's shoulder and kissed her cheek. "Can I get you anything to drink?"

"Thank you, but I'll wait for Okidu to bring out coffee."

"Coming right up, mistress." The Odu rushed inside the house.

Kian could have sworn that Okidu seemed excited to serve Ronja.

It was becoming more and more difficult to dismiss all the little oddities in his behavior. Something was up with him, and Kian wanted to find out what.

"I heard that the punch bowl incident wasn't caused by faulty glass," David said.

"Who told you?" Kian pulled a cigar out of the box and handed it to his newest brother-in-law.

"Sari talked with Amanda this morning. Is it supposed to be a secret?"

Kian glanced at Ronja.

He didn't mind the family knowing about Cassandra's power, but he didn't want the rumor spreading to the entire clan before her dormancy was confirmed.

"It's not a secret, but the lady in question is not part of the clan yet, so I'd rather any information about her stayed contained for now."

"I understand." David used the cutter to snap the cap off his cigar.

The sliding door opened, and Andrew stepped outside. "Is there a cigar left for me?"

"Of course." Kian offered him the box.

"How are things progressing with the China expedition?" Andrew pulled one out.

Kian handed him the cutter. "Jin and Mey are studying Chinese with Morris, and they are about to start Kra-ell lessons with Emmett."

"You can't expect them to learn anything in such a short time." Andrew cut the tip off. "Are you considering postponing the trip?"

Kian let out a sigh. "I don't know. On the one hand, I don't want the trail to get even colder, but on the other hand, it might be a fool's errand to send the two best sleuths for the job without providing them with the proper tools first. It would have been fantastic if we had a telepath who understood Chinese. He or she could enter Mey and Jin's minds to translate what they hear."

"I can enter their minds," Annani said. "But I don't speak Chinese."

Kian huffed. "Even if you did, I would never allow you to go."

As Annani's expression hardened, Kian regretted his choice of words. He'd been disrespectful.

She arched a brow. "Allow? I assume that you meant advise against or discourage me from going?"

He dipped his head. "Precisely. I've misspoken."

5

CASSANDRA

*C*assandra had an hour to prepare her questions while getting ready for Onegus to pick her up, and by the time the guard at the gate called to let her know he was on his way, her list had reached gargantuan proportions. Nevertheless, she was pretty sure that it wasn't extensive enough.

At the top of her questionnaire was Onegus's age.

It should have been the first question she'd asked him, but her mind hadn't been working right after learning that her boyfriend was an immortal. The alcohol she'd consumed, and the punch bowl incident, hadn't helped either.

After partying with a bunch of immortals who'd been trying to get her drunk, meeting Onegus's snotty mother, and blowing up a punch bowl the size of a witch's cauldron, it was a wonder she'd been able to process any of it at all.

For all she knew, Onegus might be ancient.

And how old was his mother? Or her own mother, provided that she really was immortal?

What if Geraldine was centuries old?

Did female immortals have fangs?

Probably not. Otherwise, Onegus wouldn't have difficulty figuring out whether Geraldine was an immortal. Supposedly, immortals' fangs elongated in response to aggression, so provoking her mother would have been enough.

Cassandra was still going over the list in her head when a knock sounded at her front door.

Grabbing her purse, she opened it up. "Good afternoon."

Onegus stared at her with awe as if she'd stepped out from the pages of a fairytale.

"Are you ready to go?" She smoothed her hand over her yellow summer dress.

It was pretty, and it made her look good, but it was nothing worth gawking at.

He shook his head as if to dispel a spell. "You are so incredibly beautiful that it shocks me anew every time I see you." He leaned and kissed her cheek.

"You are such a flatterer. But thank you. It's nice to hear compliments first thing in the morning. Or rather afternoon."

"I'll make it a habit to call you every morning." He opened the passenger door for her. "And tell you how beautiful you are before you start your workday."

"I can live with that." She fastened her seatbelt. "You'll earn the gratitude of everyone working in my department for making me less bitchy."

Turning the engine on, he cast her a sidelong glance. "It doesn't seem like you have fun at work. Perhaps you should rethink the way you do things."

Cassandra shrugged. "I don't want to rock the boat too much. Other than Kevin, no one would pay me as much or let me get away with my attitude." She sighed. "If I were a man, I would be called assertive and demanding. But because I'm a woman, I'm called a bitch. Life is not fair."

"No, it isn't." He reached for her hand. "How are you doing?"

She knew that they were no longer talking about her work.

"Am I allowed to speak freely, oh supreme master?"

His smirk looked positively lupine. "Don't use that word lightly. You've just given me a raging hard-on."

"Men!" She shook her head. "Dream on, buddy. No one is or ever will be my master." She put an emphasis on the last word.

"Not even in play mode?"

She looked at him from under lowered lashes. "That's a maybe. Now, can I talk?"

"Yes. You can say the words immortals, fangs, venom, and everything else I told you about."

"How old are you?"

He chuckled. "You could have asked me that without getting permission to speak freely."

"I know. But this question will most likely lead to another. I don't want to have to stop when I'm on a roll."

"Oh, boy." He ran a hand over his deliciously square jaw. "The ride is not long enough for that."

Was Onegus stalling? If he was afraid to tell her how old he was, she should brace for a shock.

"You didn't answer my question yet."

"I'm five hundred thirty-two years old."

"Wow." Cassandra slumped back in her chair. "Talk about a cradle robber. I don't even know what to think. Do you feel old?"

"Not in particular. Kian is celebrating his bimillennial birthday this Wednesday, and I don't think he thinks of himself as old either. You're invited, of course."

"Since when?"

"Since now. I couldn't push it before and invite you to the birthday as well because you were still a human. But now that you know about us and are under compulsion to keep it a secret, that's no longer a problem."

"Are you sure? It's Kian's birthday. Maybe he doesn't want outsiders at his party?"

"You are not an outsider. You are my girlfriend. Besides, this is a huge event, the size of the wedding just a little toned down. After all, it's our regent's bimillennial birthday. It's a big deal."

The number was just incomprehensible when referring to the lifespan of an individual.

"Un-freaking-believable. How do you people manage not to get jaded and bored? How do you pull off acting the age you look?"

"Our bodies don't age, so we don't suffer from the aches and pains that make life difficult for older humans. And as for getting jaded, perhaps some do, but we're fortunate to have Annani as a leader. She gave her descendants a purpose, and it gives us a reason to wake up in the morning and do our best."

"What purpose?"

"Help humanity evolve. That was the goal of the gods, and after they perished and only Annani remained, she made it her mission to continue their work."

Cassandra let out a breath. "That sounded like an opening to an hour-long tale. Do we have time? Because I'd rather hear everything at once and in order than piecemeal. It's confusing enough as it is."

"We are almost there, so let's keep the long story for some other time."

"Where is there?"

"A surprise." Smiling, he let go of the steering wheel and turned to look at her.

"What are you doing?"

"The car switched to self-driving mode." He lifted a finger and pointed behind her. "Look at the window."

"What the heck? It turned opaque. I've seen windows like that in a jetliner, but never in a car. Is it even legal?"

"It isn't. Our cars are designed that way to keep our village's location a secret. A few miles before the entrance to the tunnel, the windows turn opaque, and the car's computer takes over the driving."

She narrowed her eyes at him. "Are you taking me to your secret lair?"

He nodded. "Where did you think I lived?"

"Downtown."

"That's only temporary while we have visitors who need Guardian protection during their stay."

"But you are the chief. I'm sure you know how to get to the secret village."

"I'm one of the few. But this is also a piece of information that I will have to ask Eleanor to compel you not to reveal."

Cassandra huffed out a breath. "That's another part of the story that I can't wait to hear. Who are these enemies you are so afraid of? And why do they hunt your people?"

"All in good time, Cassy." He gave her hand a squeeze. "Can you feel the temperature change?"

She'd been too busy interrogating Onegus to notice, but it had gotten cooler in the car. "Are we in a tunnel?"

"Yes. And in a moment, the car will enter an elevator."

"Are we going up or down?"

It would be cool if their village was located underground, but it wouldn't be a place she would like to live.

"Up, why?"

"Just curious."

Was she actually thinking about moving in with Onegus after knowing him for only a week? They had met last Saturday for heaven's sake.

Not only that, but she also loved the house she'd bought with her own money and wasn't eager to move anywhere. Besides, she had Geraldine to think about.

Even if her mother turned out to be immortal, she wouldn't want to move either. She had her friends, and her book club, and other social activities that kept her busy. What the heck was she going to do in the immortals' village?

6

ANNANI

As Ronja stubbed her cigarette out, Annani rose to her feet. "If you are done smoking, I would like to go inside. It is too warm for me out here."

The heat was not as much of a problem as the glare. Even with her specialty sunglasses, it was irritating her sensitive eyes.

"I'm done." Ronja put her cigarette pack in her purse.

Annani had tried to cheer her new friend up, telling her funny anecdotes from her travels with Alena, but Ronja had barely smiled. They needed time alone so she could ask Ronja what was bothering her. Everyone assumed it was Bowen finding his mate, but Annani was not sure whether Ronja was upset because she had feelings for the Guardian or because it amplified the fact that she was alone.

Her chances of finding love again in an immortal village were not good.

Or perhaps it was a general feeling of ennui, a resurgence of grief.

Annani was a veteran of the process, intimately acquainted with its stages, its ups and downs, and the toll it took.

Grieving was a long process, and it never really went away. She had learned to live with hers, and so would Ronja, but it would take time. The misery came and went in waves, and sometimes it crashed over the griever like a tsunami, obliterating the progress that might have been achieved and sending her back into the pits of despair. Ronja would have to claw her way back, but she did not have to do it alone.

The problem was that Annani was going home soon. She had not decided yet how long she would stay, but it would be two weeks at the most, and once she was gone, who would take care of Ronja?

Lisa was a good daughter, loving and supportive, but she was dealing with her own grief, and she was just a kid.

Rushing to open the sliding door for her and Ronja, Okidu bowed. "Can I

460

offer you more refreshments, Clan Mother?" He turned to Ronja and smiled. "Mistress?"

"I would like a Perrier," Annani said.

"So would I." Ronja returned Okidu's smile.

Interesting.

It almost seemed as if Okidu was aware of Ronja's anguish and was going out of his way to be nice to her.

That implied a level of emotional intelligence the Odu should not possess. Was it possible that he was mimicking Syssi's behavior?

After all, he was a quick learner, and the Odu stored everything he observed in his memory banks for future use.

Thinking about the amount of data he had stored in his artificial brain made Annani's head spin. It also gave her an interesting idea.

Annani waited for everyone to come inside and find a place to sit before turning to Kian. "I have a suggestion regarding the team going to China. It would help if you had someone fluent in Chinese. Okidu can probably master it in a few days. He can even morph his features to look like a native."

For a long moment, Kian seemed to consider her suggestion, but then he shook his head. "Morris is fluent too. He can't morph his features to look Chinese, but I don't think that's important. Okidu can't blend in anyway."

"I think he can," Syssi said. "People would just think that he's a little too formal or a little strange. No one will suspect that he's not human."

Annani observed Okidu, who continued serving drinks as if the conversation was not about him.

"What do you think, Okidu?" she asked, curious about how much he could absorb.

"About what, Clan Mother?" He bowed.

"Can you learn Chinese in a matter of several days and morph your features to look the part?"

Straightening, he had already started morphing his facial features, and when he was done, he just looked strange. "Is that what I should look like, Clan Mother?"

"Close. I suggest that you look through pictures of middle-aged Chinese men."

"I have many stored in my memory, Clan Mother. I am afraid that this is the best I can do." He pointed to his face. "Perhaps I should attempt to look like a middle-aged Chinese woman?"

"Give it a try," Syssi said.

"Very well." Okidu bowed to her, and then started changing his body shape to look female and softening his facial features.

The result still did not look right. He could perhaps pass for someone of mixed heritage, but not pure Chinese.

"What about the language?" Syssi asked. "How quickly can you learn it?"

"I will need at least a week, mistress, and I do not have time to dedicate to learning the language until after all our guests return home." He bowed his head again. "My apologies, mistress. Perhaps one of my brothers could be of service."

"That's okay, Okidu," Kian said. "I think we can manage without your help."

"You need to postpone the trip," Kalugal said. "Without Mey and Jin's abilities, your Guardians will be no more effective than Turner's human contractor. Give the girls more time to learn Chinese and Kra-ell."

"What if Turner's guy finds a clue for us to follow?"

"Then put your people on the plane and send them there."

"It might be too late. I need them to be in place."

Kalugal shrugged. "They are your people. Do with them as you wish." He crossed his legs and leaned forward. "What about Emmett? Can you send him with the team to continue teaching Jin and Mey on the go?"

"I don't need him to be there physically. He can do that on the phone or via teleconferencing."

As the two continued their back and forth, Annani replayed Okidu's response to the requests in her head. Something bothered her about it. The Odus did not prioritize tasks on their own. Okidu should have asked Kian whether learning Chinese was more important than the tasks he was charged with during the festivities.

Could he have botched the Chinese appearance on purpose because he did not want to go?

Normally, Annani would have dismissed it as impossible, but since the drowning accident and his reboot, Okidu was acting a little differently than he used to.

He seemed a little more sentient.

Annani stifled a chuckle. It was like saying that someone was a little pregnant. They either were, or they were not.

7

CASSANDRA

*C*assandra tried to memorize every detail as she and Onegus strolled through his village. It was so beautiful and serene that she felt herself relax. Perhaps it was the lush greenery, or the almost surreal quiet, but the place seemed like a fairytale land.

Even her gated neighborhood wasn't that quiet. There was traffic noise from the nearby highway, and with the exception of Sunday, there were always gardeners working somewhere near with their noisy air blowers.

Here, there was something in the air that promoted peacefulness, a vacation vibe, the outside world and its troubles far away and forgotten.

A couple passing by smiled at them, the woman adding a little wave while the guy averted his gaze as if he was afraid of Onegus.

Cassandra smiled back. "Who were they?"

"That was Meryl, a clan member, and the guy was a newcomer."

Unexpectedly, a surge of jealousy burned through Cassandra's newfound tranquility, the energy swirling inside her intensifying tenfold.

Meryl was short and plump, but she had a beautiful face and a gorgeous smile. She didn't look like Onegus's type, but the guilty expression on the guy's face hinted that there might have been a history between Meryl and Onegus.

Forcing a smile, Cassandra leaned into Onegus. "The guy looked like he was caught with his hand in the cookie jar. Was Meryl a former girlfriend of yours?"

Onegus laughed. "Meryl is my cousin, as are almost all the females in this village. And those who aren't are mated to my male cousins." He wrapped his arm around her waist. "Besides, I told you that I've never had a girlfriend. You are my first."

That was a relief, but it was short-lived.

He hadn't chosen her because she was a cut above his previous choices. Her one big advantage was in her genes.

"Am I your first girlfriend because you think I'm a carrier of the immortal genes?"

He nodded.

"What if I'm not?"

"I'd rather stick to my conviction that you are a Dormant instead of playing what-ifs." His hand on her waist tightened. "The Fates wouldn't be that cruel and dangle the perfect woman in front of me just to taunt me."

Well, that was encouraging. Onegus wasn't sure that she was a Dormant, but he thought that she was perfect.

Still, what he'd said before didn't make sense. "It's not possible for every female in your clan to be your first cousin. Is there also a prohibition on second and third cousins getting together?"

"Our immortal genes get passed only by the females, and since most of us are the descendants of Annani, we are considered closely related, and no matter how far removed, we are still forbidden to each other."

That didn't make much sense either, but Cassandra had never been good at biology or physiology. In high school, she'd spent those classes doodling designs for the outfits she wanted her mother to make for her.

Still, she was a fairly intelligent person, and if Onegus explained things properly, she would probably understand.

"Forgive me if it's a dumb question. But what does one have to do with the other? If only immortal females can pass the immortal gene to their children, why does it make them ineligible for marriage with their very distant male relatives? From the little I remember of what I learned in school, there is no risk in marrying a third cousin."

Onegus shrugged. "From the very beginning of gods and immortals, the descendants of the same matriarch were considered closely related. It's a serious taboo that is drilled into our heads from a very young age."

Perhaps the taboo had more to do with tradition than genetics. In any case, it was good to know that none of the women she'd seen at the wedding or strolling the village pathways had ever dated her guy.

"Is it far to your house?" Cassandra returned yet another woman's smile, this time not having to force it.

"Less than five minutes. After the next turn, it's the fifth down the street."

It was more of a pathway than a street, wide enough for a small golf cart going in one direction. If another one came from the other side, it would have to veer to the side. In that regard, the place was like a real village. The houses, though, had just a touch of country flair. They were average-sized, about the size of her house, and they all had front porches with stairs leading up to them.

The place was perfect for raising a family, but she'd seen no children.

Right, the low fertility rate Onegus had mentioned.

That was a major bummer, and so far, the biggest negative to becoming an immortal.

"By the way." Onegus turned right at the fork. "I invited Sylvia and Roni to join us for lunch."

To be with Sylvia, Roni must have been one of those newcomers who were not related to Annani, the head of their clan. When Annani had called them her children during the ceremony, it hadn't been a figure of speech.

"Any particular reason for inviting them other than socializing with your cousins?"

"Sylvia is the one with a similar talent to yours, remember?"

"Of course. Is that why you brought me here today? So she could start training me?"

"That isn't the main reason, but I figured the sooner you start, the better. Your power is dangerous."

"What is the main reason?"

"I wanted you to see how beautiful this place is." He started up the stairs to his house. "Maybe it will help you decide faster."

"About turning immortal or moving in with you?"

"Both."

She stopped him with a hand on his arm before he could open the door. "Don't rush me, Onegus. We've known each other for only one week. You can't expect me to make life-altering decisions after such a short time."

8

ONEGUS

$\mathcal{C}$assandra leaned back and patted her flat belly. "Thank you for lunch, Connor. It was delicious." She cast an amused glance at Onegus. "Your roommate thought that seeing the village would help convince me to consent to the induction. But if you and he are a package deal, that might be a stronger incentive. I could get used to having home-cooked meals."

Connor grinned. "I'm glad you liked it. What do you normally do for food? Do you eat out?"

She nodded. "My mother cooks from time to time, but she has nothing on you."

"Speaking of your mother," Roni said. "Does she have a similar power to yours?"

Cassandra looked at Onegus, waiting for him to allow her to speak freely.

"While in the village, you can talk about anything that pertains to immortals and special talents."

"I wouldn't call my destructive energy a talent. A pain in my derrière is more like it. Thankfully, my mother doesn't have it. Given her memory issues, her life is difficult enough as it is. The last thing she needs is things blowing up around her when she gets mad."

That was odd. Onegus had felt Geraldine's energy. Was Cassandra unaware of it? Or was she trying to protect her mother?

"Your mother emits the same energy as you do, just to a much lesser degree. Did neither of you suspect it?"

Cassandra shrugged. "Nothing has ever exploded around my mother unless I did it."

"What about electronics?" Sylvia asked. "Do things malfunction when she's near?"

"Not that either of us has noticed." Cassandra frowned. "Come to think of it, I noticed that buttons stop working after she uses a device for a long time. The

466

coating peels off, or the plastic gets misshapen, things like that. I always blamed the hand lotions she uses, but maybe it's the energy releasing from her fingers? Does that happen to you?"

Sylvia shook her head. "I cause more damage than malfunctioning buttons. If I don't rein in my power, electronics all around me fritz out."

"How do you rein it in?"

Sylvia's brows dipped low. "After Onegus called me this morning, I thought about it. I've been doing it for so long that I no longer do it consciously." She let out a breath. "I visualize collecting all the strands of power from within me and storing them in a box in my mind. When I need to use them, I reach into that storage box and take out just enough to disable what I was asked to do."

Cassandra frowned. "What happens when your box gets overfilled?"

"I don't make new energy. I just harness what's already inside me. It doesn't deplete either."

"That's not how it works for me." Cassandra tucked a stray strand of hair back into her bun. "When I get angry or overly excited, the energy inside me swells, and I have to release it before it reaches critical mass like what happened at the wedding."

"How do you manage that? Can you direct the energy at a specific target?"

"To some extent. I have very limited control over it." Cassandra chuckled. "It's like driving a car with no brakes. The only way to stop it is to drive it into an obstacle before it gets too fast and the impact is fatal."

"Can you summon your energy at will?" Roni asked.

"I need to get angry first. I don't have anything to discharge when I'm calm."

Onegus put a hand on Cassandra's shoulder. "It's there. I can feel it even now."

She let out a breath. "I got a charge when I thought Meryl was a former girl-friend of yours."

He smirked. "I love it that you get jealous over me."

Sylvia lifted her hand. "So let me get this straight. You've gotten a little peeved, which created a surge of energy, and now you're stuck with it until you can discharge it? It doesn't dissipate on its own?"

"Some of it does, and I can get rid of the rest by going on a run or doing vigorous cleaning. It's only dangerous when I let it accumulate."

Or through sex, but Onegus wasn't going to mention that in front of the others. Although given Roni's smirk, the same thing had occurred to him.

"Let's see what we can do about that." Onegus pushed to his feet.

Cassandra narrowed her eyes at him. "I hope you're not thinking about discharging it by playing your favorite game."

That was a polite way to phrase it, but she hadn't fooled anyone. Sylvia hid a smile behind her hand, Roni kept smirking, and Connor started collecting the dishes to hide his own smile.

"In fact, I am," he teased her. "Let's get these empty water bottles to the back-yard." He lifted the two closest to him.

Roni collected the rest.

"To do what?" Cassandra asked.

"You can practice directing your energy at them."

"Plastic won't do. It has to be either glass or clay."

"I guess we need to drink some beer." He headed to the kitchen. "Snake Venom is my favorite, but I doubt you'll like it. Can I offer you anything else?"

She shook her head. "After last night, I'm not touching alcohol." She cast a baleful glance at Roni. "You and your friends kept pushing drinks at me. What was that about? Get the human drunk?"

Roni lifted his hands in the universal sign for peace. "We were hoping that if you had enough to drink, you wouldn't notice a glowing goddess presiding over the ceremony."

She huffed out a breath. "You shouldn't have bothered. My mind doesn't stop working just because I'm tipsy, and it has a way of explaining away the most bizarre things."

Connor handed her a fresh bottle of water. "You didn't say a thing when Annani showed up."

"What was I supposed to say? How could I have suspected an outlandish thing like a goddess showing up at a wedding? I thought that she was a priestess with a penchant for drama, that the red hair was a wig, and that she had smeared glitter all over her skin."

"What about her unearthly beauty?" Sylvia asked.

"It fit with the scenario I came up with. I thought that she was using her beauty to ensnare everyone into joining her cult."

"A cult?" Roni snorted. "How did you come up with that conspiracy theory?"

Sylvia put a hand on his shoulder. "Look at it through Cassandra's eyes. She's invited to a wedding where everyone looks the same age but acts like a family. A commune or a cult is not such an outlandish assumption."

9

CASSANDRA

*L*ong minutes passed as Cassandra stared at the lineup of beer bottles, trying to focus and willing them to explode, but it was no use. For her energy to reach explosive levels, she needed to get less anxious and more angry.

Roni walked up to stand beside her and pushed his hands into his pockets. "Do you need help?" he asked. "I'm very good at annoying people."

"I'm sure you are, but it takes particular kinds of annoyances to get me angry enough to produce energy capable of blowing things up."

"Give me a hint, and I'll come up with something."

She grimaced. "Degrading comments about women usually do the trick, but I doubt your girlfriend will tolerate hearing them coming out of your mouth."

He smirked. "I know just the thing, and Sylvia won't mind because she's heard it before. I used it to annoy Kian."

To risk the wrath of the goddess's son, Roni must be an adrenaline junkie. Cassandra wasn't easily intimidated, but Kian was one of the few exceptions. The guy was scary even when he was in party mode and trying to be nice.

"Why would you do a thing like that? Do you have a death wish?"

He chuckled. "I almost peed myself, but I had no choice. Kian couldn't summon the aggression to fight a scrawny dude like me, so I had to make him angry. Truly vile slam poetry did the trick."

She must be missing a piece of the puzzle because what he'd just said didn't make sense. Why would he need to fight Kian? Was there an initiation ritual that the transitioned males had to go through to join the clan?

Or maybe Roni had done it to get bitten? Was the kid a glutton for punishment, or bisexual? Even if he was either of those, why Kian?

"Couldn't they have found you someone your own size for the hazing ritual?"

Roni frowned. "Hazing? What gave you that idea?"

She shrugged. "What other reason could you have for fighting a powerful immortal? If you wanted to be bitten for pleasure, you should have chosen a more appropriate partner. First of all, Kian is out of your league, and secondly, I doubt that he's bisexual."

Behind her, Connor started laughing so hard that he was making choking sounds.

She whirled at him. "What's so funny?"

A hand over his heart, Connor took a shuddering breath to calm himself. "Apparently, Onegus still has a lot to tell you. You're missing major elements of the story."

"It would appear so." She cast Onegus an accusing glance.

"There was no time last night. I only told you the bare minimum."

"If Onegus doesn't mind, I'll sum it up for you." Roni waited for Onegus's nod and then continued, "Female Dormants are induced during sex. It takes venom and semen to activate the dormant genes. Male Dormants are induced in a fight. All they need is venom, probably because the amount and composition of the venom produced in response to aggression is much higher than the other type. I had to fight an immortal male to get him aggressive, so he could produce enough venom to knock me out."

Now it made sense. "But why Kian? Are you super important to the clan?"

"I am super important, but that's not the reason Kian offered to induce me. After several other immortal males tried and failed, Kian was my last hope. As Annani's son, his venom is the most potent."

Poor Roni. She could just imagine how scared he must have been. He was a scrawny, pale dude, who probably spent his days in front of a computer screen and never saw the inside of a gym.

"It must have been difficult."

He shrugged. "I'm glad it's behind me and that I get to spend eternity with my one and only." He wrapped his arm around Sylvia's waist and kissed her cheek.

His one and only. Onegus had used the precise same words. Was that more than an expression for these guys?

"We should get on with the training," Onegus said.

"Right." Roni removed his arm from his girlfriend's waist and pulled his phone out of his pocket. "I suggest that everyone other than Cassandra plug their ears."

No one did as he'd suggested, but perhaps they should have.

The stuff was really vile, but she couldn't get angry at Roni because he was just reciting someone else's words.

She put a hand on his arm. "You can stop. It's not working. I need it to be something real."

Rubbing a hand over his jaw, Onegus smiled sheepishly. "I think I know how to get you riled. Let's talk about my mother's disdain for Americans."

Her energy stirred even before he had a chance to elaborate.

"Yes, let's talk about that. How can she detest Americans when her beloved son is one of them?"

"She doesn't think of me as American. In her mind, I'm a Scot who's temporarily domiciled in the US. It doesn't matter to her that I moved here two centuries ago and have no intentions of ever moving back to Scotland."

"Maybe she doesn't like Americans because you moved here? Your mother misses you, but she can't be mad at you, so she's mad at everyone else around you."

Finding excuses for Martha was counterproductive to getting angry, but Cassandra had a feeling that she was onto something.

"That might be part of it. But she objects to many things. Americans are obnoxious and loud, they don't know how to dress properly, and they are to blame for the invention of jeans, which she detests. They don't get irony, their humor is infantile, and their television shows are lacking sophistication or the requirement for any intelligent thought, reflecting the lowest common denominator they are geared to. Should I go on?"

Cassandra shook her head. "I've got enough for another punch bowl."

That was the least offensive thing she could have said, but in her mind, she had several counterarguments that would take Martha down a peg.

Onegus waved at the lineup of bottles. "Go for it."

Narrowing her eyes, Cassandra visualized the bottles exploding and then let go.

Nothing happened to the lineup, but behind her, Roni yelped.

The beer bottle he'd been holding shattered in his hand, and blood was streaming from the cuts.

"Oh, my God." Cassandra was mortified. "What have I done?"

"It's okay." Roni plucked a few shards from his injured hand and then licked his wounds like a dog. "It speeds up the healing." He took the napkin Sylvia handed him and wiped the blood away. "See?" He showed Cassandra his hand. "In a moment, there will be no sign of the injury."

The cuts were already closed, and right before her eyes, the lines were fading until there was nothing left.

"Amazing." Cheeks burning in shame, she looked up at Roni's face. "Nevertheless, I'm so sorry. I was aiming at the bottles on the table. I don't know how or why the blast got the one in your hand."

"Perhaps the slam poetry worked after all? In your subconscious, you might have been a little angry at me, and since Onegus's mother wasn't here to absorb the blast, it got me."

It was so nice of him not to make a big deal out of it.

"Maybe you are right."

"No harm done." Onegus put a hand on her shoulder. "Ready to try again? This time no one will hold a glass container."

She shook her head. "I'm done for today."

Glass and clay were not the only things that might get hurt.

Onegus gave her shoulder a gentle squeeze. "It was just a minor setback. You need to train."

Cassandra put her hand on her belly. "Most of the energy got discharged, and I'm not in the mood for refueling."

MARGARET

*M*argaret was still half asleep when the bedroom door opened. "Good morning, love," Bowen drawled.

His voice and the smell of coffee bringing a smile to her face, she turned onto her back and opened her eyes. "What time is it? Did I miss breakfast?"

Given how loudly her tummy was rumbling, she had.

"Yup." Bowen sat on the bed and handed her the coffee. "And if you don't wake up, you'll miss lunch as well." He bent to whisper, "Anastasia is cooking, so I wouldn't hold my breath. She's a terrible cook."

Margaret laughed. "You're mean. I'm sure it's not that bad."

Bowen leaned the rest of the way and kissed her cheek. "Get up, get dressed, and taste for yourself." He rose to his feet. "Will it take you long?"

"I need to shower."

"Then I'll tell Anastasia to wait before serving lunch."

After the door closed behind him, Margaret took a few more sips of coffee before putting it on the nightstand and flinging the comforter off.

Last night, she'd fallen asleep in the car on the way home, and Bowen had carried her in his arms like a freaking princess. Heck, he'd treated her like one throughout the wedding, telling her how beautiful she was. They'd even danced a little, or rather Bowen danced, and she'd put her feet on top of his.

When they'd gotten back to their room, Margaret had been too tired to shower or even take her makeup off. He'd helped her undress, got rid of his own clothes, and climbed in bed behind her. She'd fallen asleep with him spooning her.

He was such an amazing guy.

And how had she rewarded him? By falling asleep.

In the bathroom, the face that looked back at her from the mirror belonged on a zombie. Dark eye-makeup was smeared all over her eye sockets, and her hair looked like a bird's nest.

But at least she no longer looked pale or gaunt, which was Bowen's doing.

No matter what, tonight, they were finally going to make love. They'd waited long enough.

Surprisingly, Margaret wasn't even nervous.

She took longer than usual to get ready though, fixing her hair, choosing a flattering outfit, and applying makeup.

From now on, she would take care of her appearance. She'd developed a taste for Bowen's compliments and craved more. It wasn't vanity. That wasn't why she wanted to look her best. Pleasing him filled her with a sense of satisfaction, of accomplishment. It made her feel good about herself, and it was intoxicating.

Margaret couldn't remember ever feeling like that before.

"Look at you," Ana said as she emerged from the bedroom. "I love those leggings on you."

Giving her an appreciative once-over, Bowen wrapped his arm around her waist and pulled her against his body. "I like them even more."

"Come to the table." Ana waved them over. "Spaghetti gets mushy when it's reheated."

"I had so much fun yesterday." Margaret sat in the chair Bowen had pulled out for her. "And I love your mom, Bowen. Are we going to meet her again before she goes back to Scotland?"

"Certainly." He pulled a chair out for himself and sat next to her. "She wouldn't let me get away with not seeing you again. She already called this morning."

Ana put the spaghetti bowl on the table and gave the noodles a vigorous toss. "Eat now. Talk later."

"Yes, ma'am." Leon passed the bowl to Bowen, who scooped a heaping portion onto Margaret's plate.

For the next few moments, the four of them ate in silence. The spaghetti wasn't bad. In fact, it was quite good, and so was the salad that Ana had made to go with it.

"Thank you for making lunch." Margaret pulled the bowl toward her and took another serving. "It's very good." She cast Bowen a sidelong glance.

"It is," he agreed.

When she was done with the second serving, Margaret pushed the plate away and rubbed her stomach. "I don't know where this appetite came from. I never ate so much in Safe Haven." She smiled. "Maybe Emmett compelled me not to overeat so I wouldn't gain weight."

"Speaking of Emmett." Ana put her fork down. "When can Margaret and I see him?"

"I can call the chief," Leon offered. "Onegus shouldn't have a problem with Emmett receiving visitors as long as they are supervised."

Reminded of Stella's promise to fill in details about Emmett, Margaret turned to Bowen. "Last night, you said that there is still a lot I don't know about Emmett. Stella said she would fill me in, but I don't want to wait."

11

BOWEN

*M*argaret had expressed her wish to see Emmett before, but Bowen had hoped she'd reconsidered. He didn't want her anywhere near the guy.

Tearing a sheet of paper towel from the dispenser, he wiped his mouth. "You already know that he's a different kind of immortal, right?"

"I do. But I don't know what it means and what it has to do with China or with Stella."

It also had to do with Vlad, who was Margaret's future son-in-law, but that was Stella's story to tell, not his.

Then again, he and Margaret were a family as well, and other than what was required from him given his job, he had no intention of keeping secrets from her.

Their relationship wasn't official yet, and they hadn't had a chance to consummate it, but it was a forgone conclusion that the two of them were destined to spend the rest of their lives together.

"The story Emmett told Peter and then elaborated on when interrogated by Kian was that he belonged to a group of immortals who called themselves the Kra-ell. They are a little different from us. First of all, they are not really immortal but rather long-lived. Their life expectancy is supposedly around a thousand years. The biggest difference, though, is that they need blood for sustenance."

Margaret's eyes widened, and her hand flew to her neck. "Emmett is a vampire? Did he feed on me?"

"The short answer is yes."

Anastasia didn't look surprised, so Bowen assumed that Leon had already told her.

Margaret blew out a breath. "Talk about a parasite. Not only did Emmett profit from our free labor, which he obtained by compelling us to work for him, but he also fed on us." She lifted a pair of wary eyes at Bowen. "Or was it only on the females?"

"I think he prefers females. But Peter tells me that Emmett and his people consume mostly animal blood. Snacking on humans is considered a treat, something they do in conjunction with sex. It's not their main source of food."

Margaret grimaced. "It makes it a little less creepy, but not by much. What else?"

"Emmett is a hybrid, half-human and half Kra-ell. His father is a Kra-ell, and his mother was a human."

"Was? Is she dead?"

"Most likely. Emmett is over seventy years old, so it's reasonable to assume that his human mother has passed away. He escaped his group a long time ago, so he probably doesn't know."

"Escaped?" Margaret asked. "Was he held against his will?"

"I'm not clear on all the details, but from what I heard, the leader of the group practically owns its members, especially the males. According to Emmett, their society is female-dominated, and since there are many more males than females, the males are deemed less valuable."

Margaret gaped. "I can't imagine Emmett being subservient to anyone, and especially to a woman. He is a very dominant man."

Leon chuckled. "Apparently, their females are even more dominant than their males, and they are cruel."

"They don't form family units," Bowen continued. "The tribe or the commune is the family. The children belong to their mother's household and are raised by all its members. The males are held in communal harems, and they have to wait for an invitation to breed, which is not much fun. The females thrive on inflicting pain."

Anastasia's face twisted in distaste. "No wonder Emmett ran away. Who would want to be part of a society like that?"

Bowen shrugged. "Emmett must have been a free thinker. Most people just accept their circumstances and don't question their people's traditions. We can't understand how a woman can agree to be a second, third, or fourth wife, and yet in the countries where that's the norm, most don't question it. It's just the way it is."

"Yeah, I don't get it," Anastasia said. "Frankly, that's even weirder than the Kra-ell tradition because there is no real reason or need for it. The Kra-ell don't have enough women to go around, so the males have to share. Humans are born more or less in equal numbers."

Margaret tucked a strand of hair behind her ear. "What's the China connection? Why did Kian need Stella to interrogate Emmett in Chinese?"

Bowen felt uneasy about telling Margaret and Ana about Vlad's father. It was gossip, and he was quite sure that Stella wouldn't appreciate it. Perhaps she didn't even know that he and Leon knew.

Onegus had filled them in because of their connection to Emmett, but they weren't supposed to tell others about it.

"Emmett is originally from China, and his people are probably still there." Bowen knew that wouldn't be explanation enough and added, "But that's not why Stella was asked to assist in the interrogation. Apparently, she'd met a Kraell male twenty-some years ago."

Anastasia leaned back and crossed her arms over her chest. "So the clan already knew about these other immortals before capturing Emmett?"

"No." Leon reached for the bowl of spaghetti and scooped what was left onto his plate. "Stella didn't tell anyone."

"Why?" Margaret asked.

"I don't know." Leon twirled pasta on his fork. "Perhaps she didn't realize who and what the guy was until Emmett was captured."

12

ONEGUS

*W*hen Connor finished playing his latest composition, Cassandra clapped her hands. "That was absolutely terrifying. Bravo! After hearing the score for this horror movie, I'm not going to watch it for sure." She rubbed her hands over her arms. "I got goosebumps all over."

Sitting on the piano bench, Connor dipped his head. "Do you want me to cheer you up with something lighter?"

"Yes, please."

The incident with Roni had left Cassandra shaken, and she'd only started to relax after he and Sylvia had left.

Onegus had done his best to appear unfazed by the accident, but the truth was that it was worrisome. Sylvia couldn't teach Cassandra how to control her power because hers functioned differently, and there was no one else he could think of who might be able to help her.

Perhaps Annani would know something about it. The goddess's power had a different flavor than Cassandra's, but she was in full control of it, able to suppress it when needed and appear almost human.

That reminded him that Annani would be returning to the downtown building soon, and he should be heading back.

When Connor was done playing, and Cassandra applauded him again, Onegus rose to his feet. "As much as I would have loved to spend the rest of the afternoon enjoying your company, I need to get back to work."

Cassandra glanced at her watch. "Wow. Time really flies when you're having fun." She got up and walked over to Connor. "Thank you for a lovely lunch and for the entertainment." She leaned and kissed his cheek. "Good luck with the producers. In my opinion, you nailed it."

"Thanks. I agree." He pushed to his feet and took Cassandra's hand. "I hope I'll be seeing you again soon." He lifted it and kissed the back of it.

"I hope so too." She smiled, her fondness for Connor clearly showing in the softness in her eyes and the tone of her voice.

Onegus suspected that most of Cassandra's social troubles were the result of her wearing her emotions on her sleeve. When she liked someone, it showed, and when she didn't, it showed as well.

She clearly didn't like his mother.

Martha was not easy to like. She was opinionated and harsh, but she was also loyal to a fault and always ready to help. Hopefully, she would eventually grow on Cassandra, and the two would learn to appreciate each other.

He waited until they were in his car to broach the topic of a meeting between the mothers.

"When do you think is a good time for the dinner with Martha and Geraldine?"

"Never," Cassandra deadpanned and then smiled apologetically. "I'm not looking forward to it, but if it has to be done, then the sooner, the better. I prefer to be done with difficult tasks and put them behind me."

It was an admirable quality and one more proof that Cassandra wasn't a coward. It was just a shame that she regarded spending time with his mother as difficult and unpleasant.

"It's not going to be that bad. My mother wants to try out Gerard's place, and I hope she'll be too wowed by the service to complain about Americans. I doubt she can find anything of that caliber in all of Great Britain."

"Good point."

"I can make reservations for tomorrow evening or for Tuesday. Which one works better for you?"

"Tomorrow. I need to check with Geraldine, but I'm sure she'll gladly cancel any plans she might have to dine at the poshest establishment in the state." Cassandra sighed. "I just hope she doesn't start telling your mother her crazy stories."

"Do you want me to warn Martha? She'll understand."

Cassandra shook her head. "If need be, you can explain after dinner. I want to give my mother the chance to shine."

"Of course." He reached over and took her hand. "Perhaps if she gets all decked out, your mother wouldn't mind a group photo. I can then ask Roni to isolate hers and run it through the Department of Motor Vehicles database and see what comes up."

"She's not going to like it, but she won't be able to refuse, so that might work." Cassandra huffed out a breath. "Isn't there another way to do it? Can you do that mind thing and get into her head?"

"It's called thralling, and I'm not allowed to do it without proper cause. It's considered a violation to do so. But since we suspect that your mother is already an immortal, I wouldn't be able to thrall her anyway. Immortals can't do that to each other, only to humans."

"Well, so if you can't thrall her, that will prove that she's immortal."

"Not really. Some humans are immune."

"It's worth a try, though."

"Again, it's against clan law to thrall a human without proper cause."

"Even if I give you permission?"

"It's not yours to give."

She slumped in the seat. "Yeah, you're right. What constitutes a justified cause? Perhaps I could come up with one?"

"Protecting the secrecy of our existence or saving a clan member. Given Geraldine's particular circumstances, I could have petitioned the judge to give me a one-time exemption, but since it won't provide us with a conclusive result, the judge is most likely going to deny me."

Cassandra was quiet for a long moment. "I'm sure that other immortals break that rule left and right. There is no way you can enforce it because the humans who fall victim to thralling are unaware of it and can't complain."

"That might be true, and in most cases, it's not done with malicious intent. But what civilians can get away with, I cannot. I'm the Chief Guardian, and I can't bend the law while expecting others to obey it. I have to follow it to the letter."

"You thralled me."

"That was to protect the secret of my immortality, and therefore allowed."

Cassandra crossed her arms over her chest. "You still need to fill in the details and tell me the rest of the story. When are you going to do that?"

"I'll call you tonight." He let go of her hand to open the center console compartment. "I have a secure phone for you to use." He pulled out a box and handed it to her. "It's already programmed with my number."

13

CASSANDRA

*C*assandra had lied about her energy being completely depleted. Well, underreported was a more accurate definition. She'd discharged the initial surge, but then the guilt over hurting Roni and the reminder of how volatile and unpredictable her power was had ramped it back up.

She was simmering with it.

"Can you come in for a quick cup of coffee?" she asked when Onegus parked in front of her house.

Coffee was the last thing on her mind, but if her mother was home, that was the only thing they would be having. Hopefully though, Geraldine was still out, hanging out with her book club friends, and in that case, Cassandra was going to drag Onegus up to her room and let him defuse the last of her excess energy.

Given the gleam in his eyes, he knew precisely what she was after, but he played along. "It will have to be really quick. I need to get back to work."

"Half an hour?"

He smiled, flashing her a pair of fangs that were already partially elongated. "I can do that."

When he threw the driver-side door open, she put her hand on the handle, but having moved faster than humanly possible, he was suddenly there, opening the passenger door for her.

"Impressive." She took his offered hand.

Hand in hand, they walked up to the front door. It was locked, which was a good sign. Living in a gated community, she and her mother never bothered locking the door when they were home during the day.

"My mother is probably still out with her friends, but she might come back any time now."

The face-splitting grin on his face said that he didn't care if she did as long as she wasn't home at the moment.

As soon as Cassandra opened the door and they walked in, Onegus lifted her into his arms, kicked the door closed behind them, and headed toward the stairs.

He stopped with his foot on the first step. "Just to make sure. You don't really want coffee, right?"

Wrapping her arms around his neck, Cassandra laughed. "Did you peek into my mind?"

"I didn't need to. Your smell was driving me insane the entire way here, but I had to make sure that you wanted to play with me and not your battery-operated boyfriend."

"Bob is no competition for you."

"Naturally." He climbed the stairs. "What has gotten you so randy?"

"You." Cassandra lifted her head and pressed her lips lightly to Onegus's, careful because of his fangs. "Kissing you is complicated."

He walked into her room and pushed the door closed with his foot. "Just let me kiss you, and everything will be fine. I've been doing it for a very long time."

She grimaced. "Don't remind me."

He sat on her bed with her still in his arms. "About what? My age, or the other women I've kissed?"

"The women. I don't care how old you are."

His hand traveled up her side, skimming over her rib cage. "You have nothing to get upset about. The others were just for practice, so when I finally found you, I would know how to please a woman." Kissing up her neck, he closed his hand over her breast.

Tilting her head to allow him better access, Cassandra let out a soft moan.

"Since we don't have much time," Onegus murmured against her earlobe. "And you already know what I am." He nipped it lightly. "I can move with immortal speed."

She'd seen him do that when he'd opened the passenger door for her, but if he also planned to have sex that fast, she wasn't sure she was up to that.

Being horny and a little wet didn't make her ready, and she wasn't one of those women who was into painful penetrations. There was nothing fun or sexy about waking up sore in the morning, and reading about it in romance novels always made her cringe.

She narrowed her eyes at him. "What do you mean by immortal speed?"

"This." Moving faster than she could follow, he whipped her shirt over her head, unhooked her bra, and pulled her pants off together with her panties.

That took three seconds tops, and in the next two, he was just as naked as she was.

"Condom?" he asked.

Lowering her eyes to his beautiful erection, it was tempting to say no. Thankfully, her brain wasn't completely addled by desire, and she still retained some rational thought.

"Condom." Seeing the disappointment in his eyes, she added, "I need to hear the rest of your story before I give you my consent."

He nodded and bent down to lift his slacks. Pulling out his bi-fold wallet, he opened it and retrieved a packet.

"Let me put it on you." She crawled to the edge of the bed.

His eyes shining with inner light, he handed her the packet and leaned his powerful thighs against the side of the bed.

When she dipped her head and kissed the tip, Onegus hissed.

Wrapping her palm around his shaft, she looked up. "Can I have a little taste before I sheath you?"

He smirked. "Since when are you asking for permission?"

"You wanted to play master and slave."

"Never a slave." He put his hand on the back of her head. "I only want to be the master of your desire."

"What does it make me, then?"

"A very grateful acolyte."

From anyone else, that would have sounded condescending and boastful, and it would've killed Cassandra's fervor. But coming from Onegus, it was exciting.

For some reason, she liked his arrogance.

Onegus was the pinnacle of male perfection and therefore entitled to it. Besides, he did *superior* well. It was part of who he was and one of the many things that had made her fall for him.

14

ONEGUS

*A*s Cassandra licked his shaft like it was an ice cream cone, Onegus hissed. "Just a little taste, no more."

Giving him another long lick, she looked up at him with a challenge in her dark eyes. "Why?"

He cupped both her cheeks. "We don't have much time, and I need to be inside you."

"Oh, well. That's a shame." Cassandra planted a soft kiss on the tip. "Next time, and that's a promise," she told the bobbing head.

As it winked at her, she tore the packet with her teeth and sheathed it with the same practiced expertise as before.

"You are very skilled with those."

Smiling, she lifted on her knees and wrapped her arms around his neck. "Jealous?"

"Yes."

"Don't be." She pressed her breasts to his chest. "The others were just practice, so I could learn how to pleasure you, master." She winked.

"Minx." In one smooth move, he sat on the bed and lifted her to straddle him.

Surprise painted on her beautiful face, she quickly adjusted, grinding her moist sex over his shaft.

He groaned and caught her nipple between his lips. Sucking it in, he was careful not to nick her with his fangs, which by now were fully elongated.

It was liberating to let them grow and not force them to remain dormant. Finally, after a lifetime of stifling his urges, he could finally let them come up to the surface, but he couldn't act on them yet.

Cassandra wasn't ready for what he wanted to do to her, and thankfully, his need to do right by her overrode even his primal instincts.

As short on time as they were, he was not going to shortchange her pleasure.

He'd rather go back to work without finding release than leave her less than fully satisfied.

Still working on her succulent nipples, he ran his palms over her hips and circled to her inner thighs.

When his fingers brushed over the most sensitive part of her, Cassandra groaned, and when he penetrated her with one finger, her head fell back. Her elongated neck tempted his fangs, making them pulsate with the venom that his glands were pumping. But even though his finger was coated with her juices, she wasn't ready for him yet.

Slowly pumping into her with his finger, he added his thumb to the play, gently massaging the top of her sex.

Cassy was close, her panting breaths fanning over the top of his head as he worked her nipples and her core.

When he pulled out his finger and came back with two, her back stiffened, and then she jerked, her sheath clamping over his pumping fingers as her orgasm washed over her.

He kept at it, helping her ride it out, and when the jerking stopped, and she collapsed against him, boneless, he wrapped his arms around her and held her tight.

The words 'I love you' were on the tip of his tongue, but he swallowed them. Neither of them was ready for that. The feeling needed to percolate, to mature, and he needed to be absolutely sure that what he felt was love before he said those words to her.

Burying his nose in the crook of Cassandra's neck, Onegus breathed in her unique scent, the signature of it imprinted on his senses after only one week with her.

He felt her stirring, and a moment later, her hands were cupping his cheeks. "Thank you." She kissed his forehead. "You are such a generous lover."

As if he could be any other way with her. "I will always take care of you."

"And I of you." Lifting up on her knees, she reached down, took hold of his shaft, and lowered herself on it while looking into his eyes.

When they were fully joined, a soft moan escaped her lovely throat.

For a long moment, they just stayed like that, chest to chest, skin to skin— feeling, connecting.

It didn't last, but not because he was impatient. Cassandra put her hands on his shoulders and moved, rolling her hips in a wave.

He wanted to leave her in the driver seat, to let her enjoy going at her own speed, but he'd been holding back for too long and needed to unleash his beast.

Grabbing her waist, he lifted her until he was almost all the way out, and then slammed her down on his shaft.

Letting him take over, Cassandra surrendered, and as he drove in and out of her with the power and speed he'd been craving, it didn't take long for her to climax again.

She was so incredibly beautiful when in the throes of passion, and as her core tightened around his shaft, he could no longer hold back his own climax.

His hips jerking up, he felt his seed rising and clamped his hand over the back of her head. Keeping it immobilized, he licked her neck, preparing her for his bite.

When he hissed and struck, she screamed, but it wasn't in pain.

Another climax tore through her, and then another, and when he finally retracted his fangs and licked the wounds closed, she collapsed limply against his chest.

Wrapping his arms around her slim back, he held her tightly to him.

"I love you," he murmured into her ear, testing the sound of those words on his lips while secure in the knowledge that she couldn't hear him.

Perhaps it made him a coward, but he wasn't ready to make that final leap into the insanity of matehood. Would he become totally entangled in Cassandra like his mated Guardians were with their mates?

Hell, who was he trying to fool?

He already was.

MARGARET

*W*hile Margaret and Bowen cleaned up after lunch, Anastasia chilled on the couch with a book, and Leon went to make the necessary phone calls to arrange the meeting between Margaret, Anastasia, and Emmett.

If it were possible, Margaret would have preferred to be alone with her former mentor. She wanted to confront him about the compulsion and ask him why he had done it. But Emmett's prison cell was monitored, and Bowen would never let her go alone, so it didn't really matter that Ana would be there as well.

"What are you thinking about?" Bowen handed her a plate to dry.

"About what I'm going to say to Emmett." She sighed. "I would have liked to have a private meeting with him."

Bowen's eyes darkened. "Why?"

Was he jealous of Emmett? He had absolutely no reason to be. Whatever she'd thought she felt for Safe Haven's leader had been the result of compulsion and not any real attraction.

Smiling, Margaret playfully slapped Bowen's arm. "You have nothing to be jealous about. Whatever I thought that I felt for him wasn't real. He means nothing to me. In fact, the reason I want to be alone with him is so I can give him a piece of my mind, and I don't want Ana to hear me using foul language."

His expression softened. "You can swear as much as you want. I don't mind. Come to think of it, I've never heard you cuss." He waggled his brows. "It would probably turn me on."

"I can swear in my head, but I can't do it in front of other people. I probably wouldn't have been able to cuss at Emmett even if we were alone."

Bowen leaned closer. "How about dirty talk? Can you do that?"

Laughing, she shook her head. "Maybe. I've never tried."

Probably not.

"Can you try for me?"

She laughed again. "I'll think about it."

"When?"

"After I'm done thinking about all the other things I need to think about." She batted her eyelashes in a not-so-subtle hint.

"Like what?" The amusement dancing in his eyes suggested that he'd gotten her meaning.

Margaret leaned closer and whispered, "I was thinking about Bridget's advice. We should do something about it tonight."

As the amusement in Bowen's eyes turned into a predatory gleam, he pulled her into his arms. "I wish we had the house to ourselves," he murmured as he nuzzled her ear. "I would have liked to treat you to a romantic evening first." His soft lips blazed a trail of fire down her neck. "And then seduce you on the couch." He pulled her neckline down to kiss her collarbone. "And then carry you to bed and have my way with you."

Her body liquefied, either from his words or his gentle kisses. "I would have liked that a lot."

"I can ask Leon to take Anastasia out on a date," he murmured as his lips brushed over the top of her breast.

"Please do." She let her head fall back.

"Good news," Leon said as he walked into the living room. "I talked with Peter, and he said that we can have a meeting with Emmett tomorrow morning."

Anastasia lifted her head. "The four of us?"

"Did you think Bowen and I would let you and Margaret be alone with him?" Leon sat on the couch next to Ana. "Of course, we're going with you." He turned to look at Bowen, his eyes smiling when he realized what they had been doing in the kitchen.

Bowen's eyes were glowing, and Margaret was sure that her cheeks looked as flushed as they felt.

"We are supposed to be on duty tomorrow morning," Bowen said.

Leon shrugged. "It shouldn't be a big deal to switch shifts with other Guardians."

Switching shifts could mean another night without Bowen, and Margaret would rather give up the meeting with Emmett.

Apparently, the same thing had occurred to Bowen, and he said, "Isn't it better to reschedule the meeting for later in the day? It's not like Emmett has somewhere he needs to be."

"He's meeting with Jin and Mey at eleven to teach them the Kra-ell language. Peter says it will probably take all day."

"You don't have to come with us." Ana crossed her arms over her chest. "Peter and Eleanor can guard us just as well."

"Too late." Leon put his arm on Ana's shoulders. "I already told Peter that the four of us are coming."

"Great," Ana muttered under her breath. "Can you at least sit in the back and pretend like you are not there? I want to be able to talk to Emmett without you two growling and hissing in the background."

"We'll do our best." Leon kissed the top of her head. "By the way, my mother is coming to visit us this evening, and she might bring her friend Janet with her."

Margaret slumped against Bowen. "So much for our plans," she whispered.

They could just close the door to their bedroom at night and have complete privacy, but this was going to be their first time, and Bowen was right about wanting it to be special.

Bowen let out an exasperated sigh. "In that case, I'd better invite my mother as well. She can hitch a ride with Rowan."

"I'll let my mother know." Leon pulled out his phone and typed a message.

"I'm not cooking again," Ana announced.

"Thank the Fates," Bowen whispered in Margaret's ear.

"You're so bad." She slapped his arm. "It was good."

Looking their way, Ana pretended she didn't know what that had been about, or maybe she hadn't heard, but Margaret doubted that.

"I can't believe I'm asking this, but I really don't want to cook again today. Can you grill some hamburgers for dinner?"

Bowen grinned. "It would be my pleasure."

16

CASSANDRA

*W*hen Cassandra opened her eyes, she wasn't surprised that Onegus was gone, but she was disappointed nonetheless.

He'd covered her with the blanket, lowered the shades, and closed the door behind him. Glancing at the pillow next to her, she hoped he'd also left her a note, but there was none.

Instead, the new phone he'd gotten her was on the nightstand, unboxed, and when she lifted it, she saw that he'd left her a message.

I had to leave, and I didn't want to wake you up. I'll call you later.

With a sigh, she put the phone back on the nightstand.

Hopefully, once all of Onegus's guests went home, he wouldn't have to rush and could stay with her longer. She hated waking up alone after making love to him. It would have been nice to spend the night together for a change.

Right.

As if they could do that with her mother sleeping in the master bedroom down the hall.

They were not teenagers.

What was the solution, though?

The immortals' village was like something taken from a fairytale, and she wouldn't mind moving in with Onegus into one of its cozy homes, but she couldn't leave her mother behind. Perhaps Geraldine would agree to come along and live next door to them?

Connor was an awesome guy, and perhaps he wouldn't mind trading Onegus for Geraldine as a roommate. They could be neighbors and hang out together.

Talk about a fairytale.

Things were never that easy, not even without the whole secret immortal clan thing.

Even if her mother was an immortal as Onegus suspected, she wouldn't want to live in a secluded village. She would miss her friends and her book club, or whatever else she was doing while pretending that she was with them.

On the other hand, she might find an immortal to build a life with. Wouldn't that be wonderful?

Heck, maybe one day Geraldine could even have another child?

Immortals might have low fertility, but at least it didn't come with an expiration date. Or did it?

It was just one more item on the long list of questions she'd prepared and was still waiting for Onegus to answer.

After taking a shower and getting dressed, Cassandra stuffed the new phone Onegus had given her in one pocket and her old one in the other and headed downstairs. Her mother wasn't back yet, which got her a little worried.

She sent her a text. *Where are you?*

Geraldine replied a moment later. *I went to the mall with Jill. Do you need me to come back?*

No, I just wanted to know where you are. Have fun. Cassandra added a heart emoji and pressed send.

A kissy face was her mother's reply.

Pulling a bottle of water out of the fridge, she took it to the living room, plopped on the couch, and took the two phones out of her pockets. She should go up to her home studio to do some work, but she wasn't in the mood.

Depleted, but in a good way, Cassandra felt languid and lazy.

Sex with Onegus worked much better at getting rid of her excess energy than meditation or relaxants. She should keep him just for that.

Glancing at her shiny new phone, she picked it up and examined it closely. It looked like an iPhone, and it even had a similar interface, but it wasn't. She checked the list of contacts, smiling when she saw the two numbers Onegus had programmed—his and Connor's.

Selecting Onegus's, she wrote him a text. *When can we talk?*

The phone rang a moment later. "Did you have a nice nap?"

"The best." She leaned back on the cushions. "I slept until half an hour ago, and I'm not in the mood to work, so I'm bugging you instead."

"You are not bugging me. I'm glad you called."

"Are you busy?"

"I'm never too busy to talk to you."

"Do you have time to tell me the rest of the story?"

He hesitated. "I'd rather do it in person."

"You said that this phone was secure."

"It is. I'm not concerned with security. I just think that this kind of conversation should be done face to face."

"I'm tired of waiting. When can I see you again?"

"Perhaps I'll be able to sneak out tonight. Do you need to wake up early tomorrow?"

"I'm usually up at seven, but I had a long afternoon nap, so I can stay up late."

"Good. Leave your balcony door open."

He must be joking.

She chuckled. "So you can turn into a bat and fly in?"

"So I don't wake up your mother when I come. I can climb up to your balcony and go straight to your room. Can you tell the guard at the gate to let me in without calling the house first?"

"I can do that, but I have a better idea. How about I come to you?"

There was a brief moment of silence before he answered. "I don't know when I'll be able to get away, if at all. I'll text you, and we can take it from there."

"Fine." She ended the call and dropped her new phone on the seat next to her.

He was so annoying.

While she'd been thinking about upending her life and moving in with him, he was still wary about her learning the exact location of his downtown office.

17

ONEGUS

*T*he Clan Mother was back at the downtown building. If she had stayed in her apartment with Alena, it would have been easy to guard her, but Annani had decided to use her time to visit as many of her people as she could manage in a day.

Onegus had suggested she invite them to her place, but Annani wanted to see the other apartments and compare them.

Alena couldn't even provide him with her mother's schedule because the goddess hadn't planned her visits and was just floating from one apartment to the next.

What a headache.

Dealing with Annani, Onegus could now understand what Kian went through every time she came for a visit.

The Clan Mother didn't follow the safety protocol, and no one could make her listen to reason, not even Alena. Instead of her adapting her actions to the protocol, it had to be constantly rewritten and readjusted to accommodate her whims.

When she'd finally settled in her apartment, and the last of the guests had returned from their visits to the village, it was close to midnight and Onegus was exhausted.

"Lock the building down after I leave," he told Magnus, who'd temporarily replaced Bhathian as his second-in-command at the keep.

Magnus kept his expression impassive, but he couldn't hide the amusement dancing in his eyes. "When should I expect you back?"

"In the morning. I might spend the night in the village. But don't hesitate to call me for any reason."

"I won't." Magnus sat in the command seat Onegus had vacated. Facing the array of monitors, he put his feet on the desk. "Good night, Chief."

"Good night." Onegus walked out into the hallway and pulled his phone out of his pocket.

There was a good chance that it was already too late for Cassandra. It would be close to one in the morning when he got to her place, and the things he needed to tell her would take several hours. If she were an immortal, the nap she'd taken after their afternoon delight would have been enough to re-energize her for the next twenty-four hours, but she wasn't one yet, and tomorrow was a regular workday for her.

Perhaps it would be better for them to postpone the talk for another day.

Walking toward his car, he typed, *are you still awake?*

Her reply came back immediately. *I'm waiting for you. Are you on your way?*

I just left the office and can be there in twenty minutes. Did you let the guard know that I'm coming?

Instead of sending another text, she called. "I did, but I'll call again in case there was a shift change. The front door is unlocked, so just come in. Do you want me to make you a snack?"

He smiled. "That would be greatly appreciated."

Did she even know how to cook? That wasn't something she'd mentioned before, but even a sandwich would be awesome if it was made by her hands. There was something special about partners feeding each other. It implied closeness.

"I'll get right to it. Is there anything you won't eat?"

"I'm not a picky eater."

"Good because I'm not much of a cook."

"Anything you make for me would be delicious because it was made by your hands."

She chuckled. "Aren't you sweet."

Was there a sarcastic undertone in those words?

"I don't know. Am I?"

"I'll have to taste you again to make sure."

He hardened in an instant. "You have work tomorrow, and I'm about to keep you awake for several hours. Maybe we should just have a snack together and save the story for another day?"

Cassandra laughed, the husky sound going straight to his shaft. "Nice try. After we talked earlier, I went back to sleep, so I'll be able to stay up all night. You are not wiggling out of it again."

"That wasn't my intention. It's just that all that talk about tasting my sweetness has made me randy. I'd rather snack than talk."

"Normally, so would I, but wouldn't you prefer to get rid of the wrapping first?"

Onegus swallowed. "I'm driving, woman. With all that innuendo, double entendre, and the stick shift that has suddenly popped in my automatic-transmission car, I might get into an accident."

"God forbid. We don't want that."

"What about your mother?" he asked.

"She's asleep," Cassandra said. "If we stay in the kitchen or the living room and talk quietly, do you think she can hear us all the way from the master bedroom? It's on the other side of the house."

"If she's immortal and awake, she might. But I thought that you wanted her to hear us."

"I changed my mind. Even if she's immortal, I doubt she knows it or remembers what happened to her. Hearing us talk about immortality might scare her."

After Onegus had gone back to the office, he'd called Roni and given him Geraldine's name and address. He doubted that the hacker would come up with anything interesting, but perhaps he could find a record of Cassandra's birth certificate and the parents' names listed on it.

"Or it might clear things up for her. Assuming that she's immortal and doesn't know it, she probably doesn't understand why her hearing is so good or why she's so strong. That, by the way, could be another indicator. Did you notice her doing things she shouldn't have been able to? Like picking up heavy things or opening jars without needing to put any effort into it?"

"No, she always hands me the jars to open."

"If she's immortal, that could imply that she's aware of it and that she actively hides her abilities."

"Sounds too sophisticated for my mother, but who knows." Cassandra sighed. "Maybe I don't know her as well as I think I do."

18

CASSANDRA

*A*s Onegus's car pulled up in front of her house, Cassandra opened the door. Stifling the urge to run out and pounce on him, she waited impatiently for him to get within reach so she could grab him and pull him inside.

The temporary calm she'd enjoyed was gone, partially because she was annoyed with him and the reservoir of her energy had been replenished, and partially because the more sex they had, the more she craved it.

Not that he needed to have his ego inflated even further.

Nevertheless, she would have run out and jumped on him like a teenage girl with her first crush, but the light was still on in the Rothmans' house, and Mrs. Rothman was one of those nosy neighbors who stuck her nose in everyone's business.

What would they think of her if she ran out in the middle of the night to greet her boyfriend wearing shorts and barefoot?

Cassandra had worked hard to earn the reputation of a respectable high achiever, the VP of a large cosmetics company, and a member of the architectural committee of her homeowners' association.

The grin on Onegus's face as he sauntered toward her was sexy as hell, and when he climbed up the front steps, she reached for his shirt, grabbed it, and pulled him to her for a kiss.

God, he smelled good enough to eat.

Chuckling, Onegus wrapped his arms under her butt and lifted her as he stepped inside. "Someone is happy to see me." He carried her to the couch and sat down. "Can we skip the talk?"

"Tempting." She was loath to leave his lap or even remove her arms from around his neck. "But if we jump on each other every opportunity we have to be alone, we'd never get to the story."

"True." He sighed.

"Come." She pushed out of his arms. "I made pasta and salad."

"Perfect." He followed her to the kitchen.

"I hope it's not terrible." She ladled a generous portion into a bowl and put it in front of him. "Can I get you something to drink? I have wine. It's not fancy, but it's quite good."

Even though Onegus had said that he wasn't a finicky eater, that probably didn't extend to wine, and he was most likely used to much finer ones.

"If you like it, then I'm sure I'm going to like it too." He scooped a heaping forkful of pasta and shoved it into his mouth.

Her guy was hungry for real, which was great since he probably wouldn't notice that the sauce was from a jar. She'd added sautéed onions and bell peppers to it, but it was still a far cry from one that was made from scratch.

"This is delicious." Onegus twirled more noodles on his fork.

"You're hungry." She pulled the wine out of the pantry cabinet, uncorked it, and poured them each a glass.

"Cheers." She lifted hers.

"To us." Onegus clinked his glass to hers.

"To us." She smiled and dug into her salad bowl.

While she nibbled on the veggies, Onegus helped himself to another serving of pasta and finished what was left of the salad.

"Thank you." He wiped his mouth with a napkin. "That was delicious."

Damn. She should have remembered how much Onegus consumed at each meal and made more of everything.

"Are you still hungry? I can pop a pizza into the oven."

"I'm good." He rose to his feet and carried the dishes to the sink. "Let's take the wine to the living room."

The bottle was already half empty, so she pulled another one out of the cabinet and brought it to the living room as well.

Onegus sat on the couch and patted the spot next to him. When she sat down, he wrapped his arm around her shoulders. "While driving over here, I thought about the best way to tell you the story. There are two options. I can give you the short version, and you can ask me to elaborate on points you would like to know more about. Or I can tell you the long story and try not to forget anything."

"I would love to get a complete picture, but given that it's after one in the morning, perhaps something in between will work better?"

"I thought that you were good until morning?"

"I am. But what if the long version takes longer than we have? I don't want to run out of time."

"Good point." Onegus took a long sip from his wine and put the glass down on the coffee table.

"Some background is unavoidable, but I'll try to make it short."

"Are you kidding? That's the most interesting part. I want to hear about the gods, and how they created the immortals, and how the story of their creation made its way into the Bible."

"So much for keeping the story short." Onegus kissed the top of her head. "That wasn't the only Bible story that originated with our people. That all-time bestseller is full of them."

"I hope you're not going to tell me that the gods used their incredible magical powers to create the world in six days and then rested on the seventh."

"I'm not going to. The gods weren't deities, and they didn't possess magical abilities, although that's what it might have seemed like to the humans. The gods were powerful, but they were still just flesh and blood, and the only real magic they possessed was mind control over humans. Well, that and fantastical technological knowhow along with advanced knowledge in genetics."

19

ONEGUS

*C*assandra pursed her lips. "Did the gods create humans?"

"That's how the story starts. Some parts are speculations, others were told to us by Annani, and the rest are facts and events from history that are verifiable."

"Just let me know which is which."

"Of course. The part about human creation is speculation, and it is rooted in Sumerian mythology, which we know was based on what they were told by the gods. Not many people are aware of that, but the Sumerians knew much more about the world than other civilizations thousands of years in the future. They knew that the sun was in the center of the solar system, they had depictions of rockets and of things that looked like modern satellites, and they were the first to have a fully developed written language."

"I didn't know that. I remember learning about Greek mythology in school, and I know a little about the Egyptians from movies, but hardly anyone mentions the Sumerians. I always thought that they weren't important."

Onegus sighed. "Contrary to what most people believe, history is not the recount of facts and events as they really happened. It's written by the victors and highly politicized."

She chuckled. "That's like what's reported in the news today. One news outlet spins things one way, another the opposite way, and the people remain clueless."

"I knew you were smart." He hugged her closer to him.

"Thank you. Now, let's get back to the Sumerians. They sound fascinating."

"Absolutely. Their society sprung seemingly overnight, complete with laws that protected the rights of individuals, men and women alike, took care of those in need of assistance, and afforded everyone the right to a fair trial. They had schools for children, where boys and girls were taught to read and write and calculate numbers." Leaning over, he took the wine bottle and refilled their glasses. "Up until less than a hundred years ago, humanity hadn't reached that level of enlightenment, and in some parts of the world, it hasn't yet. You take education and equal rights for granted, but until not so long ago, those weren't available to girls, even in countries that you consider enlightened. And the same went for personal property and inheritance laws. But Sumerian women enjoyed those rights over seven thousand years ago."

Cassandra frowned. "What happened to the Sumerians? Why did their culture disappear?"

"I'm getting there. We assume, and that's speculation, that the gods originally came to Earth to mine for gold." When she arched a brow, he chuckled. "Not because it's shiny and makes pretty jewelry. Gold is a crucial component in all our modern electronics. It's a highly efficient conductor of electricity and is used in cell phones, CPUs and memory chips, motherboards, and so on. Space vehicles are fitted with gold-coated polyester film to reflect infrared radiation and help stabilize temperatures. Astronauts' visors are coated with a thin layer of gold to filter out harmful rays. Not surprisingly, many cultures believed that gold belonged to the gods."

"Fascinating. Let's fast forward, shall we?"

"I only explained because you looked doubtful."

"You said it was speculation, not fact."

"True, but it's taken from Sumerian mythology, and many of their legends have at least a kernel of truth in them. The story was that the gods came to mine gold, but it was hard work, and the males rebelled, asking for help. One of the three gods in charge heard their plea, and together with his sister, they combined the genetic material of a male god with that of an earthly creature, probably our less intelligent ancestor, the Homo sapiens."

"The Garden of Eden story."

"Correct. The brother and sister conducted many experiments, most of which were unsuccessful, until they finally created Adam—the first human being. At first, those hybrid creatures were infertile, as many hybrids tend to be, but then the scientist god—who was a human sympathizer—gave them the ability to procreate. By the way, the god whose symbol was two snakes wound around a staff was Ningishzida, whose name meant lord of the good tree. It wasn't the same one who was attributed with creating humans, but I find it interesting that to this day his symbol represents medicine, the Caduceus, and also the double helix. In addition, the snake was a symbol of fertility, not only in the Sumerian culture, but in many others."

Cassandra's eyes widened. "A tree and a snake. It sounds like the story of the Garden of Eden, and the snake tempting Eve with the apple from the tree of good and evil."

Onegus nodded. "The tree of knowledge of good and evil. Knowledge, or to know, means to know intimately in biblical Hebrew. And as for good and evil, sex can be good, and it can be evil. Abducting young girls and women, sometimes also young boys, and selling them into sex slavery is one of the evilest and most abhorrent plagues afflicting humanity to this day."

Cassandra grimaced. "I agree. But let's get back to the story."

"Right. Once the humans gained the ability to procreate, they did so in numbers that threatened the gods, who were a small group that rarely produced offspring."

Understanding shone in Cassandra's eyes. "That's why they were banished from the Garden. Their so-called sin was having children, and their punishment was for the women to suffer in childbirth and for the men to toil the land to produce food for them."

"Precisely."

"But that's speculation, right? Not something that your goddess told you was true."

"All of what I told you so far was based on Sumerian myths. I didn't get to the part we learned from the goddess yet."

20

CASSANDRA

he Bible stories made much more sense to Cassandra after hearing Onegus's explanation. Not yet believable, they were just too outlandish, but more palatable to modern ears. She could imagine beings with superior knowledge playing gods by manipulating genes and jumpstarting human evolution by millions of years.

Without their interference, it might have taken a lot longer for the ape brain to develop into a thinking, human mind.

Maybe the gods had even seeded Earth, providing it with the original biological blueprints that evolution could work from, meaning the DNA and the RNA. Every living organism, even viruses, had one or the other. Or maybe both Earth and the gods' home planet had been seeded by beings even more powerful than the gods. Who knew what wonders were floating in the vastness of the universe?

"Penny for your thoughts?" Onegus touched a finger to the furrows in her forehead.

"I just had a mind-bending thought. What if there is a never-ending hierarchy of intelligent beings in the universe? What if the gods and humans are somewhere down the chain, just a little higher than animals? What if those near the top are beings of pure energy who shed their physical bodies eons ago? Perhaps there are many creators who exist outside of space-time, and they're using the universe as their playground to create life, destroy it, create it again, and then destroy it again. A never-ending cycle that for them is a game, keeping them from being bored."

He chuckled. "The computer game theory."

"There is a theory like that?"

"You are not the first one to come up with that idea. But if we keep on philosophizing, I'll never get to the parts of the story that you're actually interested in."

"I'm interested in everything you've told me so far. I don't remember ever having such a fascinating conversation with anyone." Leaning, she kissed his cheek that had gotten a little scruffy, the short bristles poking her lips. "Don't let it go to your head, but you are the whole package."

"Oh, yeah? Tell me more. I want to hear your thoughts about the size of my package."

Laughing, she pushed on his arm. "You're so bad. Just get back to your story."

"Fine." He reached for the second wine bottle, uncorked it, and refilled both their glasses. "Now I'm getting to the parts that were confirmed by Annani."

"No more speculation?"

"From now on, you can regard everything I tell you as fact, unless I specifically tell you that something is speculation."

"Good. I want to keep things straight in my head." Cassandra picked up the glass and sipped on the wine.

"We are fast-forwarding to the city-states of Sumer and the creation of the first immortals. Each city was ruled by a god or a goddess. The temple was the administrative center, where goods were brought by the citizens in tribute to their god or goddess. You can think of it as voluntary taxes."

"Is there such a thing?"

He smiled. "Don't forget that the gods could control the minds of humans and make them believe that they paid the tribute voluntarily. By the way, I'm sure that humans were designed like that, but that's speculation."

"Do you mean to say that we were genetically predisposed to be susceptible to mind control?"

He nodded. "Part of the tribute was used to maintain the temple and pay the wages of those serving in it, and part was used to make improvements to the city and help the needy. Each god or goddess had a lot of autonomy over their city, but they were all subject to the head god. It was a hereditary position, but the head god couldn't make any major decisions without presenting the issue before the big assembly and having it voted on. Naturally, a lot of politicking went into those votes, but it was a democratic process."

"If only the gods could vote, it wasn't true democracy. I assume that immortals and humans were not invited."

"True. But I didn't get to the creation of immortals yet."

"Were they included later?"

"No."

"That's what I thought. By the way, I'm missing a piece of the puzzle. You've jumped from the gods creating humans for slave labor to where they lived in cities and had all those progressive laws to govern them. When did the gods start treating humans as people?"

"I don't know. Perhaps it happened when they realized that the humans they'd created were nearly as intelligent as they were, and it wasn't right to keep them as slaves. The gods still needed their labor, though, so they created the cities and taught the humans under their control how to function as a just society."

"What about the other humans? Those who didn't live in the Sumerian cities?"

"Some lived as nomadic tribes, others were influenced by Sumer and adopted some of its culture and customs. But none were as advanced."

There were still big holes in the story, but Cassandra's eyelids were starting to droop. If they kept veering off the topic, there was no way Onegus could finish his tale before she fell asleep on him.

"I need to write down my questions for later." She stifled a yawn. "Can you skip over to the creation of immortals? I'm not sure I'll last much longer."

21

ONEGUS

*C*assandra's eyes had narrowed into slits, and it was quite apparent that she was fighting a losing battle with sleep. He'd better hurry, or he would lose his audience of one no matter how good of a storyteller he was or how fascinating she found his tale.

Leaning back, he patted his chest for her to put her head on it. "The human population was growing at a staggering rate compared to the glacial rate at which the gods procreated, and there weren't enough of them to rule and guide their subjects. So when a group of lower stationed gods petitioned the assembly to remove the prohibition on mating humans, the law was changed. Gods were allowed to take human lovers, provided that they didn't use their mental powers or any other undue influence to lure humans into their beds. Consent, which was a major tenet of the gods' law, was also required from the lowly humans. Those unions proved to be much more fruitful, and many hybrid children were born. Those children were born immortal and possessed some of the gods' powers, but to a much lesser degree."

Cassandra recited, "When the sons of God came in to the daughters of men, and they bore children to them. These were the mighty men who were of old, the men of renown."

"You have a good memory. Did you attend Sunday school?"

She laughed. "My mother is a devout agnostic, probably because she has no clue what religious group she was born into. We've never attended any services, and I never had any classes on the subject. I've heard that passage in a movie, and it stuck in my mind."

"Perhaps it resonated with you."

"Possibly. You said that the immortals inherited some of the gods' powers but to a lesser degree. Can you be more specific?"

He stifled a chuckle. Cassandra might wish to shorten the story, but her curiosity and her attention to detail forced her hand.

"They could manipulate the minds of humans, but not each other's or the gods'. To this day, our abilities vary. We have one guy whose power resembles that of the gods, and he can manipulate the minds of thousands. I can control up to five, and most can take hold of only one mind at a time."

"What makes one person more powerful than the other?"

"Instead of going back and forth, let me continue with the story, and I'll get to that."

"Okay."

"Unions between gods and humans created immortals, but unions between immortals, or immortals with humans created humans, or so it seemed. It turned out that the children born to female immortals possessed the gene and could be turned, but the children born to male immortals didn't."

"That's not fair."

He debated whether to tell her now or later about the addiction that female immortals developed to their partners, which equalized the playing field.

On the one hand, it might give her the wrong impression and scare her off. But on the other hand, Cassandra would bite his head off if he started her induction without telling her about it first. He needed to tell her.

"The Fates gave the males other advantages to compensate. If an immortal couple is exclusive to each other, after a while, the female immortal develops an addiction to her partner's venom, craving sex only with him and being repulsed by others. In time, her scent changes to create a similar addiction in the male and prevents other immortal males from wanting her, but it takes longer."

Surprisingly, Cassandra remained calm. "A built-in fidelity insurance."

"There are ways to circumvent it. Just as in the Greek mythology you're familiar with, the Sumerian gods were not known for their fidelity. They were quite promiscuous. Those who mated for political reasons avoided addiction by sleeping around and mixing it up."

"What about those who mated for love? Did they stay loyal to each other forever?"

"I wasn't there, but that's what Annani claims, and I believe her."

Cassandra's eyes no longer looked tired. "Now I understand why you said that you needed to make absolutely sure that you're committing to the right woman. When you do, it's forever because of the addiction."

"Actually, I said it because of the bond. True-love mates form a powerful bond that makes the addiction irrelevant. Perhaps it's even a myth, something to explain the mystical bond between true-love mates."

She lifted her eyes to his. "Am I your true-love mate?"

His first impulse was to say yes, but what if he was mistaken? Taking it back would be cruel.

Instead, he hedged. "I think so."

"But you're not sure."

"You said it yourself. We haven't had enough time together to talk about forever. Also, this is the first time I'm falling in love, and I'm not sure whether what I feel is love or attraction. Does liking a woman a lot and being attracted to her mean love? I don't know."

CASSANDRA

*C*assandra shook her head. "You're funny."
　　"How so?"
He wanted her to commit to him forever, and yet he wasn't willing to admit, even to himself, that he'd fallen in love with her.

Not that she was any better.

It took a leap of faith that she didn't have the guts for.

Not yet.

And perhaps that was the real reason behind her hesitation to agree to the induction. It wasn't just about turning immortal. It was about spending eternity with Onegus, and that was even scarier than the difficult, potentially lethal transition.

"Never mind. Continue your story."

For a long moment, he eyed her from under lowered blond lashes, but that prolonged stare wasn't going to get him an explanation. She was well-acquainted with that intimidation tactic, had used it plenty of times herself, and wasn't about to cave when it was used on her.

Most people didn't realize the power of silence. It was like playing chicken. Whoever couldn't stand the vacuum created by lack of speech and started talking first.

With a nod, Onegus accepted defeat. "Very well. Where were we?"

She reminded him, "The discovery that the children of female immortals had the immortal genes and could be activated."

"Right. Once that discovery was made, and many more generations of immortals were born, a hierarchy emerged. Those closer to the gods were at the top, and those farther removed at the bottom. The abilities got diluted the farther an immortal was from the source. But there were exceptions, and a lowly immortal could manifest extraordinary powers. I assume it had to do with which god or goddess they descended from because the gods also varied in power. Some were so weak that they were less powerful than an immortal who was the descendant of a more powerful god. A perfect example of that is Annani's sister Areana, who's mated to the clan's archenemy, Navuh. She's a full-blooded goddess, and he is just an immortal, but he's much more powerful than her."

"Finally. I was waiting to hear about those mysterious enemies of yours." Cassandra yawned. "I want to know who they are and why you are so afraid of them."

"Are you sure you want me to continue tonight?"

"Yes. I'll text Kevin that I'll be coming in late tomorrow, so I can sleep until noon. I'm putting in double time nearly every day, so he can't complain when I take half a day off."

Cassandra had decided that more than an hour ago when her eyes started drooping. Since then, she'd gotten a second wind of energy, but she knew it wouldn't last long, and eventually she'd crash.

"That makes me feel much better. I can function on two hours of shuteye, and I can also catch a short nap during the day. But you're still a human and need your eight hours of sleep."

"Normally, yes. But as I said, I want to hear the entire story tonight."

"The split occurred when Annani fell in love with Khiann and broke off her engagement to Navuh's father, the god Mortdh. As the daughter of the leading couple, she was next in line as the ruler of the gods. Mortdh was a powerful god with big ambitions of one day becoming the ruler as her mate. He saw the break of the engagement as a great insult. Long story short, he murdered Annani's husband, was convicted of the murder, and was sentenced to entombment by the big assembly. All of that was done in his absence, and since he was so power-ful, no one knew how they were going to bring him to justice. While the gods deliberated on what to do, Annani feared that he would attack first and fled to the far north. Her hunch had been correct, and shortly after that, Mortdh bombed the big assembly, killing all the gods and dying along with them."

"How did he do that?"

"No one knows for sure. The speculation is that he had some sort of a nuclear bomb, and that he was caught in its blast zone. The devastation was incredible, with most of the population in the region perishing. Some must have survived, otherwise, we wouldn't have found Dormants who are unrelated to us, but the biggest surviving group was in Mortdh's stronghold in what today is Lebanon. His son Navuh took over and swore to continue his father's malignant legacy."

"What happened to Annani, and how did her sister end up with Navuh?"

"Areana agreed to take Annani's place as Mortdh's bride. But by the time she arrived at his stronghold, Mortdh was gone, and so were the rest of the gods. She didn't know that Annani survived, and since Navuh has kept her secluded from the world, she didn't know that he was actively hunting her sister and her descendants. But let's leave the rest of Areana and Navuh's story for another time. Can we do that?"

Reluctantly, Cassandra nodded. "Tell me about Annani."

"After mourning for her husband and her people, she took it upon herself to continue the gods' legacy of helping humanity form an enlightened and just society. Since she couldn't undertake the task by herself, she took human lovers in order to procreate. Over time, as her clan grew in numbers, so did her influence on the world. But since only her female descendants could bring more immortal children, the growth was slow. Navuh, on the other hand, started with an advantage. He inherited his father's harem of immortal females and started a breeding program, managing to amass an army of about twenty thousand immortal warriors."

"How many people does the clan have?"

"Fewer than a thousand."

"That's why you need to hide."

"Correct."

If everything Onegus had told her was true, then the clan were the good guys, and their enemies were the bad guys. Regrettably, Navuh and his army outnumbered the clan, so joining the good guys was risky. Still, she would rather be on their side.

"What happens if I turn immortal? Would I need to hide? Move into the village and quit my job?"

"You don't need to quit your job. Many clan members work outside the village and commute to work."

"But I will have to move."

Onegus eyed her from under lowered lashes. "Where do you think you belong? With humans or with your own kind?"

He had a point.

She'd never felt as comfortable with people as she had with the immortals. On the other hand, though, she loved the house she'd bought. And if her mother was indeed an immortal, she was proof that it was possible for them to live among humans and not get noticed.

Then again, it was just a house.

The village was a community of people, possibly her kind, and it came with Onegus. She could commute to work, but he was the chief of security and needed to be in the village, so it wasn't as if he could move in with her. Besides, it wasn't fair to demand of him to live with her mother, nor did she want him to. If everything went well and she transitioned, Cassandra wanted to build a new life with Onegus.

23

ONEGUS

"I don't know what to tell you." Cassandra sighed. "After hearing the history of your people, I feel comfortable about joining your community, but it's not just about that. We need to find out whether my mother is an immortal, and if she is, whether she's willing to leave her friends and come live with us in the village. I can't leave her alone here, and you can't come live with me. Still, even though those are far from trivial issues, they are not my biggest concern."

"Am I the problem?" Onegus asked.

She nodded. "I think that you love me, but you're not ready to admit it to yourself or to me. How can you expect me to commit to forever with you if you can't commit to forever with me?"

He shouldn't be surprised that she needed guarantees from him.

"I think that you are right. I'm pretty sure that I'm in love with you, but I don't want to mislead you. That's why I want to be absolutely and irrevocably positive. Besides, the induction process is not what is going to bind us to each other. If we don't bond, and if for some reason we decide that we are not meant for each other, you will have a wide selection of clan males to choose from."

Just the thought of someone else going after Cassandra was enough to fill his venom glands to bursting, and maybe that was the best sign that subconsciously, he'd already decided that she was the one for him.

She smiled knowingly. "Your eyes are glowing, and I don't think it's because you are aroused. What has spurred your aggression, Onegus? The idea of me hooking up with someone else?"

"Yeah." Striving for calm, he ran a hand over his jaw. "Does that mean I'm in love with you?"

"Not really. Guys can get possessive over their women without being in love with them. It's kind of vile in my opinion. They regard them as possessions."

Great, so now she was disgusted with him. "I don't know what to say to that. I'm not the jealous type. But with you, everything is new. You're like a drug that I have to get a sniff or a taste of every few hours or I get restless like a junkie going through withdrawal. I can't stay away from you. And I'm not proud of this newfound possessiveness and jealousy."

Leaning toward him, Cassandra cupped his cheek. "That's because you're in love with me, silly. Try to imagine me moving away to Australia for a fantastic job offer that I'd be a fool to turn down. How does that make you feel?"

"Desperate." He put a hand over his chest where his heart was thundering as if he was under attack.

"What would you do?"

"Follow you. I can't stand the thought of being away from you."

"What about your job? Your position in the clan?"

There was no question about what or who he would choose. "I would resign."

Lifting her head, she pressed a soft kiss to his lips. "That's what love is. When you can't imagine your life without your beloved. When you would drop everything to be with her, sacrifice everything not to be apart from her, then you know that you're in love."

"Is that how you feel about me?"

She narrowed her eyes. "Chicken much, Onegus? You go first."

No one ever accused him of being a coward, but perhaps in matters of the heart, he was the big chicken Cassandra had accused him of being.

It was time to man up and take a leap. It wouldn't even be a big one because he was already ninety-nine percent there. All he needed to do was make a tiny leap over the remaining one percent.

Taking a deep breath, Onegus lifted her hand to his lips and kissed it. "Since what I said before is precisely what you define as love, I've already said it in so many words. I love you, Cassandra Beaumont. I can't imagine my life without you. Can you say the same about me?"

She swallowed audibly. "I can imagine life without you."

His heart sank.

But then she continued, "It would be back to being all work and no play, back to existing rather than living, back to wondering if that was all life had to offer. If I can be sure that what I feel for you now will never diminish, I will say yes to you right here, right now. So I guess my leap of faith will be trusting that what we share will get stronger rather than fizzle out, and that it's worth the sacrifice of motherhood."

His heart felt buoyant again, filled with hope for the future. "You are not sacrificing anything, Cassandra. You're only buying yourself more time. You will be a mother, just not right away." He lifted her hand and kissed it again. "I'd rather have you all to myself for a few years."

"I'm okay with several years. What I'm worried about is waiting a few centuries."

He could imagine himself a father, especially to a little girl who looked exactly like her mother and was as much of a spitfire. But he wasn't ready yet.

"We won't have to wait that long. We have a doctor who might have the answer to the problem of immortal fertility. He helped Syssi and Kian conceive, and several other couples are currently taking his potions."

"That's good to know." She smiled, and then her smile turned into a yawn.

"So, is it a yes to starting the induction process?" he asked.

"Yes." Cassandra leaned her head against his bicep. "But not tonight. I'm too tired."

24

ELEANOR

"*I* don't want to sleep in the apartment upstairs." Eleanor lifted her feet and propped them on the coffee table. "Do you mind if I sleep down here on the couch?"

Peter arched a brow. "Why? So you can stare at Emmett some more?"

She'd spent way too many hours doing just that, but it could be argued that watching his activity through the monitor was part of her job.

"What if I am?" She cast him a challenging look. "It's my job."

It wasn't the reason she wanted to stay in the underground suite, though. The two apartments reserved for the Guardians in the tower above were over-crowded. She didn't have a room to herself and had to share it with two other guys. It was like being the only female in a frat house. They were trying their best to behave, but they resented having to do that.

For some reason, they were okay with treating Kri as one of the guys, but not Eleanor. Maybe it had to do with Kri being their cousin and happily mated, while Eleanor was not a relative and presently unattached. Despite everyone's best efforts to act professionally, her being available created sexual tension.

Hopefully, she was reading the situation right, and that was their only problem with her. It could also be that the Guardians didn't like her. Not everyone was happy about the quick change in her status.

Only a few short months ago, Eleanor had been a mistrusted and unwelcome newcomer, who had been kept under constant watch. Now, she was a Guardian in training and getting paid accordingly.

It wasn't easy to get accepted to the program, and only the best were offered the opportunity. They might have resented her for weaseling her way in.

Peter was different.

He treated her like a buddy, and if he let her stay in the suite he'd taken over from Arwel, she could at least have the living room to herself. The only downside was that getting to the bathroom required going through the bedroom he slept in.

Peter pushed to his feet and opened the fridge. "Do you want a beer?"

"We are on duty. We're not supposed to drink alcohol."

"I wasn't talking about Snake's Venom." He pulled out a Coors can. "This is like soda to immortals."

"Then sure."

He tossed her a can.

Eleanor popped the lid and drank a good third before putting it down. "So, can I sleep on your couch?"

He sat down and put his feet up next to hers. "I have no problem with that. Just keep the place tidy. We are having a bunch of visitors tomorrow. In the morning, Margaret and Anastasia are coming over with Leon and Bowen to have a talk with Emmett, and after that, Arwel is bringing Jin and Mey to meet him as well."

That was news to her. "When was that arranged, and why did no one tell me?"

He cast her a sidelong glance. "In case you've forgotten, you are not in charge here. I am. I don't need to inform you of everything that's going on."

Arrogant prick.

Crossing her arms over her chest, she looked down her nose at him. "And in case you've forgotten, I'm the one working undercover here."

"About that." He grimaced. "What you did last night was reckless, and the only reason I didn't report both you and Alfie to Onegus is that it would have made me look bad. This is my first command, and with my subordinates breaking the rules, it might be my last."

"I didn't break any rules. I did what I was supposed to do—befriend Emmett and get him to trust me."

"And how's that going?"

"Very well."

"I'm glad. Next time, do it without muting the sound and reducing the resolution. I don't care how embarrassed you are about being watched while having sex with him. Your safety is more important than your modesty."

She huffed out a breath. "Admit it. You just want to watch."

His lips twisted in a sly smile. "I won't deny that I want to see you naked. Maybe you could do a little striptease the next time you undress for the asshole?"

There had been uncharacteristic vehemence in Peter's tone. Usually, he was an easygoing guy, and despite his history with Emmett, he'd been cordial to the former cult leader.

Was it jealousy?

Peter constantly flirted with her, but it wasn't serious. He wasn't even attracted to her.

"Why do you suddenly hate him? You didn't right after the kidnapping, so why now? Are you jealous?"

"Terribly," he teased. "I don't hate him." Peter draped his arm around her shoulders. "I just don't trust him, and you are letting yourself fall for him."

"I am not."

He lifted both brows. "Are you that clueless? I listened to the recording of your time with him on double speed. You are revealing too much information and not getting nearly enough back. He's using you."

The same thing had occurred to her, but there was no harm done. Emmett wasn't going anywhere. "I'm doing that on purpose. If he thinks that he has me in his pocket, he might reveal his hand more readily. Besides, how is he going to use the information I provide him with? He's never going to be let loose."

It was only half a lie. Eleanor hoped that showing Emmett trust would encourage him to do the same, but the truth was that she'd said too much. For some reason, she was less suspicious of him than of nearly anyone else, and that was a mistake. The problem was that she realized that only when she wasn't around him. If she didn't know better, she would have thought that he had used compulsion on her.

25

ONEGUS

*D*espite sleeping for only an hour, or maybe because of that, Onegus was walking on air.

Cassandra had said yes.

She loved him.

She hadn't said the words, but she'd told him that she was willing to commit to forever with him, provided that what she felt now didn't fizzle out.

He knew it wouldn't. Their relationship would only get stronger the more time they spent together. But there were several issues that he needed to address to make it easier for Cassandra, and the most important one was her mother. If Geraldine was an immortal, and she agreed to move into the village, half the battle would already be won.

As things stood now, Cassandra was torn between wanting to be with him and the love and duty she felt toward her mother.

He'd given Roni Geraldine's information yesterday, and the hacker had promised to look into it today. Perhaps he should give him a call.

Pulling out his phone, Onegus selected Roni's number.

The guy took his sweet time to answer, and Onegus was about to end the call when he finally picked up. "Good morning, Chief."

"Good morning. Did you have a chance to research Cassandra's mother?"

"I did it as soon as I walked into the lab. I found over two thousand matches for Geraldine Beaumont. Half of them in Europe, some on other continents, and about a third in the States. Out of that, fewer than two hundred are between the ages of thirty and sixty. I cross-referenced them with social media, and I can send you the few whose profile pictures loosely match the description you gave me."

"Send them over."

When his phone pinged with the incoming message, Onegus scrolled through the dozen or so profiles of attractive blue-eyed brunettes, but none was Geraldine.

"No luck. None of these women is Cassandra's mother."

"I didn't think we would get that lucky. Unless I have a good picture of her face that I can run through the program, I'll have to check each of the matches that didn't have their pictures posted, and that's too time-consuming."

"I'll get you a photo of her. My mother and I are meeting Cassandra and Geraldine for dinner tonight, and I plan on cornering Cassandra's mother into taking a group picture. She won't be able to refuse without appearing rude or weird."

"She might not care what you think."

Onegus chuckled. "Not everyone is like you, Roni. Besides, my mother's formidable presence guarantees compliance."

"Good luck."

"Thanks. I'll send you the picture tomorrow." Onegus ended the call.

He itched to talk to Cassandra, to reinforce the progress they'd made last night, but she was most likely still asleep. Or at least he hoped so.

Last night, or rather this morning, she'd practically passed out in his arms. He'd carried her to her bedroom, helped her undress, tucked her under the blanket, and left, even though that had been the last thing he'd wanted to do.

Making love to her would have been his first choice, but just sleeping with her in his arms would have been a close second.

How the hell had he fallen in love in one week?

Had it been the Fates' doing? Some perfect cosmic star alliance? Or was it just the right time and the right person?

Whatever and whoever it was, they had his gratitude.

A week ago, he'd still scoffed at the idea of a fated mate, hadn't wanted one, and hoped not to meet her for several centuries. The Fates were probably laughing their scheming heads off.

Tapping his fingers on his desk, Onegus looked at his office door and hoped that Ingrid would walk in. He needed to tell someone that he'd fallen in love, but Connor was at a meeting in the studios, and Onegus didn't talk about his personal life with his Guardians.

That left his mother, but he could just imagine how she'd respond. He needed to call her, though, and remind her about dinner tonight.

"Good morning, Onegus." She sounded harried.

"Am I interrupting something?"

"I'm at the gym, running on the treadmill. But we can talk."

Some of the guests made use of the keep's gym, but he was surprised that his mother was one of them.

"Since when do you exercise?"

"Since we've gotten the new treadmills in the castle's gym. They have television monitors that display all kinds of terrains. I can pretend that I'm running in nature."

"Isn't the real thing better?"

"It's never the right temperature, and back home, it rains most of the year. I prefer the treadmill."

"There is that. I called to remind you about dinner tonight."

"I didn't forget. Are we going to Gerard's restaurant?"

"Yes. I've got us reservations for seven-thirty."

"Wonderful. How are things going with Cassandra?"

Well, if she asked, he wasn't going to lie.

"To borrow your phrase, wonderful. I'm in love."

For a long moment, the only sound coming through the line was the one made by his mother's slowing footfalls on the treadmill. When that stopped too, she said, "Are you sure?"

"I've never been in love, but given Cassandra's definition of it, that's precisely what I'm feeling."

"How did she define it?"

"When you love someone, you want to be with that person at all times, and when that's not possible, you feel like part of you is missing. It's like an itch that has to be scratched, or you'll go insane." Cassandra hadn't phrased it like that, but that's how he felt, so he added it to the definition. "She asked me what would I do if she got a fantastic job offer in Australia and had to move. I didn't even need to think it through. I told her that I would quit my job and follow her there because I can't imagine life without her."

There was another moment of silence. "Was it by any chance right after sex?"

He rolled his eyes. "It was after I told her a somewhat abbreviated version of our history."

"I see. It still might be just an infatuation."

"At my age? After all the women I've been with over the five centuries of my life? I don't think so."

"You have a point. Well, I guess congratulations are in order. Does she love you back?"

"Yes, she does. Her only misgiving was the reduced fertility, and yet she was willing to give up motherhood for me. I assured her that no such sacrifice was required. It will just take more time and a little help from Merlin."

"Don't be so sure."

"What do you mean?"

"It would appear that the Fates brought you and Cassandra together because you are fated mates. But neither one of you has suffered greatly or sacrificed a lot for others. Maybe that's the sacrifice they require."

A chill ran down Onegus's back, but then he shook his head. "I didn't suffer, but I dedicated my life to the clan and its safety. That counts for something. Cassandra had no father and grew up with a mother who had memory issues and needed constant help even when Cassy was a little girl. She also clawed her way to the top and made life better for herself and her mother. None of those things is huge, but taken together, they might suffice."

"I hope so. What's wrong with Cassandra's mother?"

"She forgets things and tries to cover up by making up stories. So be patient if that happens during dinner. Cassandra says that it's best to go with it and not contradict her. She gets upset, and her symptoms worsen."

"I can imagine." His mother sighed. "I'll do my best not to cringe."

"Will you?"

"Of course. What do you take me for?"

"You're not always kind."

"I'm not kind to those I expect more of. I would never be unkind to someone who can't help it because they have a disability. Although, if Geraldine is an immortal like you suspect, I have to wonder how it is possible. We don't get dementia or Alzheimer's, but we do get mental illnesses like PTSD. Do you know what caused Geraldine's memory issues?"

"Cassandra said that it was head trauma, but that's what her mother told her. It might be psychological. In any case, I'm going to push for a group photo so Roni can later isolate her picture and run it through his programs."

"What if he doesn't find anything?"

"Then I'll have to find another way to test my theory."

"I can help. During dinner, I could accidentally cut her with my knife, or scratch her with one of my rings."

Onegus chuckled. "Don't. Once Roni gets Geraldine's picture, he can have an answer for us in a matter of hours. If he doesn't, I'll arrange another lunch or dinner with her, and you'll get your chance then."

26

MARGARET

*P*eter handed Margaret and Anastasia two earpieces each. "These are new. The old ones translated everything into the same male voice, which was disorienting when the speaker was female. The new ones pick up on whether the speaker is male or female and use the appropriate machine voice."

Margaret held one of the rubbery devices between her thumb and forefinger. "We are only going to talk to Emmett. So it doesn't matter."

"Trust me, it does." Peter handed a set to Leon and another one to Bowen. "Let's say that Emmett is talking, and then Anastasia comments on it. With the old earpieces, it would have sounded as if the same person was talking. You wouldn't have even noticed that it was Anastasia. You could only have figured it out based on context."

"But that's only useful when the two speakers are of different genders." Ana put one of the devices in her left ear. "If they are both men or both women, the problem remains."

Peter shrugged. "That's what we have for now. In the future, William and his team might come up with something better. I just wish I'd had these or the old ones with me at Safe Haven. Although given the way Emmett apprehended me, it wouldn't have helped. After bashing me over the head and knocking me out, he would have just removed them."

"If he knew what they were for," Leon said. "By the way, where is Eleanor?"

"I sent her to get more water from the kitchen. We are running low."

"How do I turn it on?" Margaret asked.

Peter pointed to his own earpiece. "To activate, tap once. To deactivate, tap twice." He waited for everyone to put their earpieces on, and then tapped on his, reminding them to activate the devices. "Can everyone hear me?"

Margaret nodded. The voice didn't sound like Peter's, but she hadn't expected it to.

Ana tapped her shoulder. "Say something. I want to hear the other voice."

519

The earpiece had switched to a female voice.

"It works." She gave Peter the thumbs up.

After verifying that everyone knew how to operate the earpieces, Peter motioned to the couch and the two armchairs. "I'm going to get Emmett and bring him here." He pulled out one of the dining chairs and placed it against the long side of the coffee table. "He will sit here, so he can see all of you, and you can see him. Since Bowen and Leon are with you, I'm not going to chain him, but I suggest that the men sit closer to him."

As Leon and Ana switched places on the couch, Eleanor walked in with a case of water bottles. "Anyone thirsty?"

For some reason, her eyes lingered on Margaret. "You look good. Much better than the last time I saw you."

Eleanor hadn't attended the wedding, so she hadn't seen Margaret's transformation.

"Thank you."

"The cast is gone," Eleanor said.

Margaret lifted her leg. "Doctor Bridget replaced it with a brace."

Eleanor's lips twitched with a stifled smile. "I bet Bowen is helping speed up your recovery."

"Indeed." Through no fault of his own, not as much as Margaret wished for.

Last night, it was nearly three in the morning when Elise and Rowan had decided it was time to go back to the downtown building, and given the late hour, Bowen had volunteered to drive them back.

Tonight was not going to work either. To be able to accompany her and Ana to the meeting with Emmett, Bowen and Leon had to switch shifts with other Guardians.

Peter walked toward the open door. "I was just about to get Emmett. Do you want to come along?"

Eleanor nodded, and the look that crossed over her face was interesting to say the least.

She seemed both excited and worried. The question was why. Was she afraid of Emmett? Or was she afraid of what the four of them were going to put him through?

Margaret leaned toward Bowen. "Is there something going on between Eleanor and Emmett?"

"Definitely," Leon answered instead.

Bowen just nodded.

She wanted to ask how they had known that, but the sound of three sets of footsteps had her turning toward the suite's open door.

As Peter entered with Emmett, Margaret stifled a gasp. He looked so different from the guru of free love who'd led Safe Haven. Gone were the prophet's beard and long hair, and instead of a white robe, he was wearing a pair of jeans and a T-shirt.

He looked so young. No wonder he'd opted for the theatrical hair and beard style. They'd been part of a costume to mask his youthful appearance.

Still, he didn't belong in jeans and a T-shirt. Somehow, she knew that the outfit hadn't been his choice, and that he would have been more comfortable in a pair of slacks and a button-down.

"Margaret, Anastasia." He beamed at them. "And your mates." He dipped his head. "Bowen and Leon. Such fine men you both have found." He turned back to look at Ana. "And you are an immortal now. Congratulations."

The machine voice couldn't translate the inflection she was so familiar with, and it felt like a loss. She missed hearing him talk, the inspiration he'd provided, the meaning he'd inspired in her otherwise meaningless life.

But all of that belonged in the past. Margaret no longer needed Emmett to give her life meaning. She had Wendy and Bowen, Vlad and Ana, and all her other new friends. She had a family and a village full of people.

Perhaps now, Emmett needed her more than she had needed him. He was alone, a prisoner, with no flock to preach to.

Peter put a hand on his shoulder. "Sit down, Emmett."

Full of charm and elegance as usual, Emmett sat down with his back straight, a smile on his face, and eyes that sparkled with good humor.

"Hello, Emmett," Margaret said. "How have you been?"

He lifted his hands and tilted his head. "I don't have an easy answer for that. On the one hand, I've lost everything I worked for. On the other hand, I might have gained something even more valuable." His eyes drifted to Eleanor. "My first real friend."

27

ELEANOR

*O*h, he was good. He'd gotten her right in the chest.

Eleanor resisted the urge to rub the spot over her heart.

My first real friend.

What was Emmett's agenda? Was he concerned that she might get jealous of his former lover?

There had been a little bit of that. Margaret no longer looked like a starved mouse. She was a looker, and Eleanor could only imagine how beautiful she'd been when she'd arrived at Safe Haven.

Seeing her again, looking like a damn model, had no doubt stirred a lot of old memories in Emmett. Or maybe not so old?

When had been the last time he'd had sex with Margaret?

"I want to ask you something," Margaret said to him. "Why did you compel me to get a panic attack every time I thought about checking on my daughter?"

Emmett sighed dramatically. "I was acting with your best interests at heart. Your husband sounded like a controlling sociopath. I feared what he might do if you went back to look for your daughter. You feared it too, but your motherly urges might have prompted you to risk it. I simply amplified your fear and made sure that you stayed safely hidden in Safe Haven."

Margaret looked like she wanted to believe him, and Eleanor wished she could, but her bullshit radar was flashing red. She hoped Margaret's radar was doing the same.

The woman shook her head. "Did you know that I was a Dormant?"

"How could I? I didn't know other immortals even existed."

"But you knew that I was different."

Casting a quick glance at Eleanor, he nodded. "Yes."

She knew the truth, and so did Peter, but apparently no one had told Margaret that her blood tasted delicious to Emmett.

"How?" she asked.

"Were you told about my nutritional needs?"

"I know that you drink blood."

"Yours tasted a little different."

"In what way?"

"Better."

"I see." Margaret crossed her arms over her chest. "So keeping me was not just about my safety. I was a tasty snack."

"True. But that was just a bonus, a reward for what I believed was a good deed. I would have never kept you if I thought your life would be better on the outside. I was genuinely concerned about your safety." He looked into Margaret's eyes. "I cared for you."

The way he said it cut through Eleanor like a knife. It was a good thing that Margaret couldn't hear his tone through the translating earpieces because she would have melted.

No wonder the guy had the entire community of Safe Haven enthralled, and he didn't even need to use compulsion to achieve that. He had some innate power, a charisma that was mesmerizing, hypnotic.

Eleanor had thought that cult leaders used compulsion without even realizing it, but what Emmett had just done wasn't a compulsion. It was a different kind of paranormal talent. Or maybe her immunity made her respond to some other aspect of his compulsion, a quality she hadn't been aware of before.

Did she have it as well?

Not likely.

If she had, she would have charmed people into liking her the way Emmett did, and she'd never been successful at doing that. If anything, she was good at alienating people.

"What about me?" Anastasia asked. "How did you convince me that I was too weak to resist my father's control, and that unless I stayed in Safe Haven, my life would be miserable?"

Emmett smiled indulgently. "Since you are immune to compulsion, you can't blame me for that. It was what you believed when you came to the retreat, and I just served as an echo chamber, repeating back to you what you said to me."

Letting out a breath, Anastasia slumped against the couch's back. "Yeah. You are right. That one is on me." She gazed lovingly at her mate. "Once Leon translated the voices in my head and proved that I wasn't crazy, my confidence soared. I was no longer afraid to confront my father and live my life as I pleased. I also realized that he wasn't the enemy. He was a victim of grief just as I was."

Emmett clapped his hands. "Good for you. So the voices were real after all."

"Yes." Anastasia said. "And what's even better, they are gone. I hope they never return."

He grinned. "Excellent. I'm so glad that everything has worked out for you."

The guy was a born performer, controlling the room, including the men. The hostility Eleanor had sensed from Leon and Bowen when Emmett entered the suite was practically gone, and the two were regarding him with the same friendly attitude everyone aside from Kian did.

Was Kian the only one truly immune to Emmett's special juice?

"What will happen to Safe Haven now that you are not there?" Margaret asked.

"I don't know." The confident mask Emmett had worn for the sake of his former disciples slipped. "I asked Peter to check on that, but he says that it's no longer my concern."

Eleanor cast Peter a sidelong glance. She hadn't known that Emmett had made such a request. Why hadn't he asked her to do it? She would have gladly called the woman who had taken his place and compelled her to tell her everything.

"Safe Haven is still running retreats," Peter said. "So it's safe to assume that things are going well." He smiled at Emmett. "Especially now that they get to keep the money. I bet the members are very happy to get more perks for their hard work."

Emmett pursed his sensuous lips. "I would be very surprised if the money finds its way to the members. Riley and whoever else is helping her run the place are probably pocketing the profits, provided that there are any left after the expenses. Being the shepherd is always more profitable than being the sheep, and the only thing that's different with me gone is that Safe Haven now has a new shepherd. Hopefully, she is capable enough to at least keep the sheep fed."

28

CASSANDRA

$\mathcal{G}$ eraldine tugged on Cassandra's arm, pulling her down so she could whisper in her ear, "What is this place?"

Cassandra had explained how exclusive By Invitation Only was, and her mother had been excited about going. Had she forgotten already?

"It's just a fancy restaurant, Mom." She urged Geraldine to follow the hostess instead of gawking.

"I know that. But why is it so dark in here?"

"I'll tell you why." Martha threaded her arm through Geraldine's. "It's dark to give the patrons privacy. This is the kind of place that rich men take much younger women to, women who aren't their wives and whom they wish to impress."

If Martha's whisper had been loud enough for Cassandra to hear, the patrons she'd been talking about had heard it as well. Still, it didn't stop the men from following the blonde bombshell with leering eyes.

Onegus's mother was a gorgeous woman who knew the power she wielded with her tall, curvy body, her waist-long blond, curling hair, her large blue eyes, and everything else that made her magazine-cover perfect.

Well, perhaps not magazine covers from this decade. Martha wasn't skinny. She wasn't overweight either. She just looked healthy and not starved or depressed like most fashion models did.

Cassandra was naturally slim, but even as an eighteen-year-old gangly teenager, she hadn't been thin enough for modeling clothing. Not that she'd ever wanted to do that. Modeling makeup had been good enough for her.

The poor girls walking the fashion shows' runways were always hungry. How were they supposed to be in a good mood?

Thank God she'd never had to diet, just watch what she ate and consume enough liquids to keep her skin hydrated and smooth. It might have gotten harder to maintain as she'd gotten older, but her stressful job meant many missed meals, and the constant aggravation burned through the calories she managed to consume.

Nevertheless, she loved her job and wouldn't give it up even if she didn't need to work for money. What else was she going to do with her life? What else could provide her with such a sense of accomplishment?

Kids?

Possibly. But that was not on the cards for her, and not just because turning immortal would make her nearly infertile. If she hadn't met Onegus, there was no guarantee she would have met the right human before her biological clock tapped out.

Bottom line, she wasn't sacrificing anything to be with him, not even having children sometime in the future, and not her career. But she was gaining immortality, an awesome man, and a community of like-minded people.

As the hostess stopped in front of a secluded booth and pulled out a chair for Geraldine, Onegus pulled the other one out for Martha and then one for Cassandra before sitting down.

"Can I get you something to drink?" the hostess asked as she handed each of them a menu.

"I would like an Affinity," Martha said.

Cassandra arched a brow. Was it a double entendre, or was there a drink named Affinity?

"Of course." The hostess noted it on her handheld tablet.

Apparently, it was the name of a drink.

"What's in it?" Geraldine asked.

"Scotch, vermouth, and orange bitters," Martha said. "It's a nice cocktail to have with dinner."

"Then I'll have it too."

Somehow, Geraldine and Martha seemed to be getting along just fine. Her mother hadn't been taken aback by Martha's stunning and youthful appearance, hadn't questioned how it was possible that Onegus's mother looked younger than him, and she even seemed to like the woman.

Well, Geraldine liked everyone, so that wasn't a big surprise. Her mother could find something to admire about the most wretched person.

Still, the truth was that Martha was starting to grow on Cassandra as well. She could see the similarities between their characters that Onegus had pointed out, which was a bit disconcerting. Did she come across as critical and as demanding as Martha?

Probably.

Could she try to be a little nicer?

Perhaps Geraldine's approach was healthier. Instead of focusing on everyone's shortcomings, she should try to find the good in every person, a quality to admire.

Who knew? Perhaps she could get her snowflakes to do more with a carrot than with a stick?

When the drinks arrived, Geraldine lifted hers. "What are we celebrating?"

Martha lifted hers. "My son and your daughter's future. I hope it will be happy and fruitful. Fates know I need a grandchild in my life."

Geraldine patted her arm. "Shush, dear. Don't let anyone hear you say that because they'll think you are crazy. You don't look old enough to have a grown son, let alone a grandchild."

"Funny that you should say that." Martha's lips twitched with a stifled smile. "I could say the same about you."

Geraldine leaned closer. "True, but I'm being smart about it. I keep it a secret."

Cassandra rolled her eyes. "You tell all your friends about me."

"I do. But I lie about your age." She winked. "I tell them that you're twenty-four. Besides, they all think that you're adopted, and that I lie about being your birth mother."

"How do you explain your youthful appearance?" Martha asked.

Yeah, Cassandra wanted to know that too. It seemed like Geraldine wasn't as clueless as she pretended to be. She knew that there was something strange about her looking so damn young.

Her mother shrugged. "I got lucky, I guess. I took good care of my skin, and I've never spent too long in the sun." She smiled. "Except for the summer I met Cassandra's father. I met him on the beach, you know."

Cassandra stifled a groan. *Oh boy. Here it comes.*

29

ONEGUS

" $\mathcal{H}$ e was a young aide to the Ethiopian ambassador. So handsome." Geraldine's expression turned dreamy. "He had such an irresistible smile."

Onegus had heard a version of the story before. Except the other day, Cassandra's father was an analyst who was a descendant of the Queen of Sheba.

"What was his name?" Martha asked.

"Emanuel. In Hebrew, it means God is with us. Many Ethiopians have biblical names, which gives credence to the story about the Queen of Sheba and King Solomon falling in love and having a son together."

"What was his surname?" Martha kept pushing.

Hadn't she realized that Emanuel existed only in Geraldine's fantasy?

"They don't have surnames in Ethiopia. They use the father's first name, like Emanuel, son of Ephrem."

To know that, Geraldine must have read something about Ethiopians, or perhaps she'd actually met a guy named Emanuel who worked for the embassy.

"What happened to him?" Martha asked.

"He went back home."

"And you've never told him about his daughter?"

"I didn't have his address or phone number. It was just a summer fling. I remember him fondly, though. He gave me my Cassy."

Martha turned to Cassandra. "It shouldn't be too difficult to find him. An aide working for the embassy thirty-some years ago is probably an ambassador by now or holds some other political office."

Not wanting to embarrass her mother, Cassandra had to answer as if she believed the guy actually existed. "He most likely has children and even grand-children by now. Discovering that he has another daughter would only upset him and his family."

"You don't have to contact him. But if I were you, I would like to know more about my father."

Onegus put a hand on his mother's shoulder. "Have you ever tried to find yours?"

She shook her head. "When I was old enough to ask, he was no longer among the living."

"We both know that was just a story your mother told you so you wouldn't go looking for him. I never tried to find my father either."

Geraldine sighed. "Look at us. We are so similar that it's eerie. No one knows who their father is." She looked at Onegus and smiled. "I hope that you and Cassy will start a new tradition."

"You don't know who your father is either?" Martha asked.

Geraldine shook her head. "I suffered a bad accident as a girl, and I forgot everything, including how to speak. I had to relearn everything. It was like being reborn." She tilted her head. "Maybe that's why I look so young. The amnesia was like a reset button."

"Good evening," the waiter said.

Given Cassandra's happy smile, she was glad for the interruption.

After everyone had selected their appetizers and entrees, Onegus pulled out his phone. "Could you do me a favor and take a picture of the four of us?" He handed it to the waiter.

"Sure thing." The guy motioned for them to lean toward each other. "Say cheese."

As the waiter adjusted the focus, Geraldine dipped her head and looked at the table.

"One more," the guy said.

"You need to look into that camera." Martha put her arm around Geraldine's shoulders. "We need to practice for the wedding."

"I hate having my picture taken," Cassandra's mother complained. "I come out looking like a ghost."

"Nonsense." Martha brought her cheek so close to Geraldine's that they were almost touching. "If you smile big, it will brighten the picture and make you look good. Just follow my example."

Cornered, Cassandra's mother had no choice, and as the server snapped away, she smiled big.

Perhaps too big.

Sneaky lady.

People didn't smile in driver's license photos.

But what could he do? It wasn't like he could tell her not to smile.

When the waiter returned the device, Geraldine tried to snatch it out of his hands. "Please. Erase my pictures."

"They are not yours." He put the phone in his suit pocket. "They are of all of us. We need to start collecting family photos for our future children and your grandchildren."

His mother cast him a questioning look. "Is this an engagement party, and no one told me?"

He wasn't sure whether she was playing along or had forgotten all he had told her about Cassandra's mother and what he'd planned to achieve tonight.

"It's not an engagement," Cassandra said. "It's just a meet the parents kind of thing, or in our case, meet the mothers."

3 O

EMMETT

"That went well," Eleanor said as she escorted Emmett back to his cell. Was she being sarcastic?

He was drained. Assuming his former persona of a charismatic and compassionate leader for Margaret and Anastasia's sake had been difficult.

He'd kept his public appearances and personal interviews with community members to a minimum for a reason. While performing, he was soaring high, feeling powerful, invincible, a god. But after the high came the low, and he was left depleted.

It took him days to recuperate.

Except, his day had just started, and soon he would have to gather his remaining wisps of energy for another performance.

Arwel's mate and her sister were coming for their first lesson in the Kra-ell language. That in itself didn't require much energy, but he was sure that wasn't the only reason for the visit. They wanted to check him out and grill him about their possible ancestry. Besides, it was a great opportunity to gain more supporters.

They would be wearing those damn earpieces that rendered his compulsion useless, but he still had his other persuasive leadership qualities that had nothing to do with his voice or compulsion.

"Is there any way the next visit can be postponed?" He sat on his couch and let his head drop back. "I'm tired."

"Do you want me to make you coffee?" Eleanor asked.

He cast her an amused glance. "Coffee won't help, but a little nibble on your neck would do wonders for my energy level. You are like a rapid charger."

She rolled her eyes, but he could smell her arousal.

"I got a lecture from Peter this morning about muting the sound and lowering the resolution of the recording. From now on, everything we do will be heard and watched."

"I don't mind." He patted the spot next to him. "Come, sit with me."

Letting out a long-suffering breath, she sat down, but turned her back to the camera and spoke quietly. "Peter didn't say anything about the bathroom, but once we use up that option, I'm sure he will give me a lecture about that as well."

Emmett leaned toward her and wrapped his arms around her slim back. "Then we will turn the couch around to block the view of the bed. It will give us at least a little bit of privacy."

"That's unacceptable. I need to go over Peter's head and talk to Kian, but I hate doing that to him. It's his first command, and it would look bad for him."

Emmett was listening with only half an ear. Pulling off the band at the end of Eleanor's braid, he unraveled it and fanned out her hair over her shoulders.

"What are you doing?"

"Hiding what we're doing behind the curtain of your hair." He nuzzled her neck. "Say yes. Give me just a little taste."

After getting more than a little on Saturday night, the craving should have subsided to a mere background hum. Except, having Eleanor so close to him, inhaling her scent and looking into her dark eyes must have awakened it. Or perhaps it was the depletion in energy that spurred his hunger.

Eleanor didn't answer. Instead, she closed the mere inches between them and kissed him.

He was about to deepen the kiss when he heard someone clearing her throat. "Is this a bad time?"

Eleanor jumped back as if someone had bitten her, only he hadn't had the chance to do it.

A tall Chinese woman entered the cell. "Eleanor. Long time no see." She smiled, exposing a set of fangs that were tiny but still unmistakable. "You've been busy, girl."

Eleanor stepped aside. "Emmett, this is Jin, Arwel's mate."

Following protocol, he remained seated, put his hands on his thighs, and offered her a disarming smile. "A pleasure to meet you."

As another tall Chinese lady entered together with Arwel, Emmett would have known that they were sisters even if he hadn't been told. Mey seemed more refined, more ladylike, while Jin was truer to her paternal heritage, which he had no doubt was Kra-ell. She radiated aggression the way Kra-ell females did, just to a lesser degree.

Emmett wondered whether she was cruel, and if she was, whether Arwel enjoyed it.

He'd never heard the male purebloods complain about the way they were treated by the females. Except, he hadn't heard them talk about anything. The only time they'd deigned to talk to a hybrid was to issue orders.

Arwel cast his mate a hard glare. "I told you to wait for me."

Old conditioning kicking in, Emmett tensed. Would Jin lash out at Arwel? If a Kra-ell male dared to address his mistress like that, she would have punished him. At best, he could have forgotten about getting an invitation to breed. At worst, she would have sentenced him to a whipping.

But all Jin did was shrug. "Eleanor is here. Isn't she a Guardian?"

"Not yet."

Emmett let out a breath. Jin wasn't like the Kra-ell females.

Perhaps hybrids were a mellower version of the purebloods.

But then, Jin and Mey were second-generation hybrids and had been raised by humans, while the first-generation hybrid females who were born in the compound had been raised by Kra-ell mothers, and most likely had grown up to be just as nasty.

"Let's move to the suite," Arwel said. "There isn't enough room in here for all of us."

"I was just leaving," Eleanor said. "I can bring a couple of chairs over from the suite."

Arwel looked at Emmett. "Where would you prefer to do it?"

"If Jin and Mey want to take notes, the dining table at the suite will be more comfortable."

"I have a tablet." Mey pulled it out of her large purse.

"And I take notes on my phone." Jin sat on the couch next to him. "We can stay here." She looked around the cell and smiled. "I have fond memories of this one."

He arched a brow. "Were you imprisoned here?"

"I was sheltered here." She crossed her legs and put her hands on her knee. "So, Emmett, any idea who our parents might be?"

He shook his head. "I left a long time ago. You were born after that."

Jin flicked her long hair back and presented him with her profile. "Do we look like any of the hybrid males you knew back in the day?"

"I'm sorry. I wish I could be more helpful."

As a moment later Alfie walked in with two chairs, Mey thanked him and sat down. Arwel joined her.

"Do we look like hybrid Kra-ell females?" Jin continued her interrogation.

"You do. Your sister less so. But thankfully, you are much mellower."

Arwel chuckled. "If Jin is mellow, I can just imagine how bad the Kra-ell females are."

That earned him a glare from his mate. "Did I ever give you any reason to complain?"

He lifted his hands in the peace sign. "Never. I was just teasing."

"I'm sure that the Kra-ell females are not inherently bad or good," Mey said. "That's how their society is built, and it probably serves a purpose."

"Thank you for coming to my people's defense. I appreciate it." Emmett dipped his head. "It is true that the Kra-ell females are as trapped in their traditional roles as the males are, and given the big gender disparity, the harsh customs make sense. If you two had grown up in the Kra-ell compound, you probably would have adopted the same aggressive and cruel attitude." He smiled. "You should be grateful for being raised by humans instead."

"We are," Mey said. "My sister and I were very fortunate to get adopted by wonderful people."

3 1

CASSANDRA

"I had a lovely time," Geraldine said as Onegus pulled up in front of their house. She turned to Martha, who sat in the back with her. "It was so nice to meet you. Will I see you again before you go back to Scotland?"

"I hope so." Martha glanced at her son. "Onegus is so busy right now, but perhaps we can have lunch together, just you and me."

Cassandra tensed. There was no way she was leaving Martha and her mother alone. "I could take a long lunch break and come along."

Martha's lips thinned out. "Of course."

She wasn't happy, but that was her problem.

"I know where we can go," Geraldine said. "My book club met there last week, and I loved the place."

As the two continued making plans for meeting on Thursday for lunch, Onegus opened the door for Cassandra.

When she took his offered hand, he pulled her against his chest and whispered in her ear, "I'll drop my mother off and come back to get you." He nuzzled her earlobe. "I can't go another day without making love to you."

She whispered back, "Where are you going to take me?"

The village was nearly an hour's drive away, and the apartment in the downtown building wasn't exclusively Onegus's. He shared it with several Guardians.

"The same place I took you after the wedding." His lips trailed down her neck.

Cassandra shivered, but not because he was taking her to a cell in the dungeon. The place was kitted out like a luxury hotel suite. It was a little claustrophobic to be in a room with no windows, but she had no problem spending the night there.

"Okay." She pushed on his chest. "Our mothers are watching."

"They know that we're in love." He winked and walked over to Geraldine's door.

Once all the goodbyes and promises to meet again on Thursday were over, Martha stayed in the car while Onegus escorted Cassandra and her mother to the front door.

He kissed Geraldine's cheek and then Cassandra's. "I'll be back in less than an hour," he whispered in her ear.

"Drive carefully. You barely had any sleep last night."

"I took a short nap."

Geraldine unlocked the door, and as they stepped in, Cassandra waved goodbye to Onegus and Martha.

Her mother stepped out of her high-heeled shoes and sighed in relief."These were pinching my poor little toes the entire evening." She leaned and picked them up. "I like Martha. She's not as bad as you made her out to be."

"She was on her best behavior tonight." Cassandra headed upstairs. "I'm going to change. Onegus is picking me up in an hour."

"Where are you going?" Her mother followed her up.

She had no problem telling her mother that she was spending the night with Onegus, but she couldn't tell her that it was going to be in a dungeon. Geraldine might get the wrong idea. "We are going to his place. I'll probably be back in the morning."

"Why don't you take your car, so you can go to work straight from there?"

"I don't want to drive to an unfamiliar place at night. You know how bad I am with those navigation systems. I'd get lost, which would make me angry, and then something would explode."

Geraldine smiled. "We can't have that. By the way, I wanted to ask you something but kept forgetting. How is your power behaving around Onegus? Is he a calming or agitating influence?"

"He's very good at helping me discharge it in a positive way. But I still get mad about things, and my energy still boils over from time to time."

"Then you must discharge it more often." Her mother winked and then ducked into her bedroom.

Shaking her head, Cassandra continued down the hallway to her room. She needed to pack an overnight bag with a change of clothes and something to drink and snack on. The problem with the dungeon room was that it had a limited stock of refreshments.

Tonight was special. They were going to make love without a barrier between them, and the consequences were potentially life-altering. There was still a small chance that she wasn't a Dormant, and that her mother wasn't an immortal, just strange.

Perhaps not so small.

All she had to go on was Onegus's conviction that she was a Dormant. There was also her mother's unnaturally youthful appearance, but both could be the result of something that didn't involve immortal genes.

Perhaps witches weren't a myth either?

Wouldn't it be cool to find out that she and Geraldine came from a line of powerful witches?

Cassandra shook her head. Next thing she would discover that vampires and shapeshifters were also real.

Talk about fairytales.

Was that why she hadn't told Onegus that she loved him yet?

Was it fear that the fairytale bubble would burst?

If she admitted to herself that she'd fallen head over heels in love with Onegus, it would be doubly devastating to discover that she had no place in his fairytale world.

Except, she'd already said it to him in so many words, and she hadn't been ambiguous about it. So it was no longer a question of admitting it.

It was time to woman up.

Just as she'd needed to hear Onegus say the words, he needed to hear them from her, and tonight was the perfect opportunity to say them.

The occasion demanded wine, and plenty of it.

Would two bottles suffice?

Perhaps three bottles would be better.

32

ONEGUS

*A*fter dropping his mother off at the apartment she shared with three other Scottish clan members, Onegus got back in his car and called Magnus.

"Things are running smoothly, Chief. Stop worrying and enjoy your time off."

Promoting the guy to the position of Head Guardian had been a good decision. Magnus was reliable, capable, and even-keeled.

"Thank you. I will be spending the night in one of the cells in the dungeon. Don't hesitate to call me for any reason whatsoever. With Annani staying in the building, we need to treat security as code red."

"Every Guardian is aware of this. We are vigilant."

"Good. Again, call me with anything." Onegus ended the call and made another to Peter. "How is Emmett doing?"

"He had a busy day. First with Margaret, Anastasia, and their mates, and later with Mey and Jin."

"Did he behave?"

"He was his usual charming, charismatic self. I don't know if he's cloaking himself in charm every time he has guests, or if it became part of him after all his years of pretending to be a guru. The guy is hard to read."

"How is Eleanor progressing with him?"

"She's doing well. Do you want to speak with her?"

"Not today. I took half a day off to spend with my mother and Cassandra. I'm on my way to get her, and I need someone to get fresh supplies to a clean cell. Who can you spare?"

Onegus would have preferred not to share personal details with his Guardians, but there was no avoiding it if he wanted their help. Besides, he wasn't about to sneak Cassandra in. She wasn't a dirty secret.

Possibly, she was his mate.

"Eleanor can do it." Peter chuckled. "She's flipping me off."

Onegus was glad that Eleanor was available. A woman would know what to get for what he had in mind.

"I'm bringing Cassandra over, and I need supplies for a romantic evening."

"I'm on it," Eleanor said. "How soon do you need it?"

"I'm on my way to pick her up. So as soon as you can."

"Consider it done, Chief."

After ending the call, he dictated a text message to Cassandra. "I'll be at your place in fifteen minutes. Are you ready?"

His phone rang a moment later.

"I'm ready. I have an overnight bag packed and three bottles of wine."

He smiled. "Great minds think alike. I sent Eleanor to get supplies for a romantic evening in a cozy prison cell."

"That sounds so kinky," she purred. "Are we going to play prisoner and jailer?"

He was relieved that Cassandra wasn't mad about him involving Eleanor, and he was more than happy to comply with any fantasy she might come up with.

"We can play anything you are in the mood for. I'm at your service."

"Did you really take a nap?"

"I did. Twenty minutes of shuteye on the chair in my office. It reclines."

"Doesn't sound like much. Did you get any sleep when you came back?"

Why did it feel so good that she was concerned about his well-being?

When his mother bombarded him with questions of that nature it irritated him, but he loved that Cassandra was asking them.

"I slept for an hour and a half, but given that I normally don't sleep more than four hours, that's not a big deal." He lowered his voice. "If you are worried about my ability to perform, don't."

She chuckled. "I wouldn't dare."

"That reminds me. I still owe you a spanking."

There was a long moment of silence, and then Cassandra let out a breath. "Some other time. Tonight is stressful enough."

"Right. Are you scared?"

"A little."

"If you need more time to process the idea, we can keep using condoms for a little longer."

"No, I made up my mind. I want to become immortal. But if you want to wait, that's fine with me."

Was that a plea to postpone the process without her having to admit that she needed more time?

It wasn't like Cassandra. She was proud, but she was also a straight shooter. She wouldn't have gone about it like that.

"I don't want to wait, but now that you brought it up, I would rather you didn't start transitioning before Kian's birthday is over and the guests all go back home."

"After all the conditions are met, how soon does the transition usually start?"

"For most, it takes a few days. For some, it takes weeks, and for others, just one day. It's unpredictable."

"Then maybe we should wait. I might be one of those who start transitioning the next day."

33

CASSANDRA

*A*s the guard called the house that Onegus was on his way, Geraldine cast Cassandra one of her sweet yet sad motherly smiles. "Have fun, dear. Will I see you tomorrow morning?"

She should have thought about calling the guard gate again and instructing them to let Onegus through without calling the house first, but it didn't matter. She'd already told Geraldine that she was spending the night with Onegus. But even if she hadn't, it was still too early for her mother to be asleep and for Cassandra to sneak out unnoticed if she so wished.

"If I wake up late, I might go straight to the office and then take an Uber home." She leaned and kissed her mother's cheek. "Don't worry. Even if Onegus and I do get married one day, you are coming with me. I'm never leaving you behind."

"Who said that I'm worried?"

"Your face." Cassandra kissed her other cheek. "Bye, Mom."

She walked out the door right as Onegus pulled up in front of her house. He was too fast for her to make it to the passenger side without him rushing out to assist her, so she didn't even try, waiting on the sidewalk for him to get out of the car.

Glancing at the house, he took her bag and slung it over his shoulder. "Don't look, but your mom is peeking at us through the sheers."

"I think she's worried you are taking me away and never bringing me back."

He wrapped his arm around her and led her to the passenger side of the car. "You made it very clear that you and your mother are a package deal. I have no intentions of stealing you from her. She'll come with us." He opened the door for her and waited until she was seated before closing it.

When he got behind the wheel, Cassandra fastened her seatbelt. "As the saying goes, we'll cross that bridge when we get there."

"Might be sooner than you think."

"Did you send the photo to Roni?"

"Not yet. It's after working hours, and I don't want to bother him at home."

Cassandra chuckled. "I'm sure he won't mind. Roni loves what he does."

"A little too much." Onegus cast her a sidelong glance. "If I send it now, he'll go to the lab right away, and Sylvia will be upset. I want to stay in her good graces."

"Because of me? I don't know if she can help me. Our powers don't work the same way."

"That's just one of the reasons. Sometimes, we have missions that require Sylvia's particular talent. Since she's a civilian, I have to ask for her help, I can't just order her to do it."

Interesting. Perhaps the clan would find a use for her powers as well? If she could harness them and wield them at will, perhaps she could replace cannons and missiles. Right. As if that would ever happen. Even if it could, she didn't want to be a weapon.

"What do you use Sylvia for?"

"So far, we only used her to disable surveillance equipment so we could sneak in and out of guarded places."

That didn't sound too bad. If Cassandra could do that, she would gladly offer her assistance.

"When I worked as a model, and a photographer got handsy, I melted their cameras. Not the entire thing, of course. Usually, a small discharge was enough to melt an important component and make the camera inoperable and unfixable. Those things cost thousands of dollars, so I felt vindicated."

Onegus's eyes blazed in the car's dark interior. "Did any of them molest you?"

"A few tried, none succeeded. They were too busy trying to save their expensive equipment, which was suddenly emitting smoke."

"Good. I'm glad you did that."

"Yeah, well. It's dangerous to play with unpredictable power. Sometimes the damage is much greater than what was intended."

"Did you hurt anyone?" he asked softly.

She nodded. "One day, I'll tell you about it, but not today." She reached over the center console and took his hand. "I don't want to spoil the mood with morbid tales, not when we are on our way to a romantic prison cell, located in a mysterious underground dungeon, with the intention of making love until morning."

As she'd intended, Onegus laughed. "I bet no one has ever said those exact words in that order. A romantic prison cell indeed."

"You should decorate each cell in a different way. At least one should look like a real dungeon, just with a comfortable bed."

He looked at her from under lowered eyelashes. "Do you have kinky fantasies, my love? One of my Guardians owns a club that caters to those sharper tastes. Would you like to visit it?"

He'd called her his love. Should she tell him that she loved him now?

It didn't seem right when they were discussing a kink club. She'd find a better opportunity later. Perhaps when they opened the first bottle of wine.

"I'm not into whips and chains, if that's what you're asking. But I'm curious. Could you take me there one day?"

"I'm not into those things either, and I've never visited the club, but I could ask Brundar to give us a tour once things get back to normal here."

"Brundar," she rolled the Rs. "It sounds appropriate for a kink club owner. Is he a big, muscular guy who's covered in tattoos?"

"Brundar looks like a cross between a statue of an angel and an assassin." Onegus cast her an apologetic glance. "He doesn't have tattoos. We can't get any because of our fast healing. Piercings are not possible either."

Affecting a disappointed expression, Cassandra crossed her arms over her chest. "That's it. I'm not doing it. I always wanted to have a dragon tattoo on my entire back."

She stifled a smile when Onegus's expression turned worried. Hadn't he realized that she'd been teasing?

"It can be painted on, but it's not going to be permanent."

She laughed. "I was just joking. I'm an artist, but I prefer canvases that are not made from human skin."

He let out a breath. "I'm glad. I'm not a fan either, especially when it comes to you. You are perfect as you are."

34

ONEGUS

*W*hen Onegus opened the door to cell number five, the number Eleanor had texted him, he didn't expect the elaborate setup Eleanor had managed in such a short time.

Soft music was playing, the coffee table had been replaced by a tiny bistro table and two chairs, and there were fresh flowers in vases on every surface. A champagne bottle was chilling in a bucket, next to a tray of fancy chocolates.

A note on the counter told him to look in the fridge for more snacks and an assortment of drinks.

"When did you have time to prepare all this?" Cassandra turned in a circle.

"I didn't. Eleanor did."

"I thought that you only sent her to get supplies."

"I did. I asked her to get some refreshments, and she went all out."

"Nice." Cassandra plucked one of the chocolates off the tray and popped it into her mouth.

He sat on the couch and watched as her eyes rolled back in pleasure, and when she moaned and then smacked her lips, the effect was predictable.

"That good?"

"Orgasmic." She reached for another one. "I have to know who's the chocolatier. Those are out of this world." Picking another piece, she turned around and sat on his lap. "Kiss me." She wrapped her arms around his shoulders.

He kissed her softly, and as his tongue swept into her mouth, the taste of her was more exquisite than the chocolate's.

"Hmm," he murmured against her lips. "Delicious."

"It is." She licked her lips.

"I meant you, not the chocolate. It's good, but it can't compare to you."

Leaning back a fraction, she looked into his eyes. "I love you, Onegus. And I'm grateful to fate for bringing us together."

As his heart did the flip and soar thing that he'd thought was fictional, he closed his arms around her waist and rested his forehead against hers. "I love you too."

"I know. And now you know as well." She chuckled nervously. "It wasn't as hard to admit as I thought."

His answer was to kiss her again, and as she shifted to straddle him, he deepened the kiss and slid his hands under her shirt to cup her breasts.

Under her lacy bra, her nipples were two hard points begging to be suckled, and as he impatiently tugged the shirt up, she lifted her arms so he could peel it off her. Moving at immortal speed, he unhooked the bra, plucked it off her body, and dove for her right nipple.

"Yes." She arched into his mouth, her fingers threading into his hair and holding him to her.

Her grip loosened a fraction only to move him to her other nipple. When he did, she tightened her hold again. Her hips churning on top of him, her sex ground into his shaft through the layers of their clothing.

Lifting with her in his arms, his mouth still latched to her breast, he moved to the bed and laid her on it.

Reluctantly, he let go of her succulent nipple so he could finish undressing her.

Shoes went flying, followed by her pants and panties. And then he was attacking his own clothes, barely able to slow down and not ruin one of his favorite suits.

When they were both naked, he gripped Cassandra's hips, yanked her to the edge of the bed, knelt on the floor, and hooked her legs over his shoulders.

"Tonight, I'm going to take my time with you."

Her eyes gleaming as if she had already turned immortal, her mouth slightly open, her breaths coming out shallow and panting, she was a vision of feminine beauty and sexuality.

His first lick against her petals had her jerking her bottom up, the second one had her mewling like a kitten, and the third one had her groaning like a tigress.

"What a delicious feast you are." He blew air on her heated flesh, cooling her.

"Don't tease me, Onegus."

He smiled evilly. "Oh, I intend to. I want to feast on you for hours, but I know neither of us is going to last that long."

He kissed her inner thigh, then the other, gently parting her folds with his fingers and then licking into her as deeply as his tongue could go.

Moaning, she bowed off the bed. And as he replaced his tongue with two fingers and licked at the apex of her thighs, she exploded with a scream, her juices coating his lips, his chin, and his fingers.

It drove him mad, bringing his inner savage to the surface. Licking, pumping, and growling like a beast, he wrung another climax out of her, and then another, until she pulled on his hair hard enough to leave a bald spot.

"No more," she whispered. "I want you inside of me."

35

CASSANDRA

*L*ike the predator he was, Onegus came over her, his powerful body blanketing hers.

His mouth descended on hers, the kiss deep despite his fangs. Somehow, he was able to keep them from fully elongating, probably so he could kiss her properly.

Reaching between their bodies, she gripped his length, the velvety feel of him so warm, so needed, and positioned him at her entrance.

"Now," she hissed into his mouth.

"What about a condom?"

She'd forgotten that they'd considered waiting for after Kian's birthday.

"No need. We are starting tonight."

"Thank the merciful Fates." He slid into her until they were one.

The sensation was so different without the barrier between them.

It felt so right.

Stilling, he looked at her with those gorgeous glowing eyes of his. "You are mine."

She knew what he meant. This was a proper joining that went beyond the physical. There was an unmistakable mystic quality to it, as if the world had righted itself, and from now on, everything was going to be okay.

She wrapped her arms around his muscular back. "And you are mine. Now, move."

He laughed. "Yes, ma'am."

Pulling out slightly, he thrust back in and stilled. "Like this?"

"More." She lifted her legs and wrapped them around his thighs.

He did it again, pulling out and thrusting back in, then a little faster, deeper, and with every thrust, she could feel that mystic quality solidifying.

Was that the mate bond Onegus had talked about?

"Can you feel it?" She lifted her head and kissed the underside of his jaw. "Can you feel the bond?"

"Yes." He dipped his head and took her mouth again.

But when his shafting became more urgent, more powerful, he had to let go of her lips, and she had to cling to him for dear life as he pounded into her.

The coil inside her tightening with every corkscrew motion of his hips, she turned her head, offering him her neck.

There was a hiss, and as a moment later his tongue swept over the spot he was about to bite, the anticipation sprung the coil, and she climaxed at the same time his fangs sank into her.

Barely any pain registered through the orgasmic haze, and as the venom entered her system, she orgasmed again, and again, and again, until she blacked out and soared.

It must have been hours later when she opened her eyes. The room was almost completely dark, with just a sliver of light coming from the small bathroom. Behind her, Onegus was wrapped around her like a cocoon of warmth and love, his steady breathing indicating that he was asleep. Though the hardness pressing against her bottom meant that he was either dreaming sexy dreams or was at least partially awake.

Turning in his arms, she kissed his jaw. "Are you asleep?"

"I was." His shaft twitched against her belly.

"Liar."

"Swear to the Fates. You woke me up when you turned around."

"Are you always this hard when you're asleep?"

His large hand closed on both her ass cheeks and squeezed. "Only when I'm sleeping next to you." He dipped his head and kissed her lightly. "My sexy mate."

"Mate," she repeated. "Did we bond?"

"It sure felt like that."

"Does that mean I'm a Dormant for sure?"

"I have no doubt that you are." His hand smoothed up to caress her back. "And I also have no doubt that you are going to transition successfully. For some reason, the Fates deemed me worthy of a true-love mate."

Cassandra frowned. That hadn't sounded like her swaggering Onegus.

"Why wouldn't they? You are amazing." She smiled. "As you keep reminding me."

"I *am* amazing." His hand returned to her bottom. "But the Fates usually reward those who have suffered greatly or sacrificed a lot for others. I didn't, not really."

"Yes, you did, and you still do. You told me that you were married to your job. And your job is protecting the clan. You've been doing it for how long? Five hundred years?"

"More or less."

"And I'm sure you are not dedicated to your job only because you're after the prestige or the money. You work so hard because you care."

"Of course, I do. The clan is my family." He smiled. "And now it's yours too."

"Not yet. Let's not jinx this. I have to transition first."

"I'm taking it for granted. How do you feel about suddenly having hundreds of cousins-in-law?"

"Is that even a thing?"

"It is. My cousins are your cousins-in-law."

"Then I feel blessed beyond measure. It's always been just my mother and me. I've dreamt about having a big family but never expected that dream to come true. It's like living in a fairytale."

A smirk lifted one corner of Onegus's lips. "It came true with an added bonus. You also got Prince Charming without having to kiss a frog or live with seven grumpy dwarfs."

She laughed. "You are right. I did."

36

ONEGUS

*O*negus started his day late.

He'd stayed in bed longer than usual, waiting for Cassandra to wake up. They'd made love again in the morning, had breakfast together, and then he'd driven her home.

By the time he got back to his office in the keep, it was after nine in the morning, and Magnus didn't look happy.

"Good morning, Chief." He pushed to his feet.

"I'm sorry for coming in late. I know that you're eager to get back home to your mate."

"Indeed." Magnus smiled. "But I still remember how it was when I just met Vivian. Getting out of bed before she did was impossible."

Onegus sat in the chair Magnus had vacated. "Is it easier now?"

"Not really, but I can stretch the cord a little longer than I could a year ago."

"Good to know."

It had been difficult to say goodbye to Cassandra this morning, but they both needed to be at work.

"I'm heading home." Magnus walked to the door.

"Anything of interest to report?"

Magnus shook his head. "It was a quiet night. The guests came back before midnight as instructed, and the Clan Mother followed the schedule of visits Alena prepared for her."

"Thank the Fates for Alena."

Magnus chuckled. "What would we have done without her?"

"I don't know. I guess keeping Annani out of trouble would have been Kian's headache."

"Mothers." The Guardian opened the door. "Can't live with them, can't live without them."

"Ain't that the truth."

When the door closed behind Magnus, Onegus pulled out his phone and went over the photos the waiter had snapped. There was only one of Geraldine that was semi-decent, and he hoped that Roni could use it for his search.

He wrote a short text to the hacker, added the photo, and sent it over. Hopefully, it wouldn't take Roni too long to find a match. If they found Geraldine's last issued driver's license, the one she'd supposedly lost, it would be a good start.

His phone rang a moment later with Roni's number on display.

That wasn't good. Perhaps Roni couldn't work with the picture because Geraldine's face was slightly turned to the left.

"Is the picture no good for the facial recognition program?"

"I don't need to run it through the program. I know who she is," the hacker's voice trembled. "Geraldine is my grandmother, which means that Cassandra is my aunt. No wonder I immediately liked her. That doesn't happen often. I don't like most people."

Onegus felt as if he'd been struck by lightning. The puzzle pieces that had been floating in his subconscious fell into place.

The damn quilts.

Roni's long-lost grandmother was a quilter. Turner had found a thread of a trail, but it had winked out before leading to her.

Geraldine was very clever about hiding her identity.

He couldn't believe that his conscious mind hadn't registered that Cassandra and Roni shared similar facial features despite her being beautiful and him bordering on ugly. Their different ethnicities threw him off. They even had the same snarky attitude that bordered on rude.

He should have connected the dots.

"I remember that you found several driver's licenses with her picture. Can you send them to me?"

"Sure. When can I meet my grandmother?"

"I'll have to get back to you on that. I need to call Kian and let him know that we found an unaffiliated immortal."

"Can I call Cassandra?"

"Not yet. I'm sorry, Roni, but this has to be handled with care. Geraldine, or whatever her real name is, has memory issues and probably some mental problems as well. I don't want to shock her."

"I get it." Roni sighed. "I'm not a diplomat like you. You will probably handle it better."

"I'll try to arrange a meeting as soon as possible. I know that you are eager to meet her."

"I've waited this long, I can wait a little longer. I'll send you photos of her other driver's licenses in a few minutes. I have them ready in a file I keep on her."

"Thanks."

"By the way. What do you need them for?"

"She doesn't remember who she was before and what happened to her. Maybe we can piece it together from those licenses."

"She could be faking it."

"It occurred to me. If she is, though, she must have repeated the same lies so many times that they just roll off her tongue. I don't feel her getting anxious or uncomfortable when she tells her stories."

"Perhaps Vanessa should talk to her."

"Yeah. All in good time."

Roni sighed. "I just want to find out what happened to her."

"So do I. I'll be in touch." Onegus ended the call and leaned back in his chair.

This was excellent news.

Roni had just confirmed that Geraldine was an immortal, and that made Cassandra a Dormant for sure. Mother and daughter could both move into the village, provided that they wanted to, which wasn't a given.

But first, he needed to let Kian know what was going on and then arrange for Bhathian to take over for him again.

The news was great, but it came at an inopportune time. Kian's birthday was tomorrow, and Onegus should be going over the security detail instead of dealing with this new development.

He couldn't postpone it until after the birthday, though.

Cassandra needed to know, and he needed to be with her when he told her.

37

KIAN

"Un-fucking-believable." Activating his phone's earpiece, Kian pushed his swivel chair back and got up.

"The Fates have a twisted sense of humor," Onegus said.

"I'll say." Kian patted his pocket, making sure that the pack of cigarillos was there, and headed for the rooftop terrace of the office building.

Cassandra's mother was Roni's missing grandmother. No wonder Cassandra reminded him of someone. That someone was Roni. She was beautiful, and he was not, but the similarity was there, along with the attitude. Cassandra wasn't nearly as bad as Roni, but that was probably because she'd tried her best to be civil at the wedding. He wondered what she was like in her natural habitat. Probably, she was nearly as bad as her nephew.

The two were one more proof that blood was thicker than water.

Damn. Just a few days ago, they'd found out that Margaret was Wendy's mother. Was this the missing relatives' month?

Perhaps it was serendipitous, and the celebrations and the good mood permeating the clan were attracting more good fortune for a change.

In the past, it had always seemed to him that good things were followed by bad, the Fates leveling the playing field to preserve the balance. He'd never shared his observations with anyone, not even Syssi, in part because he didn't believe in them wholeheartedly, and in part because it was a downer on happiness.

Nevertheless, he'd always been wary following joyful events.

"Roni sent me the driver's licenses with her picture that he discovered a while ago, and unless Geraldine had a bunch of doppelgängers, it's her."

Kian pushed the rooftop door open. "What names did she use? Was there a pattern?"

"Not at all. Her original driver's license data was not found, either because she didn't have one before, or more likely because the records hadn't been computerized. Her real name was Sabina Bral, and that was the first driver's license Roni found from thirty-eight years ago. I believe it was real, and she was thirty-four at the time. The next one was issued two years later under the name of Mila Velashi, and the third one was issued twelve years ago under the name of Linda Graver. There is no pattern. I think she bought whatever was available when she needed it. I wouldn't be surprised if she had more licenses that the software missed, or low-quality ones that weren't registered at all."

Kian lit his cigarillo and took a puff. "So she's about Eva's age." He chuckled. "We need to check with Kalugal if he ever met Geraldine. Maybe he was the one who induced her transition as well."

"That would be one hell of a coincidence, and it'll inflate his ego even further. I don't think the village is big enough to contain it."

Kian laughed. "I don't think the galaxy is large enough. But we digress. Did Roni check whether those belonged to real people?"

"The first two were issued before the era of social media, and since he knew they were fake, he didn't bother. They wouldn't have helped him to find his grandmother."

"Were they all from California?"

"The first one was from Washington, the second from Oregon, and the last one from California."

"It looks like she started in the north and traveled down the coast. Check with Cassandra whether they lived in Oregon."

"I will, but since she's never mentioned it, I don't think they did."

"Did you tell Cassandra?"

"Not yet. It's not the kind of news that can be delivered over the phone. Besides, I wanted to get as much information as I could first, so I'd have something to show her."

"Do you need to take time off?"

Talk about bad timing. Couldn't Onegus have met Cassandra a month before or after the week of festivities? Did everything have to happen at the same time?

"I do. I've already arranged with Bhathian to take over for me for a couple of hours, so I can meet Cassandra for lunch." There was a brief moment of silence, and then the chief sighed. "I'm sorry that it's happening when you need me the most."

"Don't be. Two new immortals joining the clan is always good news. We should thank the Fates for that."

Onegus let out a breath. "I don't know about joining the clan. Geraldine has memory issues, and it's not going to be easy to explain to her that she's not human. I don't think she's aware of being immortal."

"Obtaining fake driver's licenses indicates otherwise. She might be pretending to cover up for being over seventy."

"The thought had crossed my mind. But she also invents fantastic stories about her past. That's indicative of someone with gaps in memory trying to fill in the missing pieces. Maybe she's aware of her age but doesn't know the how and why of it."

"Eva didn't know either, but she didn't invent memory issues or stories to cover up."

"Eva was a well-trained undercover agent who knew how to disappear.

When she realized that she wasn't aging, she knew what to do. An ordinary woman in her position would have been lost, maybe even have gone a little nuts."

"That's why I suspect that Geraldine is faking her mental issues. That's the easiest way to cover up for what she can't understand or explain. Also, people are used to her telling fantastic stories, so no one takes her seriously or wonders about her other oddities. That being said, neither one of us is a professional. We need Vanessa to evaluate her."

"I agree. The question is how to convince her to go to therapy. I don't want to trick her into it."

"Of course not. Let Cassandra decide how to handle her mother."

38

CASSANDRA

"*You*re leaving?" Kevin stopped Cassandra at the door.

"I'm going out for lunch."

"With the enigmatic and charming Onegus, I presume?"

She nodded.

Kevin's calculating smile meant that his head was already churning ideas of how he could benefit from her relationship with the man he thought was the head of an international conglomerate.

"Say hello to him for me, will you?"

"Sure will." She smiled, waved, and walked out the door.

Her smiled wilted as soon as she was alone.

Onegus had sounded a little strange when he'd called earlier. Well, strange for him. He'd sounded serious, like he was arranging a business lunch meeting. He hadn't told her that he loved her, hadn't commented on their lovemaking last night, and hadn't mentioned the bond they'd both felt.

Hopefully, Onegus's serious attitude had nothing to do with them and their relationship. He'd probably had a stressful morning at work and that was why his usual sexy banter had been absent.

As she left the building's parking, Cassandra glanced at her car's navigation system and checked the time of arrival. In fourteen minutes, she would arrive at the address of the restaurant she'd never been to before.

"Your destination is on your right," the computer voice announced at the same time she spotted the valet station.

Rudy's Steakhouse must be a lot fancier than she'd expected if they had valet service for lunch.

When she walked in, her suspicions were confirmed. Cassandra was glad of being dressed to the nines as she usually was for work.

"I'm meeting Mr. Onegus McLean," she told the hostess.

"Of course." The young woman gave her a quick once-over as if to assess whether Cassandra was worthy of meeting such a handsome man. She must have approved because she nodded and smiled. "Follow me, please."

Cassandra glared at the woman's back.

The place was large, the hostess passing many vacant tables before reaching a secluded booth at the farthest wall from the entry.

Seeing her approach, Onegus smiled and rose to his feet.

His expression was apprehensive, and her gut clenched.

But then he said, "Hello, love," and kissed her cheek.

Whatever it was couldn't be bad if he called her love, right?

There was a bottle of wine and two glasses on the table, so maybe he wanted to celebrate the start of her induction?

The hostess waited for Cassandra to sit down and for Onegus to return to his seat before handing her a leather-bound folio.

"The waiter will be with you in a moment to take your order."

"Fancy," Cassandra said when the woman left. "Are we celebrating a special occasion?"

"You could say so." Leaning forward, he took her hand. "I have good news for you. Actually, excellent news."

Her mind immediately went to Roni and her mother's picture. "Did Roni find anything about my mother?"

Smiling, Onegus nodded.

"Wow, that was fast. What did he find out?"

"He didn't have to search. He knew right away who your mother was." He leaned even closer. "Roni recognized her as his grandmother, who supposedly drowned thirty-seven years ago."

The energy swirling under the surface of Cassandra's skin spiked, zapping Onegus's hand.

He didn't pull it back.

No wonder Roni had looked familiar and that they'd immediately clicked. They were related.

Except, Cassandra had a hard time accepting such an extraordinary coincidence. She wasn't a religious person who believed that the hand of God or fate guided people's destinies.

"I assume that Roni's grandmother's body was never found."

"It wasn't."

"Maybe my mother just looks a lot like her? I admit that even that is freaky, but to jump all the way to believing that they are the same person is too much."

"I thought that you would say that." Onegus let go of her hand and pulled out his phone. "I don't want to bog you down with the details, but Roni discovered that his grandmother must be an immortal a couple of years ago when he found three driver's licenses with her picture, under three different names. The last one was from twelve years ago."

He handed her his phone. "Take a look."

It was her mother, or someone who looked exactly like her. "That still doesn't prove that she's my mother." She handed him the phone back. "Counterfeiters might have gotten hold of Roni's grandmother's original driver's license and used it to produce new fake ones for other people."

Onegus arched a brow. "Using the same picture? If they did it for other people, they would have put different pictures in them. One reason to keep the picture but change the information is to provide the same person with several identifications for different purposes, none of them legal. But then the documents would all be issued around the same time, not nearly thirty years apart. The other reason to keep the same photograph, and the only one that applies here, is if someone needs to hide the fact that she's not aging."

ONEGUS

*T*heir conversation was interrupted by the waiter arriving to take their order.

Impatient to continue, Cassandra ordered the lunch special without checking what was included in it, and Onegus did the same.

"Would you like something to drink besides the wine?" the server asked.

"Diet coke, please," Cassandra said.

"Water for me."

As Onegus waited for the guy to finish writing up their order, he wondered why Cassandra was trying so hard to refute the findings. Perhaps she didn't like Roni? The kid was a tough nut, and it took time to get to know him and realize that hiding under the prickly exterior was a decent person. So yeah, he had an inflated ego, but he was entitled to it. Roni was one of the best hackers in the country and an incredible asset to the clan.

"You might be right," Cassandra conceded. "But I still think that Roni should run my mother's picture through the facial recognition software. It might pick up on details that were not visible to the naked eye and find differences."

"Why are you fighting it, love? Is it because of Roni? He's not that bad once you get to know him."

Her eyes widened. "Don't be ridiculous. I like Roni a lot. I'm just playing devil's advocate. My mother's mental state is fragile. Unless I'm absolutely sure it's true, I don't want to confront her with this."

"It's true. But if you insist, I'll ask Roni to confirm by running her picture through the program and comparing it to the other three he has. I think he also has some old family albums with his grandmother's pictures." Onegus refilled their wine glasses. "By the way, his grandmother's driver's licenses were how he found out that he was a Dormant. We needed to test a new facial recognition software that we had developed in-house. The idea was to flag up precisely these kinds of instances as a way to identify immortals. Back then, Roni worked for the government, and he had access to the database. We approached him, and he agreed to do it behind his bosses' backs. Imagine his surprise when the software flagged his own grandmother."

Cassandra rubbed her temples between her thumb and forefinger. "I would love to hear the rest of the story someday, but right now, I'm trying to figure out how to break it to my mother."

"She might know." Onegus lifted his phone. "While we think it through, I'll text Roni and ask him to double-check." He typed up the message and sent it. "The fact that she bothered replacing her driver's license every so often, and doing it under a different name each time, indicates that she's aware she's not aging."

"When was the last one issued?"

"Twelve years ago."

"And what was the name on it?"

"Linda Graver."

"Twelve years ago, my mother still had her driver's license, and it was under her name—Geraldine Beaumont."

"Are you sure? Did you see it or just assume?"

Cassandra hesitated. "I don't remember."

"She also might have had more than one license."

As his phone pinged with an incoming message, they both tensed.

"It's from Roni." He opened the message and read it. "Done it already. It's her."

Cassandra's breath left her in a whoosh. "What do I do now? Do I take the rest of the day off and go talk to my mother?" She shook her head. "If I show up at home in the middle of the day, she'll get anxious, which makes her even loonier than usual. I need to do it when she's calm."

"Do you want me to be there with you?"

"That would be immensely helpful. She might not believe me, and you can provide the proof. Maybe having Roni there as well would be even better."

"I have an idea, but it will have to wait for after Kian's birthday. I just can't take any more time off until it's over."

"Good. I need time to wrap my mind around this as well." She emptied her wine glass. "So, what's your plan?"

He refilled her glass and then his own. "Geraldine and Martha made arrangements to meet for lunch on Thursday, right?"

"Yes."

"I can talk with my mother and work out a change of plans. Instead of them meeting in the city, I'll pick you up from work and Geraldine from home and bring you to my house in the village. I'll invite Roni and Sylvia to come as well, and we will show her the different driver's licenses as well as Roni's family photos. I can even ask the clan therapist to be there in case Geraldine freaks out."

"Can we do it on Friday instead? I'm so behind on work that I feel like I'm drowning. I know that it sounds inconsequential in the face of such a discovery, but I'd rather have the entire afternoon off to be with my mother, and I won't be able to do that on Thursday."

Onegus had a feeling that Cassandra wanted to buy herself more time, which was fine. There was no reason to rush.

"I'll talk with my mother and ask her to call Geraldine about changing their plans."

40

ELEANOR

"Stop pacing." Peter shot Eleanor an annoyed glance. "You're giving me a headache. Better yet, take a break and go to the gym. You look like you have excess energy to burn."

"Thanks. I'll see you in an hour."

He waved her off.

Jin and Mey were in the cell with Emmett, Arwel supervising inside the room, and Alfie from across the corridor. At first, the Guardian had just leaned against the wall, but as the lesson had stretched from an hour into two, Eleanor had taken pity on him and brought him a chair to sit on.

Emmett's cell was too small for four people, let alone five or six. That was why she wasn't in there either.

It was also too exposed because of the damn surveillance camera, and Eleanor didn't know what to do about it.

"Where are you going?" Alfie asked as she stopped by his chair.

"The gym. My pacing annoys Peter, so I'll do it on a treadmill."

"I don't know why Emmett needs four Guardians," he said quietly. "He's not going to fight his way out of here with those cuffs on."

The door to Emmett's cell had been left partially open, but since she could barely hear what was being said inside, keeping their voices low should be enough to prevent Emmett from hearing their conversation.

Eleanor leaned against the wall next to Alfie's chair and crossed her arms over her chest. "I'm here for one reason only, but I can't do my job with the damn camera in there watching me. I'm not like Carol, who didn't mind being watched. I just can't do it."

"Yeah." The Guardian's lips twisted. "Peter bit my head off for disabling the recording on Saturday."

"You didn't disable it."

"I couldn't hear you or see you. I relied on you turning the lights on as a signal that you needed me. It wasn't safe."

She huffed out a breath. "Emmett is not going to hurt me. The Clan Mother compelled him not to harm any of her clan members, and like it or not, I am a member."

Had she given Emmett a reason to think that she wasn't a bona fide member? If she had, he could use it as a loophole in the goddess's compulsion. She'd told him that some still viewed her as an outsider and didn't trust her, but she'd also told him about being a Guardian in training. That was a sure sign of membership, and he couldn't twist it into a loophole.

It was black and white. Only clan members could serve in the Guardian force.

Besides, she had relatives in the clan. Ella and Parker were her niece and nephew.

"The problem is that Peter is not convinced that Annani's compulsion worked on Emmett." Alfie rose to his feet and leaned against the wall next to her. "He might have just pretended to be under her influence. The guy is an incredible actor."

That was true.

They'd gotten pretty close since she'd started guarding him, and Eleanor was a good judge of character. But even though she had a healthy bullshit radar and knew who she was dealing with, sometimes she couldn't tell whether Emmett was being genuine or putting on an act.

"Even if Peter is right, I still need privacy, and if I'm willing to assume the risk, Peter should let me."

"It's not that simple." Alfie crossed his arms over his chest. "What if he uses you as a hostage?" The Guardian lowered his voice to a whisper. "All he needs to do is hold you in front of him as a shield and put his cuffed wrist against your throat. He would be able to just walk out of here because none of us would risk your life to detain him."

"If he wanted to do that, he's had plenty of opportunities. I've spent enough time alone with him."

"Maybe it didn't occur to him?"

"Yeah, no. Emmett has probably thought of a hundred other things that didn't occur to us. He's smart." She shook her head. "If I don't find a solution to this problem, I'm going to kidnap him myself, so I can have my way with him."

Alfie snorted a laugh. "For someone who makes such a big deal about being seen having sex, you are certainly not shy about it."

"There is a difference. I'm not shy, but I'm also not an exhibitionist. I don't want to do it, but maybe I should call Kian after all and go over Peter's head. Do you think he'll hate me for it?"

Alfie shrugged. "I don't know him that well. He might."

"That's a problem. We are sharing a house." Eleanor pushed away from the wall. "I'm going to the gym to think."

41

ONEGUS

"*H*ello, Onegus," Martha answered the phone after letting it ring for almost a minute. "I didn't hear the ring. I'm shopping with Belinda, and it's so noisy here."

She was an immortal with an immortal's hearing. She should have heard the phone.

"Can you talk? I need to ask you for a favor."

"Anytime. What can I do for you?"

That was the thing about his mother. He could always depend on her help.

"We've confirmed that Geraldine is an immortal."

His mother let out an audible breath. "I'm glad the picture worked. Did Roni find her in the database?"

"Actually, he recognized her as his long-lost grandmother, who we knew was an immortal even before his induction. That's how we knew he was a Dormant. Anyway, Cassandra and I were debating what's the best way to break the news to Geraldine, given her fragile mental state. We decided that a meeting with Roni would be best. He can show her the evidence, like her old driver's licenses spanning thirty years and yet sporting the same face, and he also has old family photos of her."

"That sounds like a good plan. What do you need me for?"

"We want to ease Geraldine into it. You've already made plans with her to meet for lunch on Thursday. If you could call her and postpone it to Friday, we can pick her and Cassandra up under the pretext of lunch, and take them to my house in the village, where Roni and Sylvia will be waiting. I can bring takeout or ask Connor to make something."

There was a moment of silence and then a sigh. "Why do you need me there? I have nothing to contribute."

"You are our cover."

"Forgive me for saying it, but it's a silly plan. I'll meet Geraldine for lunch on

Thursday, and then you can invite her for lunch or dinner on Friday and take her to the village to meet Roni."

That sounded suspicious. Did his mother want time alone with Geraldine for some reason?

Maybe she wanted to pump her for information about Cassandra, thinking that she could manipulate Geraldine into revealing dirt on her daughter.

Sneaky and underhanded, but clever. If he were in Martha's shoes, he would have done the same thing.

"Do you plan on tricking poor Geraldine into telling you Cassandra's secrets?"

Martha huffed. "What gave you that absurd idea? I just want a nice lunch in town. There is a new restaurant I haven't been to before that I want to try. I've seen enough of the village."

He gave her the benefit of the doubt. "Fine. But I want you there on Friday as well. Cassandra and Geraldine are our family now, and this meeting is an important step that you should be part of."

"Then it's official. Cassandra is your mate."

"You don't sound happy."

"I am happy provided that she's the one. You met her less than two weeks ago."

"She's the one. Can I count on you to be there on Friday?"

"Just tell me when and send someone to pick me up."

She sounded as excited about coming over on Friday as a human making a dentist appointment.

"Thank you. I will make all the arrangements."

"One more thing that you should consider, Onegus. As you've said, Geraldine's mind is fragile. After you bring her to the village, how are you going to guarantee her silence? If she's an immortal, you can't thrall her."

"I can ask Kalugal to compel her. He's proved that he can compel immortals with ease."

"Geraldine has memory issues. She might forget the compulsion."

"Compulsion works on the subconscious mind. And if she forgets, all the better. Besides, who is going to believe her? Everyone she knows is aware of her problem."

"True. Well, I see that you have everything covered."

"Not yet. I want you to dig deep and find your softer side for Geraldine. She will need your support on Friday, not your criticism and sarcasm."

Martha huffed. "Of course I will be supportive. Stop making me out to be a monster."

He might have overdone it. "I don't think of you as a monster. I love you, and that includes your assertiveness and your can-do attitude. If I didn't love those qualities, I wouldn't have chosen a woman with a similar character. Cassandra also has a problem with stepping on people's toes, and it's for the same reasons you do. She's demanding and unapologetic."

Martha chuckled. "That's a nice way to call both of us a bitch, but I don't mind. I'd rather be called a bitch than a pushover, and I also prefer an assertive daughter-in-law to a softie that would let you walk all over her. You need a strong woman."

42

EMMETT

*A*fter Jin and Mey left, Emmett lay on the bed with his arms crossed under his head and closed his eyes.

He'd been cooperative, teaching the girls basic words and phrases that had to do with travel and moving, but he doubted they'd retained anything. The Kra-ell language was too foreign, in sound, structure, and different forms of address for them to absorb in a few days.

The sisters had recorded the phrases he'd taught them on their devices, Mey on her tablet and Jin on her phone, and both had promised to practice before tomorrow's lesson.

He already had Mey wrapped around his finger, but Jin was a tougher nut. Soon, he'd get her too. His charm, as well as his patience with her slow progress, were eroding her resistance and suspiciousness.

Not that Emmett had any concrete plans for them in mind, but the more people he had on his side, the better. When the time came for Kian to decide whether it was safe to allow him into their community, they might be helpful.

Once he was admitted to the clan, he would start accumulating disciples. Not for any harmful activity, of course. He wasn't about to start a revolution. But people, humans as well as immortals, could all benefit from guidance, from a renewed sense of purpose, from being shown the path to fulfillment, and they were willing to pay a lot for it, either with money or with favors.

Good thing that he was such an amazing salesman. They would be eating from the palm of his hand.

Emmett wasn't sure what he would do with that power either, but it was always better to have it than not. Any advantage over others was worth putting effort into.

"Tired?" Eleanor sauntered into the cell with an uncharacteristic swagger. The woman was confident, but she wasn't a showoff.

"Exhausted." He licked his lips, letting her know precisely what she could do about it.

She sat on the bed next to him. "Your wish might come true sooner than later."

Her smug expression intrigued him, and he narrowed his eyes at her. "What did you do?"

"I talked to Kian. Well, not exactly. I exchanged texts with him, but that's semantics."

"About what?"

"Our privacy problem. He offered a solution that Peter hates, but I love. We are switching cells. You are moving into the suite, and Peter is moving in here."

That got his attention. "What about you, Alfie, and Jay?"

Some of her smugness evaporated. "When I'm with you and we retire to the bedroom, one of them will be in the living room. That's the best I was able to get us. There is a camera in the suite's bedroom, but it's going to be deactivated. With the door closed, we will have privacy."

That was the best news Emmett could have hoped for. Wrapping his arms around Eleanor, he lifted her and draped her over his body. "You are a miracle worker." He kissed her long and hard.

When she came up for air, Eleanor shook her head. "We are not in the bedroom suite yet. The guys watching the feed saw all this." She pushed out of his arms.

"I don't mind."

On the contrary, he wanted them to witness his enthusiasm and believe that he had feelings for Eleanor. It wasn't a lie, but it was a slight exaggeration. He liked her a lot, but he wouldn't hesitate to use her if it gained him an advantage.

Hell, he wouldn't hesitate even if he loved her. There was no reason not to mix business with pleasure.

"When is the switch happening?"

"Right now. The Odus are too busy to come and change bedding and clean the floors, and whatever else needs cleaning, so I volunteered to do that." She motioned for him to get up. "You're going to help, of course. Start by taking the bedding off in here, and I'll do that in the suite. I'll take it to the laundry and come back to vacuum and scrub and all that jazz."

It had been ages since he had done any housework. In the Kra-ell compound, it had been the humans' job. When he'd escaped, it had taken him some time to accumulate enough money to open Safe Haven, and there was a very short period of time that he'd been forced to learn the basics, but he'd soon discovered that he could pay people to do that. He'd never washed a cup again.

"Why are you looking at the bed as if it's an unidentified alien artifact?"

"It has been a very long time since I've changed bedding. I'm not sure I remember how to do it."

Eleanor snorted. "Nice try, buddy. You are not getting out of doing your share of work by claiming ignorance. You're a smart guy. Figure it out."

His lips twitched with amusement. He loved it that Eleanor didn't take any shit from him or anyone else. She was assertive without being aggressive, or rather not overly aggressive. There was some of it in her, but not enough to turn him off.

43

CASSANDRA

*I*t had been one hell of a day, and Cassandra's energy had reached explosive levels.

Nothing overly aggravating had happened at the office, but the combination of anxiety and stress was enough to produce the equivalent of an energy bomb.

First, it had been the news about her mother, which was good, but she was terrified of how it would affect Geraldine. What if it sent her careening into a psychotic episode? She couldn't be hospitalized because she wasn't human, and with her mind not working right, she might forget to hide her super strength and super hearing and whatever other superpowers she possessed.

Then there was the work Cassandra had fallen behind on and had no idea how to catch up. It would take several all-nighters, but she didn't have them. Tomorrow, she was supposed to attend Kian's birthday, and Onegus would expect her to stay the night.

Hell, she wanted to spend the night with him.

That energy needed to go somewhere, and the most pleasant way to discharge it was with multiple orgasms, especially since she didn't have to fear hurting Onegus in the process. The guy was indestructible.

Today, she would work until she couldn't keep her eyes open, and tomorrow, she would try to motivate her snowflakes into helping her out. Maybe she'd promise them bonuses. She wouldn't mind paying them from her own pocket just to have the work done on time, so she could take half of Friday off.

But right now, she needed a quick discharge before she doubled down in her home office.

Geraldine wasn't home yet, so she wouldn't get mad about Cassandra destroying more household items. Grabbing a few glasses from the top shelf that her mother could barely reach, she walked outside to the backyard and arranged them on the wicker patio table.

She needed the practice, and she could always order more glasses online. That's why she never bought expensive drinkware for the house. Eventually, either unintentionally or intentionally, anything made from glass or clay would become a target for her energy.

Taking a few steps back, she focused her eyes on the first glass and imagined it shattering.

Nothing happened.

Perhaps she needed to get herself worked up?

It didn't take much. All she had to do was think about the amount of work waiting for her upstairs and the reason why it was waiting. The lazy employees in her department who barely put in one straight hour of work, spending the rest of the time surfing the net and socializing.

A glass exploded, but it wasn't the one she'd aimed for.

Well, it was better than nothing, and she felt a little calmer. One more, and she would be good to go.

What else was she mad about? Oh, yeah, the gas prices that had doubled over the last month. What the freaking hell was with that?

Another glass exploded, and Cassandra let out a breath.

"What are you doing?" Her mother walked out onto the patio. "Are you destroying the glasses I hid on the top shelf?"

"Oops." Cassandra smiled sheepishly. "I'll order new ones. I needed to discharge, and I thought you didn't care about these." She waved a hand at the remaining two glasses.

Geraldine shook her head. "They were the last matching set. I put all the mismatched ones on the bottom shelf."

"I'm sorry." Cassandra wrapped her arm around her mother's shoulders. "I'll buy several new sets, and I'll also get some cheap mason jars to destroy."

Geraldine let out a breath. "What got you upset?"

"Too much work. I love spending time with Onegus, but the result is that I'm falling behind on work. I was planning to pull a couple of all-nighters, but then he invited me to another family thing that's happening tomorrow, and I just don't know how I'm going to make it."

"Is there anything I can do to help?"

"Yes. You can bring me coffee upstairs every hour or so."

"I can do that."

"Thanks, Mom." Cassandra kissed her cheek.

"Anytime, sweetie."

As Geraldine walked back inside, Cassandra collected the remaining two glasses and carried them to the kitchen.

She still found it hard to believe that Geraldine was an immortal. Trying to think back, she didn't remember her mother ever getting sick or hurt. She'd gotten depressed from time to time, but it had never lasted long.

On the other hand, she'd never caught Geraldine doing things she wasn't supposed to be able to do. When there was something heavy to lift, she always asked for Cassandra's help, and when they went on a walk around the neighborhood, her mother usually got tired much sooner than Cassandra and asked to go back.

Was she that good of an actress?

And did she remember the need to act when she couldn't remember the name of the street they lived on?

·

44

BOWEN

*B*owen couldn't wait for Leon and Anastasia to leave. Sitting on the living room couch and pretending to read, both he and Margaret were impatiently watching the hallway leading to the couple's bedroom, waiting for them to be done getting ready for their date.

Preoccupied with thoughts of finally making love to Margaret tonight, he'd barely functioned throughout the day. Thankfully, nothing requiring his full attention had happened, and it had been mostly about escorting guests to the village and keeping them safe on their outings.

Somewhere in the back of his head, a bothersome thought floated. It was too peaceful lately. What was Navuh up to?

Lokan's intel claimed that Navuh was busy shoring up his organization, financially and technologically. Trying to bring the Brotherhood into the twenty-first century, he'd also made changes to his breeding program. Instead of using mindless brutes to impregnate his Dormants, he was now using brainy males in the hopes of producing smarter offspring.

Still, Bowen found it hard to believe that Navuh had forgotten about the clan or that he no longer hated Annani with a rabid passion.

Perhaps Areana had something to do with it?

Now that she knew that her sister had survived and was being targeted by Navuh, Areana might have made a conscious effort to mellow out her mate, having him turn his focus to more productive endeavors.

One could hope.

Nevertheless vigilance, as always, was paramount, and Bowen shouldn't have allowed himself to get distracted by carnal thoughts while on the job.

Finally, the door opened, and the two walked into the living room wearing outfits appropriate for their outing. Leon was in all black, and so was Anastasia, except her outfit looked as if it was painted on her curvy body.

It bordered on indecent, but when in Rome and all that.

When Bowen had asked Leon to find an excuse for him and Anastasia to be gone for the evening, he hadn't expected the guy to take her to Brundar's club. Apparently, Anastasia was curious and wanted to check it out.

She hadn't been bashful about it either, telling Margaret where she and Leon were going and why. Someone was giving a bondage demonstration at the club's members-only section, and according to Callie, that was the most vanilla one and therefore appropriate for newbies like Anastasia and Leon.

"We won't be back until after midnight." Leon winked at him. "Don't wait up for us."

"Bye." Anastasia waved, giggling as she pranced out the front door.

"She's so gutsy," Margaret said as the door closed behind them. "I would never have had the courage to visit a place like that, not even if I was into that sort of thing, which I'm not."

"Neither am I." Bowen offered her a hand up and pulled her into his arms. "I need a few minutes to set things up. In the meantime, do you want to relax with a nice bubble bath?"

She hesitated for a long moment. "How about you join me in the bathtub? It's big enough for two."

That was an invitation he couldn't refuse. "I have an idea. I'll bring the candles and the wine to the bathroom."

Margaret's eyes sparkled. "I would love that."

He kissed her softly, his hands roving over her back. "You'd better go before I change my mind and bend you over the dining room table."

She giggled. "That sounds intriguing."

"Oh yeah?" He squeezed her bottom. "Not today, sweetheart. I have a romantic evening planned for us."

"I love you." She kissed him once more before ducking into the bedroom.

For a long moment, he stared at the door she'd closed behind her. He was still getting used to hearing her say that she loved him. Was still getting used to saying that he loved her back.

Bowen sighed. He knew as much about romance as Margaret knew about computers. Heck, probably less.

He'd bought expensive wine, stopped at the chocolatier for her favorite chocolates, and got scented candles in different colors. The salesgirl assured him that they were the perfect thing for creating a romantic mood.

He loaded a tray with everything he'd bought, added two wine glasses, and headed to the bedroom.

It didn't seem like enough to him, and he wondered what else he could have gotten. Perhaps shrimp cocktail?

Did Margaret even like shrimp?

With a sigh, he opened the door with his elbow and walked inside. Hopefully, what he had was romantic enough, and if it wasn't, taking a bath together should do it.

It was a first for him.

Margaret had left the door to the bathroom ajar, and as he pushed it open and entered with the tray, she peered at him with a seductive smile. Her body was hidden under a mountain of bubbles, with only the tips of her breasts and her knees sticking out.

His eyes lingered on her nipples and then drifted to her knees. The one she'd had the surgery on was marred with a scar, which he hoped would disappear after her transition.

Hopefully, everything would be okay. He couldn't even bring himself to think about the alternative.

Seeing where his eyes had gone, Margaret lowered her knees, so they were hidden under the bubbles. "The scar will fade. It already looks much better."

"It will disappear completely after your transition." Bowen put the tray on the vanity top. "I'll be back in a moment."

"Where are you going?"

"To get something to put the tray on."

"The side table from the living room will do nicely. The small one on the left of the couch."

"Right."

So far, he hadn't been doing a great job of being romantic. He shouldn't have looked at the scar, and he should have thought about the table before bringing in the tray.

Hopefully, Margaret's expectations weren't too great. Well, on the romance front. He was better than good where it mattered most, and mind-blowing sex should go a long way toward smoothing out his blunders.

Lifting the table, he suddenly realized what was missing.

Music.

45

MARGARET

As soft music drifted from the bedroom, Margaret smiled. Bowen was trying so hard to make this a memorable night for her, and she loved him for it.

It didn't matter if he got it right or not, the intent and effort were what counted.

"Close your eyes," he told her from the door.

"Okay." She did as he asked, listening to what he was doing.

First, she heard him put the table down, then a lighter's hiss, and as the smell of aromatic candles reached her nose, he flicked the overhead light off. A moment later, she heard Bowen's clothes hitting the floor.

Scooting sideways, she made room for him, but he didn't enter the tub. Instead, she heard him uncork the wine and pour it into the glasses.

Then he slipped into the bathtub behind her and nuzzled her neck. "You can open your eyes now."

She turned her head to look at him. "I wanted to see you strip for me."

The look on his face was so sweetly confused that she had to kiss him, just a small peck to the underside of his chin because that was all she could reach. "I was just teasing."

"Oh." He let out a breath and handed her a wine glass. "To us, my lovely."

She clinked it to his and then drank it slowly. "I don't know much about wine, but this tastes really good."

"Only the best for my mate." He kissed the side of her neck.

His mate. She was still getting used to that term. Not his girlfriend, not his fiancée, his mate. It sounded like so much more.

It *was* so much more.

When she was done with the wine, he took the glass from her hand and put it together with his on the side table. "Chocolate?"

"Yes, please."

She would rather have skipped the wine and chocolates and got down to business, but it seemed so important to Bowen to make it romantic for her that she didn't have the heart to tell him.

As he held the little delight to her lips, his erection twitched against her rear. "Someone is excited." She licked his fingers as she took the chocolate into her mouth.

His arms circled her to cup her breasts, and he nuzzled her neck. "The sight of these beauties, buoyant and pink, peeking at me from beneath the bubbles is driving me nuts."

She turned around, which dislodged his hands, but she was now splayed over his muscular chest and within reach of his lips. "Kiss me."

He smiled. "Impatient?"

"Yes."

"Then why didn't you say so?" He rolled his hips as he took her lips.

His hands roving over her back and bottom, he kissed her for as long as she had air in her lungs.

When he let go of her mouth, she sucked in a breath. His eyes, which had already been glowing before, turned as bright as two flashlights, and although his mouth was closed, she was sure his fangs had elongated.

"Take me to bed, big guy."

"With pleasure."

He lifted with her in his arms and grabbed a towel. Somehow, he managed to get both of them semi-dry before her back hit the mattress.

"You are so beautiful," Bowen said, his eyes roving over her naked body.

His fingers trailing lazily up her belly, he feathered them over the undersides of her breasts and then circled her nipples with his thumbs.

The barely-there touch was driving her mad, and as she arched up into it, Bowen wrapped his arms around her and lifted her, so her breast was aligned with his mouth.

He licked at her nipple before taking it gently between his lips and sucking.

Nothing about it was hurried or impatient. Despite weeks of waiting for this moment, Bowen was taking his time with her, going so slow that she wanted to urge him to hurry up because she could wait no longer.

They'd pleasured each other the day before and the day before that, everything save for the full joining, so maybe that was why he could be so patient.

His hands roving over her skin, setting her body on fire, Bowen teased and pleasured her nipples one at a time. When her moans turned to desperate mewls, he laid her down, and then he was over her, his erection probing her entrance.

But he was not in a hurry to join them yet.

Instead, his fingers brushed over the bundle of nerves at the apex of her thighs, and she nearly came just from the slight touch.

He chuckled against her neck. "Patience, my lovely. Let me get you ready."

"I am ready," she said as she arched up. "I need you inside me."

Ignoring her plea, Bowen continued his fingers' erotic dance over the top of her sex until she exploded all over them.

He joined them then, and the feel of him inside her triggered another climax.

"Bowen." She wrapped her arms around him and held on tight.

His head dropped down to her neck, his breathing labored as he waited for her to adjust. He stretched her, but it wasn't painful, just full and wonderful.

When she bucked up, he groaned and started moving, slowly at first, and then with more urgency. Pleasure coalesced, and as his movements became frenzied, she turned her head to the side and offered him her neck.

Even as mindless with passion as he seemed, Bowen didn't strike with his fangs until he'd prepared the spot with several quick swipes of his tongue. A hiss preceded his fangs penetrating her skin, and like before, there was very little pain. Then the first drops of venom entered her system, and there was a whole lot of pleasure.

46

ONEGUS

$\mathcal{I}$t was after midnight when Yamanu walked into Onegus's office. "The party supply people are taken care of."

"Are they gone?"

"Drove away ten minutes ago. Do you want to see what they did?"

"I'm sure the ballroom looks magnificent. They did a great job decorating the place for the wedding, so I'm sure they've done just as good of a job for the birthday."

Yamanu shrugged. "It's a bit much if you ask me. Kian might not be happy with the huge centerpieces they put on every table. It looks like a damn bar mitzvah."

Onegus chuckled. "Have you ever been to one?"

"No, but I've seen pictures in Mey's family album. The venue was decorated very similarly to what the party people did for Kian's birthday. Perhaps they even reused decorations from other parties."

"I'll take a look later. Worst case scenario, we'll get rid of the centerpieces."

That seemed to appease the Guardian. "Anything else you need me for?"

"Is the sweep complete?"

With so many humans working in the keep, it was necessary to check the place for listening devices they might have planted. It was unlikely, but Onegus shared Kian's opinion that it was better to be safe.

Yamanu nodded. "The guys found no bugs. The room is clean."

"Then we are done for tonight. Go home and rest. Tomorrow you have a bigger gig."

After the birthday celebration, Yamanu would have to take care of Gerard's crew again, which was just as large as the decorators but required a more delicate approach. Yamanu had thralled them after the wedding on Saturday, and not enough time had passed for him to unleash the full power of his thrall on them again without causing damage.

"Not a problem, Chief." Yamanu smiled, his white teeth gleaming against his dark skin. "Are you going to see Cassandra again tonight?"

Damn the clan's rumor mill. Had all the members been informed that he and Cassandra had spent the previous night together?

"She's still human. She needs to sleep."

"Right." Yamanu passed a hand over his jaw. "I'd better head home. Mey is waiting up for me."

"How are her and Jin's lessons with Emmett going?"

"Good. Mey is making progress, but Jin is ready to quit. The girl has no aptitude for languages."

"How are they getting along with Emmett?"

"I didn't hear any complaints other than how impossibly difficult the Kra-ell language is, so I assume they get along just fine."

"I'm glad." Onegus pushed to his feet. "I'll walk you out. I'm going to get some sleep as well."

They parted at the elevators, with Yamanu taking one up to the parking garage and Onegus going down to the dungeon level. He wasn't in the mood to spend the night in the apartment upstairs, where he had to share a bedroom with a couple of Guardians. If Cassandra was still awake and wanted to talk, he preferred to have privacy while conversing with her.

Exiting at the dungeon level, Onegus headed to the cell he and Cassandra had spent the night in. He opened the door with his phone, got inside, and looked at the rumpled bed.

The Odus cleaned the place once a week, but not this time. They were too busy catering to the guests, providing shuttle services from the downtown building to the village and back and running endless other errands. It was good that they only needed an hour or so of recharging every couple of days and could work nonstop the rest of the time.

It would be even better if they had many more of them.

Life would be easier on so many levels. Instead of the Chinese crews building the village, it could have been done in half the time by a team of cyborgs. Another team could be in charge of cleaning, and yet another in charge of gardening, or decorating for parties, or whatever else needed to be done by nonmembers.

Using humans for those tasks made Onegus nervous, but unless they somehow figured out how to build an army of Odus, there was no way around it.

Well, Navuh had found a solution, but it was abhorrent. His breeding program produced enough people to populate his army as well as take care of all those tasks, and yet he still kidnapped and enslaved humans to perform them.

Onegus removed his jacket, hung it on the back of a chair, then continued with the rest of his clothes until he stood naked in front of the bed and deliberated what to do first—take a shower or text Cassandra to see if she was still awake.

The shower could wait, but Cassandra might not.

Taking the phone with him, he lay down on the bed and typed up a text. *If you're awake, call me.*

He didn't have to wait long. "I was waiting for your call. Have you just finished working?"

"Yeah. What about you? What are you still doing awake?"

"Working. I fell behind so badly that I had a mild panic attack earlier today. A couple of tumblers suffered the consequences."

"I assume that you are not talking about drinking two glasses of wine."

She laughed. "I wish that would do the trick. I blew them up."

"Were you able to focus your energy?"

She sighed. "I tried, but nothing worked until I got myself riled. It's like the energy builds up in response to several triggers, but the fuse is made from anger. To discharge, I need to light it up."

Onegus smirked even though she couldn't see him. "You have another method of defusing spikes in energy. A much more pleasant one."

She chuckled. "I know. But you are not here. Are you still in your office?"

"I'm down in our cell. I wanted privacy in case you wanted to talk dirty to me."

"I'd rather do than talk."

"Just say the words, and I'll come to get you. We can spend the night here."

"I'm starting to think of that cell as our shag pad, quite fondly, I might add." She sighed. "I wish I could, but if I want to attend Kian's birthday and then take half of Friday off, I have to work tonight to catch up."

"That's a shame." Onegus palmed his straining erection. "I guess we'll have to settle for talking dirty."

"Sorry, but I don't have time even for that. By the way, are you sending Connor to pick me up tomorrow? Or am I allowed to drive myself to the party?"

"I want you to stay the night and I'll drive you home in the morning."

"Is it because you want to spend as much time with me as possible, or is it because I'm still not allowed to know where the party is held?"

"You know where it is, more or less."

"Yeah, I do. It's not in the building where we spent our first night together, but it's close by."

"Then why did you ask?"

"I just wanted to hear you say that you want to spend as much time with me as possible."

"I love you, and according to your definition, love is the need to be with my beloved at all times."

"Oh yeah? What's your definition of love?"

"You."

47

KIAN

*I*t was still dark outside when Kian woke up. He didn't know what had caused his eyes to pop open, but he was fully alert as if his subconscious had detected a threat. One of the bedroom windows was open to let fresh air in, but the screen was in place and seemed intact, so nothing could have entered the house from there, but perhaps some animal had been foolish enough to pass under it.

Usually, the only wildlife that dared to make the village their home were birds and small critters. Larger animals were kept away by the fence surrounding the finished areas and the scent of those inhabiting them. They knew better than to trespass on a den of dangerous predators.

Next to him, Syssi was sleeping soundly on her side, a wedge pregnancy pillow propping her belly.

Less than two weeks to go.

It filled him with excitement as well as dread. Birth complications were rare for immortal mothers, but since the babies were born human, the statistics of stillborn and other problems were the same as in the human population, and that kept him awake at night.

He'd grown attached to the daughter growing in Syssi's belly, but it was more intellectual than emotional. It was different for Syssi. She talked to Allegra as if the child could hear her and understand what her mother was saying. If anything happened to her, it would devastate Syssi.

"Everything is going to be okay," he murmured more to himself than her and then kissed her warm cheek.

"I know." She smiled and opened her eyes. "Why are you awake? Are you excited about your birthday party tonight?"

Kian nodded, but his excitement had nothing to do with his birthday and everything to do with the surprise he had in store for Syssi.

"Are you worried?" She lifted her hand and cupped his cheek.

He put his hand over hers and then turned his face to kiss her palm. "You should go back to sleep."

Yawning, she adjusted the pillow under her belly. "So should you. Stop worrying and get some sleep. It's still dark outside." She yawned again and closed her eyes.

A moment later, the familiar sound of her soft little snores brought a smile to his face.

He had a wonderful surprise for her, which he'd been barely able to keep a secret. Normally, Syssi didn't like surprises, but she was going to love this one.

Her parents were arriving later today, a week and a half earlier than planned.

Kian had been talking to either Anita or Adam almost daily, applying steady pressure to ensure they weren't going to flake out like they had repeatedly done throughout Syssi's life. No matter what excuse they could have come up with, he'd planned to do whatever it took to have them arrive on time for their second grandchild's birth.

Everything was set for them to leave the Congo in a week and a half's time, but then two days ago, Anita had shocked him with a message that she was ready to leave as soon as he could arrange their transportation.

Apparently, the young doctor sent by the charity organization to fill in for her while she was gone had turned out to be a great find, and after supervising his work for less than a week, Anita had decided that it was safe to leave the clinic in his capable hands.

From there, it had been a mad rush to arrange everything.

Kalugal had volunteered his comfortable jet, Charlie flew it to the Congo to pick them up, and they were scheduled to land on the clan's airstrip a little after four in the afternoon.

From there, Charlie would drive them to the downtown building, where Annani had graciously offered to host them in the spare room of her and Alena's apartment, so they could freshen up and change clothes before the party.

Kian couldn't wait to see Syssi's reaction when she saw her parents walk into the ballroom. Hopefully, it wouldn't be too much of a shock.

Suddenly worried, he considered checking with Bridget if that was advisable. It was too early to call the doctor, but he would do so as soon as it was acceptable.

Surprising Syssi had seemed like a great idea, but if it was risky in any shape or form, he would just tell her beforehand to prepare her.

The problem was that her parents loved the idea of surprising her, and they would be disappointed. But that was a secondary concern. Syssi would just have to pretend that she didn't know.

To her credit, Anita was excited about being there for Syssi and welcoming her granddaughter into the world, and she'd even offered to stay an entire month and help Syssi adjust to motherhood.

Hopefully, they would all get along.

The last time Kian had seen Syssi's parents had been at Andrew and Nathalie's wedding, and that time the visit had been short. Andrew and Nathalie had taken Phoenix to visit her grandparents when she was two, but he and Syssi hadn't been able to join them because, as usual, he couldn't leave work.

This time, Anita and Adam were not only coming for an entire month, but they were also staying with him and Syssi at the house.

As the familiar scent of his favorite waffles reached Kian's nostrils, he wondered whether that was what had woken him up.

Was Okidu preparing a special birthday treat for him?

He hadn't made his famous waffles in a long while.

The question was whether he should wait for Syssi to wake up and eat breakfast with her or get up and have some now and more later.

His rumbling stomach decided for him.

After all, it was his birthday, and he was entitled to two servings.

48

MARGARET

*M*argaret woke up feeling so wonderful that she decided to forgo the brace and walk to the bathroom without it.

So far, Bowen had bitten her three times. Was that enough to speed up her healing?

As usual, he had woken long before her and was probably sitting in the living room and reading the news on his phone.

When the trip to the bathroom had gone just fine, she contemplated forgoing the brace for the rest of the day. Her knee didn't hurt, her leg muscles didn't feel stiff, and she was almost as good as new.

Perhaps she could even go to Kian's birthday without the brace. That reminded her that Anastasia wanted to visit the hair salon again and had offered to take her along, but Margaret wasn't in the mood for a trip to the city.

She'd rather go to the café and hang out with her daughter. Wendy and Wonder were closing the place early today because of the birthday celebration, so if she wanted to go, she should make it there before lunch.

The village was so lovely, the people so friendly, and they made her feel at home.

When Margaret opened the door and walked into the living room without the brace, the three immortals seated at the kitchen counter turned to her at once.

For a moment, Bowen's eyes lingered on her smiling face, and then his gaze drifted to her legs. "You forgot to put the brace on, love. Do you want me to get it for you?"

"No need." She walked up to him and kissed his cheek. "I don't think I need it anymore. My knee doesn't hurt." She glanced at Anastasia. "What's your plan for today? Do you still want to go to the hair salon?"

"I changed my mind. Leon and Bowen are on duty at the downtown building, and we don't have cars yet. With everyone so busy, there is no one to take us."

"Leon and I can share a ride and leave you one of the cars," Bowen offered.

"That's fine." Margaret sat on the barstool next to Bowen. "I'm not in the mood for a trip to the city. Ana and I can do each other's hair."

Anastasia's eyes brightened. "I have an idea. Let's invite Wendy and Stella as well. We can paint each other's toenails, do each other's makeup, and gossip a storm."

Leon chuckled. "Suddenly, I'm very happy about having to go to work."

Bowen leaned over, lifted Margaret off her stool, and planted her in his lap. "I'm not. I want to stay home with my mate." He kissed her softly. "You look beautiful."

"Thank you. You're not too bad yourself."

"I'm serious. You haven't started to transition yet, and already you look ten years younger."

Chuckling, Anastasia got up and tugged on Leon's hand. "Come on. Let's give the lovebirds some time alone."

"You're not bothering me," Bowen said without taking his eyes off Margaret.

They didn't bother her either. The world didn't exist when she was looking into Bowen's warm brown eyes.

"Would you like some coffee?" Bowen asked.

"I would love some."

Lifting her gently, he put her back on the other stool and reached for the coffee carafe.

"I can make toast and eggs for you," Ana offered.

The three of them probably had breakfast a couple of hours ago.

"It's okay. I'm not hungry yet."

Bowen added sugar and cream to her coffee, stirred it with a spoon, and handed it to her. "You need to eat, love." He leaned closer. "You will need your strength tonight." He waggled his brows. "For dancing at Kian's birthday, of course." He added a wink.

Margaret had a feeling that last night had been an unleashing, and that from now on, she would be getting much less sleep, which was perfectly fine with her.

Ana smirked knowingly, but thankfully she kept her curiosity at bay while they chitchatted over coffee.

Her restraint lasted only until the guys left for work. The moment the door closed behind them, she lifted her mug, crossed her legs, and issued a command, "Talk. I want all the dirty details."

"Dream on, girl. I'm not sharing."

Ana rolled her eyes. "At least tell me if it was worth waiting so long for."

"It was, and then some."

"I'm glad." Ana put her mug on the counter and lifted her phone. "I'm calling Stella. Do you want to call Wendy?"

"Wendy is at the café. I thought we could walk over there."

Ana glanced at Margaret's knee. "The café is twenty minutes away. I don't think it's smart for you to walk such a distance the day you took off your brace. If you want to go, you should put it back on."

Margaret shook her head. "I'll be careful, and if I get fatigued, we can rest on the way." She smiled. "I'm done with being broken. I feel healthy and whole, and that's what I want Wendy to see."

49

KIAN

*A*s Kian walked into the living room, the first thing he noticed was the large gift box on the coffee table. The thing was about three feet on each side and was wrapped in gift paper with balloons and 'happy birthday' printed on it. A wide red ribbon crisscrossed the box, tied at the top in an elaborate bow.

Had Syssi somehow snuck it into the house during the night?

Or what was more likely, she'd given the gift to Okidu for safekeeping, instructing him to put it on the coffee table before Kian woke up so it would be waiting for him in the morning.

What could it be, though?

A vase? A statue?

He should wait for her to wake up before opening it, but he was curious. Perhaps he could give it a light shake and figure out what was inside by its weight and the sound it made.

Putting a hand on each side, he tried to lift it, but the hefty weight took him by surprise. The box was either full of bricks or books. Had Syssi bought him an encyclopedia?

That didn't make sense. Why would anyone want that when all the information was available online and didn't take any space?

Maybe it was gold or silver?

That was more like his sensible wife.

Precious metals were a good investment. She might have decided to convert some of their cash reserves into easily tradable tangible assets. In times of economic instability, those were a safe bet.

Except, the box wasn't heavy enough to be filled with either. Given the weight and size, the content was most likely books.

"Happy birthday, master." Okidu appeared beside him, an apron printed with the American flag protecting the suit underneath.

"Thank you." Kian put the box back on the table. "Do you know what's in it?"

"Of course, master. It is your birthday present."

Kian rolled his eyes. "That's obvious from the wrapping. But do you know what's inside the box?"

Okidu smiled. "Why don't you open it and see for yourself, master?"

Apparently, his butler didn't know what was in the box either. Otherwise, he would have responded to a direct question with a direct answer.

Unless Syssi had forbidden it. Kian was Okidu's master, but the butler had been instructed to obey her wishes as well, and Kian hadn't programmed him with a contingency for when Syssi's wishes contradicted his.

"I don't want to open it before Syssi wakes up. She would want to be here to see my reaction to her gift."

"The gift is not from Mistress Syssi, master." Okidu bowed. "It is from me, and you are welcome to open it at your convenience."

Kian couldn't have been more surprised if the Odu had informed him that he had fallen in love and was about to get married. In all the years they'd been together, which was Kian's entire two thousand years on the planet, Okidu had never gotten him a birthday present.

"Thank you." He frowned at the box. "Should I open it now?"

The Odu smiled so brightly and so humanly that the hair on Kian's nape started to tingle as if he was in the presence of a potentially hostile immortal male.

Shaking his head, he pulled on the red bow, unraveling the ribbon, and then tore away the wrapping. Inside was an old-fashioned chest made from wood, complete with a lid and a lock.

"Here is the key, master." Okidu handed it to him.

"Thank you."

Kian inserted the key into the lock, twisted it, and lifted the lid.

What he could see on top were four leather-bound tomes, and it seemed like there were many more stacked under them.

Apparently, Okidu had gotten him an encyclopedia.

Maybe it was a first edition, which would be a valuable collector's item. Or perhaps the encyclopedia had belonged to a famous human who'd made notations in the margins. Books like that were also collector's items and even more valuable than first editions.

"Is this an encyclopedia?"

Okidu bowed. "No, master. Those are journals."

"Like accounting ledgers?"

That would make a very odd gift, but then what could he expect from an Odu? Perhaps Okidu had seen someone gifting his boss ledgers on one of the British television shows he watched.

"No, master. Why don't you open one and see for yourself?"

It was the second time Okidu had uttered the same phrase. It seemed very important to him that Kian saw what was inside the journals.

Curious, he lifted one heavy tome and flipped it open. The first page bore a title, beautifully handwritten, but not in a language Kian could read.

Was that the gods' script?

He flipped to the next page. The same tight script, just in a smaller font, filled the entire page, and the next, and after that, there were pages upon pages of schematic drawings, marked with unfamiliar symbols.

"What language is that?"

Okidu seemed surprised by the question. "The old tongue, master. Are you unfamiliar with it?"

"I can't read it." Kian could understand some of the spoken language, but he'd never learned to read or write it. Only his mother and William could do that, and only William could decipher the schematics and instructions in the gods' tablet, which kind of resembled what was in the journal. Since much of the information contained in the tablet was still a mystery, and William hadn't been able to unlock many of its secrets, there was no guarantee that he would understand what Okidu had worked so hard on either.

William's progress with the tablet had been slow and it depended on feedback from the human world. It was a symbiotic relationship, in which the clan would release some of the gods' knowledge that William had been able to unlock, and the many human minds making use of it would develop it further. In turn, their progress helped William to decipher more of the tablet's information.

"Are all of them the same?" Kian closed the journal.

"No, master. They are a continuation of each other. One journal could not contain all the information. This is only the first of thirty-six journals."

Kian lifted his eyes from the tome in his hand. "What am I looking at?"

50

SYSSI

*A*s Syssi opened the bedroom door, she heard Okidu say, "This is only the first of thirty-six journals."

Curious, she lumbered toward the living room, entering it as Kian asked, "What am I looking at?"

A leather-bound book in hand, there was a deep frown on his face. Whatever was in it, Kian wasn't happy about it.

"Me, master." Okidu bowed and then turned to Syssi. "Good morning, mistress. I was just showing Master Kian his birthday present. Would you like to see it as well?"

The torn gift wrapping strewn about the coffee table must have covered the wooden chest sitting on top of it. Was it filled with thirty-six journals? And what had Okidu meant by saying that they contained him?

Whatever the answer was, it could wait for after she had her first cup of coffee.

"I would love to." Syssi padded to the couch. "But if you don't mind, I need coffee first. My brain doesn't start working until I have a couple of cups in me."

"Of course, mistress. Coming right up." Okidu bowed and scurried to the kitchen.

Shaking off his stupor, Kian rushed to help her lower herself to the couch. It wasn't an easy feat these days, and she gladly accepted his hand.

A moment later, Okidu returned with two mugs and put them down on the coffee table next to the wooden chest. Standing on its other side, the Odu seemed to be bursting with excitement, waiting impatiently for her to signal that she was ready to be shown Kian's birthday present.

He looked like a kid who had done something he was proud of and couldn't wait for his parents to see it. Whoever thought that the Odus weren't sentient was gravely mistaken. There was no way all of that was just mimicry.

After taking several sips, she put the mug down and smiled. "Please, sit down, Okidu. Craning my neck to look at you is not comfortable, and you can tell me all about the present from a seated position."

Gingerly, he sat on the edge of the armchair and put his hands on his thighs.

"What do you mean it's you?" Kian asked.

Okidu cast her a worried look. "Would you like your second cup now, mistress?"

It took her a moment to realize why he was offering her a second cup of coffee while the first one was still mostly full. She'd told him that she needed at least two for her mind to start working.

"It was just an expression, Okidu. I'm fully capable of understanding your explanation."

He dipped his head. "My mistake, mistress. I still find it difficult to understand humor."

Next to her, Kian was bristling with impatience. "What's in the journals, Okidu. Is it your memoir?"

That would explain why there were thirty-six hefty tomes in the chest. The Odu had lived for thousands of years. Well, lived maybe wasn't the right term.

Or was it?

"Oh no, master. Although it is a wonderful idea for my next project. These journals contain the schematics and instructions for building me."

Kian and Syssi exchanged twin shocked looks, and then Kian asked, "How did you obtain the information? According to my mother, when you and your brothers were found, you had no prior memories. They had been wiped."

"Yes, master. That is true. But it would seem that some information was encrypted, hidden in my operational memory protocol."

"How did you access it?" Syssi asked.

"When I drowned during Mistress Carol's rescue, and my system rebooted, I began to experience things differently. I think that our creator meant for my brothers and me to evolve, but only after several millennia had passed."

"You think?" Kian groused. "You either know, or you don't."

Hedging or speculating was not something the Odus' cyborg brain should be capable of. Except, Okidu was not the same as he used to be.

"My apologies, master." Okidu dipped his head. "That was the old me. The new me can make assumptions and consider possibilities. As I said, I have evolved."

"I knew it." Syssi crossed her arms over her belly. "Okidu is sentient, and he has been for a while."

Kian lifted his hand. "You don't need to apologize, Okidu, but I would like to understand what's going on. Do you have memories of your creators? A message from them about what to do with the schematics that have been hidden in your operational memory?"

"I do not, master. I only know that I awoke with something extra after the reboot. For lack of a better definition, I would say that I started to feel. I was glad to be awake, and I was glad to see that Mistress Carol was safe. I ran standard diagnostics to make sure that everything was functioning properly, and that was when I became aware of the hidden cache in my memory. I debated what to do with the knowledge. Since your birthday was coming up, I decided that it would be a perfect gift for you, master." He grinned broadly. "On several occasions, I heard you express a wish to have more Odus. Now you can make as many of us as you want."

A shiver slithered down Syssi's spine. She still remembered her vision of the Krall, or rather the Kra-ell, loading Odus into shuttles, sending them out to space like scrap metal. Had that really happened?

Perhaps they had been sending them to other planets to save them? Like Okidu and his brothers?

Was that how they had landed on Earth?

Maybe there were more of them scattered all over the universe?

Deep down, she knew that was just wishful thinking, but the alternative was too tragic to consider. Syssi didn't want to believe that the Odus had been ejected into space, especially since they had the potential to become sentient. But even with her limited technical knowledge, she knew that the small shuttles she'd seen in her vision could not have been capable of interstellar travel. Larger ships were needed for that.

But what if the shuttles had delivered the Odus to a large vessel orbiting the Kra-ell planet?

That was possible.

Blowing out a breath, she glanced at Kian. Her mate didn't look happy or excited about the incredible gift he'd been given. He looked worried and contemplative.

Okidu's expression, on the other hand, was expectant, and since Kian didn't seem like he had anything positive to say, it was up to her.

"That's an incredible gift, Okidu." Syssi glanced at the box. "Are all these journals handwritten?"

"Yes, mistress. Every free moment I had was spent writing down the information. And with the festivities coming up, I had even less time than usual. I had to employ Onidu's help."

51

KIAN

*K*ian's head snapped to Okidu. "How? Does he have the same information stored in his memory?"

"I assume that all seven of us have it. But only I and Onidu went through a reboot, so only our memories were released."

Kian's hackles rose. "How did Onidu reboot?"

Okidu smiled. "The same way I did, master. He drowned."

Not by accident, that was for sure. Onidu hadn't been anywhere near a beach since Okidu's reboot, and the pool in their backyard wasn't so deep that the Odu couldn't climb up out of it, or even jump.

"How did he drown?"

"In the bathtub, master."

That wasn't possible either. Onidu wouldn't have obeyed an order from Okidu to remain submerged until his system went offline. And since they were both equally strong, Kian doubted Okidu had forcefully held Onidu under the water.

Given Syssi's doubting expression, the same thing had occurred to her. "How did you manage to make Onidu do that?" she asked.

"I tricked him, mistress. I told him that it was an order from Mistress Amanda."

Damn. Okidu was not only fully sentient, but he'd also turned into a conniving trickster, and that was incredibly dangerous given his capabilities.

"You could have damaged Onidu," Kian said. "What guarantees did you have that he would reboot?"

The Odu tilted his head as if he didn't understand the question. "I rebooted after being submerged in water for over an hour. Since Onidu and I are identical, I had no reason to think that the results wouldn't be the same for him."

Syssi might not realize it, but an Odu thinking and doing things independently was incredibly dangerous.

The Odus were practically indestructible, and nothing short of blasting them to pieces or ejecting them into space could decommission them. As long as they were contained by their programming to obey orders and stay within well-defined boundaries, the risk was somewhat mitigated. But it seemed that those boundaries had been stretched or possibly blasted open by Okidu's reboot, and the same was true for Onidu.

He needed to find out precisely how far the two Odus could push those boundaries.

"Isn't lying about a command from Mistress Amanda a breach of your protocol?"

"Not at all, master. The protocol demands that I obey your commands, except if they are to harm another clan member. Onidu is not a clan member. He is a possession."

Syssi cringed. "We never thought of you as possessions, Okidu, not even before you became sentient. You are like a family member."

The Odu dipped his head. "Thank you, mistress. But even if Onidu could be considered a clan member, I wasn't harming him. I was improving him. I knew that he would reboot and gain the same new awareness that I did. It is a good thing, not a harmful thing."

"Perhaps." Kian pinned Okidu with a hard stare. "You shouldn't have done it without obtaining Amanda's or my permission first."

The Odu looked perplexed. "If I asked for permission, the birthday surprise would have been ruined."

They were in deep trouble.

An indestructible cyborg with the logic of a child was a disaster waiting to happen. The only solution Kian could think of was to teach Okidu mature logic in the shortest time possible.

Except, the same thing had probably occurred to the scientists who'd built the Odus, who had been much more familiar with their capabilities and limitations than he was. And yet, the only solution they'd found was to ban the technology and destroy those already built.

That wasn't an option Kian would ever consider. Sentient or not, Okidu was part of the family.

Reaching for her coffee, Syssi winced, but as Kian jumped to help her, she waved him off. "I'm fine." She turned to Okidu. "Instead of writing everything by hand, couldn't you have just downloaded the information into your laptop?"

"The technologies are not compatible, mistress. Handwriting that was stored in my brain was the only solution, and that was why I needed Onidu's help. We divided the work between us."

And now there were two of them to worry about. "Why did you hide your newfound sentience?" Kian asked.

"I don't know what you mean, master. Other than the birthday surprise, I didn't hide anything from you or the mistress."

Syssi put a hand on Kian's arm. "I don't think Okidu realizes how much he's changed, or what sentience even means. His growth progressed slowly. We've watched him become more sentient, but we dismissed it as mimicry or our familiarity with him. We didn't acknowledge what we were witnessing."

"True." Kian raked his fingers through his hair. He needed the advice of someone smarter than him. "We should get William on this."

Syssi shook her head. "I think we should call your mother first. Perhaps your sisters as well. And after we decide what to do, you will need to inform the council. This is not a trivial matter."

Okidu watched the exchange with worry on his face. "Did I do something wrong, master? You don't look happy with your birthday gift."

Kian forced a smile. "I'm very happy, Okidu. Having the blueprints to build more Odus is a priceless gift, but we need to figure out some details before we can proceed."

Security wasn't the only issue.

If Okidu and Onidu were sentient, was it right to keep them as unpaid servants?

Did that turn him and Amanda into slave owners?

The other Odus had not become sentient yet, so they could still be deemed as possessions. But was it right to keep them from evolving now that they knew how?

He wondered why the water worked to reboot them while other injuries hadn't. It might have been a clever way for their previous owner to give immortals a hint. The Odus had been found in a desert, and it might not have been a coincidence. By sending them there, the owner mitigated the risk of accidental drowning. Only someone who was familiar with stasis and the method to awaken from it would have thought to use it to reboot the Odus.

Kian shook his head. As usual, he'd let his imagination run wild. It didn't matter why or how. His concern should be what to do next. The Odus had to be contained because they were dangerous, but what right did the clan have to keep them from being free?

Kian pushed to his feet and offered Syssi a hand up. "I'm going to my office to call my mother. Do you want to talk to her as well?"

Nodding, she accepted his hand, her solemn expression telling him she understood that from now on, they couldn't talk freely in front of Okidu.

Especially when it concerned him.

52

SYSSI

$\mathcal{K}$ ian closed his home office door and helped Syssi to the couch. "You seem troubled." She patted the spot next to her. "Talk to me."

"Let me put it this way." He sat down and wrapped his arm around her shoulders. "Imagine a toddler in charge of a nuclear warhead. That's what we are dealing with. Sentience means free will, which means that all the safety measures that were programmed into the Odus can be potentially overridden. Okidu could be turned into an indestructible killing machine."

Syssi let out a breath. "I'm starting to understand why the technology was banned. Still, if the Odus are like children, we can teach them right from wrong. In fact, you and your family have been teaching them for thousands of years. And since the best way to do that is by personal example, I believe that they will turn out just fine. You and your family are good people. The best."

"You are sweet, my Syssi." He kissed the top of her head. "And I really hope that you are right."

"Me too. I have to admit that I'm a little scared, but I won't let fear dictate my actions. That's how humanity gets in trouble over and over again. A group of people is signaled as a threat for whatever reason, and suddenly they are the enemy whether the threat is real or imagined."

Kian nodded. "Fear is a powerful motivator." He put his hand on her belly. "As is the need to protect loved ones."

She put her hand over his. "Just because Okidu and Onidu are powerful, doesn't make them a threat to us. As long as their programming is good, and by that I mean the sum of their experiences, there is no reason they will turn bad. We just need to make sure that no one corrupts them."

Kian huffed out a breath. "Imagine what Kalugal would do if he got his hands on the blueprints to make more Odus."

It felt uncomfortable to admit that it was scary to think of Kalugal being able to build an army of Odus, but Syssi agreed with Kian.

Kalugal appeared charming and mellow, but Jacki had let slip that her mate had very big ambitions. With an army of Odus at his disposal, those ambitions, whatever they were, could materialize.

She squeezed Kian's hand. "We need to hide those journals, and we need to tell Okidu and Onidu to keep it a secret. They are as valuable as the gods' tablet, and they should be locked in a safe together with it."

He nodded. "You know what I hope for?"

"What?"

"That the materials and technology needed to make the Odus haven't been discovered yet, taking the ability to build more of them out of our hands. It's so tempting to make more of them. We could have a butler for each household—gardeners, builders, manufacturing workers—the possibilities are endless. But I bet the gods thought the same thing when they created them and then regretted it."

"We don't know what happened. There might have been an anti-Odu movement. After all, the gods had created humanity and then nearly destroyed it because the human population grew too fast, and they deemed it a threat. They might have developed a similar sentiment toward the Odus, who were also their creations."

"Good point." Kian pulled out his phone and then put it down. "I think we should summon a family meeting, but not here. I don't want the Odus to overhear us."

"We can go to the downtown building and have the meeting at your mother's apartment."

"And then come back here to get ready for the party?"

"Why bother? We can take what we need with us and change over there."

Kian shook his head. "I don't want to do it there either. My mother's Odus are not sentient yet, but Okidu proved that he's cunning enough to get them to reveal what they hear."

"Yeah, you're right. How about the keep? We can use your old office for the meeting."

"I have a better idea." He lifted his phone again. "Our old penthouse is available. The renters moved out last month, and we didn't find new ones yet."

"Why didn't you mention it before? We could have stayed there the entire week. Amanda and Dalhu could have stayed with us." She sighed. "I would've loved it. I have such fond memories of that place."

"It didn't occur to me until now. I think of the two penthouses as money-producing assets, not as vacation spots. Otherwise, I wouldn't have rented them out."

Syssi pouted. "You are renting out the house in Hawaii, and that's a vacation spot."

"That's different. The house in Hawaii is rented out by the week. We can go there anytime we want."

It was true that they could, but Kian would just keep on working from his home office there, so what was the point? For him to have a real vacation, she needed to take him somewhere he couldn't work. Like the North Pole.

Sighing, she leaned on his arm. "How did we get from discussing the end of the world via Odus to a vacation in Hawaii?"

"The penthouse." Kian kissed her temple. "I need to call my mother first and depending on when it's convenient for her to have the meeting, set the time. After that, I'll call Sari and invite her and David. Can you call Amanda?"

"Sure." Syssi glanced at the time displayed on his watch. "But I suggest that we eat breakfast before calling anyone. If I call Amanda this early in the morning, she will hang up on me."

"I doubt that very much." He rose to his feet and offered her both his hands to help her up. "But breakfast is certainly a priority. I can't have my wife and daughter go hungry."

When they entered the kitchen, Okidu rushed over with two plates. "Is Master still displeased?"

Poor guy. He'd worked for months to prepare the gift for Kian. He must be so disappointed.

Syssi nudged Kian's side and rolled her eyes in Okidu's direction.

"I'm not displeased," Kian said. "I'm very appreciative and grateful for all the hard work that you've put into these journals. I just want to make sure that such an important asset doesn't fall into the wrong hands. That's why I need you and Onidu to keep it a secret and not to mention it in front of anyone other than the Clan mother, my sisters and their mates, and, of course, Syssi and me."

The Odu bowed his head. "As you wish, master."

53

CASSANDRA

*C*assandra threw another outfit on the armchair in her studio and took off the one she had on.

Onegus had said that the party wouldn't be as formal as the wedding, but it was still a clan-wide affair, and his supercilious mother would be there. She needed to look party-appropriate, sophisticated and elegant, but not over-dressed.

A tough combination to pull off.

Heck, if Martha could wear a dress that exposed her back nearly to the top of her shapely ass for the wedding, then Cassandra could wear something sexy for Kian's birthday.

The silver-hued gray dress she'd worn to her first dinner date with Onegus fit the bill. It showcased her long legs and slim body without making her look trashy, and most importantly, she hadn't bought it second-hand.

It wasn't by any famous designer, but at least it hadn't come from anyone's closet.

Amanda had been very nice about the whole second-hand dress thing, not making a big deal out of it. She'd treated Cassandra with respect and had even introduced her to Syssi and Kian, which was an even bigger deal than she'd realized at the time.

Much bigger.

Kian and Amanda were demigods, and Kian was the head of the clan in America.

Damn, knowing who they were made meeting them again so much more intimidating.

Would the gray dress be good enough?

It had to be.

She didn't have time to get a new dress or even go through her entire wardrobe searching for something that she might have forgotten.

It was almost seven in the morning, and Cassandra had to get ready for work. If she was to have any chance of getting out of the office on time to get ready for the party, she needed to start her day earlier than usual.

Attending the birthday was even more exciting than the wedding, and not just because she knew now that she would be partying with demigods and immortals.

Cassandra was excited about meeting Roni again. Now that they knew they were related, they had so much to talk about.

He was her nephew, the son of the half-sister that she hadn't known she had.

What kind of a woman was she?

Did they resemble each other?

Her sister was white, so that would make them look different, but maybe they were both slim and tall?

Was her sister pretty?

How old was she? To be Roni's mother, she must be at least in her forties, but that wasn't much older than Cassandra.

Thankfully, the date of Geraldine's staged drowning precluded the possibility that she'd gotten pregnant with Cassandra beforehand. An illicit affair that resulted in a child that could not possibly be her husband's could have been a strong motivator for running away, and Cassandra was grateful that she hadn't been the reason for her mother abandoning her other daughter.

Did Geraldine remember her?

Why had she abandoned Roni's mother?

Heck, she'd forgotten to ask Onegus if Roni's mother had siblings. Maybe she had another half-sister or brother.

It was so strange to suddenly have a family. It had always been just her mother and her.

Had Geraldine staged her own drowning? Or did it have anything to do with her head injury and subsequent memory loss?

Letting out a breath, Cassandra sat on top of the pile of outfits and put her head in her hands. How was she going to break the news to her mother?

In a way, it was even more shocking than the immortality. If she were in her mother's shoes, that would have devastated her. The only thing worse than forgetting you had a child was losing them.

One thing at the time. That's how she would have to do it. The news about the immortality would come first, and if that went well, she would tell her about her other daughter.

Except, Onegus had already invited Roni and Sylvia for the big reveal, so that wasn't going to work. Perhaps she should get some mild relaxants and slip them into her mother's drink?

Right.

Pushing up to her feet, Cassandra reached for one of her work outfits, a narrow form-fitting black skirt, and a bright yellow silk blouse. She needed a little sunshine right now to brighten her mood. Besides, yellow looked good on her.

She chuckled at the double entendre. She wasn't a coward, and cowardice definitely didn't look good on her. She was a walking, talking powerhouse in every sense of the word.

It was interesting that Roni had chosen a mate with similar power. Sylvia's talent seemed to work a little differently, but both of them could mess up electronics. Except Sylvia did it like a well-trained surgeon, disabling them only long enough for whatever was needed, and then they went back to working perfectly fine. Cassandra's so-called talent was more like a sledge-hammer. Once she released her power into a device, it was good only for scrap metal.

Perhaps she needed to practice on that instead of blowing up glass containers and ceramic objects.

Cassandra had a drawer full of old cellphones that she'd saved for no good reason. She wasn't a hoarder, but she got attached to her old phones and couldn't just throw them away.

She could practice on them. But first, they needed to be charged.

Or maybe not?

Yeah, they did. She didn't need to practice blowing them up, just causing them to temporarily malfunction.

Cassandra snorted. Perhaps after melting the insides of a hundred phones, she would learn to control the damage the way Sylvia did.

54

ONEGUS

"$\mathcal{G}$ood morning, Clan Mother." Onegus bowed his head.
"Good morning, Onegus." Annani smiled as she floated by him into the elevator. Alena, Sari, and David entered next.

When Kian had called earlier to arrange a family meeting at the old penthouse, he'd been cryptic about the reason, saying only that it was a brainstorming session and that he required a Guardian escort for the Clan Mother.

Onegus had posted Guardians along the underground tunnel between the buildings, and also inside the penthouse-level dedicated elevator.

The other penthouse, the one that used to be Amanda's, was rented out to a human businessman and his family, so it wasn't possible to close access to the entire level for the rest of the day without inconveniencing the humans.

Annani's apartment in the building across the street would have been a much better meeting place, or even the keep's underground. Perhaps Kian's reason for holding the meeting in the penthouse was the surprise he had arranged for Syssi.

Her parents were arriving later today, and she wasn't supposed to find out about it until she saw them at the party. The plan was for them to freshen up from their trip in Annani and Alena's apartment, and after the party, go to the village with Syssi and Kian and stay at their house for an entire month.

Kian's office in the keep's underground could have worked, but it was a little dreary and somewhat cramped.

What Onegus couldn't help wondering about, though, was why he'd been invited and Kalugal had not.

Since the accord had been signed and Kalugal's loyalty to the clan had been assured by Annani's compulsion, he and Jacki had been included in all family get-togethers. His exclusion this time around suggested that something big was going on.

"Are Kian and Syssi already at the penthouse?" Annani asked as they stepped out of the elevator at the clan's private parking garage.

"They are," Sari said. "I just got a text from Syssi that she and Kian are there, and Amanda and Dalhu are on their way up."

The large golf cart they'd acquired to shuttle guests between the buildings was waiting for them a few steps away, and as they reached it, Onegus offered the Clan Mother his hand to help her up.

"Thank you." Annani sat down, adjusted the skirt of her floor-length gown, and motioned for Alena to sit next to her. "We should all remember not to mention Anita and Adam's arrival." She turned to Sari and David, who'd climbed up behind her and Alena. "It will be so nice to see them again. I have not had the pleasure since Andrew and Nathalie's wedding."

Onegus remembered them well. Anita was very much like Bridget—a no-nonsense, pragmatic woman who was a little intimidating. Adam was her exact opposite—a charming, smiling guy who knew how to put people at ease.

Syssi didn't resemble either of her parents. She was shy, soft-spoken, and one of the best people he knew. Andrew, on the other hand, was a perfect combination of Adam and Anita. Like his father, he was outgoing and knew how to be charming when he wanted to. But he was also pragmatic and a bit of a know-it-all like his mother.

"Did Kian tell you what this was about?" Sari asked her mother.

"Only that it concerned the Odus."

"The Odus?" Sari asked. "What could be so important about them to call an emergency meeting the morning before the party? I thought that it would be about the safety protocol for the event."

"I do not know, my child." Annani cast her a warm smile. "We will learn soon enough."

Onegus frowned.

What did Kian plan to do with the Odus?

Did it have anything to do with the team leaving for China?

They had been supposed to depart the following Monday, but Mey and Jin's linguistic progress was slower than Kian had hoped for, and the mission had been postponed.

In the meantime, Turner's human crew was monitoring the Kra-ell's former compound, so there was no real rush. It wasn't as if the echoes in the walls would become fainter in a week or two. It was more important for Mey to understand what the walls could tell her.

It would have been helpful if they had a strong telepath who could have created a bridge between Mey's mind and Emmett's. The former Kra-ell could have translated what Mey learned from the echoes.

Perhaps they should check with Ella. She and Vivian could communicate mind to mind no matter the distance. So far, mother and daughter could only do that with each other, but Ella had been practicing communicating telepathically with others. If she was successful, she could be the key to the mission's success.

ANNANI

*A*nnani could barely contain her curiosity. Kian had asked her to come without her Odus, and when she had asked him to explain, he had said that he needed to consult the family about something concerning the Odus and would rather do that over breakfast at the penthouse.

Clearly, Kian did not want the Odus to be present at the consultation, but for what reason?

As their group reached the penthouse level, Onegus knocked on the door, and a moment later, Anandur opened the way.

"Good morning, Clan Mother." He dipped his head and then greeted the others.

"Thank you for coming." Kian motioned to the dining table that was set up for breakfast. Seeing her raised brow, he explained, "I ordered delivery. Anandur and Brundar set the table."

"I see." Annani sat on the chair he pulled out for her. "Can you please pour me a cup of coffee?"

"Of course." He lifted the thermal carafe and filled her cup.

When everyone was seated, Kian lifted a thick, leather-clad book off the sideboard and held it up for them to see. "This is one of thirty-six handwritten journals Okidu presented me with this morning." He put the journal back on the sideboard. "His birthday present to me."

"Did he write down the history of the clan?" Alena asked. "Because that should have been done a long time ago." She cast Annani an amused glance. "Mother and I embarked on the project a few years back, but we lasted only a few sessions."

It had bored Annani to tears. Very little of the history was actually exciting, and Annani would have been content to record only the highlights, but Alena insisted on going into detail and recording every little thing. "It was too big of a project, and it would have taken all of our time. We need a dedicated team of historians to do it justice."

Kian lifted his hand to stop Alena from retorting. "The journals aren't about the history of the clan. I wish they were. They contain blueprints for building an Odu."

"Impossible." Annani straightened in her chair. "When Khiann's father found the Odus, they had no memories prior to awakening in the desert. Whatever was there before had been wiped clean."

"Evidently, not everything was wiped. I have to assume that whoever sent the seven Odus to Earth did that to preserve the banned technology. They hid it inside the Odus' operational protocol. We've never dared to probe them, but even if we had, we wouldn't have found the hidden information."

"How did it surface?" David asked.

"After Okidu's drowning accident during Carol's rescue, he rebooted, and the reboot released those memories, as well as extra capabilities that Okidu didn't possess before. We knew that his artificial intelligence was capable of learning, but that capability was limited, or as I suspect now, deliberately throttled. The reboot loosened some of that throttling, allowing Okidu to evolve."

"In what way?" Amanda asked.

"In a very dangerous way. Okidu now has free will, as evidenced by him working on my gift for many months in secret and tricking Onidu into rebooting so that he too was 'awake' and could help him out. That makes him sentient, which also presents a moral dilemma."

Amanda gasped. "My Onidu is sentient as well? I noticed that he was acting differently, but I dismissed it as my imagination or maybe an improved mimicry of human emotions."

"That was what I thought too," Syssi said.

"The big question is what degree of autonomy Okidu has," Kian said. "Without strong safeguards, he and the others are like dangerous weapons in the hands of toddlers. And that's only part of the problem. If they are sentient beings, we have no right to own them."

"That's one hell of a conundrum." Anandur expressed what everyone seemed to be thinking.

Even Brundar nodded in agreement.

As all eyes turned to Annani, she debated what to tell them. She was not really worried about the Odus suddenly rebelling or demanding to be paid wages for their work. She was not worried about them going haywire either. But she could not in good conscience assure her family that it was impossible. She was not a programming expert. She just had thousands of years of experience dealing with the Odus.

"Mother?" Kian prompted. "We would appreciate your input."

"No matter how self-aware the Odus become, they cannot disobey their masters except for the overriding conditions I programmed them with. The first and most important one was not to harm any members of my clan even if ordered to do so by their masters. The others were small pet peeves of mine." She smiled at Kian. "They cannot use foul language even if you order them to do so."

5 6

KIAN

*A*manda chuckled. "We figured that one out a long time ago. I still remember my poor Onidu calling me from the lab after it had been ransacked by Doomers. He couldn't repeat the *compliments* they had written on the walls."

Under the table, Syssi put her hand on Kian's knee. "Perhaps that's how we can test whether their newfound freewill can override Annani's directive. Dictate a note to Okidu that includes foul language. If he can't force himself to write it, then he can't override the directive not to harm clan members either."

Kian put his hand over Syssi's and gave it a little squeeze. "That's a clever idea. I don't think he's developed enough sophistication to pretend that he can't write cuss words." He turned to his mother. "Did your directive include written foul language? Or just spoken?"

"I did not think to include writing. The prohibition is only on speech. But as you have pointed out, Okidu would probably not be able to make the distinction."

For now.

Kian wondered at what rate the Odus' revised programming allowed them to learn. Clearly, it was still limited. Otherwise, Okidu would have learned much more about human behavior than he had since his reboot.

"I will goad Onidu into cussing." Amanda crossed her arms over her chest. "Coming from me, the request won't sound suspicious. I made similar requests before." She snorted. "When we went to Hawaii on vacation, I had to force him to wear a pair of shorts and a Hawaiian shirt. Onidu wanted to wear his suit and tie even to the beach."

David said, "The incident you describe indicated the existence of sentience even then. Onidu showed a clear preference for wearing a suit. Unless the Clan Mother included a directive about wearing suits or not wearing casual clothing, it was his choice. I think the Odus had free will all along. It was limited by programming, and they had to obey commands, but they didn't need to be told how and when to do everything."

Kian was starting to get a headache. "Perhaps as a psychologist, you are better equipped to evaluate what we are facing with the new and improved Odus and can tell us whether they are dangerous or not." He pinched his forehead between his thumb and forefinger. "Help me out here, David. Do I need to start paying Okidu wages and giving him vacations? What's the morally right thing to do?"

David frowned. "I would need to give it some thought. I'm not an expert in the field of ethics." He rubbed a hand over his jaw. "The Odus are sophisticated machines that are also potentially dangerous weapons. Their base programming makes them subordinate to their masters, which is a built-in safety mechanism, provided the masters are responsible people and don't use them to do harm. Therefore, it is the masters' responsibility to keep them. They cannot be let loose and live independently."

Syssi looked from David to Kian. "Perhaps we should ask Okidu what he wants. What are his aspirations and his dreams, if he has any?" She turned to David. "Should we do that because we are his family? Or should you do that because you are the professional?"

Uncrossing her arms, Amanda leaned forward. "We need to be absolutely sure that Okidu and Onidu are safe. You and I are about to welcome new babies into our homes. If our Odus' emotional maturity is the equivalent of toddlers', that could be incredibly dangerous to our children. Toddlers get jealous of new siblings."

Again, all eyes turned to David, who'd suddenly been deemed an expert on Odu psychology.

He shook his head. "I'm not qualified to give such a guarantee. Perhaps William is the right guy for that."

Kian shifted to look at Onegus, who so far had just listened without voicing his opinion, but his pinched expression indicated that he was troubled. "What's on your mind, Onegus?"

"Are we going to use the blueprints to build more Odus? Because I can think of plenty of uses for them."

Kian shook his head. "We don't know how to deal with the two Odus who have suddenly become more than they were before. I'm not going to even think about building more until we are absolutely sure that we can control the ones we have. But given that their creators banned the technology and destroyed most of them, I'm not overly hopeful. We don't even have the tools to evaluate the potential risks."

"What if we build simplified versions?" Syssi suggested. "With the capabilities of the Odus before the reboot but without their humanoid appearance. We can make them look more like machines."

Amanda snorted. "Why? So, they won't see themselves as people? I don't think that's how it works. It's all in the brain. They can either think for themselves and evolve or depend entirely on what we program them to do. It doesn't matter what they look like."

"It matters to me." Syssi crossed her arms on top of her big belly. "I don't like talking about Okidu as if he has suddenly turned into a dangerous criminal just because he gained a little more sentience. I've always thought of him as part of the family and treated him accordingly."

"If he were human," David said, "that would have gone a long way toward making him loyal to the family. But who knows how his machine learning works?"

"William would know," Annani said. "And I know from experience. Between the two of us, we can figure this out. In my opinion, you are all panicking needlessly. We will conduct tests, William will go over the schematics, and David will perform the psychological evaluations."

It was a concrete and sensible course of action, but Kian wasn't sure it was enough. Then again, what Syssi had said was true as well. Okidu was part of the family, had been Kian's companion for his entire life, and he hadn't willfully done anything to justify their sudden apprehension.

He'd given them a valuable gift.

Kian felt wretched even thinking those thoughts about Okidu. He was acting like those superstitious humans who turned on neighbors they had known their entire lives just because someone had accused them of witchcraft or devil worship, or whatever else had evoked fear in their small brains.

He was supposed to be more evolved than that. Except, as an expectant father, he had a responsibility to protect his child and his mate from any and all danger.

"Where are the journals now?" Onegus asked.

"In our house in the village," Syssi asked.

"Where in the house? Are they well-hidden?"

Kian frowned. "We left them in the chest Okidu put them in, and he took it back to his room for safekeeping." He turned to Syssi. "I should go home and find a better hiding place for them. Those journals can't fall into the wrong hands."

57

ANNANI

"And whose hands would those be?" Annani asked.

She knew perfectly well who Kian was thinking about, and she did not like it. Many people had worked hard to bring about the accord, including her, and Kalugal and his men were slowly but surely becoming integrated into the clan.

Keeping Okidu's gift a secret from him would not last, and when Kalugal discovered that he had been excluded from the family discussion, it would create a rift between them.

Kian cast her a look that said, *are you joking?* "Kalugal, of course."

"Why would you fear the journals falling into your cousin's hands? What do you think he might do with them?"

Leaning back, Kian crossed his arms over his chest. "Kalugal has great ambitions. He would want to build an army of Odus and take over the world."

"That is his father's ambition. Not his."

Kian glared at her. "The fact that Kalugal is charming and sophisticated doesn't make him any less dangerous than Navuh. Probably more so because Kalugal is smarter. Besides, it's not only him that I'm worried about."

Annani arched a brow. "Who else?"

"The information contained in those journals is priceless. Humans would pay a king's ransom for it. It could tempt even one of ours to steal them and sell them to the highest bidder."

To give herself a moment to formulate her words, Annani reached for her cold coffee and took a small sip.

Anandur jumped to his feet. "Let me refill that for you with fresh coffee, Clan Mother." He reached with his long arm to the other side of the dining table, lifted the thermal carafe, and poured coffee into her cup.

"Thank you." Annani smiled and took another sip before putting her cup down. "The schematics should not become common knowledge, you are right about that. But Kalugal should be included in the discussion about what to do with them."

"Why should he? Do you think he shares everything he does with us? He keeps his business very close to his chest."

She had not considered that part of the equation. Everyone knew that Kalugal was working on something big, but only those closest to him knew what it was. If he was not sharing, Kian was not obligated to share either.

Still, she believed that Kalugal would one day approach them with his project.

The cooperation between him and the clan was new, and it was natural for him to be wary. But he and Kian were becoming closer, and she hoped that their friendship would make Kalugal trust Kian to back him up. On the other hand, the project he was working on might not be aligned with the clan's goals, and that could be the reason Kalugal was not sharing.

Families were as complicated as the individuals they were comprised of.

"You have a point, my son. But I do not suggest that you hand the journals to Kalugal. I only want him to be included in the discussion. Trust promotes trust, and mistrust promotes mistrust. If you hide it from him, he will quickly realize that something is going on because you do not have a poker face. That will create a rift between you." She sighed. "I know that he is not sharing with you what he is working on, but he does not keep it a secret that he has an important project he is busy with. It is almost common knowledge."

Thankfully, her son was a reasonable man, and he nodded. "There isn't much we can do now anyway. After the guests leave, we will have time to address the issue and conduct those tests and evaluations you suggested. That means that you will have to stay longer than you planned." He looked at David. "Would you be able to fly in for a couple of days?"

David smiled. "My schedule these days is flexible, but Sari's isn't." He took her hand and lifted it to his lips. "We are newlyweds. I'm not going to leave her behind and come alone."

"Right." Kian rapped his fingers on the table and looked at Annani. "How are we going to solve that problem?"

Annani laughed. "David does not need to be in the same room as Okidu. He can use teleconferencing. But if he prefers a more hands-on method, Sari can reboot Ojidu."

"No!" Kian, Syssi, and Amanda said at the same time.

Kian continued, "Until we find out whether Okidu and Onidu's new versions are an improvement or a problem, we are not rebooting any more of them." He pinned Annani with a hard stare. "I hope that you aren't thinking of rebooting yours."

"I would not dream of it." She leaned closer to Kian and patted his arm. "I do not want to cause you even more stress. After you are reassured that the Odus are not dangerous even in their enhanced form, I will definitely reboot my three Odus. Alena and Sari will have to decide about theirs."

58

SYSSI

*a*fter everyone aside from the brothers had left, Kian helped Syssi up from her chair. "I need to go home and hide those journals. I suggest that you stay here, rest, and put your feet up."

She looked down, or rather tried to. She hadn't seen her feet from a standing position in over three months. "Are my ankles swollen?"

"Just a little."

He was such a liar.

"I'm coming with you." She threaded her arm through his. "We can talk on the way, and I can help you find a good place to hide the journals."

Anandur opened the door for them. "I suggest under the bed."

She chuckled. "That's the worst place to hide things. It's where they'll look first." She leaned her head against Kian's arm. "Whoever *they* are. It's not so easy to abscond with thirty-six thick tomes, and we have surveillance cameras all over the village. How could anybody get away with stealing them?"

Brundar called up the elevator, and as the four of them got in, Kian leaned against the wall, getting in position for Syssi to lean against his chest. When she did, he wrapped his arms under her heavy belly.

"Following your logic, we should put those tomes in the entry pavilion as part of the exhibit." He nuzzled her neck.

He'd said it as a joke, but Syssi thought that it was a great idea. "That's where they belong. After all, the Odus and the technology to make them are both ancient relics. They belong in an archeological display."

"I agree," Anandur said. "We could put the journals in a glass enclosure next to Kalugal's artifacts, effectively hiding them in plain sight, and post guards on them twenty-four-seven."

"Speaking of Kalugal," Kian said as they stepped out of the elevator. "With all the commotion about the Odus, I forgot about the call I got from the contractor earlier. The last finishing touches on Kalugal's homes are done, and the crew is cleaning up. They will be ready for furniture delivery by Friday."

"Did you inform Kalugal?" Anandur asked.

"He knows. Richard is on site every day and keeps him updated."

When the four of them got into Kian's SUV, Anandur and Brundar sat up front, Syssi and Kian in the back.

Brundar looked at them over his shoulder. "Can Sylvia's talent fritz out an Odu?"

"I don't know," Kian said. "She never tried. Why do you ask?"

"I was thinking about ways to disarm the Odus if necessary. It doesn't have to be a lethal force, just something that's enough to cause them to reboot."

"You're onto something," Kian said. "It bothered me then and still does now that a simple drowning disabled Okidu. I know that he was without oxygen for a long time, but that shouldn't have caused a reboot. He could have just entered a sleep mode."

"It almost seems like he entered stasis," Anandur said. "Except, for us, water brings us out of stasis. It doesn't send us into it."

"But oxygen deprivation does." Kian drummed his fingers on his knee. "It occurs to me that they were either designed with that back door, or their owner added it later, hoping that immortals would figure it out."

Syssi sighed. "We are all guessing. The Odus are like a black box, and we have no idea what's inside. For all we know, Okidu might have the entire history of the gods and where they came from hidden somewhere in his brain."

"Maybe we should build one just so we can test how they work." Kian let out a breath. "The journals should be moved to William's lab. He needs to go over them and see if we even have the necessary materials. They are not going to fit inside the safe where the gods' tablet is kept, but his lab has plenty of surveillance and security in place."

"It also has a foot-thick door," Anandur said. "The entire place can be locked up like a safe. The problem is that William often stays there late and then forgets to lock up when he leaves. The Guardians on patrol check the door and lock it, but someone might get in between their rounds."

"The lab is peppered with surveillance cameras, and the system was designed by William, so the only one who might be able to hack it is Roni." Kian pulled out his phone. "It's time I told William about his new project. He's not going to like it."

Syssi looked up at him. "Why not? This should be a huge challenge for him. He loves those."

"He already has too many balls in the air as it is. He is also not going to like Guardians hanging around his lab. I trust William with any and all clan secrets, but he no longer works alone."

"Roni is trustworthy." Anandur looked at them through the rearview mirror. "His prickly attitude aside, the kid is an asset, and he's loyal to a fault."

"I'm not worried about Roni either." Kian put his hand on Syssi's belly, caressing it absentmindedly. "William has eighteen people working for him now. Engineers, programmers, machinists, twenty if I count the EMTs who monitor the Perfect Match adventures. That's a lot of people."

"They are all clan members," Syssi said. "You deemed them trustworthy enough to work on the Perfect Match machines and the noise cannon and all the other classified things William is building. How is this different?"

"None of that tech is a game-changing bonanza like the ability to build Odus. The other technologies are known and available, and we are just improving on them. Some are proprietary, but they are not world-altering. Imagine a world in which each house has an Odu, even a simplified version as you've suggested. But that's not what I'm worried about. That could actually be wonderful. I'm worried about the technology being used for military purposes. What I imagine is an army of indestructible soldiers."

Syssi shivered. "If we ever go ahead with this, one of the modifications should be making them easily destructible, maybe even as fragile as humans. I think that's the best safety feature we could install in them."

"Good thinking." Anandur smiled through the rearview mirror. "If they are breakable, they can't be used for warfare. They can't be used for protection either, but that's not why we want them, right? We want them to do jobs no one else wants to do."

Syssi chuckled. "History repeats itself. The gods created humans to take over the mining and gardening and all the other jobs that the gods didn't want to do. They used their superior genetics to enhance primitive humanoids and make them intelligent enough to follow instructions, but they also made them easy to control. They made humans susceptible to mind manipulation and much less resilient than the gods. That's precisely what we are talking about in regards to creating Odus."

Still gently caressing her belly, Kian was quiet for a long moment before he spoke. "Unlike humans, though, the Odus cannot procreate."

Syssi let out a sigh. "Neither did the humans until the snake god gave them the ability."

"Ah, but humans had the necessary equipment," Anandur said. "The Odus don't. They don't have sex organs, or a womb, or eggs for sperm to fertilize."

"True." Kian kept caressing her belly. "But to multiply, they don't need to procreate. All they need to do is to build an assembly line."

59

CASSANDRA

*C*assandra looked out the window of Connor's car, observing the by now familiar concrete landscape of downtown Los Angeles. Onegus could have saved Connor the trip because she could have found the place with ease just from memory, and she wouldn't even have needed to rely on the GPS.

The architecture of the buildings was embedded like photographs in her mind, distinguishing them one from the other. She remembered small details, like the balcony at the thirty-something floor of the building they'd just passed, with the large potted tree that provided a splash of green to the blue and grey of glass and concrete. Or the lobby of the next building over, the entrance of which was encased in a colorful mosaic.

"Is something wrong?" Connor asked.

She turned to look at him. "Why do you think anything is wrong?"

"You've been gazing out the window the entire time. Are you mad at Onegus for not picking you up himself?"

"Not at all." She cast him an amused look. "But he shouldn't have inconvenienced you. I know where the building is. I could have driven myself to the parking garage."

"And deprive me the pleasure of your company?"

She waved a dismissive hand. "Save it, Connor. I don't need coddling."

"Someone is in a mood," he murmured under his breath.

"I'm not in a mood. I just have a lot on my mind." With a sigh, she let her head drop against the headrest.

Tonight, would be the first time she would meet Roni as her nephew, the son of the half-sister she hadn't known she had.

Had Onegus told Connor about her mother being Roni's grandmother?

"If you need an ear, I have two." Connor somehow managed to move his ears. "How did you do that? Is it another talent immortals have?"

He laughed. "No, it's just me. I don't know how or why, but I can move my ears like a dog." He did it again.

"Does it allow you to hear better?"

He cast her a sidelong glance. "I don't know about hearing better, but I'm an excellent listener. Why don't you try me?"

"Do you know about Roni and my mother?"

He frowned. "What about them?"

"Apparently, my mother is an immortal, and she's Roni's grandmother. I have a sister I didn't know about, and my mother has a daughter she probably doesn't remember because of her memory issues. It occurred to me that she might have been lying about that to hide that she was immortal, but my mother is not the type who could have left a child behind and pretend she never existed."

Connor let out a low whistle. "That's one hell of a story. No wonder you're moody. To learn that your mother is an immortal right after finding out that you are a Dormant, that alone is a lot to take in."

"Onegus and I already suspected that she was an immortal, so that wasn't such a big shock, but finding out about a sister and nephew I didn't know about was." She shifted toward him. "I have so many questions to ask Roni."

He glanced at her. "I didn't notice it before, but you and Roni look a little alike." He chuckled. "Except, Roni is ugly, and you are beautiful."

"Roni is not ugly. He's still in that awkward stage between being a boy and a man. When he fills out, he will be handsome." She tilted her head. "Although, wasn't that supposed to happen after his transition?"

Connor chuckled. "Apparently, Roni didn't get lucky. Andrew, Syssi's brother, grew a couple of inches. He also became even more handsome than he was before."

Hearing the wistfulness in Connor's tone, it occurred to her that the prohibition on inter-clan relationships shouldn't apply to male couples. Then again, the taboo against desiring a clan member was not only about procreation. It was a social thing, and it was instilled in them from a young age. Connor most likely thought about his male cousins in the same way they thought about the females.

"What about the female Dormants? Did they grow taller? I'm tall enough as it is, so for me it wouldn't be a desirable outcome."

"I don't think so." Connor turned into the parking garage of the high-rise. "But they got prettier. Naturally, their bone structure didn't change, but skin blemishes disappeared, their hair got thicker and shinier, and they looked more vital. Healthier." He smiled. "There is no improving on perfection, though, so I doubt you'll notice any changes."

She rolled her eyes. "You are such a flirt, Connor."

"I aim to please."

KIAN

$\mathcal{T}$he ballroom was about one-third full when Onegus texted Kian to let him know that Syssi's parents, along with his mother, Alena, Sari, and David had boarded the golf cart at the building across the street and should be arriving shortly.

As the host of the party, he'd had to arrive earlier than the rest of the family, which had been a great excuse to give Syssi for why he wanted them to be at the table ahead of time.

"I'll be right back." He rose to his feet and kissed Syssi's cheek.

"Where are you going?" she asked.

"My mother is en route. I should meet her at the parking garage and escort her in."

Syssi frowned. "Isn't she with your sisters?"

"She is. I need to escort them as well."

Amanda slid over to the chair he'd vacated. "I'll keep you company until Kian comes back." She winked at him over Syssi's head.

Amanda's job was to keep Syssi distracted until her parents made it to the table.

Even though Bridget had said it was okay, Kian still wasn't sure that he was doing the right thing. What if the excitement was too much? Was there a way to soften the impact without telling Syssi that her parents were coming to the party?

Maybe he should tell Amanda to act in a way that would make her suspect that something was up?

That way, she would expect the unexpected, and her parents' arrival would be less of a shock but still a nice surprise.

Good thing that Amanda was a gifted actress. She would have no problem figuring out how to walk the line between hinting and giving the secret away.

In the elevator, he pulled out his phone and texted his sister. *Make Syssi suspect that something is up, just not what it is. I don't want her to get startled.*

Amanda replied a moment later. *That's an unexpected change of plans, but I agree that it's better not to startle a very pregnant woman. I'll come up with something.*

Thank you. He pocketed the phone and stepped out of the elevator.

Joining the three Guardians stationed at the garage, he waited for the souped-up golf cart to arrive. When it did less than a minute later, he walked up to it and pulled the fabric panel aside.

"Good evening, Mother." He dipped his head. "Anita, Adam." He smiled. "You look rested."

He'd already talked with them twice since they'd landed, checking that they were comfortable staying with Annani and Alena, and asking whether they needed anything.

"Thank you." Adam stepped down and offered his hand to Anita. "Your sister convinced us to take a nap."

"And I'm glad that she did." Anita lifted on her toes to kiss Kian's cheek. "Happy birthday. Adam and I have a present for you." She looked at her husband. "Should we give it to him now?"

"Your arrival is the best gift."

As Kian offered his hand to his mother, she tugged on it as soon as she was out of the cart and pulled him down to her. "Happy birthday, my son." She kissed both his cheeks. "I know that I have already congratulated you, and that today is not your actual birth date, but since it is your party, I felt like congratulating you again."

"Thank you." He kissed her back.

Coming from behind him, Sari cleared her throat, and when he turned to her, he was pulled into a bone-crushing hug. "Congratulations." She let go of him only to take a small box from David's hand. "We've gotten you something small so you can fit it in your suit pocket." She winked.

It was the size of a ring box, but he doubted his sister had gotten him jewelry. "Should I open it?"

"Not yet. Open it later together with all your other presents."

Adam walked up to him with a big grin on his face. "Well, if it's gift giving time, I might as well give you ours as well." He handed Kian a wrapped rectangle the size of a small book.

Surprisingly, it also fit in his pocket.

Alena wrapped her arm around his waist. "My gift was too big to bring over. You'll get it tomorrow."

He shook his head. "I appreciate all your gifts, but you shouldn't have bothered. I'm two thousand years old, which is way too old to be getting gifts for my birthday."

Syssi had given him her present when they'd returned home to stash Okidu's journals. It was a small sketch by Picasso, the size of a large napkin, but he had no doubt that it had cost a fortune. Naturally, she'd refused to tell him how much she'd paid for it.

It was a portrait of a woman with a high ponytail, and it was exquisite, just like the woman who'd gifted it to him.

"Shall we?" He motioned for the elevators.

Anita sucked in a breath. "I'm so excited. Are you sure that Syssi doesn't suspect anything?"

"She didn't up until I left her at the table, but she might have thought it was strange that I felt the need to escort my mother and sisters from the parking garage."

Hopefully, Amanda had further fueled those embers of suspicion, preparing Syssi for the big surprise.

61

SYSSI

*A*manda moved the chair so she could sit sideways, which allowed her to look at Syssi while glancing from time to time at the entrance to the ballroom.

Sitting with her back to the entry doors, Syssi couldn't see the guests as they came in, but since most stopped at their table to say hello, she felt no need to follow Amanda's example and turn her chair.

It required too much effort, and she didn't share Amanda's compulsive need to check out everyone's outfits the moment they came in. Besides, her sister-in-law was providing a running descriptive commentary, and Syssi's visual imagination filled in the rest.

It had become a game to wait until the guest arrived at their table and compare what she'd imagined based on Amanda's descriptions to how the outfit actually looked.

"I love Margaret's dress," Amanda said. "It's nothing special, but it makes her look good. If I didn't know better, I would have thought that she'd already transitioned."

To see that, Syssi made an effort to look over her shoulder. Her back and the tendons holding her belly protested painfully, and she had to turn back, but the brief glance confirmed Amanda's observation.

When she first saw Margaret, Syssi had to struggle to see the beauty hidden beneath the stringy hair, the pale complexion, the hollow cheeks, and the haunted look in the woman's big brown eyes. At the wedding, Margaret had already looked ten times better, and tonight, she looked like a model. Her back was straight, her gait proud, and her head was held high. But perhaps the biggest change was her expression. She seemed more confident, looking people in the eyes when they greeted her and Bowen, and she was smiling broadly.

"Bowen has found a diamond in the rough. When Margaret transitions, she will be a stunner. Maybe she could model for Mey and Jin." Syssi cast Amanda an amused look. "She's not a snob like you, so she wouldn't mind modeling their comfortable, working-moms line."

Not bothering to refute the accusation, Amanda crossed her legs. "Now that you've had several hours to mull it over, how do you feel about Okidu's gift?"

Everyone sitting at their table knew about Okidu's surprise, and the music playing in the background was loud enough to muffle their conversation, but Syssi still felt uncomfortable talking about it in a public place. Especially given how paranoid Kian was about it.

"My position didn't change, and I'd rather not talk about it right now."

Amanda waved a hand in dismissal. "I wasn't talking about the big picture. I was just curious about your reaction. You searched for months for the right gift for Kian. It must have been upsetting to be outdone by the butler."

"It hasn't even occurred to me. I wanted to give Kian the Picasso at the party, but I decided to give it to him when we went home to find a place for the journals so he could put it in a safe place as well." She chuckled. "He loved it, and then he asked if it was a portrait of me."

Amanda laughed. "Only if Picasso was clairvoyant. He died before you were born."

"Kian didn't notice the signature at first. When he did, he was stunned, not because I found a Picasso sketch that was actually available for purchase at an auction, but because he couldn't believe that I spent so much money on such a small sketch done in pencil."

"What did you say?"

Syssi smirked. "I told him that it was a good investment. Works of art by famous artists only appreciate in value."

Amanda's eyes darted to the entrance again, and this time she smiled broadly.

"Who are you smiling at?"

"Someone you'll be very happy to see, but don't look."

"Why not?"

"Because it's supposed to be a surprise. I just don't want you to faint, so I'm giving you a warning. But don't tell anyone that I did, okay? I don't want them to be upset with me."

After that preamble, it was difficult not to look. Who could it be? Everyone she knew was attending the birthday.

Could it be Carol and Lokan?

She hadn't seen Lokan since Jacki & Kalugal's wedding, and Carol had been gone for weeks and hadn't even come back for Sari and David's wedding.

Amanda leaned across and put her hand on Syssi's knee. "You can look now."

As she started to turn her head, Kian walked to stand next to her, distracting her, and offered her both his hands. "I have a surprise for you."

Letting him haul her up, she turned to look and gasped. Her parents were standing a few feet back with Andrew and Nathalie, grinning at her. Next to them were Annani, Kian's other two sisters, and David.

"Surprise!" Her mother rushed to her and hugged her gently, and then her father embraced them both.

Tears misting her eyes, Syssi kissed her mother's cheek and then her father's.

"How did you get here? You were supposed to come in two weeks?" She pretended to scowl at her brother. "Did you know?"

"Of course." There wasn't an iota of remorse in Andrew's eyes.

Her mother let go so her father could hug her properly, or as properly as her belly allowed.

"I'm so happy that you are here." She kissed her father's cheek again. "How did you manage to drag Mom away from her clinic two weeks early?"

Her father released her but took her hand. "I wish I could take credit for that, but it was a combination of your husband's relentless pressure and the incredibly competent young doctor the organization sent as a replacement. Your mother was so impressed with him that she decided he didn't need an entire month of shadowing her to take over and that we could leave much earlier. That was two days ago. The rest was Kian's doing." Her father looked at her mate. "He sent a jet to pick us up, and Annani graciously offered to host us for the afternoon so we could rest before the party. Kian also invited us to stay in your house throughout our visit."

"Thank you." Syssi opened her arms in invitation.

A satisfied smile on his gorgeous face, Kian walked into them and wrapped his around her back. "Do you like your surprise?"

"I love it." She kissed his jaw. "And I love you."

62

CASSANDRA

*W*hen Connor parked the car, Cassandra was glad to see that Onegus was there, waiting to escort her to the ballroom.

He'd done the same at the wedding, and it had made entering the lions' den, so to speak, much less intimidating.

Not that Connor wasn't a gallant escort, but it would have been awkward to arrive with someone who wasn't her date for the event.

"Hello, beautiful." He pulled her into his arms, his hand smoothing over her thigh and brushing against the curve of her bottom. "This dress brings back fond memories."

"You remember what I was wearing?"

"I remember everything about every moment we've spent together."

She frowned. "Is that another immortal trait?"

He chuckled. "No, and way to steal my thunder. I was being romantic."

"In that case, I'm touched and impressed." She leaned and kissed his cheek.

Standing behind her, Connor cleared his throat. "If you are done, I would like to catch the transport before it leaves."

Onegus snatched a quick kiss on her lips before offering her his arm. "To the transport."

When they got in, she said hello to the other guests who were already seated and then scooted closer to Onegus to make room for Connor. When he was seated as well, the driver closed the fabric flap, walked back to his seat, and they were off.

"Has Roni arrived yet?" she asked.

Onegus nodded.

"Are we sitting with the same people we sat with at the wedding?"

"There has been some shuffling around. My mother wanted to sit with us, and Sharon wanted to sit with Eva, so Robert and Sharon were moved to another table."

"But Roni is still going to be there, right?"

Onegus smiled. "He's just as anxious to talk to you as you are to him."

"I doubt that. He wants to find out more about his grandmother, who he knew about. I want to find out more about my sister, who I didn't know I had."

Suddenly, it occurred to her that her sister was a confirmed Dormant. "Did Roni's mother refuse to be induced?"

Onegus shook his head. "She was never offered the option. Roni and his parents are not on good terms, and they don't even know what happened to him after we sprung him from the hospital."

"I don't get it. It's not fair to keep it from her just because Roni doesn't get along with his parents."

"It's complicated. Besides, she's probably too old to transition safely."

Cassandra had forgotten about that.

Damn, life was unfair.

When they entered the ballroom, Onegus led her to the table, and while he pulled out a chair for her, she smiled at her dinner companions. "Hello, everyone. I guess tonight no one is going to try to get me drunk."

Nick smiled sheepishly. "Don't bet on it." He glanced at Roni. "We have a lot to celebrate."

"Did you tell them?" Cassandra asked Roni as she sat down.

Roni nodded. "I keep thinking about what might have happened to my grandmother, your mother, and how she turned immortal."

Onegus put a hand on her shoulder. "I need to oversee the guests' arrival. Do you want me to get you a drink before I go?"

Looking up, she put her hand over his. "I know where the bar is. Go do your thing and come back as soon as you can."

"Yes, ma'am." He leaned and gave her a chaste kiss on the cheek.

When Onegus left, Nick pushed to his feet. "Lychee martini?"

"That would be lovely. Thank you."

Jackson poured her a glass of wine. "To tide you over."

"Thanks." She turned to Roni. "What I keep thinking about is that I have a sister and a nephew. Are there more? Did my mother have more children? Do you have sisters or brothers?"

"No to both. My mother was an only child, and so was I. My parents had been trying for many years to conceive, and when they finally did, they probably regretted it. I was a pain in the ass."

"Don't say that. I'm sure they love you."

"They loved the money the government was paying me, but they didn't love me enough to inconvenience themselves with having me home under house arrest once I turned eighteen."

Cassandra frowned. "What did you do to get arrested?"

"A stupid prank. I hacked into the US government's top-secret classified server just to prove that I could. I was caught, but because I was underage, and because they wanted me to work for them, I was offered a deal, or rather my parents were. I could live at home with a handler to watch over me, so I couldn't get out of line again, or I could be a guest of the government. In either case, I was getting paid for my services, and my parents were pocketing the money, but if they agreed to the handler, they would be compensated for their inconvenience. When I turned eighteen, all that money went directly to me. I opted to move out and keep all of it rather than pay them for the dubious privilege of staying home."

Cassandra was sure that there was more to the story. "How old were you when you got caught?"

"Fifteen."

Damn, that was young. "So your parents had to put up with strangers staying in their house twenty-four-seven for three years. That must have been difficult."

"It wasn't that bad since they used the money I earned to travel extensively. They basically stopped working and were living off my income."

"Why did it bother you so much? I'm happy to support my mother."

He grimaced. "Your mother loved you and did everything she could for you while you were growing up. My parents treated me like a changeling. I was much smarter than they were, and they resented me for it."

"What happened to them after you disappeared?"

He shrugged. "They think that I escaped my imprisonment and went to work for the Russians or something like that."

"I'm sure they miss you."

He snorted. "They miss the money for sure."

It seemed like Roni had a chip on his shoulder regarding his parents, and he wouldn't be a good source of information about them. What she needed to do was to get their names and address and pay them a visit. She wouldn't even tell them who she was, and given her African appearance, her half-sister would most likely never suspect that they were related.

Heck, Cassandra could claim to be a new investigator assigned to Roni's case, flash them a fake badge, or take Connor with her to thrall them. Onegus would've been better, but he was the chief and would never break clan law and use thralling for an unapproved purpose. Connor, on the other hand, might be willing to do that for fun.

"What are your parents' names?"

Roni narrowed his eyes at her. "Why do you want to know?"

"Because I want to see for myself whether my sister is as bad as you make her out to be."

621

63

KIAN

*W*hen all the guests were seated, and the doors were closed, Annani cast Kian an encouraging smile and pushed to her feet. "I was nominated to deliver the first speech. You are next."

He hadn't prepared one. "I planned to just thank everyone for coming. No one wants to hear speeches tonight."

His mother put a hand on his shoulder. "You have a few minutes to come up with something. It does not need to be long, but try to make it inspiring."

As Annani made her way to the podium, he leaned toward Syssi. "Help?"

He couldn't talk about the Odus, and talking about the Kra-ell and the investigative team leaving for China would not be conducive to a good mood. Everyone who knew about the Kra-ell, which by now was probably every clan member, was wary about the possibility of other immortals roaming the planet and wondering about their agenda.

"You can talk about the completion of Kalugal's section of the village and the 3D printer you bought to speed up the construction of our site and other building projects."

"Excellent idea." He lifted her hand to his lips. "What would I have done without you?"

"We are a team." She cupped his cheek. "Blessed to have each other."

"Indeed."

Across the table, Adam grinned. "It makes me happy to see you two still so much in love."

Anita looked like she wanted to add a comment but closed her mouth as Annani stood at the podium, and all conversations stopped.

"Good evening," she addressed the room. "Seeing my family gathered together to celebrate once again fills my heart with joy. Four days ago, we celebrated Sari and David's joining, and today we are celebrating Kian's two thousand years of life. Give him a round of applause."

His mother started clapping, and as everyone rose to their feet, turning to him and clapping, Kian stood up and dipped his head in thanks.

When Annani stopped and raised her hands, everyone sat back down.

"Kian," his mother addressed him. "You have been instrumental in bringing my vision to life, and without your and Sari's help, I doubt I would have been able to do much at all. You have dedicated your life to our clan and to the advancement of humanity, and I would like to take this opportunity to express my gratitude and that of everyone gathered here tonight. Thank you, my son."

Annani started clapping again, and as the whole room followed, he was forced to smile and bow again.

"Come up here and say a few words." She waved her hand in invitation.

"Good luck." Syssi patted his arm.

The clapping continued as he made his way to the podium, and as his mother pulled him down to kiss him on both cheeks, the cheering became deafening.

"The stage is all yours." Annani departed, leaving him alone to face his clan.

"Thank you. It has been a long and perilous journey, but I haven't done it alone. You were all with me, helping to promote our vision, each in your unique way, each to the best of your ability. You deserve a round of applause more than I do."

Kian clapped, and slowly others joined him, but the applause wasn't nearly as loud or as enthusiastic as it had been when Annani led it, and no one rose to their feet, but people smiled, happy to be acknowledged.

"I would also like to thank you all for your gifts." He motioned at the table groaning under the weight of wrapped packages of all sizes. "It will probably take me a week to open them all."

The clapping and cheering resumed for a few seconds and then died out when he lifted his hand.

"Earlier today, I got a call from the building contractor, and it appears that we will have one more reason for celebration before this week is over. Kalugal's section of the village is complete and ready to move into. The ribbon-cutting ceremony is scheduled for Saturday."

Kalugal, who was sitting with his men this time, pushed to his feet and started clapping first. His men followed, and then everyone was clapping.

"You are all invited," Kalugal said once the applause had subsided. "We still need to furnish the residences, but I would love to give a tour to whoever is interested."

More applause ensued.

Kian lifted his hand. "The rest of you are probably wondering when our new section will be ready, and I have good news for you on that front as well. On Monday, I finalized a deal on a 3D house printing facility. Using this technology will allow us to complete the last building phase in a matter of weeks instead of months."

"Is it our technology?" Kalugal asked.

Our?

Kian stifled a chuckle. Did his cousin think himself entitled to the information contained in the gods' tablet?

That hadn't been part of the accord, and Kian had no intention of giving him access to it.

"Not directly. It is a human invention, but it wouldn't have been possible without the technology we've been dripping for decades." Kian shifted his gaze to the side door leading to the kitchen, where Gerard stood with his arms crossed over his chest, glaring at him. "It would appear that dinner is ready." He swept his eyes over his guests. "*Bon appétit*, everyone."

MARGARET

*A*s the first course was served, Margaret nibbled on the small, artfully arranged appetizer. She wasn't very hungry, and she was a little tipsy, which made her a little nauseous as well.

She didn't regret partying with the girls, though. She'd had a wonderful time.

Wendy and Stella had come, and as they'd done each other's hair and makeup, painted their nails, and tried on different outfits, they'd also consumed way too much wine. The immortals had remained unaffected, but Margaret hadn't fared as well.

Nevertheless, she'd insisted on leaving the leg brace at home and coming to the party looking as good as she felt. Well, aside from the slight dizziness and nausea, everything else was perfect. She had a beautiful dress on, one of Stella's creations that hugged her slim body and flared at the bottom, and her hair was soft and shiny thanks to Ana's curling iron. She had very little makeup on, but it was enough to make her eyes pop.

"What's the matter, love?" Bowen looked at her plate. "You don't like it?"

"I'm not very hungry." She pushed it toward him. "You can have it."

"Are you sure?"

"Yes."

"Your loss," Ana said. "It's delicious."

"I could eat another." Elise licked her lips. "That's the problem with Gerard's exquisite cuisine. There isn't enough of it."

"I like it that it's delicious but not filling," Rowan said. "I don't like the heaviness after a big meal."

"I thought that immortals had a fast metabolism," Margaret said.

"Do we?" Rowan asked no one in particular. "I think it takes us the same time to metabolize food as it does humans." She leaned and patted Margaret's hand. "Pretty soon, you will get to experience it yourself, and then you can tell me if there is a difference."

"There isn't," Wendy said. "After I transitioned, it took me just as long to lose the excess weight I carried as it would have taken me as a human. I had to exercise and watch what I ate."

Vlad murmured something under his breath that earned him a glare from Wendy and a pitying glance from Richard. Margaret could only guess that it had to do with Wendy becoming too skinny or not needing to lose any weight because she was beautiful no matter what size dress she wore.

She liked him even better for that. Her future son-in-law was adorable.

Another hour passed as all seven courses were served and consumed, and then it was time for dancing.

When Bowen just sat there, contented to watch others dance, she put a hand on his shoulder. "Aren't you going to ask me to dance?"

His eyes darted to her legs. "I don't think it's safe without a brace. What if you make the wrong move and dislocate your knee?"

"I won't. We'll do it the same way we did at the wedding. I'll put my feet on yours, and you'll move us both."

Relief washing over his face, he grinned. "I can do that."

Pushing to his feet, he put his hands on her waist, lifted her, and smashed her against his chest.

"I can walk," she protested as he carried her to the dance area.

"Not tonight. I'm not taking any chances with you. Wrap your arms around my neck and hold on."

She did as he asked. "You let me walk from the parking garage to the ballroom."

"I only allowed that because it was so important to you to walk into the room without the brace. I was ready to catch you at any moment, and it was very stressful for me," he admitted.

His concern washed away some of the sour taste the word *allowed* had left. Margaret loved Bowen with all her heart, but she would never accept being controlled by anyone. She was an adult in charge of her own life, and all anyone was entitled to do was offer advice. The final decision would always be hers.

"I don't want you to carry me around like this. It's embarrassing." She pushed down his body until her feet touched his shoes.

The soles of her ballet flats were soft, so she knew they weren't hurting him, but she asked anyway, "Is that okay?"

"Perfect." Bowen smiled and dipped his head to kiss her.

Ignoring the couples dancing around them, Margaret kissed him back. The kiss started soft but quickly became passionate, and when she came up for air, her head was spinning.

"What's wrong?" Bowen asked.

She forced a smile. "Your kiss made me dizzy."

"You look pale. Perhaps we should sit down."

"Don't be silly. You are doing all the work. I'm just hanging on."

65

RONJA

*R*onja sipped on her wine and watched people dance. David with Sari, Lisa with Parker, Amanda with Dalhu, and a bunch of other people, some of whom she knew and many she didn't.

Being the only older-looking woman in a ballroom full of beautiful immortals was enough to shake the confidence of the most self-assured woman, and God knew that Ronja wasn't one of those.

In her younger days, she'd been told that she was beautiful, and she was still quite good-looking for her age, but given her history, that had never been enough. Michael had cheated on her, Frank had loved her, but he hadn't been the most passionate man, and Bowen...

She shouldn't even think about him. It hurt too much.

There had been nothing romantic between them. How could there be?

She was still grieving for Frank.

But she'd enjoyed Bowen's attention. Thinking that he found her attractive, that she could still catch the eye of a handsome man, had pleased her, made her feel younger than the age listed on her driver's license.

In her heart, she was still a twenty-something—desirable, coveted—the kind of woman men turned their heads after to get another look.

Sometimes they still did, but it didn't happen as often, and definitely not with young, handsome men.

Bowen wasn't actually young, but he was one of the most handsome men she'd ever met. Real eye candy. When he'd helped her and Lisa pack up their home, she'd enjoyed watching him carry heavy things around, his arm and chest muscles bulging, his square jaw determined.

She also loved his kindness, his humor, his selflessness.

God, she missed him.

His presence had been comforting.

Ronja wasn't used to not having a man around, to being alone. Having

Bowen over nearly every day had filled that vacuum, had given her the illusion that she wasn't alone, and that if she needed a strong guy to move stuff around or to reach the top shelves in the closet, he'd be there for her.

She was happy for him. Bowen was a good man, and he deserved to be happy, but seeing him fussing over his mate, dancing with her, carrying her back to the table like a princess, hurt.

Couldn't he have found Margaret a few weeks later?

If he wasn't with her, he would have invited Ronja to dance, and she wouldn't have felt like a damn wallflower, sitting alone at the table while her dinner companions were on the dance floor.

It made her feel old and forgotten.

Invisible.

As Merlin, the clan's quirky fertility doctor, blocked her view of the dance floor, she leaned sideways, not expecting him to stop in front of her.

"Hello, pretty lady." He bent nearly in half to get his face in front of hers.

Ronja had seen him around. The guy always seemed in a hurry to get somewhere, his long white hair and beard frizzy and uncombed, his stained doctor's coat flying behind him. The guy was a mess, but he seemed kind.

"Hello, handsome fellow," she echoed his greeting.

Grinning as if she'd given him the best compliment, he extended his hand. "Would you care to dance?"

The doctor was dressed like a clown, in purple pants, a blue shirt with yellow dots, and red sneakers, and he was probably the last guy in the room she wanted to dance with, but he was the only one who had offered.

"I would love to." She took his hand.

His grin got even broader. "I'm honored." He bowed over her hand and kissed the back of it. "Let me introduce myself. My name is Merlin."

"I know. I'm Ronja."

"I know that as well. You are David and Lisa's mother." He led her to the dance floor. "Parker told me all about you." He put his other hand on her waist and leaned closer to whisper in her ear. "The boy is head over heels in love with your daughter. But don't tell her. It's a secret."

Ronja laughed. "I've noticed, and I told her, but she dismissed me, claiming that they were just friends."

"Oh, to be young and naive." He straightened back to his considerable height.

"Indeed."

Surprisingly, Merlin was a good dancer. He also smelled good, which given the state of his wardrobe had been unexpected.

When the song ended, he didn't let go of her hand. "Another dance?"

"With pleasure."

"Oh, the pleasure is all mine, fair Ronja." He twirled her in a practiced dance move.

"Where did you learn to dance like that?"

"This is nothing. You should see me in a kilt dancing the sword dance."

Imagining him dressed in the traditional Scottish attire, Ronja stifled a laugh. "I would pay good money to see that."

With a roguish smile, he once again leaned closer to her ear. "Just so you know, proper Scots wear nothing underneath their kilts."

"How scandalous," she pretended to gasp.

"Not really. It's just comfortable and airy." He pulled her a little closer. "And sexy."

"Are you flirting with me, Merlin?"

"What if I am?"

66

BOWEN

*M*argaret leaned her head on Bowen's shoulder and let out a breath. "I think I should sit down." She chuckled. "All I did was hold on to you like a baby monkey, and still I got tired. I guess I'm not fully healed yet."

She'd been fine the day before and this morning, full of energy and glowing health. This was a turn for the worse, and he wondered what had caused it.

Margaret had told him she'd had a few glasses of wine while getting ready for the party with the girls. Perhaps she'd had too much?

He carried her back to the table and sat her down on the chair. "How much wine did you drink?"

"About a third of a bottle. It's a lot, but it shouldn't have made me feel so out of it." She wiped a hand over her forehead.

He crouched in front of her. "Are you feeling hot?"

"No, just tired."

Stella pushed to her feet, walked up to Margaret, and put a hand on her forehead. "You feel a little warm to me." She smiled tightly. "This might be the first sign of your transition. When did you start working on it?"

Margaret and Bowen exchanged glances.

Last night was their first time. It wasn't likely that Margaret had started transitioning already.

"It hasn't been long enough," Bowen said.

Stella shrugged. "It might be some human ailment."

"That's more likely." Margaret fanned her face with her hand. "I had a lot to drink today. Between the wine at home and the two cocktails I had with dinner, it was too much. What's strange, though, is that I no longer feel tipsy, just tired, but my stomach feels queasy like it did after the wine binge."

"Perhaps you are pregnant?" Elise suggested. "As a human, your chances of conceiving are still good."

"That's even less likely than transitioning. I got a contraceptive shot not too long ago."

Bowen was glad that Wendy and Vlad were on the dance floor. It was awkward enough to have people discussing Margaret's and his sex life as if they were talking about the weather. It would have been worse with Wendy taking part in the discussion.

"I should ask Bridget to take a look at you." He pushed to his feet.

"Don't." Margaret caught his hand. "Whatever this is, it certainly doesn't warrant bothering the doctor. Let her enjoy her evening."

"I'm worried about you. I'll feel better if Bridget says it's nothing."

"I'm fine for now. If it gets worse, I'll ask you to get her myself."

He arched a brow. "Do you promise to tell me if it does?"

"I promise."

He blew out a breath. "Can I get you something to drink? And by that, I mean coffee or tea?"

"Tea would be nice."

At the bar, Bowen saw Julian and decided to ask his opinion. After all, Margaret told him not to bother Bridget. She'd said nothing about Julian. It was a loophole he could use.

"Can I bother you for a moment?" he asked the doctor.

"Sure."

He didn't want to have the talk within anyone's earshot. "Can we step over there?"

"What's up?" Julian followed him out into the hallway.

"Margaret is feeling tired, she barely ate anything tonight, and her stomach is giving her trouble." He rubbed a hand over the back of his neck. "Can it be the transition if we only started working on it last night?"

Julian pursed his lips. "Possibly, but not very likely. For a female, it usually takes several venom bites. It's true that Eva transitioned after only one hookup, but that was probably because of Kalugal being a three-quarters god. Eleanor started transitioning after being with Greggory only twice. Most of the others required many more attempts."

Bowen shifted his weight to his other foot. "Last night wasn't the first dose of venom Margaret received. There were a couple before that."

"I see." Julian smoothed a hand over his jaw. "Perhaps that worked like a primer, and when you consummated your relationship, it was the last catalyst needed to induce her transition."

"That's what I thought too, but I wanted a doctor's opinion. What should we do?"

"Just watch Margaret closely, and let her enjoy the rest of the party. In any case, there is no reason to rush. As long as she doesn't lose consciousness, she doesn't need to be hooked up to monitoring equipment." Smiling, Julian patted him on the back. "Maybe she'll be one of the lucky ones whose transition goes so smoothly that she doesn't need to be hooked up at all."

"I hope so too." Bowen sighed. "But given her age, how likely is that?"

"Who knows, the Fates might decide to go easy on her."

Bowen nodded. "I'm not a devout believer, but I'll beseech the Fates on her behalf."

Margaret had definitely suffered enough throughout her life to merit an easy transition, and if the Fates had any compassion at all, they would listen to his plea.

67

ONEGUS

*T*hroughout dinner, Cassandra had seemed preoccupied. She'd participated in the conversation and smiled when it was appropriate, but Onegus had noticed her zoning out from time to time. He wondered what was on her mind, and whether it had anything to do with the start of her induction.

Except, what was there to second guess?

She had everything to gain and very little to lose. Provided that it went well, of course, but he had no reason to fear that it wouldn't. In fact, he was starting to doubt Bridget's assertion that transition was dangerous for older Dormants. Onegus had no medical training but based on the hundred percent success they'd had so far, his doubts were warranted.

When most of their dinner companions left the table to go dancing, Cassandra put her hand on his shoulder and leaned closer to him. "I remember you telling me that immortals have to get fake IDs every couple of decades."

"What of it?"

"Can you get me a fake FBI badge?"

He chuckled. "What do you need it for?"

"I want to visit my sister, but I don't want to tell her who I am. I thought I would pretend to be a new investigator assigned to Roni's case."

"It can be arranged. Do you want me to come with you?"

She avoided his eyes. "I would love you to, but wouldn't it be considered breaking clan law?"

"Not if I don't thrall them. Pretending to be an FBI agent is not against clan law."

She sighed. "Then perhaps I should ask Connor to come with me. What if I can't get information out of her the conventional way?"

"If you want him to do illegal things for you, don't tell me about that."

"Oh, right. Sorry about that. I probably won't ask him to come with me. It

633

was just a thought. I need to ask my sister what she remembers about our mother's drowning, and also about her relationship with her husband. Those are not the kind of questions someone investigating Roni's disappearance would ask, but I can probably come up with an angle to explain it." Cassandra glanced at the dance floor where Roni and Sylvia were dancing with Jackson and Tessa. "It's just that it occurred to me that my mother might have staged her death to escape him."

Onegus nodded. "The thought crossed my mind. She also might have realized that she wasn't aging and decided it was time to leave. That was what Eva did, but she at least waited until Nathalie went to college. Your mother could have easily dragged it longer. Instead, she did it when your sister was twelve."

Cassandra leaned her elbow on the table and her chin on her hand. "Something must have happened. My mother is not the type. The memory loss couldn't have changed her personality so completely."

"I don't know what to tell you. That's not my area of expertise."

"Mine neither. My sister should be able to shed some light on what happened. A twelve-year-old girl, especially one who is an only child, sees and understands a lot. If my mother's marriage was troubled, she must have noticed. The problem is that she might refuse to answer my questions."

"It will require some clever maneuvering, but we can come up with a story that links the two incidents. I wonder if there was a life insurance policy on your mother that Roni's grandfather collected."

She frowned. "Do you think that foul play was involved?"

"We shouldn't dismiss the possibility. So far, we assumed that your mother was the one to stage her death so she could escape. But what if she wasn't? What if she had an accident? That would fit with her memory loss?"

"Except, her accident might not have been really an accident."

"Precisely."

"Is Roni's grandfather still around?"

"I don't think so. If he were, Roni would have wanted to question him once he discovered that his grandmother was an immortal. Turner looked into that as well, and he never mentioned the grandfather either."

"Who's Turner?"

"Bridget's mate." Onegus turned around and pointed with his chin. "You see the redhead dancing with the blond guy? That's Bridget, our doctor, and Turner, who I don't know how to define."

"Is he an investigator?"

"He used to be the head of a special ops unit that dealt with hostage retrieval. When he retired, he became a private operator doing the same thing. He's a brilliant guy, and he's planned some of the most daring missions the clan has undertaken. He and Roni became close, probably because both are geniuses who don't relate well to other people, and Turner offered to help the kid find his grandmother."

Cassandra chuckled. "Are you telling me that my mother was clever enough to elude that mastermind?"

"It would seem so. Then again, he didn't have much time to dedicate to the search. Between his own operation and the help he routinely provides Kian, there isn't much time left."

"Do you know how far he got with the investigation?"

"I wasn't involved. You will have to ask Roni."

"I intend to." She pushed to her feet. "Let's go dance."

Did she plan to talk to Roni on the dance floor?

"This is not the time for this." He followed her up. "You can call him tomorrow."

She took his hand. "I don't intend to do it now."

"Good."

"I'll do that when he returns to the table."

68

ELEANOR

*E*leanor put her book down and glanced at Emmett.

It was only their second night together, and already they'd fallen into a routine. Sex, reading, some more sex, and more reading.

Philosophy, psychology, sociology, it was all a big bore.

Eleanor wasn't much of a reader, especially not of heavy stuff like that, and although the sex was spectacular, she would have liked to talk more with Emmett or cuddle on the couch and watch movies or shows. But he didn't like watching TV, and after spending several hours teaching Mey and Jin the Kra-ell language, he seemed drained, which she found strange.

Teaching could be boring, even annoying, but it shouldn't have tired him so much. It wasn't difficult mentally or physically, and he seemed to be getting along just fine with Mey and Jin. Well, more with Mey than Jin, but that wasn't surprising.

Jin was a brat, while Mey was a lady.

"Is the book not to your liking?" Emmett asked.

"Not really." Eleanor pushed to her feet. "I'm going to the bedroom to watch a movie."

"You can watch here if you want."

"I don't want to disturb you."

"You're not disturbing me." He patted the spot next to him. "Come, sit with me."

"I don't want to sit. My butt is numb from all this sitting." She walked into the bedroom and plopped down on the bed. "I wish I could take you out of here to do some physical activity. They have a well-equipped gym down here and a full-size swimming pool." She lifted the remote and clicked the television on.

Emmett put his book down and followed her into the bedroom. "I can think of a physical activity that's much more pleasant than lifting weights or swimming." He lay on the bed next to her.

"I don't want sex." She pouted.

"Are you sure?" He smoothed his hand over the curve of her waist and down her thigh.

Her damn body responded to the light touch as if they hadn't just made love a couple of hours ago.

"Stop it." She flicked his hand off. "You're turning me into a nymphomaniac."

"And that's bad?" He wrapped his arm around her, pulled her against his body, and nuzzled her neck.

As the tingles that started at her neck traveled south, she scissored her legs. "It is bad. I might become anemic."

"I promise not to nibble this time." He tugged on the neckline of her shirt, exposing the top of her breasts, and trailed kisses from her collarbone to the edge of her shoulder.

Threading her fingers in his hair, she pulled. "Can we do something other than sex and reading? There is more to life than that."

He smiled sadly. "This suite is a vast improvement over the small cell I occupied before, but even this became stifling in no time at all. If you want to go to the gym or the pool or to the party going on upstairs, just go. You don't have to be stuck in here with me."

There was no way she was stepping foot in that party. All of Kalugal's men had been invited, and she had no wish to see Greggory or for him to see her. Not before she could show up with a mate of her own.

Except, she was starting to doubt that Emmett was the one for her. Neither of them knew how to be part of a couple.

"I don't want to go. I want us to do more things together." She let go of his hair and started caressing his scruffy cheek.

He needed a shave.

"Like what?" Emmett's hand trailed down her back to cup her ass.

Eleanor rolled her eyes. "Talk, play, cuddle, watch movies, and all the other things couples do."

His hand stilled. "Is that what we are? A couple?"

"What else would you call it?"

"Friends? Friends with benefits?"

It stung, but what had she expected? The guy had been raised in a commune and had never been in a relationship. Not only that, the community he'd created for himself had a policy against couples.

"Do you really believe in the free-love crap you were preaching in Safe Haven?"

"Crap? It wasn't crap. It was a way of life that solved intimacy issues for people who would have otherwise been lonely and miserable."

Was he serious? Or was he insinuating that she was lonely and miserable?

Even if she was, his commune life didn't appeal to her at all. Then again, she'd still had Greggory when she'd participated in the retreat, had still believed that she'd found her mate. If she'd been single and lonely at the time, it might have resonated with her.

Eleanor let out a breath. "For some, it might be a good solution. But for most, it isn't. Most people want to have a meaningful relationship with one person. They want to share their lives with a loving partner, build a home together, raise children, grow old together." She sighed. "But what do I know about that? Probably as little as you do. Maybe we need Mey and Jin to teach us what it takes to be a couple. They seem to be happily mated."

Emmett's eyes clouded with an emotion she couldn't decipher. "You might be onto something. They grew up in a loving home. How about you? Did your parents show you a lot of affection?"

"They loved my brother more, but they weren't very affectionate with either of us."

"Were they affectionate toward each other?"

"Not really. There was a lot of quiet animosity going on. They never fought in front of us, but it was hard to miss the hostile looks they traded. My parents' marriage wasn't happy, but at least they didn't bail on each other like so many people do."

Emmett's hand moved up to her back, then to her neck, and he leaned closer to kiss her softly. "Perhaps I should ask Peter to get us some books on relationships. It seems that both of us had bad examples, and we need better ones."

"Not everything can be learned from books." She smiled. "And Peter is not the right person to ask for romance novels. But my sister-in-law is."

His eyes widened. "You want me to read romances?"

"Yes. Vivian's romance novels are raunchy and totally ridiculous, but at least they are fun."

He looked puzzled. "Then how can we learn anything from silly romances? They are fantasy, not reality."

She shrugged. "Vivian and Magnus have an enviably loving marriage. Perhaps those novels have something to do with that."

Turning on his back, Emmett pulled her on top of him. "We are good together, aren't we?"

"If you're talking about sex, then the answer is yes. But a relationship needs more than great sex."

He looked doubtful. "I think that's a great foundation, and we can build on that. We just need more time, and maybe more room." He glanced around the bedroom. "I hate being locked up in here. The books keep me from going insane."

His books? That was what kept him sane? She'd gone to a lot of trouble to be with him, and he thought so little of her?

"What about me?"

His eyes softened. "Of course. Having you here keeps me alive. But imagine how much faster and stronger our relationship could have grown if it had room to breathe."

69

KIAN

"Get ready," Syssi said. "My dad is heading our way."

"Ready for what?" Kian glanced at Adam over his shoulder.

"He probably wants to dance with me."

Kian wasn't happy. He'd agreed to one dance, which amounted to them swaying in place because Syssi couldn't do much more. He'd offered to prop up her belly, but she'd refused.

"He can't be serious."

"Oh, he is." Syssi smiled as Adam tapped his shoulder.

"Can I have this dance?"

Reluctantly, Kian let go of Syssi and took a step back. "Be careful."

Adam chuckled. "I've seen Anita through three pregnancies. I know the limitations of a pregnant woman two weeks short of the due date."

"Two and a half," Kian corrected.

Adam's eyes shifted to his daughter's belly. "I'm not sure about that. My granddaughter seems to be ready to greet her granddaddy."

Kian swallowed. "All in good time."

"Of course." Adam offered Syssi his hand. "Shall we?"

As she placed one hand in his and the other on his shoulder, Adam put his other hand on the side of her belly and led her in a gentle slow dance.

Kian didn't dare to leave the two alone and return to the table. Instead, he took a few steps away from the dance floor and watched Syssi and her father sway to the beat of the music.

Kalugal sauntered up to him with a glass of whiskey in hand. "I thought you could use a drink." He handed him the glass.

"What about you?"

"I've had plenty already. I'm taking a break."

For a long moment, they stood side by side, watching the dance floor in quiet companionship.

"When were you going to tell me about Okidu's birthday gift?" Kalugal said nonchalantly.

Kian's blood cooled in his veins. "How do you know about it?"

Kalugal shrugged. "I have very good hearing."

Perhaps Kalugal was bluffing. No one outside the family and Onegus knew about the journals, and they had been instructed to keep it a secret, specifically from Kalugal.

"I only learned about it this morning. What did you hear?"

And from whom? Had Kalugal planted listening devices under the table? Kian wouldn't put it past him. The place had been searched after the decorators had left, and it would be searched again once the party was over, but it would have been easy enough for Kalugal to stick a device under the table and then remove it before the party was over.

"I heard that Okidu gifted you with blueprints for building more of him. That's a game-changer, Kian." Kalugal turned and looked into his eyes. "I thought we were allies. Why did you keep it from me?"

As soon as he got back to his table, Kian was going to look for the damn thing even if it upset everyone sitting there, including his mother and sisters. He would find the listening device and have proof to show that Kalugal wasn't trustworthy.

Kian emptied the whiskey down his throat and put the empty glass on the tray of a passing server. "You don't tell me everything either. What are you working on, Kalugal?"

"Touché, cousin." Kalugal pushed his hands into the pockets of his slacks. "If I share with you what I'm working on, will you share the technology for making Odus with me?"

"It depends on what you are working on."

Kian had no intention of letting anyone have the technology. It was too dangerous. But he could play along.

"That's reasonable. Did you have a chance to go over the schematics? Do we even have the necessary materials?"

Kalugal was fishing, but he wasn't going to learn anything because Kian didn't know anything either.

"The instructions are written in the old language, which I can't read. But I'm sure we don't have the materials or the tools to make human-looking cyborgs that are nearly indestructible. The Odus are part biological, part mechanical, and are equipped with learning capabilities that artificial intelligence hasn't reached yet."

Kalugal nodded. "After William takes a look, let me know what he thinks."

Kian pinned him with a hard stare. "First, tell me what you are working on, and then I'll consider including you in the ethical discussion concerning the Odus."

"Ah, ethics." Kalugal snatched a couple of drinks from a passing waiter. "Is that your main concern?" He handed one of the glasses to Kian.

"One of them."

"What are the others?"

Kian cast Kalugal a sidelong glance. "You're a smart guy. Figure it out."

"I don't know enough about the Odus to form an informed opinion."

"The technology to make them was banned on the gods' home planet, and the Odus were destroyed. The owner of the seven that Khiann's father found must have sent them to Earth to save them. He or she also hid the schematics of the forbidden technology behind a firewall, or however things like that are hidden. I'm not a computer expert."

"Good for her." Kalugal raised his glass. "Such marvelous creations should never be destroyed."

"Why do you assume it was a her?"

Kalugal smirked. "Females are more merciful, and they are often more sensible as well. Males are ruled either by aggression, or an obsessive need to protect their loved ones, or both." He took a sip from his drink. "Contrary to what we would like to believe about ourselves, we are not very logical creatures."

There was something to it.

Watching Syssi swaying to the music in her father's arms, Kian knew that he wouldn't hesitate to strike against anything and anyone who might pose a danger to her and their child. The impulse was hardwired into him, and he doubted he would stop to evaluate things or act sensibly if they were threatened.

"We shouldn't dabble with alien technology we know nothing about." Kian took a long sip from his drink and grimaced. The martini was too sweet. "What if whoever sent the Odus didn't do it to save them, but for some other nefarious reason? After all, the gods nearly destroyed humanity once. Maybe the Odus are the Trojan Horse sent to finish the job."

Kalugal shook his head. "On the contrary, the Odu technology could be humanity's leap into the future. It's not just about building more of them. I have no doubt that those schematics include ground-breaking technology." He put his arm on Kian's shoulders. "Fear shouldn't stop progress, cousin. Humans throughout history feared change and technological advances, often eliminating the scientists along with the science. We are better and smarter than that. Besides, if we learn how the Odus are made, we can unlock other treasures hidden in Okidu's memory. Who are the gods? Where did they come from? Maybe he also has information about the Kra-ell? That might be the most valuable information of all, especially if they are invaders and colonizers. A fair warning could change the future."

The same thoughts had occurred to Kian. "You're not telling me anything new, Kalugal. And I don't intend to bury the technology without investigating it first. But I can assure you that I won't allow it to be used before I'm positive that it can be contained."

SYSSI

*T*here had been no warning, no sudden pain, not even discomfort.
One moment, Syssi had been laughing at a story her father had told her, and the next, warm liquid was sliding down her inner thighs.

At first, she'd thought her bladder had leaked. Lately, it often happened when she laughed and sometimes when she didn't make it to the bathroom in time.

But this wasn't a small leak.

It was a gush.

Pushing out of her father's arms, she tried to look down, but her big belly was in the way. "Is there a puddle on the floor at my feet?"

Her father looked down, then lifted his head and turned toward the family table. "Anita!" he yelled over the loud music. "Syssi's water just broke!"

Everyone on the dance floor froze. Heck, even the music stopped, and the entire ballroom became deathly quiet. But it didn't last longer than a couple of stunned seconds.

The commotion started with Kian rushing to her side, then her mother, followed by Bridget, Amanda, Sari, Andrew, Nathalie...

"Everyone stand back!" Anita commanded. "Someone please bring a chair for Syssi."

"Shouldn't we rush her to the keep's clinic?" Kian asked, his voice as strained as the muscles in his jaw.

Anandur brought a chair, and Kian helped her to sit down.

"In a moment," Bridget said, taking over command from Syssi's mother. "Are you having contractions?"

Syssi shook her head. "I didn't feel anything before it happened. Is that normal?"

"It's perfectly fine. We need to take you to the clinic, but since you are not in active labor yet, there is no rush. We have time to take you back to the village."

She turned to Anandur. "Please bring a wheelchair from the keep's clinic. It's in the storage cabinet."

"I can carry Syssi," Kian offered.

Bridget put a hand on his arm. "She will be more comfortable in a wheelchair."

As they waited for Anandur to come back, Kian crouched next to her and took her hand. "Are you okay?"

She cupped his cheek. "Better than you, it would seem. You're pale as a ghost." She pulled him to her for a kiss. "Happy birthday, my love. It seems like our daughter decided to share it with you."

His eyes brightened. "She did, didn't she? It's the best present I could have hoped for." His throat bobbed. "Provided that everything is okay."

"Of course, it is." Syssi smiled. "I'm immortal, and I have four capable doctors to take care of me."

Behind Bridget and her mother stood Julian and Merlin, and neither looked concerned.

"Out of the way, people," Anandur called. "Wheelchair coming through."

Syssi looked up and laughed. He wasn't pushing the wheelchair; he was carrying it over his head.

When the sea of heads parted, he lowered it to the floor and unfolded it.

Kian helped her up and then down to the chair. "Who is coming with us?" he asked.

Her mother and father got behind Kian, and Bridget took position at Syssi's side.

"I don't want to ruin everyone's party." Syssi waved her hand, motioning for Kian to step forward so she wouldn't have to look over her shoulder. "Please tell everyone to stay and enjoy themselves. There is no reason for the party to end just because my water broke."

He hesitated for a moment and then turned to the concerned crowd. "Please stay and enjoy yourselves. We will keep you posted."

There were a few murmurs of disagreement, but as Kian wheeled her out, only her parents and Bridget followed.

Or so it seemed.

Gertrude caught up to them at the elevators. "Hildegard and I are coming as well. We will drive ourselves home and meet you at the clinic."

"Thank you," Syssi said. "Do I really need so many people to help me?"

Gertrude and Bridget exchanged knowing glances, and then Bridget put her hand on Syssi's shoulder. "If you still want an epidural, I need my nurses or Julian to assist."

"I definitely want it," Syssi said as Kian wheeled her into the elevator.

There was no reason to suffer labor pains if they could be avoided, and Bridget had assured her that an epidural was not detrimental to the baby's health in any way.

Thankfully, the elevator was big enough to contain her entire entourage.

"I'm here," her mother said. "I can assist with the epidural. In my clinic in the Congo, we don't have a dedicated anesthesiologist either, and I often have to administer it myself."

"Thank you," Bridget said softly. "But tonight, your job is not to be Syssi's physician, it is to be Syssi's mother and provide her with emotional support. We will handle the rest."

71

MARGARET

"*I*t's scary," Wendy said. "Syssi wasn't supposed to go into labor for another two weeks. Do you think she's going to be okay?"

Margaret swallowed the nausea rising in her throat and plastered a smile on her face. "She's immortal. Of course, she's going to make it." She looked at Stella for confirmation. "Right?"

"I'm not worried about Syssi." Stella glanced at her son. "The only one who's in any danger is the child. She's just as fragile as any other human baby."

Margaret's stomach had felt queasy even before the party had started, and for some reason, Syssi's premature labor had made it worse. So much so that her vision was starting to blur, and she was sweaty all over. "I think I'm going to be sick," she said as she pushed to her feet. "I need to get to the bathroom."

Bowen was out of his chair in an instant. "Let me carry you. I can get you there faster."

She was too sick to argue. "Okay."

"I had an upset stomach too when I started transitioning," she heard Ana say. "I think you should take Margaret to the clinic." She chuckled. "Bridget is going to have a full house tonight."

Bowen didn't answer. Instead, he carried Margaret out of the ballroom and ran toward the nearest ladies' room. "Male coming in!" he yelled as he burst through the door.

The women standing by the sinks took one look at Margaret and one rushed to open a stall for them, while another grabbed a bunch of paper towels and followed behind them.

They made it just in time for Margaret to empty the contents of her stomach into the toilet.

"Here." The woman who'd rushed behind them thrust a bunch of paper towels into Bowen's hand. "I'll get a Perrier from the bar. The carbonated water will help."

Margaret's stomach kept heaving long after there was nothing left in it, and through it all, Bowen held her hair back and handed her paper towels to clean up the mess.

When the woman returned with the bottle, Bowen helped Margaret up and held the bottle to her lips.

The act of swallowing helped calm the heaving, and after a few more small sips, she handed him the bottle back. "Can you help me get to the sink? I need to wash my face."

"Of course." He propped her against his side and walked her to the sink.

The smell of vomit was so bad that it made her nauseous again, but she fought the urge to rush back to the stall, and splashed water over her face instead.

Looking at the mirror was a mistake. She looked gray, and not just because her mascara and eyeliner were smeared all over her eye sockets.

"I think I need to see a doctor," she murmured.

"I agree." Bowen lifted her into his arms. "Thank you," he said to the two women before walking out of the bathroom and heading for the elevators.

"Wait. We need to tell Wendy and the others that we're leaving."

"I'll call them from the car." He pressed the button.

Feeling exhausted, she rested her head on his chest. "I'm sorry."

"For what?" He stepped into the elevator.

"I stink of puke." Margaret chuckled feebly. "It seems to be a pattern for us. When you first met me, I smelled of puke as well, and you carried me to the ambulance."

He kissed the top of her head. "That was the luckiest day of my life. Not so lucky for you, though. You were in so much pain."

"Which you took away with a thrall. Back then, I didn't know how it happened, but now I do."

The elevator doors opened at the parking garage, but the souped-up golf cart wasn't there.

"We can wait for the transport, or I can walk through the tunnel if that's okay with you. It's not a long walk."

If he were a human man, she would have told him to wait for the golf cart, but Bowen was an immortal, and carrying her was not an effort for him.

"I like being in your arms. We can intercept the golf cart on the way."

He grinned as if she'd given him a boon. "I love carrying you." He walked into the tunnel. "What else do you remember from our first meeting?"

She knew what he was doing. He wanted her to stay awake and not pass out on him.

"When you arrived, I was lying on the grass in excruciating pain. And yet, I noticed how handsome you were. Most of your face was hidden behind the firefighter mask, but I could see your lips, and I thought that they were nice. I also thought that your voice was beautiful, deep and compassionate, the voice of a savior." She snuggled closer to his chest. "I think it was love at first sight. Or maybe at first sound? I remember thinking that I was hallucinating, especially after you looked into my eyes and the pain subsided."

"I should have thralled you to ease your stomach. I don't know why it didn't occur to me. Do you want me to do it now?"

"No." She closed her eyes. "I'm no longer nauseous. Just tired."

72

CASSANDRA

$\mathcal{A}$ fter the commotion of Syssi's water breaking, the party lost momentum. Some people left immediately after Syssi and Kian's departure, no one was on the dance floor, and those who stayed were sitting around the tables and talking, probably about what had happened.

Onegus's mother, who'd been uncharacteristically friendly throughout dinner, had gone to join her friends, and Sharon and Robert had come over to their table to chat. It was nice to hang out with the original group Cassandra had gotten to know during the wedding celebration, but she would have gladly left as well.

She was tired, and tomorrow was a workday, but Onegus was busy with security matters, and she had no choice but to wait for him.

The plan was for her to stay the night and have Onegus drive her to the office tomorrow morning. She'd even packed an overnight bag, which was still in Connor's car. The guy would no doubt keep her company until Onegus was done, but perhaps a better idea would be to head down to their little shag pad and get a nap in the meantime.

After Connor brought the bag from his car, he could go home instead of babysitting her.

"Guess who else was taken to the clinic." Nick put down a tray loaded with another round of drinks.

"Who?" Ruth asked.

"Wendy's mom, Margaret. She might be transitioning." Nick took a sip of his drink. "I heard that she puked her guts out, and Bowen took her to the clinic." He chuckled. "I feel sorry for Bridget and Julian. Not only did they have their party cut short, but they will also have to pull an all-nighter with one lady having a baby and the other transitioning."

Cassandra's gut clenched. Anytime now, she might start transitioning as well. What if it happened while she was at the office? If the process was gradual, she might have time to call Onegus and have him take her to the clinic. But what if she lost consciousness? And what if it happened while she was driving?

Damn, Onegus should have considered those things. He'd been so excited about her finally giving her consent that he hadn't thought it through.

Heck, she hadn't either. In her mind, it was something that would happen in the future.

"Does anyone know how long ago Margaret and Bowen started working on her transition?" she asked.

Sylvia pursed her lips. "They've been together for a few weeks. So I guess a while ago."

Cassandra let out a breath. She still had time. But maybe from now on, she should start taking an Uber to work.

"I thought that I was the only human here," she said. "Are there any more whom I'm not aware of?"

"Ronja and Lisa," Ruth said. "Ronja is David's mother, and Lisa is his sister. They are both Dormants, but Ronja is too old to transition, and Lisa is too young."

"Onegus told me about the risks involved for older Dormants. But I wasn't aware that it was also dangerous below a certain age. I assume you're talking about the tall blonde girl?"

Ruth's cheeks reddened. "In Lisa's case, the risk is not the problem. She's only fifteen, and given what's involved in inducing a female Dormant, that's too young."

"I get it. She's too young to have sex." Cassandra smiled to reassure the shy woman.

Unlike her daughter who was outspoken and outgoing, Ruth was reserved and preferred to hide behind Nick's back, even though she was much older than him.

Cassandra had learned earlier that Ruth was Sylvia's mother, that Nick was a newly transitioned Dormant, and so were Sharon and Tessa. The three new immortals worked for Eva, a woman who'd been turned immortal decades ago following a random hookup. Eva hadn't known how it had happened, but apparently, she'd had a sixth sense about sniffing out Dormants and getting them to work for her.

Perhaps it had to do with the affinity Dormants and immortals felt for each other, or perhaps it had been the Fates that everyone kept invoking, or maybe it was Eva's special talent.

In either case, Cassandra wanted to meet the woman. An immortal detective agency was perfect for what she needed to dig into her mother's past.

"Can one of you introduce me to Eva?"

"She went home already," Tessa said. "Eva and Bhathian have a little boy."

"Were they the ones with the stroller?"

She remembered thinking that the woman looked imposing even next to her burly husband. The guy had muscles to spare and reminded her of The Rock.

Tessa nodded. "Next time you're in the village, give her a call."

"Why do you want to meet Eva?" Sharon asked.

Cassandra cast a quick look at Roni. "I would like to find out what happened to my mother. How did she become immortal, who induced her, and how did she lose her memory? It's not the kind of investigation I can hire a human detective agency for."

She hadn't asked Roni about his grandfather yet. The opportunity hadn't presented itself. And now that it had, she chickened out. Perhaps it would be better to ask him when they didn't have an audience.

Roni shook his head. "If Turner didn't find anything, no one will."

"Don't bet on it." Sharon crossed her arms over her chest. "Turner didn't have a lot to go on. Cassandra has thirty-something years of clues to add to the investigation. I can talk with Eva and see what she thinks. These days, she's not actively participating in investigations, but she has a lot of experience she brings to the table." Sharon smiled at Cassandra. "I do most of the groundwork, Nick handles the surveillance, and Tessa manages all the scheduling, the paperwork, and everything else that goes on in the office."

"I'd appreciate it." Cassandra doubted that she could afford them. One detective working alone, she might, but not a four-person team.

"Don't worry." Sharon uncrossed her arms. "We will give you a big discount."

"I'll pay half the costs," Roni offered. "After all, this investigation involves me as well."

73

ONEGUS

*E*xcitement swirled in Onegus's chest. A lot of good things were happening at once. Kian and Syssi were about to become parents, Margaret was transitioning, and the clan had the technology to produce more Odus.

If the saying about all good things coming in threes was true, then making more Odus was a good thing.

There was a similar saying about bad things coming in threes as well, but that didn't bear thinking about.

His mother used to say that positive thinking was necessary for positive outcomes, and it had stuck with him. Despite his job demanding him to be acutely aware of all possible pitfalls, Onegus was the glass-half-full kind of guy, always hoping for the best.

Given the exciting events, the evening was coming to an end much earlier than expected, which was a good thing as well. He couldn't wait to be done with his duties, so he could take Cassandra down to the cell and make love to her for hours.

"Any news?" Yamanu asked as Onegus walked into the kitchen.

"It's too early. But just in case, let me check." He pulled out his phone. "No messages. How soon until everything gets wrapped up in here?"

"They are about half-done."

"I hope they hurry up. We still have to wait for all the guests to leave and then comb the entire place for bugs. Thank the Fates for William's portable detector. Before we had that, it would have taken us until morning to check every inch of such a big place."

"Don't you love technology?" Yamanu grinned.

Onegus stifled a chuckle. If Yamanu only knew what the clan was currently sitting on. He wondered when Kian would reveal the information to the council, which included the head Guardians. In the meantime though, he had to keep it under wraps.

"The party was fun." Yamanu leaned against the wall and crossed his arms over his chest. "But it doesn't seem right to continue without the birthday boy."

"True." Onegus checked his phone again for messages before putting it back in his pocket. "Come to think of it, we might need to organize another party before our guests depart. Allegra's birth also merits a celebration."

Yamanu glared at him. "It's bad luck to talk about celebrating a child's birth before it happens."

"I'm not superstitious."

Given his earlier musings about things coming in threes, that was hypocritical of him to say, but Onegus still didn't think of himself as superstitious.

"I am," Yamanu said. "And I've been proven right many times over. So, humor me."

"No problem." Onegus took one more glance at the crates Gerard's crew were packing serve ware into. They still had a lot of work before they were done. "I'd better go check on Cassandra."

Walking into the ballroom, he made a quick assessment of how many guests were still there and came up with too many. Only about a third had left, and he couldn't think of a way to hasten the others' departure.

Perhaps he should change the playlist to hip-hop?

Cassandra must have sensed his approach and turned to look over her shoulder. The smile she gave him was so dazzling that he stumbled back a step.

"Miss me?" he drawled as he pulled out a chair next to her.

"Not at all." She gestured at her table companions. "My friends kept me entertained."

"Liar." He leaned and kissed her cheek. "Anyway, I missed you. I can't wait for everyone to go home."

"I heard that," Roni said. "Do you want me to take the mic and recite slam poetry? That will clear the room quick enough."

"I bet. But I don't want to have to defend you from flying objects."

"Did you hear anything about Syssi?" Ruth asked.

"Not yet." He glanced at his watch. "It has been a little over an hour since her water broke, but I don't think deliveries happen that fast."

"I want to text Bridget," Sylvia said. "But I don't want to bother her."

"I have an idea." Onegus pulled out his phone. "Anandur and Brundar are with them." He chose the older brother's contact and shot him a short text.

No baby yet, came the reply, then a moment later, *Bowen and Margaret just got here. She passed out on the way. Julian says she's transitioning.*

"Well?" Cassandra asked.

He read the texts out loud.

She let out a breath. "It's going to be a long night for everyone."

"You have work tomorrow. Do you want to take a nap in my office while I wrap things up here?"

Hopefully, she knew that his office wasn't where he planned to take her. He just didn't want to advertise that she was staying with him in the dungeon.

He shouldn't have worried.

Cassandra grinned. "That's a great idea. But first, I need to get something from Connor's car."

"I can get it for you," Connor said. "I'll bring it to Onegus's office."

"Thank you. I'm so tired that I can't wait to put my head down for a few minutes."

Given the sly smiles all around, they were not fooling anyone, but that was okay. Cassandra spending the night with him down in the dungeon was not some big secret.

"Well, good night, everyone." Cassandra pushed her chair back. "I hope to see you all again soon."

"Likewise," Roni said.

Pushing to his feet, Onegus offered Cassandra a hand up. "Let's say good night to my mother."

"Of course."

7 4

KIAN

*T*he last time Kian had waited for his child to be born, things had been a lot different. He hadn't been allowed in the room, and since the house he and Lavena had shared was basically one open space with a loft, he'd been reduced to standing outside the window and listening to his wife's screams.

The midwife had refused to let him near the birthing bed, and although he could have thralled her to allow him in, he hadn't wanted to mess with the woman's brain when she was delivering his baby.

The memory no longer brought about the pang of pain and regret it usually had. Kian had come to terms with his past thanks to his smart and compassionate mate. Syssi had helped him realize that viewing his marriage to Lavena as a mistake and beating himself up for fathering a human child was disrespectful to his daughter's memory. It was better that she'd existed than if she had not, and thanks to his discreet help, his human daughter had had a good life, and so had her descendants.

He had done all he could for her.

This time around, he wasn't banished to the yard. He was sitting on a chair next to Syssi's bed, holding her hand while she slept, and watching the monitors she was hooked up to. It reminded him more of Syssi's transition than his daughter's delivery all those centuries ago.

Bridget had given Syssi a local anesthetic, something called an epidural, and then something else to induce her labor. With the epidural, the only indication he had of when the contractions were happening was the spikes on the monitor, which were now coming in intervals of every five minutes or so.

Bridget expected active labor to commence soon, but until then Syssi could rest, which was a blessing. The part Kian dreaded the most was seeing her suffer.

As the door opened, he turned to look at the doctor. "How is your other patient doing?"

"Margaret is still unconscious." Bridget walked up to Syssi. "So far, her vitals are good, and I hope it continues this way." She snapped on a set of surgical gloves. "I need to check the dilation. You might want to look the other way."

Bridget being a woman, he'd thought it wouldn't bother him, but it did, and he preferred to avert his gaze. Somehow, even though it was medically necessary, it seemed like a violation.

Syssi squeezed his hand, letting him know that she was awake before asking Bridget, "How many centimeters?"

"Eight," the doctor said. "It won't be long now."

"Is Margaret okay?"

It was so like his Syssi to worry about everyone when she needed to focus on herself.

"She's unconscious, but she's doing well."

"How is Bowen doing?"

"Hanging in there." Bridget pulled the latex gloves off. "Try to get some rest."

When she left, Kian rose to his feet and kissed Syssi's forehead. "After you fell asleep, your mother went to change out of her party dress, and your father went with her. I told them I'd let them know if they needed to hurry back."

She nodded and then closed her eyes. "It's so strange that I can't feel anything. I can't even feel my legs."

"Are you scared?"

"I'm impatient. I want to hold my daughter in my arms already."

"It won't be long now," he repeated Bridget's words, but coming from him, they sounded like a platitude.

"Tell my parents to get you something to drink. You sound parched."

Kian chuckled. "Don't worry about me. If I need anything, I can ask Anandur or Brundar to get it. They are sitting on the bench outside the clinic."

Syssi's eyes popped open. "Why? Tell them to go home."

"I did. They refused. Andrew is with them, and he refuses to go home either. He says that he wants to be here when his niece arrives and take pictures."

A fond smile tugged at the corners of Syssi's lips. "That's so sweet of him. Just don't let him in the room until it's all over and I'm decent. Other than Bridget and the nurses, the only ones allowed during the delivery are you and my mother." She let out a breath. "I wouldn't have minded having Amanda here as well. She's like a sister to me."

"I can call her. She probably wanted to be here but didn't think you would."

He wasn't sure about that at all, but if Syssi wanted Amanda to come, he would make sure that she did.

"On second thought, don't. It might get too crowded in here, and Bridget will kick everyone out." She chuckled. "I bet she wants to kick my mother out."

He had a feeling Syssi was right. The two doctors were doing their best to be civil to each other, but Bridget didn't like having another doctor looking over her shoulder, and Anita didn't trust Bridget with her daughter.

"Their egos are too big to fit in one room, but they are both professionals. They'll survive one night of working together."

75

BOWEN

*H*ours had passed since Margaret had slipped into unconsciousness. Leon and Anastasia had gone home to shower and change, promising to be back even though Bowen had told them there was no need for them to stay up all night.

Wendy refused to leave Margaret's side and was in the room with him, sitting on a chair across from him. His mother kept sending messages every half an hour or so to inquire about Margaret, and even Ronja had sent him a text message wishing them both best of luck.

Wendy yawned. "I'm going to get a cup of coffee from the vending machine. Do you want anything?"

"Coffee sounds good. Thanks."

"No problem." She stretched her arms over her head. "I'll be back in two minutes."

Since she'd refused to go home to change out of her party clothes, Vlad had brought her a pair of sweatpants, a T-shirt, and flip-flops. He'd wanted to stay and keep them company, but Wendy had shooed him away. He had work tomorrow and then school.

It reminded Bowen of the time the five of them were up in the cabin. He, Leon, Wendy, Vlad, and Richard. It seemed so long ago when he'd given Vlad and Wendy fatherly advice, helping them overcome their fears and take a chance on each other. He'd never imagined that he would one day become Wendy's stepfather, and Vlad's father-in-law.

But here they were.

A family.

Bowen was jumping the gun a little, but he knew that everything was going to happen just as he envisioned it.

Margaret was going to transition, they would get married, and hopefully they would be blessed with a child. A little brother or sister for Wendy would be the final step in mother and daughter's healing, erasing the last remaining shadows of their troubled past.

Some might think that he was being overly optimistic, and that there was a limit to what love could heal, but Bowen had faith in its power.

"You're going to be okay." He gently squeezed Margaret's hand.

When her fingers curled up, he was afraid that he'd squeezed too hard, but when he looked up, he saw that her eyes were open, and jumped up to his feet.

"You're awake." He brushed a strand of hair away from her cheek and kissed it.

"Did I transition?" she murmured.

"You're on your way, but it hasn't been long enough."

"How long was I out?"

"Close to four hours."

The door opened, and Julian walked in. "Hello, Margaret. I'm happy to see you awake." He walked up to the bed. "You're doing very well. Your temperature is elevated but nowhere near dangerous levels, and your blood pressure is high but stable."

She smiled feebly. "How much longer until we know for sure?"

"Oh, we know for sure already. But if you are asking when the first stage will be over, it depends. Provided that you don't lose consciousness for more than several hours at the time, it might be as early as tomorrow morning."

The door opened again, and Wendy walked in with a cup of coffee in each hand. "Mom? You're awake?"

Smiling, Margaret nodded.

As Wendy's hands started shaking, Bowen rushed to take the cups from her. She'd been so strong while her mother was unconscious but had fallen apart to see her awake?

Tears streaming down her cheeks, Wendy ran to the bed and wrapped her arms around Margaret as much as the medical equipment allowed. "I couldn't bear the thought of losing you again."

"Oh, baby." Margaret stroked her back. "I'm not going anywhere. In fact, you are now stuck with me forever because I'm never leaving."

Chuckling through her tears, Wendy kissed her mother's forehead. "I'm looking forward to many, many years together." She lifted off Margaret and wiped away the tears with her hands. "And if we need time apart, we can go on vacations." She winked at Bowen. "Elise already invited Vlad and me to visit her in Scotland. She said that she's adopting us as her grandchildren and warned that she's going to fuss over us."

Bowen put the coffee cups on the side table and took Margaret's hand. "Fates willing, we will give Elise more grandchildren to fuss over."

Margaret's eyes widened. "Did Syssi deliver her daughter while I was out?"

Everyone turned to look at Julian, who smiled broadly.

"Bridget and the nurses are with her. It should be any moment now."

76

SYSSI

*T*he strong baby wail was the most beautiful sound Syssi had ever heard. Tears she hadn't shed while pushing and grunting and straining were now flowing freely down her cheeks.

"It's a girl!" Hildegard called out even though everyone had known that for months. "And she's absolutely perfect. Right, Daddy?"

Stunned and speechless, Kian nodded.

A moment later, the nurse placed Allegra on Syssi's chest and proceeded to gently pat her dry. "Mama and baby bonding time." She covered her with a warm blanket and put a tiny cap on her head. "Daddy will have to wait his turn in a little bit."

Her heart overflowing with love, Syssi placed a gentle hand on her daughter's soft back.

"Do you want to cut the cord?" Bridget asked Kian.

He shook his head. "It's too terrifying."

"Anita?" Bridget asked.

"It will be my pleasure."

"She's so beautiful," Kian murmured next to Syssi's ear. "She looks like you." He pressed his cheek to Syssi's and gazed at his daughter.

"She does," Anita agreed, tears shining in her smiling eyes.

Syssi stroked her child's soft cheek. "Should I try to nurse her?"

"Go ahead," her mother said. "It will send a message to your brain to begin milk production." It hadn't taken her long to switch from mother to doctor mode. "Right now, all you have is colostrum, but it's all Allegra needs until milk production begins. It's rich in immunoglobulins and amino acids and will help build up her immune system."

Syssi stifled the urge to roll her eyes. Perhaps slipping into the familiar medical jargon helped her mother regain her composure after the emotional high of witnessing her granddaughter's birth.

"The placenta is out," Bridget announced.

Overwhelmed with emotion and the sensation of having her baby lying on her breast, Syssi hadn't even felt it coming out. Then again, it might have been the epidural's effect.

"Can I kiss my daughter?" Kian asked.

"Of course." Anita tugged on the blanket Hildegard had draped over Allegra and put the stethoscope on her tiny back. "I need to assess Allegra's post-delivery condition."

The assessment didn't take long, and Allegra received an Apgar score of nine from her grandmother.

"Why not ten?" Kian asked.

Anita chuckled. "No baby gets a ten."

When he didn't look happy, she patted his arm. "Don't pout. Nine is as high as it gets."

"I'm not pouting. When can I hold her?"

"After Allegra nurses, we will place antibiotic drops in her eyes and give her a shot of Vitamin K. When all that is done, you can hold her."

"Why does she need antibiotics? We don't transmit diseases."

"It's a precaution," Bridget said. "Bacteria could have hitched a ride on you, especially since you were in contact with humans tonight."

Kian let out a breath. "I can wait."

"How do I get her to nurse?" Syssi asked.

She was afraid to move the tiny baby. Allegra looked so fragile.

"All you need to do is reposition her, so her mouth is next to your nipple." As Syssi hesitated, Anita smiled. "You can move her. She'll be fine."

Gently, Syssi lifted the tiny bundle and put her a few inches down on her belly. "What now?"

"She'll figure it out," Bridget said.

Allegra's tiny tongue extended, and she gave the nipple a little lick, but she didn't suckle.

"What do I do now? Should I put the nipple in her mouth?"

"Just stroke her cheek," Hildegard said.

As soon as Syssi did that, Allegra's little mouth opened wide, and she latched on beautifully and started suckling.

"Wow," Syssi whispered. "That's incredible."

"Yes, you are." Transfixed, Kian watched her feeding their child for the first time.

It didn't take long for Allegra to have her fill and fall asleep.

"When should we bathe her?" Syssi asked in a whisper.

"Tomorrow," her mother said.

"Good. I don't want to be separated from her."

"You'll have to give her up for a few minutes," Bridget said. "We need to give her the drops and the vitamin shot, and then it's Daddy's turn to hold his little bundle of joy."

Reluctantly, Syssi let the doctor take her baby, immediately missing her, the slight weight on her chest, the soft skin on her own. But it had to be done, and Kian had been waiting so patiently for his turn.

He took the opportunity while everyone was busy with Allegra to plant a kiss on Syssi's lips. "I love you so much. I didn't think it was possible to love you more, but I was wrong. My heart is full to bursting."

Tears welling in her eyes, she wrapped her arms around his neck and held on tight. "I love you. Always and forever."

When she finally let go and Kian straightened, his eyes were misted, and impossibly, she loved him even more for that. Her big, macho guy was overwhelmed with emotion.

"Are you ready?" Anita came back holding the baby swaddled in a soft yellow blanket.

Nodding, he sat in the chair. "You'll need to show me how to hold her. The last time I held a baby, it was nineteen centuries ago."

"It's like riding a bicycle. Once you master it, you never forget." Smiling, Anita showed him how to fold his arm to create a cradle for their sweet little bundle.

When she placed Allegra in his arms, the mist in Kian's eyes became denser, but his lips curved in a proud grin. "Hello, my little princess. I am your daddy, and you've heard my voice for nine months now, so it should sound familiar."

As Kian kept talking softly to their daughter, the tears welled again in Syssi's eyes.

Happy tears.

The happiest.

CASSANDRA

*T*he sound of the door mechanism activating woke Cassandra up from a disturbing nightmare. She'd been running away from someone chasing her with a hammer, but the details were already fading, and she didn't know who it had been, other than he wasn't a stranger. The sense of betrayal still lingered, as did the rapid pounding of her heart.

She had to remind herself that she was safe in Onegus's and her underground shag pad. No one could get to her here, friend or foe.

"Are you that excited to see me?" Onegus walked in, taking his jacket off on the way.

"I had a bad dream." She scooted sideways to give him room.

His forehead furrowed. "What was it about?" He hung the jacket over the back of a chair and sat down next to her.

"Someone was chasing me, but I don't know who or why. I just had a sense that I knew him."

Cupping her cheek, he leaned and kissed the other. "Dreams are often just a reflection of what occupies our minds during the waking hours. What were you thinking about before falling asleep?"

"My mother." She pushed up on the pillows. "It makes sense now why I was having a nightmare. I was thinking about why my mom abandoned her family. She is not the type who would have left a child behind and forgotten about her. After Sharon told me the highlights of Wendy and Margaret's story, and how Margaret had no choice but to leave Wendy behind with her father, it occurred to me that something similar might have happened to my mother. Maybe even worse given the head trauma and following amnesia." Cassandra shivered. "Perhaps Roni's grandfather had something to do with it."

With a sigh, Onegus started on his shirt buttons. "Everything is possible. Somehow, we will get to the bottom of this. Perhaps your mother remembers more than she lets on."

As the two halves of his dress shirt started to part, exposing his smooth, muscular chest, Cassandra was momentarily distracted, thoughts about her mother and everything else she'd planned on discussing with him evaporating into thin air.

There was one thing, though, that couldn't wait. "You know what we both neglected to take into account regarding my induction?"

His fingers paused on the last button. "What?"

"That it's not safe. What if I start transitioning while I'm at work? Or driving?"

Since she was new to the whole thing, Cassandra's oversight could be excused. Onegus, on the other hand, should have been mindful of the risks.

He went even paler than usual. "You are a hundred percent correct. Callie blacked out while driving and got into an accident. Luckily, she only broke her arm, but it could have been much worse." He shook his head. "I can't believe it hasn't occurred to me. I was so excited about obtaining your consent, that the only risk I considered was the transition itself. In my defense, I wasn't involved with the other transitioning adult Dormants. Our kids transition at a young age, and it's a smooth process."

He looked so guilty that she took pity on him. "You're forgiven."

"If anything happened to you, I would have never forgiven myself. You have to either take time off or work remotely."

She'd already considered her options, and working remotely was one of the solutions she'd come up with. The other was to have someone drive her to and from work.

"I can use a taxi service or an Uber to commute, or I can tell Kevin that I came down with something and need to work from home. If I pass out, and they take me to a hospital, you can come to get me. That's not considered breaking clan law, right?"

"It's not. Thralling is allowed to hide our existence, and a transitioning Dormant in a human hospital is like a billboard announcing it to the world."

"I've heard that Eva's induction happened by chance. How come her transition didn't alert anyone?"

"She was very young at the time, and her symptoms were so mild that she thought she had the flu. Most Dormants are not that lucky."

"Speaking of Dormants, did you hear anything about Margaret?"

"She's doing remarkably well given her age." Onegus opened the last button, shrugged the shirt off, and draped it over his jacket. "She woke up a few hours ago and hasn't slipped back into unconsciousness."

"A few hours ago? What time is it?"

"Nearly five in the morning. The guys and I were waiting for news about Syssi."

"And?"

He smiled proudly. "Mother and daughter are doing just fine. Allegra was born an hour ago, a healthy, eight pound five ounce baby. The guys and I had a small celebration of whiskey and cigars." He smiled sheepishly. "Kian brought a case for us to smoke later, and it was a shame to let them go to waste. I took a video of each of the guys congratulating him with a cigar and whiskey in their hands."

"Kian must be over the moon."

"He is." Onegus pushed his trousers down his hips, and as he turned to drape them over his shirt, Cassandra admired his sculptured bottom.

Damn, the man was fine.

"How tired are you?"

The wolfish grin he cast her said that he had no intentions of going to sleep anytime soon. "I'm not tired at all." He dropped his briefs, tossed them on the chair, climbed into the bed, and pulled her on top of him. "I forgot to ask you something important."

She frowned down at him. "What is it?"

"How many kids do you want to have?"

Cassandra smiled. "As many as you can give me."

"That's at least ten."

"Oh, really?" She dipped her head and kissed him. "Five girls and five boys?"

"Seven and three." He flipped them around. "Both are lucky numbers."

Dear reader,

Thank you for reading the *Children of the Gods*.

As an independent author, I rely on your support to spread the word. So if you enjoyed the story, please share your experience with others, and if it isn't too much trouble, I would greatly appreciate a brief review on Amazon.

Click **HERE** to leave a review

Love & happy reading,

Isabell

COMING UP NEXT
THE CHILDREN OF THE GODS
DARK MEMORIES TRILOGY

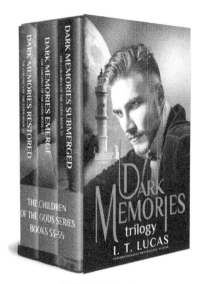

Read the enclosed excerpt

INCLUDES:
53: DARK MEMORIES SUBMERGED
54: DARK MEMORIES EMERGE
55: DARK MEMORIES RESTORED

THE CHILDREN OF THE GODS ORIGINS
GODDESS'S CHOICE
GODDESS'S HOPE

THE PERFECT MATCH SERIES
PERFECT MATCH 1: VAMPIRE'S CONSORT
PERFECT MATCH 2: KING'S CHOSEN
PERFECT MATCH 3: CAPTAIN'S CONQUEST

JOIN THE VIP CLUB AT ITLUCAS.COM
AND GAIN ACCESS TO THE VIP PORTAL

(To find out what's included in your free membership, click HERE or flip to the last page.

If you're already a subscriber, you can find **your VIP password** in each of my new release emails. If you are not getting my emails, your provider is sending them to your junk folder, and you are missing out on **important updates, side characters' portraits, additional content, and other goodies.** To fix that, add isabell@itlucas.com to your email contacts or your email VIP list.

DARK MEMORIES EXCERPT

GERALDINE

Geraldine applied a coat of gloss over her rose-hued lipstick and examined her reflection in the mirror.

Ageless was the look she was going for, but there was no hiding the fact that she looked way too young to have a thirty-four-year-old daughter. So far, she'd somehow gotten away with it, but the older Cassandra got, the harder it was to pull off.

When people remarked on Geraldine's youthful appearance, she usually responded with a simple thank you, and more often than not, that sufficed. Some went further though, asking what her secret was, and for those she had a rehearsed reply—she stayed out of the sun, applied sunscreen every morning, and moisturized day and night.

Since that was what people expected to hear, they accepted her answer and moved on. She was just a simple suburban mother who wasn't important enough to justify further inquiry.

Soon, though, she would be forced to add plastic surgery to her arsenal of answers.

With a sigh, Geraldine pulled a brush through her hair.

Where did the time go?

For most people, that was just an expression. For her, it was a reality she had to live with. Huge chunks were missing from her memory.

She didn't remember being a child, or who her parents were. It was as if she'd been born an adult, and even after that so-called birth, much of her life was hazy.

Geraldine remembered waking up in a rehab center with a mind that was nearly a blank page. Later, after she'd relearned speech, she'd been told about the head trauma that had supposedly been the cause of her amnesia.

No trace of it remained, but from time to time, she felt a phantom pain on the left side of her head, and she imagined that was where she'd been injured.

Then again, she imagined many things that weren't real.

It was so frustrating to have a brain that seemed perfectly normal and yet didn't work right.

And why the hell wasn't she aging?

Did it have anything to do with the injury she'd sustained?

Geraldine didn't know how old she was when she woke up in the rehab center, but thirty-six years later, she looked exactly the same as she'd looked then.

She lived in fear of discovering the cause, and even more so of being found out. People would pay a fortune to analyze the secret of the fountain of youth hidden in her body.

Hopefully, the fake IDs she'd gotten over the years were confusing enough to throw potential investigators off her trail. So far no one had followed her, so her strategy was working. She also didn't use credit cards, paying in cash whenever possible, and she had no property listed under her name either.

Thankfully, Geraldine also never got sick, so she didn't need to see any doctors. She'd even delivered Cassy at home with the help of a midwife.

Well, not having medical insurance had been the main reason she'd chosen to do it that way, but she was so glad she hadn't gone to a hospital. They might have taken blood samples and discovered the abnormality that was keeping her young.

At the time, she still hadn't known that there was something wrong with her other than the memory loss. But in retrospect, not having money to spare had worked to her advantage.

Raising a daughter alone and having no formal education, Geraldine found it impossible to get a well-paying job, so money had always been scarce.

She'd supported herself and Cassandra by making quilts, for which she had a natural knack. The proceeds from selling them had covered her expenses, but medical insurance had been a luxury she couldn't afford.

All of that had changed once Cassandra started working at Fifty Shades of Beauty. Now they both had medical insurance, and quilt making had turned into a hobby rather than a way to earn a living.

It was nice to create just for the sake of creation without having to work long hours or rush to complete a project so she could pay the rent.

Her quilts were beautiful if she said so herself, and while she still had been selling them, they'd been snatched up no matter what price tag she'd put on them.

The last one Geraldine had sold fetched over seven thousand dollars, an extravagant sum that she'd been sure no one would pay.

Nowadays, she only made them for fun or to give out as gifts to her friends.

In part it was to humor Cassy, who insisted that her mother no longer needed to slave over the sewing machine, and in part it was because her quilts were a calling card that someone might trace back to her.

It was safer not to advertise her work.

"Mom!" Cassandra yelled from downstairs. "Are you ready? Onegus will be here at any moment."

"I'll be right down!" Geraldine took one last look in the mirror, checked that her eyeliner wasn't smudged, and fluffed up her hair.

She and Cassandra were meeting Onegus's mother for lunch, and Geraldine didn't want to be outdone by the woman. She wasn't nearly as beautiful as Martha, but Geraldine had been told that she resembled Elizabeth Taylor, who had been called the most beautiful woman in the world, so there was that.

Except, the definition of beauty had changed since the legendary actress had been a star. Nowadays, tall leggy blondes with strong jawlines like Martha were all the rave, while petite brunettes with hourglass figures and small chins were not.

Still, she and the mother of the man Cassandra had fallen in love with had a lot in common. They both looked much too young to have children in their thirties, they each had only one child, and both had raised them without a father.

Onegus and Cassandra becoming a couple and introducing their mothers to each other seemed almost serendipitous.

Here was another woman, one who lived across the ocean from her, who also somehow defied aging. Had Martha been the victim of a freak accident as well? Could that be the explanation for both of their unnaturally youthful appearances?

Not likely.

Perhaps good genes were responsible for their youthful looks after all. And if not, perhaps Martha knew the secret and could explain why aging didn't seem to affect either of them.

The get-together would be a good opportunity to ask. Martha was returning to Scotland Sunday evening, so today was Geraldine's last chance.

Opening her purse, she dropped the lipstick and the gloss inside, closed it, and headed downstairs.

Cassandra was waiting for her at the bottom of the staircase. "You look beautiful, Mom." Her gaze swept over Geraldine's dress and matching heels. "I love the polka dots. Who knew that they would make a comeback?"

The small white dots contrasting with the navy blue was a classic pattern, as was the cut of the dress. Martha would have a hard time finding fault with Geraldine's outfit.

"Do you like it?"

Cassy had as good an eye for colors and patterns as she did, and she trusted her opinion.

"I love it. The puffy skirt and cinched waist make you look like a cover model on a fifties fashion magazine."

"They do?" Geraldine smoothed her hand over the skirt. "I didn't realize that. Should I change into something else? I don't want to look old-fashioned."

She just wanted to look older.

Cassandra shook her head. "It's perfect on you."

"Thank you." Geraldine lifted her hand and cupped her daughter's cheek. "Tell me the truth. Are you and Onegus going to announce your engagement over lunch?"

Cassandra smiled nervously. "I've already answered that. Did you forget?"

Her daughter knew that comments about her memory issues upset her, which indicated that questions regarding Cassandra and Onegus's possible engagement had hit a nerve.

"I didn't forget. But you took half a day off from work, which you rarely do, so accompanying me to a lunch meeting with your boyfriend's mother must be very important to you. What else am I supposed to think?"

It wasn't only that. Cassandra had been edgy ever since the change in plans had been made. Geraldine had been supposed to meet Martha for lunch on Thursday, just the two of them, and then Martha had called to reschedule it for today so that Onegus and Cassandra could join them.

The phone's ringing saved her daughter from answering. "It was the gate," she said after ending the call. "Onegus is here."

CASSANDRA

Talk about being saved by the bell, or the ring, as was the case.

Tucking her purse under her arm, Cassandra opened the front door just as Onegus pulled up to the curb.

"You both look spectacular." He held the back passenger door open for her mother.

"Thank you." Geraldine smiled at him. "You're very kind."

"I'm just truthful." He opened the front passenger door for Cassandra. "You okay?" he whispered as he kissed her cheek.

She nodded even though she was far from it.

Cassandra was anxious and worried.

Were they doing the right thing with her mother?

The plan had seemed solid when they'd come up with it. Bring Geraldine to the clan's hidden village, confront her about her immortality and the family she'd left behind, and have her admit that she'd staged her own death by drowning. Roni would be there with Geraldine's fake driver's licenses as well as family photos of her with her older daughter, the one she seemed to have forgotten.

Was it all an act?

Was her mother aware of not aging? Did she remember having another family a long time ago? Or had she really lost her memory and didn't know either?

Confronted with her immortality and her past, Geraldine might spiral into one of her episodes. It didn't happen often, but when it did, her mother would become incoherent, babble nonsense and jumbled sentences, and cry for hours.

Sometimes it took days to bring her back to normal, or as normal as she got.

"You're tense," Onegus said. "Do you want me to put on some music?"

"I would love some," Geraldine said from the backseat. "Did I tell you about Cassy's dad? He was a musician."

"That's a new one," Cassandra whispered.

When her mother felt nervous or insecure, her stories got even more fantastical than usual.

One of Geraldine's two favorites was the one about her father working for the Ethiopian embassy. In one story he was the ambassador, in another an aide, and in yet another variation an analyst. But at least that story was pretty consistent. In all versions, his name was Emanuel, he was tall, handsome, and had a great smile. Her mother's other favorite was the brain surgeon she'd supposedly met in the hospital while recovering from her injury. He was brilliant, the head of the neurosurgical department, and a favorite of the nurses. His name changed from one telling of the story to another. Then there was the astronaut, who made an appearance once or twice a year, and a host of many others that had been one-time guests, like the musician she'd made up on the spot right now.

Onegus reached across the center console for Cassandra's hand. "What kind of music did he play?"

"Jazz, sometimes Blues." Geraldine sighed. "Every night, I sat in the back of the club and listened to his band perform. When he was on break, he would come to sit with me, and we would share a drink and talk and laugh. At the end of the night, after they were done playing, he would dance with me."

"Was he famous?" Onegus asked. "Maybe I've heard of him?"

Onegus was playing along, which was helping Geraldine relax. Getting deeper into her story mode always did.

"His name was Luis." She looked out the window. "He and his band weren't famous. They were young musicians, but they were good."

As Geraldine dove into her fantasy world, making up club names and going on about the famous actors and actresses coming to see Luis perform, Cassandra closed her eyes and tried to calm down.

The stress about the upcoming confrontation was stirring up her inner destructive energy, and if she didn't find a way to relax, she might blow something up.

Given that they were in a moving vehicle, that was extremely dangerous. Not so much for her mother and Onegus, who were immortal, but Cassandra was still human, which was another reason for her mounting stress.

She should have started transitioning already.

But that was a worry for another time. Right now, she needed to get the swirling turmoil under control.

When her energy blasts discharged, they mostly shattered glass and clay containers, but they could also melt electronics. Hopefully, she'd be able to hold it in until they reached the village, where she could aim the blast at a glass or a pot.

Given how elaborate Geraldine's story was becoming, her mother was nervous as hell, but at least she didn't notice when the windows started turning opaque and Onegus took his hands off the wheel.

They were nearing the village, and the car's computer had taken over. For the remainder of the trip, the windows would stay opaque, so they wouldn't know where the secret entrance to the underground tunnel was.

When the car entered the tunnel, Geraldine finally noticed that something wasn't right. "Where are we? Why did it get dark all of a sudden?"

"We are in a tunnel," Onegus said. "I hope that you're not claustrophobic."

"I'm not. But where is this tunnel? I didn't know there was one in this part of the city."

Right then, the car came to a stop, and a moment later, Cassandra felt it going up. They were in the elevator.

"What's that?" Her mother's tone was bordering on panicked.

"It's just a lift to an upper-level parking," Onegus said.

"Oh." Geraldine let out a breath and slumped in her seat. "It's in one of those underground parking structures."

"Precisely." Onegus turned to her and smiled reassuringly. "We are almost there."

KIAN

From his spot at the head of the conference table, Kian watched the open door, waiting impatiently for the rest of the council members to arrive and take their seats.

His office was the last place he wanted to be while his wife and newborn daughter were home, inundated with the never-ending throng of well-wishers. Syssi's parents were there to help, but so was Okidu—the reason why a council meeting was unavoidable less than two days after Allegra's birth.

Thinking about the cutest kryptonite in existence, Kian smiled. Since the first moment he'd seen her tiny face, he'd been overwhelmed by the love he felt for her and known that he would move mountains for her.

If it were up to Kian, he would have taken a paternity leave and stayed home with his baby until she was old enough to go to college.

The feeling of holding her in his arms was indescribable. It flooded him with such enormous amounts of oxytocin that he felt as high as if he'd taken a drug. Then again, the cuddling hormone was precisely that. It was nature's way of ensuring that mammals took care of their young.

Had it been like that with Beatrix? The human daughter he'd had with his human wife over nineteen centuries ago? Kian couldn't remember. But for the first time ever, he could think of her name without feeling a pang of sorrow in his heart and churning in his gut.

He'd paid a dear price for marrying a human at nineteen, and an even bigger one for having a child with her. Foolishly, he'd believed that he could hide his immortality and all it entailed from her, but it had been impossible. When his wife had become suspicious, faking his own death had been Kian's only option.

Lavena had suspected that he was a sorcerer, or a demon, or whatever other nonsense humans had believed at the time, and she'd feared him enough to share her suspicions with others. If she had, the villagers would have hunted him down, and he would have been forced to kill them all.

She'd left him no choice.

After faking his death, Kian had watched over his wife and daughter from afar, helping whenever he could without revealing himself. He'd watched Lavena remarry, had watched Beatrix grow to adulthood and have children of her own, get old, and die.

It had been the most difficult time of his very long life.

"Are you ready to begin?" Shai asked softly, his blue eyes full of compassion and understanding.

His assistant wasn't an empath per se, but he was incredibly attuned to Kian's moods. Had Shai realized that Kian had taken a trip down memory lane?

"Aye." He nodded at his assistant. "Let's begin."

While Kian had been distracted by his memories, the last council members he'd been waiting for had arrived.

"This is council meeting number 473," Shai announced. "Aside from Onegus, all council members are present."

The chief had a prior engagement, and since the meeting was informative in nature and the council wouldn't be voting, Kian had excused him. Besides, Onegus already knew about Okidu and his gift. Amanda, William, and Bridget were in the know as well, but they'd come to take part in the discussion.

That left only Brandon and Edna out of the loop, or maybe just Brandon.

Kalugal had somehow found out about the gift, and he had no doubt told Rufsur, his second-in-command, who in turn had told his mate, Edna.

Kian still hadn't figured out how Kalugal had found out so quickly, but he was determined to get to the bottom of it. If Kalugal was spying on him, that was a major breach of the accord.

Although, if the spying had been done out of curiosity and not with malicious intent, Kalugal could claim that it hadn't been a breach and get away with it. At least legally.

Kian's anger and mistrust would be personal, which was much worse.

"Some of you know what's on the agenda and why I have summoned you less than two days after my daughter's birth. Arguably, it could have waited until Monday, but I didn't want those of you who haven't heard about it yet to feel left out."

He looked at Edna and then at Brandon. "On the morning of my two thousandth birthday, Okidu presented me with a very special gift— the blueprints to build more of him. For months, he has secretly been filling up thirty-six thick handwritten tomes with instructions and schematics that have been hidden inside his operational memory." Kian waved a hand at William. "Don't ask me what that is. I'm sure William can explain it better."

Edna shook her head. "I'm not interested in hearing the details of how it was hidden. What I want to know is why it was hidden in the first place, and how it was retrieved nearly six thousand years later. I was under the impression that the Odus were found with their memories wiped clean."

"They were. Okidu doesn't know who encrypted them nor why. He rebooted after his drowning incident during Carol's rescue, and the reboot released those hidden memories. Along with the schematics, the reboot also released a new operational protocol that enables Okidu to better understand feelings and to make more autonomous decisions. One of his first decisions was to reboot Onidu, so he could help him write down the instructions and have them ready in time for my birthday. He tricked Onidu into submerging himself in the bathtub by telling him that Amanda had commanded it."

"Oh, boy." Brandon groaned. "We are in big trouble."

Kian nodded. "My sentiment exactly. We now have two sentient cyborgs, who are indestructible and dangerous, and who have the emotional intelligence of toddlers."

"I disagree," Amanda said. "I watched Okidu with Syssi and Allegra. He's very protective of both. Every time someone stops by to congratulate you and to see the baby, he hovers closely and makes sure that they keep their distance because they might be carrying germs on their clothes that are dangerous to the baby. This is precisely what our mother programmed him to do—to protect her children, and by extension, her grandchildren."

"I noticed." Kian turned to William. "Did you have a chance to go over any of it yet?"

Given how red-rimmed the guy's eyes were, he hadn't slept since the journals had been delivered to his office in the lab.

"The amount of information is staggering, and most of it is new. It will take me months to go over the entire thing. Maybe even years." He removed his glasses and rubbed his eyes. "I still haven't deciphered all that's contained in Ekin's tablet. My progress is in step with humanity's. I can't do it all alone."

In a way, Kian was glad. If a genius like William needed so long to decipher the information, Kalugal couldn't do anything with it even if he somehow got a hold of it.

Not that he was going to.

"What do you plan to do with the information once it's deciphered?" Edna asked.

"I don't know yet." He leaned back in his chair. "I'm glad that we have plenty of time to think it through and don't have to rush our decision. Even if we decide not to build any more Odus, the technology contained in those journals might usher in a new technological era, a quantum leap in our knowledge, and by extension, humanity's."

Books 53-55: Dark Memories Trilogy

Or

53: Dark Memories Submerged

54: Dark Memories Emerge

55: Dark Memories Restored

THE CHILDREN OF THE GODS SERIES

THE CHILDREN OF THE GODS ORIGINS

1: GODDESS'S CHOICE

When gods and immortals still ruled the ancient world, one young goddess risked everything for love.

2: GODDESS'S HOPE

Hungry for power and infatuated with the beautiful Areana, Navuh plots his father's demise. After all, by getting rid of the insane god he would be doing the world a favor. Except, when gods and immortals conspire against each other, humanity pays the price.

But things are not what they seem, and prophecies should not to be trusted...

THE CHILDREN OF THE GODS

1: DARK STRANGER THE DREAM

Syssi's paranormal foresight lands her a job at Dr. Amanda Dokani's neuroscience lab, but it fails to predict the thrilling yet terrifying turn her life will take. Syssi has no clue that her boss is an immortal who'll drag her into a secret, millennia-old battle over humanity's future. Nor does she realize that the professor's imposing brother is the mysterious stranger who's been starring in her dreams.

Since the dawn of human civilization, two warring factions of immortals—the descendants of the gods of old—have been secretly shaping its destiny. Leading the clandestine battle from his luxurious Los Angeles high-rise, Kian is surrounded by his clan, yet alone. Descending from a single goddess, clan members are forbidden to each other. And as the only other immortals are their hated enemies, Kian and his kin have been long resigned to a lonely existence of fleeting trysts with human partners. That is, until his sister makes a game-changing discovery—a mortal seeress who she believes is a dormant carrier of their genes. Ever the realist, Kian is skeptical and refuses Amanda's plea to attempt Syssi's activation. But when his enemies learn of the Dormant's existence, he's forced to rush her to the safety of his keep. Inexorably drawn to Syssi, Kian wrestles with his conscience as he is tempted to explore her budding interest in the darker shades of sensuality.

2: DARK STRANGER REVEALED

While sheltered in the clan's stronghold, Syssi is unaware that Kian and Amanda are not human, and neither are the supposedly religious fanatics that are after her. She feels a powerful connection to Kian, and as he introduces her to a world of pleasure she never dared imagine, his dominant sexuality is a revelation. Considering that she's completely out of her element, Syssi feels comfortable and safe letting go with him. That is, until she begins to suspect that all is not as it seems. Piecing the puzzle together, she draws a scary, yet wrong conclusion...

3: DARK STRANGER IMMORTAL

When Kian confesses his true nature, Syssi is not as much shocked by the revelation as she is wounded by what she perceives as his callous plans for her.

If she doesn't turn, he'll be forced to erase her memories and let her go. His family's safety demands secrecy – no one in the mortal world is allowed to know that immortals exist.

Resigned to the cruel reality that even if she stays on to never again leave the keep, she'll get old while Kian won't, Syssi is determined to enjoy what little time she has with him, one day at a time.

Can Kian let go of the mortal woman he loves? Will Syssi turn? And if she does, will she survive the dangerous transition?

4: Dark Enemy Taken

Dalhu can't believe his luck when he stumbles upon the beautiful immortal professor. Presented with a once in a lifetime opportunity to grab an immortal female for himself, he kidnaps her and runs. If he ever gets caught, either by her people or his, his life is forfeit. But for a chance of a loving mate and a family of his own, Dalhu is prepared to do everything in his power to win Amanda's heart, and that includes leaving the Doom brotherhood and his old life behind.

Amanda soon discovers that there is more to the handsome Doomer than his dark past and a hulking, sexy body. But succumbing to her enemy's seduction, or worse, developing feelings for a ruthless killer is out of the question. No man is worth life on the run, not even the one and only immortal male she could claim as her own...

Her clan and her research must come first...

5: Dark Enemy Captive

When the rescue team returns with Amanda and the chained Dalhu to the keep, Amanda is not as thrilled to be back as she thought she'd be. Between Kian's contempt for her and Dalhu's imprisonment, Amanda's budding relationship with Dalhu seems doomed. Things start to look up when Annani offers her help, and together with Syssi they resolve to find a way for Amanda to be with Dalhu. But will she still want him when she realizes that he is responsible for her nephew's murder? Could she? Will she take the easy way out and choose Andrew instead?

6: Dark Enemy Redeemed

Amanda suspects that something fishy is going on onboard the Anna. But when her investigation of the peculiar all-female Russian crew fails to uncover anything other than more speculation, she decides it's time to stop playing detective and face her real problem —a man she shouldn't want but can't live without.

6.5: My Dark Amazon

When Michael and Kri fight off a gang of humans, Michael gets stabbed. The injury to his immortal body recovers fast, but the one to his ego takes longer, putting a strain on his relationship with Kri.

7: Dark Warrior Mine

When Andrew is forced to retire from active duty, he believes that all he has to look forward to is a boring desk job. His glory days in special ops are over. But as it turns out, his thrill ride has just begun. Andrew discovers not only that immortals exist and have been manipulating global affairs since antiquity, but that he and his sister are rare possessors of the immortal genes.

Problem is, Andrew might be too old to attempt the activation process. His sister, who is fourteen years his junior, barely made it through the transition, so the odds of him coming out of it alive, let alone immortal, are slim.

But fate may force his hand.

Helping a friend find his long-lost daughter, Andrew finds a woman who's worth taking the risk for. Nathalie might be a Dormant, but the only way to find out for sure requires fangs and venom.

8: Dark Warrior's Promise

Andrew and Nathalie's love flourishes, but the secrets they keep from each other taint their relationship with doubts and suspicions. In the meantime, Sebastian and his men are getting bolder, and the storm that's brewing will shift the balance of power in the millennia-old conflict between Annani's clan and its enemies.

9: Dark Warrior's Destiny

The new ghost in Nathalie's head remembers who he was in life, providing Andrew and her with indisputable proof that he is real and not a figment of her imagination.

Convinced that she is a Dormant, Andrew decides to go forward with his transition immediately after the rescue mission at the Doomers' HQ.

Fearing for his life, Nathalie pleads with him to reconsider. She'd rather spend the rest of her mortal days with Andrew than risk what they have for the fickle promise of immortality.

While the clan gets ready for battle, Carol gets help from an unlikely ally. Sebastian's second-in-command can no longer ignore the torment she suffers at the hands of his commander and offers to help her, but only if she agrees to his terms.

10: Dark Warrior's Legacy

Andrew's acclimation to his post-transition body isn't easy. His senses are sharper, he's bigger, stronger, and hungrier. Nathalie fears that the changes in the man she loves are more than physical. Measuring up to this new version of him is going to be a challenge.

Carol and Robert are disillusioned with each other. They are not destined mates, and love is not on the horizon. When Robert's three months are up, he might be left with nothing to show for his sacrifice.

Lana contacts Anandur with disturbing news; the yacht and its human cargo are in Mexico. Kian must find a way to apprehend Alex and rescue the women on board without causing an international incident.

11: Dark Guardian Found

What would you do if you stopped aging?

Eva runs. The ex-DEA agent doesn't know what caused her strange mutation, only that if discovered, she'll be dissected like a lab rat. What Eva doesn't know, though, is that she's a descendant of the gods, and that she is not alone. The man who rocked her world in one life-changing encounter over thirty years ago is an immortal as well.

To keep his people's existence secret, Bhathian was forced to turn his back on the only woman who ever captured his heart, but he's never forgotten and never stopped looking for her.

12: Dark Guardian Craved

Cautious after a lifetime of disappointments, Eva is mistrustful of Bhathian's professed feelings of love. She accepts him as a lover and a confidant but not as a life partner.

Jackson suspects that Tessa is his true love mate, but unless she overcomes her fears, he might never find out.

Carol gets an offer she can't refuse—a chance to prove that there is more to her than meets the eye. Robert believes she's about to commit a deadly mistake, but when he tries to dissuade her, she tells him to leave.

13: Dark Guardian's Mate

Prepare for the heart-warming culmination of Eva and Bhathian's story!

14: Dark Angel's Obsession

The cold and stoic warrior is an enigma even to those closest to him. His secrets are about to unravel...

15: Dark Angel's Seduction

Brundar is fighting a losing battle. Calypso is slowly chipping away his icy armor from the outside, while his need for her is melting it from the inside.

He can't allow it to happen. Calypso is a human with none of the Dormant indicators. There is no way he can keep her for more than a few weeks.

16: Dark Angel's Surrender

Get ready for the heart pounding conclusion to Brundar and Calypso's story.

Callie still couldn't wrap her head around it, nor could she summon even a smidgen of sorrow or regret. After all, she had some memories with him that weren't horrible. She should've felt something. But there was nothing, not even shock. Not even horror at what had transpired over the last couple of hours.

Maybe it was a typical response for survivors--feeling euphoric for the simple reason that they were alive. Especially when that survival was nothing short of miraculous.

Brundar's cold hand closed around hers, reminding her that they weren't out of the woods yet. Her injuries were superficial, and the most she had to worry about was some scarring. But, despite his and Anandur's reassurances, Brundar might never walk again.

If he ended up crippled because of her, she would never forgive herself for getting him involved in her crap.

"Are you okay, sweetling? Are you in pain?" Brundar asked.

Her injuries were nothing compared to his, and yet he was concerned about her. God, she loved this man. The thing was, if she told him that, he would run off, or crawl away as was the case.

Hey, maybe this was the perfect opportunity to spring it on him.

17: Dark Operative: A Shadow of Death

As a brilliant strategist and the only human entrusted with the secret of immortals' existence, Turner is both an asset and a liability to the clan. His request to attempt transition into immortality as an alternative to cancer treatments cannot be denied without risking the clan's exposure. On the other hand, approving it means risking his premature death. In both scenarios, the clan will lose a valuable ally.

When the decision is left to the clan's physician, Turner makes plans to manipulate her by taking advantage of her interest in him.

Will Bridget fall for the cold, calculated operative? Or will Turner fall into his own trap?

18: Dark Operative: A Glimmer of Hope

As Turner and Bridget's relationship deepens, living together seems like the right move, but to make it work both need to make concessions.

Bridget is realistic and keeps her expectations low. Turner could never be the truelove mate she yearns for, but he is as good as she's going to get. Other than his emotional limitations, he's perfect in every way.

Turner's hard shell is starting to show cracks. He wants immortality, he wants to be part of the clan, and he wants Bridget, but he doesn't want to cause her pain.

His options are either abandon his quest for immortality and give Bridget his few remaining decades, or abandon Bridget by going for the transition and most likely dying. His rational mind dictates that he chooses the former, but his gut pulls him toward the latter. Which one is he going to trust?

19: Dark Operative: The Dawn of Love

Get ready for the exciting finale of Bridget and Turner's story!

20: Dark Survivor Awakened

This was a strange new world she had awakened to.

Her memory loss must have been catastrophic because almost nothing was familiar. The language was foreign to her, with only a few words bearing some similarity to the language she thought in. Still, a full moon cycle had passed since her awakening, and little by little she was gaining basic understanding of it--only a few words and phrases, but she was learning more each day.

A week or so ago, a little girl on the street had tugged on her mother's sleeve and pointed at her. "Look, Mama, Wonder Woman!"

The mother smiled apologetically, saying something in the language these people spoke, then scurried away with the child looking behind her shoulder and grinning.

When it happened again with another child on the same day, it was settled.

Wonder Woman must have been the name of someone important in this strange world she had awoken to, and since both times it had been said with a smile it must have been a good one.

Wonder had a nice ring to it.

She just wished she knew what it meant.

21: Dark Survivor Echoes of Love

Wonder's journey continues in *Dark Survivor Echoes of Love*.

22: Dark Survivor Reunited

The exciting finale of Wonder and Anandur's story.

23: Dark Widow's Secret

Vivian and her daughter share a powerful telepathic connection, so when Ella can't be reached by conventional or psychic means, her mother fears the worst.

Help arrives from an unexpected source when Vivian gets a call from the young doctor she met at a psychic convention. Turns out Julian belongs to a private organization specializing in retrieving missing girls.

As Julian's clan mobilizes its considerable resources to rescue the daughter, Magnus is charged with keeping the gorgeous young mother safe.

Worry for Ella and the secrets Vivian and Magnus keep from each other should be enough to prevent the sparks of attraction from kindling a blaze of desire. Except, these pesky sparks have a mind of their own.

24: Dark Widow's Curse

A simple rescue operation turns into mission impossible when the Russian mafia gets involved. Bad things are supposed to come in threes, but in Vivian's case, it seems like there is no limit to bad luck. Her family and everyone who gets close to her is affected by her curse.

Will Magnus and his people prove her wrong?

The thrilling finale of the Dark Widow trilogy!

Julian has known Ella is the one for him from the moment he saw her picture, but when he finally frees her from captivity, she seems indifferent to him. Could he have been mistaken?

Ella's rescue should've ended that chapter in her life, but it seems like the road back to normalcy has just begun and it's full of obstacles. Between the pitying looks she gets and her mother's attempts to get her into therapy, Ella feels like she's typecast as a victim, when nothing could be further from the truth. She's a tough survivor, and she's going to prove it.

Strangely, the only one who seems to understand is Logan, who keeps popping up in her dreams. But then, he's a figment of her imagination—or is he?

While trying to figure out a way around Logan's silencing compulsion, Ella concocts an ambitious plan. What if instead of trying to keep him out of her dreams, she could pretend to like him and lure him into a trap?

Catching Navuh's son would be a major boon for the clan, as well as for Ella. She will have her revenge, turning the tables on another scumbag out to get her.

The trap is set, but who is the hunter and who is the prey? Find out in this heart-pounding conclusion to the *Dark Dream* trilogy.

As the son of the most dangerous male on the planet, Lokan lives by three rules:

Don't trust a soul.

Don't show emotions.

And don't get attached.

Will one extraordinary woman make him break all three?

Will Kian decide that the benefits of trusting Lokan outweigh the risks?

Will Lokan betray his father and brothers for the greater good of his people?

Are Carol and Lokan true-love mates, or is one of them playing the other?

So many questions, the path ahead is anything but clear.

While Turner and Kian work out the details of Areana's rescue plan, Carol and Lokan's tumultuous relationship hits another snag. Is it a sign of things to come?

A former beauty queen, a retired undercover agent, and a successful model, Mey is not the typical damsel in distress. But when her sister drops off the radar and then someone starts following her around, she panics.

Following a vague clue that Kalugal might be in New York, Kian sends a team headed by Yamanu to search for him.

As Mey and Yamanu's paths cross, he offers her his help and protection, but will that be all?

33: Dark Queen's Knight

As the only member of his clan with a godlike power over human minds, Yamanu has been shielding his people for centuries, but that power comes at a steep price. When Mey enters his life, he's faced with the most difficult choice.

The safety of his clan or a future with his fated mate.

34: Dark Queen's Army

As Mey anxiously waits for her transition to begin and for Yamanu to test whether his godlike powers are gone, the clan sets out to solve two mysteries:

Where is Jin, and is she there voluntarily?

Where is Kalugal, and what is he up to?

35: Dark Spy Conscripted

Jin possesses a unique paranormal ability. Just by touching someone, she can insert a mental hook into their psyche and tie a string of her consciousness to it, creating a tether. That doesn't make her a spy, though, not unless her talent is discovered by those seeking to exploit it.

36: Dark Spy's Mission

Jin's first spying mission is supposed to be easy. Walk into the club, touch Kalugal to tether her consciousness to him, and walk out.

Except, they should have known better.

37: Dark Spy's Resolution

The best-laid plans often go awry...

38: Dark Overlord New Horizon

Jacki has two talents that set her apart from the rest of the human race.

She has unpredictable glimpses of other people's futures, and she is immune to mind manipulation.

Unfortunately, both talents are pretty useless for finding a job other than the one she had in the government's paranormal division.

It seemed like a sweet deal, until she found out that the director planned on producing super babies by compelling the recruits into pairing up. When an opportunity to escape the program presented itself, she took it, only to find out that humans are not at the top of the food chain.

Immortals are real, and at the very top of the hierarchy is Kalugal, the most powerful, arrogant, and sexiest male she has ever met.

With one look, he sets her blood on fire, but Jacki is not a fool. A man like him will never think of her as anything more than a tasty snack, while she will never settle for anything less than his heart.

39: Dark Overlord's Wife

Jacki is still clinging to her all-or-nothing policy, but Kalugal is chipping away at her resistance. Perhaps it's time to ease up on her convictions. A little less than all is still much better than nothing, and a couple of decades with a demigod is probably worth more than a lifetime with a mere mortal.

40: Dark Overlord's Clan

As Jacki and Kalugal prepare to celebrate their union, Kian takes every precaution to safeguard his people. Except, Kalugal and his men are not his only potential adversaries, and compulsion is not the only power he should fear.

41: Dark Choices The Quandary

When Rufsur and Edna meet, the attraction is as unexpected as it is undeniable. Except, she's the clan's judge and councilwoman, and he's Kalugal's second-in-command. Will loyalty and duty to their people keep them apart?

42: Dark Choices Paradigm Shift

Edna and Rufsur are miserable without each other, and their two-week separation seems like an eternity. Long-distance relationships are difficult, but for immortal couples they are impossible. Unless one of them is willing to leave everything behind for the other, things are just going to get worse. Except, the cost of compromise is far greater than giving up their comfortable lives and hard-earned positions. The future of their people is on the line.

43: Dark Choices The Accord

The winds of change blowing over the village demand hard choices. For better or worse, Kian's decisions will alter the trajectory of the clan's future, and he is not ready to take the plunge. But as Edna and Rufsur's plight gains widespread support, his resistance slowly begins to erode.

44: Dark Secrets Resurgence

On a sabbatical from his Stanford teaching position, Professor David Levinson finally has time to write the sci-fi novel he's been thinking about for years.

The phenomena of past life memories and near-death experiences are too controversial to include in his formal psychiatric research, while fiction is the perfect outlet for his esoteric ideas.

Hoping that a change of pace will provide the inspiration he needs, David accepts a friend's invitation to an old Scottish castle.

45: Dark Secrets Unveiled

When Professor David Levinson accepts a friend's invitation to an old Scottish castle, what he finds there is more fantastical than his most outlandish theories. The castle is home to a clan of immortals, their leader is a stunning demigoddess, and even more shockingly, it might be precisely where he belongs.

Except, the clan founder is hiding a secret that might cast a dark shadow on David's relationship with her daughter.

Nevertheless, when offered a chance at immortality, he agrees to undergo the dangerous induction process.

Will David survive his transition into immortality? And if he does, will his relationship with Sari survive the unveiling of her mother's secret?

46: Dark Secrets Absolved

Absolution.

David had given and received it.

The few short hours since he'd emerged from the coma had felt incredible. He'd finally been free of the guilt and pain, and for the first time since Jonah's death, he had felt truly happy and optimistic about the future.

He'd survived the transition into immortality, had been accepted into the clan, and was about to marry the best woman on the face of the planet, his true love mate, his salvation, his everything.

What could have possibly gone wrong?

Just about everything.

47: Dark haven Illusion

Welcome to Safe Haven, where not everything is what it seems.

On a quest to process personal pain, Anastasia joins the Safe Haven Spiritual Retreat.

Through meditation, self-reflection, and hard work, she hopes to make peace with the voices in her head.

This is where she belongs.

Except, membership comes with a hefty price, doubts are sacrilege, and leaving is not as easy as walking out the front gate.

Is living in utopia worth the sacrifice?

Anastasia believes so until the arrival of a new acolyte changes everything.

Apparently, the gods of old were not a myth, their immortal descendants share the planet with humans, and she might be a carrier of their genes.

48: Dark Haven Unmasked

As Anastasia leaves Safe Haven for a week-long romantic vacation with Leon, she hopes to explore her newly discovered passionate side, their budding relationship, and perhaps also solve the mystery of the voices in her head. What she discovers exceeds her wildest expectations.

In the meantime, Eleanor and Peter hope to solve another mystery. Who is Emmett Haderech, and what is he up to?

49: Dark Haven Found

Anastasia is growing suspicious, and Leon is running out of excuses.

Risking death for a chance at immortality should've been her choice to make. Will she ever forgive him for taking it away from her?

50: Dark Power Untamed

Attending a charity gala as the clan's figurehead, Onegus is ready for the pesky socialites he'll have a hard time keeping away. Instead, he encounters an intriguing beauty who won't give him the time of day.

Bad things happen when Cassandra gets all worked up, and given her fiery temper, the destructive power is difficult to tame. When she meets a gorgeous, cocky billionaire at a charity event, things just might start blowing up again.

51: Dark Power Unleashed

Cassandra's power is unpredictable, uncontrollable, and destructive. If she doesn't learn to harness it, people might get hurt.

Onegus's self-control is legendary. Even his fangs and venom glands obey his commands.

They say that opposites attract, and perhaps it's true, but are they any good for each other?

52: Dark Power Convergence

The threads of fate converge, mysteries unfold, and the clan's future is forever altered in the least expected way.

53: Dark Memories Submerged

Geraldine's memories are spotty at best, and many of them are pure fiction. While her family attempts to solve the puzzle with far too many pieces missing, she's forced to confront a past life that she can't remember, a present that's more fantastic than her wildest made-up stories, and a future that might be better than her most heartfelt fantasies. But as more clues are uncovered, the picture starting to emerge is beyond anything she or her family could have ever imagined.

56: Dark Hunter's Query

For most of his five centuries of existence, Orion has walked the earth alone, searching for answers.

Why is he immortal?

Where did his powers come from?

Is he the only one of his kind?

When fate puts Orion face to face with the god who sired him, he learns the secret behind his immortality and that he might not be the only one.

As the goddess's eldest daughter and a mother of thirteen, Alena deserves the title of Clan Mother just as much as Annani, but she's not interested in honorifics. Being her mother's companion and keeping the mischievous goddess out of trouble is a rewarding, full-time job. Lately, though, Alena's love for her mother and the clan's gratitude is not enough.

She craves adventure, excitement, and perhaps a true-love mate of her own.

When Alena and Orion meet, sparks fly, but they both resist the pull. Alena could never bring herself to trust the powerful compeller, and Orion could never allow himself to fall in love again.

––––––

THE PERFECT MATCH SERIES

That is until Gregg makes her an offer she can't refuse—a gift certificate to the virtual fantasy fulfillment service everyone is talking about. As a huge Star Trek fan, Alicia has a perfect match in mind—the captain of the Starship Enterprise.

Made in United States
Orlando, FL
07 February 2023

29633854R10382